the
OLD
GARDEN

the OLD GARDEN

HWANG SOK-YONG

Translated by Jay Oh

Seven Stories Press
New York

Published and translated with kind support from the Korean Literature Translation Institute.

Seven Stories Press
140 Watts Street
New York, NY 10013
www.sevenstories.com

In Canada: Publishers Group Canada, 559 College Street, Suite 402,
Toronto, ON M6G 1A9

College professors may order examination copies of Seven Stories Press titles for a free six-month trial period. To order, visit www.sevenstories.com/textbook or send a fax on school letterhead to (212) 226-1411.

Book design by Jon Gilbert

Library of Congress Cataloging-in-Publication Data

Hwang, Sog-yong, 1943-
   [Oraedoen chongwon. English]
   The old garden / by Hwang Sok-yong ; translated by Jay Oh.
      p. cm.
   ISBN 978-1-58322-899-9 (hardcover)
   I. Oh, Jay. II. Title.
   PL992.29.S6O7313 2009
   895.7'34--dc22
                                    2009018095
Printed in the USA

9 8 7 6 5 4 3 2 1

The little rose, oh how should it be listed?
Suddenly dark red and young and near?
Oh we never knew that it existed
Then we came, and saw that it was there.

Unexpected till we came and saw it
Unbelievable as soon as seen
Hit the mark, despite not aiming for it:
Isn't that how things have always been?

—Bertolt Brecht

1

The sound of footsteps far off. Heels hammered on the concrete floor in a martial rhythm.

It was the chief guard making his last rounds.

"All clear," the watchtower reported.

To reach this section, he would have to pass through two iron gates. I emerged from the quilt tightly wrapped around my shoulders and sat up. In that position I felt the cold dawn air cut into my back. I took off the felt slippers I wore at night over thick wool socks, and then the cap I'd made out of another sock. I put on my prison uniform stenciled with the numbers of my building, my cell, my registration. Number 1444 had been my name for a long time. I'd almost forgotten my real one. When did they give it to me? At roll call, mail call, on work detail, when I had a visitor or was getting a penalty, it was always with that number, preceded or followed by an insult, that they conceded that I did exist.

Standing on a low table, I pulled down the cardboard that, in violation of the rules, shaded the fluorescent bulb that shone day and night. The prisoner had to be observed 24/7. Daylight never ended, daylight with no sun. I'd torn apart a cardboard carton from ramen noodle packets, covered it with writing paper, then attached it to the light fixture with sticky tape. I attached a broken chopstick to this shade to raise and lower it. Of course, I took it down during every inspection. These little things made my life a little easier. Everything I had in the cell was made by me or my fellow inmates, bit by bit.

I folded the quilt, stacked it with the blankets in one corner, and made a square with the dark green sponge mattress, which folded into three. This was my seat. I decided not to take a cold shower today. Yesterday, I had selected things I wanted to keep and packed them into two small toiletry bags. They were the remnants of my imprisoned life.

I stood up. I stretched, then spread my arms wide as I often did and pushed the two walls on each side with my open palms. The cement walls were white with frost. On the ceiling where my breath reached while I slept there were little droplets of water, as always. In this cell, with the single mattress spread out across the width of the room, a little gap of about two feet was left. You could take one step and reach the door to the bathroom. There was a water bucket in front of the bathroom door, and on that side of the wall was a three-level plastic shelf where I stored my personal belongings and dishes.

There was a thin layer of ice in the water bucket. Today I poured three scoops of water into the basin and scrubbed my hairless cheeks, chin, and neck. I had taken a bath yesterday, I even got a haircut and a shave. I asked the prison assistant for a bucket full of warm water and got permission to use the common sinks. I mixed the warm water with cold, and took a bath in lukewarm water.

The middle-aged chief of the prisoner-run barbershop was said to be a hardened criminal already here fifteen years, but as they say in here, everyone becomes a gentle lamb after about ten years. Another barber once told me the chief barber had robbed a train, but in here it was forbidden to ask each other the cause of imprisonment, so I never heard the full story. After serving thirteen years, the chief barber was recently allowed a furlough. There was a mutual respect shared among us long-timers, and he was exclusively in charge of my haircuts. The chief barber's technique was so good, he received a gold medal from the National Vocation Training Competition for Prisoners. He didn't ask me how I wanted my hair done. Everyone at the barber shop knew that I was a political prisoner. A public security offender did not shave his head. This way, he was easily distinguished from other ordinary criminals.

"I'll trim just a little."

Expertly handling his scissors, he clipped the hair underneath my ears. After I sat down on the chair, I closed my eyes and did not speak. He lowered his head.

"It's tomorrow?" he asked softly.

"So it seems."

After shaving my face, the chief barber slathered my cheeks and chin with scented aftershave he'd gotten who knows where. Then he gently wiped my neck and ears with a dry towel, like they do outside.

"All done."

"Thank you."

As I was getting up, the chief barber quietly set his hands on my shoulders and whispered again.

"Mr. Oh, mind if I say a little prayer?"

I was perplexed for a moment. I was no Ca-Bud-Pro believer, I had never prayed before. Inside, a Ca-Bud-Pro believer was a disparaging term for those people who switched their religion regularly in order to attend every gathering thrown by Catholics, Buddhists, and Protestants—each religious group came here with armloads of food in the name of rehabilitating the criminal minds. But at that moment, I thought of our long, long solitude. The barber would leave here with me, because I would remember his prayer for a long time.

"May I?" he asked. He pressed my hands in his.

"Dear God, this brother is about to return to the world after serving eighteen years of imprisonment. Please let him bury everything that has happened here in his heart, and please take care of him outside as you've done until now. Let his future be full of hope and joy. And please allow him a happy, humble life where he is grateful for even the smallest thing. And most of all, do not let him forget those of us still left behind in here, I pray in the name of my Lord, Jesus Christ. Amen."

I took the thick Chinese dictionary from the desk and opened it. I took out my hidden private property, a palm-sized mirror. Because of the threat of suicide, a solitary prisoner was forbidden to own a piece of glass, any type of string, or a sharp piece of metal. I'd bartered for the mirror with a prison assistant. I cannot remember if I gave him ramen noodles or an egg cake. Hidden among the leaves of thick books were my treasures. In the bible, there was a small knife as long as my finger, made by sharpening an aluminum can lid on the cement wall of the bathroom. I used it to peel fruit or cut kimchi. A comb was hidden in an envelope at the bottom of a paper folder stuck to the wall.

I raised my head to the fluorescent light and faced the mirror. A sad-looking fifty-something man appeared there. Hair graying from the bottom of the ears to the top of the head, deep lines etched around the mouth, and more around the eyes and forehead. There was darkness behind the face in the mirror. What was there? Was there really a world outside? I combed my hair, a tangle of fading threads. It shone even paler under the fluorescent light.

The iron gate opened, and I heard the screeching sound of the steel bolt and steps approaching from the corridor downstairs. I quickly put my books, mirror, and comb into their places and sat down meekly on the mattress.

Again, I heard the sound of the iron gate on the second floor of the maximum security area and the steel bolt clacking, followed by the iron gate crashing into the iron pillar. The guard on duty reported the number of inmates, and the sound of the chief guard's steps were muffled now. He was probably walking on the long carpet in the corridor along the cell row. He arrived quietly in front of my cell and showed his face in the little window. It was about a foot long and covered with plastic. I could barely make out his face.

"Number Fourteen Forty-Four, leaving today?"

"Yes."

The visor tip of his cap tilted down, "It's past four o'clock. Let's go," he said brusquely.

The door opened with a clear clanging of steel, just like it did every morning before the exercise hour. The vastness of the corridor suddenly seemed to pour into the tiny cell.

"Get your things."

"Beg your pardon?" I asked him, bewildered.

"You're going home."

"Home? Ah, yes . . ."

I picked up the two little bundles placed where my head used to lie, and white rubber shoes from the shelf above the door. I placed them in the corridor and put them on. I took a step. I stood with two feet out-side the cell. My cell was second from last, and every second cell held a political prisoner like me. I knew they were awake, waiting for this moment. I was about to walk along the row when the guard directed me from behind my back.

"This way."

Before turning, without thinking, I shouted:

"Oh Hyun Woo is leaving now. Take care of yourselves, everyone!"

As I finished, the corridor was in commotion.

"Goodbye, Mr. Oh!"

"It was tough, Mr. Oh!"

"Goodbye, Oh, keep in touch!"

"Good luck!"

Annoyed, the chief guard clucked his tongue and pushed my shoulder. I turned toward the staircase on the opposite side. The guard from our block shook my hand.

"Take care, Mr. Oh. Don't ever come back."

"Thanks for everything."

Like bygone history, I turned. The chief guard and I didn't exchange a word as we stood in front of the iron gate. It closed behind us. There was another gate in the middle of the corridor leading to the main building. A young soldier, who was serving his mandatory military service as a guard at the prison, opened and closed the gate, shouting *Loyalty!* I had walked back and forth along this wing thousands of times, whenever I went to the clinic or the security office or the visitation room or the administration office. The wing disappeared behind my back, one sec-tion after the other.

We finally passed the third iron gate leading to the main building. Beyond the iron gate was the bare ground where the guards assembled every morning. For no reason, I looked up at the sky. It was still dark, but something cold came down, soft and delicate. It was snowing. As I always did, I walked one step ahead of my escort. Like a well-trained animal, I knew where to go. I stepped up into the building and turned right.

An unfamiliar heat enveloped me when I walked into the security office. On top of the blazing gas stove, a kettle was whistling as water boiled. The chief administrator on duty was dozing off, seated deeply in a swiveling chair. He took down his feet from the opposite chair and slowly stood up.

"Fourteen Forty- . . . ah . . . Mr. Oh Hyun Woo, you're being released today, right?" He glanced at his wristwatch then pointed toward the chair where he had placed his feet.

"Please, take a seat."

I walked over to where he sat comfortably in front of the stove and bowed awkwardly.

"Sit down, sit down. You met with the warden yesterday, didn't you?"

"Yes."

"Actually, your official release began at midnight, but we've been waiting for your family and transportation, things like that." Then he asked the chief guard standing behind me, "What about his personal effects, did you retrieve them?"

"His nephew deposited clothes yesterday. Money and other things are over here."

"His nephew? He must have stayed overnight somewhere nearby, then."

"Yes, he phoned yesterday to say he'd be here at five o'clock."

When I heard that my nephew was here, my heart finally began to race. I saw him every few years or so, most recently a couple of years ago when he came for a visit with my sister, telling me he was about to start his military service. He was a five-year-old, a little boy, when I came in here. Watching that little boy grow into an adult, I kept track of time passing. Inside here, the changing seasons seemed indistinguishable, and I was never sure what year it was, but little incidents marked time in my memory like growth rings on a tree. I remembered one year by the winter when the black cat I fed day and night died, and another year by the long autumn night when Mr. Yang, an eighty-year-old man, wept all through the night, saying he did not want to be released, and another by the night when the man we called Toothless Mouth suffocated and died in the middle of the night, one week before the end of his prison term.

"Please come over here."

The chief guard had piled up a suitcase and envelopes on another desk. I was stifling by the overheated gas stove, so I promptly moved over to his desk. When the chief guard opened the suitcase, the first thing that caught my eye was a pair of black leather shoes. The toes of the slip-on shoes were slender and shiny, reflecting the light. They looked too perfect to wear. Also in the suitcase were a wool shirt and a jacket, which looked so warm, and a leather belt, something I had not seen for years. There was new underwear and socks, price tags still attached.

"Change your clothes."

I took off my prison uniform as if I were shedding my skin. First I took off the unshapely, quilted jacket, which we jokingly called the Chinese Army uniform. Then the pants with no belt, held together by short strings about the length of a little finger. When I had taken off the old knitted thermal underwear with baggy knees I stood there in only my underpants and T-shirt, yet I did not feel cold. Instead, my sweat finally began to dry.

"No need to hurry, we have a plenty of time."

That's what the chief guard said, but I moved quickly yet precisely, just like I had during the physical examinations. I folded the prison clothes neatly and stacked them in front of me, then began to dress in my new clothes in reverse order, starting with the new underwear. I put on the wool shirt and pants, put the leather belt around my waist, tightened and secured it, then took one deep breath. I looked down at the sharply creased line of my slacks. They were ironed like a bureaucrat's. When I put my shoes on, my feet appeared so small it was as if they were drowning under my slacks. The last item I put on was the warm, loose jacket. The clothes I took off were piled under my feet like rags, the pair of white rubber shoes neatly placed on top, like relics of a dead person.

"You look pretty good, Mr. Oh."

"Ha ha, you look like our warden."

The administrator and the guard each commented. Without saying anything, I put my two bags in the suitcase. The chief guard took money out of a large envelope.

"Here, your money deposited before, and the receipt . . . and I think those are your personal properties."

I simply folded the bills and stuck them into an inner pocket of my new jacket.

"Count them. I don't want to hear later that you're claiming anything missing."

"It's fine."

My old belongings tumbled down into a small plastic basket. There was a gold ring decorated with leaf patterns. There were letters from my sister, a picture of my mother before she passed away, and a brown wallet, faded and wrinkled. I opened the wallet. One ID card, the photo on it discolored yellow. In that picture, the younger me had wavy long hair and glared. Seeing the address reminded me of the house surrounded by forsythias near Buk Han Mountain. Then I opened another part of the wallet fastened with a snap. I held my breath a moment to control my breathing, but my heart was beating hard. I knew very well what was in there: a talisman my mom had given me when I left home, of Avalokiteśvara, the Buddhist Goddess of Mercy, and a small passport photograph. I unsnapped the small compartment. There was the talisman, wrapped in red silk, and the photograph. I pushed the snap down and closed it again. I didn't want to remember anything in there. I put the wallet in the other pocket. As I put the gold ring on my ring finger, she appeared to me, finally, her fingers, her voice, her white calves wearing white rubber shoes with jutting toes. *Look here!* she said, her voice breaking slightly. *A single moss rose has blossomed, the first one!* And she touched her mouth with one raised finger and gestured toward me. *Hush, can you see? Underneath the apple tree, there's a hoopoe!* The telephone rang.

"Hello? The front entrance? Got it."

The chief guard put down the receiver and told the chief administrator on duty, "His relative is waiting at the front gate."

"Mr. Oh Hyun Woo, come over here please."

The chief administrator thrust a piece of paper toward me.

"This is the official certificate of your release. You're still considered a security risk and a subject of surveillance. When you get home, you'll have to report to the local police within one week, is that understood?"

The chief administrator stood up and formally shook my hand.

"Congratulations on your release. It is my sincere wish for you to become a productive member of society."

He saluted and I bowed deeply. I left the main building with the chief guard. It was still snowing and windy. The chief guard looked up to the sky and mumbled, "You have a long way to go, I hope the road condition is okay."

We passed through a small opening in the corner of the front gate and walked toward the guard station near the prison's outermost wall. Armed soldiers were guarding the station, and in front of it in an empty field was a lone passenger car with lights on. When we reached the guard station, the chief guard stopped walking and said, "From here on, it's the real world. Best of luck."

"Farewell."

We said our goodbyes like that, him inside, me out. I moved the little suitcase from one hand to the other, and I entered the world.

The car door opened, and a man who must have been my nephew jumped out and walked fast toward me.

"Uncle!"

First, he embraced me tightly.

"The things you had to suffer . . ."

"Well . . . I managed."

He took out a piece of tofu and shoved it into my face.

"Eat this. Mom said you have to."*

"Tofu? That's all superstition."

"Mom said from now on, you do what others do."

I understood that as her most sincere wish. The tofu was cold and unseasoned and dry; it was hard to swallow. My nephew opened the back door.

"You can spread out in the back, maybe get some sleep."

I looked around the car with awe, as if I was touring a luxurious mansion. My nephew started the car and took the road in front of the prison to a highway. The highway was already lined with cars with lights on, coming and going. So many cars. He took out a small object that looked like a transistor and began talking.

"Mom? Yes, Uncle just got out. We're already on our way. Yes, sure, he's fine. Yes, yes, I'll put him on."

---

* In Korea, it is a custom for a just-released prisoner to eat tofu. They say this will prevent him from going back to prison again.

He handed me the object. I felt timid and waved it off.

"What is that thing?"

"It's a cell phone. Don't worry. It works just like a telephone."

I touched the thing and put it against my ear. I tried to speak.

"Hel . . . Hello . . . ?"

"Hyun Woo? My God, after all these years . . . how long has it been? Is this real? Are you really out?"

"Yes, I'm in the car, on my way."

She was unable to talk, and began sobbing.

"Fine . . . fine . . . soon we'll talk as much as we want. I'll see you at home soon."

"Yes, I'll see you soon."

I replied evenly. My nephew turned on the radio. A young woman cheerfully introduced light instrumental music. Because my sense of space had not fully recovered yet, it tired me to look out the window.

"It'll take at least three hours. The road condition is bad today."

Through the window, snowflakes blew onto the glass, some melting away, some forming a thin white line at the bottom. As the car entered the freeway, my ears were slowly deafened by the muffled noise. I was in a deep forest and the sound of the city seemed to be coming from somewhere far away. My basic instinct, the only thing that I had in solitary confinement, was self-protection. The scenery outside the window kept changing, but I couldn't feel the car moving or tell how fast it was going. I drifted into sleep.

"Wake up, uncle."

The car had stopped. I looked around.

"Let's take a break at this rest stop."

I walked toward the rest station, already full of people traveling since dawn, trying not to be separated from my nephew.

"May I go to the restroom?"

My nephew turned and laughed, startled.

"Of course you may, you're free to do whatever you want!"

I was not yet confident enough to navigate this large space without hesitating. Looking at me frozen to the spot, my nephew reached for my hand. After using the toilet I touched the faucet to wash up and I panicked. I had never used something that looked like this. I didn't know what to do with the hook-like handle that jutted upward, and I realized it was not something to be easily mastered when my nephew lifted it up lightly to let the water out and then twisted it precisely to get the right temperature. Then there was this machine that dried hands without towel or paper, from which warm air gushed out if you pressed something somewhere. An hour and a half earlier, before I left prison, it never occurred to me that I would have difficulties living outside. Stepping out of the restroom, my first encounter with outside culture, I was drowning in helplessness. I didn't know what to do with my hands and feet. My nephew saw the state I was in.

"Sit here for a minute. You're not hungry?"

"I'm fine. I don't eat breakfast, even in there."

"Mom has been preparing a feast for a few days. We'll eat at home. Would you like something to drink?"

I surveyed the people eating and drinking. I saw a young woman slowly licking a coiled ice cream cone, using the tip of her tongue.

"I want that."

"What, the corn dog or the fish cake?"

"No, ice cream."

My nephew came back with a cup of coffee and an ice cream cone.

"By the way, when was the last time you had something like this?"

"Maybe about eleven years ago?"

"Where?"

"A prison officer bought me one during my furlough."

I took the cone and, like that young woman, began licking the end of its coiled tail with the tip of my tongue. As the cream melted into cool liquid in my mouth, I saw an open window and billowing drapes printed with small flowers. The scent of acacia drifted in from outside, and honeybees buzzed by the glass window. Then came the taste of the American gum drops my mother left for us during the war while she went out to earn money. There were red, yellow, blue, purple, and green ones, but the black one, it had a scent so exotic and distinctive. What did they use to make it so fragrant? I knew that world was gone now yet I missed it all.

The sun was coming up. The sky was frosty and opaque, but it was no longer snowing. The streetlights on the freeway went out. Only the lights on the cars coming and going were still illuminated, like the eyes of wild animals. The landscape told me we were near Seoul. As the dawn slowly emerged, I was beginning to adjust to my surroundings. I fumbled around my inside pocket and took out the wallet.

Like a blind man fingering braille, I stroked the outside of the wallet with my fingertips, hesitating a little. Yes, my mother had been alive then. The talisman was smeared with her worries and tears. I could not get annoyed and throw it away then, but what use was a talisman to a man of science? Mothers are not logical. Maybe I was now ready to throw it away. I took out the talisman and rubbed it between my thumb and index finger, then put it back again. I knew very well there was something else, the passport photo. The photo was stuck to the wallet. I took it out with my fingertips.

In the photo, she is not smiling. Imprisoned with me for almost twenty years, the little thing had yellowed. But she was still there, with her hair, slightly curled up at the ends, framing her face. Her hair coiled as if chemically treated but I knew it was natural. Right here, her round forehead, her almond-shaped eyes with lightly creased lids, her high cheekbones, her mouth stubbornly closed, her air of cleverness and thoughtfulness. Without realizing, I whispered to her, *it's been a while.* There had been a few letters exchanged a decade ago, but all contact was blocked after I was transferred to another prison. I lost all her letters. Other than immediate family members, no visitation was allowed. Only harmless, meaningless greetings were allowed in letters, and those from acquaintances had to be returned to the authorities after reading. The photo was taken away with the wallet when I was arrested. I knew very well where this photograph had been hibernating. Whenever the weather changed, I would go to the depository to return woolen blankets or retrieve winter clothes. There were perforated aluminum panels divided into sections like a bookcase, each compartment bearing the inmate's number like a dog tag. Sorted into each slot were the worldly possessions of the now imprisoned owner, still smudged with his life, the smells of his body. An old pair of shoes with worn heels held the dirt of unknown streets and alleys the owner had passed through. A faded jacket with traces of rice wine still visible, an eyeglass case, summer clothes threadbare like rags, woven summer sandals that were once the height of fashion, thick hiking boots, assorted hats, rings, necklaces, and watches. Frozen at the moment the owner was caught, they lay there tied with string like a dead man's memories.

For a while, I held onto her letters by copying them onto a piece of paper, but even that disappeared during the search and inspection before my transfer. I still remember how the last letter ended.

When will you join me in Kalmae? We're still there.

Maybe I reversed the sentences. I put her passport picture beneath my mother's talisman and closed the wallet.

"Uncle, we're entering Seoul now."

Cars were lined up, moving and stopping. I assumed we were near the tollbooth entering Seoul. I recognized the place from the days I traveled via express buses all around the south region for the organization. The entrance seemed a bit larger than it was then. After the tollbooth, cars were crawling.

After the Olympic Bypass, the car sped up again unlike those in the opposite lane, going to work. There was Youido district.* Sprouting across the river was a small forest of concrete buildings. When I was a child, I could cross a dyke there and go swimming in a pool underneath the Ghost Rock every summer evening. Neither the pool nor the rock remained. The Yang Mal Hill was blasted when I was still outside. No more reed fields, no more peanut fields. I remembered the evenings I gazed at the Sam Gak Mountain colored by the sunset on the way back from fishing in that thin stream of river with my brother. From pink to red to purple, the Sam Gak and In Wang mountains changed colors and then became submerged in darkness. I sat there and watched for a long time, sitting on a warm gas pipe from the American base, until my little brother complained he was starving. Sometimes, practice planes with propellers rose from Youido Airport and flew by, shining like toys.

My sister was living in a new development at the outskirts of town. My head swam when I looked up at the twenty-story building. I followed my nephew as closely as possible, surrounded by tall buildings in every direction. We took an elevator to the fifteenth floor, and my sister ran out as soon as he rang the doorbell. My brother-in law was standing behind her. She hugged me by the neck and burst into tears.

---

* A neighborhood in Seoul.

"My God, you're here in our house! Am I dreaming?"

It had only been a year since I'd seen my sister last. After my mother's death she had come to visit once or twice a year. Both my sister and her husband were professors, and it was difficult for them to leave Seoul unless it was a holiday or a vacation.

Inside, my aunt and cousins were waiting for me. I didn't feel like myself yet. Halfheartedly, I managed to break into a smile and exchange pleasantries, but their words only reverberated in my ears, and I couldn't make out one single word properly. My brother-in-law gazed at my face and understood.

"Tired? Go lie down and rest," he said.

"Without eating anything?"

"Uncle doesn't eat breakfast, even in there," my nephew answered for me.

"Is that so? Then go take a nap."

"I guess you didn't sleep very well last night. Go ahead."

My brother-in-law gently pushed my back, and my sister took me to her son's bedroom. She drew the curtains and quietly closed the door. The room was so much larger than what I was used to, I somehow felt afraid of the empty space next to the bed. I turned toward the wall. It was not a bare cement wall, but covered with wallpaper. The wall was one thing I was used to. In the middle of that wall, I pictured many things. I clearly remembered the stains all over the cell walls. There were stains on the ceiling, too. I used to remember my childhood, when I would lie in a field of grass by the river, looking at the clouds moving about on a summer sky, swept by wind, gathering and separating. I remembered imagining many stories based on their shapes.

Sometimes I had wet dreams. Women I did not know appeared. One night, bright with moonlight, I was barely asleep and opened my eyes just a slit. There was a slender woman, her body wet like a fish, standing upright and looking down upon me. Where did she come from? I was wandering around the empty, winding corridors, because I wanted to leave here, this desolate place, but I always returned to a place that looked just like the first floor of the prison building. Around the staircase was a small store like those you find in train stations, where teenage girls were gathered. They were chattering and nibbling on something. None of them looked at me as I approached. A woman in her forties, perhaps the owner of the stand, was looking at me. Her face was only darkness. When I asked her where the exit was, she laughed out loud and shouted, her voice echoing through the corridor.

Why don't you stay here with us for a while? You wanna leave already?

That faceless woman was probably the owner of the building. But seldom did the face of someone I knew appear. I would think of one person right before going to sleep, missing her, but I never saw her.

I got up late in the afternoon. I tried to taste each dish they laid out in front of me, but the seasoning was too strong, unfamiliar. They were all cautious, gently probing to see whether I felt comfortable. I was not able to give them long, detailed answers, just yes or no. Is it tasty? Yes. Are you tired? No.

I talked to my younger brother, who had immigrated to the United States. It was a long phone call, him talking about his family and his business, while I just listened. My aunt, out of the blue, wanted to talk about the possibility of my getting married soon, emphasizing that it was my mother's dying wish to see me paired with someone suitable. I didn't have to come up with an answer, thanks to my sister's intervention. The first day out of prison I was in a stupor, like someone suffering from chronic fatigue. I kept seeing myself as if from a distance. When I tried to open a door, I had to tell myself, you're about to open the door. Only then could I do it.

For three days and nights, I stayed at my sister's house, going back and forth between the living room and my nephew's room. My sister and her husband decided that I needed a full physical examination after observing my odd sluggish behavior. Except for the first day, I wasn't able to sleep for more than a couple of hours each night. When the time to rise approached, I became anxious and stood out on the terrace for a long time. Looking into a mirror in the bathroom, I found a strange man gazing back. With my nephew's help, I went out to the neighborhood stores or to the public bathhouse, but I didn't even think about going out the door by myself.

They packed my underwear and toiletries. I was admitted to a university hospital. They paid for a deluxe single room with an attached bathroom. The small room was furnished with a single bed with my nametag on the headboard, two chairs, one love seat, a television, and a small refrigerator. I walked in there and thought I had returned to my prison cell. Finally I was comfortable and relieved to be alone. I followed all the rules, obeyed the nurses without question. I was an exemplary patient; I found it so easy to do as I was told and stick to the schedule, to skip a meal or take medicine or follow someone to somewhere else in the hospital. I had no major illness, doctors told me, but my eyes had deteriorated a great deal and my gums were in even worse condition. Because of gum disease that was now almost impossible to get rid of, my molars were no longer anchored in place. One doctor told me the possible causes were stress and malnutrition. A neuropsychiatrist thought I was about to have a nervous breakdown, common for those who spent years imprisoned. I would be insomniac, claustrophobic, and unwilling to talk or make physical contact with others. If I was lucky this should last only about three or four months and then the symptoms should disappear, but there was a possibility the condition would last for more than a year. I was getting old, but I did not want to lose my mind; I took the prescribed medicine every day, twice a day.

About a week into my hospital stay, my nephew called just before lunch hour. He was in the neighborhood with his mother and asked me to join them for lunch. Without asking for permission from the nurse in charge, I changed into my own clothes and left the hospital. I walked down to the street without any incident. People passed me by and none of them seemed to stare at me.

I came to a crossroads. Without thinking, I took the one in the middle. I was on the university campus, and the road I took was the central avenue from the main gate to a cluster of school buildings. I took a few steps and realized I was headed in the wrong direction, but I could not turn around. Students going to their classes clogged the street. I was a salmon swimming upstream. I bumped shoulders with them, blocked one student's way while trying to avoid running into another. I became too conspicuous. Some kids glanced at me, others avoided me and walked around. I saw the main gate and told myself this ordeal would be over once I got there. I took one step at a time, deliberately and slowly. I became nauseous and couldn't stop sweating. Beyond the main gate was a grand avenue full of traffic. Cars whizzed by, leaving dusty fumes behind. I thought every bus and truck was about to run over me. Holding on to a tree, I stood on the sidewalk for a while, then collapsed. My stomach was queasy and I spat onto the ground. I took a few more steps, then took a rest, counting the roadside trees one at a time. Finally, I got to a busy neighborhood full of restaurants, but I couldn't even attempt to look for the one where I was supposed to be. I sat on the steps of an overpass and waited for my nephew to find me.

"Uncle, what's wrong? You're not feeling well?"

He came to me and reached for my hand, pulled me up.

"Well, just a bit dizzy . . ."

"I guess it's still too much for you to go out."

We walked to the restaurant where my sister was waiting. I finally calmed down after sitting in a corner for a while.

After lunch, it was decided that my sister would take me back to the hospital along a different path, over a quiet hill behind the hospital. My nephew, who walked so fast, strode ahead of us for a while, then came back. He looked at his mom, then turned to me.

"I have to go back to work. I'll see you later tonight."

"Sure, sure. I know you're busy. Go ahead."

We walked through tall trees still holding onto a handful of dry leaves. Once in a while, a car went by slowly. The air was refreshing and cool and clean. A couple of magpies flew up and down, joyfully screaming. My sister opened her mouth.

"You should go to the countryside and relax."

"The country?"

I had nothing, I owned nothing in this world, other than those random, humble things that I had made in my prison cell.

"I guess you didn't hear about Professor Han in there."

At first, I did not know who she was talking about.

"Professor Han . . . who are you talking about?"

"Han Yoon Hee. You've forgotten?"

My heart stopped for a second as if it was frozen, and my arms and legs loosened up, as if my body were slowly submerging into warm water. I did not forget. I was afraid. I was afraid of hearing something bad. Where was she now, what was she doing? Her last letter had been confiscated eleven years ago.

"I haven't heard from her since I was moved to Choong Chung."

My sister seemed to hesitate for a moment, she was examining my face. She asked softly, "Did you . . . love her?"

I did not answer. I kept walking, with my head down, my feet rummaging through dry brown zelkova tree leaves. When I spoke again, it was not in answer to her question but a mumbled soliloquy.

"I still have her letters."

"She wrote to you?"

"A long time ago. Maybe three years ago."

We were standing side by side on top of the hill overlooking the hospital.

"You'll be discharged tomorrow?

"Yes, after some test results come back in the morning."

"Your brother-in-law will come and get you. Go, go back in there."

I went back to the hospital, changed into hospital pajamas, took my pills, and lay down in bed. I felt like smoking. I wanted to lock the door and smoke at least a couple of cigarettes back to back. I turned toward the wall.

From the bus, I can see the town below and far away. A church steeple, gray Japanese-style two-story buildings, old gabled roofs and newer slate roofs, all the way down the steep road. Darkness is falling. The main road leading to the town has yet to be paved. It is at the southern tip of the peninsular, not far from the ocean. Although it is the middle of winter, the wind is warm and green bamboo trees and camellia plants are everywhere. When the bus finally reaches the main station in town, the central avenue is illuminated with fluorescent lights and bare lightbulbs in every store along the way. I take a crumpled envelope from my coat pocket and make out the scribbled letters under a store light. I ask a man standing by the bus station. He gives me directions. "Walk along the central avenue until you see the junction in front of a pharmacy. Take a right. You'll see the police station and the local office of the department of education facing each other. Go up the road toward the girls' high school. That's the entrance to Soosung village." Around there I see the town mill. In front of the mill, I ask someone else for directions, this time reading the address out loud. Across the street on an empty field, children are celebrating the First Full Moon. They make a hole in an empty steel can, attach a string to it, fill it up with dried debris, light it, and spin it around. Sparks dance in circles in the air. There is a long, narrow pathway lined with low stone walls. The warm voices of happy people, chatting and laughing softly together and snacking on walnuts and chestnuts, escape into the street. Soon the full moon rises, clearly showing the low stone walls and the narrow pathway. As I was instructed, I stop in front of a pair of tall persimmon trees. They seem to sprout from the long stone walls. Instead of a gate, there are wooden pillars standing in front of a courtyard, and behind that a house with a gabled roof and a barking dog tied in front.

"Who is it?"

The house is southern-style, long and rectangular. A woman appears from the kitchen on the right side.

"The school teacher? She went out and hasn't come back."

I write down the house phone number.

"And whom shall I say came to see her?"

"Her brother's friend."

I walk out the way I went in. I eat a bowl of rice and broth for dinner and walk into the Hometown Café that I noticed before across the street from a pharmacy. I order coffee. I allow myself to be persuaded by a flirtatious waitress to order a cup of herbal tea, which costs a lot more than coffee. I waste at least two hours before I call the house. I give the phone number to the operator and wait. The person who answers the phone hollers her name several times. Finally I hear her voice. As always, she sounds calm and restrained. Based on her voice alone, I guess she is older.

"Mr. Yoon told me about you. I'll be there soon."

When she arrives, it looks like she didn't have time to change her clothes. Her trench coat is unbuttoned, and underneath she is wearing light brown knits. She finds me right away since I sit facing the door, and walks straight over to me.

"Are you the one who phoned?"

"Yes, I am."

"I'm Han Yoon Hee."

I pause for a second, then manage to utter some words while I swallow.

"I'm . . . Kim . . . Jun Woo."

A faint smile appears at the corner of her mouth.

"Of course that's not your real name. Let's get out of here."

Yoon Hee gets up, pays my bill without asking, and walks out the door. Afraid to lose her, I hurry and run down the stairs. She is already walking toward the pharmacy, each step deliberate. As I approach her, she walks faster. Near the marketplace full of pubs and cheap restaurants, she finally glances back to make sure I'm following her, then walks into one. When I reach her, Yoon Hee is sitting in a corner and looking at me. It is the most inconspicuous spot. I want to appear relaxed, so I smile.

"I've never seen a woman walk so fast!"

Yoon Hee answers in a low voice.

"Do you have any idea what kind of place that is, the Hometown Café? It is right in front of the police station. Half of their clientele are police. The waitresses blabber about whatever they see and hear."

"I didn't know."

"How long have you been underground?"

"Since last fall."

"It's about time you got tired of it."

"To be honest, yes."

"Did you eat dinner?"

"The first rule of a runaway is do not skip a meal."

"Then let's just order a bottle of soju and we can go."

"To where?"

"Where you're going to sleep tonight. You don't have anywhere else to go, do you?"

We drink in silence. Raw oysters are served with soju, and some broth, too. I still remember the old wooden table at that watering hole, its surface worn and marked. She walks and walks until we have left the town center and reached a solitary road. We stand and wait.

"There's a village near the temple, and there are many inns. Check into the Camellia Inn. I'll come see you tomorrow afternoon, so you should be in your room by then. It's the weekend, so there're going to be a lot of tourists. I'll call you when I'm nearby, and you come straight to see me. By the way, do you have money?"

She takes some money from her pocket and places it on a table. My fingers sneak up to the thin papers and enfold them, as if I won them in a bet. I catch the last bus, which is completely empty. Yoon Hee is still standing there, radiant under the full moon, now in the middle of a dark sky.

2

After I was discharged from the hospital, I went back to my sister's high-rise apartment building. I hated the place. When every family member went into their own room and closed the door, it was just like a prison, everyone perfectly locked down. There was no trace of the old village left in that neighborhood. All I could see were the interiors of cars, paved roads, and sidewalks overlaid with colorful blocks in various shapes.

One day I remembered a comrade who had finished his sentence seven or eight years ago. I asked around and found his phone number. When I called, at first he could not say a word. I patiently waited for him to calm down.

"Everyone has already heard that you are back. I called Seoul and everywhere else, but they kept saying we should leave you alone, let you rest a bit. We have a place for you here, too, we were just waiting for you to contact us."

"So how's everyone?"

"Good. Well-fed, a roof overhead . . . the world has changed so much."

He mumbled, somewhat like an old man. He was in his mid-forties. All my friends would be almost fifty or older. A generation was gone.

Kwangju. The word did not thump my heart any more. Before, whenever I envisioned that city's name, my whole body became enflamed as if there was a ring of fire around that word. Now it sounded like a famous tourist attraction. How many years had passed by? I began counting by nodding. One, two . . . seventeen, eighteen, nineteen. Would I recognize anyone? In my mind they were still babyfaced and gawky and so young. The dead are forever young.

I decided to take a trip and first unpacked my bags from the prison, spreading the contents all over the room. There was shabby underwear, a couple of winter sweaters, thick woolen socks, a muffler and knitted mittens, a few books, an unfinished tube of toothpaste and a new toothbrush with its bristle still stiff, a hand exerciser, and a golden turtle made by nonviolent criminals. The hand exerciser, along with the Buddhist prayer beads, were made by those who worked at the wood shop during their spare moments. A Chinese juniper stick was carved into an oval shape, then cut wooden pins were densely wedged in. On chilly mornings when my hands were frozen, they said, I should put it in one hand and roll it around inside my palm. It would be like getting an acupuncture, which would prevent frostbite and help blood circulation. I put the well-worn thing in my hand, then opened and closed it. The golden turtle was a large piece of laundry soap skillfully carved and painted glistening gold. It had a place of honor on top of the shelf next to the toilet, for good fortune. As soon as I had come outside, these things turned into shabby and pathetic junk.

"Why don't you throw it away, all of it."

My sister was looking in from behind.

"I will . . . later."

"Are you going somewhere?"

"Yeah, I want to see some old friends."

"Yes, I think it'll be good for you to change your environment. We'll look for a place for you while you're gone."

"My own place?"

"You know, you have to start preparing for a real life, get married, all that. Mother made me promise again and again before she passed away. There's something she left for you, too."

"Do you happen to know . . . Professor Han's address?"

"I told you, didn't I? I have her letters. I guess it'll be okay . . ."

She came closer and sat down.

"I wasn't going to tell you until later, but . . . she's dead."

I took a deep breath, broken in two, then slowly exhaled.

"At first, I just put them away, but we didn't know when you'd be out, so I opened and read them."

My head down, I just stared at the floor. My sister silently left the room then, a little later, opened the door and passed me a handful of letters.

"I'm not sure this is the right thing to do. I thought I'd give them to you much later."

The door was closed. There was the familiar circular handwriting of Yoon Hee. The envelopes, bearing the address of a small city college where she once worked, had become discolored and yellow during the last few years. The letters were sent to my sister's university. There were three of them. One was dated November 1995, the next February 1996, and the last simply Summer 1996.

Dear Hyun Woo,

It has been so long since I wrote your name down. I feel like I'm addressing someone who is no longer in this world. It breaks my heart.

Yes, it's been fifteen years since you left Kalmae. Did you receive the letter I sent to the prison on the year of the Olympics?

I'll tell you later, but that was a very difficult time for me. After that, I left the country for five years. Thanks to you, I painted a lot. I quit after two solo exhibitions, and now I don't want to paint any more. I guess I'm sick of this greedy world so full of cultural products. Meanwhile, you're hanging in there in the middle of it all like an icicle hanging from the slate roof of a shed, precarious but pure.

This letter is written by me, not your wife, not your child. I am no one to you. Perhaps it'll never reach you in prison. I wonder when you will be able to read my letters. So I thought of Professor Oh. At least, I knew the address of her university. Your comrades once told me your sentence would be reduced one day, but I can no longer welcome any change at this point. I'm not saying I don't want you to be released. The world has changed, and people are beginning to see errors, too late. And it's so lopsided. Then from the other side, those who caused many of those errors are now saying, 'see, we were right!' Ah, my precious one, what are you thinking now?

I'm not well. I know it's nothing serious, but I'm going to the doctor today. I want to quote what you used to quote often. "Even during the tempest, time passes." It's quite windy today. The glass windows are rattling. I would like to believe that even the tiny window of yours might let in many days of wind and rain and sunlight, nights of starlight and moonlight, the sound of birds and maybe even of people living in the distance.

I dream about you once in a while. But you know what's strange? You're always the person I knew in Kalmae. In my dreams you never answer me, no matter how many times I ask you to. I run around the kitchen, trying to prepare something delicious for you, but when I come back, the door to the terrace is wide open, so is the entrance. A strong wind has come into the house and the window drapes are fluttering. Already you're gone. Sometimes we are at the beach. Remember what you used to say? *Let's go to the last village on the peninsula, where there is no checkpoint. We can weave fishnets and harvest seaweed, spend a few days, bake some potatoes for dinner.* At the beach, I gaze at the boundless horizon. When I turn around, you are returning to the mountain, swinging your arms. You don't turn around, not even once, though I call for you again and again. Was that your imprisoned spirit?

I'll write again after the doctor's appointment. I think it's nothing. I am a prisoner here until you return to this side of life, a life of dust. I'll be perfectly healthy again.

November 1995, Yoon Hee

Ah, I'm shocked how long it has been since the last time.

So I wrote to you the day before I came to this hospital. I haven't forgotten you. I was a little surprised at first, but not too sad. They said I have cancer. It's already quite advanced. My body is shrinking, like a taut balloon losing air. But I still think clearly, and I think of Kalmae during the terrible long nights here. I think of everything, every facet of it, until I'm satisfied that I have collected my memories, down to the last, tiny fragment, then I fall asleep. The next evening, however, there are still things I've forgotten that must be added.

Do you remember that outdoor bathroom in the spooky bamboo field behind the fruit shed? The one with mud walls and ridiculously long and wide wooden supports and inhabited by monstrously big crickets. There was a piece of wooden board with a hole in it, and the container underneath was so deep. You used to joke that it took a while to hear something land at the bottom when you did your business. Once I had a stomachache in the middle of the night. I think I had eaten a bad watermelon. I begged you to escort me with a flashlight. I felt like I had returned to my childhood. You know that I am the eldest daughter. Once I turned ten, I had to go to the bathroom by myself and guard the door for my siblings, suppressing my own fear. Father at the time was always drunk, mom was out selling things and came back just before the curfew began. So when I say childhood, I mean before I started school. *Daddy, are you there? Yes, I'm here. Don't worry, take your time. Daddy, daddy! I'm here.* I kept calling you like I used to then. You said to me, *If you're scared, leave the door open. There's a cool breeze, and the stars are bright.* I peeked through the slightly opened door. There really was a night sky full of stars, like golden sand scattered everywhere. *Look, there goes a shooting star.* I saw it, too. A long, delicate line of light stretched across and then disappeared into darkness. I remembered a night like that while lying in this hospital bed and receiving painkillers.

Jung Hee has been taking care of me. It has already been three months. Of course, she is married now and has two children. Mom visits from time to time, but I begged her not to come too often, because she just sits over there and quietly weeps. Jung Hee will mail this letter for me.

I wish you were near me. Maybe it is better this way, I look so awful now. Flowers are still beautiful when dried out and dying, there's beauty while they fade away. Why does a person's body get so terribly destroyed?

February 1996, Yoon Hee

The doctor notified my family of something today. I read everything in Jung Hee's uncontrollable sobs. He must have told her to be prepared or something like that. Around noon, mom came by with a minister and a couple of her fellow churchgoers. Are you still a materialist? I'm not being sarcastic. I adore their faith. Who knows if there is something beyond the darkness. Still, if I could carry on longer. I want to see you once.

The hospital grounds were once filled with acacia flowers, so familiar from my youth. They are gone, swept away, and the world is covered with dark green.

After we left that place, I once painted your young face. Later, in the empty space I painted myself, older, as I looked then. You looked like my son.

Here's a lyric from a popular song. "Why can't love survive time? Why is love just like death?"

I once read in a Buddhist scripture. When the body dies, the part one was most attached to deteriorates first.

You in there, me out here, that's how we spent a lifetime. It was tough, but let us make peace with all the days. Goodbye, my darling.

Summer 1996, Your Yoon Hee

P.S. My sister passed away three days later, on the evening of July 21. According to her wish, her body was cremated. Before she died she said these words to me: *I'm going to Kalmae, tell Mr. Oh, if you see him later, tell him to please come there.* She made me promise, so I did. I do not know when Mr. Oh will be able to receive this letter, but I wanted you to know.

Han Jung Hee

After persevering in solitary confinement for a long time, your small emotions are mostly hidden deep underneath a thick layer of insensitivity. Showing them helps no one. In the beginning, you forget words. It's an easy one. You can't remember when last you actually wanted to use them. More words disappear from your mind, even the names of those around you. The next step is when you cannot recall names of everyday things that are right in front of you. *Wait a minute, what was that thing called?* Then comes the symptom of muttering to yourself. *Hey, it's time to sleep*, or *that guard is such a stickler*, or you fart and complain to yourself, *gee, that stinks.* Among the prisoners, those with long sentences rarely smile or cry. During the audio-visual education lessons, when they show you movies, prisoners shed their tears in darkness and cry to their heart's content. Their eyes are red and bloodshot when they walk out of the room. For those who have spent too much time in solitary confinement, however, their ability to express feelings is taken away. It is impossible to empathize. You forget words, feelings. Even your memories get bleached away.

I sat there in the room in a daze, her letters in my hand. Collecting myself, I put the letters back in their envelopes, then put them in the innermost pocket of the travel bag I had packed. My nephew was not home yet, he would probably be working late again. My brother-in-law and I sat in the living room while my sister prepared dinner. We sat a little apart on a sofa and stared at the television without talking. In between programs there was a cooking segment. A prim woman in her thirties wearing an apron brought out pots and pans and began cooking.

"In this hour, we'll make a soup with dried pollack. As many of you know, it is made in many different regions, a very well-known cure for hangovers. It's easy to make, and it is very soothing, a perfect soup to comfort those troubled stomachs the morning after."

Her hair was neatly pulled into a ponytail, a few strands falling to the side secured by a simple barrette in the shape of a butterfly. The neck of her sweater was modest, and her apron had blue stripes and was edged with frills. She looked like a proper housewife, an ordinary woman such as are found everywhere in the world.

"Here are the ingredients. We need dried pollack, ginger extract, chopped garlic, and some pepper for seasoning. Fifty grams of ground beef, and to season the meat we need one teaspoon of soy sauce, three tablespoons of chopped garlic, a little bit of pepper and one teaspoon of sesame oil. Also needed are one scallion, chopped, one egg, and a little salt."

Staring at the television and thinking of a warm pollack soup for a family, my eyes welled up and a tear rolled down my cheek. My brother-in-law saw this and was about to say something, but he turned around and lit a cigarette, pretending he did not notice anything. I stood up surreptitiously and sneaked into the bathroom. For the first time in a long time, I looked at myself reflected in a big mirror. My closely cropped hair was half gray, which made me look tired. Both eyes were bloodshot, and underneath them were two crescent bags deeply creased and shadowed. Without the prison uniform I looked like the old man I was. I washed my face with cold water. I dried my face, took a big breath through my nose, and went back to the living room. Both my sister and my brother-in-law pretended not to have noticed anything and remained silent. That was how I said goodbye to Han Yoon Hee.

3

The airplane was slowly descending. They no longer told us to lower the window shade as they used to. I looked down at the familiar landscape of fields and streams around the airport. Far away toward the downtown area of the city, something gray like smog or a fog was hovering, and the freeway was lined with bare trees on both sides.

As I left the gate, I saw him. He'd been pacing, and he raised his hand high when he saw me.

"Mr. Oh, here!"

"Kun! It's been too long!"

I hugged him tightly. Then I began to study his face. There were many strands of white hair from his temples to almost the top of his head, and many little lines around his eyes. I had seen Kun briefly at the detention cell, then we were separated. He finished his sentence and was released a few years before me. He was probably five or six years younger than me. I had escaped from Kwangju, but he took up arms as part of a civilian militia. Later, he was arrested for his underground activities. If he had been captured earlier at the state capital, Kun would have led a much easier life. Kun found me at my hiding place in the slums two days after the last crackdown at the state capital. His cheeks were hollow and his face haggard; he was wearing a shirt stained with dirt; he grimaced and burst into tears as he tried to hold on to us. *Sang Woon is dead. Young Joon insisted I get out first, later I saw he was gone, he got shot just once.* Ah, we would never be able to embrace each other again as we did that dawn. About one week later, the comrades who'd somehow flown from that city gathered, then spread out again, each looking for his own hole. Some people openly ignored us, some gave us a little money and begged us to go someplace else. Some accepted us as family and hid us.

"It's an old car. Someone gave me this."

Still a little proud of his car, Kun chattered on as he put on the seat-belt.

"You wanna go to the inn first?"

"No, let's go to Nam Soo."

"Of course."

Instead of taking the highway downtown, Kun half-turned the wheel.

"I'm going to take another way around. It's so congested."

"It has changed so much, hasn't it?"

"It's busier than the old Seoul. Every country bumpkin bought a car, it's swarming with cars."

"Is your sense of direction a little bit better now?"

We laughed together. It must have been better, since we avoided the traffic and drove around downtown. Soon we reached a quiet part of the town near the Mang Wal Cemetery. He stopped the car near the Moo Dung Mountain.

"You sit here and wait. I'll go get some flowers."

In one corner of the three-way road was a flower shop. I followed Kun out of the car. Pushing the glass door we entered the shop. I felt instantly better when I breathed in the fragrance of fresh flowers and moist, warm air. There were roses, gypsophilas, which had become common but since when I did not know, carnations, and different shades of mums. Kun was nodding his head, counting something in his mind. He bought different flowers and prepared four bouquets.

"Why are you buying so many?"

"Once you begin, there's no end. Just think of those you were really close to, how many there are."

I remained quiet and did as Kun suggested, and stood and walked behind him. The temperature had not dropped, but the wind was cold. We climbed the overhanging hill on the way up the mountain.

"Those up here, they're noninstitutional, and down there are institutional. Even the graveyard is divided into two."

Muttering under his breath, Kun climbed and found Nam Soo at once. Someone had brought him flowers, wilting away in a glass liquor bottle. Kun murmured as if he was talking to someone standing next to him.

"Hey, good to see you. I brought Mr. Hyun Woo today. You guys have a lot of catching up to do."

There was a little mound covered with dry grass shivering in the winter wind. *So . . . how are you*, I said without opening my mouth. I could see Nam Soo's tanned face breaking into a wide grin.

It's been more than twenty years since Nam Soo first went into hiding after the Reading Group incident. He was imprisoned for ten years because of a case involving another organization and was released before I was. During the bloody uprising in Kwangju he was already in prison, and by the time he was released I was in prison. When we first met in the seventies, I was a high school teacher in a small southern town and was preparing to leave the country to study abroad. We both were young and opposed the Yushin regime, which changed the constitutional law in order for General Park to continue his dictatorship. I read him a poem by Sergei Yesenin, handwritten in an old notebook. I do not remember where I got that notebook.

> Still around, old dear? How are you keeping?
> I too am around. Hello to you!
> May that magic twilight ever stream
> Over your cottage as it used to do
>
> People write how sad you are, and anxious
> For my sake, though you won't tell them so
> And that you in your old-fashioned jacket
> Out onto the highroad often go

I could not clearly remember what followed next. It was something like, *Don't go eating your heart out with worry that I am now an unknown drunk at a tavern for fear that someone will stick a knife into my chest.*

> I'll return when decked in white the branches
> In our orchard are with spring aglow

I recalled the night Nam Soo left for Seoul, sometime in the late seventies. At the time, I was renting the wing of an old-fashioned house. It had a sliding door that opened to a small porch, and next to the stone wall stood a magnificent zelkova tree. When the wind came, its branches shook and the leaves rubbed against each other, and it sounded like the sea. We turned off the light and lay down, listening to the waves of leaves. Nam Soo was restless, turning left and right, unable to fall asleep.

"You know what? The first time I was caught distributing the underground newspaper, when I was taken handcuffed to the interrogation room and slapped around, someone pretty high up from the Intelligence Office came in. He handed me the printed leaflet that I wrote and ordered me to read it out loud. So I stammered but read it. Then he slapped me really hard, and he screamed, *you bastard, my son goes to a good school, too, and do you think he's behaving himself because he doesn't know as much as you do?* Then he took out a gun and put it to my forehead. The muzzle looked so big, my knees gave out and I just knelt down in front of him. Whenever I think of that . . . it's just humiliating."

Nam Soo got up and sat. I fumbled in the dark and found a cigarette and lit it.

"Can't sleep?"

Suddenly, Nam Soo pushed the sliding door open. He looked out at the zelkova tree, its branches quivering in the dark.

"I want to be a real fighter now. This is the end of my half-heartedness, as of tonight."

"They say a road is made after many people walk on it."

"There's always someone ahead of everyone else."

Early the next morning, Nam Soo left for his hiding place in Seoul. All he had was a battered travel bag full of worn-out underwear and unwashed socks. When I walked with him that early morning, caged dogs barked and wailed all around. He left me a piece of paper onto which he had copied a letter from Che to Fidel, written when he had given up all his power and position in the party and had left for Bolivia. On the back was another letter from Che to his children about the future.

"Look, there are many more waiting for you over there," Kun said as he stepped away from Nam Soo's grave. I passed by the grave where Ki Soon and Sang Woon were buried together. They were married in a posthumous ceremony.

"Sang Woon is buried in the 5.18 cemetery down there. This is a temporary one. So you can see him again there."

We said hello to many different names. In the 5.18 cemetery were Sang Woon, Young Joon, and Chul Young, who passed away more recently. Chul Young, unlike me, spent nineteen years in a psychiatric hospital, his brain injured during torture. He lived his whole life stuck in that day. He lost his mind because the memory was frozen. Whenever his struggling wife came during a visitation, Chul Young asked her about the safety of those already dead and what was happening in front of the state capital. He'd been the last of the civilian militia in solitary confinement at a psychiatric hospital. Decorated with marble, the 5.18 cemetery looked more like another kind of prison. Where Nam Soo was resting was a real, older cemetery, where myriad friends gathered amiably. There, even the dry grass seemed warm and comfortable.

Kun took me out to dinner downtown. Nothing much had changed there. Some people had gathered at a Korean restaurant and were waiting for me.

The whole evening was a tedious performance, and I have no specific memory of it. I kept saying no, but despite my objections the gathering continued on to two subsequent bars and I lost consciousness in between. It was my first night out drinking since my release and I was cautious until someone at the first bar provoked someone else and began a fight. I think I took shot after shot at that point. What I remembered from the conversations we had that night played out like a strange movie that was shot slowly but projected at a furious pace.

"I guess there's no way to bail out Yang Hoon from his bankruptcy now, is there? How much did you put in there?"

"Just a couple, but it's just not right. What am I supposed to do, he just ran away after things went kaput!"

"Listen, listen, everyone from Kang Wook to Duk Hee took the parachute and got something but you? What are you doing, just looking after everyone else? What's the use of all these committees and boards and memorials when you can't even get a seat on the local assembly?"

"It gives me a headache, I want nothing to do with them. How come there are so many organizations related to the Kwangju Uprising?"

"The revolution is short but life is long, I guess. To be alive is to be ashamed."

"Look who's talking! Take care of yourself and don't fool around."

"It's a disease caused by too much to eat and too little to do."

"Don't just think of your business, think about others, too! Help some of them, at least show up for special occasions like funerals and weddings. Look what happened to Hyo Shin. We ignored him until his liver dried up and his face went totally black. What kind of community is that? Where's Bong Han tonight?"

"Well, well, look who's talking now. Community? It was shattered once compensation began."

"We always end up bickering when we get together. Why? Why is that?"

"Is this living? I am just empty and bitter inside, that's why."

I could not remember whose words turned the table upside down. It was quite certain that I was there, based on the red pepper sauce splattered all over my shirt. I climbed up the stairs of the inn, wobbling and supported by someone. I guess others staggered toward taxis or climbed into their cars, held up by their chauffeurs. Maybe they dozed off in the back of their taxis. Or maybe some felt lonely and stopped by a street bar and had another glass. What were they thinking, with a cold glass of soju on a stained table? Would they be as devastated as I was? There was a woman who came with me. I would presume someone who owned a business sent her with me, like he would do for a client or a government official he wanted to butter up, take care of me in bed. I yelled, I kicked the door, the bellboy was annoyed and pleaded with me to be quiet, the woman ran away, I vomited in the bathroom, in the sink. My mind was blank, I was sitting down on the bed in my underwear. Like I used to in solitary confinement, I spat out the words in a garbled mumble, "No one can win against time."

The telephone rang. I let it ring for a while before picking up.

"This is Bong Han. Kun called me and I'd like to take you out for lunch."

"Well, I'm still hungover . . . I guess I can leave now."

"You should take better care of yourself. Why did you drink so much?"

"They started it."

"How long are you staying here?"

"I don't know . . . I don't have a schedule. I have someplace else to go."

"Whatever, hurry up. I do want to see you."

He was a man of principles. He counted every bean, and he rarely trusted anyone but himself. He divided things into black and white and then cut them with a knife. Many people complained that he was hard-hearted. His life was locked up in Kwangju in 1980. In the middle of the massacres, he had escaped to Seoul and hidden in an attic for two years before he was smuggled out of the country. Kang Won, who wrote poetry, met him accidentally during his underground days, and the little study group they organized together became a network of spies. After serving five years in prison, Kang Won struggled to make ends meet and died of cancer like Nam Soo. I liked Bong Han and loathed him, equally. It would have been better if he had remained a revolutionary, like those of the Japanese occupation cra, but he was lucky enough to survive and unfortunate enough to live past the end of his own legend. For ten years he was in exile and managed to build several well-organized youth groups in Europe and America. I heard of him from time to time when I was in prison. Maybe he was now a scrapped vessel, his propeller gone, anchored at shore. But is there really anything you can devote yourself to for your whole life? I remember a phrase from a song.

> I know in my memory
> lies my strength

Slowly, very slowly, like a mound of earth dissolving little by little in the wind, what we wanted to accomplish was now leaving its mark on the world in a shape quite different from that we expected. But what could we do? There were still so many unknown days left.

"This town has gone to shit."

That was the first thing he spat out when I pleasantly greeted him.

"Maybe that's for the best. Now this city has gone back to normal."

Every fire in the world goes out eventually. What is left is ash. Perhaps some things are salvaged, but most are swept away by the wind.

"How's your health?"

"I think I'll be okay. And you?"

"Pretty bad. I once had a problem with my lungs, now it's back. I have to do these breathing exercises.."

"Are you . . . making ends meet?"

"I manage somehow. Have you ever seen me worry? You need to go somewhere and rest for a few months, figure things out. What are your plans?"

"I don't know . . . I guess I should look for a job."

"Kun didn't say anything to you?"

"About what."

"His wife died."

"How? Was she ill?"

Bong Han, watching his own words, turned his head toward the window and looked out toward the street.

"Hit by a car."

"What . . . ?"

"She was crazy, she jumped in front of it."

We stopped talking. He took the bowl of beef broth, bent his head down, and slowly sipped from it while blowing. I took a few spoonfuls in silence. Grasping the edge of the bowl, Bong Han's fingers looked like a bird's feet. Thin black lines of dirt were visible underneath his fingernails.

"I'm exhausted. This city wears everyone out."

"There should be new things to do, different from what we used to do. No more commemorations."

"Hyun Woo, do you have a line you follow?"

"A line?" But I did not laugh. Was there hope somewhere? If something like that still existed, that would be the line I would follow. I changed the subject.

"First of all, you have to get your life back. You're anonymous now. You're no one. You're no longer on the most wanted list, all of that is over. Everyone lies . . ."

I realized he could no longer get along with others now that he had returned home. Lunch was done. I wanted to part ways with him.

"Well, I better get going. I need to go somewhere."

"Where to?"

"Somewhere . . . if you see Kun, tell him I'm sorry I didn't say goodbye. I may come back on my way back to Seoul."

Bong Han seemed like he had more things to say, but I waved to him and walked toward the traffic. He shouted to me as I climbed into a taxi, "Take care."

The day I met Yoon Hee I was staying in a small inn, a traditional building with a gabled roof among the storefronts in Saha village. When you opened the sliding rice paper door, there was a small porch, and a few steps further, a ravine. It was pretty steep, and the waterfall was quite loud. The first night lying down on my futon, my ears were ringing but I got used to it quickly. It had already been five months since I'd fled. The advantages of Seoul were that it was my original zone of activity and I had many friends there. It was easy for me to find places to hide, but for the same reason it was more dangerous.

Bong Han had just switched his hiding place for the second time. He was at the top of the wanted list, and it was the most dangerous period for him. We were to meet in Miari in a billiard hall with two exits, one leading onto the main street, one into a back alley. It was around three or four in the afternoon, when there were plenty of people coming and going. I got the only empty table and pretended to play by myself, while I continuously watched the two exits. I did not see him come in, but Kwon Hyung was sitting there on a long bench under the scoreboard right behind the billiard table. He smoothly took a cue and hit a red ball as if it was now his turn.

"Bong Han is not coming. I dissuaded him. His pictures are everywhere."

"He should not meet with anyone from his hometown."

"Of course not. We're discussing the situation. He'll have to leave."

"Where will he go?"

"Wherever, he can't stay here."

We concentrated on our billiard game. I won both games. Perhaps because I was nervous, I played better than usual. As we climbed down the stairs from the billiard hall, Kwon Hyung gave a signal.

"Wanna stop at the restroom?"

I followed him into the restroom silently, we stood next to each other, looking into a mirror, and peed. He handed me a piece of paper.

"Read it over and memorize it. Don't forget to destroy it later."

I walked out of the alleyway first. He may have taken another way out; I did not see him. I was able to guess where Bong Han was hiding. Right before the whole thing blew up, around the tail end of martial law, three of us had searched for previously unknown places. After checking out the last one, we walked into a fortune-teller's place at a corner of a market. The owner was a female shaman. The three of us were totally embarrassed, but we obediently sat around the little table covered with raw rice. I think it was Kwon Hyung, who sometimes reminded me of an ascetic monk, who insisted that we have our fortunes told. The shaman kept mumbling and sucking on her teeth, as if she had been interrupted during her meal. She looked at me first. Out of the blue, she imitated a little child with a high-pitched voice. I forgot most of what she said, but I still vividly remember a few words.

"Mister, you'll be okay. You'll wander around in a faraway place, and then you'll be sick for a while. You'll stay put and suffer through it, then you'll be okay."

Next was Bong Han's turn.

"Mister, you were in prison, weren't you? And that's when your father passed away. Your father is still wandering around, he can't go to the netherworld. I can see blood right in front of you, sir, blood like a river. If you want to be released from your crimes, you must make a clean suit for your father and burn it in front of his grave."

It was March or April of 1980. I could never forget her word, blood like a river. I read the piece of paper from Bong Han.

One day, their crimes will be divulged, but it'll take some time. We have to stay alive in order to be witnesses. Do not hurry, be circumspect. I have sent words regarding your safety. I hope you find peace.

I tossed and turned for a while listening to the sounds from the ravine. With the first full moon of the year beaming down, the rice paper door was iridescent, and the shadow of bamboo trees draped elegantly on the back window facing the yard. I heard the wind chime hanging from the roof. For an instant, I tried to picture Miss Han Yoon Hee, my new protector. Because I'd only seen her briefly, I could not remember what she looked like. I do not remember how I spent the next day. I went up to the temple, I wandered in the forest . . . ah, now I remember. Right by the first entrance to the temple where pine trees were abundant, I sat on a rock to cool down. Underneath the rock where it was shaded, snow had frozen into ice, which was in turn slowly melting from the bottom, forming an endless little stream of pure droplets. I could hear a man and a woman talking to each other gently from down the hill. I guessed they were having a picnic. They were young. The man began singing in a high clear tenor. *I return to the hill where I used to play, the old poet lied when he said that nature does not change. The grand pine tree that once stood here is now gone, cut down.* I cannot forget their mindless singing. Just like an old movie. The girl laughed, the sound of water tumbling down a valley. They soon began singing in harmony. *Walking along the pasture in the evening, with my darling coming home, walking along the pasture in the evening . . .* I sat on the pine hill until late in the afternoon, until the wind became too cold. The singing youths had left the hill a long time before. I was already in my thirties, and maybe I envied their youthful energy.

Walking past an unfamiliar village in the rain, you can sometimes see a family in a lighted room, sharing dinner and conversation. You move from under the eaves and keep on walking, just glancing at them once. You can sometimes hear a mother call to her children who have gone too far to play. Or observe, from afar, a farmer and his wife sitting on a porch looking out onto their courtyard. The wife is shelling beans, the husband has just taken off his muddy boots. The farmer absentmindedly glances at the stranger, only half of his body visible over the low mud wall. The dog loses interest and stops barking. A night train passes over a bridge, the sleeper cars dimly lit. A black silhouette passes from one train car to the next by the train's outer steps. After dropping a cigarette butt between the fluid wheels, you check if there's someone in the next car. Walking into a vacant motel in a small village, there is a wanted poster right next to the door. All the programs on the black-and-white television are over for the day, its washed-out screen snowing with little specks of black and white light, and the woman at the reception desk is sleeping, leaning against the wall. The vinyl-covered floor has black holes here and there, and on top of a seat is an unbearably red fleece blanket. The fluorescent light bulb is making a *zzzzz* sound. In the guest register book, you write clearly the identification number that friends obtained for you. At night, you are too tired to wash your dirty socks, but you know it is important to appear clean and proper, so you wash your windbreaker and hang it up by the window. When you go on the road again in the morning, the wheels of the everyday world are obliviously turning as usual, nothing changed.

I went to see Han Yoon Hee, trusting the address Bong Han had gotten through numerous layers of contacts. I was going to quietly disappear if I detected any hesitation from her. She came to the inn around sunset. Yoon Hee was wearing a turtleneck sweater, a down parka, and a pair of casual pants. She did not look like someone going to work. In fact, carrying a little backpack, she looked more like a traveler than me. When Yoon Hee arrived, I had briefly fallen asleep in my room at the very back of the inn warmed by the wood furnace. Still, even in sleep, I felt the gentle movement and opened my eyes. The footsteps stopped on the porch, followed by a muffled cough. The sliding door cracked open silently. I stayed lying down, I just lifted my elbow from my forehead to turn my head and looked through the crack.

"Did I wake you?"

She opened the door a bit more but did not come inside. She sat down on the tiny porch and talked to me from there. I lazily stretched and got up.

"Get your stuff," was all she said and closed the door. I put on my jacket and socks and packed my bag. She was waiting for me standing outside the main gate of the inn.

"You didn't eat dinner yet?"

"No, I had a late lunch."

"Good. I'm very hungry."

Four or five hikers with huge backpacks passed us by. We went down toward the village, where stores and restaurants lined the street. There was a bus stop. The tourist bus stood still, while the local bus let out blue smoke, waiting for its scheduled departure. Three taxicabs, their drivers gone, were lined up.

"We'll go somewhere," Yoon Hee said. "We'll take the car from over there. After we eat, that is."

There was no one in the restaurant.

"What did you do all day?"

"Went to the temple, took a nap, things like that. Are you coming from work?"

"I went home and changed. Tomorrow is Saturday, so I have no class to teach. I don't have to go back to school until Monday."

"At school, what do you teach?"

She grinned a little, a bit bashful. From the first moment I met her, I liked Yoon Hee's mouth when she gently smiled.

"Art, painting."

"That's cool."

"What is?"

Then Yoon Hee took out a cigarette box from her parka pocket, put a cigarette to her mouth, and lit it.

"You can never trust an artist's talent. That's something I found out accidentally among the ruins of other numerous trials. You realize that at once at a school out here in the countryside. There're always a couple of students who have amazing potential."

"Who would believe in a self-deprecating artist?"

"Oh no, I'm not one yet. I'm thinking maybe I should try. There was this one girl, a real genius, and she dropped out of school last semester and went to the city. Something about working at a beauty salon. She never had a brush or anything for the class, so I bought her some. Her grades were awful. Her parents are farmers, she has three older sisters, and they all left to work at a factory or be a maid."

When Yoon Hee concentrated on talking, she pointed her index finger like a gun and swung it.

"Of course, her talent would be ruined if she went to art school."

"Are you from around here?" I asked her. I had been wondering. It was very important for me to know where my protector was from. If someone who knew her well saw me with her, there would be questions.

"Unfortunately I'm from Seoul, born and raised. Now, aren't I allowed to ask some questions, too?"

"Go ahead."

"That name is really . . . are you really Kim . . . Jun Woo?"

"What's wrong with my name?"

"That's the name of the guy who disappeared into the Hwarang cigarette smoke, like the one in that song?"*

I almost burst into laughter. Instead I asked, "How do you know Mr. Yoon?"

"I don't know him that well. I can't tell you how or where, but I met him once, just once. You should know this: I'm not an activist."

"You should know—you may get into trouble later if you help someone in hiding."

Yoon Hee replied with her usual gentle smile. Her teeth peeked through her lips for a second and then disappeared again.

"I saw the tape from Kwangju. The NHK version. The local priest lent it to me."

Her expression had changed. There were shadows under her eyes, and she opened her mouth a little and shook her head as if she was weary.

"I can't forgive them. And I could finally understand my father."

"Your father?"

"No . . . he drank his life away."

"What happened to him?"

"He was a casualty of history. Let's change the subject. Why are you avoiding answering my question?"

"Which was . . ."

"If you are trusting me with your safety, you should tell me about yourself. Your real name, and since you don't look like a student, what your job was, what did you do, meaning why did you go into hiding? Isn't it natural for me to be a little curious?"

---

* The word "Jun Woo" means a fellow soldier or a "war buddy" in Korean. The Hwarang cigarette was a brand of cigarette specifically supplied to the military. There is a famous song from the fifties that ends with the following lyric: "My dear fellow soldiers [jun woo] who disappeared into the smoke of Hwarang cigarette."

"Yes, of course."

I felt a bit apologetic as I answered.

"My name is Oh Hyun Woo. I'm thirty-two years old. Until a couple of years ago I had a teaching post in a middle school in a small village, like you, Miss Han. I got involved in the student movement while I was at university. I went to prison briefly, then I was forced into military service and served at the DMZ zone. And the rest I'll tell you later."

"My goodness, too much information for such a short time!"

We left the restaurant. We climbed into the backseat of a taxicab, the driver's seat still empty.

"Is it okay to do this?" I asked. Uneasy, I looked around. Yoon Hee smiled.

"He'll be here soon. And you're single, of course?"

"Until now."

The taxi driver, wearing only the top of his uniform, was walking slowly toward us. Yoon Hee added quickly, "From now on, I'll do all the talking."

The driver checked out his passengers and climbed into his seat. Yoon Hee told him the destination, and I closed my eyes and pretended to sleep. The taxi traveled on an unpaved road, clouds of dust trailing behind, and crossed a hill. Our destination was the next village. It took about twenty minutes. We arrived at a tiny depot that looked like any other depot in any other town and got out. Yoon Hee left the taxi stand and walked down the main street, again just like in any other town.

"I think it'll be better to take a bus from here. We could have continued in the taxi, though. With a direct bus, it takes about forty minutes to my school."

"Where are we going now?"

"Just follow me. I'm taking you to paradise."

There was a movie theater, its door tightly shut and looking more like a dilapidated warehouse. Maybe it opened only in the evening. We waited for a bus at a stop in front of the movie theater. Yoon Hee opened her mouth.

"I found it while I was roaming the countryside to draw. I have a studio there."

"Then why don't you move in, too? You said the school is not too far."

"I'm going to."

The bus approached slowly. It was not a market day, and there were not many people in the bus. A few students here, a few women there, each occupying a seat. As soon as we sat down, the bus left. A driver's assistant tottered over to collect our fare.

"Where to?"

"Two for Kalmae."

From the main road the bus took a narrow pass between mountains. On one side was a deep valley, where melted snow from the mountaintop formed a stream and flowed down, bubbling up here and there. Up on the rolling hills, farmhouses and neatly trimmed fruit trees stood in rows. This village was so affluent because it had the most orchards in the province. On both sides of the valley were narrow rice paddies in steps, and around the stream were eulalias that had flowered last fall but were still holding on to their white tufts, gently dancing in the wind. Yoon Hee and I got out of the bus above the valley, in front of a cement bridge, before the bus clattered away into the distance.

We crossed the bridge and, after the bend in the mountain, what had been hidden by the valley was finally exposed. Directly in front of us, a round hill sat like a person with both arms and legs wide open. Scattered on the southern end of its foot were a handful of houses. No one from the other side of the valley would have guessed that there was a hamlet like this across the bridge and down the narrow path. A small stream slowly glided down from the valley, and on its bank there was even a water mill with a thatched roof. Behind the orchards was a dark green bamboo forest. We were at the threshold of spring, the wind was warm and murmuring, and it carried the fragrance of earth. A couple of magpies cheerfully chirped while flying up and down a persimmon tree with only a few, dried-out fruits left. Yoon Hee took a deep breath, as if she was tasting the wind, and she whispered:

"This is Kalmae."

4

Now, I am going back to Kalmae.

Eighteen years ago on the night a typhoon arrived, I left for Seoul. Yoon Hee followed me to the bridge, holding onto an umbrella. Her peasant skirt with printed flowers was wet, her pointy rubber shoes kept coming off. The headlights of the last bus appeared out of the darkness. What looked like the eyes of a beast got bigger and bigger, reflected in the pouring rain. I turned around once before climbing up into the bus. Yoon Hee was going to say something but instead raised one arm halfway and meekly waved her hand. As soon as I got in, the bus departed. I tumbled and hurried toward the back window. For an instant I saw a trace of her body holding the umbrella, but it quickly disappeared into darkness.

The local route was now neatly paved, and the bus made only infrequent stops. When the familiar village came into view, I was somewhat depressed and bewildered by the changed scenery. The tiny depot had become a full-fledged bus terminal located at the outskirts of what had become a small city. The main street was much wider and lined with four- and five-story buildings. At intervals there were higher buildings with almost twenty stories, jutting like uneven teeth. I got into a taxi waiting at the station.

"Where would you like to go?"

"To Kalmae, please."

The chauffeur seemed a little flabbergasted. He had not started the car yet.

"Why . . . is there a problem?"

The chauffeur clucked his tongue and started the car.

"It's not a problem, it's just not far enough."

"But shouldn't it take at least twenty minutes?"

He glanced at me through the rearview mirror.

"Maximum ten. I'll have to double the fare."

"Fine."

I began to feel uneasy. Passing through the downtown area, I looked at the new buildings, so straight and rectangular, the high-rise apartment buildings hovering where rice paddies and vegetable fields used to be. Would Kalmae still look like what I remembered? I could not ask the chauffeur. The sleek cement road extended to the outskirts, the traffic line clearly marked in the center. Passenger cars and trucks busily passed by. Was there still a stream coming down the valley? There were pillars and railings painted to glow in the dark. There were rice paddies and fields, but up on the hill where an orchard used to be was a factory.

The bridge was still there! But it looked different. The railing was now stone pillars, sleekly carved into flower buds. The taxi turned nimbly into a smooth and flat street, not a narrow passage in between mountains. As soon as we entered the hamlet, a pair of wooden pillars greeted us. The first thing I noticed was black words written on a plank announcing "Kalmae Garden," a Korean barbeque restaurant. The orchards on the right side of the mountain were gone. Instead there was a new development with colorful rooftops and a few more billboards. There was a log house, a white house with a terrace and panel windows, even a thatched house, the color of its roof a strange, bright yellow. Cars were parked everywhere, and in front of the taxi I was riding a black passenger car moved slowly. Through the window I could see the heads of a man and a woman sitting side by side.

On the left there were still orchards, but half the size they used to be. There was a billboard with "Todam, Traditional Tea Salon" written on it. The house of the vice principal, the old house with trifoliate orange trees, was hidden behind this new building. I got out of the car and slowly climbed the hill. Passing by the tea salon, I looked in and saw some guests at a few tables. The newly paved road went up to the new building, but beyond it the old dirt trail remained. There was a house still surrounded by trifoliate orange trees. My heart was beating fast. I approached the house little by little, savoring the suspense. A yellow dog tied to the pillar wagged his tail and barked at the same time. There was a spigot where a hand pump used to be, but the house was the same, a long rectangular, Southern-style house with a long side porch made of wooden panels. The courtyard was empty and there was no sign of people in the house. I stood by the entrance and looked around. "Who are you looking for?"

The voice had come from behind me suddenly, and startled, I turned around quickly. There was a familiar face, but a changed one, like gradually chipped and worn household items I had seen. Suspicious, she narrowed her eyes and studied me slowly, from top to bottom. There she was, the wife of the vice principal, the Soonchun lady.* I bowed.

"How are you, ma'am?"

"Who are you? I think I know you but I can't quite place you."

"I'm . . . I'm the one who was preparing for the big exam."

I was sure she knew everything by now, but Yoon Hee had introduced her companion as her boyfriend who was studying for government exams. The Soonchun lady's mouth was wide open, she clapped her hands lightly. Finally, a sound came out of her mouth.

"My goodness, my goodness! Are you really . . . ? Mr. Oh? Mr. Oh Hyun Woo?"

She grabbed my hands and stroked them with hers.

"What you must have gone through. But when were you released? My God . . . and you never got to see Miss Han."

The Soonchun lady pulled me to the porch and made me sit down. For no reason, I looked at a photo frame on the wall. In it were a number

---

* In Korea, some elder women are referred to with the name of her hometown, not by their own names. Soonchun is the name of a small city in South Korea.

of old and yellowed pictures. Her eyes welled up, she gazed at me for a little while.

"Miss Han's sister came here once. I thought it was strange that she waited a year, but I just assumed she'd been abroad. And she closed her eyes without seeing this day . . ."

I humbly bowed my head and waited for her grumbling to end. Finally I turned my head toward the house and blurted out, "This place has changed a lot, too."

"It's a different place now. The power of money."

"And your husband . . ."

"He had a stroke. He suffered for a while and passed away a while ago. My first and second sons went to the big city, and I live with my youngest now. He runs the tea salon over there. He's trying to make a living."

Her husband had been the vice principal of the neighboring village's elementary school. He was a man of few words, badly nearsighted, always wore a pair of thick glasses, and if he had one weakness it was that he loved to drink. I liked him, with his stubby nose and squinting eyes, and on several occasions we went fishing together in the levee over the mountain. He never asked me anything, but he had an idea I was not staying there to study. Once, when the local government was doing a survey, he covered for me by saying that I was a distant relative.

"Let's go inside. Did you eat lunch?"

"Yes, I already did. I just want to go see the house in the back."

"Oh yes, it's still there. Miss Han fixed it up nicely about three years ago. She bought the house and the yard a long time ago. Her sister looked in on it, but we don't know what she plans to do with it."

The Soonchun lady took the lead and walked out the door. She turned onto a narrow path next to the trifoliate orange trees. Behind the bamboo forest I glimpsed the house surrounded by the familiar sight of persimmon trees, chestnut trees, and alders. Entering the courtyard, I saw a spigot connected to the water supply. It was standing on cement ground, the edges raised to form a barrier, complete with a low basin and a drain. It was unnecessary, but the Soonchun lady turned the water on to demonstrate that it worked. Water gushed out.

"Look, this winter's been so warm it didn't freeze. I think it was done about ten years ago. The village collected money to dig a well and install a motorized pump and all that."

The courtyard was covered with tall weeds, dried yellow and trembling in the wind. There were remnants of my own renovation of the place so many years ago. The house was originally used as a fruit shed. When we moved in, we divided it into two and remodeled one side as living quarters and the other as Yoon Hee's studio. After laying a foundation for the wall, I inlaid the leftover stones from the front porch around the house to the outdoor restroom to act as stepping stones and a gutter. Over time, they had settled into the ground nicely, surrounded by weeds. Originally the wall of cement blocks was bare, but now it was insulated with bricks and painted white. The front porch and the latticed entrance door were still there, even the glass panel between rice papers still remained. I opened the door. The window that looked out onto the mountain was now made of glass, instead of a board one pushed up. The linoleum floor was no longer there; it had been replaced with traditional paper treated with bean oil, which retained a subtle sheen. What did remain was a double shelf supported by a pair of triangular brackets on the eastern wall. It was something I made when I bought a piece of board and logs in town and smoothed them with a plane. On top of the shelf were old books and odds and ends wrapped in a cloth. I turned toward her studio. Instead of the old wooden door was a sliding door with glass panels, which allowed me to look inside. The studio previously had a hard, concrete floor, with a tiny door and a raised wooden floor so small it could only fit one person. Now the whole floor was covered with wood, and the old-fashioned hearth was replaced by a modern kitchen sink. I also saw in the studio a coal briquette stove, a sofa and chairs, an easel and canvases, pails and wooden boards covered in paint. I turned to the Soonchun lady who was following me around.

"Would it be possible for me to stay here for a few days?"

"Of course, as you wish. This is your house, too. We need to heat up the room, though."

"Is there a furnace?"

"No, she wanted to keep that as it used to be. We got rid of the hearth in the kitchen, but put a new fuel hole in the back."

I went around the house to the right. There was a small shed with beams attached to the house and topped with a slate roof. The fuel hole was covered with blackened aluminum. The shed was protected from the wind by a simple wall on the northern side and inside were stacks of logs and kindling.

"We used the room from time to time, when our children came to visit or if we had a guest. It's been empty for a few months, though. It needs to be cleaned."

"If I can borrow a broom and a mop, I'll do it."

"No, no, no, you shouldn't do that. Go for a walk or something, I'll do it as quickly as I can."

"That's okay, I can do it by myself."

Then I added, a bit forcefully, to forestall the Soonchun lady from prevailing, "I want to think about her while I clean."

As I expected, she gently gave in.

"Of course . . . I understand."

I took off my shoes outside the studio, pushed the glass sliding door to the side, and entered. The chill of the floor traveled up my feet, and the subtle scent of pine resin lingered in the air. Wait, I remember. What was that smell? It starts with a T . . . turpentine. Yoon Hee used to pour it onto her palette whenever she tempered her colors from the tube, holding two or three brushes in one hand. She always smelled like turpentine, the scent clinging to her clothes and apron with its numerous colors. I picked up her palette. There still remained traces of her brush where it had smoothed out paint after she squeezed it onto the palette. I could see the traces of bristles. The hand holding the palette was trembling weakly, and I felt her touch. Her fingerprints were left on the squeezed paint tubes, their openings hardened with dried paint. I looked through the neatly stacked canvases in the corner, as if leafing through a book. At the bottom I found a small canvas and placed it on the empty easel. Two heads painted close to each other. The face on the left is mine. I am wearing a white short-sleeved shirt with a blue checked pattern. It was the last summer I spent outside. Everyone wore their hair long then, and the painted me has hair long enough to cover the collar of my shirt. There is a dark shadow around my eyes, and my hollowed cheek hints at the anguish of that time. The background is painted mainly in a dark red with dark cobalt blue stripes added lengthwise, emphasizing the melancholic tone. At first she painted a latticed door with rice paper next to my face, but Yoon Hee later painted over it with gray and put her own face in, as she wrote in a letter. After so long, I studied her face. Yoon Hee expressed herself with a rougher and thicker touch, layering paint, unlike how she painted me. There are gray patches on her head, and her eyes are only a few black lines, which made it hard to read their expression. Her cheekbones are emphasized, and slightly different hues of paint were applied to her cheeks, indicating both her disappearing youth and the richness of her soul. And there it is, that mysterious smile of hers that I always loved, perfectly captured in the lines of her lips and chin. She meets my eyes with a smile on her face. A young man of thirty-two years of age and a middle-aged woman are looking at me, each with a different colored background.

I remained in front of the easel long after the Soonchun lady brought me cleaning supplies. Feeling cold, I remembered the Soonchun lady telling me I should get briquettes from her if I wanted to light the stove. I got up from the chair and walked down the dirt path. The Soonchun lady looked toward me from her kitchen and gestured.

"These briquettes are already lit, take them."

She showed me a tin pail that would fit two briquettes and a pair of tongs.

"Start with those two and put some wood in the hearth. It'll be warm enough. I'll tell my son to bring you more later."

"No, that's okay. I can just bring a couple at a time."

"And you should have dinner with me."

I put the two lit briquettes in the tin pail, picked up a new one with the tongs, and walked back. I returned to the kitchen, this time piling four briquettes into the tin pail. Little by little, I brought up a dozen briquettes to pile in the shed. I put two lit briquettes in the hearth and added a couple of unlit ones on top. The hearth still had plenty of space left, but I thought four would be enough. Soon, the house was warm. I searched through the kitchen cabinets to see what was in there. Maybe I wanted to find more remnants of Yoon Hee. I took out a kettle with a blackened bottom and filled it with water, to make use of the fact that the kitchen sink was now outfitted with running water. I put the kettle on the stove, then filled the sink with more water and wet a cloth. I bent down on the floor and pushed the wet cloth from one end of the room to the other, like I used to at school when I was a child. The cloth became black and dirty after only a few wipes. I gathered up canvasses and palettes and brushes and dried tubes of paint and put them in one corner. I gathered sketch pads piled on a table, then stopped. I wanted to see the traces she left with pencils or crayons. There were quick sketches and writings, compositions being worked out. People or similar-looking objects were depicted with lines like spider webs, from different angles and in different positions, overlapping. Like a strange comic strip, there was a peculiar figure with only eyes and stick legs. Many scenes stood among various tools and instruments, its story a riddle waiting to be solved. A book filled with graffiti went on for page after page. And sometimes gibberish was scribbled at the bottom of the page, like lines for a play.

> There they put you in a regular cage consisting of two layers of wire mesh; or rather, a small cage stands freely inside a larger one, and the prisoner only sees the visitor through this double trelliswork. It was just at the end of a six-day hunger strike, and I was so weak that the Commanding Officer of the fortress had almost to carry me into the visitors' room. I had to hold on with both hands to the wires of the cage, and this must certainly have strengthened my resemblance to a wild beast in the zoo. The cage was standing in a rather dark corner of the room, and my brother pressed his face against the wires. "Where are you?" he kept on asking, continually wiping away the tears that clouded his glasses.*

Ah, sometimes I wish he would visit me. So I clean the dusty glass pane, the one he so painstakingly fitted himself, and look through the trees and down the dirt path, to the road to the orchard. Wishing he was walking toward me.

* A letter from Rosa Luxemburg to Sophie Liebknecht, dated February 18, 1917.

I wish I had lived with firmer convictions.
Always on guard and covered with honorable wounds.
I regret the days I've wasted because of fear.
I was exiled only once.
I wish I had lived more courageously!*

Rosa once wrote in a letter that she wanted this poem to be her epitaph. But later she corrected this, as if she were mocking herself.

Mathilde, you don't think I'm a serious person, do you? Do not laugh at me. I don't want a lie written on my tomb. All I need on my grave are two words: twit twit. A sound of a little bird chirping. That little bird is flying to me now, I am so used to that sound. It is always clear and pretty and shiny like fish scales. Think about it. One day, you'll hear the little sound of twit twit. Do you know what that means? It is the sound of an early spring. When it's snowing outside, when it's covered in frost, when we're lonely, the little bird and I believe that the spring will come. If I cannot wait until then, if I die before the spring comes, please do not forget to write just 'twit twit' on my tombstone.**

Rosa Luxemburg fell down like a dog when the Freikorps officials struck her head with rifle butts. A lieutenant put a bullet into her head, although she was already unconscious. They put Rosa's dead body in a truck and drove around, then threw it into the Landwehr canal near the Tiergarten. There is no twit twit, no song of a little bird on her epitaph. Only a few dying red carnations, a symbol of Rosa, left by someone. In Berlin, I used to have light snacks at the Tiergarten. I remember eating little bread rolls called Brötchen while sitting on a bench not far from her grave.

---

* A poem by Conrad Ferdinand Meyer, quoted in a letter from Luxemburg to Mathilde Jacob.
** Ibid.

I will always come back here. And I will prepare something delicious for the fledgling poet. If he comes back, and if I could last until I can sit next to his deathbed. But what was it, what does it mean now, the first step we took together? All the vivid dreams have disappeared like smoke, and there is not a scene I can recall clearly. Do I call this state of vagueness love? An old woman once told me, *If I dream, I can't remember anything when I wake up. I guess my brain is not working as well as it did when I was young. What is this, why am I dreaming about this? But then I can't make heads or tails out of it. I think and think, but I can't figure it out. I wish I could see the dead people. But you know what? When you see the dead in your dreams, it's kind of boring. It's like looking at a vegetable, so dull. Look at that dog over there, he wags his tail when he sees someone he knows, right? It's not even close to that! You can't communicate.*

I traveled far away and I came back here. But Kalmae has disappeared. I decided to fix the house. Found my old letters high up on a shelf and reread them for a long time. So childish and full of dreams. I was about to throw them into the fire but decided to keep them. Like a passing monsoon, those two people. That young man and young woman do not exist today.

Can such direct opposites exist? Looked at monographs on Bosch and Bruegel all day. Bosch's nightmare of a despondent hell and Bruegel's valiant living human beings. In fact, they are the front and back of the same body. The scene is filled with a vast field, and a cow and a farmer plowing. In the left hand corner is a tiny ocean the size of a palm, and there, I can barely make it out, the two legs of a man who fell headlong into the sea. This is called the Fall of Icarus. Compared to everyday life, the fall of an idealist who flew too high with candle-wax wings is an unremarkable tragedy.

I walked around the courtyard, stepping on the stones that he'd laid one by one. I stopped and decided to flip one of them. It was repulsive and fascinating. There were three earthworms, a handful of sow bugs, a few clumps of green moss. I even saw deeply embedded in that moist earth the white root of a violet that had stubbornly sprouted under the stone. I regretted disturbing this little universe. I thought of the world a little bit while carefully placing the stone back exactly has it was.

Art, what the hell. Will never paint again. Meaningless innumerable mistakes. The word "mistake" is quite amusing. In Chinese, it means the tracing of a lost hand. Today, I continue writing the old letter to him.

I closed Yoon Hee's sketchbook and finished cleaning the room. I kept thinking I should warm up the room more, so I went out and walked toward the fuel hole. First, I stacked a handful of thin branches and ignited them with a lighter. Like a wriggling little animal, the flame spread to the top. I picked a few thicker branches and broke them. They were stacked over the flame, crossing each other to support a couple of logs on top. They were so dry that they caught easily without emitting too much smoke. I put a couple more logs in. The fuel hole was soon filled with warm yellow light, and the warmth spread to my lower body. I stared blankly at the flame. It looked like the tongue of a live creature, licking the fuel hole and spreading toward the kitchen.

The first day we arrived here, Yoon Hee did not go back. She started the fire with me in front of this fuel hole. Each of us insisted on starting the fire and finally agreed to do it together. One of us said, *Do you know how much fun it is to start a fire?* The other said, *Who doesn't know that?* And we coughed and cried because of the peppery smoke from the pine tree branches that were still fresh. The smell of smoke, the darkness, so warm, our bodies getting closer.

There was no electricity at the time, only one candle to light the room. A month after living there, we brought in cables from the main house and installed a fluorescent light. We decided that we liked the candle better. We borrowed two flannel blankets from the owners that first night. The floor was burning up, it was so hot. Each of us took a blanket and slept on opposite sides of the room, maintaining a careful distance from each other.

After filling up the fuel hole I went back to the room to finish mopping. By the time I was done, the sun had set and darkness had fallen. Under the fluorescent light, the paper window was an even paler shade of white, and the glass window darkened to black.

5

After dinner I walked down to Todam, the Traditional Tea Salon, run by the youngest son of the Soonchun lady. I became reacquainted with the Bunny Boy, who was now in his thirties. Yoon Hee and I had adored the youngest boy at the main house. We frequently sent him on errands to the village in order to give him pocket money. Yoon Hee nicknamed him the Bunny Boy because his two front teeth protruded and his eyes were so round. It is inevitably disappointing to see someone you knew as a child all grown up. A child has a future full of possibilities, yet there is no shadow of greed. All too soon, however, the childish ingenuity and innocence are gone without a trace. As the face matures, layers of tired guile are added. The Bunny Boy was not shy at all. Instead, he seemed to be guarded or sneering at me, this old man who had returned. When I said how sorry I was to see Kalmae changed so much, he said, quite firmly, that I did not know the reality, that the village needed to be developed further. His wife, the youngest daughter-in-law of the Soonchun lady, only went to village schools and had never lived in a big city, but she still looked like a woman who enjoyed more urban surroundings like Kwangju. They called me Uncle, a small gesture they offered to acknowledge my connection to his parents in the past. As I left, I bought a pack of cigarettes for the first time.

I opened the packet, pulled out a cigarette, and held it up to my mouth. In prison, on snowy days when the cement wall was covered with water droplets as frost melted and the chill from the bare floor penetrated my knees, I would think of warm sake. I imagined the guard on duty having a psychotic episode and secretly pushing a cup of it through the little slot they put the meals through. I walked into the bathroom and looked at the sky, the heavy snow falling through the tiny window cross-cut with bars. My breath dissipated into the air like cigarette smoke. If only I could have had one shot of sake and one cigarette on nights like that.

In the middle of the night, I was awoken as the calm valley began to stir slowly with the sounds of the imminent spring. I heard the little stream flowing, the endless sounds of lonely wind grazing the bamboo leaves. Trying to calm my fluttering heart, I found myself sitting in front of a bundle wrapped in cloth, which I had taken down from the shelf.

In the bundle was something I recognized. Recently, it had become possible to get elegant holiday cards with various designs from the outside world, but for a long time only a limited number of cards of poor quality printing and paper were available to prisoners. This was a card with a picture of a pine tree and a crane. I was certain I sent this to her from the holding cell shortly after I was arrested. I opened the folded card. The thirty-two-year-old me was still in there, frozen in the discolored writing.

Dear Yoon Hee,
    The first night I came here, I stood on top of a paint can and saw a few bright stars in the empty darkness far away. Or I thought they were stars. The next day I realized that those were lights from the ghetto up on the hill. In the early evening the hill was covered with lights, but close to dawn, they disappeared one by one. There is one over there, and all the way over there another. Eventually I began to wonder why the window would become a star. As a sleepless heart becomes a star, mine would become another.

There were also a few postcards that I had sent around that time. Perhaps she wrote back to me, but I never received a reply. I did not receive anything until the new president was elected.

My dearest Yoon Hee,

The trial is over. I am sure you already heard what the outcome was. They sentenced me to life. It didn't feel real. When I returned from the court, the chief guard called me. He is a devout Christian, and I am told that he did this not just to me but to murderers who received death sentences. He held my hand and prayed. I don't remember exactly what he said. After returning to my cell, I read scribbles left on the wall by previous prisoners and began to ponder. There was one phrase, 'existence is happiness.' It seemed time was standing still. I slept for two days and nights, but it seemed like the same day. The third night I paced around the whole night and didn't sleep. I felt like I had no life to live anymore, but then I braced myself with the thought that in order to persevere for a long time I would need to consider this my home.

I stopped reading my own postcard and thought of Mr. Huh and the young Mr. Choi. Already I could not recall their first names. They were both on death row. Mr. Huh was in his early forties. Since he had been on death row for eight years by the time I got there, I presumed he had begun his sentence when he was around my age. He was in a solitary cell like I was, and our cells were right next to each other. While others washed up in the communal bath, the two of us brought two big barrels of hot water into the staff restroom and had a steam bath. Mr. Huh was a big guy with powerful hands, and he knew how to scrub well. He used to soak his lower body in water and quietly chant Buddhist prayers. Every spring Mr. Huh was depressed and withdrawn, rarely talking to anyone. This was because they usually carried out executions when the seasons changed, especially in the new spring after a long winter. A few mornings I saw that his eyes were swollen and bloodshot, perhaps because he cried alone at night worrying about his daughter, who he entrusted to a Buddhist temple before he came in here. I would put on a concerned face and lie, *You've been waiting for so long, I'm sure you'll be pardoned.* He would contort his expressionless face in an attempt to smile and mumble as if he did not care, *I should go soon, I trouble too many people.* The young Mr. Choi, who came later, was a smart and gentle guy. His widowed mother visited him often, and encircling his wrist were Buddhist prayer beads, carved out of bo tree, that his mother had made. The reason I cannot forget them is because I found out about their deaths the day before they happened. The chief guard for our block wanted to see me, so I went to his office, skipping my afternoon exercise. He was leaning over his desk, intently reading some papers. Without realizing that I was waiting right behind his back, he did not take his eyes off of them. Inadvertently, over his shoulder, I saw a list of names, among them Mr. Huh and the young Mr. Choi. Sensing someone was behind, the chief hurriedly turned the paper face down and turned his chair around to face me. *What is it?* I asked casually. Still nervous, he looked around then raised one hand. He made the hand as stiff as a knife and motioned cutting his throat. Quickly understanding, I mouthed the word *when?* without making a sound, and he mouthed back *tomorrow.* I returned to my cell and had to witness with the eyes of death the everyday life of two men. After dinner, when we were allowed to visit each other's cells, the young Mr. Choi asked me the date and hour of my birth. He told me about his own fortune which he'd read in a book. He talked about his old age as it would unfold a few decades from now, whereas I knew he had only a few hours left to live. That memory has been engraved on my heart for a long time. Early the next morning, as soon as the wake up call rang, Mr. Huh began beating his wooden gong and chanted his morning prayers. I got up as well and paced around, whispering the name of Ksitigarbha bodhisattva over and over again. I went out first for my daily exercise; they did theirs right before lunch. Maybe everyone sensed something from the guards, maybe we all have a sixth sense. Everyone, from the old-timers to the petty criminals, was nervous without knowing why, and the entire block sunk into silence. I sat in my cell cross-legged with my back straight. There was no sound, not even the usual greetings we shouted to each other when the meal arrived. They say they feed you first because the well-fed ghost is prettier. As soon as lunch was over, the men with red hats rushed in. It was eerily quiet. They must have gotten Mr. Huh first. I heard him grumbling, *Why did you fill me up? It's going to be ugly. If I knew, I would have had only fruit juice.* He paused in front of my door. *Mr. Oh, I'm going first. See you again later, but take your time.* After he walked away, it was the young Mr. Choi who quietly stood in front of my door. *Look, here . . . Take this. And please write a letter to my mother.* What he handed me was the prayer beads. I could never forget Mr. Huh and the young Mr. Choi. It was as if they were my family. I understood early on what time meant for a lifer.

My dearest Yoon Hee,

I am being transferred to another prison the day after tomorrow. Once I am there I won't go anywhere else, they say, since I am a lifer. I will stay there for a long time. Don't be sad. I know I am being cruel, but I have to say that my prison cell will become my coffin. Only immediate family members are allowed to visit and write letters, and what I read will be censored, too. The lawyers said that this affair of our organization was pretty hopeless from the beginning, yet it could be quite useful to paint us as political casualties. I can't write about it too much, I know it'll be censored.

In here, when a woman finds new life, they say she puts her rubber shoes on backwards. That's what they said when a thief with numerous criminal records came back to the cell with his head down, his face covered with tears and crushed, that his wife put her rubber shoes on backwards. Don't hate me. I have too many hours to spend in here, so please, Yoon Hee, I want you to turn your shoes around.

Now I regret that didn't I stay in Kalmae longer, even only for a few months. Or a few weeks. Even only for one day.

There were a handful of postcards that I had sent and about twenty notebooks of similar sizes but different paper quality and binding. Each notebook was numbered with a sticker; perhaps she had organized them later. I opened the first notebook.

It was exactly one year ago that you left. I went through some changes, too. First, I quit school. I am no longer a teacher. I resigned during the last winter break. The school found out that I had provided refuge for you, and it became a big issue all the way up to the ministry of education. I have become your common-law wife. The police did not treat me too roughly. But because of my father's past, they wanted a thorough interrogation, which lasted fifteen days. I have decided that I do not want to do anything here, just rest for a while, then apply to graduate schools. I will need to do something to dissipate the eternity. One half of this notebook was written while I was living here alone. The latter half was written much later, when I was visiting Kalmae twice a year, summer and winter.

Like a preface, this was written on the first page. She must have written it after she finished this notebook.

A woman I knew from my university sent word that someone connected to the Kwangju Incident would come see me. How unlucky I was. Nothing ever happened when I breezily passed through the southern provinces before. I graduated and took the exam to become a teacher. I found a job, and it wasn't easy, and all of sudden I had this responsibility. Not just any but an enormous responsibility that put me at risk. If I hadn't stopped by her studio in Seoul, if I hadn't copied the videotape from the priest, if I hadn't been in the Cholla province during the massacre, I would have been able to live through this age effortlessly. I had no luck. But when was I ever lucky? As long as I was my mother's daughter, there is no way I could be lucky.

When I first met you at the Hometown Café, I was nervous because it was right in front of the police station. But the lighting was so bad in there, I did not get to see your face clearly. Only after we moved to the pub near the market was I able to really look at you. I already knew your name but you came up with such an obviously fake name that I had to suppress my laughter. My first impression was that you reminded me of my father in his youth. Of course, I was not born when he was a young man, I mean the portrait I painted of him based on his photos and what my mother had told us. At first, I could not tell you the story of my father. I vaguely referred to him as someone wounded by history. I still cherish two photos that capture his youth. One was taken when he was studying in Tokyo, and he is wearing a college cap and gown. Everyone in those old, discolored photos looks so mature and illustrious, don't they? He would probably have finished Kant and Hegel or maybe Feuerbach, and around the time the photo was taken he had begun Engels and Marx. He would have found paperbacks of *Capital* and *The Communist Manifesto* at the used bookstores in Kanda.

The other one is the picture in question, taken during his stagnant period just after the October insurrection in Daegu in 1945. Men usually had short hair at the time, but my father has long hair parted in the middle, a symbol of intellectuals, and he is wearing what looks like the uniform from the Japanese occupation period, buttoned all the way up his neck. According to my mother, he was not able to return home for about eighteen months at that time. So he took the picture at a photographer's studio in an unknown city where he was active and sent it home around New Year's Day. I was not yet born, but my older brother was. I do not know what he looks like, he died at the age of five in the countryside. Later, my father would cry out his name when he got drunk. In this photo, my father looks like a professional revolutionary from Russia or Ireland, his cheeks shallow and his eyes blazing intensely. That was the end of his youth. After he took that picture he was arrested, then he escaped and went into the mountains. Naturally, I found all this out many years later.

I guess it is natural that I somehow saw in your face my young father. I grew up hating him, and later I hated myself for that and became reconciled with him. Remarkably, I got to understand him perfectly while I nursed him as he was dying of liver cancer. In your face, I saw what was imprinted in the face of my father, photographed in a studio—in a setting that looks like a makeshift stage with curtains and white fences and a window and a painted background of a gas lamp and the moon—in an unfamiliar city; the youthful hunger and the determined heroism, something like a fever. I do not know why, but just like you have said, the classic activists have an air of a consumptive or a rejected writer. Why can't they look like a practical engineer or a professional, a doctor or something like that? Ah, I'm sorry, I am not being cynical. What I mean is that I felt close to you that way.

When we first went to Kalmae, I actually had no plans to move there. In an old-fashioned agricultural community, a female teacher cannot live as openly with a man without a job or known history. But if we were not so explicit, who would believe our story? The first night, we started the fire together. The kitchen fireplace was so warm and cozy. Without realizing, I found I was humming. The melody came from a song my father sang while in the mountains. You were quietly watching the fire and said to me, "Miss Hahn, I am a socialist."

Even though the term was not quite fashionable at the time, I wasn't too surprised, as I had already gone through so much within our family. Mischievously, I asked cheekily, "Well, are you sure about that?"

"I am leaning toward that," you replied sheepishly. I guess you felt you had said too much and you were embarrassed about using that word. It doesn't look too bad when men do that. Looks a bit immature, but somehow reassuring.

When I went back to work after that first weekend, the little foxes at the girl's school smelled something. They kept commenting that I looked different or something. Ah, really. You asked me a few times, but I really didn't feel anything special toward you at the beginning. Just friendly. I don't know why, but I just could not wait to tell you about my father and discuss all the issues with you.

I went back the following weekend. You had already turned that storage house into a living space, you also did the floor for my work space. I was so uneasy about my decision to move in.

I remember us going to the village to buy pots and pans and food, and having dinner across from each other. How could I tell you about my father without becoming truly intimate with you? I remember a friend at school once saying, don't share a meal with any man, you become intimate when you eat together. Remember at the beginning how we slept far apart from each other, with the two fleece blankets borrowed from the owners of the house? We lay there like that, our backs turned to each other, and talked until late, unable to sleep. I think I began to mention my father after a few days.

When I was in elementary school, we lived in Seoul and moved around a lot. My mother was the sole breadwinner, and we could afford to buy a house only years later. Jung Hee was too young to go to school, so whenever my mother was out I made breakfast and woke my father, since he always went to bed drunk. Since we moved around so much I went to many different schools. One day at a new school, my teacher told me to go to the principal's office. There was a stranger waiting for me.

"You're Han Yoon Hee?"

Then he said my father's name and asked if that was my father. When I said yes, he asked if I knew our address, and I said no I didn't. The principal told me, "Go pack your book bag and come back here. You can leave early today."

I was afraid that something had happened at home, and I was scared of the man in the leather jacket with piercing eyes. As I walked home, the man followed me. As we walked together, the man asked me questions.

"Do any men come to your house?"

"No."

"Does your mom still sell clothes at the market?"

"Yes."

"What does your father do?"

"He just stays home."

"What does he do at home?"

"Nothing."

"You have a radio at home?"

"Yes, we do."

"How many? Do you have a really small one?"

"We only have one."

"Who gives your father money for drinks?"

"Mom does before she goes to work in the morning."

When we got home, on that particular day, my father was sober. He saw me coming home unusually early, and the man who was following me, and got angry.

"I told you I'd contact you! You went to my kid's school? Do you really have to do this?"

"My bosses want a report and I couldn't get in touch with you. What's the use getting mad at me?"

My father left with the man and came back late that night. He was even more drunk than usual and could not walk straight. I heard my parents screaming and fighting, and though I couldn't hear the full details I found out that the man was a detective and that my father had to report to him whenever we moved.

When he was sober, my father always read books. He collected paperbacks in Japanese and English from used bookstores. We were proud of him because he knew so much more than we did, though we didn't like that he drank too much. He was never affected by hot or cold weather. In winter, he never wore long johns, always just a pair of pants. During the hottest days of summer, he sat quietly in his room all day, cross-legged and slowly fanning himself. He always sat straight and upright, and once he settled down he did not move. His feet were grotesque and ugly. There were only three toes on his right foot, and his left foot was missing its little toe. Plus both his ankle bones protruded like a hard rock. When we were little, Jung Hee and I used to pinch and scratch the hardened calluses on his anklebones and giggle.

When I told you about my father's feet, you calmly interrupted me. You said his feet looked like that because he spent years in prison during difficult times. That we would know why if we spent one winter on a cold cement floor.

There were so many anti-Communist rallies and events. At school we were constantly assigned to design an anti-Communist poster, write an essay about crushing communism, or prepare an anti-Communist speech for a contest. I was in seventh grade when I was painting a poster as homework. Since elementary school I had always been praised for my artwork, but I never received any serious training. My mother was against it. Only in my senior year in high school was I sent to a drawing class for a few months to learn how to draw and prepare for a college entrance exam. Anyway, I was doing this homework, and at that age I was mostly familiar with comic books, so I did a picture like something from a comic book. On top I wrote in red 'Crush the Commies!' There were three adults, a muscular soldier and two civilians—a man and a woman. Arm in arm, they trampled on a red monster with horns and canine teeth and hair all over his body. For a while I was concentrating on painting the monster's entire body in red, so I did not realize how long my father had been looking at my picture from behind me.

"What are you doing, Yoon Hee?"

I replied proudly.

"Our homework is to make an anti-Communist poster."

"I see . . . so who is that monster with horns down there?"

"This is a Communist."

"He's really grotesque."

"Because he is a Communist."

At the time, he did not say anything more. But later, it all blew up. My painting was selected as one of ten the school sent to the national competition, and I won a prize. I received a letter of commendation with gilded decorations and as a prize a sketchbook and an expensive set of water-colors in many different shades. As I entered our courtyard I saw my father sitting on the porch, so I shouted in delight, "Father, I got an award!"

He was drunk, and when he saw the letter of commenda-tion, his hands began to tremble. At once, he tore it in two. Then in four, then into many little pieces. He threw them away, scattering them all over the courtyard, and threw away the sketchbook and watercolors too. The sketchbook flew across the courtyard, landed in a water basin, and quickly sank while the watercolors were scattered all over the court-yard. Speechless with shock, I collapsed onto the ground and cried.

"What, you think you did the right thing? You think that the Northerners are not our people? Award? For what?"

I was so hurt and embarrassed by his drunken frenzy that I just went to my bedroom and cried under the covers. My mother probably heard what had happened from Jung Hee when she came home. But instead of shouting and getting angry at my drunk father, she was unusually silent that night. I felt betrayed by her.

I finally became aware of his past, little by little, when I was in high school. My mother told me one story after another, as if she was unwinding a long skein of thread. I knew that my father had had a tough time and faced many dangers during the Korean War, but I just assumed that he was "on our side." Ah, but my father was that hideous, scary, red guerilla. From then on, I could never forgive him. He was the root of all our problems.

I was a senior in high school the first time I defied my father. Finally my mother had bought a store of her own in the marketplace and a small gabled house for us to live in. We wanted a more stable life. After school on certain days of the week, I went to an art studio to practice my drawing instead of going home. On those days I got home after nine at night. My mother was always late, usually coming home past eleven after closing the store, so either Jung Hee or I cooked dinner, whoever was home first. Normally Jung Hee had dinner ready when I came back from the art studio, but that night she was late as well and just had a bowl of ramen for her own dinner. I was starving but decided to cook some rice for my mother, who would come home later, and my father, who had not returned home yet. I was washing the rice by the faucet in the courtyard when my father came back. He was completely drunk, as usual, and stumbling. Looking at my staggering father, I felt sad and annoyed and angry. I glared at him while I stayed seated in front of the water. He stumbled and stopped in front of me.

"What is this, you're making dinner now? There are two grown-up girls here, and dinner is not ready?"

If he had just passed me by and gone into his room, if he had fallen asleep turned toward the wall and scrunched like a shrimp as he usually did, then I would have made sure he had his blankets and a glass of water to drink when he woke up. I slowly got up and faced him.

"Since when were you so worried about this family that you're now concerned about dinner? All you need is alcohol, you don't care about us."

He stood there, his face vacant. I could not stop myself.

"Have you ever done a decent thing in your life? Have you ever acted like a head of our family that we could be proud of? We want our mom to stay home like everyone else's moms. I'm not asking for a father I could boast about to other people, I just want a father who works hard for his family."

My father slowly sank down and sat on the porch, his shoes still on. He looked at me, silent. I had finally managed to spit out the words that always lingered in my mouth but that I had been unable to speak before.

"All you can give us is the label that we're children of a Commie, is there anything else?"

Then he walked slowly toward me without stumbling,

without saying a word. He slapped me once, on my face. His shoulders were trembling as he walked to his room. He went in and closed the door quietly. Maybe he went to sleep, the room remained dark. I wept silently, not because my cheek hurt or I was ashamed to be slapped, but because I felt guilty that I had done something unforgivable to my own father. The next morning, I went to the door of my parents' bedroom and whispered, "I'm going to school."

My mother was still in a deep sleep, exhausted. The sliding door opened quietly.

"Yoon Hee, come closer."

Through the slightly opened door I saw my father's long and thin face. As if he was trying hard to smile, he crinkled his eyes with dark circles and looked at me. He handed over a slender book.

"I went to Kwanghwamoon yesterday . . . I bought this for you."

Once in a while, my father went to a foreign bookstore in the Kwanghwamoon neighborhood to look around and sometimes he came home with a book or a magazine. What he gave me was a Japanese paperback. It is now one of my most cherished books. A book on Goya's etchings. That world full of scary, extraordinary disasters and pain. You can feel the hand of an absolute master. As I received the book, I became more embarrassed by what had happened the night before.

"Father, I am so sorry about last night."

"I know. Hurry, go to school."

A few days later, I heard from my mom why he was so extremely drunk that night. After the Revitalizing Reforms of October 1972, the Law for Society's Safety was introduced. Under this new law, anyone who once infringed on the Anti-Communism Law was to be reinvestigated, some of them imprisoned depending on the outcome. My father needed a sponsor. I guess it could have been a lot worse. All his life, my father lived in disgrace because of the old scars he carried. I found out much later, when I spent many hours nursing him, that he had already "converted" years ago, that he had denied his belief in communism and socialism and had pledged loyalty to the government of South Korea. He was alive thanks to my mother's family. When he was captured in the mountains and sent to a detention camp in Namwon, my mother's oldest brother took action and made sure that my father received a more favorable classification. Thanks to that, my father received a five-year sentence instead of being executed without trial. My uncle was a lawyer when he passed away, but he passed the bar exam during the Japanese occupation and was a prosecutor of political offenders after the liberation. My father hated seeing his powerful, eminent brother-in-law, but my mom frequently went to his house for a sobbing session. I remember going to my uncle's house with her when I was little. While she knelt in front of her screaming and scolding brother in the library, I would snack on sweet rice cakes or red bean jellies that my aunt brought out.

Ah, I can picture that day, my father meeting my mother at the market and together going to my uncle's law office to beg for clemency. I can imagine my father's return home. After sending my mom back to the market, he walks down the busy, unheeding street in the middle of the day, in the world where no one believes in his future. On the grand avenues full of government buildings, where the whole street would freeze during the daily ceremony of lowering the national flag, my father tries to breathe and wander around the dark corridors of foreign bookstores and used bookstores. And he buys the book on Goya for me, feeling the same way he did when he first saw the Goyas in Tokyo as a young man from a colony. Those black-and-white images are like fearful groans issuing from war and oppression.

I will write later about our reconciliation, the year I was able to go back to his past. I already told you I was with him from the moment we found out about his incurable condition to the moment he died.

Now that I think about it, I was waiting for you. Maybe I blamed myself. When I was young I did not try to understand my father, and when I grew up and became a college student I did nothing about the military dictatorship. I read as much as I could about the other side. Then one day, you appeared. I remember the day we first kissed. It was one spring day, on a weekend, when you finished remodeling our room and my studio.

6

I closed Yoon Hee's notebook and lay down for a bit. Most of the stories about her father I already knew because I had heard them from her. Yoon Hee talked about her family whenever she had a chance. I could picture her father even better than Yoon Hee, like adding light and shadow and background to a drawing with only thick lines.

When I became involved in the organization in the late seventies, it did not happen by accident. The summer Nam Soo left for Seoul, I was invited to a certain gathering. Around that time, several Christian groups were actively working all over the country, and this gathering was for both Christians and non-Christians active in various fields, from the labor movement to factory night schools to street protests, to share information and encourage each other. Most people involved in the youth and labor movements had started while they were students, and many had been to prison already. In reality, the gathering was pretty harmless. People presented field cases that were already well-known throughout the country, and we would debate in groups about current events and just get to know each other and socialize. After dinner I left the building to smoke a cigarette, and a man approached me. He was short, with a square head and sparkling eyes, a young man of my age.

"I wanted to introduce myself. My name is Choi Dong Woo."

"I'm Oh Hyun Woo."

"Ah, I know you well."

"How . . . ?"

"You went to prison during the October Struggle. You were one of the first to oppose the Reforms in '72, right? I was in the same class with Park Suk Joon."

"Wow, I see. So glad to meet you. What are you doing now?"

"After the military, I went to work at a factory in Inchon. But I'm going to quit soon."

That was how I met Choi Dong Woo. We didn't say much more there, but I did mention the small village where I was teaching and found out Dong Woo was born and raised there. He said his eldest uncle still lived there. After the gathering was over, we automatically walked home together. He spent two nights in the house I was renting in the countryside. Something he said on one of those nights deeply reverberated with me.

"Don't you think that our history post-liberation is just like the game of stacking up Korean chess pieces? You start with a couple, then more, and you think you've finished building this tower. But there's this irresistible force that slams the board, and the chess pieces fall like a sand castle. On top of ashes and bloody ruins we start building again, one by one. We all know the ultimate limitation, but instead of overcoming it we just keep building and collapsing and building and collapsing, again and again. What do you think that ultimate limitation is? It could be something you can see, something tangible, or it could be a metaphysical concept. It is the division of our country and foreign influence."

We returned to the question we used to debate endlessly, the question of radical versus popular politics. I was still hesitant. I remembered how I wasn't able to say anything when Nam Soo said he wanted to be a real fighter. After he left, I met Nam Soo several times in Seoul. He was much calmer than he'd been before. Once I met him in a park, and he was carrying a huge bundle. We went to a big mansion where a young couple lived and spent the whole night talking, just the two of us. He was in the middle of an operation. The organization he belonged to had begun a new project in different parts of the city, and Nam Soo was in charge of the western section, distributing leaflets on each university campus. Earlier that day he had studied his routes around that part of the city. From his bundle he brought out a roller and a mimeograph. He put them into another bag. He said they were trying hard to get a more efficient printer. I told him that I knew a missionary who might be able to locate one for them. Nam Soo whispered to me, "I am just going crazy inside because I'm so nervous. We all started at different points, but we're all walking the same road, so there isn't that much conflict. When you go up a mountain, there's a little path, there's a wide road, then there's a steep path covered with thorns. You'll only find out which one is the right path when you're standing at the summit."

After I began to get close to Choi Dong Woo, I ended my stay in the country and moved to Kwangju. Once there, Nam Soo urged me to join the organization. In order to do so, I first needed to form my own group and prove myself by writing and distributing leaflets and training others. Dong Woo did not like the idea. We had already begun our own study group with almost twenty people. We were not an official group recognized by a bigger organization, but our work progressed with seriousness and depth. By the end of the seventies, our membership had grown to over thirty. Of course, other than the first five founding members, each was contacted and managed separately.

Nam Soo's group ended up being arrested first. When I thought about it later it was a great pity. If they had been active during May of 1980, the resistance in Kwangju might have evolved exponentially.

I escaped Kwangju on the twentieth of May 1980. Two days before, soldiers stormed into my friends' houses and dragged them away with guns pointed at their heads. Many in Seoul were also arrested early in the morning. Choi Dong Woo and Park Suk Joon both begged me to return to the capital.

I was not able to take the direct train; instead I took a bus all the way to Masan, then took a night train. As promised, I got out at Youngde-ungpo Station. First we went to Dong Woo's house. He was staying in an empty sweatshop factory that his brother used to run. There was a spacious factory building, a storage house, and even a bedroom for people doing night shifts, a perfect hiding place. We didn't need to debate, we immediately began the work of publicizing what had happened in

Kwangju. We obtained a professional printer with hand levers. I wrote the leaflet, Dong Woo printed it, and Suk Joon filled two duffle bags with leaflets and distributed them among our members.

In the late seventies, at the end of President Park's regime, the police were on high alert, so we had to be even more precise and cautious. We carved incendiary slogans on a rubber pad and inked and stamped them on the thin paper used in typewriters. Most of the slogans were short and intense, mottos of less than ten words. All work was done with our fingers covered by rubber thimbles from the pharmacy, and the printed paper was cut into thin strips with scissors. We put them in the inner pockets of our jackets or coats like money and went to busy markets and streets full of people on weekends. The inner pocket would be torn, and we walked around leaving trails of paper strips. Sometimes we hastily wrote slogans with felt-tip pens on stickers and put them on the backs of bus seats or inside telephone booths. One member actually put a sticker on someone's back in a packed bus.

But by the time of the Kwangju Uprising it was different. We knew very well we would fail, but we believed that the truth would be revealed, even if it took a long time, and we believed in a future where the world would be transformed into a righteous place. A tiny stream of water can make a crack in a formidable stone, which becomes a hole, which becomes bigger and eventually causes it to collapse. We formed teams, two in each, and divided Seoul into four zones. The A Zone was where many government and business offices were, a southwest corner of the downtown area within the four gates of Old Seoul. The B Zone was the university area, the C Zone was the industrial area on the outskirts of the city and around the slums, and the D Zone was the corner stores in various neighborhoods. Each zone was divided into four quadrants, and each team was responsible for each zone. Among them, the A Zone was considered the most critical and perhaps the most dangerous, but we considered the area—with many high rises and big companies full of the more educated office workers—as an important strategic target. We thought the leaflets would have the most impact in the B and C Zones, and that these would be much safer than the A Zone. The D Zone would act as a buffer between the other zones, a safe station where we could gather before and after each operation. There were some grander operations in which all of us spread leaflets at the same time all over the city, but most of the time each team took a day and distributed leaflets irregularly, at several times. Dong Woo and I were a team, Suk Joon and Kun another, and we took turns studying the area or checking other teams when they were in action.

Dong Woo was used to doing these sorts of things. When President Carter visited Korea in June 1979, Dong Woo teamed up with a religion student to burn the welcome arches erected for the occasion, as a protest against the United States' acceptance of the military dictatorship. There were two teams of three, one taking an arch on the second bridge of Han River. Dong Woo's team took an arch in Kwanghwamoon. The operation was to begin at 7:00 p.m. the night before Carter's arrival, but unfortunately it rained that night. Although it was just a soft drizzle, it was enough to soak the sheets of plywood that made up the arch. The team responsible for the bridge prepared gasoline, but no matter how much they poured on, the fire would not light and they failed to accomplish the mission. Dong Woo's team at Kwanghwamoon waited until the operating hour at a bakery next to the old Kookje Cinema. Inside his parka, Dong Woo was carrying two cans of lighter fluid. His team members were the seminary student and an unemployed man who had just finished his military service. First, Dong Woo climbed the steel structure that formed the spine of the plywood arch. When he reached a certain height, he poured both cans of lighter fluid onto the plywood. After Dong Woo sneaked down, the other two climbed up while he kept watch. They hadn't rehearsed, so no one knew how explosive the lighter fluid was. The moment they lit the fluid, it blew up. Caught off-guard, the seminary student fell down to the ground, followed by the unemployed man whose hands were both red. People on the street stopped and gathered around. Dong Woo rescued the seminary student from those trying to capture him by hitting them with his umbrella, and the two of them ran to the alleyway behind the Kookje Cinema. The unemployed man was in such a hurry he ran across the road full of speeding cars and toward Mookyo-dong. He became even more disoriented with cars screeching to a halt and honking. That night, about half of the arch was burnt and scorched. But the restoration began early the next morning, and by the time people were going to work there stood a welcoming arch, its color even more vivid and fresh. Our work was as useless as throwing an egg against a rock.

During the precarious weeks following the Kwangju Uprising in May 1980, our usual gathering points were bakeries or, quite common at the time, casual restaurants with lots of booths serving Western food on the outskirts of Seoul. The chosen bakeries were frequented by housewives, not businessmen or people in law enforcement. Furthermore, most bakeries were empty around dinnertime. And the Western-style restaurants were usually dark, playing loud music, and full of young people out on dates. In the back corner booth of one of these places, we could talk safely. Dong Woo was usually my companion, and we were sometimes joined by Park Suk Joon. We would order a pitcher of beer and wait for hours for Kun, who manned the phones in another location, to contact us. The password for the all-clear was simple: "going home." If a team needed to be summoned, Kun met the captain elsewhere and brought him to us. The operation was usually carried out during the evening rush hour, and once everything was done and our members had moved to a safe zone, it would usually be around 8:00 p.m. Kun was usually in charge of safety check, but sometimes Suk Joon did it. Each of us wore the only suit we owned, always clean and nicely pressed, and a white dress shirt and a tie. To anyone watching, we looked like a group of fine young salaried men who had just left work for the day. I remember the waiter would call out a name when someone in the restaurant had a phone call.

"There's a phone call for Mr. Kim!"

I leave the booth to talk on the phone.

"This is Kim."

"Hey guys. Hae Soon wants to go out with you."

"Bring her over, then."

Dong Woo and Kun get up and disappear, and I wait for them by myself. Around 9:00 p.m., two people finally make an appearance by the door and search around. I remain in my seat patiently until they circle the restaurant to find me. Hae Soon finds me first and she collapses into the other side of the booth. Suk Joon finds another table by the entrance and sits there facing the door. Hae Soon's short hair is wet and plastered to her forehead.

"Is it raining outside?"

When I ask her, she brushes her bangs back.

"This is sweat. Ugh, it was really bad."

"Something happened?"

"I want a new partner."

"Where's Duk Hwa?"

"Don't mention his name. Do you know how much money I spent on taxis today?"

"You were in Myung-dong today, right?"

There had been two teams operating that day. We had already heard from the other team that they had finished work in Shinchon and gone to a safe zone.

"We were almost caught. I told you I didn't want some nerd who went to college!"

Hae Soon was a factory worker who was fired from her job. She was working with Dong Woo, and it was impossible for her to find another job because she was on a blacklist. Some members collected money to buy a few knitting machines for them, but among the five who were fired from the same factory, Hae Soon and Jung Ja joined our organization. We put the two in separate teams and made sure they didn't run into each other too often. Hae Soon was not happy with this arrangement in which she had to work with college students.

Hae Soon was teamed up with Duk Hwa. During the Kwangju Uprising period there were too many checkpoints and inspections downtown, and it became too conspicuous to carry a big backpack or a duffle bag. Hae Soon made a sack out of cloth that she could put around her waist under her skirt. She could stuff about a hundred leaflets in there. Duk Hwa opened his shirt and put leaflets inside and put a barn coat on top. Their assigned spot was an underground passageway at the entrance of Myung-dong. Following our rules, they surveyed the area first and decided to carry out the operation during rush hour, after sunset. At first, each of them would go down the underground pathway from different entrances, then spread the leaflets as they passed each other and run away. But, as she told us, "Duk Hwa insisted that this was too risky. He told me to get a cab and wait for him while he distributed them at the entrance of Myung-dong by himself, and then we could get away in the cab. I guessed he wasn't confident because I was a woman. And of course, I was right. He was scared." Hae Soon said she squatted, took out the leaflets she was carrying, and handed them over. Duk Hwa took the ones from his shirt and clutched them in each hand. But Hae Soon did not go to get a cab. Instead, unable to trust him, she watched from behind, anxious. Duk Hwa appeared to take a peek under the passageway stairs, then suddenly threw down the leaflets and ran away without turning back. Hae Soon saw the leaflets, still in a batch, lying there in the middle of the stairway, perfectly positioned for someone to pick them up and report to the police. Without thinking, Hae Soon ran down the stairs and picked up the batch, spread it out like a fan, and threw the leaflets into the air in two handfuls. Fortunately, there were only a couple of people walking up and down the steps at that moment. Hae Soon went up and searched for Duk Hwa in the direction he ran, but there were too many people. She grabbed a taxicab that was approaching slowly and went toward Uljiro. "While in the car I saw him running toward the end of Uljiro with his hair flying. I lowered the window and called him as I passed, but he didn't hear me. I couldn't stop the taxi, there were all these cars behind. I looked back and saw his face, it was so red. He should have been walking, that would have made him less conspicuous."

"So where did he go?"

"I don't know. He didn't show up at the first meeting point. I waited for half an hour, just as the rules dictate, then I called Suk Joon and came to the second convening point."

I considered this for a moment. It was clear that Duk Hwa was under too much pressure, and the work we were doing was too much for him to handle. I decided to exclude him. I left Kun, who found him, to take care of the rest.

In Seoul that May, different teams were active. Without talking to each other, we were all aware of each other's operations and activities. There were a couple of incidents where the word spread underground, when a demonstration was planned in front of the Youngdeungpo market or in Chongro. Different groups waited at both sidewalks and alleys. When the time came, a small group in Youngdeungpo ran into the wide traffic lane shouting slogans, and was captured almost immediately. In Chongro, the activist leader climbed to the top of the Christian Association building, from which he shouted slogans and distributed leaflets and threw himself down, but those waiting on the street didn't know what was going on and were unable to turn it into a bigger protest.

Early one morning we received word that the last battle and the crackdown in the state capital in Kwangju were over. Dong Woo and I had left his brother's factory building and rented a two-room house in a slum. Only Kun and Suk Joon knew about it. We stayed up all night. Around seven in the evening, those who escaped from Kwangju had contacted their bases in Seoul. We clung to each other and cried. The uprising was over but the operation continued for about a month. In the summer of 1980, we decided on a period of dormancy, and the number of members dwindled notably. They went back to work or switched to running night schools. Only about fifteen responded to our regular roll calls. Nam Soo received a fifteen-year sentence. He had already been arrested once before and survived horrific torture, having his fingernails pulled off. Some got life sentences, some death.

We collected all records of the Kwangju insurrection, various leaflets, and reports on our organization's efforts and results. We got together to organize everything and held a reading. It was held for three days at a private prayer house near the highway connecting Seoul and Choonchun. The government had published the outcome of its investigation on the Kwangju Incident, and a wanted list of three hundred people suspected of inciting social instability. Of course, Kun was on the list, and Dong Woo and I were included as well. Fortunately, Suk Joon was still unknown to the authorities. On the last day, we named the organization and chose a platform for a preparatory committee. We lit candles as we criticized ourselves and cried, feeling guilty for escaping and regretting our survival. We ended the gathering by pledging to be fully operational by fall. As soon as summer was over, Suk Joon left for Tokyo to join his uncle and study there. At first, we were sad and didn't want him to go, but Dong Woo encouraged him. We needed to make connections overseas, he said, and ask for assistance. This would become the legal case against us.

There were numerous other organizations and groups like ours. First, those from the farming movement, who went up to the rooftop of the

American Cultural Center in Kwangju in the middle of the night, destroyed the roof, and started a fire by throwing lit bottles. Hyun Sang, who later set fire to the ACC in Busan, was persistently laying the groundwork in Seoul and the Youngnam region. Everyone had seen or heard of the cruel massacre of innocent civilians in Kwangju. It was the beginning of the eighties, the age of fire. There was no way to beat this brute force with the lukewarm thoughts and actions of the past; it seemed impossible that the people could take power in our generation. Everyone talked about a revolution. And we thought a lot about the power of the working class. Naturally, the leaders of the movement rushed into ideological studies in order to train the leaders of revolution. Becoming a radical was the only way to overcome despair and shame.

7

I heard the long crow of a rooster, soon followed by all the other roosters in the neighborhood, as if they were in competition. I stayed lying in the darkened room and watched the back window become lighter. By my head was a small, low table with her notebooks stacked on top. Inside them, Yoon Hee's monologue, written in tiny script, was waiting for me.

As it was written in her notebook, Yoon Hee packed her things and moved in from the neighboring village the day I finished renovating the house. Together the two of us unpacked various household things and her art supplies. We put a cabinet on top of the kitchen fireplace in her studio. We didn't dare cook in the huge cast iron pot secured to the fireplace, so we decided to only heat water in there. We cooked rice on a portable gas burner she brought with her and lit two candles, since we had no electricity. In the candlelight we really felt like we were in the most remote corner of the world. We sat facing each other and ate dinner. All we had was rice, a tofu stew, and sour kimchi, but after more than a year of wandering around, I felt like I had come home. Yoon Hee sat in front of the kitchen fire and washed her hair. She combed it dry and hummed.

"So what do you want to do in the future?"

"I should go back."

"No, not that. Don't you have something you want to do?"

"A long, long time ago, I thought about writing poetry."

"But now?"

"I'm a runaway."

Yoon Hee stood up then sat on the tiny porch that connected the two rooms.

"I think you should become a poet. Otherwise, when the struggle loses its direction, you'll have my father's life."

"For humans or, you know . . . even for wild flowers, there's a best time for everything, isn't there? For your father, his twenties was the shining moment of his life, and if you survive you just go on living."

"I don't understand people like you. You're all the same. You're like horses with blinders on, only looking ahead."

"Because we need to go a long way."

Yoon Hee did not say anything any more. Her hair was combed back, and she raised her head, her profile so sharp, to stare calmly at my face. She walked into the bedroom and closed the door. She took out a futon and comforter and spread them out.

"I only have one set. The blanket was so dirty, I had to wash it. We'll have to sleep together," Yoon Hee declared and climbed into bed first. A bit flustered, I remained seated on the other side of the room.

"Recite one, if you still remember."

"What . . . ?"

"One of your poems."

"I do remember a few verses. When I was young, my friends and I would drink some rice wine and take bets who could write a better poem. Once, it happened to be raining lightly at the time, so we decided to compose something about that."

"Please, go on."

"The wind is coming. The air is wet. I call it the spring rain."

"Is that it?"

"There's one more. I did the first one, the next one is better."

"Are they all called 'The Spring Rain'?"

"The spring rains. Yet it is not enough to wet the potato field."

"So each of you came up with a verse. Not bad."

"My friend died early, in a car accident. A poetic sensibility is never enough. Or maybe it never existed. During your adolescence, it is even more mysterious, like a labyrinth."

"Why don't you lie down and talk? My neck hurts."

I lay next to her, about a foot away. We remained there, looking at the shadows from the candlelight dance on the ceiling. From the backyard came the sound of bamboo trees rustling in the wind. An owl flew in and howled hauntingly, pausing intermittently, but we could not tell from where.

I fell asleep while reading Yoon Hee's notebook, but I was awoken early by sparrows chattering in the bamboo field. As soon as I got up, without knowing why, I put my face against the glass window and looked out. The morning fog had descended everywhere, filling the courtyard. I could not see the tops of the trees. As I was used to doing here now, I took my shirt off and went out to the water faucet in the courtyard. I poured cold water over the top of my head and slowly positioned my back under the faucet. An unbearable chill covered my back and chest. Then I rubbed my torso with a wet towel until I felt heat. As I walked to the main house, the Soonchun lady, watching from her kitchen, gestured to come in.

"Come inside!"

In her long, rectangular, Southern-style house, there was a pantry on the left side connected to the kitchen. A narrow porch was attached from the front of the pantry to the other end of the house, and all the rooms were lined up behind it. Next to the pantry was the master bedroom, with the fuel hole for the kitchen underneath it. Next to the master bedroom was a large room with side doors, followed by a children's bedroom and a study for the man of the house at the end. When he was still alive, the vice principal had me over to the study, to play a game or just to talk. A door on that side opened and the youngest son of the family, the Bunny Boy of the past, came out to the porch.

"Good morning, come on in."

We went into the pantry, each of us offering passage to the other. There was a round table in the pantry already covered with little dishes. The daughter-in-law was helping the mother in the kitchen. The kitchen floor was now covered in tiles, not the bare dirt floor of the past. A sink was installed with running water indoors, and they were using a gas stove. They brought in soup and put cooked rice from an electric rice cooker into little bowls.

"Hope this suits your palette. You like this soup with dumplings?"

"Of course I do. You're still a great cook."

"No, I forgot everything, I don't know how to cook a single dish."

I could tell the son was dithering about something, and he finally opened his mouth and whispered so that the women in the kitchen could not hear him.

"Well, Uncle, someone wants to see you later today."

"Who . . . me?"

"Well, yeah, how should I . . . someone is coming from the police station. He just wants to ask a few questions."

I guessed that the son had called the police last night. Perhaps it was the Soonchun lady's idea. Why wouldn't they be worried? When I was arrested, Yoon Hee was not the only one here to be interrogated. I am sure the vice principal and his wife had to endure much more than they deserved.

I was planning to go into town to shop after breakfast, but after hearing the youngest son's words I decided to stay close to the house and take a walk to kill time. I strolled down to the lower part of Kalmae village. It was too early in the morning for the restaurant and the café to be open, and only the village dogs stirred and barked loudly as I passed. The dirt road that had cut through an orchard full of apple and pear trees had disappeared. Instead I circled the village on a paved road and walked back toward our house, thinking I should hike up the little mountain behind it. An old, black car that hadn't been washed in a while though it was covered in dirt passed me by and went toward the vice principal's house. I glanced into the car for a second, and I presumed the man who was looking for me was inside. From a distance I saw a man getting out of the car and climbing the steps to the café Todam. I walked leisurely down the paved road and went up to the café. The youngest son, who was peeking outside through a slightly opened door, met my eyes and smiled. He opened the door a bit further and stood in the doorway.

"Come inside and have a cup of tea."

I climbed up the steps, smiling back. Inside, the walls were covered with traditional rice papers, the lamp shades were made out of bamboo baskets, and the wooden tables were quite rustic. They tried hard to conjure a Korean provincial style, but the window was a huge glass panel, and it just seemed so incongruous. The man was sitting by the window, and he glared at me as I walked in. He could have been simply looking at me, but his eyes were so sharp I got an unpleasant impression. The youngest son gestured toward him with one hand.

"I told you earlier, right? He is from the police station."

The man half rose from his seat. I nodded my head and stood there, not sure what to do.

"Mr. Oh Hyun Woo, correct? Please, take a seat."

The youngest son escaped over to the cash register. I sat in front of a man who looked like a detective. He gave me his card.

"This neighborhood is my area, so . . . I just have a few questions, for official purposes."

He took out a notepad and a pen from inside his jacket.

"It's been about ten days since you were released, right?"

"Almost two weeks."

"Released on parole?"

"No, I finished my sentence. It was reduced while I was inside."

The man grinned.

"Of course. Anyhow, you are now a subject of the Security Observation Law. Did you report to the local police when you arrived?"

"I did not break any law, so I did not report anywhere."

"In fact, you broke the law by not doing anything. It is okay. What is the reason for your visit?"

"I just wanted to relax."

"From what I hear, that house up there is owned by Han Yoon Hee, so what is your relation to her?"

Inside, I repeated his question to myself and thought about it for a moment. Well, what was our relationship? Like I was in the habit of doing in prison when I was not able to answer a question, I looked up to the ceiling and smiled.

"She's not your wife . . . but I heard you were engaged?"

"Something like that."

"How long do you plan to stay here?"

"Ten days, or maybe a couple of weeks, I think."

"And you plan to return to Seoul after that? Naturally, you'll stop by in Kwangju, no?"

"No, I'll go back directly."

He put the notebook and the pen back into his inner pocket and cast a glance behind me. The youngest son came over and asked, "What kind of tea would you like?"

"Well, what do you have?"

"Quince tea, green tea, citron tea, date tea . . ."

"How about a cup of date tea?"

"Uncle, what would you like?"

I got up from my seat and said to the detective, "I think we're done here, so if you'll please excuse me . . ."

As I turned around and walked away, the man followed me.

"Look, I know this is awkward. I didn't want to do this, but my bosses told me I should."

"Of course, I understand."

I walked up the dirt path leading to our house, swinging my arms. The Soonchun lady's youngest son followed me, almost running. I guess he was flustered.

"Uncle, Uncle, just a minute!"

I turned my head to see him and stopped walking.

"Actually, I called him last night. My mother was so nervous, so . . ."

"I'm glad you did." I had guessed correctly, and I was truly sorry for all their troubles. "I'm so sorry, but this is the situation I have to deal with."

His face brightened when I said that. "You are too kind. There was nothing else I could do, we need to make a living. Now you can rest without worrying about anything!"

I returned to my room. Lying with my head resting on my arms, I decided that I should start cooking for myself from now on. I should go into town to order gas and do some grocery shopping, I thought. No, if I do that today it'll be too obvious. I should start doing my own cooking tomorrow. The world had not changed that much. I was not completely free, and who knows, maybe there was still something left for me to do.

I went grocery shopping in the afternoon. I scrubbed and cleaned inside the dust-covered refrigerator and stocked it. I bought rice and ramen noodles, and the propane gas I ordered for the stovetop was delivered and connected. My appetite had been suppressed for such a long time, but now it was back, and I wanted to cook everything I bought myself as soon as possible. But I knew I shouldn't hurt the feelings of the family in the main house, so I would walk down there tonight and have dinner with them.

I wanted to be with Yoon Hee again. I opened the notebook. As in her sketchbook, she had written down her thoughts as letters to me.

Today I went up the hill behind the house. No matter what, I wanted to see what was behind this ordinary mountain. It was so densely covered with thickets and weeds that it was hard to walk through at first, but there was the beginning of a path, as if people walked through there from time to time. Remarkably, it became a lot easier to hike once I got on the path, and I walked up following the natural line of the ridge. By the time I reached what could be called the summit, the sweat had soaked through my T-shirt. There were trees, but not as many as at the bottom, and a few bulging rocks. I looked through the trees and into the distance. It's not like there was a wide ocean to relieve my heart. There was another narrow valley, and behind it a mountain higher than this one, blocking the view. At the end of the slowly descending ridge on the right, I could just see a newly constructed highway, the one I was pretty sure I had driven on. I knew this, because there was a tributary of a stream running along the road. I sat on a rock to cool myself down. A few steps down was an empty clearing, so I went down to see and found a pretty grave. Well, there is no such thing as a pretty grave, is there? It had been abandoned for such a long time that the mound was flattened, there was no tombstone, not even a mark. The only reason I knew it was a grave was that the land was not as flat, but deflated like an old woman's breast.* There were many weeds growing, but nothing like the tall eulalias and scouring rushes and foxtails down below.

* A traditional Korean grave is a dirt mound with grass growing on it. The fancier the grave, the higher and larger the mound.

In the grass were little patches of violets and clover. There was a soft breeze blowing from the valley. It was so comforting, and I lay with my back against the grave and whispered, hello. I thought of the grave's occupant, who was disintegrating only a few feet below. Of the streets and villages he had walked through and of the people he had loved. They say flowers in a cemetery grow with the tears from those who come and cry. That's a lie. In this peaceful stillness and wind, I find proof there is something good beyond life.

After coming back from the mountain at night and reading the newspaper, I realize the death I met up there was just my sentimental response, far from the objective reality. I am copying down records from the Spanish Inquisition, strangely familiar.

Hands and feet cut off from the body. Eyeballs expelled from the head. Ankles detached from the legs. Muscles wrenched from the joints. Dislocated shoulder blades. Arteries inflated, veins popping. Victims are raised up to the ceiling, then crashed down to the floor. Spun around, hung in the air upside down. I saw the torturers whip, beat, break fingers, hang the body high up with heavy weights, tie with rope, brand with sulfur, throw hot oil, singe with fire. When a woman finally confessed after enduring the unendurable tortures, the inquisitor told her, if you are going to deny what you have just confessed, you should do it now. Then I'll write a report in favor of you. But if you deny the truth in court, you'll be returned to me, and you'll receive an even harsher treatment. I can make a stone cry tears.

My goodness, that was the Middle Ages, but it is the dreary voice you hear so much of here and now. I heard from his sister about the forty-five days he spent in hell. We cannot even face the wild flowers we meet on the mountain, we should be so ashamed. How unfortunate we are.

Let's go back to painting. There is no permanent impression in this world. A painting is from the beginning an illusion produced by the one holding the brush. As he recited that spring rain was named by someone. I'm positive a socialist would say the class determines the perception. I'll never praise a landscape again. A painting is a way of seeing.

Go your own way, let the others talk!
Reflected in these words are a determination to transform the world and, in the inverse, a loneliness. And he was never free from the noise of others' endless chatters. A stubborn exile suffering from poverty and hunger, he went to the libraries and listened to the speakers at Hyde Park. Later, a bald Russian walked back and forth in the same space. But they fared better. So many unfortunate revolutionaries were destroyed under unknown circumstances, crushed like ants under raging feet. But what's really strange is that although those crushed have left no body, no trace, no memory, the ones who crushed them can never forgive and must keep loathing the dead and any thought related to them. A guilty conscience? No, they're afraid of themselves. This kind of tenacity lasts as long as anything they inflicted on their victim.

From now on, we live separately, him inside, me outside. Is there really an inside and an outside? Or is it me who's inside and he's the one out? This is my record, a memento of my life. He will have his own in that little room. Years from now when our long parting has ended, how are we going to reckon our own time?

I know why a hungry thing digs the earth for seemingly no reason, from what I heard about my father's days in the mountain. Why hungry dogs or wolves or horses aimlessly use their front legs to rake the earth. They have already forgotten how famished they are, but they realize that if they don't move, they are not alive. I heard many times my father's story of how he was the only one of three who came down with a fever, how he lay between rocks for a few nights before he was captured. Even later, my father was afraid to look at stars. His eyes were dry as if they were filled with sand and the dark night sky slowly and heavily weighed on him like his fever. Hunger extends time to infinity.

One day, when he was sick, he said to me, "I could never imagine myself in old age."

He also said, "How can you predict November, so far off, when you've just taken down the first couple of pages of the calendar?" How could he, as a dying young man, lie next to the corpse of a comrade who slowly expired anonymously, in a place where he knew no one? "You can talk about them and you can think about them, but in the middle of the action, you don't realize death, prison, and war are anything more than games. Everyday things, like a vase, breaking when it falls from a table. Hey, look over there. What did I tell you, he's really dying. Old age is like the taste of dried persimmons that remains in your memory after you've finished the whole box. Maybe there are a couple left, after all, and you sustain yourself by nibbling on the past." I told you about my father's last days, and we grew closer.

8

I remember that night. The Saturday we first kissed. On Sunday we went into town, because we wanted to buy a few things. There was so much we needed, from tableware to pots to bedding. After waiting for the bus for a while at the bridge, we simply began to walk toward the dusty road, each of us taking turns leading the other. A small truck gave us a ride. We sang together until we were able to see the town. I think it was a Russian folk song called "A Sailor's Farewell" I had taught you, one I learned from my father when I was a child. You sang it first, then I followed.

> Let's sing a joyous song
> Let's sing tonight
> For tomorrow we'll leave the port
> Piercing the early morning fog
> My beloved hometown, but tomorrow to the sea
> Early in the morning on the gunwale
> A familiar blue handkerchief

You must have been suffocating. For more than two weeks you did not leave Kalmae while I was gone. Watching you enjoy the outing so much, I felt so sorry for you. Your long hair fluttered in the wind. Now there is an agricultural union's storage house, with ugly cement walls painted yellow, but at the time, at the entrance to the village, do you remember the mill with a thatched roof? There were always mounds and mounds of grain stalks, and it was always so dusty, with grain kernels floating in the air. Behind the mill was a dense forest of reeds and cat-tails, and further behind was a large pool where streams from the mountains gathered before they flowed into the river in the neighboring village. Now it is a reservoir.

It was not a market day, but there were plenty of people in town. It was the weekend, so working people like me were running errands or going to church. Just like in any other sizable village, there was a public market. Next to it was an empty space with makeshift storefronts for the big market that opened every five days. The public market was small, but there was everything anyone could hope for. There was a hardware store and a housewares store with all sorts of kitchen supplies. And there were a dry goods store, a stationery store, an electrician's, a general store, a bakery, a rice cake shop, a snack shop, a cotton gin place, a barber shop, a beauty salon, a movie theater, and a public bath. We waved goodbye to each other and walked into the male and female baths. Since I took more time to bathe, you got a much anticipated haircut, too. We had to shop, but we were so hungry. We bought a lot of things, each of us carrying bags in both hands, and looked around by the entrance to the market. Marveling, you once more looked back at the market that we had just left.

"Let's come here every market day!" you said.

"What about my school?"

"Ah, that's too bad."

"You can come without me, enjoy it for me."

"What fun would it be to do it by myself? Anyway, I love country markets."

We walked into a noodle house that looked like a tavern from a fairy tale. There were wooden tables and stools, and the owner, without asking, drained a fistful of noodles in a bamboo basket and added them to hot broth for us. It was a typical country noodle soup, the broth made by boiling radishes cut into rectangles and dried anchovies as long as fingers, and garnished with seasoned zucchinis and scallions and red pepper. The type of food farmers eat as a midday snack. I gave you some of mine; you did not leave a drop of broth in your bowl.

"When I was a kid, I sometimes shoplifted when I followed mom to the market."

You said that, but I didn't understand what you meant.

"When passing by a dried fish stall or a fruit stall, I would take a few dried anchovies or a few pieces of dried squid, or a few grapes or strawberries. It was so much fun!"

"I did that, too."

With all our bags, we did not want to ride the crowded bus full of people going home after a day's outing, and we did not want to be too conspicuous. Inevitably, we took a cab. Ah, through the open window, the fragrance of newly sprouting young grasses blew in with the wind. Where humans live, the pleasant activity of the life and the wind danced together. At that moment, we thought everything would be fine.

After we came back home, we organized our new house. You brought water from the main house while I washed the dishes and bowls. There was no water carrier, so you brought two buckets and came back staggering with a bucket full of water in each hand. I told you to slow down and take a break if you needed, but you were in such a hurry, the water ended up spilling everywhere and your pants got all wet. You were so funny—of all the delicious things you could have asked me to cook, your favorite was stir-fried fish cakes, something our mothers would have packed for us in a lunchbox. I was going to ask another teacher who lived near the town for some pickles and side dishes, but you said not to.

"I'm not a permanent resident, I'm still a wanderer. All I want is something that can be packed in a lunchbox."

I remember our humble but warm dinner. We brought in cables from the main house, and instead of a fluorescent light we put a sixty-watt light bulb into the socket. You said our house was illuminated like Edison's lab.

"I still like candlelight better when it's time to go to bed."

"We need to take turns making sure that the candle is out. Otherwise, we'll burn the house down."

I was against it, but in the end I lit the candle myself. With the candlelight, we were isolated from the world and transported to a place far away from it all. That night, we made love together for the first time. Do you remember what I said after we lay down at first, awkwardly, at each end of the room?

"Do you want to come closer? I can't sleep."

You didn't even hesitate for a moment! You just slipped under my comforter and held me tight. And with no talking. It wasn't rough. Your lips were a bit chapped. And I could smell cigarettes. Until the sun came up the next day, we had so many things to talk about. From time to time I was worried. You would open the door and lay down on your belly with your chin on the pillow and stare blankly out into the darkness. Your thoughts were somewhere else. Were you thinking of your comrades in danger, or of your duty, I wonder?

I had a boyfriend when I was in college. He was a couple of years ahead of me, majoring in sculpture at the same school. I think I once mentioned him to you, too. I began to notice him one winter.

It was around the time the doctors had given up on my father. He had left the hospital to come home, and he spent his days in bed while Jung Hee and I nursed him. I spent many nights curled up next to him. After a night like that, I usually woke up too early in the morning. And the pathetic sight that greeted me in those early mornings! As the window onto the street became light, I would see bottles of painkillers and syringes scattered around the top of his bed. The patient was so thin I could see the bones beneath his skin. His eyes were hollow and his cheekbones protruding. As if he had lost all his energy, my father slept with his mouth half open and without sound. I would get up, frightened that he had already passed away. I would sit up straight and debate whether I should touch him or not, and then finally gather up enough courage to gently shake his arm. He would sigh weakly or flinch or give me some other sign. Anyway, it was another morning like that. Suffocated, I could not stand it any longer; I just wanted to scream and run outside. With nowhere to go so early in the morning, I went to school.

There was no one at school. The trees were bare, the windows of the school buildings black, and the streetlights still dimly lit. My footsteps echoed throughout the stairwells and hallways. I walked into the art

studio. There was a gas stove and packets of coffee and green tea supplied by students. As I walked into the studio and turned the light on,
there were folded easels standing guard and unfinished canvases waiting
for their creators' touch. Behind them, I thought I saw the studio floor
rising up, but it turned out it was just two desks joined together. And
something was moving, something that looked like a dark beast. I was
scared out of my mind. I just stood there with my mouth open, unable to
say anything, and watched. With a sound of *zip!*, a human head emerged
from what appeared to be a sack.

"Oh my God!"

As I screamed, the person was also taken by surprise and screamed
almost simultaneously.

"What? What . . . ?"

I was finally able to see that it was a man in a sleeping bag. I knew who
he was. Of course, I had never talked to him before. He was two years
ahead of me, and except during the summer when he wore dirty shirts,
he always wore a military coat dyed black. Naturally, his shoes were a
pair of black combat boots, their toes worn white.

"Well, good morning! Did you come to treat me to breakfast?"

I was flabbergasted. *What am I, a social worker?* I almost said it out
loud.

"Did you sleep here?" I managed to say back, and he replied without
shame.

"Recently, this has been my bedroom."

"Are you on a deadline?" I said, thinking that he had been working all
night, feigning indifference.

"I have nowhere else to go. For a student, school is home."

He had probably run out of money to pay his rent. On his black
fatigues were white chicken feathers from the army sleeping bag. They
made him look worse than dirt.

"Is this yours?"

I picked up a sketchbook that had been tossed on the floor near his
feet and leafed through the pages. It was a good thing he did not reply,
because I was astounded by his drawings. We were still drawing from
plaster casts or models hired by the school, but he was doing something
completely unexpected. Now that I think about it, what he did was nat-

ural. He went out onto the streets. He drew a man carrying a load. Alive in his drawing was the man's straining face, the lines on his face, his clenched hands holding onto a stick, and the bulging veins on his hands, his feet and his calves as he walked. Then there was a mother and a daughter, drawn perhaps near the central station, walking with bags and bundles. A man slept on a bench with a newspaper as a blanket, and the paper had slipped off to reveal half of his face, especially the angular cheekbones. Behind him a man was lighting a cigarette butt. His cheeks were gaunt from sucking on it, his eyes cast down to the tiny flame of the match, his hands cupped to shield the flame from the wind. Next was a young woman breastfeeding her baby while sitting on a bench in the train station. She was followed by two boys, perhaps vagabonds, wearing jackets that were so big on them that they look like long coats, their hair spiked and tangled like bird's nests, happily chattering away and snacking on what looked like baked sweet potatoes. They were so refreshing that I was mesmerized.

"They're really great," I mumbled as I kept turning the pages of his sketchbook.

"What is? How are they great?"

"They're alive." He smiled listlessly. I didn't know how but he seemed to be sneering and my cheeks burnt. "The reality . . . that's the most important thing."

I was only in my second year in college, but I was already bored and tired of what was being taught there. I mean, what was the point of drawing, no, copying plaster casts of foreigners who looked nothing like us, people not from our own time, but from thousands of years ago? And we were graded on that? And the closest we got to something alive was a nude. A body away from real life is just another object. So you draw that a few times, and you apply some paint, and you are an artist. His eyes were bloodshot like those of someone suffering from chronic fatigue, but I thought they were intense.

"I'll buy you breakfast if you let me have one of your drawings."

"Go ahead."

I chose the drawing of the cheerful vagabonds. I liked the breast-feeding woman, too, but those boys were so animated and vivid. I took him to a tiny restaurant in the nearby market where they sold soup with stuffed pig intestines. He shuffled after me. I had been there only once before, when I followed the men in our class there after some sort of a gathering. That's how I found out men like soju and soup with stuffed pig intestines. Hanging over the door was a banner made from pieces of cloth, like a shredded skirt, and written on it in irregular handwriting were things like pig intestines stuffed with tofu and vegetables, head meat, pork belly, and rice wine. Inside were a couple of dirty wooden tables with makeshift chairs made of plywood, and also tables made out of barrels with fires burning in the middle to cook pork belly at the table, with round stools. I ordered one bowl of soup.

"Why are you just getting one?" he asked, sulking.

"I already ate breakfast."

"That early?"

"Of course, I got up even earlier."

"Well, this is no good, I'm not a dog you feed. I'll eat on the condition that you drink a bottle of soju with me."

"I don't drink soju."

"Then it's written over there, a bowl of rice wine per person."

I glanced back to the wall with the menu.

"Fine."

He slowly ate his soup. Then he picked up the rice wine that came in an astonishingly large bowl and drank the whole thing in one gulp. Beads of sweat appeared on his nose and forehead.

"You know the saying that you haven't drunk anything unless you've had three glasses, don't you? What a tease . . ."

"Fine," I replied, fingering my purse. "On condition that you take me with you when you go out to draw."

So each of us drank three bowls of rice wine. Without hesitating, he burped really loudly. His face was a little flushed, but he seemed to be relaxed. And I was, after all, my father's daughter, and after having what amounted to about a kettle full of rice wine I was perfectly fine, except for some throbbing around my eyes.

"You can drink," he commented curtly, then quickly left while I paid. I ran after him into the street, which was full of students walking to the campus. As I kept pace behind him, I thought, now everyone will talk. Do you know where he took me to? The top of the Yumchungyo bridge near the central market. Lined up on the street toward the South Gate were ironworks and hardware stores. To the north of the bridge was a market selling all sorts of things, and to the south was a tangle of railroad tracks where steam engines came and went, passing by dirty open sewers and shacks. There were many crows around the railroads. There were so many things to draw, I did not know where to begin. He was sitting on the bridge railing and sketching, already on his third page. I began sketching the steam engines and railroads under the bridge and the roofs of the shacks behind, and he came over to take a look.

"You learn how to react instantly only when you draw living things."

I studied his sketchbook full of freshly caught people, their animated postures, and I turned from the railing and crossed the street to walk into the central market. I found two men unloading fruit boxes from a hand-cart and drew them. They were moving so fast and their gestures kept changing moment to moment, but I tried to stick to my first composition and kept adding lines. Next, I turned to a woman selling sticky rice cakes, whose movements seemed to be repetitive. Her face did not move, but her hands moved quickly. It was difficult to capture, so I repeatedly drew her wrist. I continued until I had filled about twenty pages in my sketchbook. I left and walked down the large avenue, quickly sketching the street vendors and the passing people and the crowd. I did not know where he had gone, I could not find him. I waited for him at the bridge for at least half an hour, and he finally came back trudging in his old boots.

"I need a break. I think I'll go back to school."

"Go ahead. I need to go someplace nearby."

"What do you mean? You should at least escort me back to where we started."

I did that on purpose. The truth was, all classes would be done even if we went back to school, and it was time to go home to take care of my father until my mother came back from the market. But Jung Hee would be home, so I had until nine and could keep him company until then. But he obediently nodded and took the lead.

"No problem, I'll take you to the bus stop."

This time, I stopped walking and shook my head.

"No, I don't want to go. You are in charge of me until nine tonight. I'll buy the dinner, though."

"Well, what can we do."

He did not seem annoyed, he was really thinking about it while scratching his head. Out of the blue, he said, "Show me all the money you have right now."

"For what?"

"Let me see, let me see your bag."

How preposterous! He abruptly snatched my leather bag from my shoulder. Reflexively, I grabbed onto the handle and took a few steps back, shaking him off.

"How much do you have?"

That day, I happened to have a lot of money for a student. I was working as a private tutor for a high school student who was preparing for the art school entrance exam, and my monthly pay, received the week before, was still untouched in my bag.

"I have enough, don't worry."

He gestured to me to follow him and walked back into the market. From the butcher he bought a few pounds of pork belly. And he bought rice, tofu, scallions, red pepper flakes and other seasonings, and four 1.6-pint bottles of soju. Every time he bought something he simply pointed at me with his chin, as if he was ordering me to settle the bill. With grocery bags in both hands, he walked up the narrow, winding alleyways in the crowded slum of Manli-dong.

We were headed to the second floor of a building that looked like a barrack with no courtyard and no kitchen. He climbed the rickety steps made of thin wooden boards that bent under his weight to the point of breaking, and he gestured again with his chin to tell me to do the same. So I took off my shoes, as he did, and climbed the narrow, steep stairway. It reminded me of a ship's cabin or an attic.

The room was unbelievably messy and musty. The door, made of plywood, was open, and there were shoes in a tiny space about one foot wide. But the first thing I saw was a blue porcelain chamber pot right next to the door. It was covered with a piece of newspaper, the lid gone somewhere else, and its foul smell filled the air. On the right was a window, and under it a cupboard, a portable gas stove, and a bucket half-filled with water. Further inside the room, a man with disheveled gray hair sat leaning against the wall on a dirty blanket. A young boy, about seven years old, was devouring cookies that he must have just received. The artist was kneeling as if he was in a church, his head down and his face grave. Confused, I did not know whether I should sit down or not, so I just stood there. He finally pulled at my clothes.

"Sit here," he said.

Unnerved by his brazenness, I slowly descended to kneel.

"Bow."

Again, I followed his order as if I was under a spell, and bowed down deeply from my head to the waist. Then I heard him say, "Father, this is my fiancée."

I hadn't yet raised my head from the bowing position, and after hearing this incredible lie I could not. The gray-haired man straightened himself a little from his leaning position and mumbled in a hoarse voice, "I'm just so grateful that you're in a university and met someone like this young woman . . ."

My cheeks were flushed and I was losing my patience, but I could not say a word. Instead, I just pinched him as hard as I could. He did not scream, just coughed a little.

"How's your mother in the countryside?" the gray-haired man asked.

"They're all fine. How's your back?"

"Well, it's been two months, but it's not getting better."

"She hasn't come back?"

The gray-haired man did not answer, his eyes pointing at the young boy still eating cookies.

"I have to get better before I can ask someone to take care of him."

Ah, how did I fall into this deep hole? I felt like I had walked into a cave about ten times darker than my own home. But the ordeal was far from over. Do you know what he said?

"She did some grocery shopping to cook your dinner."

He sprang up and said to me, "I'll go get water from the communal faucet. You start with the rice."

I did not run out the door. Without saying anything, I put some rice into a pot and poured some water in to rinse it. I looked for a place to throw out the water. His father said, still half-sitting and half-lying there, "My dear girl, you just throw the water out the window."

I somehow managed to put a pot of rice on the stove, which was black with soot. Thankfully, the fluorescent light worked. He came back with water and prepared to make a stew, using a tiny cutting board about the size of a palm and a rusted knife to mince the meat and scallions and garlic and cut tofu. He cut some kimchi from the store, opened a bottle of soju, and filled an aluminum bowl. He placed the open bottle by his father's head and offered him the bowl.

"Father, here's your drink."

I could not believe my eyes. The man was as crumpled as an empty sack a minute ago, but he suddenly got up as if by reflex, snatched the bowl and emptied it into his mouth in one motion. *Kaa!* he exclaimed, then he picked up the bottle and poured the contents directly into his mouth. He put the bottle down and wiped his mouth only after he finished more than half the bottle.

My eyes welled up. My father was not as bad as he was—at least he was cleaner and neater—but they were in a similar desperate state of a declining life. And my father was slowly dying. The artist watched his father without saying anything. When the rice was done, he put the stew on the stove. His father had already finished the 1.6-pint bottle and smacked his lips. He asked his son, "Get the salt jar from the cupboard for me."

The artist got the salt jar and gave it to his father while remaining silent. His father took a pinch of salt and sprinkled it into his open mouth. The artist set the dinner table without saying another word while his half-brother galloped around the room with a spoon in his mouth, excited for no apparent reason. Deep inside me was a mixture of pity and empathy. We sat around the circular table and ate dinner like one big family. The artist opened another bottle and slowly poured one bowl at a time for his father. After we were done I washed the dishes while he continued to pour drinks for his father. Later, the gray-haired man who looked like an empty sack hummed a couple of songs, and at one point slowly fell to his side. The artist carefully tucked the sleeping boy in next to his father, gave me a signal with his eyes to leave the room and turned off the fluorescent light. We carefully climbed down the stairs. We walked back toward the Yumchungyo bridge. It was late at night; the market's lights were out and it was empty. Instead, the once-quiet neighborhood around the railroad and the slum on the opposite side was full of life. I think there was a red-light district nearby. I learned much later that the artist's father was a ruined landowner who did not adjust to the changes in the postwar period. He had sold his land to open a distillery, started and bankrupted a number of small manufacturing companies, then met a young woman and left home as if to run away. We walked to the South Gate without talking. I was the first one to speak when we saw the bus stop.

"Where are you going now?"

He no longer scratched his head.

"Going home."

"Home?"

"I mean school."

I ran to the bus stop and hopped onto one without looking back, like I was angry. This was the beginning of my first love. I never asked if he went back to see his father, but he started to work at an art studio run by an alumnus of our school. We were still really poor.

For the rest of the year, we were very close. We left behind the remains of our homes and traveled to draw the living, sweating people of our time. That winter, we went on a short trip to an island on the west coast. It was very windy; there was a storm warning and ferries stopped running. We were staying in a boarding house not too far from the coastline, and there was no electricity on the island. We spent the night in candlelight, as you and I did in Kalmae. We had brought hiking supplies like a camp stove and a gas burner, but the last night we hung a cast iron pot over the fuel hole in our room and made a soup of fish broth cooked with little pieces of torn dough. It was snowing hard outside, and so dark that we could not see the inside of the pot. We sat in front of the fuel hole with our heads touching, each of us with a handful of dough that we threw in little pieces into the boiling broth.

As soon as he graduated he began the mandatory military service. Like other women at that time, I went to Yongsan Station early in the morning to say goodbye as he got on the train to Nonsan training camp. But he was luckier than others. He had won the grand prize at the national competition around his graduation. He was extremely talented, and his worldview was much more mature than that of others his age. His father had passed away by that point. He found the abandoned body at a civic hospital and brought it back to his hometown. My father passed away the following year, and I think it was around the time of his death that I went to the eastern front to visit the artist.

Deep in the valleys of Kangwon province, the winding one-lane road went on endlessly. On the way I saw soldiers wearing dirty padded suits and laboring, cutting down trees or digging. At the entrance to a minor unit, I gave the guards his name. Walking down the road from his unit, his face was so burnt and caked with dirt that he looked like an old farmer. I couldn't stop myself from crying. It was past April, but there was still snow in the valley, and azaleas were blooming only in places where the sunlight reached.

He said he was allowed to stay out overnight, meaning he was allowed to sleep out of the unit. Don't you think that was really crude of them, that a soldier was allowed to sleep outside for one night, no questions asked, if a young woman came for a visit? We had to walk for a few miles to get to the nearest village. We walked without saying much. He was always like that, but he was devoid of all emotion during his army days; he was like a burnt, dry piece of coal. His hands were cracked from the cold like a turtle's shell. I felt like I was his mother.

It was a small town, the main business district only about twenty yards long. We went into a small motel. The room was newly wallpapered, though the pattern was too loud for my taste. The floor was covered in vinyl, and part of it had been burnt away by the heat radiating from beneath. I guess they had seen many couples comprised of soldiers and visitors, as the owner seemed to be unsurprised by our appearance. She told us to take a bath. The communal bathroom was next to the kitchen, a huge, old-fashioned iron tub heated with logs from below. It was a Japanese-style tub lined inside with wood, so one could submerge one's body in hot water. There were wooden boards on the floor of the bathroom, too, so one could pour water without slipping, and a number of buckets and dippers of various sizes. I washed myself first and then took him in there. I'll spare you the details, but I saw his naked body for the first time that night. The short bristles of his hair were stiffer than a brush. I washed them with fragrant soap, not the laundry soap he asked for. From his head and body came the odor of a lonely man, different from that of sweat. A bit like an animal, a bit like the odor of steamed rice gone bad, with a dash of soy sauce added to it. The odor of a man worn out by solitude. I scrubbed his back, and dirt came off like grains of rice. I forced him to soak his hands in hot water and scrubbed them with a red scratchy cloth. He screamed in mock agony and he kept pulling his hands away, I kept hitting his back but did not stop scrubbing.

I held him in my arms that night. Tears rolled down my face when I thought of saying goodbye to my father. He apologized in a faint voice, thinking that I was crying because it was my first experience. I had a hard time suppressing my laughter. The sun was rising, and he fell into a deep slumber, softly snoring with his back turned toward me. I doodled with my fingers on his back as I watched the paper door becoming lighter behind his shoulder. Looking back after all those years, I was still not ready to be freed from my father. What I loved was the vague image of his beautiful youth. To me, the artist's dark youth was not unfamiliar, and maybe I was trying to soothe myself by comforting him.

I graduated, took the teacher's license exam, and took a teaching post in a suburb in Kyunggi province. That same year, he was discharged from the military. The moment he was discharged, he came to see me. For him it went without saying that of course he wanted to marry me. But I did not really care. As I expected, he took the art world by storm. He was quick to figure out the trend of the moment and the audience's taste. Within eighteen months, he swept three grand prizes.

His work was no longer the powerful and vivid art of the days when he slept in a sleeping bag at the school studio. His praised works were mostly based on other artist's concepts, nimbly adapted to his own style. In my mind, his paintings were now just concepts. He called me after we had not seen or spoken to each other for months. He wanted to introduce me to a new friend. So I met him for the first time in quite a while. He told me to meet him at a coffee shop in a hotel. When I walked in, a neatly dressed executive popped up from his seat. I almost didn't recognize him, he had changed so much in a few months. His once disheveled hair was now trimmed tidily and slicked back with a hair product that made it shine. And there was no sign of stubble on his face. He was wearing a double-breasted suit with a tie.

"It's been a while."

He sounded rather solemn. I slowly looked him up and down, and I could not stop myself from laughing.

"You look like a CEO!"

He did not laugh. He added quite seriously, "So, doing well these days?"

It made me laugh even more, he sounded like a stockbroker or something like that. But I tried not to make fun of him. I was expecting it, too, and I did not want him to misunderstand, I did not want him to think that I was hostile toward him because we were about to officially break up.

"And your friend?"

"Coming. So how are you, how's your work?"

"So so. I saw the last National Art Exhibition."

"What did you think?"

I thought it was a bit shameless to ask me what I thought of his painting, but I decided not to reveal anything.

"Well, you got the big prize, good for you. And you know yourself what's best."

"I think you're right. The biggest weakness we painters have is that we're so skilled with our hands but have no philosophy."

I did not say anything. He hesitated, but finally said, "The thing is, I got engaged last week."

Inside, I told myself that it did not matter, but the aftershock made me tremble a little. But you know what? Human relationships can be very lonely. There are so many pop songs about it, how once all the feeling and sentiments have been removed, our naked selves emerge. It's like a child making clothes for a paper doll. She designs and colors all the dresses she wants, then she cuts them out and stacks them in a box. She spends hours changing the clothes on the paper doll, trying different dresses. Later she opens the box for the first time in a while. The colors and designs of the past are now tired.

"Great! Congratulations."

As I said these words, I did not think of his sleeping bag filled with chicken feathers or the cracked backs of his hands. He was just beginning to be rewarded.

"Next month, we leave together to study abroad."

He described his fiancée with sincerity. Well, it was a typical story you see all the time in soap operas. Maybe these stories were so prevalent because they reflect the reality after all. A union of a poor young man with tremendous potential and a little rich girl, a marriage, time studying abroad, and a farewell to his past. Just about when we were running out of things to say, his fiancée arrived. I guessed she must have just graduated from college. There was something about her that reminded me of graduation parties. She was dressed in a pink silk dress with a row of buttons, and her eyes and cheeks were perfectly shaded. The fiancée nodded her head, but she seemed to be waiting for a proper introduction from her man. I quickly opened my mouth.

"I'm Han Yoon Hee. We went to the same university. Nice to meet you."

"I heard a lot about you from him. I really wanted to meet you."

We went somewhere else for dinner. We each had a glass of something alcoholic, too. He seemed to be gradually growing more uncomfortable, so I got up first to leave. He followed me down to the lobby of the hotel. As I was looking for a taxi, I heard him say from behind, "Thank you."

I stared at him for a while, then I asked him quietly, "For what?"

"For being so kind to me."

I told him with real sincerity, "Be brave. Best of luck."

That's how our movie ended. The reason I wrote a story like this in detail is because I wanted to show once more the silliness of this life, no matter how much we talk about our dreams and ambitions and success.

9

The evening wind hissed through the forest, and the barking dogs quieted. As I walked toward the main house, the Soonchun lady looked out from the kitchen; she seemed delighted to see me. "Come in! I went up to your house a while ago but it was so quiet, I thought you were sleeping."

I walked into the pantry and found a table set for one.

"Where's everybody?"

"We already ate."

The Soonchun lady came back from the kitchen with rice and a bowl of soup and sat next to me.

"This is a soup with young barley sprouts. You like this, right?"

"Wow, I haven't had this in a long time."

"That's the taste of spring."

The Soonchun lady sat there quietly for a while, but soon she sighed and began talking.

"You know, how should I say this, about this afternoon . . . I'm really sorry."

"Huh? What do you mean?"

"Well, didn't you meet with someone from the police?"

"Ah yes, it wasn't a big deal."

The Soonchun lady lowered her eyes and rubbed her finger against the edge of her skirt.

"I know this is difficult for you. When my husband was alive, after what happened to you, we all got into big trouble. Miss Han was the first one, she was sent all the way to Kwangju, and we were interrogated by the district police, too."

"I caused too many troubles for you all."

"So I was just nervous about everything this time. But I thought about it, and you've done your time, and what else can happen at this point? So I told my son to report you."

"You did the right thing. It was my fault, I should have called them."

"My goodness, I just felt awful about all this. When he left, he said there will be no more trouble as long as they know when you leave here."

"I'll give him a call when I leave."

"I have to say, it is so much better now. Before, they would want you to go here and there, it would have been a huge hassle."

I somehow managed to finish dinner. I kept quiet and took out a cigarette. It tastes best after a meal.

"Did Miss Han visit here every year?"

"Well now, more than once a year. Every vacation, summer and winter, she spent months up there. Never got married, just waited for you. No, wait, she skipped a few years around the '88 Olympics. Let's see, she didn't come here for about five years, that's right. We got postcards from Germany, here and there. And when she returned, she came back first with her sister. And then she bought the house."

Her eyes suddenly welled up, and she touched her eyes with her stubby fingers.

"I think the last time she came here was the winter of '96. She was already sick by then. Maybe she knew something was going to happen, but the summer before that she came here and renovated the whole house. I heard why she was sick, but I didn't know how quickly she would . . ."

I sat there with my head down and listened to her rambling on. She continued.

"I had to say something. I asked her, why are you spending so much money fixing up an ordinary hut? It'd be better to tear it down and rebuild a new house. What did I know? You know what she said? She said Hyun Woo will not recognize it when he comes back. I didn't know, we didn't know what she was really thinking about."

I got up without saying anything. I wanted her to stop talking without being too obvious. I sat on the narrow porch and put my shoes back on, and she continued from behind, "By the way, I saw that you had gas delivered and you're buying all these things, but really, it's no trouble to us, all we do is add another place at the table. Eat your meals here."

I had no choice but to tell her, "No, you really don't have to. Frankly, I have to catch up on reading and organize a lot of things, so my daily schedule is very irregular. I can take care of myself. There are many things I want to cook, too."

Walking up the narrow path, I realized the nighttime breeze was quite warm now. Kalmae was not as quiet as it was in my room. It was weak, but I heard the driving beat of a pop song coming from somewhere. In between the branches of the orchard, I saw the flickering red neon sign of the Korean barbeque restaurant at the entrance to the village.

I returned again to Yoon Hee's voice. Her handwriting in ink was so familiar by now, I could see it shifting and turning into a gentle voice. Captured in her handwriting was the tide of her emotions. When she was sad the flow of ink was faint and weak, when she was happy her letters were round and free. And when she was swept away in violent emotions, there was the imprint of her pushing the pen down hard onto the paper at the end of each stroke. Sometimes on the back of the notebooks were rough drafts of letters she wrote to family and friends. I sorted through them carefully and read everything.

Dear Jung Hee,

How are you? I am spending this summer in Kalmae. I think my life as a teacher is over at this point. The truth is, I got married in secret last summer. I am truly sorry that I did not even tell you. But there was nothing I could do. He is a so-called activist. You guys would call him a militant. But he's neither too theoretical nor hardened. He's not like those young men from poverty who want something back from society, who form a small group and practice power control rather than quickly transforming themselves into something. He's, how should I say it, a bit tentative. With his circumstances it's too late, but he hopes to become a poet. I think he's very stubborn. Ah, I knew this relationship wasn't going to be easy. As soon as he left here last year, he was arrested. He may not be able to come back to this world for a long, long time. Yet I volunteered to be his wife. Why? He has no one but me. I've decided that I need to study more, since I'll have to live by myself for a while. I am thinking of applying to graduate schools. I don't think you remember the last year of dad's life. You were a senior in high school applying to universities, it was too hectic for you. I used to spend day after day with him. Because it was liver cancer, his head was clear until the day he died. We talked so much. Later, I felt I wanted to write down every detail of the last few days and what happened just before he passed away. I want you to remember, too. I'm not alone here in Kalmae. I haven't told Mom yet, but I'm going to ask you for a lot. You have to help me. I know you'll be curious, but you'll soon find out, perhaps by this fall. If you promise that you'll not rush to come here, I'll tell you. I didn't know before, I thought all women lived the same way, but that's not true. A caterpillar pops out of an egg, and that caterpillar builds a cocoon and becomes a chrysalis. The chrysalis sleeps in the cocoon for a long time. By the time it breaks the cocoon and sheds the shell and becomes a beautiful butterfly who flies away in the blue sky, this butterfly is no longer the caterpillar of the past. A woman who has become a mother is not the woman of before.

Dear Jung Hee,

I begged you not to do this, but if you must, I'm not going to stop you. The sunflowers and China asters I planted in a corner are now in full bloom. The rays of sunlight aren't too strong. In the early evening, red dragonflies fly at an angle into the sunset, and I think of snowy winter. They say it is really cold in prison. We're fine. The changes that have happened to my body are truly amazing. I had no idea that so much liquid could gush out from my body, like a maple tree. I have gotten bigger. I eat a lot, and I am always sleepy. Ah, I wish I could show him once, just once, the little angel's face when she sleeps. She looks into my eyes and smiles. At first, her head seemed so flat, she looked like a baby owl. The contours of her face became clearer, her eyelids have come down, and now she looks like a little girl. You have to promise me. I'll tell Mom later, you really cannot say anything. There are so many things I worry about. Mom will have to take care of her until I finish graduate school. Yes, I worry about many things, but my worries are always about others. As for me, I am full of energy and courage to go on. And I am passionate about my work, too. Also, when you come here, can you bring some baby clothes and bedding? I did prepare, but I didn't find anything here that's good quality. Nothing synthetic, only cottons and natural fabrics. I am happy to hear that Mom expanded her store again. Really, she should have been born a man. She was never once depressed while being a breadwinner her whole life, and she has never been indebted to anyone. And that's not all! We were never late to pay our tuition fees, not even once. I am determined to be as tough a mother as she was. I don't think I can say anything when I am face to face with you, so I am writing this all down beforehand. As your older sister, I am so sorry. But I hope you understand.

Dear Jung Hee,

It has been already a month since you were here. Winter has come already. Migrating birds carry winter in their wings to the southern provinces. I can hear mallards crying from the reservoir and the lake. The tips of bamboo leaves are drying yellow, and only a few persimmons remain on top of the tree for the magpies.

I found our baby's name while scanning through a dictionary. It's Eun Gyul. It means the sunlight reflecting on a river. She is crawling everywhere now. The room is too small for her to ride the walker, but I can't leave her on the floor of my studio. The bedroom is filled with her stuff. We'll get through this winter here and will go to Seoul by next spring. I remember you saying that it may be less of a shock to Mom if you tell her gently, before I show up. I was against the idea at that time, because I didn't want her to run down here. I'll send you a letter a few days before our departure. Would you please talk to her around then? You also said that we should tell Mr. Oh, but I'll never allow that. He has too many things besides himself to protect for the rest of his life. I do not want to disturb him. Incidentally, he sent me a card. It has been confirmed, he got life. I expected it, but I sat there in a daze, breastfeeding the baby and reading his card over and over again. We don't know how the world will change in the future, and maybe he'll come back at one point. No matter what, I am not going to tell him until he's back. Or until he somehow finds out himself. Why do I have this premonition? I get startled sometimes with the ominous thought that I'll never see him again. If that happens, I want you to tell him about Eun Gyul.

The last few months of my father's life was a serene period of reconciliation for me. Except for the last month, he didn't stay in bed that much. He sat on a futon, wearing a T-shirt and a pair of wide-legged Korean pants, and read books. His face got darker and darker, and he was not able to eat much because his digestive system was failing. We could only offer him liquids. Later, he slept a lot. Once, he looked for me in the middle of the night.

"Yoon Hee, are you sleeping?"

"No, Father . . ."

"Open that door."

"Why, is it too hot in here for you?"

"No, just open it."

I got up, still half asleep, and pushed the sliding door of the room. The cold air drifted in from the empty living room, and we looked past the steps to the little courtyard of our house.

"Is there someone who came to see me?"

"Who's going to come at this hour?"

"Right . . . close the door."

Not understanding what was happening, I shut the door again.

"Father, did you . . . dream of someone?"

"I guess it was a dream."

"Who came to see you?"

"My old comrades came. They were all wearing tattered American military uniforms and had long hair and beards, like animals."

"You mean, your friends in the mountains?"

"There was a student, a factory girl, and my closest friend, the captain of cultural affairs—they were the people who were also sick and spent ten days at the infirmary with me right before I was captured. The two younger ones died before me, but the captain left us. He promised to come back and walked out of the tent, but he never returned. I guess he must have died, too."

"Look, Father, drink some fruit juice. You must be thirsty."

"I think I don't have much time left. I think they came to take me."

"What are you talking about? You don't even look like a sick person."

"I smell something fishy from my mouth. I know roughly what's going on. Your mom's not back yet?"

"No. It's right before the Lunar New Year, things are really busy at the market. She said she'd stay at the store until tomorrow."

"I should apologize to you both."

"Why do you say such things? We are so grateful to our parents. We went to good schools without worrying about anything. I'm already a senior at university, and Jung Hee will be a university student next year."

"That's what your mom did. Dear Yoon Hee, just after the liberation, I worked with my friends with the hope of making our country a place of freedom and equality. But look where we are today. I still can see the mountains where we ran around, making our way through snowstorms. But I was captured and sent to the Namwon detention camp, I wrote the letter of conversion like your uncle ordered me to, and my younger self died right there with that generation. I somehow persevered with this shell of myself until today."

"No, you did your best, Father."

"You resented me for that."

"Yes, when I was younger, because I didn't know anything. I thought people like you were evil."

"It seems I just waited in silence until you read many books and learned about history and all that. Yes . . . the world will keep changing. We were a tiny part of that change."

As he spoke, my father's voice became lower and thinner, and he began to fall asleep.

"This is not our world."

"What, Father, what did you say?"

"Walk your way, no matter what they say . . ."

"Where are you going?"

"I have to go . . ."

Then he fell into a deep sleep. Until a few hours before he passed away his mind was sound, he drank lots of fruit juice and, although his voice was weak and almost a whisper, he talked to me for a long time.

"Listen, when you face the end, you know exactly what your mistakes were, and you can also forgive yourself. I will never regret that period of my life. But I do wonder a lot if that was the only way. Yes, the Buddha said all of creation is bound by our own limitations. The world imagined by my friends was just a shining star up in the sky. Now looking at both sides, it's like looking in a mirror, the left and the right are reversed, but that's it. While fighting, they began to resemble each other. But don't you think that this incompleteness of our world is quite splendid? Before anything is accomplished, everyone from the same era all die. How do they say that in Buddhism . . . In one hundred years, none of us who exist today will remain. People of that age are all new. It just repeats over and over."

My mother brought the minister and deacons from her church. When they walked into the room, my father barely managed to sit up, but looked directly into the minister's eyes and said, "I have no prejudice against any religion, but I hate doing what I've never done before. I am repenting my sins, but I don't think there's any time left to correct them now. I'll allow you to pray quietly if it is for yourselves, not me."

It was a cold-hearted gesture toward my mother, but I thought he seemed so dignified. As the minister prayed for his pain and suffering and for peace of mind, my father lay there in silence with his eyes closed. When the prayer was over, the churchgoers quietly left the room so as not to disturb this dignified patient. My mother and I stayed up the whole night watching him. He withered away like a burning candle. Then he suddenly opened his eyes wide and screamed:

"I cannot die like this!"

My mother gathered his clenched fist quivering in the air and folded his hands on top of his chest.

"Please, my dear, some peace of mind . . ."

Sometimes, he muttered a song he used to sing when he was young.

"We're the fire that burns down the world, we're the hammer that shatters the iron chain. The sign of hope is the red flag, what we shout for is the battle . . ."

"My dear, please, no more, please, let's pray together . . ."

My father's breathing became difficult, and he was in pain

as he coughed with blood pooling in his throat. My mother burst into tears.

"Go now, please. Go!"

That night, my father was placed in the coffin my mother's congregation had prepared. According to the men who prepare the bodies for funerals, they can work out the life of the dead by looking at the corpse. And they also say the body of someone who dies from liver disease has the worst appearance, because all the other organs become filled with liquid and the body tends to decompose quickly. The body slowly deflates to about half the size it used to be and the arms are so stiff that they need to be broken with force when placing the body in the coffin. Fortunately for us, my father was put into the coffin as soon as he passed away, and his body was slipped in whole. But the problems began afterward. It was still cold outside and the room with the coffin was kept unheated, but it was springtime, after all. The body began to decompose soon after, and we could not get rid of the stench no matter how many sticks of incense were burnt. If I borrow the words of Christianity that mother believed then my father definitely went to hell, based on what his dead body looked like. Until the end, he was holding onto something and unable to let go, I think. When the pallbearers went to lift up the coffin, it would not budge. There was a commotion, and my mother ran into the room, wailing, to comfort the dead.

"My dear, please, you need to rest now and go where you have to go. Don't worry about me or the girls. I won't hate you, so please get up and go!"

People rushed into the room and pulled the coffin from the floor. Some sort of liquid had trickled out of it, and the coffin had stuck to the floor. I was standing outside the living room, facing the house. The pallbearers were carrying the coffin with strips of cotton cloth, but the one on the front missed a step as he was stepping down from the living room to the courtyard. The coffin slid toward me, and I fell backwards while trying to catch it. The people who were supposed to be in charge of running the funeral were so inexperienced that they didn't know what do, and I began to cry from shock and fear. Then I felt something wet running from my chest to my legs. I looked down and found dark blood that had collected in the coffin and oozed out from it. My two hands soaked in the blood of my dead father, I fell to the ground screaming and writhing and crying as if I had become a ghost myself. My mother was wailing, too.

"Dear God, how can you do this to us? How can you do this to your most beloved daughter? If you still hold onto all your sorrows and bitterness, you won't be able to rest anywhere, not underground, not in water, nowhere!"

That was how my father left us. I do not think that all those incidents were just accidental, as my mother tried to explain to me. Did he know that I would meet you and live the way I do now? Is that why he could not let go and leave in peace?

Later, I found a few curious things in a hidden drawer in my father's stationery case. There were three books and a bullet shell. The books were published in the years following the liberation, printed on what we called horse shit paper. You know, there was a shortage of everything at the time, so many books were printed faintly on dark recycled paper with speckles.

There was a collection of poems by Yi Yong Ak called *The Old House*, Goethe's *The Sorrows of Young Werther*, and Chekhov's *In the Ravine*. Inside the front covers, written in small, dainty handwriting, was a name Kim Soon Im and a date of Dan Ki year 4281. It was fashionable at the time to note the year starting from the founding of the first dynasty in the Korean peninsular, so Dan Ki year 4281 meant 1948. The ink had smudged and faded, but in that name the owner's touch still clearly remained. On the rusty and crumpled cover, a small piece of paper was attached with scotch tape. Something was written on it in tiny letters. *While hiking the Jiri Mountains, Spring 1969.* Where did it go, the bullet once attached to this shell? I'm guessing there's no connection between the books and the shell, based on the long period of time between the two dates. I just wonder, what was his relationship with the books' owner, Kim Soon Im? Did they meet after the liberation and fall in love? Or were they just comrades who belonged to the same organization? My father once said they shot the wounded when they had to retreat urgently, because those in pain would not survive at the infirmary. Maybe my father, on a hike years later, found the remnants of those old battles, in which one could not distinguish an enemy from a friend. Something made him want to pick up that shell and keep it. What triggered this, I'll never know. Now I safeguard the shell and the books that my father held onto.

However . . . ah, I do remember something! While he was sick, he once asked me, out of the blue, to get persimmons for him. It was too early in the season for persimmons, so I asked again, "Do you want the ripe ones or the sweet ones?"

"Try finding the unripe ones. If you soak them in salt water, they taste good."

We were told that vegetables and fruit were good for him, so my mother was buying case after case of not only the seasonal fruits but also sweet pineapples and other imported tropical fruits. I went to the market and tried to find the unripe persimmons that my father talked about, but all I could find were the sweet ones nicely packaged.

"Father, there's no unripe persimmons these days. They use chemicals or something like that to ripen them all."

"I guess they have to in order to sell them. Maybe we'll find them in the rural areas."

"Kids these days won't eat things like that."

My father held a sweet persimmon on his palm and opened and closed his hand several times while staring at the fruit.

"You just wanted to look at it, didn't you? "

"Why not? You can see the autumn."

He looked at the fruit for a long time. Finally, he spoke again.

"You're an artist, you want to hear a funny story about one autumn?"

My father told me that after the liberation, as soon as he came back from Japan, he joined the Preparation Committee for Founding the Nation and the Communist Party of Korea. At the time, although he was eager, there wasn't much for him to do, so he worked as a translator for publishers or a lecturer at factory night schools. My father got more involved during the movement against the new laws governing Seoul National University and the October Incident in the province of Kyungsang. Around the harvest time of that year, my father went down to his hometown to get some rice, which was becoming more and more scarce in Seoul.

He spent two days in the village and was coming back to Seoul. It was right after the railroad workers' strike, and there was a rush of passengers who had been delayed for days. Too many people were getting in and out of the train, breaking the glass windows, and even climbing up into the baggage compartment. At first my father rode the train by the exit, hanging onto the door, and slowly he was able to push inside until he ended up in a little corridor in front of the bathroom. When he sat down, he saw a young woman with bobbed hair squatting on her own bag. He assumed she was a student who had gone to her hometown to get food, just as my father had. Before they exchanged words, he knew, he said, he could feel that she was an intellectual. She was reading a pocket edition from Iwanami, the legendary Japanese publishing company.

"It's only been two days since the train started running again, I think that's why there's such a crowd."

He put his backpack on the floor so she could sit on it.

"I heard that a few thousand railroad workers were arrested."

He asked her once again, looking at the pocket edition in her hand.

"What are you reading?"

As if she was a little embarrassed, she flipped the book and showed him the cover. It was *The Origin of the Family, Private Property, and the State* by Engels. My father quickly realized what kind of person she was.

"Which . . . organization do you belong to?"

"The Coalition of Democratic Youth."

"Ah, really? So glad to meet you. In the city of Daegu, a civilian resistance has begun. I'm sure it'll soon spread throughout the country."

"We're also participating in the protest against the Seoul National University situation. It began within the campus, but now it is all over the country."

"The liberation is still far away. We have to start from the beginning again."

"And you . . . are you in school?"

"No, I gave that up a long time ago in Japan. At the moment, I'm working in other provinces."

They didn't talk too much, but they understood each other. They arrived at the Seoul central station at three o'clock in the morning, hours before dawn. The only public transportation available at the time was the streetcars, which were not running at that hour. Furthermore, in the city and the rest of country, a state of emergency had been declared, and a curfew was imposed for the hours before daybreak. The waiting room in the station was packed with people sleeping with a sheet of newspaper as a blanket. The two young people stood by the exit waiting for the sunrise, when a woman approached them.

"Come stay at our boardinghouse! The price is reasonable, and it's very close."

"I do think it'll be better if we can rest a little."

My father got up carrying her bag, and she followed silently. They followed the woman through little alleyways behind the station and arrived at a Japanese-style boarding-house. She seemed to think that they were a couple, and showed them to a room without asking them any questions. It was a room divided into three sections, the floor covered with *tatami* mats and the bedding neatly folded on one side of the room. In the middle section was the sort of Japanese-style heater that looks like a table covered with a blanket. The two sat facing each other with the heater in between them and waited for the sunrise. It was tedious, but above all, they were starving. Since dinner the night before, they had eaten nothing, and had stayed up all night in a train. My father fumbled inside his backpack and found the sticky rice cake his grandmother had packed for him. He offered it to her.

"Try it. You must be hungry."

"But this is for your family!"

"I think there's water in that kettle, so eat slowly and don't choke on it."

So each of them ate three pieces of rice cake. But the sun still did not come up, so they sat there for a long time. This time, my father found persimmons from his backpack.

"I took it down from the tree in my hometown. Taste it."

The girl accepted it as there was no other way to handle the situation, and she began nibbling the persimmon. My father told me he thought it was understandable that she was trying to be modest, but the way she was eating it didn't look so pretty, because she was eating it like a mouse, holding it with two hands and taking tiny bites with her front teeth. He thought, maybe she's savoring every bite, not wanting to finish it too quickly. Feeling a little sorry for her, he took another persimmon out of his backpack and offered it to her.

"Take one more."

The girl accepted it and sat there holding the persimmon. At one point, my father dozed off, and when he woke up he was alone in the room and the sun was way up in the sky. He had no idea when she had left. In the place where she had sat was a note, folded like a ribbon.

Dear Sir, you were in such a deep slumber, so I decided not to awake you. Wishing you the best of luck in all your endeavors. I do hope to meet you again, wherever that may be . . .

When he got back home, my father took a bite of one of the persimmons, but he had to spit it out because it was too bitter. He and my mother were still in their newlywed phase, and she couldn't stop herself from laughing when she saw his face distorted with pain.

"You can't eat unripe persimmons just like that! You have to soak them in water with salt or rice for a few days."

"What did you call this?"

"An unripe persimmon. It ripens and softens if you leave it under the sunlight for about three weeks, but you can eat it in a few days if you soak it in salt water."

Only then did my father realize why the girl from the train nibbled on the persimmon he gave her. Isn't that unbelievable? She finished the whole persimmon, something inedible, enduring it without once mentioning anything because she knew he was being nice. I don't know if my father was telling me the truth, but he said she wasn't so pretty. He didn't say she was ugly, but he just described her as admirable.

He did meet her again the following spring. On March 1, 1947, there was the biggest clash yet between the Left and the Right since the liberation, followed by the Jeju Island incident in April and widespread strikes, uprisings, and violent clashes throughout the country. The leftist organizations held a celebration at Nam Mountain in Seoul, in memory of the peaceful uprising against the Japanese occupation on March 1, 1919. After the event was over, they walked from Nam Mountain to the South Gate market, while the rightist organizations who had their own event at the Seoul Sports Complex were marching past the Chosun Bank, and the Department of Police and Firefighters toward the South Gate. The opposing sides crashed into each other at the five-lane street in front of the South Gate. That day, my father was not among those marching in the crowd, but walking on a sidewalk, and he saw her, in the middle of the crowd, marching with a placard. My father rushed to her and walked fast alongside her.

"How are you? Do you remember me?"

"Of course I do."

"I'm so sorry I forced you to eat that unripe persimmon. I really didn't know."

He said she laughed, her hand covering her mouth. The marching stopped right at a point where they could see the South Gate, and soon an attack from the right began and the line was demolished. There were gunshots, and the crowd scattered to the roads diverging in many directions, the wounded falling onto the streetcar rails covered with blood. It all happened so suddenly, and my father was separated from the girl from the train in an instant. He said he worried for a long time if she was safe. So I asked him, "So this is your story about one autumn. Did you meet her again later?"

"Of course I did, we were on the same side."

"How many times?"

"She died . . ."

That was his answer, and he would not say anything more. Once he shut his mouth, he gave me the same answer no matter how many times I asked. Maybe the owner of these books, Kim Soon Im, is the girl from the train, and the memory behind the shell has something to do with her. But these are only my best guesses.

I think I have said everything I wanted to about my father. Several times I painted my father's unripe persimmon, with a broken branch and dying leaves still attached to it.

10

Yoon Hee confessed to her sister about the baby, but she tried very hard for all those years not to have that piece of information reach me in any way. Perhaps she was determined not to lean on me, not even for psychological support, while I was imprisoned. I have a daughter. A child of Kalmae, brought into this world by Yoon Hee.

Ever since I came here, I have not been able to fall into that deep, death-like sleep, not for one night. Another day passed by. My sense of space was slowly recovering. As soon as I woke up, I got ready to cook. From the packed little refrigerator, I took out fish and vegetables and prepared them for a stew, and put rice into an electric rice cooker. I was keeping myself busy in front of the stovetop for a while when I heard a pair of shoes dragging on the ground. When I looked out, I saw the Soonchun lady walking in, carrying a big, round basket on her head.

"Good morning, ma'am."

"Did you sleep well? I just brought this little bit over. Try it."

The Soonchun lady sat on the little porch, put the basket down on the ground, and showed me what was under a sheet of newspaper.

"Some pickled garlic stems, some pickled sesame leaves, and this is young radish kimchi, really fresh. And I also brought you some bean paste and pepper paste, just to taste, not too much."

"Really, you didn't have to do this."

"You should put the kimchi in the refrigerator. Garlic stems and sesame leaves are salty so they should be okay at room temperature. The pastes should be stored with other seasonings. By the way, this smells good!"

The Soonchun lady opened the pot lid and nodded in approval.

"So, you're a chef! This looks good."

"Would you like some?"

"No, no, I was just talking. I already had breakfast."

I pulled a chair over and sat down facing her. Even a moment of silence was too awkward for her, and she hurriedly got up.

"Goodness, I forgot all about it! I have all these vegetables in salt and I forgot to prepare scallions. I should get going."

"Wait, ma'am, just one second."

The Soonchun lady gazed intently at my face and waited.

"I have something to ask you, please sit down."

"What do you want to ask?"

I could no longer hesitate.

"After I left, the following year, Miss Han . . . she gave birth here?"

"Phew . . . I was so nervous, I've been wondering when you would bring that up. I delivered her, you know, since there's no midwife in this town. She had a noble face, just like her mother. They came here together, maybe not every year, but at least every other summer vacation, and we didn't see her for years while her mother was in Germany. I almost didn't recognize her when she came back about three years ago! She was a big girl then, as tall as her mother."

"I had no idea. My sister didn't say anything, either."

"I guessed that was the case, and since it was none of my business I kept quiet. You see . . . no matter what, legally she was unmarried, and I can't imagine what Miss Han must have gone through. Only her immediate family members knew, and they kept it under wraps, I think."

"It's . . . all my fault."

"What could you have done in your situation? As my late husband said, it's because you were born in the wrong era."

"Then, does she live with her grandmother now?"

"No, I heard that she was registered as the sister's child."

"You mean Han Jung Hee?"

"I think so."

I had never met Jung Hee, but had heard so much about her from Yoon Hee that I could picture her face and personality.

"I heard she has her own practice in Seoul, I think her husband is also a doctor. I have their address and phone number written down somewhere. Would you like me to find out?"

"Yes, please, but no need to hurry."

"Well, I really should get going."

The Soonchun lady got up from the porch and walked out to the fence around the house, but I could not say a thing, and I sat on the chair blankly.

If Eun Gyul was born in 1982, she was almost eighteen now, a young woman. I thought there was nothing left for me in this world, but Yoon Hee gave me a child. Suddenly, I felt impatient and I wanted to run down to the main house and make the phone call. But I was worried about what, if anything, Eun Gyul knew about her father. What did Yoon Hee tell our daughter about me? Maybe I shouldn't meet her, I thought, and my heart ached. I now realized why Yoon Hee insisted on writing down every little thing about her father's youth and kept reminiscing. She was probably worried about the love-hate relationship between a father and a daughter that Eun Gyul and I might continue on this earth.

Until the fall of 1980, Choi Dong Woo and I spent time confined to a small room we rented in a slum. Once in a while, Kun came by to inform us what was going on around us. Suk Joon left for Japan before the new semester began, and Kun seemed to be overburdened by managing the members by himself. One day, Kun came over and told us, "This neighborhood is no longer safe. I heard that there's going to be a major shakedown."

"There's nowhere else to go! They are holding community meetings to inform people about the wanted list, there are checkpoints just to cross the Han River, and they are even searching Buddhist temples."

"That Gymnasium President?* He announced that he has formed

* Chun Doo Hwan, the army general who became the fifth president after the Kwangju Incident, held an election by committee and an inauguration at a gymnasium. Hence, he was nicknamed **Gymnasium President**.

something called the national security committee, and that it will arrest all criminals who commit harm against society."

"Harm against society? What the hell is that?"

"They say people prone to commit crimes, like gang members, but I bet they will include anyone antigovernment, like us."

"Isn't massacring innocent civilians the biggest harm against society?"

Dong Woo was being cynical, but Kun was seriously concerned. He sighed.

"We need to find a new place as soon as possible. Any ideas?"

"How about you? You should take care of yourself first."

"I'm fine. I'm with Jung Ja."

Hearing this, Dong Woo, who was lying on the floor leisurely with his arms crossed under his head, sprang up.

"What? What did you say?"

"Why are you so surprised? Hae Soon already gave us her blessing."

"Who said that dating between members is allowed?"

Listening to Dong Woo flaring up, Kun simply smiled as he looked into space.

"Hmm, this is not dating, this is life, everyday life. We are going to get married. You should congratulate us. I actually came here today to tell you that. I also started a knitting factory. I'm the manager."

"You think people collected money to buy knitting machines for you? That was for those who lost their jobs!"

"There are four workers, and I run around getting business."

I was listening to their conversation, and I wanted to encourage Kun.

"Good for you. Good luck, too! But you'll be very busy because of our work."

"It's not a problem, the gatherings are usually after business hours. Anyhow, that's my problem, but you still have to move . . ."

"We should talk about it. Let's say we'll leave here by sometime next week. Why don't we ask our sponsors?"

It was exactly two days after Kun came to see us. Dong Woo had gone down to the main street to buy groceries, but he came running back out of breath. He banged shut the door in the kitchen that led directly out to the alleyway, then he put the lock on and secured it with a long spoon. He was still standing there with his ear attached to the thin plywood door, trying to figure out what was going on outside. I opened the door from the room to the kitchen and asked, "What happened, were you followed?"

"Shhh, be quiet. And turn the light off."

I became nervous hearing his frozen voice, so I turned the fluorescent light off as quickly as I could. He was still standing by the door in the same posture. Soon, we heard the footsteps of several people, and voices talking. The voices got louder.

"This way!"

"There are so many little alleys, who knows where he hopped to?"

There were sounds of footsteps. Flashlights wavered. They slowly walked away. Someone was calling from far away, "Detective Yi, come over here."

Police! Only then I was truly shocked and scared. I sat in the darkness without moving, as if my back was glued to the wall. Dong Woo sneaked into the room and sat next to me, his knees touching his mouth and his back straight against the wall. His breathing was even now.

"What happened?"

As I whispered, Dong Woo answered in a whisper, too.

"Phew . . . I almost got caught. You know the little market by the street down there, right?"

I knew it well. It was more like a gathering place for street vendors at the entrance to the neighborhood. Throughout the summer, I walked there to buy watermelons and melons and vegetables, and it was the place where the men in this neighborhood bought special treats for their families when they had money left over from the pubs and bars.

"I was walking down there when I saw both plainclothes and uniformed policemen, a lot of them, inspecting everyone, I mean everyone. So I just stopped there. They even had those chicken coop buses parked by the street."

"Kun was right. It's a crackdown. The police and the military are working together to round up as many people as possible, and didn't he say that they send the criminals for some sort of purification or reeducation?"

"That's it. If they find us, it would be like catching lobsters while looking for anchovies. I was trying to be inconspicuous, but my eyes met those of a plainclothes officer. *Hey, you over there, come here,* he said.

Me? Yes, you, come here, and he walked fast toward me. So what else could I do? I ran!"

"And he's thinking, why would he run unless he had to? You're busted!"

"I know, I know. It doesn't look good. Think about it, they'll soon go around the neighborhood and ask everyone about renters and tenants, and somebody could rat us out by saying something like, over there in that house are two young men."

"Let's stay up through the night and leave early tomorrow morning. We might lose time, but they'll have to change guards at some point and dispatch from various points downtown."

Dong Woo and I waited in darkness for things to quiet down. Far into the night, there was no signs of people walking around, and the sound of whistles in the distance had died down, too. It seemed they had all returned to the local police station with the chicken coop bus. Dong Woo opened his mouth first.

"I'm hungry."

"Shall we make some ramen?"

"Yeah, turn the light on."

I fumbled for the switch and turned it on. The room became too bright, and I had to sneeze. With the return of the light, the darkness disappeared at once, and with it our fear. Once we had quickly fed ourselves ramen noodles and sour kimchi, we were ready to push aside every worry and trouble of the world. I opened the back window and looked outside. About an arm's length away, there was the neighboring house's cement block wall, and connected to it was the slate roof of the house.

"Why don't we just sleep? I don't think anything will happen tonight," said Dong Woo as he took down the bedding and jumped onto it. I agreed with him.

"I guess we can worry about it when the sun rises again tomorrow. And hey, don't forget the contact point."

"No, I won't."

We fell asleep with our clothes on and important papers packed in our backpacks and placed by our head. I don't know how long we slept. We heard someone knocking on the door. I sprang up first, followed by Dong Woo. We were also wearing our shoes.

"Hello? Open the door, please!"

The back window was already open, too.

"Who is it?"

Dong Woo asked as he signaled to me with his eyes. I stepped up to the window and put one foot on the neighboring wall.

"I'm the head of this neighborhood's association."

Dong Woo shouted back as he followed me and stepped up to the window.

"Give me a minute, I need to put some clothes on."

I was already up on the roof of the neighboring house, using the wall as a stepping stone.

"What are you waiting for, break it down!"

Someone yelled, and I heard several feet kicking the plywood door. Dong Woo climbed over the neighbor's wall. I lay down flat on my belly under the deep shadow of the roof. Someone flashed a light out the window and shouted, "The alleyway behind, they ran toward there!"

"I knew they were on the wanted list!"

There were footsteps running all around. There seemed to be at least seven or eight of them. They left the light on and searched our room, through our books and clothes and all our things. It was almost four in the morning when two of them who stayed behind packed everything up and finally left. I looked around to make sure there was no one around, and when I was certain of it I jumped from the roof to the alley. I ran toward the pine forest at the edge of the neighborhood. It was fortunate that we had packed at least one bag each. As I left the residential area I came upon a crumbling hill and a weed bush filled with chirping crickets. I struggled to walk up the hill without a path. At first, the hill was overrun with acacia trees, and my pants legs kept catching on their branches. I forced my way into the forest and found a place to sit where the pine trees grew more sparsely. I had not exercised in a while, so I was out of breath and sweat covered my forehead and chest. From the hill, I saw the gloomy rooftops of the slum below and the streetlamps and lights of the city further down. A blue and red neon sign continued flashing a word I could not make out on top of a high-rise with no lights on. For the hunted, Seoul was as foreign as a city in a different country. There were many different houses imbedded in the darkness like pebbles, but there was not one room for me to lie down in. As I caught my breath and calmed down, I belatedly realized that the forest was filled with a chorus of insects. I still remember clearly that early fall morning, listening to little insects singing and understanding the small creatures' joy of life in the midst of a world full of pain and danger. For years in my solitary confinement, I would hear the sudden appearance of crickets, usually on the first day of autumn or around then, and I would always think of that early morning on that crumbling hill waiting for the sunrise just after I had barely escaped capture.

When the sun came up, I went down the other side of the hill and into a busier neighborhood. This was at least three or four bus stops away from where we used to live, so I was not too nervous. I went to our contact point. I took a bus downtown and walked to a Catholic church near a university hospital. We chose this place because the garden of the church had three different exits, each connected to three different commercial districts. The backyard was also nicely wooded, and there were wooden benches all over the place. Once seated, it was possible to observe the church building without being too conspicuous. As I walked onto the church ground, I saw Dong Woo emerging from the wooded area and waving at me. I was relieved. I had been anxious not knowing whether he had been caught after he climbed down the wall. We sat next to each other on a bench in the most secluded area under some wisteria trees. Dong Woo took out a small carton of milk and a piece of bread from his backpack and smiled as he handed them to me.

"First, eat."

"What happened? I thought you were caught in the alleyway after you climbed over the wall."

"Don't ask. I climbed over to the neighbor's house but they were already guarding every alley. So I climbed another wall and went to the next house, but this house's yard was small and there was no place to hide. Then I saw a big plastic container with a lid next to the door. I opened it, and thank God, it was almost empty except for a couple of used briquettes. So I climbed in and closed the lid and crouched down. Ugh, my legs were cramping, my feet were numb, I almost wanted to go out and turn myself in!"

"We have papers, but our books and everything else we owned were taken."

"What can we do now? Anyway, there must be traces of our real identities in there, and they'll begin to tighten the net."

Quickly, I fumbled around inside my shirt and found a pocketbook. I took out the ID card that was hidden in the inner flap of the pocketbook and put it into the inner pocket of my jacket.

"We need to burn the pocketbooks first. There are too many phone numbers and notes."

"Just memorize the most important numbers. If we need them, we can always ask around, and most of all, we should not contact anyone directly."

"You do have an ID card, don't you?" I asked Dong Woo.

"It's not mine. It was made somewhere near Inchon. There was a factory worker who's good at photos and government seals."

"Is it safe?"

"Of course. I was searched several times outside of Seoul and had no problem."

We each took out our datebooks and tore out every page, including the vinyl covers, and we made a pile under a bench and set them on fire. The papers flared up quickly. There was a little bit of smoke, but there was no one around so early on a weekday morning in the garden of a Catholic church. The vinyl burnt with a stench, leaving only a handful of black ash. Dong Woo patted my backpack.

"What should we do with these papers?" he asked. "We can't get rid of them."

"This is our organization, right in here. We have to protect it. How about safekeeping it at Kun's factory?"

Dong Woo paused for a second.

"Wait a minute, it's not like they knew where and who we were and came to raid us. It was a coincidence that we were caught during a crackdown."

"But that will change from now on. Our case will be sent to a different department. I bet they realized right away that we are wanted. There were books. And our names may be written somewhere in one of those books."

"At the very least, they'll figure out our real names. Not to mention what we look like."

"For a while, we need to remain inconspicuous. Let's call Kun and talk with him."

I paused.

"We have to be careful not to cross paths with those from Kwangju."

As soon as we left the church, we found a public phone near the bus stop and called Kun. He came immediately to meet us near the East Gate market. We walked into a twenty-four-hour café in the market and gathered around a corner table. There were a few store owners from other cities and truck drivers sleeping sprawled on chairs. As soon as we sat down, Kun scolded us.

"You know, it's really frustrating. What did I say? Didn't I tell you that they'll be looking everywhere and that you should move as fast as you can?"

"We were just putting it off for a few days. It's our fault."

"Well, no more of that. Now, this is a real emergency. It's October now, so let's break up for a couple of months."

Dong Woo shook his head when he heard Kun's opinion.

"Two months is too long. Let's say we'll take a break for one month. We'll need to start running the organization again in the new year. What are you going to do?"

I realized Dong Woo was talking to me, but I could not think of a single place to go so quickly.

"How about you?" I replied.

"I'm thinking of leaving Seoul."

"We'll remain in contact?"

"Of course. I'll call Kun once a week and report back that I'm okay."

"Okay, there's a place I'm thinking of going, too."

I was the first one to go through my pockets and take out money.

"Okay, let's do some accounting right here. I have about . . . 500,000 won right now."

Dong Woo also pulled money from his pants and jacket pockets and put it on the tea table.

"I have . . . 400,000 won. Kun, you should contribute some, too."

"Oh, shoot. All I have right now is money to buy yarn. Fine, I'll put down one half of what I have."

The total was 1,200,000 won.

"We should set aside an emergency fund for the organization," suggested Dong Woo. "We can't waste money like water. After all, it was collected by our sponsors. We can get by with half of that."

"What are you talking about? We can start an emergency fund among the knitting factory club members. You should split that money between the two of you."

I took out 500,000 won from the pile and handed it over to Kun along with my backpack filled with papers.

"We'll work for a living. You'll need money to organize a meeting next month."

"Wow, I got interest of 200,000 won within a minute!"

Dong Woo got up first and patted my shoulder.

"Okay, let's get going. I'll leave first."

We did not ask each other where we would go. Dong Woo left the café and I remained a bit longer, seated facing Kun.

"How's the factory going?"

"It's so busy we may need extra hands. It's fun, too."

"Do you live there, too?"

"We found a monthly rental, a two-room place, and it is the biggest house in the slum! In one room, Jung Ja and Hae Soon and I eat and sleep, and we put the knitting machines in the other room and on the porch. It's livable. By the way, where do you plan to go underground?"

"Somewhere near Seoul."

"Report back to me at the beginning of each week, please. And leave a name."

"Fine, let's use Kim Jun Woo, it's the one I used before. I should go, too."

I left Kun in the café and walked toward the market. It was past the early morning rush hour and somewhat in between the busy times of day, so the storefront was pretty quiet. I had decided to go to Anyang. We all learned the rules of the runaways from a little book, a collection of European experiences, and those rules were quite beneficial in urban areas. It was Kwon Hyung, the one who was helping Nam Soo and supporting Bong Han's hiding, who found the book from a street vendor selling foreign books from the US army base. Kwon Hyung spent ten days translating it, and we typed it, made it into booklets, and distributed them to various groups. I still remember some of the basic principles from the book.

When an activist goes underground, this means he is walking into the life of faceless people, disconnecting himself from familiar surroundings and identities. He should have no name, nothing distinctive. He should also learn the basic skills of making a living, just like any ordinary citizen. He should be ready to function in any job that is offered to him. A person without work loses his ability to survive, and furthermore he cannot be trusted by many who might have provided assistance to him. So find a job, and find as soon as possible neighbors and friends who can surround the weakened self in that unfamiliar territory he has just entered.

Disconnect any communication with the past. No telegrams, no letters, no personal deliveries, but above all, no telephone calls. When there is an absolute need for communication between two runaways, they must go through a third party connected to both of them, and the third party needs to double check everything. The third party in charge of communication needs to check safety before everything. The organization should be aware of the runaway's situation from afar, and it should never attempt to assign the runaway to any position or to communicate with him.

The runaway should avoid built up areas. His appearance and speech should be ordinary. It is not advisable for the runaway to walk through the downtown area. When walking in the city, use the inside of the pedestrian passages and utilize storefront windows. When walking across a pedestrian crossing, wait behind the crowd for the signal to change. When among the crowd, do not walk too fast or too slow. When using public transportation, do not travel long distances. If there is a need for a long trip, divide it into several segments and switch modes of transportation. When riding a bus in the city, the safest spot is right behind the driver, the row toward the traffic and closest to an exit. The rows toward the pedestrians, and especially the window seats, are dangerous. Move around mostly at night; the next safe time is early in the morning, but avoid rush hours when there is a surge of crowds. Be invisible and inconspicuous so that no one can remember you.

The rules continued endlessly. But there was one thing that stuck with me for a long time.

The first duty of a runaway to his peers is that he should never be captured. For a runaway, hiding is the most important activity. He is a germ carrier who can spread danger to the others. Therefore, he needs to isolate himself and fight with himself until all danger is cleared.

Discipline, integrity, self-sacrifice, faith, courage . . . there were many words like that hidden between the lines, and they constricted my whole body. It was like panting with a hot, dry tongue. Such dry, overheated sentences made me thirsty, so that I wanted to drink cold ice water streaming down between rocks until my chest was frozen.

The grapevines from the old days were no longer there in Anyang. Instead, there were small sweatshops, bars full of hookers, and an open sewer full of dirty waste water. I was actually happy to see overgrowing reed canary grass by the open sewer. I presume this is gone by now, replaced by high-rise apartment buildings.

I found the woodworking shop owned by Sergeant First Class Yim. He was about ten years older than me, and he was the staff sergeant in charge of my barrack when I was serving in the military. I met him once by chance after I was discharged, when I was almost forced by friends in the movement to teach at a night school in an industrial area. The night school usually ended around ten at night, when the night shift began. I met at a street-side bar with a friend who was also teaching at the night school, as we were hoping to fill our stomachs with a bowl of noodles and a bottle of soju. A few men were in there, already tipsy, drinking soju and grilling a plateful of chicken intestines and cow's heart. We were late and we did not have a lot of money, so we squashed into a corner and ordered. The three middle-aged men were loud. Two of them were wearing uniforms from an electronics company while one was in a suit, and the one in a suit called the ones in uniforms sir and poured them glass after glass of soju. I knew a few girls at the night school who worked long hours at the electronics company and were paid ridiculously low wages, and I glared at the men at the bar from time to time, taking the girls' side. At one point, the man in the suit glanced at us and met my eyes. He first turned away then looked back at me. I had also recognized him. He leaned over and asked me, "I was just wondering, where did you do your military service?"

"Sergeant Yim, it's me. I'm Oh Hyun Woo."

"Hey, you bastard! You're Corporal Oh! I was thinking from the moment you walked in that you looked really familiar!"

That night, Sergeant Yim and I went on to another place. Within a few months of my discharge, Sergeant Yim had also quit the military as a career soldier. Soon he found a job as an entry-level worker in the woodworking department of an electronics factory, and it did not take long for the manager to realize that there was a professional soldier in his charge. Within a year, Yim was promoted to a foreman position. He received more training and proved himself to be a good manager of other workers, so he rose again to the head of his department in five years. By that time, he was well aware of the workings of the woodshop, and he was able to figure out where to get supplies and how to find a job as a subcontractor. He left the factory with a few skilled workers and opened his own, and so he had become a success story after being discharged from the military, so to speak. That night, completely drunk, he dragged me all the way to his home right next to his factory in Anyang. He had this vague idea that a night school teacher like me could only be seditious, doing things that could not be beneficial to our nation. He was afraid to get involved, but he confessed that somehow he was in awe, too.

"What do we know about what you're really doing? I just know that you believe in something. There are those who fight, then there are those of us who have to feed the family and survive."

Whenever he was drunk, Sergeant Yim repeated something similar to that.

I walked along the Anyang stream. On top of the furrows alongside an unpaved road was the cement block structure that housed the woodworking factory, and behind it an almost identical structure that served as living quarters. Piled up in front of the factory were raw materials and waste, and I could hear from outside the piercing noise of an electric saw. I looked around in front of the factory, then finally pushed open the plywood door and looked inside. I saw Sergeant Yim in a vest, his head wrapped in a towel and his mouth covered with a mask, concentrating on his task. I pushed the door open further and walked into the factory, the air filled with sawdust. I could not hear what he was saying because of the noise, but I did see him waving at me from his station. He walked over and yelled into my ear, "Hey, Corporal Oh! I haven't seen you for years! Let's go outside."

He pulled my jacket and dragged me outside. He grabbed my hand and shook it, and studied me from head to toe.

"Look at you, you look awful. Are you still doing that stuff?"

"Well, I guess so."

"Wait, it's lunchtime soon, I'll be right back."

Sergeant Yim came back with an air force jacket over his vest and his hair covered with sawdust.

"Let's have lunch at home. Hey, do they offer you lunch or dinner when you run around protesting? Get a grip! How old are you now, thirty?"

"I came here to ask you for a job, Sergeant."

"Listen to this! Do you want me to get into trouble, too? Anyhow, let's go in."

We walked into his cement block house. Inside, the walls were plastered nicely with clean wallpaper, and the entrance was covered with sleek linoleum. He shouted, "Honey, I'm home!"

A sliding glass door to the kitchen opened quietly, and a woman who appeared to be older than Sergeant Yim peeked out and put a finger to her mouth.

"Shhh . . . the baby will wake up! Don't go into the master bedroom, he just fell asleep."

"Hey, you remember this guy? It's Corporal Oh!"

Mrs. Yim's hair was permed curly like ramen noodles, and she was wearing a pair of red rubber gloves. I bowed to her while holding her hands.

"Yes, I remember the smart university student. Why do you still call him a corporal? I am so sick of your military talk."

"Can we get some lunch? I'm so hungry, I'm about to die."

We walked into the smaller second bedroom. It looked like a room for a child in elementary school, with a desk and bookcase built by the father, and children's books neatly stacked.

"I thought one was enough," Sergeant Yim said. "But she said it's not enough. So now we add one this late in our lives, and we can't sleep well at night. I can't even watch TV when I want to! By the way, are you serious about finding a job here?"

"Yes, I am. I don't know if it's going to be for a month or several months, but I need to make a living."

"You bastard, you're running away, aren't you? I know everything. Are you in big trouble?"

"It's not me, I just have to disappear for a while for the others' sake."

"I hope I'm not gonna get into trouble because of you."

"It really isn't a big deal."

"Okay, fine. What can I do, there is something called loyalty. But I can't pay you much. You'll have to be a trainee, so I can't use you as anything other than an assistant. Still, you'll be able to eat three times a day. And here, I'm not your sergeant, so call me Mr. Manager. And I'm sorry to do this, but you're my employee, so I'll just call you Oh. Agreed?"

"Agreed, one hundred percent."

The lunch table was brought in. It was not one of the slapdash meals prepared by the clumsy hands of Dong Woo and me, it was a real home-cooked meal. The kimchi tasted good, and the seaweed soup was silky. Sergeant Yim, who had been concentrating on his lunch for a while, raised his head.

"By the way, do you have a place to stay?"

I shook my head.

"Of course you don't."

"Would it be okay if I stayed at the factory after work? I'll clean up nicely."

"No, that wouldn't work. It's a fire hazard, and I don't want the others to talk. Let's see, you have no luggage? You left with nothing other than what you have on?"

"Yes, early this morning."

Flabbergasted, Sergeant Yim looked up to the ceiling with his mouth full of rice.

"Bastard, why are you doing this to me? Okay, fine, listen, I'll find someone who can take care of you, and you should stick close to them, be joined at the hip, that's how you're going to survive."

After lunch, we went back to the factory. Sergeant Yim searched through his jacket and found a 10,000-won bill and gave it to me.

"Well, this is just a first day thing. There's a movie theater over there showing two movies for one, so go watch both of them and come back here around seven. You're going to be such a hassle!"

I smiled sheepishly and walked down the unpaved road to the business district. There was not a single young man at the movie theater, only a few old people and a couple kids who were let out of school by noon. I took a seat in the middle in front of a wide aisle and stretched my legs out. I spent hours watching the movie and dozing off. I could not stay awake.

I saw two movies in a row, but it was not even five in the afternoon by the time I got out. I walked out of the theater and into the traditional market. I bought underwear and socks and toiletries, and also a duffle bag to pack them in. I got a pair of pants and a new shirt. I decided to take a bath, since I might be conspicuous if I looked too disheveled. There was no one at the public bath; the whole place was mine. I used a disposable razor to shave my stubble cleanly. I changed into my new underwear and socks, and I felt like I was back home. Lastly, I walked into a restaurant and ordered a spicy beef stew for dinner. I pledged that I would support myself with my daily earnings.

"Oh, say hello to Mr. Park, the best employee at our factory."

Sergeant Yim introduced me to a tall young man blanketed with sawdust. Park readily offered his hand, as if we were meeting at a social occasion, and shook mine.

"I heard a lot about you from Mr. Manager here. Welcome."

"Good. Oh, I need to talk to you before you leave."

He took me into the factory where the machines had stopped running.

"Listen, I told that guy that you're a brother of a friend of mine from the country. I thought you should know that. That guy, he's really cheerful and he's a good guy. You should be roommates. They all do that to cut the living costs. You pay half the rent and meals, things like that. Now, go."

"Thank you, Sergeant."

"Bastard, I told you! Call me Mr. Manager!"

I followed Park along the Anyang stream. A cluster of barracks was standing on a hill, and next to them was row after row of long storage structures that together looked like a weird chicken farm. Later, I learned those were called the honeycomb houses and were common in an industrial area. Around the entrance to the village were a handful of little stores, all lit up, and it looked like the marketplace in the slum I had just left.

"So where in the countryside are you from, Mr. Oh?"

"Not too far, in the Kyunggi province."

"It's hard to make a living in the country these days, isn't it?"

"Yeah. I wasted too much time after high school, and then I had to do my military service, and now it's too late. I thought maybe I should at least learn some sort of a skill before I get married."

"Let's go grocery shopping. We need something for dinner."

"I already ate."

"You did? Okay then, you want to get a drink?"

"Okay, I'll buy you one tonight."

"Why?"

"Call it a newcomer's bribe," I said cheerfully, trying to match his spirit. "Hopefully you'll be nice to me."

Park laughed out loud.

"I wonder if one drink will be enough. Let's see."

He walked into a little pub among other little stores and restaurants at the entrance of the honeycomb village. As he sat down on the long wooden bench he said, "I come here a lot."

The pub was about sixty square feet. There were three tables, and the kitchen was just big enough for one person to turn around. Still, on the wall was a menu neatly written in calligraphy, and the smell of grilled fish permeated from the kitchen. Inside, a group of three men were drinking soju.

"The usual, please."

"Okay."

I was curious and asked Park, "What's the usual?"

"Well, there's a sequence. First, a bottle of soju and a grilled mackerel. Then poached tofu, but since I haven't had dinner yet, I'll add one order of ramen."

"Sounds pretty substantial!"

A whole mackerel, scored and grilled with a little salt, arrived on the table still sizzling, soon followed by a bottle of soju. With his finger-tips, he lightly shook off my hand reaching for the bottle, poured the liquor into my glass first, then handed me the bottle. I poured him a glass. Park raised the glass and said, "Cheers! Congratulations on your new job."

"Great to meet you."

We emptied the glasses in one shot. Park poured himself another glass and finished it again. His head was still covered in white sawdust, and his fingers holding the little glass were dirty and stubby; they looked like a bunch of little twigs. But his neck muscles, exposed whenever he poured the alcohol down his throat, seemed so healthy and impressive. His eyes were bleary with exhaustion, but his fatigue was that of a satisfied man who had finished the labor that was assigned to him.

"Mr. Oh, do you have a girlfriend?" he asked me, without pausing from stuffing himself with the mackerel's flesh.

"No, I don't have one, it's too much of a hassle."

"You want me to introduce you to someone?"

"Not really—I mean I can't even support myself."

Park winked at me.

"Don't worry. Whatever you earn as a daily wage, it'll never be enough. You know, I'm considered a technician, but I'm always in the red at the end of the month. I can never save a penny. How can I get married and have a family?"

"So why do you need the additional headache of a relationship?"

"Girls have the same problem as we do. But we can't spend this golden age in our lives just working all the time, what kind of life is that?"

In no time we had finished a bottle of soju, so we ordered a second bottle and another order of grilled mackerel.

"Fine, I get it, one day it'll get better. We're just trying to somehow make it with subcontracts from the electronics factory, but if we want to make real money we need to change direction and do furniture. Manager Yim knows that, too."

Then Park asked me, out of the blue, as if it just occurred to him, "Mr. Oh, are you really a brother of Manager Yim's friend from the countryside?"

"That's right."

"I think that's a lie. You don't look like a country bumpkin. You smell like a bookworm."

"I hear that a lot. In the army, too."

"It doesn't mean that I think you look like a obedient boy. And look at your hands!"

"Hands of a lazy man."

"No, hands that write."

"That's why I want to learn from you, Mr. Park."

"There's nothing to learn. From tomorrow morning, you start cutting the things that are allotted to you."

Before he finished the sentence, he sprang from his seat. He hurried to the door and shouted outside, "Hey, Maeng Soon, where are you going?"

I could not see the woman, but I heard her voice.

"Where do you think I'm going? I'm done with work, and I'm going home."

"Come in here. Have a drink."

A woman's white face peered in. She looked around the pub.

"I haven't had dinner yet."

"Just come in. I'll buy you something good to eat."

They sat next to each other, facing me. He punched her back playfully and said, "Introduce yourself. This is a new guy who will be my room-mate starting tonight."

"Hello."

"Hello."

"Mr. Oh, this is my girlfriend."

"Girlfriend? Since when?"

She searched the menu on the wall.

"You didn't have dinner yet, right? Excuse me, one order of ramen noodles, please, with kimchi and scallions, as fast as you can!"

"I don't want ramen. Do you have any rice here, ma'am?"

"Yes, we do. Would you like a walleye stew?"

Park's eyes widened.

"What are you doing, Maeng Soon? Do you know how much a walleye stew costs?"

"If you don't want to pay for it, fine. And why do you call out to me like that? Call me Miss Yi Myung Soo, say it properly."

Amused, I watched the affectionate tug-of-war between a man and a woman after a day's work. Park asked, "Hey, Maeng Soon, you know your roommate?"

"Which one, Kyung Ja?"

"No, not that one. I'm talking about the skinny one."

"Ah, Soon Ok."

"Yeah, where does she work?"

"She's a seamstress at a dress shirt factory."

"Yeah, that one. Let's introduce her to our Mr. Oh here."

"And what's in it for me?"

"Tonight's dinner. How about that?"

"Hmmm, I think she's worth more than one dinner."

"Okay, fine, I'll take you to a movie in Youngdeungpo next week."

Myung Soon calmly gazed at me over the table.

"Hey, I have a better idea! Why don't you bring Soon Ok over to our house later?"

"No, she's working overnight tonight. I was doing overtime, too, but managed to get away."

While she ate dinner, we finished the second bottle of soju. Then we started the third bottle, ostensibly ordered for Myung Soon, who had finished her dinner. Park was getting drunk and his voice was becoming louder.

"I don't think I can work with Manager Yim any longer! Listen Mr. Oh, you don't know us. Well, I don't care if you tell him. Since when is he the manager? We started working almost at the same time, and he said we should do our own business, and he said all he can count on is my skills. Then what happened? I don't get a monthly salary, I get daily wages— this is not the way to treat a technician, is it? I can't stand it any longer, I'm going someplace else."

He was full of hot air, but he changed his tone when he turned to me.

"What do you think, Mr. Oh? Friendship is one thing, but money is scarier, isn't it?"

"Have you looked around to see if anyone will hire you?"

"Sure! I have so many options. Furniture factories are in desperate need of skilled carpenters. You can't compare that to this subcontract work, making television and radio frames. The most profitable thing for us is a record player, do you know why? Because it needs lots of decorations. With furniture, you make money by charging for its design."

Myung Soon had been quiet, but she could not resist any longer. She took a glass and emptied its contents down her throat, then opened her mouth.

"Even if you end up leaving, you should remain quiet until you actually do. Why are you such a big talker? You just don't think about things first."

"Hey, Maeng Soon, I'm doing all this to take care of you. You need to get married someday."

"Wow, I am about to weep, I am so grateful. Why don't you take care of yourself first? I don't need your help, I just want you to stop pestering me for money to pay all your debts at the end of every month. Phew, I should go home now."

As Myung Soon got up from her chair, Park stood halfway to stop her.

"Are you leaving already? Come on, have another glass. So far, it's been our Mr. Oh's treat, but I'll buy the second round."

"I want to go home, wash up, and go to bed. I have the first shift tomorrow morning. Excuse me."

"Hey, you're not listening to me . . ."

After Myung Soon left, Park did not say much. I felt that he regretted what he had told me before, that he was thinking about switching jobs. Without saying a word, he pushed around little pieces of fish on the plate with his chopsticks.

"Actually, I came to see Mr. Yim looking for something to do for the next couple of months," I said as I poured more soju into his empty glass. "Once I get the hang of it, I guess I'll look for a better job."

"There's not much of a prospect here. You'd be better off finding work at the industrial complex, doing something electrical or working on a lathe. You're a high school graduate, you'd become a technician within a year."

Park and I left the pub and climbed the hill. On the slope were row after row of long rectangular structures, hastily built with cement blocks. Like a train, there were windows of the same size and shape punched through the long wall, many of them still lit. There were tiny skylight windows on slate roofs, too. Park walked into one of the rectangular houses and gestured with his chin to follow.

"Come on in. This is the 0:50 train from Daejun."

As soon as he pushed open the plywood door, I heard water gushing from a faucet. Just beyond the door was a small courtyard the size of a single room with a communal faucet and draining floor in the middle, a suitable place for washing clothes or dishes. One woman was cleaning a chamber pot, while another was using a small bucket to pour warm water down the back of a half-naked man who was frozen in a push-up position on the ground. Park spoke to them as though he knew them well.

"You're home already? You came back early tonight."

The man remained in his push-up position but lifted his head to talk back.

"I didn't feel good today, so I came home early."

"It's one thing to make money, but he hasn't slept for the last three nights."

His wife, standing next to him, sounded like she was pleading.

In the middle of the house was a narrow corridor, wide enough for one person to pass from one end of the building to the other. On both sides of the corridors were identical sliding doors, connecting rooms that really did look like honeycombs. On the ceiling of the corridor was a blackened fluorescent light that seemed to have little time left. I found it baffling that there were no shoes in front of any of the rooms. Park opened the door of the room at the end of the corridor and fumbled for a light switch on the wall. Above the sliding door was a wooden plaque with the number sixteen. He took off his shoes and entered the room carrying them. The room was stuffy with the smell of unwashed feet and sour kimchi. It also smelled of briquettes, and I guessed there was a fuel hole right under my feet. I entered the room, too. From other rooms came the sound of a man and a woman bickering, an old man coughing, and a baby wailing almost out of breath. Park kicked away a futon and blanket, both which had clearly not been washed for a long time, to make space for me to sit.

"Take a seat, make yourself comfortable. This is how we live," said Park, comically. There was one mirror and one plastic shelf on the wall where dishes and food containers and toiletries were all piled up. There was a blue chamber pot in the corner next to the sliding door. There was one small vinyl wardrobe in the middle of the room and hanging from it, up in the air, was a laundry line with socks and underwear. He took the blanket and gently spread it out in front of the door.

"For tonight, this is your bed. Ask Manager Yim if he can lend you a blanket."

Looking up from my seat, I saw the skylight. The one on the wall was so small, I doubted any air would circulate even if it was open. Without a trace of modesty, Park took off his clothes and turned on a transistor radio on a small desk. A popular music program called *The Starry Night* was on.

"How many people live here?" I asked. He nodded his head to count them.

"Let's see . . . there are sixteen rooms, and each room has at least a couple, and some of them a family of four or five, so I guess about fifty?"

"They all work?"

"I think so. Some are factory workers, and the man who was bathing outside, he's a substitute bus driver. In fact, there are three substitute bus drivers here. Some of them work in construction, some of them are street vendors. They persevere here for a few years and then they move out when they can afford to lease a house somewhere. Even the house-wives, none of them are wasting time. They make beaded bags or glue envelopes."

Just wearing his underwear, he wrapped a towel around his neck, stuck a toothbrush into his mouth, and walked out of the room calling to me, "Do you want to wash yourself? My whole body is itching because of sawdust."

"I'm okay, I took a bath earlier."

I breathed a long sigh after Park left the room and fell back onto the blanket. From the radio an R&B song continued that sounded like someone crying. *Dying leaves falling one by one, he said he'd come back last fall but there's no news; broken heart, and the leaves are falling again, frosts and wild geese honking as they fly away.*

The once noisy corridor was quiet and I could no longer hear the sound of drunken men outside, yelling and screaming as they walked home. It was quiet everywhere. Park was in a deep sleep, snoring loudly. Seeing the dawning of another day through the ceiling window, I could not fall sleep. The living conditions at the honeycomb house were worse than the slums. Everyone in this house lived from day to day, earning barely enough to eat for one day. I had thought I was used to this, as I had traveled to many places in the past few years, calling myself an activist. But all of a sudden, I was struck by an unbearable sense of helplessness. Had Dong Woo found a place to settle down? Was it really possible for us—and there was not even a handful of us, and we were so young—to change the world with nothing but our noble intentions?

At seven o'clock in the morning, Park got up from his slumber like clockwork and woke me up. I followed him to the communal faucet, which was already chaotic. It seemed like everyone at the honeycomb house was out there. Park, holding a red plastic bucket tightly in one hand and a plastic wash basin in the other, charged to the faucet.

"Hey, everyone's busy here. Wait for your turn!"

"Oh come on, it won't take long."

"Look, you're splashing!"

"Can't you wash the chamber pot outside? Do you have to do it when it's so busy here?"

"Now, move if you've got your water!"

This complaining continued endlessly. Outside the house was the same, the narrow alleyways in between houses clamoring with people in underwear washing their faces and brushing their teeth. The ground was muddy with water that had been unable to drain for a long time. Following Park, I brushed my teeth and ended the morning ritual by scooping up some water from the bucket and rubbing it on my face a few times. There was a long line in front of the outhouse not too far from our house, and grumblings and complaints continued there, too. Park glanced over.

"Don't ever go there unless you absolutely have to," he told me. "It's much better to do your business at the factory where you're not rushed."

I felt pressure to go, but gave up. I had to deal with this nightmare again later when I was arrested, in the ancient jail built during the Japanese occupation period. It really hurts for the first two or three days, but after about ten days you get used to it. Eventually, you can eat three meals without batting an eye while the stench from collected filth surrounds you. What is bothersome and irritating lasts for a few minutes, but the warmth between people in the same harsh environment somehow continues.

I began working at the factory. In the morning, Manager Yim assigned the day's allotment to each worktable. There were six at the factory, including Yim, and now there were seven with my arrival. There were three technicians, Yim, Park, and another man named Nam. The other three were apprentices who were younger than me. As for machines, there were three electric saws, a plane, a sander, a drilling machine, and a table with a huge round saw. The shape of the saw blade changed depending on what was cut, whether it was a plane board or a plywood board or a square wooden peg, and also depending on whether it was cutting a curved or a straight line. I became Park's assistant. After he received the order from Manager Yim, he first made a model based on a specification. He showed it to me.

"Today, your job is to cut 1,500 of them. You have to hand me at least 150 per hour."

The stick was about a foot long, and it tapered at the bottom.

"What is this?"

"Legs for a television set."

He taught me how to use the table saw.

"Push the valve under there, under your foot, the saw comes up. Push it again, it goes down. Can you see under the table? Touch it with your finger. You push that, the saw starts spinning. Push it again, it stops. Try. You see the graduations? That's how you meet the specifications."

I practiced, following his directions step by step, and began working. When I handed him the square wooden stick that I cut to the specifications, he smoothed it off diagonally with a wire saw. In about thirty minutes, I got used to the work. The weather was cool, but everyone was working either with his top off or wearing a short-sleeved T-shirt. I assumed no one wanted sleeves flapping around their wrists. They were wearing masks and safety goggles with rubber headbands, but they all worked in bare hands with no gloves. It was more dangerous for the fingertips to be dull. Mr. Nam was in charge of the circular saw to cut large lumber into small pieces. Others were working on cutting plywood to fit the backs of radios or making the holes in the front for speakers and additional decorating. Making television legs was not that easy. Once the horn-like shape was done, Park was in charge the second day of rounding it off and hollowing out a groove at the bottom. Then the finishing team took over to apply glue and attach a rubber pad.

During lunch, Yim went home to eat while the rest cooked and ate together, except for Mr. Nam, who always packed a box lunch. There was a scruffy cupboard on one side of the hallway to the restroom, where pots and bowls and other things were stored. We took turns cooking, and those not cooking went out front to smoke cigarettes and chat or play volleyball. As for food, all we had was rice, kimchi from Yim's house, and a stew consisting of whatever was around. On top of the worktable covered white with sawdust, we spread out newspaper and placed the stew pot in the middle, and we stood around with rice bowls in hand and ate, sweating. I really liked life at the factory. There was no time for distractions, and I was quickly becoming better at what I did. Park said it usually took at least six months of apprenticeship, but the way I progressed, all I would need was three months, tops.

After a couple of weeks, I reported to Kun that I was safe. Hae Soon answered my phone call.

"Hello? May I ask who's calling?"

I lowered my voice and talked with my mouth pursed, trying hard to pronounce each word thickly.

"This is Kim Jun Woo."

"Kim . . . Jun Woo?"

Hae Soon had no idea that it was actually Oh Hyun Woo calling, and she seemed a bit suspicious. After a pause, I heard her calling Kun to get the phone.

"Hello?"

"It's me, Kim Jun Woo."

"Hey, everything alright?"

"Sure, I'm fine."

"Really? Are you really okay?"

I decided to ask him about Choi Dong Woo.

"How's the Inchon guy? He's good, too?"

Kun understood immediately to whom I was referring.

"Yeah, yeah, he's fine. The Inchon guy's name is Han Il Goon, remember? Hey, you know you really made me nervous. You were supposed to contact me at least once a week."

"I'm sorry, I've been busy trying to make a living. Fine, until next time."

"Wait, wait a second. Il Goon wants to meet with you where we parted."

"When?"

"Call me the beginning of next week."

I was planning to stop at the market on the way home. Park went with Manager Yim to the industrial complex for a delivery, and he was coming home late. I asked him again and again, as he left riding a truck with Manager Yim, to come home as soon as possible, as I was preparing dinner. Park would not forget it, either. Today was his birthday. I had noticed a few days before that he had drawn a red circle on today's date in the calendar.

The market at that hour was so crowded with housewives and female factory workers who had just finished work that it was impossible to walk around without knocking into everyone's shoulders. I bought three pounds of pork belly, scallions, garlic, green peppers, lettuce, and for the bean paste stew, I got tofu, zucchini, and potatoes. Carrying plastic bags in both hands, I walked out of the market and all the way to the bakery in the commercial district. I chose the cheapest cake with the least tacky decoration and asked for four candles that would signify his age of thirty-one.

The birthday party was not being held at our house, but at Myung Soon's place. I went there for the first time with Park the week before, so this would be the second time. The Sunday before that, Myung Soon, Soon Ok, Park, and I went all the way to the Youngdeungpo theater to see a movie and have dinner. Soon Ok was a tall and slender girl from Daejun. From behind, the way she wore pants appeared too sleek for a country girl. But she was not like Myung Soon, more of a quiet type, and I thought she was too straitlaced. There was another girl named Kyung Ja, a bit heavyset, whose face was flat and wide, her eyes thin. When we first met and exchanged hellos, her face got so red it looked like flowers were blooming in her ears. Among them, Myung Soon was the most assertive and energetic.

Further up the hill, past the rows of honeycomb houses, there were small houses hastily and carelessly built with cement bricks lining the narrow alleyway in clusters. Each house was somewhere between 550 and 725 square feet, with a slate roof and a thin plywood board that served as a door. Still, there was a kitchen and a restroom, and a little courtyard with a faucet to do laundry. People were still poor in this neighborhood, but one could live like a human being here, better than at the honeycomb houses. When I pushed the plywood door open and walked in, I was soon enveloped by the smell of hot oil wafting from the kitchen near Myung Soon's room. I peeked into the kitchen.

"What are you all doing?"

"Hi, welcome!"

Myung Soon, wearing a billowing peasant skirt like a farmer's wife and with her head wrapped in a towel, was frying little pieces of meat and vegetables in a small pan on top of a gas burner. Soon Ok took the plastic bags from me. I put the cake in their room.

"What is that?"

"A birthday cake."

Myung Soon was not at all touched.

"Mr. Park doesn't like sweets," she said evenly.

"Still, it's his birthday. What does he like, anyway?"

Myung Soon grimaced with her entire face, as if she were sick of it. "All he thinks about, asleep or awake, is liquor. Especially the harshest soju."

"Oh no, I forgot to buy a bottle!"

"Don't worry about it, he'll bring some. We also have a couple of bottles here."

I went into their room and sat down while the two women continued cooking.

"Where's your other roommate?"

Soon Ok answered, "Kyung Ja hasn't come back from work yet. They're doing overtime tonight."

The table was set with the cake in the center, out of its box and with the candles in place. Now it looked like a proper birthday party.

"Okay, I'm getting nervous. When is he coming?"

Myung Soon sat down with her arms crossed and mumbled. By the time I craved a cigarette, we heard someone whistling and walking toward the house. Park walked in.

"Sorry, sorry. I made you wait for a while, didn't I?"

"The food is cold now. We were going to eat everything without you, but we didn't. By the way, there's nothing for you to drink."

Undeterred by Myung Soon's gruffness, Park raised the paper bag he was carrying.

"Ta-da! I bought four half-liter bottles!"

"Ugh, bastard."

"Mr. Park, come here and sit down. Let's start the party!"

"Wow, this is the first time someone has treated me to a birthday cake. Isn't that a little girly?"

We sat around the table. I lit the tall and short candles with my lighter. Myung Soon sprang up and moved so quickly, her skirt fluttered.

"Wait a sec, if we're going to do it, we might as well do it right."

She turned off the fluorescent light so that only candlelight remained in the room. Park calmed down and muttered, "Looks good."

"Now, blow them out."

Park sat there blankly, staring at the candlelight. Myung Soon urged him on.

"What are you waiting for? Blow!"

He blew the candles out and the room became dark. We clapped, but we did not sing "Happy Birthday." At that moment each of us was following his or her own thoughts. Soon Ok whispered in the darkness, "With no light, it feels like we're back in the country."

"Yeah," Myung Soon added, "I was also thinking of my younger brothers and sisters."

I did not say anything, but Park sighed.

"One year older." Then, as if shaking off his own thoughts, he shouted, "Hey, turn the light back on. Let's drink!"

Myung Soon cut the cake, and we opened the soju bottle. As we all got drunk, we took turns singing, then sang as a chorus with chopsticks serving as drumsticks. Myung Soon began to cry, Soon Ok soon followed with tears in her eyes, Park kept banging the glass on the table and angrily screamed at someone, and I fell sideways from the table and passed out. When I opened my eyes the next morning I smelled perfume on the blanket, and right next to me was someone, definitely a woman, sleeping under another blanket. When I rustled around, Soon Ok said, in a sleepy voice as if she had just opened her eyes, "The other two went to his place."

"Ah, I see."

My head was aching like it was about to break open, and my stomach was burning so that I wanted to drink ice water, but I decided to suffer through it all. I fell asleep again. After that night Park teased us mercilessly, saying that Soon Ok and I had become a couple. I knew it would be even more embarrassing to protest that nothing had happened, so I just smiled back at him like a fool. Park often teased Soon Ok, "You can't treat the man you've slept with like that!"

One day, I think it was the following week, I called Kun as I had promised and was told the scheduled time to meet with Choi Dong Woo, whose alias was Han Il Goon. After work was done I skipped dinner and went to the Catholic church where I had seen him the last time. From Anyang, I took a bus and crossed the Han River to the northern part of Seoul. It was a long journey. It took an hour and a half. I switched buses at Jongro and got out one stop before the closest one to the church. To make sure that no one was following, I crossed the street twice. I bought a newspaper from where I could see the church and watched the entrance for five minutes before I crossed the street again. We did not have support from the organization as before, so we had to be careful on our own. I finally entered the church grounds and walked slowly to the back. I saw in the darkness the bench where we had sat last time. I walked to the last bench and sat down facing forward. Dong Woo emerged from the shadow made by the corner of the building and sprinted over to sit next to me.

"You just arrived?" I asked, and Dong Woo nodded without saying a word.

"You're well?"

"Um, I'm alright. And you?"

"I'm actually having fun."

Dong Woo said, "Suk Joon in Tokyo sent something via a friend. Some books and a letter."

"What did he write?"

"He had good news. He met some new people."

"New people?"

"Well, that's all he wrote, so that's all I know. I'm guessing Korean-Japanese."

"And what kind of books?"

"You can read them later. We need to strengthen the educational program within the organization."

Dong Woo handed me a large envelope containing books.

"It's too early for everyone to get together. It's still dangerous."

"We can do it through correspondence. Kun's factory could be the center where we distribute materials to each team."

"Who will produce the material?"

"I'll do the first month, you can do the next. They'll form a new government by next spring."

Choi Dong Woo stopped talking and got up.

"Let's get out of here. Someone's coming."

I turned around. I did not know who it was, but the shadow of a person was walking around the church building and approaching the backyard. We walked out on the other side, onto the wide boulevard where I had gotten out of the bus before. We only turned around once we were among the crowd of pedestrians, and no one seemed to be following us. Dong Woo whispered, "We have to make sure we're not being followed. Let's cross the street."

We walked toward the crosswalk and looked into the shop windows while waiting for the green light. We saw the changing light reflected in the window and crossed the street with a crowd. As soon as we reached the other side we turned into a little alleyway a few steps from the crossing. As though it was choreographed, as soon as we jumped into the alleyway we began running. As expected, we heard the tapping noise of other shoes running behind us. It was too dark to see clearly, but I figured there were at least a couple of them. The alleyway split into two, and we took the closest way, where we could see another major street at the end.

"That way!"

Dong Woo squeaked under his breath as he ran. "Let's cross the street as soon as we get there!"

I ran right behind him. We headed toward a well-lit, busy intersection. Dong Woo and I ran into a busy traffic lane where cars were speeding past. They honked and screeched and spun, but we managed to cross the street and find another side street to run through. Looking around, I spotted a little café at the corner of the street. It was an old two-story Japanese-style building. I climbed the stairs and Dong Woo followed without hesitation. The café was quite large but only two tables were occupied. First we walked over to the back window draped with curtains, to study the layout of the neighboring side streets, then we took a table next to a window overlooking the street. It was the middle of November and the weather was quite cool, but sweat streamed down my neck and chest. Puffing and gasping for breath, we were still unable to relax, and we stared at the street down below. The waitress approached us, yawning.

"Would you like to order?"

"Two coffees, please."

Dong Woo showed her two fingers and turned his back to the window.

"We were being followed, no doubt."

"Yeah, they followed us at least up to the alleyway over there."

But then I thought of how they had urgently pursued us through the side streets after we crossed the street, and I realized something.

"No, they weren't just following us, they were ready to pounce."

"I think you're right. One came into the church to confirm our location. We happened to see him first."

"And the other one was waiting outside. How many do you think there were?"

Dong Woo was nodding his head, as he was in the habit of doing when trying to figure something out.

"Two or three? I don't think they're from here. If the national security people were following us, there would have been layers and layers of nets. Where do you think we got the tail?"

"Either you or me."

"Yeah, someone near us must have reported us to the police. There's someone suspicious, maybe a spy, so why not find out for sure? So they follow him, and he walks into a darkened church garden. And meets someone. Even provincial police would quickly realize something dubious was taking place."

Dong Woo's deduction was logical, and I reached a conclusion.

"The solution is simple. We need to move from our hideouts."

"I guess that's the only thing we can do. Ugh, here we go again."

"I don't have much, all I have are underwear and toiletries. I don't even have to go back there."

"I'll send someone to stay in my room for a few days, and if nothing happens I'll go back there. I'm sure they'll come tonight if they are coming at all. If you were in their shoes, would you be able to wait one more day? Their hearts must be racing now."

Dong Woo sounded like he had calmed down, and I reconsidered the situation.

"I guess that would be a natural way to survey your surroundings. The more I think about it, the more I think it was on my side. I have a hunch."

We swallowed the too-sweet coffee in one gulp. Before he got up, Dong Woo took the package of books back from me.

"I think it'll be safer for me to take that."

"What's in it, anyway?"

Dong Woo wavered a little and answered with a faint smile on his face.

"The fastest shortcut is to break the forbidden law. It's from over there."

"What, *Capital*? I read that a long time ago."

"Not from the West, from over there."

Dong Woo pointed upward. He got up with the envelope tucked under his arm.

"Okay, I'll go first. Call Kun tomorrow morning. I'll call him, too."

Dumbfounded, I sat and thought about the meaning of over there. That was the last boundary, and the thought made my mouth dry and my whole body tingle with anxiety. And I was so curious. One half of our people lived in their own way in a completely different world. What did they talk about? What did they think about? Where were they headed? About twenty minutes after Dong Woo left, I descended the stairs of the Japanese-style building. I walked as far as I could and caught a bus far from where we had been.

 Back in Anyang, I got off the bus two stops before the one nearest to the honeycomb house village, at a busy commercial district full of shops. It was late at night. I walked toward the neighborhood up on the hill, taking the path on the other side of the mountain. I had come back there to confirm something. It was something that needed to be done, the one thing I had to do before I went underground again. I had thought about it during the bus ride and decided to see Soon Ok. Instead of taking the main road, I climbed the far side of the mountain and dipped down near the cement walls and cement blocks. Along a narrow passage, tiny houses that looked like little boxes stood right next to each other. When I reached the house of Myung Soon and Soon Ok, I stood as close to the wall as possible and looked inside. There was a barely audible sound from a transistor radio but no voices, so I figured someone was listening to the radio alone. I walked into the house and gently pushed the kitchen door. It was locked from inside. I waited for a minute, than knocked on the door lightly. There was no answer, so I knocked again, a little louder.

"Who is it?"

It was Soon Ok's voice. Thank God.

"This is Oh."

"Goodness," she exclaimed softly and said, "wait just one minute." She bustled around for a while, then finally turned on the light in the kitchen. The door opened a bit, and I pushed it and jumped in. Soon Ok was wearing a sweatshirt and a pair of sweatpants, and a red cardigan on top, unbuttoned. It looked like she had just changed. I brazenly crossed the threshold from the kitchen into the bedroom. I turned to Soon Ok, who was still standing in the kitchen, nervous and confused.

"Turn off the kitchen light and come in, please," I said. "We need to talk."

I took a seat by the door, and Soon Ok came in and sat upright by her bedding in the corner of the room. Like all men would do in such a situation, I sucked on a cigarette and blew smoke toward the ceiling, taking my time.

"The truth is, I'm in hiding right now because I am wanted by the government. But it's not because I did something criminal. I went to university, and since then I've been . . . involved in the student movement."

"What kind of a movement?"

"I protested against the government."

"Ah, the protesters."

Soon Ok's face changed, as if she understood what I was talking about.

"There are many people who are like me, and if one gets caught everyone else will get caught, too. I won't be the only one in trouble. So, have you heard Mr. Park say anything? Where's Myung Soon? And Kyung Ja?"

"Kyung Ja is on night shift these days. Myung Soon left a while ago to have dinner with Mr. Park. I think they're in that little pub down there."

"Some people followed me all the way to Seoul. I think they were detectives. Are you sure Mr. Park didn't say anything?"

Soon Ok thought about it for a while before speaking.

"I haven't heard much from Mr. Park. But yesterday, Myung Soon said something. She said you didn't look like someone who would do hard labor. The way you talk, the way you look, she didn't think you looked like someone who belongs here. I thought so, too. There was a similar incident in our factory. A female college student got a job under false pretenses and was later arrested."

Something heavy was welling up inside me. Ah, I was still so far behind. I still hadn't gotten rid of the air of an intellectual. I looked down and my eyes were filled with hot tears. I did not want her to see it, so I kept my head down and stopped talking.

"Why do you do such things?" she asked. "There are people who want to go to universities but they can't because they have no money, so they go to Seoul to make some."

"Your parents, you, Soon Ok, and your friends, you all work so hard, yet you barely make a living, right?"

"That's because . . . we're poor."

"Why are you so poor?"

"We had nothing from the beginning."

"If you work so hard, you should be able to save and have some money, no?"

"Well, we had no education and we can't find a good job."

"Wouldn't it be great if we lived in a world where, even if you had no education and no money, everyone could live well if they worked hard?"

Soon Ok remained silent, unable to find words.

"My friends and I, we hope for our world to be like that."

Soon Ok shook her head meekly.

"I don't know, that is . . . that will be too difficult."

I did not want to torment her anymore, so I changed the subject.

"Can I stay here tonight until the curfew is over?"

Soon Ok nodded her head.

"Kyung Ja will be back tomorrow morning and I think Myung Soon will stay with Mr. Park."

"Thank you. But I have one more favor to ask you. Can you go down there and get Mr. Park for me around midnight?"

"Bring him here?"

"No, to the empty lot up there with the horizontal bar."

"Okay. But do you think that's a good idea?"

She was sincerely worried, and it was something I had been wondering about since the dangerous incident near the church and throughout the bus ride coming here. They would choose me. If I trusted them, they would not desert me. In a way, I had come back to validate that belief. Soon Ok rose from her seat.

"You haven't eaten dinner yet, have you?"

"I'm fine."

"I bought lots of ramen noodles for night snacks. It won't take long."

The room was soon filled with fumes as Soon Ok lighted the portable gas burner. I opened the window. As I looked out through the open window, I saw a pale half moon.

Around midnight, at the beginning of curfew, I sent Soon Ok down to fetch Park, and I went to the empty lot by the rock at the top of the hill. It was an open-air gym for people in the neighborhood to use, a place they went to in the midst of their busy daily life to stretch and relieve stress. The main flaw was that it was a desolate place where no trees grew; it had only weeds and piles of used briquettes. Instead of going to the middle of the lot, I chose a spot by the wall opposite from where Park would probably climb up.

A dark outline of a person appeared from the alleyway. He was staggering, a little drunk. He looked around the empty lot then walked toward the rock and collapsed on it. Wearing a pair of sweatpants and a military parka that I had seen him wear at the factory, I was sure it was Park. I could even hear his voice muttering that he was freezing and grumbling. To make sure that he was not being followed, I waited for about five more minutes until I was certain he was by himself. I left the corner and walked toward the center of the empty lot.

"Oh?"

"Yeah, it's me."

I did not give him a chance to talk back, I got right to the point.

"Why did you do it? How can you stab your own roommate in the back?"

Instead of answering back, Park dropped his head and sighed.

"I know, I am sorry I deceived you."

"I don't know if you'll understand, but I was involved in the democratization movement, and now I am underground. Yes, I am wanted. Did you report me because you thought I was a spy?"

Park raised his head.

"That's not what I thought. I never thought you were a spy." Then he continued in a weaker voice. "I just happened to be drinking with some people from the neighborhood at the pub down there, and you were mentioned. I can't remember very well what I said, I was a little drunk."

"When was this?"

"The day before yesterday, after work."

"Try to remember what you told them."

"Well . . . just that it's a nasty world. If you say righteous things, they come and get you, something like that. That my friend is now working as a lowly assistant to a woodworker, but it's certain that he's highly educated."

I put my hand on his shoulder.

"That's enough, Mr. Park. It's all my fault."

"After you left, four detectives came, around nine. They went through everything in the room and took all your stuff. I had to go to the police station to be questioned."

"Did you say anything about Manager Yim?"

"No, I'm not that dumb, and I won't jeopardize someone unnecessarily. I told them I met you by chance at a pub, that you said you were working at the industrial complex and looking for a room, so I told you to pay me 30,000 won a month so I could save some money. I said I didn't know you very well."

"And they let you go?"

"There are a lot of factory workers at the honeycomb house who become roommates that way. They told me to cooperate. They told me to let them know when you come back home, tonight or tomorrow."

Suddenly, my eyes welled up with tears. I lifted my head toward the empty sky, but the liquid rolled down anyway and reached all the way to my chin. I wiped my face and under my chin with my jacket sleeve.

"Mr. Park, I need to ask you a favor. I'll never come back here again, so please, make sure that no harm is done to Manager Yim. Just stick to the story that you told them. I told Soon Ok to be careful, and you should tell Myung Soon, too."

"I promise. I am so sorry. I had too much to drink and I made a big mistake. Every wall listens and reports back, especially when you're so poor."

"Now, let's go. I'm going to wait for the curfew to be over in Soon Ok's room. I think I'll feel better if you stay with me."

"Let's go. We should drink our last glass."

"No . . . no more liquor."

We stood up together. Park took a long sigh again and murmured, "I hope you'll understand, Mr. Oh. If you report someone suspicious, they give you rice as a reward."

"How much?"

"At least three quarts."

My eyes welled up again.

"Yeah, that's okay. Three quarts of rice is worth something for a family."

I said that, but I could not get rid of my sense of helplessness. Park and I walked back to Soon Ok's room, where she had turned off all the lights though her bedding was neatly folded away. She was waiting for us. Park followed me into the room, but I stopped him at the threshold.

"Let's say goodbye here. I'll leave when the curfew is over."

"No, I want to stay."

I extended my hand toward him.

"Go back. Someone at the honeycomb house may be watching."

Unable to disagree, he took my hand.

"Goodbye. I'm really sorry about everything."

We shook hands. Park disappeared beyond the kitchen door, and I collapsed to the floor in front of the door, away from Soon Ok. She remained silent for a while, then handed me a pillow.

"You have a few hours until 4:00 a.m. Why don't you lie down and sleep a little?"

"I won't be able to get up if I lie down. It'll be better if I stay up all night."

Soon Ok put the pillow on top of the rest of the bedding, folded and stacked.

"Like Mr. Park said, please try to understand. Everyone here barely makes enough to survive."

I nodded, but did not say anything. I wanted to leave holding onto the belief that my neighbors had not turned on me, those who slept next to me snoring loudly, those who were grateful for the most humble food, those who got drunk with me and laughed and joked with me.

Soon Ok and I did not talk much. I think we talked about her hometown. About the fifty acres or so of rice fields that her family labored on, about the death of the family bull whose belly was stretched like a drum with gas, about the failed attempt to grow strawberries in greenhouses and the mounting debts, and about the few months she worked as a beautician's assistant. And she talked about her little dream, that with a little money saved and her sewing skills she would be able to open a dressmaker's shop outside of Daejun, something with a really pretty sign. Because of her many younger siblings that she needed to support, she thought she would not be able to afford getting married until later.

We heard the siren indicating the end of the curfew. Aiming to get the first bus, I waited another half hour or so.

"I think I should go now."

When I got up, Soon Ok followed me, putting her shoes on.

"I actually want to go by myself."

"I need to make sure that you leave safely. Only then can I tell Mr. Park and Myung Soon that you did."

I thought she had a reason. It was early winter, the frosty morning air blew down my neck. We walked up the hill and down the other side. Once in a while, a garbage cart passed us. One of them was pulled by a man with his body bent down almost ninety degrees, while a woman in baggy pants pushed from behind, her head shoved to the ground. Soon Ok and I reached a busy street. Far away, buses parked at the end of the line were starting their engines. I stopped in front of a signal light in order to cross the street and turned toward Soon Ok.

"You should go back home now."

Soon Ok wavered, touching the pavement with the tip of her shoe and her head bowed down.

"Do you have . . . money for the bus?"

I smiled and tapped the chest area of my jacket.

"I have a lot of money. Well, then . . ."

But before I crossed the street, Soon Ok raised her voice, speaking quickly to my back.

"If it becomes too hard, just turn yourself in."

I pretended I did not hear her and ran across the street. Just in time, a bus was coming toward me, so I waved my hand to stop it and got on. The bus was completely empty. I glanced back as I took a seat, and I saw the red of her sweater still standing at the street corner. The bus soon took a right turn, and she disappeared.

Later, in prison, I thought of them often. I had forgotten most of the dangerous situations in Seoul; I did not want to remember those days anyway. For me, those dreamy months in Kalmae were everything that I had, but that one month in the hellish honeycomb house lingered deep in my mind as well. It was awful, but the confirmation of trust from the few young workers I met there sustained me. It was one of the reasons I did not give everything up during the years of imprisonment. I wondered where they were now. What happened to the willful Myung Soon and the nice but weak Mr. Park? Were they able to rent a better place and get married, as they had hoped? And did Soon Ok realize her little dream of going back to Daejun and opening her dress shop with a pretty sign? Did she make money, support all her siblings, and finally find time to get married herself and have babies? And those young girls at the factory who I met while teaching at the night school, all of them so scared and hungry, were they now mothers in a different world?

The police were closing in, so it was too dangerous for me to see Choi Dong Woo again. The organization had to give up the plan to keep me near Seoul for a while. When Kun told me, I accepted it without protest. Until the end of that year, I stayed at a boarding house in a middle-class neighborhood near a university in Seoul, and the only connection I had with the organization was an occasional notice Kun somehow managed to send through a third party. I decided to leave Seoul and ask for help from other organizations who managed those on the wanted list in different regions. Winter in the city was colder and more desolate when spent alone. No one was surprised when Chun Doo Hwan was again nominated as the sole nominee for presidency and as the head of the new party. The emergency martial law was withdrawn.

It was the first snowy day of winter. I was passing by a gift shop full of high school girls and it occurred to me to buy a number of cards for the holiday season. Remembering my childhood, I walked into a bakery, took a seat in the back corner, and ordered a roll filled with pastry cream, bread with sweet crumble on top, and a glass of milk. I began writing on the cards in tiny script.

Dear Mother,

It's already the end of the year, and it is snowing. I am well, so please do not worry. And do not waver no matter who comes to see you and what they tell you. I sincerely believe that you understand your own son's intentions. I once read somewhere about a woman who had a son in a similar situation to mine. She was caught while distributing leaflets, and she said this:

"I do not know politics. I begged my son not to do what he did. But he did not listen to me. He knows how much I love him. I think he disobeyed me for something that is bigger than the love between us. Therefore, I decided to join him."

Dear Mr. Park,

I wonder how everyone is. I've been regretting the hasty way I left you all. I am sorry. It's time to take down the calendar in your room. I remember you wrote on there this verse: "Should this life sometimes disappoint you, Don't be sad or angry at it." I hope you write that again in your new calendar. Hope you're well. Please give my regards to Maeng Soon and Manager Yim.

Soon Ok, Myung Soon, Kyung Ja,

I hope you're all doing well. Wherever you are, life can be tough. Once the time goes by, however, you look back on your past and find there were good days, and you're proud that you made it so far. I've met many different people in many different places, but the most beautiful ones are those who work hard.

11

In darkness I groped for his skin, his hair, the outline of his
bones. But I could not clearly recall the familiar odor of his
armpits, his protruding Adam's apple, the coarse texture of his
shaved chin and his most private parts. In the dim gray of the
morning I woke up, still resting my head on his arm, and
touched him to confirm his presence. Sharing a bed became
a daily routine for us. According to that melancholic scientist
who interpreted dreams, the earliest hour in the morning is
the moment when suppressed thoughts rise to the surface.
We could not tolerate the sordid and evil world before us. It
was like the backdrop of a surrealist painting, and in the fore-
ground was the two of us, distinct figures. In my head, I black
out that background. We'll never have a child together. I inject
all my feelings and emotions into him and create another me.
That becomes the familiar image of myself. He and I have
become each other's reality. Would it be possible for us to
remain confined forever? Just the two of us in hiding?

Spring passed before we knew it. About three months after
we met we finally became used to each other. They say a

baby is accepted as a real human being one hundred days after birth, and you should pray for one hundred days if you want to move heaven. We had created our own unique world. It was a four-poster bed draped in white cotton, like those in a tropical climate. Our own little world separated from the rest. He and I, we really didn't think about anything, we did nothing. We would lie down next to each other and we were lazy, or we might go out to the backyard to watch insects. Once we decided for no apparent reason to climb up the little path behind the house. Panting like one body, we hovered around each other. Sometimes our eyes would meet, sometimes we would lift our fingers in slightly different gestures. We would turn our heads or scratch with the tip of an index finger the itchy spot on our cheek.

Looking back, every day in our life as lovers was a new beginning. Birth, togetherness, aversion, weariness, understanding, death, hatred, anger, yearning, tediousness. All of it passed by like an endless parade of clouds during the rainy season. Like the scene in a documentary where flowers sprout from a tree branch and grow and bloom and bloom too quickly and wither and droop and each petal falls away and finally only one petal is left, and it flutters and gives up in slow motion. Then the film is rewound and starts over again. Each start is new, every time. I am sometimes anxious, like in those paintings from the fin-de-siècle. A farewell, too, could be a new start. Perhaps he will steal himself away from me.

We have to last for a long time here in the valley. One year, or two? Or tomorrow, the day after tomorrow, and the following day? But how should we continue? Have children, live happily ever after? In order to do that, he'd have to vanish from himself forever. Perhaps everything feels so vivid and we're so nervous because we are taking refuge from battling that enormous power. If we were no longer suffering from trials and tribulations, would we love each other like we did at first? Standing on our two feet in this world with nothing in our hands?

You said you liked our mountain. Not the majestic peaks, but the humble, ordinary rolling hills one finds in every neighborhood. One morning while we were having breakfast, you suddenly spoke.

"Yoon Hee, why don't you skip school today?"

"They'll fire me if I don't work today. I already did that once."

Then you stuck your lip out like a petulant child and put down your spoon.

"Okay, what do you want to do if I don't go to work?"

"Let's go hiking with rice rolls. I can make rice rolls."

It was such an absurd idea, I had to laugh out loud. Yet I could not help myself.

"It is very tempting," I said. "I should just quit my job."

"I hope that school burns down."

"My goodness, you want to be a poet and you want a school to be torched?"

As you usually did, you pushed relentlessly once you got started.

"We can come up with a new way to educate our children without schools."

"Look, I may have just begun but I am still a teacher."

We brought in a chopping board to make the rice rolls. You insisted that you did not like the nice-looking ones rolled up with various fillings and cut into a nice round shape, that you wanted to do it your way. You spread out rice on a rectangular sheet of dried seaweed, then added little pieces of kimchi, torn with your hands, of course, and seasoned dried anchovies. You rolled it all up into a long log.

"You hold the whole thing in your hand and chomp on it from the top. It is the best!"

That kind of rice roll was prevalent during the war, when

you were a toddler, or during those difficult times after the war that our generation experienced. I ate something like that during the annual picnic at school. They were rolled in newspaper sheets, and the smell of ink had permeated here and there. The seaweed was dehydrated like tree bark and the filling was mostly coarse barley, and each bite had to be taken with a sip of water. Otherwise, it stuck to my throat and I could barely swallow it. You insisted, but certain things had improved, so we packed our rice rolls with plastic wrap. And we did not forget to brush the rolls with sesame oil.

We went up the hill behind our house, carrying a little backpack with the rice rolls and a small water bottle. I've written in this notebook how I went up there once in a while after you left. Every few months or so. At the top, it was connected to another ridge. Turning to the right there was a lonely grave that seemed neglected, and to the left was a descending path that led to the summit of the next mountain. We were sweating and out of breath, and we walked through thorn bushes to climb up. It took us about an hour to reach the summit, and from it we saw the other side of the valley, where we had never been, because we usually turned and walked around the mountain when we got out of the bus. And we saw the blue ridge of the faraway mountains and the upper reaches of the stream that passed through Kalmae toward the big town.

"Hyun Woo, let's take a break and eat lunch here."

"Here? Now? We can go higher, to our left."

"No, this is the end of the hill behind our house. We have reached our destination."

I was about to sit down on the grass, but you grabbed my wrists and pulled me up.

"What destination? We can't see anything from here."

You dragged me along the edge of the ridge.

"Maybe we can see something really fantastic from up there. What kind of an artist are you?"

I thought I was going to die hiking another mountain. I lagged behind you because I rested for a while, and even after that I could not walk well. I heard you shouting from the summit, "Look! There's the world!"

It still took me quite a while to reach where you where. The sky was wide and open. The fields seemed to extend endlessly, and there were pale white and pink patches of flowers blooming in orchards across the curve of the hills. Here and there, little villages were nestling into the hills, and beyond them was the haze of the city. Cars were crawling down there like tiny insects.

"This is refreshing!" I exclaimed as I sat down on a rock, but you remained silent, contemplative. I took out a water bottle from our backpack, took a gulp, and handed it over to you. "I'm starving. I'd say breakfast has been digested. Let's eat!"

Still, you did not turn around, you just kept staring beyond the horizon. You finally opened your mouth. "What day is it today?"

"Wednesday, May 27th. Three hours for the ninth graders and two for the tenth graders."

"What do you mean?"

"My art classes. Since I skipped them today, they would be doing study hall now."

"It was exactly a year ago," you said, still without turning to look at me. "The last massacre at the state capital."

At that moment, your young friends had been transferred from the jail at the military academy to a local prison, where they protested by kicking the iron bars and singing and refusing their meals. The dead people had yet to have a proper burial. But I wondered why you had to bring it up there, on that day? I wanted to console you, so I casually blurted out, "Let's have a memorial service tonight."

"Yes, let's do that."

The truth was, I was worried. I had a feeling that your eyes were wandering toward the world over there. We ate the rice rolls. It reminded me of past picnics, and you seemed to be in a better mood.

Since we decided to hold a memorial service, I went to the village market to buy some fruit and fish and beef. I also got some sheets of rice cakes, one with embedded flower patterns made out of dates and beans, and another with red bean flakes. That night I prepared the food we were craving, the memorial service being an excuse. I cooked in the kitchen, while you set up a table in the bedroom. The candles were lit, but we had no incense to burn. We opened a bottle of soju and poured some into the lid of the rice bowl, and we knelt down next to each other. I was a little embarrassed—your somber silence made me feel uneasy. But honestly, all I wanted to do was to hold still your restless heart. I was just helping you, it was not like I was keeping you captive as if we were characters in some kinky story. But I was feeling guilty, and I did not know why. You took out a piece of paper and began reading out loud. You started with a year and month and date, some long sentences that I can no longer remember. But I do remember the last sentence, about longing for a new, different world.

"From Baekdoo to Halla, I can see the beautiful land of Korea as one. But you are all gone now. What kind of world did you picture in your mind?"

Now that I think about it, leaflets containing similar sentences were frequently circulated at the time, and most of them sounded hackneyed. Yet my heart was aching and my blood was boiling. Being a radical meant inclining toward the Left, but it was only after the massacres that you and your friends began to read books and study the other side. We no longer had a home. The classic revolutionary age was already finished. Still, ideas can be renewed and move forward as much as the world will let them, and I never once had any intention of dissuading you from your choices.

The next day, when I returned from school, you were not there, just as I had feared. You did take a look at the world when you were up on the mountain. After all, Kalmae was not your reality. On the low table pushed against the wall was your note.

I'll be right back. I won't go all the way to Seoul, just to Kwangju. I can't bear it, I keep seeing my friends' faces. I think I'll be back by late tonight at the latest. Please, don't worry even if I have to stay one night away. I promise I'll be back by tomorrow morning.

That was what you wrote, but you did not come back on Thursday, Friday, Saturday, or Sunday. Do you have any idea how much I cursed you during those days? The thing I feared the most was parting from you without preparation or warning. I used to wake up in the middle of the night covered in cold sweat, did you know that? I was afraid that it did not matter how we felt for each other, that one day you would be captured in some unknown place and taken away with no way to let me know where you were. I used to think that what we wanted, what we dreamt of, was something similar to the simple and peaceful existence in Kalmae. But the world you pictured while reading books, the world you wanted to create, would never be simple or peaceful. It would be a place of nervous turmoil with endless struggles and determined, forceful battles for equality among different classes. There will always be enemies of the revolution. Do not criticize yourself over life in Kalmae being the luxury of a libertine. It's all I ever wanted. No matter what system took power, our humble hiding place would remain. Ideology is not an issue for me, if you are by my side.

She was right. When I stood on that summit, my heart was about to burst with the burden of self-exile. They flourished as a mighty military power through brute force, while our dead friends were secretly rotting in shallow graves surrounded by the hushed cries of their loved ones.

We needed power and structure to control it correctly. No matter how long it took. Somebody had to take the first step, the shortcut through the mountains that Nam Soo spoke of. It was also the long way of Bong Han, who told us to survive by all means and to somehow gain back the people's power one day. Dong Woo dreamt of a new solidarity among the people. The Kwangju Uprising was the crossroad where our path became clearly separated from the others.

I waited until Yoon Hee left for work, staying under the blanket and pretending that I was still sleepy and unable to get up. As soon as she left, I sprang up to change my clothes and I left the house. I walked to the edge of town and took a bus near the bridge to the next village. Then I took a cross-country bus to Kwangju. I got off the bus on the outskirts of the city by a railroad crossing. It was a clear day, and sunlight bathed the empty ground with white light.

First, I decided to go see Choi, a preacher, to get information regarding the current situation in Kwangju. I walked to Yanglim-dong, following the railroad. I had once rented a room in that neighborhood, so I was familiar with its narrow alleyways. It was an old neighborhood with a low roofline, and the houses were so close to each other that it would have been considered a slum in Seoul. I stood where I could see the two-story house of Preacher Choi, and I made sure that there was no corner store or telephone booth from which someone could observe the house easily. I walked up the iron stairway outside the house to a small veranda where I could look into a window and see inside. His new wife was cooking something in the kitchen while Preacher Choi was reading a book, lying on his belly on the floor. With my fingertips, I tapped on the window right behind him. He turned his head reflexively and his mouth dropped to the floor. He jumped up and hurriedly opened the window.

"My God, is it really you? You are safe, Hyun Woo!"

"Yeah, how are you?"

As I walked into their house, the first thing his wife did was to draw the curtains. We sat facing each other, and Preacher Choi's eyes reddened in an instant. He wiped away tears with his shirt sleeve.

"Did you come down from Seoul?"

"Yes, I did. How are the rest of the people here?"

"What rest of the people? They are all dead or in prison or have no jobs. It's not a living. We can't even say hello when we see each other, we're so ashamed. In fact, we avoid each other."

"What are you ashamed of?"

"The fact that we are still alive. How about the Kwangju people in Seoul?"

"I think they are okay."

"From what I've heard, they are arresting group after group, accusing them of being secret agents."

"I can imagine. In South America, revolutionaries were accused of being Communists."

"It's almost like they are pushing us to go over to that side. And I believe in Jesus!"

"If we're against the US, we must be red."

His wife had been preparing lunch just then. She brought in a full table for two. The green of the baby lettuces and crown daisies was so vivid.

"You need protein for energy, but all we have are leaves."

"Don't worry, I eat meat all the time in Seoul."

With enraged voices, they told me stories. Stories of bodies found on the northern outskirts of the city, secretly buried in the mountains. Stories of someone witnessing a garbage man carrying bodies in his truck and dumping them in a park pond. Stories of dead bodies thrown into the reservoir, which was then filled with a powerful disinfectant. Stories of how people could not drink the water from the faucet throughout the summer. For them, the situation was not over yet. On the street, they avoided meeting others' eyes, as if they were accomplices in a crime. They told me stories from the deepest part of their hearts.

"Can you take off for a couple of days?"

He knew right away that it was a serious proposition, and he got nervous.

"Today's Thursday? It should be okay until Saturday."

"Good. I want you to come with me tonight. Let's go to Seoul."

"I thought you just came from there."

"I really need to see Kun. But I'm a stingray, submerged and swimming at the bottom of the sea."

"So you want me to contact him?"

Preacher Choi quickly understood the situation. He once went to prison while serving in a ministry in an impoverished neighborhood.

"The thing is, I have this bad feeling. I think the phone's been disconnected."

When I'd left Seoul in February, I'd contacted Kun. Hae Soon had been there to make sure that our meeting place was secure, and he waited at least twenty minutes before appearing. Throughout the winter, the organization was managed via correspondences, but information was somehow leaked and a member was arrested. They did not know all the details but had heard that one member, a graduate student, had accidentally left his backpack filled with papers and leaflets at a pub in front of his school. Both of them were extremely nervous. Dong Woo had severed any contact with them, and he had ceased his monthly safety report. Whenever I went to the next village I tried calling Kun, but there was no answer.

"Why not? Thanks to my minister, I've been well fed and safe."

When darkness had fallen we prepared to leave. His wife approached us with eyes full of fear.

"You were interrogated so many times already . . . why are you doing this?"

"Don't worry, darling, nothing will happen. It won't take too long."

"Yes, don't worry too much. We'll be back by tomorrow."

We went to the train station. At the time, the police frequently inspected ID cards at the station, searching for the wanted. They would stand by the entrance and target young men. Before we entered the station, we looked around to see if any detectives were standing outside, and we decided to separate.

"Buy two tickets and go to the platform. I'll use another way to get inside."

I checked my watch; there were still fifteen minutes left until the train's arrival. After sending Preacher Choi into the station, I walked around the building and approached a fenced area where baggage was handled. There was no one around, so perhaps it was dinnertime. I found a cardboard box for fruit or ramen noodles and stealthily went into the baggage area, the cardboard box secured under my armpit. If someone asked, I was going to say I was looking for the place where I could send a parcel. Fortunately, no one approached me while I hopped over several tracks. I hid under the dark shadow of a freight car waiting for a go-ahead signal at the far end of the station. The cardboard box was a perfect seat once I flattened it. I resisted the urge to smoke and waited. Soon I heard the announcement and saw people rushing to the platform. I strolled over the tracks again and stood among the crowd. Preacher Choi quickly stood by my side. We did not exchange one word until the train came. It wasn't a market day, so there weren't too many passengers. With many empty seats in the car, we chose a middle section and sat facing each other so we could watch the corridor in both directions.

When we arrived at Youngdeungpo Station in Seoul, it was almost five o'clock in the morning. Although we had not planned to, Preacher Choi and I decided to find a public bathhouse with a sauna. Each of us took a shower and fell asleep on the floor with a wooden block as a pillow. Preacher Choi tried calling Kun around seven o'clock, but again we did not get through. It was not yet the morning rush hour, so we decided to move quickly and headed toward the slum where Kun's knitting factory was. We got out one stop early and walked to a modest restaurant that specialized in soup with stuffed pig intestines, close to the entrance of a market. We decided to meet there later, and Preacher Choi went to Kun's house according to my directions. I could not just sit there at the restaurant, so I ordered a bowl of soup and pretended to eat. Hae Soon came in, lifting the drape by the door, which also served as a menu board. Preacher Choi followed her, and both of them sat across from me silently.

"Are you out of your mind?" She whispered, but it was clearly a rebuke.

"Something happened?"

"Yeah, something happened. Kun was arrested."

"When did that happen?"

"Over a month ago."

"Well, that explains your telephone situation."

Hae Soon let out a long sigh and began to cry. It was not violent, just a few tears asking me to take her side.

"We disconnected it. We visit the stores in person to get orders."

"Where is he now?"

"No one can figure that out. Could be Namyoung-dong,* could be Namsan. Jung Ja is running around like a madwoman, but everyone says they don't know."

"Contact the Catholics. They'll help."

"People are being killed for no reason. All organizations are scared stiff."

Hae Soon explained what had happened over the last few months. Right before I left Seoul, the graduate student was arrested, as Kun had feared. They quietly investigated for more than three months, using the list of names they had obtained. They must have put everyone on the list under close surveillance. A meeting between one of the members and Kun was witnessed, and the tail was moved to Kun. They monitored the knitting factory for a few days.

"For some reason or other, we were inundated with peddlers. It didn't matter what time of day it was, they would just push the door open and come in, and they would linger even when we refused to buy anything."

Then they came, almost twenty of them, in the middle of the night. Everyone was asleep when the plywood door was suddenly broken into pieces with a great noise, and men in work uniforms jumped into the house. Caught off-guard, Kun sprang up from his bed, but a man who seemed to be the leader put a gun to his forehead.

"Someone turned the light on, and they began to beat everyone with bats. They didn't care who was there, they just beat us. Then they dragged us out to the alley and made us put our hands behind our head and kneel. They kept beating us even after they handcuffed us from behind and even when we were walking to the traffic lane. Then they stuffed all of us into a tiny chicken coop car."

While being interrogated, Kun named a few members, but Jung Ja and Hae Soon and everyone else who worked at the knitting factory persevered, insisting that they had no connection to the organization and that they did what was told to them by Kun because he paid them.

"This is not over," I whispered to Hae Soon.

"This is only the beginning. Did you have any papers in the house?"

---

* A neighborhood in Seoul where the Anti-Communist Department of Public Safety Division was located.

"They found everything except for the organization's roster. Jung Ja said they have enough to sentence him for many, many years."

I knew that Choi Dong Woo kept the most important papers. Still, they must have found the mimeograph and the minutes of our meetings and other information. The brain may not have been revealed but the intestines were laid bare. Preacher Choi, who had been quietly listening to us, opened his mouth.

"Well, everyone, I don't think we have much time. We need to separate."

"Yes, we'll go first. You should eat something here, though."

We looked around and found the owner sitting on the threshold of her living quarters, absorbed in a soap opera on television. When I got up, Hae Soon burst into tears, covering her face with both palms and doing her best to muffle the sound.

"Don't worry, everything will be okay," I whispered to her, lightly stroking her back.

"I don't know why I keep going," she managed to utter. She lowered her hands and regarded me, her face stained with tears.

"Hyun Woo, why don't we just give up? Let them enjoy their power for the next ten thousand years."

Preacher Choi and I were weeping, too. We left the restaurant feeling like we had been kicked out. From behind, I heard Hae Soon's voice.

"Don't ever come back here. Goodbye, Hyun Woo."

And I never saw her again. During the long years Kun was imprisoned, Jung Ja found another job and ended up marrying someone else, another worker who shared a similar background. I think I once heard that she lives in Ansan. Their situation was even worse than ours, the so-called intelligentsia, and they were soon forgotten. They coped on their own and withstood hardships, but no one cared to remember them later. But no one can take away from them their generosity and their youthful dignity, despite their anonymity in history.

You came back to me late on the Sunday night. I was not sleeping. I knew it was you when I heard footsteps approaching from beyond the fences. The door quietly opened, and there was that familiar scent of you. Like a dog who had returned home, you gulped down water from the yellow tin kettle on the table. I waited for you to fall asleep, lying there with my back to the light from the desk lamp, but you had to look over my shoulder at my face. I could not resist it any more, so I talked to you first, trying to sound like I was just waking up.

"When did you come in?"

"A while ago."

You were lying. I knew you had sneaked in just then. But I was determined not to show any sign of the agitation I had felt staying up every night for the past few days, worrying about you. I got up, rubbing my eyes, and pretended to be indifferent.

"How was your visit to the world?"

"It is just as it was before."

"What kind of answer is that?"

You took off your clothes and went outside. I heard the sound of running water and splashing. I did not say anything when you came back into the room, fell on your back, and finished a cigarette.

"We've been crushed," you mumbled, but I pretended I did not hear you. It took a while for you to say something again, still looking at the ceiling.

"There was a guy who got lost deep in the Himalayas. He found a crevice between rocks and he went in there to escape from the snow and wind. Inside, it was spacious and it was a different world, a gentle world where there was neither pain nor separation nor sadness, nor poverty nor hunger. There was a garden blooming with flowers of every radiant color, and fruit trees. None of the bad things in the real world existed there. No one fought, no one got sick . . . somehow, this life of harmony continued. But one day, he began to wonder what was going on outside and how his family was, so he left the cave. He returned to the country he was from and lived the rest of his life there, going crazy with a desire to return to that different world. He went back to the Himalayas to look for it, but he never again found the little crevice under the snow."

You were murmuring as if you were talking to yourself, and you came into my bed. You were not wearing a shirt, and I felt your firm shoulder blades when I put my hands around your back, almost automatically. We shared a long kiss. With one hand you grabbed one of my breasts while with the other you took my underwear down. Your touch was rougher and more forceful than usual. When it was over, I didn't mean to cry but tears rolled down my face. You had not just visited the world outside, you had rooted yourself in it again. The choices you and my father made caused you to look down on what we shared as insignificant, the domain of the petit bourgeois that created a false sense of freedom. Yet we were on a ship together, raising the sail and about to leave the port to cross the ocean through countless storms and rough waves. And our love had only just begun.

We got back into the old routine, an ordinary daily life where nothing really happened. And I came up with a cunning plan to grow vegetables. It happened to be a market day, so I went to the next village to buy young eggplants and peppers and tomatoes. I wanted to plow the little field and plant seeds for lettuce and crown daisy, and to dig a hole for compost and grow pumpkins, too.

"How about we grow a vegetable garden?"

"Yeah! Why didn't we think of that before?"

I had no idea that you would like my idea so much, but I was relieved to see you jump at the suggestion and grab a shovel. You dug the field and turned over the earth, and I followed behind you, breaking the bigger clumps of earth with a hoe. All afternoon, we made furrows and ridges in the field. We even decorated our little vegetable garden by building a low stone wall around it.

"It might be too late," you said, "but let's plant the seeds anyway."

"Sure! We just have to water them twice a day, they'll grow like crazy. Let's plant some flowers, too."

We went to the next village to buy the young plants, we got little branches to use as a support, and we seeded various annuals. Morning glories, four o'clocks, rose mosses, balsams, zinnias, even cosmos and asters. We were going to have a garden where all these flowers would bloom in sequence from early summer to late autumn.

How can I describe that feeling when you see the very first sprout coming out of the dry soil where nothing used to be? At first, there are only a couple, and I cannot tell if they are buds or weeds. Then, as if the first couple whispered to the rest that it is okay to come out, the field is covered with numerous sprouts the following day. They are almost transparent light green and look like they would be broken by the softest wind or the thinnest drizzle. The shifting appearance of our garden was a calendar. They used to grow so rapidly that I would not recognize them if I didn't look at them for a couple of days. You went out to the field every morning with a bucket and a watering can.

By early summer, our field was full of abundant green leaves. Do you remember the first time we picked lettuce for lunch? The leaves were not fully grown, but it was about half the size of my palm. If we overlapped two or three of them, we could wrap a spoonful of rice. Eating young lettuce leaves, my mouth was filled with the fragrance of life.

I was happiest when I watched you tending our vegetable garden. Every farmer can become a poet. Whenever you caught an insect on crown daisy leaves or picked up a snail, or even when you shook aphids from a plant, you touched them gently and made sure that you did not hurt them. You put them on a leaf and took them away. I loved that you did that. It comforted me and made me think that maybe nothing bad would ever happen to us, that heaven was watching out for us, too. People from the city get bored quickly with the stillness of the countryside and its scenery, and they run back in a few days. But open your eyes and look around! Nature is ever changing; it is alive and shifting. When the grasses and leaves dance, they look so different depending on the wind. In a soft breeze they flutter a bit, in a gentle wind they rustle, and when the wind becomes strong they sway and wave and shiver. Even in silence when the wind chimes are still and the air is not moving, it is soon altered by a grasshopper or a locust jumping out of the grass forest and hopping over the path. Or a frog jumping into water. The summer in Kalmae was a concert stage for the chorus of everything alive. I remember the evenings when we sat out in the courtyard with a straw mat on the ground. We burned dried wormwood from the main house to repel mosquitoes, and ate rice wrapped in steamed pumpkin leaves for dinner.

The rest of our lives would be dominated by those three months, and that summer was our life. It rained so frequently then.

Plump rain clouds of the blackest shade graze the mountain tops and rush toward us, and you run around the fence and shout, "Rain's coming! Get the laundry!"

By the time I find a pair of shoes and get down from the porch, big, fat drops of rain are falling already, on my head, on my arms, on the dry ground. A lightning flash crosses the sky, followed by a loud noise that shatters everything around. That noise spreads far and wide, echoed by the grumbling sound of thunder. When the rain begins, the hot earth cools down and releases the fresh scent of soil. A cool wind arrives and a delicious scent of air fills our noses. We hurry, gathering what needs to be gathered and putting away what needs to be put away, and then we stand on the porch or by the kitchen door to watch the rain come down, filling up the void. A flash again, lightning, and again the shattering noise.

"Let's make pancakes," one of us would suggest. I love the dark sky right before the shower begins, I love the peals of thunder that sound loud but are in fact gentle and lonely, and I love the fragrance of wild flowers and soil and the chill that brings goosebumps to my skin.

On rainy days, I sometimes went outside to burn little branches in the fuel hole, and I would hear you humming inside. By the time the rain's fog was pushed down the hill, the moist air was mixed with the scent of burning pine tree branches. It would make me feel cozy and warm. It felt like I was returning from the long gone past. I could hear the rain drops pattering on fluttering pumpkin and bamboo leaves, knowing soon my ears would be filled with the constant sound of rain, and I became sleepy. Sometimes we would be hiking when the rain began. We would return home wet through, and the first thing we did was wash our rubber shoes caked in mud by pouring water on them. Then we'd rub our wet hair with dry towels, take off our clinging shirts, pants, and skirt, and change into new, dry underwear. Then we'd wrap ourselves together in one blanket and lay flat on our stomachs, our chins supported by our hands, and look outside where it was still raining. Shivering once in a while, we listened to the rainwater collecting in the gutter and flowing down. When the rain stopped, the sunlight would drape itself across everything like a gauzy cloth and then disappear. The wet blades of grass would shine, and the birds shaking under the tree would begin to hop from one tree to the other, chirping. In Japanese, an oriole cries "ho-oh-ho-ke-kyo." Listen carefully, it really sounds similar to that. Like a miracle, a golden handkerchief hovers and darts around in the forest after the rain stops. First, it says "ho-oh" and extends the vowel as if it is hesitating a bit, and raises its voice to a higher octave for the "ke."

I remember you once said that the nicknames of all the birds crying at night from late spring to early summer have something to do with eating. Around this time of the season, food in storage is almost gone, yet it is too early to harvest barley. Waking up in the middle of the night because his stomach is empty, the farmer cannot fall asleep again, thinking about how to survive, how to feed his hungry family, and fearing for the future. I always thought *sotjoksae*, the scops-owl, would be small and pretty, based on its melancholic, delicate cry. But I once saw a picture of it in an illustrated guide and it looked just like any other owl, except it had a pair of horns. They say a scops-owl's cry sounds like someone complaining how small his rice pot is, *sotjok, sotjok, sojokda*. The great tit is called the farmhand's bird in the southeast regions, because its short cries, *tst, tst, tst*, sound just like the sound a farmhand makes as he clucks his tongue when driving a cow. When he hears the farmhand's bird at night he must think of himself earlier that day, plowing the field under the blazing sun with an empty stomach. And how does a short-eared owl cry? Here's a rice cake, *hoot-hoot*! Here's a bowl of rice, *hoot-hoot*! And in the northern regions they call a woodpecker a *zokbaksae*, a tiny bowl bird. It is said to be the reincarnation of a daughter-in-law who starved to death. She cried to reproach her mother-in-law for giving her the tiniest bowl of rice. So when the *zokbaksae* cries, it is the daughter-in-law asking the mother-in-law to exchange her little *zokbak* for a bigger one, *zok, zok, zok, zok*.

Do you remember the day we went to the little stream to wash our clothes? It was a gloriously sunny day after another downpour, when the sky seemed so high and masses of thick clouds hung here and there. I didn't go to work, so it must have been a Sunday or a Saturday afternoon.

We gathered the quilt covers and sheets and pillowcases and our underwear into a huge wooden bowl. On top of that we put a wooden laundry stick, a washboard, and a couple of laundry soap bars, which at first appeared to be too soft and dark in color, but cleaned clothes beautifully. I carried the vessel on my head while you packed our lunchbox, a portable stove, and charcoals in your backpack. You followed me holding in one hand a big tin tub to boil clothes, which we had to borrow from the main house, and in the other you held your fishing bag, packed with a fishing pole, a case of bait, and a net.

We took the path away from the orchard up the hill toward the upper stream of the creek, which widened by the time it reached the next village. Here, however, both shores of the river were covered with sand and pebbles, and there were a few little bays where the stream curved and the speed of the water slowed down. It was quite a distance from the main street and the residential area, so there weren't loud kids splashing about or farmers busily irrigating. They have built a cement dam and turned it into a swimming pool in recent years. Anyway, it was you who found this tranquil place with clean water during one of your many walks around the neighborhood while I was at work.

Past the sandy shore and down by the pebbles was a flat rock that looked like a swimming turtle, its back big enough to hold three or four people. I always wondered who brought it there. I put the vessel down near the rock and positioned myself with my skirt hiked up. You placed the other things on top of the pebbles and changed into swimming trunks, then walked into the water holding your fishing bag. The water rose from your ankles to your knees, and then to your belly, and I could not resist yelling out to you, "Don't go too far! Do you know how to swim?"

But you pretended you could not hear me, and you kept on walking, the water rising to your chest.

"Really, what is he thinking . . . ?" Nervous, I stood up, and you disappeared underwater, the plastic fishing bag left floating on the surface. I didn't think this was really happening, but still I was scared. I didn't know what to do, so I walked into the water until it reached my thighs and yelled one more time, "Don't be so childish. Come out now!"

But it took a while before your head reemerged. Your upper body followed and you stood up, and I saw that the water only came to your belly button.

You took a place across from the laundry station and began to fish. I began to wash the clothes by taking each garment out, one by one, and soaking it in water. I started with little things, soaped and scrubbed them on the washboard. The big sheets were folded in half and swirled around in water. I soaped them in parts and beat them with the laundry stick. The rhythmic sound echoed across the valley.

We placed the tub on the sandy area, then stacked and lighted the charcoal. We filled the tub with water and ashes, then neatly folded and stacked the little things together with the sheets in the tub and boiled them. I thought I had to be the last one from our generation to wash clothes like that. Doing laundry in a washing machine is really dull. As I rested, soaking my feet in the stream while the laundry was boiling, little rice-fishes gathered and tickled me, perhaps trying to eat salt from my feet and calves. Among the horsetails and foxtails growing here and there I found little sprouts of bilberry trees. I pulled them up to find the white roots, which tasted sweet. I looked for Indian strawberries and sandburs.

You had pierced a couple of worms on your hook and thrown them into the water, and now you were intensely watching the fishing line. When you pulled something shiny out of the water, I could tell even from far away that it was tiny, because you put it in the fishing net without saying anything. If you happened to catch something larger, like a stone moroko, you hooted and howled. Later I found out that even those were only about the size of my hand.

"Wow, it's a big one! And strong, too!"

I ignored you no matter how excited you seemed. After boiling the laundry for a couple of hours, I took it out, rinsed it in water one more time, and put it away back in the wooden vessel.

"Let's eat!" I shouted.

"Wait, they've just began to bite."

"I'm hungry. Fine, I'll just eat by myself."

You reluctantly gathered your things and walked across the stream to me. You opened the fishing net and proudly showed me the catches of the day.

"These are just minnows . . . you thread them on a stick, salt and grill them, they taste really light and delicious. A stone moroko, here . . . isn't it big? This one is called a floating goby. An ugly looking fellow, isn't he? And look, I got one slender bitterling. But I think we should let this one go."

"Why? It looks like the best tasting one."

"It's rare these days to find one. It looks like a butterfish from the ocean, doesn't it?"

You fingered its flapping tail for a while as if you couldn't decide what to do, but then you finally picked it up and threw it back into the stream.

"So, shall we eat?"

"Not yet. You have to help me first."

I picked up one end of the dripping bedsheet and you took the other without complaining. We wrung it out until there was not one drop of water left. We opened it flat and kept hold of the opposite sides, raised it high as if we were cheering someone, then lowered it, shaking it as the moisture evaporated into the air. We laid it out on the pebble beach. The sunshine filled the white sheet. In a line next to it, pillow cases lay next to each other like friends. We placed our underwear on top of a large, flat rock, already hot from the sun, which dried the clothes quickly. We surrendered the best spots to the laundry and ate our lunch by the sand. What seems so insignificant, the everyday tasks of a simple life, are in fact the most important part, aren't they?

12

It was the beginning of the rainy season, sometime in the second half of June. I had gotten into the habit of going fishing in our little pool behind the hill almost every day, either early in the morning or just before sunset. At first I would dig in the moist part of our backyard to find worms for bait, but one day Yoon Hee bought me a box of paste bait. I diluted it with water and sometimes mixed in ground shrimp shell, and some days I caught maggots and washed them in clean water. In time, I figured out a few places where the fish gathered, and I began to catch good-sized stone morokos. Once, I caught a foot-long catfish.

One day, I went as soon as I finished breakfast, carrying the fishing rod on my shoulder. It was a cloudy day with no wind; the water's surface was calm, and it was easy to watch the float. As soon as I sat down I caught a goby minnow. It was so impetuous, it stiffened and died as I pulled up the rod. I sat there until almost eleven o'clock, but I only managed to catch three or four minnows. I thought about moving to another spot, but I suspected it would rain soon so I packed up and left. As I headed home down the hill past the orchard, I noticed someone in front of me, walking in between trees while pulling a bicycle at his side. I sped up to follow him. He was wearing a dark yellow jacket and a pair of the camouflage pants of the reserve army, and his hair was shaved short. I thought maybe he was going to the main house, but he passed it by. I deliberately slowed down and watched him from a distance. As I suspected, he disappeared behind the fences surrounding our house, and I heard his voice clearly.

"Hello? Anyone home?"

I tried to slow down my racing heart and tried to think. There was no plan, no preparation for a situation like this. First of all, Yoon Hee and I had never discussed a cover story that we could present to others, and all we had told the family at the main house was a vague statement about me being Yoon Hee's fiancé. The excuse for the fact that I did not have a job was that I had been preparing for the bar exam for the past couple of years. I decided to avoid this stranger. I quickly walked away from the fence and went into the orchard, squatting behind the trees. A minute later, I saw the man leaving our courtyard and mounting the bicycle. He held onto the brake and went slowly down the hill. He stopped at the entrance to the main house. Again, I heard every word that came out of his mouth.

"Good morning, ma'am. How are you? Is the vice principal at school?"

"Yes, he is. And what brings you here?"

"Who lives in that house up there?"

"Why? The art teacher at the high school is renting it."

"I heard there is a man living there, too."

"Oh yes, her fiancé. He came down to study for the bar exam, but I also heard he's not well."

"So he's here to recuperate, is that it?"

"Sure, to rest and to study."

"I need to meet him. When do you think I can come back and find him?"

"Why don't you come around dinnertime?"

The bicycle emerged again and went wobbling down the hill. I sat among the trees in the orchard listening to the bees buzzing until everything was quiet.

I closed all the doors and windows except for one back window and waited, flipping through books, for Yoon Hee to come home. There was the familiar sound of her footsteps, followed by Yoon Hee, muttering to herself.

"Are you home? Has he gone fishing again?"

I stayed down on the floor with my chin on a pillow, and Yoon Hee absentmindedly opened the door, surprised to find me in there.

"My goodness, you were in here! Were you sleeping?"

"Just come in."

She saw my face and lowered her voice.

"Did something happen?"

When I told her about the man who came by the house before noon, the color of her face changed.

"Did the Soonchun lady know him?"

"I think so. He said he'd return in the evening, so he should be here soon."

"Wait, wait, wait. I don't think it's a big deal. I mean, think about it, if he knew who you were, would he have come like that, by himself on a bicycle? I'll go to the main house and ask who came by earlier."

"What are you going to say when she asks you how you know someone came by?"

"Well, I'll say you were napping and heard something while you were sleeping."

Without changing her clothes, she went straight down to the main house. Maybe she thought I would be going crazy, because she came right back within five minutes.

"No need to worry. Only the chief of a substation at the next village."

"Still, you never know. We should be prepared."

"Okay. We got engaged last year. You were studying for the bar exam, but you became ill, something with your lungs. The early stage of tuberculosis. Have you memorized your ID card? What's the name on it?"

"Jang Myung Goo. Age twenty-nine. The home address is in Inchon."

"Let me see. Hmm, it's not even Kim Jun Woo! Whose is this?"

"Don't know. A friend got it for me."

Right on cue, we heard a bicycle bell ring behind the fence. Yoon Hee quickly threw the ID card back at me, whispering, "He's here!"

"Excuse me . . ."

Yoon Hee deliberately pushed the door wide open and walked out. Beyond her legs I saw the dark yellow jacket out in the courtyard. Taking a commanding position on the porch, she called out to him.

"Who are you? And what is this about?"

"Ah, yes, I'm from the substation. There's something to be cleared up. What is the number of family members in this house?"

"Two."

"So . . ."

The chief of the substation searched beyond her and hesitantly looked toward me. I went out to the narrow porch where Yoon Hee was standing and sat down with my legs hanging.

"So you teach at the girl's high school, and this is . . ."

"My fiancé," Yoon Hee replied sharply, without giving him a chance to continue.

"I would like to see your ID cards, please."

"Both of us?"

The chief nodded meekly, as if he was somewhat flustered at having to do this. Yoon Hee turned to me and I handed her my ID card. She stacked it on top of her Teacher's Identification card and fanned herself with them.

"Wait a minute, what is this for? What needs to be cleared up?"

"Please, there's no need to get upset. We just to need to know who the new residents are in our neighborhood. That is the basic duty of our substation."

He carefully studied the two ID cards that Yoon Hee handed to him.

"You're from Inchon? And what do you do?"

"I was studying, but I've not been feeling too well."

"Do you plan to stay here for a long time?"

"He'll be here for the summer vacation," Yoon Hee replied quickly, "and he'll return home as soon as it's over."

He gave us back the ID cards and awkwardly raised his right hand to his forehead to salute to us, even though he was not wearing a hat.

"Beg your pardon, sorry to have inconvenienced you. We're in a state of emergency, you know."

He climbed onto his bicycle, and Yoon Hee walked to the opening in the fence to watch the bicycle leave.

"It is a state of emergency, you know," Yoon Hee imitated the chief's manner of speech as she walked back in. I guess I was quite nervous, since this was the first inspection I had to go through in Kalmae. From then on, a sense of uncertainty surrounded me like a fog. I was not worried about getting caught, but I feared that the peace of this little house would cease to exist. There were no more lunchboxes and hiking, no more tranquility at our laundry spot, staring absentmindedly at the smooth water's surface while fishing, no more long afternoon naps and the sound of night birds and rain. Yoon Hee went all the way to the city and bought a suitcase full of law books from a used bookstore. She stacked them neatly on the low desk, which was the first thing you saw when you opened the door. When Yoon Hee was at work, after lunch and before a nap, I made an effort to actually read them. Reading about different laws, the world seemed to be filled with things you should not do. It was as if the sky and the earth and the mountains and the village were covered with an invisible net. Feeling helpless, I would fall asleep.

I went into the next village one day while Yoon Hee was working. I avoided it during the weekend when it was full of people running errands. I was craving a bowl of noodles with black bean paste, and I needed to contact Preacher Choi, who was now in charge of my security. There was no point eating lunch while I was nervous or worried, so I decided to head to the Chinese restaurant first. It was full, even though it was not market day. A woman with three children was sitting at a table covered with bowls of noodles in spicy broth and noodles with black bean paste, busily cajoling her kids to eat. The delivery bicycles came and went, and from the kitchen came the sound of someone kneading dough. I liked the chaotic liveliness at the Chinese restaurant. Of course, I ordered a double portion of noodles with black bean paste, the same thing I always got. Sitting at an empty table, I stared absently at the man at the next table until something in the newspaper he was reading caught my eyes. The headline "A Network of Spies Captured" was printed in big white letters against a black rectangle. There was a list of names, including Choi Dong Woo, Kim Kun, and other familiar names, but the rest of it was covered by the man's hand. The customer's food was brought out, and he threw down the newspaper and began eating. I could not wait, I reached for it.

"Do you mind if I borrow your newspaper?"

The man glanced at me and nodded once. I picked up the newspaper and sat down, turning my back to him. I spread the paper out on the table and began reading. There were mug shots of Choi Dong Woo and

Kun, and other familiar faces. The number of those arrested was somewhere between seventy and eighty, less than a third of the whole
organization. Still, what the investigation had uncovered was quite close
to the truth. At the bottom, I recognized a photograph of myself, which
I had not noticed at first. Shocked, I inhaled and looked around.
Everyone was busy eating; no one was paying attention to me. It was an
old photograph taken before I went into the army, the one used on my
ID card. My hair was longer, my cheeks were hollow, I looked unsophis-
ticated. I comforted myself by thinking that no one would recognize me
here based on this photograph. My bowl of noodles came, so I closed
the newspaper and mixed the noodles and paste and ate, bewildered. I
kept pushing noodles into my mouth with chopsticks, but my head was
filled with what was in the newspaper.

According to the diagram, I was the chief operator and the principal
offender. That was about it: a simple label of "wanted," no mention of
specific charges against me. Dong Woo was the vice chief who established a base in Inchon and Boopyung to persuade and influence
laborers. There were names I had never heard of before, and they were
described as field agents of Dong Woo. Books and papers from North
Korea were discovered with him, and Park Suk Joon in Japan was named
as a contact. Kun was said to be the manager of the secret base of our
operation, with the names of Jung Ja and Hae Soon and other factory
workers included. I did not return the newspaper to the other patron; I
left it on my table and stealthily got up to leave. As I paid the cashier I
glanced back, and the man still had his back to me, busily eating and
showing no interest in the newspaper. I had already decided to keep this
information to myself and not tell Yoon Hee about it. First of all, I
needed to contact Preacher Choi and ask him how bad it was. I did not
go into the pair of telephone booths in front of the post office, even
though there were not many people around. I walked all the way to the
bus station. It was busy as usual with buses continuously streaming in
and out, and there were four telephone booths in front of the station
building. There were a lot fewer people there compared to the weekends,
and all the booths were empty. I walked into the furthest one. I dialed,
and I heard Preacher Choi's voice.

"Hello? Hello?"

"It's me. I saw the papers."

"Is that you? It's all a mess. The Inchon guy was dug up, and everyone else became potatoes."

Just as when I'd read the newspaper, I did not blame Dong Woo. If you were caught first, it was customary to dump everything onto those who had not been caught yet, to lessen the burden and buy more time. The problem was that people who were outside of our organization were mentioned. Maybe there was something else that he had to protect. No matter what, Dong Woo was the potato vine, and when he was pulled, all the bulbs underground followed him into the light.

"I can't imagine what it must have been like for you."

"Listen, I can't talk to you for too long. We worry about your health, more than anything. Consider yourself a hermit. Take care of yourself."

I tried to whisper farewell but the words never left my mouth. I hung up without saying anything.

I found out later that Choi Dong Woo deserved to be criticized. The first rule for an activist who had gone underground was not to be captured, but it was the hardest one to follow. You are isolated from daily life, and as the pursuers tighten their net, you become more militant and begin to hallucinate that you are fighting against the whole world. You are prone to being impatient and ever more radical. Dong Woo had been staying at the rented place of a laborer comrade in an industrial zone, where he had continued to run a study group. At first, he only used practical books published legally, but he gradually moved onto illegal ones from Japan, and eventually introduced books from the other side. He distributed the books by copying them into a notebook by hand and having his students copy them again. After Kun was arrested, Dong Woo had not left. He'd gone further, distributing leaflets in the industrial zone. A supervisor who used to be a technician saw one of those leaflets at his factory, and he took the laborer, who happened to be Dong Woo's student, to a pub to buy him drinks and gently question him. The student proudly told him everything. It is not clear whether the supervisor directly informed the police or not, but there was no question that the agency was secretly investigating in that area and had a widespread network of agents.

They descended on Dong Woo at three o'clock in the morning. He must have been exhausted; he had gone into hiding long before the Kwangju Incident, during the last years of the previous administration. He had a steel pipe on hand for self defense, so he resisted at first, swinging it around. When he had a chance, he took the back window and climbed over the neighbor's wall and roof to run away, as he had done before. But they were more experienced and prepared now—they had surrounded him in layers—and as soon as he got out of the alleyway and ran toward the major boulevard, a motorcycle was waiting for him. There were two men on one motorcycle, one driving and the other brandishing a bat. It soon caught up with Dong Woo, who was running, and as it inched ahead of him the man in the backseat wielded the bat and hit the back of Dong Woo's head. He bounced off like a ball, spun around, and fell to the pavement on his back. Naturally, he was unconscious. Before he was dragged in for interrogation, he was brought to an emergency room where his head was stitched and he was hooked up to an IV until he regained consciousness. It was the only lucky break we had. Because he was injured during the capture and because it was their fault, he was able to insist on his right to remain silent for four days. Time was golden. During those four days, Dong Woo rearranged and cleared his thoughts. First, he erased the names of laborers who were barely surviving and replaced them with the names of intellectuals who were managed by Kun through correspondences, even though they had little to do with what he was doing at the moment of his arrest. He also tried to minimize the damage by remembering only a few names of laborers from where he was staying. He followed the new picture he had composed, surrendering only a name at a time, and faced two months of torture. I cannot even begin to describe it. You would never know how sensitive your penis and anus are to electric shocks, and you would never know how it feels when your eyes jump from their sockets, as if they are about to burst. Dong Woo was a boy from the sea who could always see the smallest fishing boat out on the horizon, but after that he became terribly short-sighted and had to wear thick glasses.

He spent twelve years in prison and got out before I did. His last three years were split between a regular prison and one in the south, where there was a psychiatric ward. Once there, he would stay at least six months in the psychiatric ward. I heard about him from time to time from other students who were transferred to my prison.

We were together in the same detention house before the trial—not in the same section, since we were coconspirators, but in the same compound, his building right in front of mine. From the window in my bathroom, I could see his building's public bath. Whenever he went out for exercise or for lunch, or whenever he left the building to attend hearings or visitations, he would call for me.

"Oh Hyun Woo! Hyun Woo, where are you?"

I looked out through the bars on the bathroom window and waved to him. Dong Woo climbed on top of the washstand, squatted down in front of the grilled window, and gave me news from outside and about people who came to visit him. The prison guard sometimes interrupted.

"Who's talking to the other prisoner? You know it's not allowed."

"Shut up, you fool. You're the one who should be quiet."

A little later, the chief guard would appear beyond the grilled window with his cap on.

"Get down! Hey you up there, get back inside! Who told you to talk to each other?"

"Hey, I'm doing my business here. Man's gotta go when he's gotta go."

We did not care, we told each other to eat well and take care, and finally said our goodbyes. After the final sentencing, before we were transferred to different prisons, both of us put in a request so we could say farewell to each other. We sat side by side at a table, drinking barley tea and looking out the window. It was snowing. We saw a corner of the female prisoners' exercise ground, and there was a lone woman in a gray prison uniform kicking a ball. The ball she was using was sold in the prison store, a soft volleyball. The snowflakes were quite big, but she kept kicking the ball against the long, high wall, skillfully catching it with her chest or foot and kicking it back repeatedly. Her action seemed so futile, kicking the ball again and again against the wall in the empty playground. Maybe she was killing time. Both of us watched her for a while in silence. Of course, Dong Woo and I each knew one another's thoughts, as well as the recent news regarding our other friends. Dong Woo spoke first.

"Kun left already."

"You saw him?"

"Yeah, he came to see me while he was being transferred. He happened to pass our section, so he just ran in with his bags. The guards knew we were saying goodbye, so they pretended not to notice."

At the time we were called "prisoners of public order crimes," and this was signified by a red triangle on our chests. Sometimes other ordinary criminals would taunt us as we passed their cells by calling out simultaneously, "Hey you, Commie bastard!" The red triangle was gone by the time we were transferred to our prisons, but we always stood out because our heads were not shaved as other prisoners' were. He was sentenced to twenty years, I to life.

"I am so sorry."

Dong Woo dropped his head.

"For what?"

"I didn't do it right, the interrogation."

"What's the difference? One way or another, it's either you or me, nothing else would be different."

"We won't be able to exchange letters ourselves. Let's keep in touch through those outside."

That was how we parted. For the next three or four years he did well, and he sent his regards a couple of times a year through our families, the only ones who could exchange letters with us. About five years later, I heard news about him from another prisoner of public order crimes who had been transferred from a southern province.

"Choi Dong Woo is in the hospital ward now."

"Really? Why was he sent there?"

"My last prison has a tuberculosis ward and a psychiatric ward. He was sent there last year."

"Are his symptoms serious?"

"That's usually the case. They only transfer the worst cases. I heard he doesn't recognize anyone."

I remembered things I had seen in the prison I was in before, and I could easily guess his condition. I had been on the second floor, a special section for prisoners of public order crimes, and below me was the infirmary. The long corridor was divided into two by a partition; closer to the entrance were patients with normal illnesses, and inside, behind another set of iron bars, were mental patients. The mental patients' cell was immediately beneath mine, and I knew their activities and movements very well. In the cells closer to the iron bars were the relatively benign patients, while more violent ones were housed in the innermost ones. There was a man, another lifer, who stayed in the cell right underneath mine for a long time. I had heard that he was from the notorious boot camp in Samchung, where gang members and other "menaces to society" were sent in the name of purification. He rebelled against the guards and injured some of them, and in return he was beaten just enough so that he would live and then be transferred to our prison. After he arrived, he suffered a psychotic episode while working in the prison factory and killed a fellow prisoner with a hammer. Even when he had those episodes, he continuously proclaimed his innocence and protested against his enemies. He would debate passionately, and he gave a speech every night. His screams at night were wretched. In the middle of the night, the whole building would be in commotion: other prisoners, awakened by his howling, screamed back at him to shut up so they could sleep, while guards shouted commands. I had permission to use the tiny courtyard, which faced south, as a little vegetable garden and as a place to dry my bedding. The mental patients' windows looked out onto it, and their sewage tank was in the corner of that courtyard, so I ran into them from time to time. One day I was watering my lettuce when, out of the blue, someone began shouting behind my back. It was him, the guy from Samchung, making another speech, starting with "My dear fellow citizens." He ended it by asking people to vote for him in the next parliamentary election; I do not know how he knew the name of the president at the time, but he named the president and shouted, "Down with the presidency!" In the beginning, the prison guards would get angry and try to stop him, but after a while they let him be. This sort of thing was actually uneventful compared to his more serious episodes. One time when he was edgy he remained quiet for a while, then collected his feces in a bowl and threw it at the chief guard during his regular inspection. Once in a while I saw him from the courtyard as he stared out the bathroom window. He was always looking far away and did not seem to notice me. He would stand there for a long time without moving. When he received meals, sometimes he ate them, but most of the time he threw them all over his cell and painted the walls with his feces. The prison assistants, who had to bathe him and clean his cell and clothes every three days, detested him. Every six months he was sent to another prison with a psychiatric ward, then he would come back a bit subdued. For three years he went back and forth, until one day he never returned. I once mentioned him to a prison guard, who snickered and mumbled, "I guess he left."

"How? He was a lifer."

"Therefore, he left because he died."

I remember another guy, the one nicknamed Daddy Long Legs. He was in his early twenties, and he seemed perfectly normal at first. He knew my name and the charges against me, and he even asked me if I would lend him books. He was bony and tall like a basketball player, and whenever there was a prison championship, everyone said, *What a shame, if only he had a clear mind, he would be the best player we had.* Daddy Long Legs made scenes only when the warden or the prison board or someone high up came for an inspection. As they stood in line to take a look, he spat and swore.

"You assholes, am I a zoo animal? What are you looking at?"

Naturally, the important people would hurry up and leave, but his swearing trailed them into the corridor.

"You fucking asshole, you think you're so important? All you have is a shitty cap on your head! You bastards, you browbeaters, you black-mailers!"

As he banged the door and got hopping mad, it took three or four prison guards to overpower him, tie him up with ropes and leather straps, and put a muzzle on his mouth. When they left his cell, utterly exhausted, he continued to kick the door with his foot.

Daddy Long Legs was also sent to the other prison every six months, and he gradually stopped talking. His cheeriness was replaced by silence, and his body grew even thinner. The youthful energy that had filled his eyes disappeared, and he began to look like a middle-aged man. One day I was watching the group of men from his section doing exercises and drying their bedding out in the courtyard, and I spoke to a guard in charge of the exercise.

"That guy, Daddy Long Legs, he's changed a lot. He's in such low spirits."

"Isn't he a gentleman now? Well, he'll have to be. He has to change if he wants to survive when he leaves this place."

"No, I mean he seems worse."

"I heard he's much better now. He doesn't talk nonsense anymore, does he?"

I did not think he had gotten better. I thought he had gone to the other world, from which he could never return. Over a couple of years, after he had done three round trips, he turned to stone. He did not remember me. He finished his six-year sentence and disappeared.

For everyone, there is a line that should not be crossed. It does not matter whether you are inside or outside. During imprisonment, it went without saying that everyone would go through several crises: the first day after sentencing; facing your fourth year in solitary; going from your ninth to tenth year. When your wife leaves. When a family member, especially your mother, passes away. When your child is sick. When the guard you hate is put in charge of you. When you are punished unfairly. When you are handcuffed from behind and your feet are tied, when you have to eat like a dog in a dark windowless cell. At that moment, you cross the boundary from this side of life to the other. Unable to bear it, your spirit leaves the space around the body and creates a world of its own.

Dong Woo survived the first four years of imprisonment, but he lost it in his fifth year. Like others, he was sent to a psychiatric ward every six months, which only made him worse. I got word that when Dong Woo was released his older brother and mother took him to a house they had bought in the countryside. Chul Young remained trapped in the moment of the Kwangju Incident, and he still remembered the situation and the names of friends, but Dong Woo did not remember anything. I think I am going to go see him one day, even if all there is left of him is his aged face.

The tranquility in Kalmae had been shattered. The rainy season was over, the mosquitoes in the bamboo forest became fat, and everywhere things grew tired and dark green. Yoon Hee's school was on vacation, so she no longer went there. We spent most of the time in our house, only going out when it was absolutely necessary. We did not want to be seen by anyone. But during that July there was something that Yoon Hee and I had to accomplish.

On the first day of vacation she was crouching in the kitchen, stretching a canvas. I was moving about in the room, pacing, then lying, then sitting, then reading, all without meaningful intention.

"Why are you making so much noise so early in the morning?" I asked Yoon Hee.

"I'm making my frame."

She always referred to her canvas as her frame.

"What are you doing?"

"I want to paint."

I did not probe further, as I normally would, but rather left her alone. Yoon Hee did not explain either; she simply stretched the canvas cloth over a wooden frame and nailed it. She studied it to make sure the cloth was taut. Afterward she turned to me.

"Can you help me?"

I thought she wanted me to lift something heavy or put the canvas somewhere high up, so I jumped up and went to the kitchen. Yoon Hee picked up a small chair and placed it in front of me.

"Sit there."

Without knowing why, I perched on top of the chair. Yoon Hee came toward me. Without saying anything, she turned my body sideways toward the window, then turned my head toward her.

"What are you doing?" I asked, embarrassed.

"I want to paint you," she replied calmly. "So that you can remain in that frame for a long time."

I grinned.

"Well, that's unnecessary . . ."

Yoon Hee glared at me with unforgiving eyes.

"Unnecessary?"

She began to squeeze oil paints onto her palette.

"Hyun Woo, you've already left this place. I want to keep you here in the painting."

I knew she was not joking around, so I closed my mouth. Yoon Hee did not say much after that. She picked up her brush and began painting. I thought perhaps she was doing an outline, sometimes narrowing her eyes to gauge the light and shadow, but she never stopped moving her brush, continuously looking back and forth between the canvas and me. She did not stop when she spoke again.

"It shouldn't take long. You're not going anywhere until the summer vacation is over."

I could not tell if she was talking about her painting or our life together. A little angry, I shot back, "I'm leaving this place before summer is over. I do not want to inconvenience anyone."

Yoon Hee stopped painting.

"I can barely capture your shadow now. I cannot paint your face without looking at it, not yet. Maybe I won't be able to finish painting you before the end of the summer."

"Can I move?"

"As long as you keep the same basic posture, it's okay. But your thoughts should remain in the same place."

"What thoughts?"

She stopped painting again. This time, she held up the brush and narrowed her eyes, measuring the distance between us. I felt a little tired and powerless, but I stared back at her sharp gaze, poised on the tip of her brush.

"Just think about this place, nothing else," Yoon Hee mumbled as she began painting again. There were times when she had sketched my likeness in her sketchbook with charcoals or crayons. She was not satisfied with any of the drawings. If you are an artist, I guess the most basic skill is to depict the likeness of a person as closely as possible. Some of her sketches did indeed look like me, capturing what I considered to be the distinctive features I saw in pictures or reflected in mirrors. But most of them looked a little different from me. At first, I pointed out the ones I thought were a faithful depiction of my likeness and told her that I liked them, but Yoon Hee felt the opposite. She said she did not like them for that very reason.

"A person's face is not an object like a kettle or a glass or an apple. A face is an expression. It is a vessel projecting one's heart. The artist should be able to see that. Moreover, we're together all the time. Who knows?" Yoon Hee mumbled as she kept painting. "Maybe I'll finish it after you're gone."

In an instant, I thought of the past few months, the peaceful days when nothing happened, yet much did, the clear recollection of the little things that happen in everyday life. I thought of the sense of spring's arrival, and the deepening of that season as it enriched the land around us. I thought of the rain and the wind and the thunder, the sound of birds and water, the laundry and fishing spot we found, the pool and the fish and the smell of water plants.

"It's like you're pushing me away." Yoon Hee kept moving her hand and then uttered in an indifferent voice, "I saw the newspaper."

When we first began living in Kalmae, we had agreed that there was no reason to bring in the outside world. I listened to the radio news once in a while, but we decided not to subscribe to newspapers. Above all, we did not want someone to visit us regularly to deliver them. At first I felt a little uneasy, but soon I got used to it. Listening to the radio became a cumbersome and burdensome exercise, so I stopped that, too.

"I saw it at the school, purely by chance . . ."

I had to say something now.

"I saw it, too. When I went to the Chinese restaurant in the next village."

"I thought you did. Why didn't you say something to me?"

"Because you'd worry."

Deliberately, I tried to sound cheerful and indifferent. Yoon Hee put her brush down and got up from her chair in front of the easel. Suddenly, she rushed at me, grabbing my head in both her hands and hugging it to her chest. Coming from her body I could smell turpentine, like pine trees.

"Is that why you said you'll leave before the summer is over? Is that it? Tell me."

I kept my head against her chest and waited quietly. Her lips traveled down through my hair to the crown of my head, to the temples, to my cheeks.

"When I read the newspaper, I had this premonition that if you leave this time I will not see you for a long, long time. Why summer? Stay through the snowy winter, think about it again when the new spring is here. I can quit my job, we can go deeper into the valley."

"Everybody has been caught, so how much longer can I last? And they'll leave the others alone only when I surface."

"I'm not going to just sit here and do nothing if you have to go."

"What are you going to do?"

"I'll find those still in hiding. I'll fight against the military dictator-ship."

"You're already doing that."

"No . . . please, wait just a little more. You never know when things will change."

From the day she began painting my portrait, Yoon Hee became quiet. Sometimes she asked me to go into the next village and get her green apples. Now that I think about it, she must have already been pregnant with Eun Gyul by that time. I was so foolish, I had no idea. She seemed so vulnerable and sensitive, yet, for my own convenience, I simply assumed that she was conflicted because of my dangerous situation and her desire to keep me there. I thought, *Ah, this woman really wants me to stay*. Until then, Yoon Hee was never weak. She fit into the stereotyp-ical image of an artist, independent and self-centered, and she rarely showed her inner emotions. Looking back, Yoon Hee was pregnant with our baby. The reason she desperately argued for next spring was because that was when Eun Gyul was to be born.

I have been looking at the portrait of me that she left behind in Kalmae. At first it was only of me, but after a long time she added her self-portrait to the same canvas, as though she were looking at my youth from behind. There is dark shadow around my eyes, my cheeks are hollow and my face is thin, revealing the anguish of that time. The background is the dark red of dried blood. That must be the world surrounding me. On top of that dreadful red there are vertical stripes of cobalt blue, and that transparent blue somehow manages to make my gloomy and tired face still appear youthful. From mid-July to early August, while she painted the portrait, there were more hours of nervous silence than we had had in the preceding few months of languid comfort. But it was then that we realized how deep our relationship had become. We gazed at each other without speaking, and I discovered Yoon Hee's mysterious smile. It was not a big smile, but a very faint one that was barely a smile at all, as if she was about to say something. Yes, now that I thought about it, she was not looking at me by herself, she was looking at me with our baby. There used to be a latticed window in the portrait, but it was gone now, and a little further back Yoon Hee emerged. She said she painted it before she became ill, so she must have done the self-portrait three or four years ago. Unlike the dark background I had to bear, hers was a thick coat of light gray paint, close to the color of a dove. Her brushstrokes appeared to be a lot rougher and more mature. Her high cheekbones, the little lines under her eyes and the gray in her hair, her cheeks painted with overlapping colors, together they betrayed her withering youth and her solitude. But her eyes were calm and collected, and there was that mysteriously tender smile. Here were a thirty-two-year-old man and a woman in her forties, depicted in different colors and distinctive tones, standing side by side and watching the world beyond the canvas. She was right behind me, not looking at what was right in front of her but staring at something far away, over my shoulder. Where was I looking, so nervous and pained? And where was she looking years later, with the hindsight of her age? Which way in the world were we going?

In our garden, asters and cosmos began to bloom. Yoon Hee's school was about to start again. Our friends in Kwangju, those who had somehow survived and gone through humiliating trials, were released from prison on the thirty-sixth anniversary of the liberation, some pardoned, others paroled. Either way, they should have been grateful to be alive, but they also had to live the next decade with the guilt that came from owing their lives to others. Around that time, Yoon Hee was almost done with my portrait. It became all that was left of my youth.

Before the season changed, it was rainy and windy. During the rainy season of early summer, the atmosphere was filled with sticky, hot, humid air, but on a rainy day on the cusp of autumn, a gloomy chill filled the sky. Even the still green leaves left the violently shaking branches and floated away as if they had been kicked. The thunder in spring comes from far away, in summer it is impatient and close by, and in autumn, even thunder disappears from the low sky, as if the world is sinking.

> I didn't know why, but I didn't feel good. I felt dizzy all the time, I had to take breaks when I climbed stairways. If I left the school building after being in there for a while, or if I stepped out of a shadow into the sunlight, the sky would turn from yellow to dark black. You know that I decided to take a

leave of absence soon after school began. My health was one issue, but above all, I knew for sure by then that you would leave. The day I handed in my notice, I bought a fat chicken from the next village. It was a cute hen, its comb small and dainty like a flower and its feathers reddish brown with a light brown tail. I chose her from the chicken coop at a butcher's stall in the market. As soon as I pointed her out, the female owner in a rubber apron took up a crude cast iron knife and adroitly turned around. It did not look like she was doing much, but in a few minutes she presented to me a naked piece of meat, whose wings and legs stuck out like branches on a bonsai tree. Like my mother used to, I bought a small bag of sweet rice, garlic, dried dates, and a handful of young ginseng roots. The truth was, I thought I would throw up if I even caught a scent of cooked chicken, but do you remember how poor our diet was that summer? All we had were greens we grew ourselves. Oh yes, I forgot, there were those stone morokos you caught. They were good. You told me how to cook them with seasoning and pepper paste and honey, how to combine them all in old soy sauce and braise them at low heat for a long time till the bones melted away. Whenever I stopped at the market on the way home, you acted like a little child, checking each bag to see what I had bought. Sometimes I bought sweet rice cakes with bean flakes, or wormwood cakes covered in sesame oil, and you would be so happy that you would hum a song while devouring them.

"Let's make a chicken stew!"

When I said that, you pushed your stubbled face into the kitchen and said something silly.

"What are you trying to do, fatten me up?"

"Isn't it too late for that? Tomorrow, I'll make spicy beef soup."

"What's going on? Did you get a raise?"

"No, we didn't eat properly during those dog days of summer, so I decided to cook everything over the next three days."

I filled the cavity inside the chicken with ginseng roots and sweet rice, and I closed it up with white thread. When it began to boil, however, I began to feel queasy and I could not bear it. I did not want you to notice, so I shut my mouth and covered it with my hands and went outside. I vomited before I could find a place to squat down. It was not like there was anything left to come out, just liquid, but the nausea would not go away. I was worried and decided to go see a doctor. I had to be extra careful that you would not notice anything. I would have told you if we were going to be able to continue our life in Kalmae, if you were not suffering from the guilty feeling that you were the only one in a comfortable hideout. I knew what the two of us would have to face after sending you away. I thought about contacting my sister, but what was most important to me was for you to go through that process with no reservations. I was encouraged when those who had armed themselves, fought with weapons, and been fortunate enough to stay alive were pardoned on Liberation Day. I did not know that you were about to fall into a dark, bottomless pit. They were hostages freed to show the newly formed government's mercy, but you and your friends were the new sacrifice made to justify a new wave of repressions to come.

"Hyun Woo, I've decided to take a leave of absence from school."

You did not appear to be too concerned.

"Well, that's good. Why don't you start preparing for the national competition? You should concentrate on painting now."

I remained cautious for the next few days, trying to control my emotions. And then the typhoon came, signaling the beginning of autumn. I did not want to look at the orange asters shaking under the cold rain as soon as they bloomed; instead I cut an armful and put them in a round clay jar that we used to store pepper paste. We stood on the porch together and watched the leaves blow away in the rain and wind. And I remember us sitting next to each other on a torn cardboard box in front of the fuel hole and building the fire. You start by placing a bunch of twigs in the fuel hole and lighting them. At first, the weak flame makes a crackling sound as it moves from one twig to the other, then, all of sudden, the whole bunch catches on fire. We put dry logs on the fire and watched as the resin still stuck to the log smoldered. Sometimes the twigs crackled and sparked, and a little piece of burnt wood landed on my bare foot. I would scream, and you would put your finger into your mouth and rub my foot with it.

"Saliva is the best cure for burns."

"That's disgusting."

One night the fuel hole was glowing, touching our faces with warmth and light as darkness fell. I felt so relaxed and languid, I put my head on your back. Through your back, I heard the air moving in and out of your lungs, and your heartbeat. Silhouetted in the glimmering light, I saw your shaggy long hair sticking out and felt somehow helpless. I grabbed the back of your head where hair spread out like a sparrow's tail and jiggled it.

"Look how long your hair is. You need a haircut."

"Hey, that hurts."

Remember how it rained all through the night as I cut your hair? I took off your shirt and made you sit on the floor covered with newspapers, draped a sheet around your shoulders and gave you a mirror to hold, so that you would not be too bored. I used to cut my friends' hair, so I was pretty confident. All I needed was the double-sided blade that you used to shave, held between my thumb and index finger. I opened my left hand like a comb and raked it through your hair, and I held onto a handful as if to bite it with my hand, then sheared the ends lightly. When you use a blade instead of scissors, the tip is not cut off, but sliced at an angle, and it made your hair shine. It twinkled as you moved your head.

"Hmm, not bad, not bad at all," you said, while looking at your own reflection in the mirror and shaking your head. "But why is it so shiny?"

"Because I used a blade. I think it looks good. It's as if stars had showered down on your head."

I was kneeling behind you and you were sitting on the floor holding the mirror. In it were our faces, mine hovering on top of yours. You looked into the mirror for a while without saying anything. Perhaps it was the same composition as that of our portrait I finished many years later. I wonder what you were looking at. Whenever someone gets a haircut, nice and neat, it means there is going to be a change in his everyday routine, in his appearance. You quietly put the mirror down and turned around to face the real me behind you.

"I'll be leaving soon."

My heart dropped. I thought I would say it first. I wanted to tell you to leave the two of us here, but hurry back.

"When?"

"Maybe the day after tomorrow or the following day."

I raked your hair scattered on top of the newspaper with my hand. I collected it all, but there was barely a handful. Do you know what I did with it? Without thinking about it, I went out and opened up the tin shield of the fuel hole and threw it in, little by little, onto the red embers that remained. They burst into flame with a scent of burnt skin. I flicked off every tiny particle of your hair from my hand into the flame. Later I read in a book that soldiers, before going to the front line, cut their hair and nails, wrap them in a clean piece of paper, and leave them for their mothers or lovers. And what did I do? They say you burn the hair when you say goodbye to those who have already passed away.

The following evening, the western sky was the unlucky shade of dark gray. There was not a single line of color, it was dark as far as we could see. Meanwhile, the sky above us was red, as if draped with a piece of cloth, its color fading.

"I think it's going to rain," you said, looking at the sky from our porch. "The old farmers always said that it would rain when there was no sunset in the western sky."

"No wonder, the red dragonflies were flying really low," I said as I gathered the laundry hanging on the clothesline. The sun had not gone down completely when we sat down at our dinner table, but suddenly it became dark. I had to get up and turn on the light. A cool wind came like a rising tide, and the rain came down in large drops all over the courtyard and on the roof. It was not the noisy, driving summer rain, but the slowly escalating rain of the early autumn that falls continuously. From that night, the wind became stronger.

The bamboo forest outside was thrashing violently in the wind, and I lay there with my head on your arm, nervously listening to the gloomy sound of an approaching storm.

I imagined that by the ocean all the boats and ships were tied to the port, and there was a typhoon warning. No seagull dared to fly, and dark waves with white teeth charged up the shore endlessly, shattering into white droplets as they crashed into a wall. In the complete darkness, where we could not find one flicker of light, we were tied to a broken, listing raft, scared. The waves rose up like walls around us, as if they would devour us. At that moment, I saw far away a few specks of light, perhaps a big ship, perhaps a little village on the shore. I cut the rope that tied us. I let you go, the brave one, to swim there first.

The rain and wind continued all the next day. I took out and ironed your clothes, from underwear and socks to shirts and jackets and pants, and I folded them neatly and packed them in a bag. At first, you said you were going to leave in the afternoon, after lunch, but I did not say anything, and neither of us could walk out the door. Was it because it was still raining?

The wind had died down, but the rain poured on, and unlike other days when the twilight would last for a while, the darkness came in quickly.

"Why don't you eat dinner before you go?"

I did not say that to make you stay one more day. You know that, don't you? I cubed the new potatoes we pulled up from our garden, sliced the zucchinis and green peppers that had grown throughout the summer, and cooked them together in a broth with bean paste. I braised salty mackerel, one of our favorites, in a peppery sauce with radishes, accompanied by the sesame leaves pickled in bean paste that they sent from the main house and the young radish kimchi that I had made. You used to say that salty mackerel with young radish kimchi and hot rice in cold water accompany each other perfectly. I always presented mackerel with its flesh exposed, but you insisted on turning it over to show-case its skin and dark meat, saying that it looked more appetizing that way.

We ate together in good spirits, as if nothing was out of the ordinary. Suddenly, the electricity went out; we lit two candles, but it took a while for our eyes to get used to the darkness. It was comforting to light the candles, just like it had been in the first days we came here, when we felt like we were so far away from everything. A little later, after I sent you away, I lay in the empty room, unable to fall asleep as the candles melted away.

"Would you please tell me where it is?"

Out of the blue, you used the respectful form of speech, as if we were strangers. Of course I understood that you were not doing it to distance yourself, you were just concerned that I would be too distraught before we parted.

"I once saw it stuck inside a book," you continued.

"What are you looking for?"

"The passport photo."

"I don't like it, I look weird."

You went through some books on the low desk and managed to find my passport photo, hidden in a book of poems either by Heine or Neruda.

"Here it is!"

I did not try to take it away from you, I let you have it. As soon as you put the photo in your wallet, you got up, as if the idea had just occurred to you at that moment. You picked up the bag I had packed. Powerless, I was going to follow you, but then I remembered to go to the kitchen and find a flashlight and an umbrella we could use together. I returned to the room to blow out the candles, and darkness enveloped us again. You held up the umbrella and walked in silence, and I held on to your arm, illuminating the path with the flashlight.

The raindrops felt cold on my bare feet, and I saw them clearly as they landed on that familiar pair of shoes of yours. The apple trees in the orchard stood there like dwarf monsters, their limbs shaking. At the bridge where Kalmae began, you embraced me with your free arm and kissed me. Both our lips were cold.

"It won't take too long. I'll come back soon."

How presumptuous! You'd be back soon? Still, at that moment, a year or two later seemed not too far away. The last bus was approaching slowly, driving on the newly paved road along the stream. Suddenly, I decided to take my ring from my finger and give it to you. I did not say anything.

Before you climbed into the bus you turned around for a second to look at me, and I waved back to you meekly. The windows on the bus were too dark, and all I could see was black.

13

The bus rattled as it drove along the unpaved road. As soon as I got in, I ran along the narrow corridor with unsteady steps. The last glimpse I caught of Yoon Hee through the back window of the bus lasted only a moment, a fleeting moment, but it was an image I pictured repeatedly over the years I spent in solitary confinement.

The umbrella covered her face so I could not see her well, but she was holding a flashlight in one hand and I saw her skirt fluttering in the wind. She had bought it at the open market, a cotton skirt with a flower pattern, something a middle-aged woman would wear while she worked in the kitchen or did laundry. But when Yoon Hee wore it, the little flower patterns were beautiful, and she looked like a newly wed bride. I loved the carefree look of Yoon Hee when she wore the peasant skirt and a pair of white rubber shoes on her bare feet.

Whenever the season changed and it rained at night, I would open up the tiny window of the prison bathroom and look up through the bars into the sky. My cell was at the end of the corridor, and I was able to see behind the building opposite mine to where we had been, to the mountains and the open fields to the west. There was a narrow road that circled the mountain, and there I watched the seasons change as it rained and snowed. Around the bend magpies cheerfully croaked in a persimmon tree. Sometimes there would be a cultivator parked underneath the tree, or farmers taking a break in its shadow during the summer, or village women resting on their way home. And sometimes, when the space was empty, I placed Yoon Hee under the persimmon tree. Yoon Hee's cotton skirt with flower patterns fluttered in the wind as she stood there in a pair of white rubber shoes with pointed toes, no umbrella, her long, straight hair dancing in the wind. I stared for a long time until the sun came down, until the darkness enveloped everything except for that road, remaining pale in the darkness. Still, a trace of her remained. The guard would look in through the tiny viewing window and remind me where I was.

"Number Fourteen Forty-Four! What are you doing?"

Embarrassed, I silently turned around and smiled at him.

"Have you been somewhere else?"

I just nodded and smiled. I got used to doing it, and later I was able to place her there at night, too. On rainy days, I stood by the bars and reproduced her cotton skirt with flower patterns. In my dreams, I was standing next to her.

After leaving Kalmae, I arrived in Kwangju before eleven that night, the perfect time for a someone on the run like me to move about. I took the night train and fell asleep as soon as I collapsed into my seat. I woke up and dozed off repeatedly, listening to the endless noise of the iron wheels. Still half asleep, I raised my head to look out at an unfamiliar station in an unknown town where a couple of people left the train with their luggage and a couple got in, their friends and family waving and smiling outside. And there were small, empty stations, lit by a single bulb, slowly passing by like in a dream. For me, there was no longer an exit. In my mind I was returning to Seoul, but there was no place for me to go. When I thought of returning home I clearly pictured the little house in Kalmae. It took me a while to picture the house by Bukak Mountain, surrounded by forsythias, where my mother and brother lived, and where I had not been in years. I had to go there now to see my mother for the last time.

Like that morning a few months before when I had gone to look for Kun, I arrived at the Youngdeungpo station early in the morning. I had decided to go see Myung Hun at his art studio in Shinchon first. After the incident in Kwangju, some people came to Seoul looking for somewhere to hide. I volunteered to help place a few of them, and I asked Myung Hun to take in Ho Sun. Both of them are no longer alive. Myung Hun lived his life as an alcoholic bachelor and was hit one night by a taxi speeding through the city. Ho Sun died last year of liver cancer.

In Shinchon, there was a narrow street along the railway that connected the campuses of Ewha Women's University and Yonsei University. Running off that street were little alleyways lined with tiny, prefabricated houses. Myung Hun was lucky to find an old Japanese-style, double-story house, and he was renting the second floor as his studio. I walked down the empty alleyway, pushed open the thin wooden door, and climbed up the creaking steps. On the worn-out door was a rough handwritten sign that read "Studio." I pushed the door quietly, but unlike the other times I had been there, it did not budge. When I knocked on the door I heard someone moving behind it, but he seemed to be waiting without answering. I had no choice but to talk.

"Myung Hun? It's me, Hyun Woo."

As soon as I said my name Ho Sun opened the door, as if he had been waiting. He squinted his eyes as he turned the light on.

"Jesus, what are you doing here?"

"I thought I'd drop by to say hello."

Looking around the studio, I heard someone snoring behind a screen by the window facing the street. The room was a mess, littered with easels and tubes of colors and papers. Ho Sun had a wooden bed, like those used in the military, and an upside-down wooden crate as a table. Instead of chairs, similar-sized wooden boxes, the kind used as seats in small, poor theaters, surrounded the table. Ho Sun and I sat on them, facing each other.

"He's drunk again, no?"

"Yeah, yeah, yeah. He came back a little while ago and just dropped dead."

"And how are you?"

"Thanks to you, I'm doing relatively well. We're all worried about you."

"I know, thank you. How's Bong Han? Is he well?"

"I think so."

"It seems like you guys will be okay, after all."

"Some civilians and a few who were connected to Kim Dae Jung were released, but they are still searching for those wanted as the leaders of the uprising. By the way, should I make some ramen for you?"

He went over to the little kitchenette in a corner, filled a pot with water, and lit a flame underneath it. While the noodles cooked, Ho Sun continued to talk in his usual sulky voice, as if what he was saying was not a big deal.

"It seems like you've committed a major crime, according to the newspapers. Looks like you'll be going away for a long time."

"What can I say. I have no luck."

"Don't act like this isn't happening to you. Do you have a plan?"

"What would you do?"

He brought over to the crate table a steaming bowl of ramen noodles. It looked so good, with a cooked egg and chopped scallions added on top.

"What else can you do? Run for as long as you can, or try to leave."

"Those already caught must be going through hell right now."

"The worst is over. They should be at the detention house now."

"Maybe I should start my life over."

Perhaps our voices woke him up. Myung Hun appeared from behind the screen, still drunk, with his hair disheveled.

"Who's here? What time is it?"

"You drink like this every day?"

"Hey, watch your mouth, you bastard. Where do you think you are? I should call the police."

Ho Sun brought a bottle of barley tea from the refrigerator and handed it to him. Myung Hun gulped it down straight from the bottle and shook his head violently, trying to wake up. I continued in a more serious tone, "I am sorry to have troubled you."

"Shut up. It's Ho Sun you've troubled. He already has to take care of me, a drunk. By the way, where have you been?"

"Underground."

"Why not stay here on the second floor, with us? Your sister came here once looking for you. Your brother's immigrating to the US. He wants to see you before he leaves."

"He's moving to the US?"

"That's what she said. All the paperwork is done."

Ho Sun, who had been listening in silence, spoke up.

"In that case . . . you'll want to go home? I bet it's surrounded. Or at least there'll be someone watching."

I put my head down on the crate table.

"I think it's time to finish up," I said quietly. "There's nothing left for me to do. I have no intention of turning myself in, though."

Neither of them replied for a while.

"Well, we should get some sleep," Myung Hun yawned. "We can think about it afterward. Look, it's still dark out. You may think differently once the sun comes up."

We were startled out of our slumber by the loud sound of a locomotive passing by. It was already noon. Ho Sun was not there. Myung Hun drew open the thick drapes on the window, and sunshine rushed into the room.

"Man, my stomach hurts. Let's go get some broth."

"Where is Ho Sun?"

"Went to work."

"What kind of work can a wanted person do?"

"Over there some new apartments are being built. He was bored out of his mind, so I asked an architect friend of mine for a favor. It's not hard labor. I don't think it's too much for him."

We did not have to leave the alleyway. Across the street from the double-story house was a small diner. It was lunch hour, but there was exactly one person in there, eating a bowl of rice and broth made out of beef bones. We ordered the same thing. As we sat facing each other, waiting for the food, Myung Hun regarded my face for a bit.

"Your face has changed. It's more relaxed."

"Why, what did I look like before?"

"Well, your eyes were filled with fear and anxiety and nervousness. You looked pretty ferocious. And your cheeks were so hollow . . ."

"And now?"

"Your cheeks are fatter and your eyes, they are so soft and mellow now. Are you . . . are you in love or something?"

"What kind of bullshit is that?"

I browbeat him into shutting his mouth up, but inside I was a little bit surprised. I guess you cannot hide from the eye of an artist.

"He turned a corner, too."

"Who are you talking about?"

"Ho Sun. For a long time he was so restless, he made me nervous. One day, he told me he had decided to leave. I didn't try to stop him. That bald-headed minister, he was the one helping Ho Sun."

It was only then I realized why Ho Sun had mentioned my leaving. Minister Hyun was friendly with a diplomat from a European country, and they had made plans for Ho Sun to hide in the embassy. At the appointed time, the minister and Ho Sun arrived at the embassy, and Minister Hyun pushed Ho Sun into the elevator, saying everything would be fine. People in the embassy had suggested that he could stay there until an opportune moment, when they would take him to the port in the official embassy car and put him on a ship for their country.

"Faced with leaving everyone behind, he said he could not make up his mind. He asked if he could smoke a cigarette."

While finishing the cigarette, Ho Sun made a decision on his own. He decided not to leave the land where his friends had died. That story touched somewhere deep inside me, and I felt like I was being electrocuted. Was it repentance? I had a bitter taste in my mouth, and I mumbled aloud, "Yes, I think I will start over. I should find others who will work with me."

After lunch, we had nowhere else to go but back to Myung Hun's studio. He could not work since I was there, so we spent the afternoon talking about our friends, whom I had not seen in a while. No matter what, I was going to visit my mother, and I needed to wait until nighttime.

Myung Hun was not really one of us. He had an aversion to any discussion involving words like dictatorship, democracy, foreign influence, autonomy, capital, or revolution. But he certainly agreed with us in principle. He said he ought to help those of us who were being hunted, he believed in an artist's freedom of expression, and he opposed those who killed innocent civilians. He had no interest in the prevalent style of painting at the time, and he had no desire to depict reality in his art. He was a modernist, what my friends would call a decadent. He wanted to live according to his own wishes, and a world in which someone like him could not be free was the one I myself opposed, so I guess we were on the same side. If Ho Sun and Myung Hun had met each other under normal circumstances, they would have called each other names and never seen each other again. But now they were brothers.

I did not want to wander around the city. I decided to climb up the mountain near Suyuri and wait there until late that night before I went home. It reminded me of the days when I was still in school, when my friends would come to see me late at night. We would go up the mountain and have a picnic, or rather a drinking party, waiting for my mother to fall asleep.

I got off at the last bus stop, in plain sight, and bought a bottle of soju and a bag of shrimp crackers like I used to. I avoided the alleyway that led to our neighborhood and took a roundabout way up the mountain beyond it. I walked on the familiar trail and passed the vegetable garden where my mother used to grow cabbage. There was an old grave right above the vegetable garden that used to be the spot where I hung out with my friends. The air was damp and cool, but I was undeterred. I made myself comfortable on the grass and took sip after a sip from the bottle. After a couple of sips, my cheeks and neck began to burn up. I could see down to the forsythia fence around our house and our neighbors' high stone wall. A dog was barking. It was definitely our dog Mary. Maybe it was the alcohol, but my eyes were burning up, too. My mother had adopted Mary, a half-spitz mongrel, when she was a little puppy, and she would be an old person now in human years. Mother used to say Mary understood everything. After ten o'clock, the lights started to go out in many windows, until only a streetlamp in front of our house remained lit. Cautiously, I approached the house. Mary barked a couple of times at first, but she quickly recognized me. She moaned and pulled on her chain, jumping around. I chided her quietly as I walked around the house. The light at my brother's window was still on. I used one finger to tap on the glass panel.

"Who, who is it?"

Caught off-guard, my brother opened the window a tiny bit but did not show his face.

"It's me. Open the front door."

I heard the sound of him running to the living room, and he opened the front door as he ran out barefoot.

"Hurry, come inside."

"Is Mom sleeping?"

"I heard her television on a little while ago, I think she just went to bed."

The living room was dark. My brother and I went into his room and sat down.

"You want me to wake her up?"

"No, I'll go see her before I leave."

"You're not going to stay the night here?"

"I can't. I just dropped by."

Finally, it hit him. He gave out a little cry and raised his arm to cover his eyes. All I could do was sincerely apologize.

"I am so sorry. I know you were all worried."

"We're doing fine, really. The thing is, I've decided to move to the US."

"What do you think you'll do there? I guess, no matter what, you'll get paid more."

"I can't live here. Whatever happens, it'll be better than this."

I did not want to, but shamelessly I asked him, "What about Mom?"

My brother was being too nice. He did not bark back at me as he used to, he did not say that if I were truly worried about our mother I should stop wandering around getting involved in the useless business of protesting and teaching laborers at night schools.

"Her sister has decided to move in with her."

My aunt was a widow. My brother had majored in engineering, but he quit school to work in the Middle East as a technician. After toiling in the desert for a few years he came back with a small amount of savings. He had just turned thirty. There was a girl he had been involved with since college. Out of consideration for me, who had never settled down and was always wandering around, they never got officially engaged. Her family had decided to immigrate to the US, and they had been separated for the past couple of years.

"Will you get married there?"

"I guess so. On paper, it's all done."

"What did Mom say?"

"All she does is worry about you. She also . . . she read the newspaper, too. She says everyone in the neighborhood says you're a Commie."

"Is that what you think?"

My brother seemed conflicted. He dropped his eyes to the floor.

"You and your friends . . . The ones you're fighting against are powerful . . . What can you do now?"

"There are many of us."

"Maybe."

"There is going to be so much to do, and a lot more people like me."

Both my brother and I were silent for a while. Then I said, "I should get going. I'll go see Mom, you stay here."

I walked across the living room and quietly opened the door to her bedroom. I saw a dim red nightlight and the outline of my mother's tiny body curled under the blanket. I sat down by her head and held her thin fingers poking out next to the pillow.

"Mom? Mom . . . ?"

"Umm . . . who is it?"

"Mom, it's me, Hyun Woo."

"Who?"

Still half asleep, she got up and pushed the blanket away. She reached for her glasses and looked at me.

"Turn the light on."

I stood up quickly and turned the light on. She regarded me from behind her glasses and gestured.

"Come, sit closer to me."

I sat right next to her. She was wearing pink pajamas that were too big for her. I had bought her the pajamas when I had made a little money after working on a translation.

"Where have you been?"

"At a friend's house in the countryside."

"Did you eat well? You were not sick?"

"Of course not. I never once even caught a cold."

"I know what you're doing. I know everything now. I don't have the energy to put a stop to it, but I do wish you could stop it before you get hurt. Look at your brother. He's moving to the US. You're the eldest son in our family. You should get married and have children!"

"I'm sorry, Mom."

"You're going to disappear again?"

"Yes. Give me some time, I'll wrap things up."

"Can you at least call me once in a while?"

"I'll do that."

She opened a drawer and reached into it until she finally found a small plastic bag and handed it to me.

"Keep this."

"What is it?"

From the bag she pulled something rectangular the size of a matchbox, wrapped in red silk.

"I normally don't believe in these things, but this is a scary time."

Without saying anything, I lifted the top part of the folded red silk with my fingernail. There were intricate letters in red ink and a picture of Avalokiteśvara, the Buddhist Goddess of Mercy, in gold. I almost laughed out loud and threw it back into her lap, but I managed to control myself and ask her again, as if I did not know what it was.

"Really, what is this?"

"Well . . . it's a talisman. A group of women from the neighborhood were going to see a fortune-teller, so I went with them. The fortune-teller made it. I know you think it's only a superstition. That's what I thought before. But I've changed, I've changed a lot. Things don't always work out the way you want them to."

"Fine, Mom. I'll keep it."

I used both my hands to hold it as if I was receiving a prize, then I took out my wallet and opened the coin compartment. In it was the picture of Yoon Hee. Before my mother could see, I quickly put the talisman on top of her picture and closed it, and I put the wallet back into my jacket. When I got up, my mother suddenly grabbed my hand and began to cry. Tears streamed down her deeply lined face.

"Please, please take care of yourself. I think I'm going to die before I see you again."

"Please, don't say such a thing. It'll all be cleared up in three, four months, then I can come back and take care of you."

"No, I know everything. Your brother and sister are lying to me, but I know what's going on. I know you betrayed the government. But remember this. If you truly believe in what you believe, one day even the government will realize that it was wrong and change itself. It'll take some time, but it can happen."

I could not stand it any more. I turned around to hide my face and she put something in the back pocket of my pants. I took it out and saw a roll of cash.

"I don't . . . I really don't need it."

"No, you do. It's getting colder every day, so you need to get some new clothes. And eat meat once in a while to stay healthy. Okay, go now." She gently pushed me.

"Stay inside, please."

"Why can't I see you leaving?"

This time, I pushed her back.

"I don't want any neighbors to see when I leave."

"I guess you're right."

Helpless, my mother stood behind the slightly opened door to her room and watched me walk across the darkened living room. She kept gesturing as if she were pushing me away, silently telling me to hurry up. I no longer hesitated. I put my shoes back on and deliberately closed the front door with a loud bang. As I walked down to the courtyard, my brother followed me.

"Are you leaving?"

"Yes."

"To go where?"

"Why do you ask?"

My brother took his hand from his pocket and put something in my back pocket. I glanced back and saw a white envelope. Like my mother, he was giving me money.

I decided to simply accept it as I had with my mother. I did not want him to be seen, so I decided not to go out through the gate, instead taking the trail leading back up the mountain. Just I was about to walk through the forsythia trees, Mary began to wag her tail like crazy and bark violently. I quickly sat down next to her, stroking and scratching her head and neck, waiting for her to calm down. Mary finally relaxed and lay down on the ground. I could not wait any longer. I got up and offered my hand to my brother, who had been watching me in silence.

"Good luck in the US . . . and don't worry about me."

My brother held my hand, still not saying a word. Deliberately, I took my hand from his, and I walked through the forsythia trees and past the vegetable garden. All the dogs in the neighborhood were barking now. I passed the old grave and took a trail past another neighborhood and toward the bus stop. I waited in the darkened alley, then ran to the bus as it was just about to leave. As I took the seat right behind the driver, I realized that I had been so preoccupied with visiting my family and leaving without anyone noticing that I had no idea where I was going next. I thought of going back to Myung Hun's studio, but I gave up on the idea, not wanting to burden Ho Sun. I pictured the bus route in my head: it was headed toward Shinrim-dong, and I thought of a friend I knew from the night school who rented a room in that neighborhood. I figured I could crash with him, if only for one night. Everything else I would think about in the morning. All of a sudden, I was exhausted. I folded my arms, lay across the empty seat in front of me, and dozed off. In my sleep, I heard the rattling sound of the iron bridge over the Han River.

"Hey, last stop."

The bus was empty. An attendant who had come to clean the bus was shaking my shoulder. It was almost midnight. Even the bars and restaurants were closed, and there were only a couple of drunkards pestering each other in the narrow alley.

As I walked up the alley lined with identical houses, I tried to remember which one was my friend's. It did not take me too long to find the rusted iron gate draped with grapevines. I hesitated for a while before I rang the door bell. I could hear birds chirping, but the house remained quiet and dark. Once again, the sound of a chirping bird. A light was turned on near the foyer, and a woman's sleepy voice came out of the speaker.

"Who is it?"

"Excuse me. Is Hyup in?"

"Huh? Jesus Christ! Do you know what time it is? Hyup has moved back to his hometown, he doesn't live here any more."

There was a clicking sound, and the light in the foyer went off. I could picture her yawning and cursing under her breath as she returned to bed.

I slowly walked down the alley and returned to the commercial area near the bus stop. There was a red neon light. On top was the symbol of a hot spring, a circle with three curving lines, and two blinking syllables below, Rim Inn. I knew what the missing first syllable was; I think its full name was Hak Rim Inn. I remembered staying there one night when we all had gotten too drunk but were still unwilling to go home. I walked into the motel. The face of a middle-aged woman with heavy eyes appeared behind a glass panel.

"Is there a vacancy?"

"Are you alone? Someone just left, so we have one empty single room."

She walked in front of me, carrying a towel, a pitcher, and a registry book. I humbly followed her. Yes, here was Room 401 of Hak Rim Inn. It was supposed to be a good class of motel, but the room was the size of a bathroom. In order to meet its classification, there was a bed that filled up the room and left a tiny space on the side you could barely walk through. The woman put down the tray with the water glass and pitcher and handed me the registry.

"Write down your information, please. In detail. There are so many crackdowns these days."

I took out the ID card that was given to me for situations just like this, and I wrote down the number and the address on it. I could not remember the last time I had stayed at a motel. After she left, I went into the bathroom and turned on the water. As I expected, just like it did the last time, dark sludge came out of the faucet. I waited for a long time with the water on, and finally the sludge turned the color of light coffee. At least the water was pretty hot. I could not bring myself to take a bath in that water, so I washed my face and feet. I lay down on the bed but could not fall asleep. I stared at the black rotary phone on the bedside table. If I called one number I would be connected to the outside world. In my mind, I called Kalmae and had a long conversation. Yeah, it's me. I arrived in Seoul, I'm still safe. I went home and saw my brother, my mother. I miss you. Should I come back?

I did not know what time it was. Later, when I thought about that day, I figured it was around three in the morning. Someone knocked on the door. The woman from the front desk spoke.

"Sir, open the door, please."

"What is it?"

This time a thick male voice, accompanied by aggressive banging on the door, yelled, "It's an inspection!"

I sprang up from the bed. I looked around. I saw the room with its ridiculous bed, the hanger where I had hung my clothes, a small window. And this was the fourth floor.

"Hurry, open up!"

"Yes, yes . . . I'm coming."

I tried to sound as groggy as I could and put some clothes on. Meanwhile, I quickly recited to myself certain facts. The address, the name, the ID number, the job, the reason I was there. I took a deep breath and slowly exhaled. I turned on the light and opened the door. The woman had already removed herself to the background, and facing me were two policemen, one in uniform and the other in plainclothes. The plainclothes one stood glaring at me with penetrating eyes and held out his palm.

"Your ID."

I took my wallet out of my pocket, pulled out the ID card, and handed it to him. He studied it carefully, front and back.

"You live in Inchon?" he asked, still holding the ID card.

"Yes."

"What do you do?"

"I work for a company."

"What company?"

I had memorized the name of the factory where the real owner of the ID card had worked, so I told him that, adding the department and the position. I did it confidently and stared back, and he smirked.

"And what are you doing here at this hour?"

"I came to see a friend from high school, but he wasn't home, and it was late, so . . ."

"Where does he live?"

I had to pause a bit there.

"It's nearby."

"Really? Then I guess we'll have no problem finding it. That's your bag? Bring it."

"What is this? Don't I have a right to stay a night at a motel?"

The plainclothes officer kept smirking, and the uniformed one said, "It shouldn't take long. We just need to verify a few details, so let's go."

I picked up the duffle bag and walked out of the motel as they followed behind me. As soon as we were outside, the plainclothes put his hand underneath my jacket and grabbed my belt.

"Hey, what are you doing?"

"Pardon me, but I don't want the hassle of chasing you if you run away."

They took me across the street to the police station. The plainclothes officer, never letting go of my belt, took me to a tiny holding cell in the back of the station. He pushed me in, locked the gate, and grinned through the bars.

"You know what? My nose is very sensitive. I know you're a wanted man. It won't take long to verify that."

I could not sit on the dirty cement floor, so I stood there next to the iron bars. I heard people bustling about, but he did not return. Not knowing what else to do, I squatted on the floor and wrapped my arms around my legs. I put my head down and let my mind wander. Ah, it was time to end my long journey. I'd been arrested.

There was more noise from outside, and the plainclothes officer came back. This time he did not say a thing as he took me out of the holding cell and began putting a pair of handcuffs on me. I was determined to do everything I could until the end, so I pushed him away as I yelled, "What are you doing? Do you arrest innocent people? Is that what you do here?"

"Asshole, wanna die now?"

He struck my belly, and all of sudden I could not breathe or even stand. I bent over and collapsed, and he put the handcuffs on me and pulled me up by the neck.

"Bastard, don't be such a crybaby."

I had been in a room with no windows, so I did not realize that it was already light outside. A van from the main police station was waiting for me. I was taken to an interrogation room, where the plainclothes officer handed me over to another officer. But he did not leave the room; instead he took a seat where he could observe me. The new officer was a stocky man with short hair wearing dark green fatigues. He talked to me as he flipped through the paperwork.

"Name?"

"Jang Myung Goo."

"Listen to this bastard!"

The plainclothes, who was sitting across from me, sprang up from his chair and kicked me. I tumbled over backward in my chair.

"You still wanna do that, huh? You really wanna do that?"

The dark green fatigues gazed down at me, then told the plainclothes, "I am too tired to humor this guy. Bring in the other bastard."

The plainclothes left the room. The fatigues took out a cigarette and slowly tapped it on the armrest before he lit up.

"Hey, why are you doing this? You think we can't figure you out?"

The door opened. There was the factory worker from Choi Dong Woo's club in Inchon, also handcuffed, followed by the plainclothes. First, the plainclothes slapped the factory worker's cheek, and then he asked, "Tell me who this is."

The real owner of my ID card quickly stole a glance at me and put his head back down. The plainclothes struck him again, this time kicking his shin.

"What did you say a little while ago, you bastard? You gave him your ID card because Choi Dong Woo asked you to. So who is this bastard?"

"This . . . is . . . Oh . . . Hyun Woo."

The fatigues roared.

"Was that so hard to say, you dirty little Commies? You know what? First, charge this bastard with obstruction of justice and faking official documents."

After the real Jang Myung Goo was taken away, the fatigues finished his cigarette in silence. He finally turned to me, speaking in a calm, smooth voice, "Oh Hyun Woo, it's all over for you. You're not under our jurisdiction, you'll be transferred shortly. So let's not make it more complicated than it needs to be, shall we? All you need to tell me is what you did while you were in hiding. The case against you guys is already completed, and you are the principal offender."

I did not reply.

"Remaining silent? A Commie does not have that right. We don't have time to waste. In order to report your capture, we need to know where you've been all this time, and only then can we hand you over. We can't just give you to them with nothing, we all have to save face. So, shall we start? Where were you after May 1980?"

They interrogated me for three days and nights at the main police station, not letting me close my eyes for even one minute. Then three men in sharp, dark blue suits came to take me away. As they walked into the interrogation room, they did not even bother to cast a glance at me. The detectives stood to attention and yelled something in unison as they saluted. The middle-aged man who came in first kept his hands in his pockets and simply gestured to them with his chin.

"You're the chief?" he asked the fatigues.

"Yes, sir!"

"We're from Namsan. So, this is Oh Hyun Woo?"

Only then did he look at me, sitting on a chair in a corner of the interrogation room. He sized me up with his eyes, as if I were a package that needed to be shipped.

"Give me all the relevant paperwork . . . And I assume you've been doing something with him?"

"We did some basic interrogation."

"Yeah, make sure you give me all that."

When the man in fatigues handed him the file he had prepared, the man in the dark blue suit did not bother to flip through, he simply gave it to another man in a suit. Leaving behind the chorus of their salutes, the three men in suits took me out, pushing and pulling. Outside, a black sedan was waiting, its engine on. I sat in the middle of the backseat, flanked by two men, while the man in dark blue took the passenger seat in front. As soon as the car began moving, one of the men struck the back of my head, snarling.

"Put your head down, bastard."

So began my forty-five days in purgatory.

14

Darling, which notebook are you reading now?

You will know it all by now. The reason I took a sabbatical right before you left Kalmae was because of our baby.

My body was changing. There was no place for me to go. As the new year began, I couldn't take it any more. I resigned from the school altogether. That year, time seemed frozen. The only reality I wanted to experience was the growth of our baby.

By that winter, anyone could see that I was pregnant. I was fortunate that the Soonchun lady came to see me several times a day to make sure I was okay and to help me in any way she could. They are really nice people. After you were arrested, we were all summoned to the local police station, then to the state police department, to be interrogated. We brought them so many troubles, but they never once blamed you. Actually, they just wanted to comfort me.

We worked out that the due date would be sometime in March. That was around the time we arrived in Kalmae, remember? I cannot express in writing what I felt when I first noticed the baby moving inside me. Carrying a living being inside your body feels quite different from simply having a full stomach. It was like there was a new cavity, a deep one, in between my pelvis and my vertebrae, and it contained a brand new organ. And that new organ wiggled and squirmed, touching and kicking my sides and my lower abdomen. It vibrated throughout my whole body, made my heart burst.

"My goodness, it's alive!"

I know it sounds a bit absurd, but I did talk to myself. Feeling her every little movement, I desperately wanted to take your hand and place it on top of my belly. It was like watching the silent surface of a vast lake, out of nowhere a pebble or a droplet of water drops in, and delicate waves spread across the lake, slowly but surely altering the whole surface. I put my hands on my stomach.

"Thank you, my baby," I whispered.

Yes, I was grateful. Imagine what it was like for me being left here alone after that rainy night. People say it is easy for the one who left to forget about where he used to be, but the one left behind suffers because she has to live with the emptiness. Whenever I felt the movement inside my belly, I quickly placed my hands on top and clenched my teeth to keep from crying, even if my eyes were already tearing, and promising myself that I would be brave. I ate well, too, swallowing big spoonfuls of rice and finishing all the side dishes the Soonchun lady brought to me, until I scraped the plate. Time flew by, just like it does in the movies. The pages on the calendar fell away, the leaves on trees changed from green to red and gold, fell from the branches, and the world was covered in white snow, and then all of a sudden new buds sprouted up. Time never stopped, it just kept going.

The day Eun Gyul was born, I did not feel anything in the morning. It was around four in the afternoon when I started to feel pain in my lower abdomen. It was already the end of March, and I was about a week overdue. I had never experienced it before, but I knew instinctively that this was the beginning of labor. I was scared. There was no one around, and I did not know what I needed to prepare. Hugging my belly, I tried to stand up. I was still able to walk and I tried to, slowly, supporting myself with the wall. About a month before, the Soonchun lady had told me to organize everything, so I had neatly folded everything I had collected for the baby—receiving blankets and little cotton handkerchiefs, a blanket made out of soft fleece and a little comforter, loose baby shirts and a waterproof pad—and stacked them in the corner of the room. I walked down to the kitchen and started to boil water in a big barrel, and I placed dried seaweed in a place where the Soonchun lady could easily find it.

I told myself, surely someone will come to check on me, at least one single person, before it is all over. But the truth was, I was so scared I was shaking. I thought of you, sitting in a darkened cell all by yourself, and tried to be as strong as I could be. My situation is much better than Hyun Woo's, I told myself. Wasn't it? I was with our baby, our strong baby. It was like a spiral, as the interval between contractions narrowed, the circle becoming smaller and smaller. The first circle took a while, but then it came faster and faster. I guessed that the tiniest circle at the end meant the birth.

I do not know where I found the strength to do it, but I got up again and walked toward the door, groping against the wall with my hand. It took a long time for me to climb down from the porch to the ground. First I squatted at the edge of the narrow porch and put one foot down, then placed the other right next to it. I hung onto the porch as I turned my body and raised myself up, and I was finally able to take steps. One by one, faltering, I walked down the narrow path toward the main house. When I got to the bamboo fence around the main house, I touched it with my fingertips and walked like a blind person. The Soonchun lady, who happened to be in the courtyard, saw this pathetic scene and ran to me.

"My goodness, Miss Han! What is going on?"

She told me later that I grabbed her hand so hard it hurt her, but she could not shake it off. I mumbled in a voice that somehow came from deep down in my throat, "Ma'am . . . please, please help me."

"Of course! Don't worry, let's get inside."

She grabbed my arm and tried to pull me in, but according to her, I resisted stubbornly.

"No, not here . . . Back to our house, please."

"Fine, fine. Just wait a second."

The vice principal rushed out, too, and each of them took an arm and brought me back home, almost carrying me. The Soonchun lady glared at her husband and kicked him out of the room, then changed me into a nightgown. She put the waterproof pad on top of the futon and draped a bath towel on my knees, then massaged my legs and told me to breathe in, breathe out. The pain was unbearable when the baby's head came out. I do not remember what happened after that. I think I blacked out.

From far away, I heard a baby crying, the Soonchun lady shouting. I lay there with not an ounce of strength left in my body, while she washed and swaddled the baby and placed her next to me. I turned to my side and touched her hand, so fragile, like water. It moved, writhing softly. Two eyes tightly shut, and what seemed to be just a trace of a mouth flinched and winced, as if she were smacking her lips. Sometimes a low, weak moan escaped. I was caught off-guard by something dribbling down onto the baby's blanket. I was not thinking, I did not feel it, but tears were rolling down my cheeks. I turned again to look up at the ceiling and put an arm over my forehead to shield my eyes from the light. I cried again without feeling.

"What are the tears for? You just gave birth to a beautiful, healthy baby."

The Soonchun lady had already prepared the seaweed soup and was bringing in a bowl on a small tray. I did not mind her chiding me a little, but I kept my arm where it was and cried a little more, although to do so was meaningless.

"I know, it's because of the baby's father, but . . . you'll chase away all the good luck."

Really, it was not like I felt that tragic or sad. Yet they were not tears of joy and happiness either. I remembered a woman I saw once, at the end of a market day. She was sitting there vacantly, and she made no effort to sell her sesame plant leaves, which were divided into little batches and placed on a small wooden board. Her face was deeply tanned, and she was breastfeeding a baby, who seemed to have fallen asleep while still sucking on her nipple. The baby was naked except for a dirty, ragged T-shirt. It looked like both the baby and the mother were frozen in time, in a daze. Why were they just sitting there? There was neither reason nor meaning; they did not try to sell and they did not attempt to leave the marketplace. I can't imagine them ever smiling or crying. I do not know why I was reminded of that woman when I was lying there, soon after giving birth to Eun Gyul.

"You should eat first. Your milk will start only after you eat some seaweed soup."

She helped me by putting her hands under my armpits and pulling

me up. I looked down at the little tray for a while without saying anything, then I picked up the spoon and devoured it, as if I were starving.

That was how our little baby came into this world. Soon after you
were confined to your little cell, heaven provided us with a small but
beautiful bridge that would forever connect us. I did not tell anyone, and
I spent the first three months of the baby's life with her alone. And soon
we returned to the most peaceful season you and I spent together, the
beginning of summer. I carried Eun Gyul on my back and brought her
to our laundry spot by the stream. I placed her under a tree and spent
the whole day there, washing clothes and eating and smoking and talking
to her.

"Eun Gyul, look! This is a frog. I think he wants to be your friend."

It hopped over to the blanket she was lying on, and Eun Gyul stared
back at the cute little frog. So I talked to the frog as well.

"You must be the good frog who listens to your mom.* Did you come
to see Eun Gyul?"

It was marvelous to see two newborns finding each other. We are all
born alone, but some of us manage to run into each other's lives.

A year after you left Kalmae I was beginning to feel restless, like a wolf
during the full moon. My stomach was constantly in knots, I was filled
with anxiety from my heart to my belly, and I kept fretting. I could not sit
still next to Eun Gyul, so I would pace around the room. I would open
the door to look outside at the view that never changed. Or I would put
her on my back and walk to the edge of town and watch the buses that
came and went for a long time, sitting on the bridge railing.

After a few anxious days, I finally decided to write to my sister. I
could not bear the loneliness any longer, I had to tell someone that I had
a baby. And I could not bear the fact that my memories of you were
gradually fading too, leaving behind just enough so I could manage.
There was no reply from Jung Hee. Of course, there was no reply
because I did not tell anyone the address of our home in Kalmae. When
I occasionally called my mother or Jung Hee, I always did so from the
school, and all I ever told them was that I was fine. I also told them I
was not able to go to Seoul for a while because I was working on my
first solo exhibition. Jung Hee told me later that she had been going

* There is a Korean folk tale about a green frog who never listened to his mother.

crazy. Out of the blue, she got a letter saying that I was going to be someone's wife, with some vague reference to the change in a woman's life when she becomes a mother. Jung Hee was old enough to guess what was going on.

I just wanted to make sure that I was not completely alone in this big, big world. I regretted sending such an incomprehensible and absurd letter as soon as I sent it. I meant to write again to tell her more clearly what had happened and to let her know exactly where I was, but she wrote to me first. I got her letter when I finally made my way to the school to hand in my resignation.

My Dear Sister Yoon Hee,

I could not believe what I was reading. You were always like that, even when you were a little kid. I know you are an artist and all that, but really, there are too many gaps in your story. What do you mean you got married in secret? And this happened not recently, but a while ago? And you don't explain anything?

To tell you the truth, we were getting a little worried about you. Mom just bought two more stores, so she's really busy. And I'm busy because of school and my boyfriend, so yes, I admit that it's not like we were thinking about you all the time. Nevertheless, you did not call, you did not write for months. We called the school and all they could tell us was that you were on sabbatical, no one knew where you were staying or how to get in touch with you. You're a grown-up, but you're also a daughter of this family! Even our mom, the busiest, the most intrepid person there is, was worried. She told me that I should go down there to find you if you remain elusive after school starts in fall. So, as soon as you read this letter, I want you to turn yourself in!

I am still worried about you, but I always believed in your judgment. Father always said, and I know this sounds horribly old-fashioned, but . . . he always wished that you were a son. Also, Mom always said you were the most considerate and patient person. When Father was sick, he didn't ask me to do much when I nursed him. He just kept asking when you were coming home.

You are in love, are you? And he is an activist who went to prison. Indeed, there are many of them around us. Last year, I joined a volunteers' club. There was a man who had one year in medical school left, and I really liked him. Once a month, he took us to the poorest neighborhoods to volunteer at free clinics, but I have not seen him this semester. I don't know where he is now. Somebody told me that he quit school and is working at a factory. I think he's going through a phase and I'm sure he'll come back to school more mature and experienced, and become a better doctor. Sorry if I sound too callous.

By the way, your last sentence was quite mysterious. You wrote it as if you are a mother now, that it was based on your own experience. A woman who has become a mother is not the woman of before? I read your letter and read it again and again so many times. My dearest sister, did you really have a baby alone in a small village deep in the mountains? What are you, a tragic heroine? Why are you doing this to me? You always treated me like a child. I'm old enough to have finished school if I didn't go to medical school, and I have lots of friends who are engaged and married. Please, please write back to me as soon as you read this. And write clearly on the envelope your current address.

I sent her a short letter saying that I'd soon let her know where I was, but I delayed until it was almost October. Then I wrote to her again, this time writing that I would not stop her from coming for a visit. As she had requested, I wrote my address in Kalmae clearly on the envelope.

I think she must have left the moment she received the letter. Within a week, she appeared. I had fed Eun Gyul and put her down for a nap, and I had a rare moment to sit in front of my easel, when I heard the Soonchun lady calling from outside.

"Miss Han? Eun Gyul?"

I got up and looked out through the glass window. Jung Hee and the

Soonchun lady were already kneeling on the porch to take a look inside the bedroom. I just stood there, my arms crossed, and watched them instead of saying anything. I saw Jung Hee step into the room, so I went back to the studio and quietly opened the door that connects it to the bedroom and peeked in to see what she would do. Jung Hee bent over to look at the sleeping baby, her head slightly tilted, and she carefully studied Eun Gyul's face. The vice principal and his wife walked into the room and sat right behind her, as if they wanted to observe the baby's face from the exact same angle as Jung Hee's.

"Look, isn't she adorable? Not a single thing in that face that is not pretty!"

I could not wait any more. I pushed the door open a little further and called my sister's name in a small voice.

"Jung Hee . . ."

As it was in her nature, she did not hurry, she simply raised her head slowly and quietly met my eyes. I saw her eyes fill with tears.

"Yoon Hee . . . she is so pretty," she whispered.

Thanks to Eun Gyul, we did not have to say much. I just sat next to Jung Hee and looked down upon our baby, too. Jung Hee did not take her eyes off the baby, but her fingers moved across the floor and found my hand and covered it with hers. She held my hand tightly, and I smiled at her. The Soonchun lady spoke, almost to herself.

"Her complexion is a bit dark. Maybe she takes after her father. Although I hear that tanned skin is fashionable these days."

We two sisters just sat there, saying nothing. Maybe she thought she should not have mentioned him, or maybe she realized that we did not want to chat. The Soonchun lady exhaled and got up.

"Well . . . we should get going."

"Are you going back to your house?"

She replied in a whisper, matching the mood of the room.

"Yes . . . you know what? Your sister is here, so why don't you join us for dinner tonight?"

"Thanks for the invitation, but we have so many things to talk about, and . . ."

"Oh, alright, don't worry, I understand."

After they rushed out of the room, Jung Hee opened her mouth.

"How are you?"

I just smiled back at her, meaning, how else could I be?

"Did it hurt a lot?"

"No. Everyone does it."

"So you named her Eun Gyul."

"Yeah, I spent the whole day with a book."

"Maybe I should name my daughter Geum Gyul."

Finally, she released every question that she had been holding inside.

"What on earth . . . why didn't you let us know what was going on? What were you waiting for? Where is that so-called poet? Does he know?"

I wanted her to stop talking, even if it was just for a little while, so I changed the subject.

"You want a cup of coffee? Let's go over there."

I got up first and opened the small door to the studio, and I offered the makeshift chair to Jung Hee. While she looked around the room and studied unfinished paintings, I made coffee. I handed a cup and saucer to her, and she took them and sipped as she studied your portrait.

"Is that him?"

"I was going to paint it. It's not done yet."

"I'm sorry. I still don't really understand."

"No, that's okay. He's just begun serving his sentence."

My sister kept sipping her coffee and sat silently for a while.

"It's really weird."

"What is?"

"I once read in a book that children not only inherit their parents' limitations, but they end up embracing their parents' flaws as their own. I wonder if you became like this because of our father."

"I see your point."

"Did you also believe in his ideology?"

"Not everything, but I did agree with a lot of what he thought. We all have principles, don't we? Even the rich and the dictators."

"Hey, watch it. Is that the way he talked?"

"No, this is the way everyone talks. I just want this world to be a place where there is respect for things like freedom and people's basic rights, their lives. That's all he wanted, too."

"I know, I know, I met a lot of student activists at school, too. And I know they're okay, they're fine, but I hate that they think they're somehow different and better. And I don't like their war games, their struggle for power."

"I've been reading Buddhist scriptures lately, and there was this one sentence, that a Bodhisattva is someone who performs good deeds without realizing it. When you fight with evil, you begin to resemble it, and there is no way to uproot all desires and ambitions. That's the limitation of human beings. But don't you think they are beautiful because they risk everything?"

"I don't know, I really don't know. Why you? Why do you accept a life with him when there is no promise for tomorrow?"

"I guess that's my life. Out of nowhere he came to me one day, and I lived with him for six months. What's left of our time together is Eun Gyul. And paintings that I want to finish. I guess I'm talking like him now. He once said the thing that is so special about people and the world we live in is how it changes. From now on, although for how long, I don't know, I'll experience those changes from outside while he does so in darkness. I want to do my best."

Before my father passed away, we spent days and nights together for months, and we became so close that we could understand each other by simply looking into each other's eyes. Later, I had to untangle all the knots by myself. I guess my mother had already done that when my father was in the mountains. But I was his daughter, not his wife, so it took longer. Yes, there is no bargain in life. In order to find answers to the mysteries of life, one has to suffer and endure pain. Only then the answers are revealed, one at a time, and you only find out as much as you have gone through. That's the truth.

"What are you gonna do now?"

Jung Hee seemed to be frustrated. She was gesturing with large movements, and she raised her voice. I tried to indulge her.

"I just told you. I'll do my best."

Jung Hee fetched her purse and took out a cigarette. She appeared to be quite used to it, inhaling the smoke deeply and exhaling as if she was the woman with too many stories to tell.

"I have no choice but to support you, I guess."

After a pause she added, "You are . . . amazing."

"Thanks. You'll help me, right?"

"What, in dealing with our mom? Don't worry, I'll do more than that. Eun Gyul is, so to speak, a daughter, just like us."

There was a little spark in my heart, as if I was being electrocuted. Right at that moment, Eun Gyul began to wake from her nap and cry. I sprang up and went into the room to pick her up. Her diaper was wet. I put her down again and changed her diaper.

"Hi, sweetie . . . I know, it doesn't feel good, does it? You're such a good girl. Mommy will clean you up and Mommy will give you something yummy, too, okay?"

As I murmured to the baby, Jung Hee moved to the narrow wooden porch in front of the door and sat down to watch us. I had done it so many times at that point, I could do it with my eyes closed. I put some baby powder on her and picked up both legs to secure the cloth diaper under the rubber band. Then I put her legs down and secured the front of the diaper. I carried her in my arm, then mixed a precise amount of formula in a bottle already filled with water and shook it with one hand. Still seated behind the threshold, Jung Hee watched my movements, dazzled.

"You feed her formula?"

"Yeah. I breast-fed her for a while, but I don't think it's enough."

"I don't know . . . does this happen to everyone? You do it so effortlessly, you look like a woman who has raised a half-dozen babies."

"Anyone can do it, it comes to you naturally."

After Eun Gyul finished her bottle, I placed her upright against my chest and patted her back. She burped. I put her down again and sang her a lullaby, the one passed down from our grandmothers to our mothers to us, the one with a monotonous melody.

> Sleep, sleep, our little baby
> Don't bark, little dog, don't crow, little rooster
> The mouse is sleeping, the birds are sleeping, even the stars in the
>   sky are sleeping
> Swaddled in her mother's arms, whining while still asleep
> Return to sleep, little baby, sleep well, sleep well

I felt more at peace after Jung Hee's visit. Eun Gyul began crawling, and she smiled at me, too. As the baby grew, time seemed to speed up as well. The first snow came down in the middle of November. It was just a dusting, but people in Kalmae said an early snow meant a better harvest the following year. I had made a decision that I would leave there with Eun Gyul in the spring, for our new life. I told you I had decided to go to graduate school. Thanks to my questionable personal life, I could no longer be a teacher in a small town. But most of all, I needed to find a way to survive on my own. I guess I had become tougher than I used to be when I was with you.

Eun Gyul was fine throughout the day, she ate well and she played well. But one night, she was crying and made a strange noise whenever she coughed. And her forehead was covered in cold sweat. I touched it, and it was burning. I knew nothing and got scared. Above all, I was terrified that if something happened to this child I would be left alone in this world. I wrapped her in a blanket and put her on my back, then put another blanket on top of her. I ran down to the main house.

"Ma'am . . . I think there's something wrong with our baby!"

The Soonchun lady and the vice principal came out to the room and studied her, touching her forehead.

"She's burning up and wheezing. It doesn't sound good. Let's call a cab, fast!"

The vice principal called the taxi company, the Soonchun lady put her coat on and got ready to go to the hospital in the next village. As we waited for the car to arrive, I suddenly became a devout Christian, like my mother. I did not know any other prayers, so I just kept repeating the Lord's Prayer over and over again. By the time the headlights appeared on the narrow road between the orchards, I was crying. We rushed to the hospital. Already, the downtown area was empty, all the stores along the main street closed. Just a few neighborhood dogs were prowling around. Years later, after hearing about other people's similar experiences, I realized I was not the only one who felt so helpless in a situation like this, and that it was not just because I had been alone with our baby. But at that time, I felt sorry for Eun Gyul, that she had to have me as a mother in a world like this. I pitied her and felt so helpless, I just wanted to sit down somewhere. I felt that way even more when we arrived at the hospital and had to bang on the tightly closed door of the darkened building. The Soonchun lady tapped my shoulder.

"I don't think anyone is here," she said. "But I bet the house behind the building is where the doctor lives, so I'll go get him. You stay here and wait."

The Soonchun lady walked into a narrow alley next to the hospital building and knocked on the gate of a house. The light came on, there was a mumbling sound of people talking, and I heard her calling for us.

"Eun Gyul! Eun Gyul!"

I ran over there as fast as I could. It was an old, Japanese-style house. The light at the entrance was on and the gate was open.

"Everything will be fine now," the Soonchun lady said. "The doctor's coming."

"I feel so bad, it's late at night."

"What do you need to apologize for? I bet he was just watching base-ball on television."

A bald-headed man in a sweater came out and told us to come in. We walked across the courtyard and entered the hospital through a back door. On the second floor was the waiting room, and we rushed through to the doctor's office. I placed the baby on the examination table and was ordered to take off the blankets. Before he placed the stethoscope on her delicate skin, he questioned me.

"She has a high fever, and her glands are swollen. Any other symptoms?"

"She was fine until dinnertime, she finished her bottle, too. For the last couple of hours, she's been coughing, her breathing has been labored, and she's been very hot."

The doctor listened through his stethoscope, he opened her mouth to examine her tongue and throat, he took her temperature.

"Has she received all the vaccinations after birth?"

"No . . . not yet."

"Hmm, how old is she?"

"Nine months old."

"She's got whooping cough. So she is not vaccinated for measles?"

"No, we live out in the boondocks."

That was what everyone said if they did not live in town.

"Fortunately, we caught it in the earliest stage. I'll give you something for tonight, but you need to come back tomorrow."

I was a little relieved. Eun Gyul was not even crying any more; she whimpered like a puppy once in a while but remained quiet otherwise. She got shots, I received medicines, and the doctor cracked the door open from inside so we could exit through the front door. Outside it was even darker than before. We walked to the taxi station where cars were waiting for passengers late into the night. The Soonchun lady patted Eun Gyul, who was wrapped in blankets on my back.

"Wow, you are so lucky! You get shots and medicines for that? Listen, Miss Han, whooping cough or measles were not considered serious illnesses when I was raising kids. Every kid got them at one point or another, just like catching a cold! It just means she's growing up."

I made the decision that night that I had to leave Kalmae. And somehow I knew that I could never be a good mother.

Years later, when I spent a lot of time in front of a television, I once saw a documentary about of lions in the wild. You know what? The male lion does nothing! He is needed for a few minutes in order to procreate, but that's about it. He is useless at raising cubs and helping them to survive. He looks great with his golden mane and he wanders around in a dignified manner, but he spends most of the time yawning or taking a nap. He growls when he wants to assert his power over females and to confirm rank in his family, and he fights with other males to rule more females, but that's it. When hunting for food, the lionesses work together to catch their prey while the lion stands back and watches. When the food is ready, he strides in and takes the best part. He takes no interest in his cubs, and sometimes he kills them so he doesn't have to be bothered. Only the lionesses feed and raise the cubs, and they take care of one another's babies, too. But the lions fight and kill each other. When a lion kills a rival, he kills everyone that belonged to his rival, including any cubs and lionesses who defy the new leader. It has something to do with preserving the purity of the bloodline.

I wasn't thinking about the lions because I wanted to talk about men and politics and civilizations. It's just that one cannot help but pity a mother and her baby. Nature binds them together, yet it can also be cruel

and careless toward them. And there are times when they have to be separated mercilessly. Speaking of the lions, what about their prey, the
buffalo? The mother buffalo watches her calf from afar as he is captured,
and when his legs, pointing to the sky, stop convulsing, and the lions begin
to devour his body, the mother simply sniffs and walks back to her herd.

Ah, I have become a mother like that.

The winter ended, and the spring of '83 arrived as the frozen streams
slowly melted away, the pussy willows turned green, and the yellow
flowers of the spice bushes bloomed.

I have mentioned that I had already decided to go back home on that
winter night Eun Gyul was rushed to the hospital. Home? You're not
with us, but our home is really here. I decided to go back to my mother's
house and beg for her help. Eun Gyul needed a family who would love
her and take care of her. I informed the Soonchun lady of my decision
and sorted through my art supplies, books, other important items, and
necessities for Eun Gyul. I packed them in boxes and shipped them first,
so all I carried for the bus ride with Eun Gyul was a diaper bag. Eun Gyul
was almost a year old then. As I promised, I sent a letter to my sister a
few days before our departure. She replied with an express letter, which
encouraged me.

> Dear Jung Hee,
>
> Finally, I am ready to go back to Seoul. I can't thank you
> enough for all the wonderful things you sent me. The
> clothes, the pacifier and baby food, how did you know to
> find such things? I realized how uninformed and foolish I
> was as a mom after reading the baby book you sent. And
> thank you for the book of poetry and other books I had
> requested. There is a passage that caught my eye, so I am
> writing it down for you:
>
> *The echoes of a shaken tree branch remain in the heart of
> a flying bird. The trees on top of the mountain are swinging
> wildly in the wind, but there remains in the falling leaves the
> warmth of a touch.*
>
> So, have you prepared our mother for the surprise? I will

dare to ask for everyone's help. I told you I want to go to graduate school. There is no special reason, I just think I need a better foundation in order to become self-sufficient and raise my daughter on my own. I need some time before I can do that. I will tell her everything, you just drop a hint or two. I hope you meet a normal, ordinary person and make up for everything that I have done and will do to her. I think we'll arrive in Seoul by next weekend at the earliest.

I think I wrote in my last letter that he sent me a postcard informing me that he had received a life sentence. But didn't people come back alive from death row during the last administration? Maybe he'll be back in about three years. Maybe it'll take a little longer than that. Or maybe he'll never see this world again, as long as it is divided into two and there is no earth-shattering change.

My dearest sister,

I was so glad to receive your letter. I knew Eun Gyul's birthday was coming up, so I was getting nervous. As soon as I got your letter, I began to look for the right moment. On Saturday, I invited Mom out to dinner. I just got paid—I told you that I've been tutoring? And I just got a raise, too, so I asked Mom if I could treat her to dinner at a nice restaurant. She kept saying she was too busy, so I went to see her right before dinnertime. The wedding season is coming up, and her store is actually busier on weekend evenings with brides-to-be and their mothers buying fabrics and traditional dresses. As I expected, the store was full of customers, but I waited patiently. Around nine at night the store suddenly emptied. When I reminded her of my promise, she seemed to be pleased. I dragged her to a restaurant I had in mind. It was not too busy by then, since the earlier diners had already left. We were seated at one of the best tables, by the corner window with a view of Nam Mountain and the city at night. I started by informing her that you had resigned your position at the school, that you were planning to attend graduate school.

But you know what? It's really uncanny, she's so quick. Remember? She was always like that when we were growing up, too. Our father would spend the whole day with us, playing and sharing meals together, but he was still clueless about a lot of things. But her? When she came back from the market, she took one look around the house and just looked into our eyes, and she knew exactly what had happened that day.

She was listening carefully, nodding, and she just waited, looking at me with these patient eyes asking for more details. I hesitated, not knowing what else to tell her or how. She goes, *Is that it? I don't think you dragged me here to tell me that.* In spite of myself I said, *Mom, she said she wants to get married.* Mom remained calm and replied, *Really, that's great. Who is he? I don't know him well,* I answered, *but he writes poems.* Her face broke into a faint smile. This is what she said: *I thought I was done with bookworms. It is one thing to read poems, but writing them really doesn't help with everyday life. Well, that's not the case these days! You can be a teacher or work for publishers or newspapers, there are lots of jobs that you can have.* Mom is our father's wife, after all. She shook her head and said, *I'm not worried about employ-ment. During the period of crisis, a man who writes poems cannot stand it. Every book tells him that the world should not be like it is.* I seized that moment to slip it in, *The truth is, the man she wants to marry . . . he is in prison right now.* She put down her fork on the plate and gazed outside for a long time.

You went to see Yoon Hee a few weeks ago, didn't you? You said she was fine and well. I just sat there with my head down and waited for her bubbling emotions to subside. Then, the thought of your loneliness and pain came to me, as well as the sleeping face of Eun Gyul. I know our mom went through a lot, but I thought our pains were part of her life, too. After all, she chose and remained with our father, didn't she? I decided to be honest. *Mom, she married him in secret. They lived together for six months. She sent me a letter saying that she'll come back to Seoul.* I decided to stop there. Mom looked like someone with a headache. She put two fingers on her temple and laid her head down. When she came back from the ladies' room she looked perfectly fine. There was not on smudge on her makeup. Since then, she has kept silent.

After we returned home, she did not once ask about you again. She's really strong, isn't she? I haven't told her about Eun Gyul yet. I am guessing that I won't be able to stop myself after sending this letter, I'll be telling her soon. All I am going to tell her is how important Eun Gyul is to our family. I just want our formidable mother to want to see her granddaughter as soon as possible. Now I think about it, I'm still so young. You and Mom and Father, you're all so unbelievably similar. You have no fear of life. Hurry home, do not worry about anything.

15

The first winter in prison was harsh.

I was placed in the strictest solitary confinement. I was not even placed in the section where political prisoners were usually sent. Instead, I was locked into the very last cell of the corridor among ordinary criminals. It was a small cell divided into two by a partition, about the size of a torture cell. The next door was supposed to be a single cell, too, but it was always empty. I was completely alone. Even when I was transferred, the cell, about six feet in every direction, remained the same. I got used to it.

The winter in solitary confinement begins early in October. Not one ray of sunlight comes in, and the tiny viewing window on the iron door is purely decorative. There is another slot on the door, through which meals come in three times a day. Those are the only times it is opened, otherwise it remains locked from outside. Right next to the door is a narrow space for a low table, which blocks about half of the door's width. If there is occasion for me to go out, I have to walk sideways. Above the desk is a fluorescent light. This light never turns off; it is on 365 days a year. There is no "lights out" in prison. Inside, the prisoner needs to be watched at all times, whether he is eating or defecating or sleeping or masturbating. The four walls and ceiling are, of course, bare cement walls. Only the floor is covered in wood. If you spread out the thin futon on the floor, there is a gap of about a foot to the side. Sitting down, my hands touch the walls without my spreading my arms. At the foot of the bed is a narrow space about three feet wide, which I use to store my toiletries and other items. And then there is the bathroom. Its door is a wooden frame covered with plastic, so the guard can look through the viewing window and clearly see the inmate squatting. The toilet needs to be flushed with water, one scoop of water for urine, two for feces. It stinks, so I have an empty plastic bottle filled halfway with water stuck upside down in the hole on the floor. Some old-timers use a rubber glove, filled with water to the size of a soccer ball. Tied to a string, it works as a makeshift cover for the hole. You just pull on the string before you go.

In the bathroom is a real window, a small single-pane one. During times when the prison had enough in its budget, these windows were covered with acrylic, but the older ones were simply covered with ordinary plastic nailed into the frames. The bathroom window is the only place through which you can leave the cell, a place where you can see a corner of the sky, a tip of a mountain, a little part of the road the moon travels, or a handful of stars. We spend a lot of time standing in front of it. The small rectangular frame always holds the same view, but it is possible to change the picture in your mind. The tiny bathroom became so familiar to me that I can still picture in my head the closed-in walls and the spots on the ceiling and the peeling paint. Hunkered down in there, I would move the spots and patterns around in front of me like pieces of a puzzle to create new images. There was a rabbit and a dog, or a woman with long hair, or the private parts of a man and a woman. If it looked close to, but not quite, what I imagined, I scraped it with my nails to complete the picture. After a few months, the stains and traces would shift into different shapes.

I would wear a thick sweater and a vest underneath the prison garb, but, still shivering in the cold mornings and nights, I wrapped myself in a blanket. Then I learned from the old-timers how to chase the chills away by washing my body with ice cold water. I also got a hot water bottle, which was usually distributed only to the sick and the model prisoners. It was actually a waterproofed army surplus cartridge box. I filled it up with hot water and closed the lid tightly, put it in a sack and placed it by my feet, where it remained warm until the next morning. To get out of the bedding warmed by my own body at the coldest time of day took real determination. But if I could not resist the temptation to stay under the blanket, the whole day was shot. Your state of mind during these critical hours before breakfast determined the rest of the day. If I stayed under the blanket, feigning illness, I would miss the exercise hour, which meant I would not see the sun and breathe fresh air outside for the whole day. The sun would go down quickly, and as the evening chill rushed in and the four walls closed in, I would begin to feel I would go crazy if I did not smash my head against the steel door and scream.

To survive the day, I run into the bathroom naked. The water bucket by the door has a thin layer of ice on top. I break it with the plastic dipper and scoop out water into another bucket, then wet a towel and begin rubbing my body with it. When the wind comes in through the plastic window and grazes my wet body, it feels like my skin could crack and split open. After rubbing for a while, the skin is flushed with energy, and warmth courses through my whole body. I wash my face, pick up the bucket, and pour whatever water is left over my head. My teeth chatter. I dry myself well, especially my ears, since they tend to get frostbite easily. I breathe in and out several times, then I support myself on the iron bars over the viewing window to do push-ups or run in a stationary position. In prison, only two seasons exist, winter and summer. Spring and fall are too short and fleeting; they're gone before I realize they are here, and they only exist in calendars.

After the workers leave for the prison factory, breakfast is delivered. *Ready to Deliver!* scream the inmates who work as the guards' assistants. The dull sound of cart wheels and the smell of food drift in. In the corridor they post a menu that seems edible and varied, but in reality every single thing looks and tastes the same. Mostly, it is a pool of liquid in a bowl. The only way to figure out whether it is supposed to be a soup or a stew or braised meat is to see what is left at the bottom. A couple of morsels are always there, and on a lucky day I can find a piece of tofu or some mackerel, pike, or pork. In the earliest days of my imprisonment, I felt like crying whenever the meal was pushed in through the slot at the bottom of the door. I felt like an animal, like I had plunged to the very bottom of the world. To eat and survive seemed too tiring and hopeless.

Finally, exercise time! After breakfast, after I wash the dishes, fill the water bucket, empty out the trash can, and mop the floor clean, I get ready to go out and wait for the guard in charge of exercise. I hear his footsteps approaching, followed by the familiar voice saying, *Want some fresh air? Let's go outside!* With a clank, the steel gate is opened and the corridor looks like a grand lobby at a fancy hotel. As I walk out the building, the air is cool and the freezing wind slices my ear like a knife. There are inmates exercising and doing sports out on the large ground used by common criminals. Some are doing laps around the yard wearing only their underwear, some are swinging from parallel bars. There is a group of people kicking balls, others playing volleyball or a simplified version of baseball. Some just sit there in the sun, like sunflowers. And there are the old-timers and those at the top of the inmate hierarchy who are dressed in nice workout clothes and play tennis with help from a group of ball boys. But I pass by them and walk through the fenced-in passageway to an empty space between two buildings. There used to be an exercise field exclusively for political inmates, but they built an assembly hall on that site. Maybe someone did not want someone like me to have the benefit of open space. Even when I was transferred to another prison, there was no large ground where political prisoners were allowed to go.

When I was housed in the detention cell, our exercise ground was a circular building that was divided into fan-shaped pieces, just like a pizza or a cake, and modeled on that infamous Panopticon model devised by Jeremy Bentham. Within the structure, each inmate could be surveilled, but he himself could see no one else. Bentham got the idea for his prison from the zoo at Versailles. Each section had a door, and the inmate was locked in, surrounded by cement walls. There was a two-story circular tower in the middle. Not as high as the outer wall, this tower was the hub. There was a row of numbered doors in the outer wall, like on a flying saucer. When a number was called an inmate opened the corresponding door and walked into the fan-shaped space. The guard at the top of the tower watched all the sections from above. I never saw a guard walking around up top, diligently observing us inmates. I was pretty sure he was somewhere up there, sitting comfortably and smoking a cigarette or chatting with other guards, turning his head or stretching out his neck to observe who was doing what in each section. The structure was heavily symbolic. Our activities were as exposed as mice in a lab.

I could hear a guy on the other side of the wall mumbling and kicking a ball against the wall again and again. Someone else just paced, counting numbers out loud. Some people stood there blankly and stared at the mountains and the sky beyond the wall. I looked at the sky, mostly. There were clouds and birds flying. And there were different airplanes, always flying on the same path. After a while, I was able to differentiate between southbound ones and southeast-bound ones, and I could guess based on the size and shape of the planes whether they were international or domestic flights. The returning flights seemed much larger, perhaps because they flew lower. I imagined the people in them. A passenger who had pushed his seat back and was sleeping comfortably, or rummaging around for something to eat. A mother soothing a child, a businessman reading a magazine or a newspaper, a student listening to music. The flight attendants walking back and forth along the aisle, someone sitting on the toilet, a man turning his head to kiss his girlfriend, and all the oblivious people in the world. Underneath, I am alone in my concrete cell.

While spending time in that Panopticon structure, there were two activities I actually enjoyed. I raised wildflowers and I took care of ants. From spring to summer, little wildflowers and weeds grew under the shadow of the cement walls. Mostly they were dandelions, lettuce flowers, and violets. I watered the ones that seemed prettiest. I carried water in an empty milk carton and fed the delicate flowers that somehow managed to grow. Inmates also pulled up weeds and used them to write messages on the cement wall. At first the writings were green, but they turned white by the next day, and they did not wash away even with rain. Students and laborers arrested for political reasons wrote slogans and messages for their comrades. *Down with the Military Fascists! Power to the People! Yankees Go Home! Long Live Democracy!* Whenever there was an inspection, the first things the guards did was wash all the walls and pull up the weeds. They did not simply pull them out with their hands, they ordered other inmates assigned to menial labor to uproot everything with weeding hoes. The flowers I raised so carefully were mercilessly pulled out and left on the ground to dry. They were so delicate, there was barely a trace of them left behind.

There were various species of ants living within the cement walls. There were the smallest ones with jet black bodies, those with a black upper half and a reddish plum lower half, those who were smaller and fast, and the army ants, who were big but not as rare. My favorites were the little black workers who were good at digging tunnels and did their job with such enthusiasm. It was the other flying insects who flew in from the outside who actually led me to study and befriend the ant colony. Many flying insects came in without realizing where they were. Some of them never found their way out; they kept spinning around and crashing into the walls until they slowly died. There were usually grasshoppers and long-headed locusts, some beetles, and once in a while perfect dragonflies. When we found a trapped insect, most inmates picked it up carefully and helped it fly away over the walls. It reminded us of our situation.

One day, during my walking exercise, I noticed a group of ants gradually moving the body of a dead grasshopper. It was so much fun to watch them. When one ant found something to eat, it surveyed the surroundings and then quickly went back to the tunnel to fetch other ants. They returned to the spot, and it was fascinating to watch each one post itself automatically at every strategic point. If the food was big enough, they all came out and formed a line stretching from the food back to their colony to transport it that way. If another species of ant approached, they brazenly attacked as a group. Even the biggest army ant ran away in a flurry if it mistakenly approached the other ant colony. I took a couple of candies from my pocket and sucked on them a little before I placed the moistened morsels not too far from the ant colony. I crouched down by the wall and remained motionless for a long time. Sometimes the guard on the watchtower asked me what I was doing, and I would simply turn around and show him my grinning face. I was pretty sure that he already knew what each inmate was in the habit of doing within those walls. When the ants found the candy, they either spent hours sucking the sugary juice and melting it, or they dug up another tunnel from below and stored it underground. Little pieces of sugar were

carried away one by one with their unbelievably small teeth. In fall, the
ant queen made an appearance in order to branch off and start another
nest. Nothing, absolutely nothing, seemed to remain in winter. But even
in the cement box the beautiful survival of tiny creatures continued, and
bit by bit I became stronger.

The exercise space designated for me at the prison outside of Seoul
was just a piece of empty ground between two buildings that were
vacant, as the inmates had gone to work at the prison factory. Later, I
got permission to cultivate a little vegetable garden there. It was surrounded by bathroom windows, and there was a half-buried cement
septic tank in the middle of the ground. It smelled bad, but the cold air
was still quite refreshing. I had come up with a walking route that followed the inner walls of the prison, taking a turn around one of the
buildings and arriving at the window of an administrative office. I walked
fast. There were piles of snow in the shade, but the slope reinforced for
erosion control was always sunny, and little but tenacious weeds were
always sprouting out from the yellow grass. I tried not to start a conversation with the guard during the exercise hour. To whatever he said, I
nodded and smiled like a child learning for the first time. In various corners on this path, I encountered many living and breathing creatures that
varied depending on the season. There were grasshoppers and sow bugs,
praying mantises and really big crickets. Frogs hopped over from somewhere, too. During the rainy season, a small green frog came all the way
into my solitary cell through the bathroom window. Around the septic
tank were numerous holes where enormous and fearless rats lived. They
were not like house mice with gray fur, these were wild rats with brown
fur who had settled down here. They did not run away when inmates
saw them, they just stared back. I once caught a really fat one with my
foot. They searched the dark and fetid septic tank for food waste thrown
away by inmates while washing dishes. Of course, their natural enemy—
feral cats—came too, and there were hordes of them living in the
emergency bunker near the prison buildings. During breeding season,
the prisoners could not sleep because of their mating calls, and we would
curse and throw things at the cats. But some cats were so used to having
gotten food from the inmates since they were kittens that they depended
on handouts even when they were grown. At meal times, they came to

the building they had always come to and meowed by the windows, asking for food. The inmates would then throw them a leftover fishhead or a piece of cuttlefish or sausages, which they bought from the prison store. Some inmates named the cats, who responded when called. During my exercise hour I ran into them often, and once I selected one to be my pet and raised it for a few weeks.

I served my sentence at three different prisons, and I grew fond of several animals over the years. The long-timers called prison home, and the guards who transferred easily from one prison to another were called guests. The warden, whose appointment would usually last from about six months to, at the longest, a couple of years, was called a traveler. A prison in the central part of the country held many political prisoners and repeat offenders serving long sentences. The inmates there knew how to grow various plants and vegetables. Some people grew potatoes, sweet potatoes, and onions throughout winter in plastic soda bottles cut into half, and some grew wild orchids found while working in the fields. Someone saved the seeds from a summer watermelon and planted them in spring. He showed it off by hanging the vines and the little fruits on the window sill. Of course, they were mercilessly confiscated before inspections, because they obstructed the guards' field of vision.

I knew a man there who had tamed a mouse. Mice were commonly found in buildings with inmates who worked in prison factories. They made holes in the bathroom or underneath the floor boards to let them in and out of the cell when it was empty during the day. Another inmate in a solitary cell like me realized there was a mouse visiting his cell and decided to capture it alive. He put margarine on a piece of biscuit, placed it on the floor, and waited. The mouse appeared from an open gap between the floor and a wall, and as the mouse crawled across the room toward the biscuit, he blocked the gap with a strip of sticky tape. When he saw the mouse curled up under the desk, he did not attempt to capture it, he simply made sure he closed all the gaps the mouse could escape through. He acted as if he had no interest in what was underneath the desk, but he saved a little bit of food from every meal, placing it on a piece of torn cardboard he used as a table for the mouse and kept at a fixed spot. He pretended to sleep so that the mouse, who would not move from under the desk while the inmate was awake, crept out and ate. After a few days the mouse was afraid of him no longer. The moment he placed the food down, the mouse came over and sat down and used two front feet to hold onto its food, just like a squirrel. The inmate always talked to the mouse. He named the mouse Popi after a rabbit in a commercial for toilet paper, and it came to its new owner and climbed up on his lap whenever it was called. The owner built a tiny house for his mouse with cardboard, and even lined the inside with a piece of material torn from his own blanket. I watched him many times whispering to the mouse as it climbed up and down, from his knee to his hand to his shoulder to his head to his back. As the new year approached, the little mouse grew to the size of an adult's hand, and maybe because it had become so friendly with its owner, it looked quite smart, rather than repulsive. The owner gave the mouse a bath from time to time and made a necklace out of red yarn for it. If not for that long tail, it would have looked like a perfect pet.

Before the cells were locked up for the night, there would be a few minutes for me to look over the iron bars into another cell and talk to another human being. One day, when I looked into his cell, the mouse's owner was looking up into the empty space and crying. Tears were streaming down his face.

"What happened? Why are you crying?"

When I spoke, he wiped away overflowing tears with his knuckle.

"Popi's gone," he said.

"Well, he's big now, it's about time you let him go."

"No, they came here for an inspection today. They took him in his house."

"What are they going to do with a mouse?"

"They took him to the incinerator."

Popi was cremated just like that.

When we went out near the tall walls of the prison in order to work or exercise, we often found newborn baby tree sparrows. The young ones had come out from their nests on top of the roof or a tree in order to practice flying, following their mother. First, they would sit on the wall, then come down to the ground, and some of them were bound to fail to fly back to the top of the wall. They tried again and fell again, knocking into the slick, tall wall. Noticing their failed attempts, someone would run over and catch the baby tree sparrows with his bare hands, simply by cornering them against the wall. On top of the wall, the mother tree sparrow darted around, worried and impatient. The inmates captured the little birds to raise them.

I saw a number of domesticated tree sparrows in other solitary cells. The birds hopped around the narrow cells or found a place to doze off on top of their owners' shoulders or heads. During meal times, the birds shared the meals with their owners, picking food right out of the rice bowls with their beaks. When the owners came back from outings, the tree sparrows cried merrily and landed on their owners' bodies and rubbed their beaks. When I asked one owner why the tree sparrow did not fly away through the bathroom window, he replied simply, "Because I cut his wings."

He opened his tree sparrow's wings and showed me. The tips of the fan-shaped wings were neatly trimmed into straight lines.

"If it grows, I just cut it right back."

I thought the tree sparrow was just like the inmate in solitary confinement. I tried to raise a little bird once when I found one fallen by the wall during my exercise hour. I cupped both my hands just enough to contain it, but I still felt the little one gasping for breath on my palms. I carefully brought it back to the cell and trimmed its wings before I let it go. It was stuck to the floor and constantly flapped its broken wings. No, it was not even flapping, shivering would be a more accurate description. The sound of its shivering wings was really loud, like that of an insect, a cicada, or a fly. I found out later that I was supposed to bind its wings with bandages for a few days. The little bird did not eat one grain of rice or one drop of water, it just made that shivering sound. Even when I was falling asleep, I heard the sound of his broken wings trembling. As soon as I woke up the next morning, I saw the bird lying on its back, feet and beak pointing upward. It was already stiff and cold. I could still clearly remember the warm and pulsating heart beating the night before. It was killed by the irresistible instinct to fly away freely. I held the dead bird in my hand and took it outside to bury it under a little patch of grass. And I was depressed for a while. That sound of shivering wings, like that of the vibrating weather strip around the window, remained in my cell. I kept hearing it and thinking I heard wrong, and as I tried to listen carefully the sound would disappear.

The cats around the prison usually gave birth in early spring. There was one particular cat called Blackie because her fur was jet black except on the belly. She was so healthy and fertile, she had three litters in two years. Ever since she was a kitten, she ate her breakfast with the inmates studying for exams and then received her lunch from the barbershop. Her breakfast usually consisted of one sausage from the snack bar, but her lunch from the barbershop was pretty substantial. There were many old-timers working at the barbershop, and it was close to the kitchen, so they always set a side a piece of fish or dried anchovies to feed her. Of course, the best food was in the kitchen, but that territory belonged to the king of all feral cats, the one named Spot, whose fur was a mix of black and white. A vagabond cat named Viking, the one with brown fur and stripes, lost one eye to Spot when they fought over the kitchen territory.

On a snowy night when Blackie was a kitten, I was told, she sat under a window on the first floor of our building and cried so sadly that she woke up everyone in that section, which was full of people who were selected to study for various equivalency tests. The head of the section took her into his blanket and let her sleep there. Since then, the ones in the exam preparation section took turns taking care of her and named her Blackie. When someone higher up came for an inspection, they hid Blackie deep underneath the desk. When that winter season was over, however, Blackie was suddenly an adult cat. She left the room and came back shortly after with her belly bulging. Each inmate in the exam preparation section had a different response, some disappointed, others content. It was as if a daughter whom they had married off had come back.

"Oh my, we devoted ourselves to raising you, and you get pregnant by some playboy?"

"You whore! How dare you to come back here like that!"

"No, no, it's fine. I don't care if they are brown or spotted, I just want them to be healthy!"

They threw her sausages and a cuttlefish leg that they bought from the prison store. When fish was served as a side dish, they collected the pieces in an empty instant noodle cup for Blackie's breakfast. We knew she lived in an underground bunker below a watchtower, because a lot of people witnessed her going in and out of an opening there. Blackie gave birth in there. Her distended nipples swinging from her belly, she came to the front yard every morning and meowed. Now she did not eat the sausage she got; instead she carried it back to her bunker and then came back. We knew that she was feeding her kittens so we prepared three or four sausages every morning. Blackie slowly ate the last sausage while sitting in the front yard. And as soon as she heard the staff pushing the lunch cart, she quickly ran across the front yard, climbed over a barrier wall as tall as a man, crossed the path, climbed over another wall, and arrived at the prison barbershop located at a corner of the exercise field. The lunch would already be delivered to the barbershop. They said because the barbershop was first, they got more solid pieces than liquid in their meal. There was a young apprentice designated to prepare lunch for Blackie, so her food was fatty and fishy. She had so many kittens, but she never let them live off of the same people. Once they were grown, she kicked them out of her territory, biting and scratching and yowling.

She died when she was three or four years old. After the cells were locked down, after dinner and the music broadcast were all done, an inmate went to the public bathroom and found Blackie stretched out on the front yard.

"Blackie is dead!"

Within a minute, the news traveled throughout the building and inmates fought over who got to look out the window to see her dead body. The building was soon buzzing and clamoring with people calling Blackie. Surprised, the guards ran around the building blowing whistles.

"Bedtime, bedtime! Get back!"

Some old-timers approached the guards through the iron bars and asked them for a favor.

"Listen, listen, you know what this is all about, right? Blackie is the eldest daughter of this building, but we think she just stopped breathing. Who knows? Maybe if you bring her in and warm her up a little by fire, she'll come alive again!"

But the guards did not give a damn. If we did not break major rules, they did us a favor by simply pretending they did not notice anything, and they had been tolerant for a while when it came to Blackie. We were finally allowed to go outside the next day during the exercise hour. It snowed through the night after Blackie died, and her body was buried deep below. Only after digging in the snow did we find her body. There was a large wound on her neck and blood everywhere around her. Maybe she got into a fight over her territory, maybe she was attacked by a male cat. An old-timer who worked in the repairs department wanted to cook and eat her, saying it would be good for his arthritis, but the other inmates would not allow it. They wrapped her body in the lining from a winter coat and put her in a cardboard box, and they never stopped berating the old man.

"No wonder no one ever visited all the years you spent rotting in here, you evil man."

"Hey, did you say something to me?"

"Yeah, I said the old bastard is losing his mind because it's about time he dropped dead. We raised her, we treated her like a precious child, we even married her off! She's like a granddaughter to you. And now you wanna eat her to live a few more years? For what? To contribute more to the septic tank?"

It was curious to see men who had committed various crimes outside becoming so attached to unimportant little creatures around the prison. Once a man spent months growing a black beetle-like insect with a horn like a rhinoceros's, and I even knew a man who diligently caught live flies to feed his frog, whom he kept in a plastic container.

I once got a kitten from the prison assistants on the way back from the public bath. It was a female cat with gray fur and black stripes. They were convinced that it was one of Blackie's kittens. When I brought her back to my solitary cell, she turned round and round the tiny cell, then cried loudly, scratching the door. I guessed she felt suffocated, locked in a small cell after running around outside. I tried to comfort her by feeding her and putting her in my bed to sleep. I kept her for about a week, but one day, when I came back from the exercise field, I found the string that tied her to the desk broken and the little door on the meal slot open. She was gone. Being an inmate, it was not possible for me to go around the building to search for her, so I went to bed alone, trying to ignore the sudden emptiness in my heart. I did see her a few days later while I was out in my designated exercise area. She was skulking around the wall, the string around her neck still attached. Happy to see her, I called and approached her. But she took one glance at me with cold eyes, and without any acknowledgment, disappeared beyond the fence. The cat's indifferent reception made me feel to the bone how insignificant my existence was.

Later, when I was moved to a cell at the end of an empty row for stricter solitary confinement, I found something else to grow attached to. There were almost one hundred pigeons living within the prison wall. They traveled in groups, moving freely in and out of the prison to find leftover food or gleanings on the furrows. I sprinkled bird food on the ground right below my window as other inmates did, and pigeons began to gather regularly there, even sitting on my window sill. In order to prepare their food, I bought a few bags of peanuts from the prison store. I peeled the skin from every nut and pounded them with a wooden block to break each into four or five little crumbs. Cooked barley could be dried under the sun by spreading it out on the bathroom window sill. After a couple of days, they dried up and became hard, and I mixed them with the peanuts. Of course the pigeons preferred peanuts, but it was too expensive to use them alone. For the first few days, the pigeons did not know what my day was like, but the smarter ones soon realized I had a very regular schedule and started to appear right before I spread out their food. The first shift was the thirty-minute period between breakfast and exercise hour, and the second shift was around dusk after dinner, when the prison was filled with piped-in music. But as soon as I felt attached to a handful of pigeons, they forced me to change my schedule. The new shift was right after I woke up, before breakfast arrived, and in the late afternoon, before dinner came. They actually lived in a cage as a unit, just like us, built on the exercise field by the prison factory. There were other coops and a small pond where fancy carps were farmed. Two long-term inmates were designated to take care of them. They woke up early to open their cages, and at night they fed the pigeons and collected them back in there. The pigeons also had a schedule to follow.

The pigeons came in many different colors, and if you looked closely, every one looked distinctive. The more common pigeon had gray feathers mottled with a whole variety of colors, from different shades of gray to brown to purple to black. There were pigeons of one color too, gray ones and black ones, and also black ones with white spots, brown ones with white spots, and pure white ones. Before they got to know me, they came to the front yard and stayed to find bread and cracker crumbs, usually thrown by the prisoners still under trial who were housed right below my cell. After they got used to my peanuts, they waited for me on the tin roof of the storage facility across from my building, then flew at once to my window when I appeared. I poured their food on the window sill. The pigeons trusted me, and some of them would even sit on my palm.

There were a few pigeons I was particularly fond of, and I named them. The first one I called Captain. He was a male pigeon with pure white feathers. It was easy to distinguish male and female birds by their size, physical appearance, and behavior. The male pigeon's breast was wider than the female's, and his belly slimmer. When he drew his neck in and out and swaggered, he looked like a weight lifter showing off his muscles. The male pigeons always fought over territory with rival males; they pecked and pushed and smacked each other with their wings. In front of a female, however, the male walked around in a circle, puffed up his body, and coo-cooed. The second pigeon I named was a female one, also pure white. I called her Sooni. She was smaller and more slender than Captain. At first, I did not notice her among the group of birds. When she came to the window, she was pushed away by the others. I studied her carefully one day as she sat facing the window, and I noticed that one of her feet was lame. There were quite a lot of pigeons who were crippled because some inmates would try to catch the birds. Some caught them to keep as pets, but many used to catch various creatures to eat. Mice and tree sparrows were also targets, but many caught pigeons just to kill time. During the weekends or on national holidays, there was no exercise hour, and that made the day unbearably long. On a day like that, the inmates spent time hunting for pigeons and other little animals. First they made a tool, using a peanut as bait. A piece of peeled peanut was firmly tied to the end of a long string. Some used it just like that, and some attached another string to it and held it from inside. At one time the inmates would unweave a sock or a glove and use the cotton thread from it, but most of my fellow inmates could now afford synthetic thread, which did not break. Years ago, when the inmates were always hungry, they grilled or boiled the pigeons. They tore off about half an arm's length of toilet paper and twisted it between two palms to make kindling; it was possible to cook a bowl of ramen noodles with one roll of toilet paper. A pigeon could be plucked, salted, and grilled in the bathroom with that fire, and there would be no smoke. During winter, I was told, they boiled them at the prison factory on top of a heater. But no one killed the pigeons to eat anymore—now they did it for sport.

It was a game, cruel revenge against the pigeons who led a life of leisure and freedom right outside our windows. There was no need to hold onto the string and wait; all they had to was throw the trap with peanuts and watch the unsuspecting pigeon flounder. The pigeon pecks at the peanuts, attached to a strong, thin length of synthetic fiber, and as it does so the string dangles in the air from its beak. The pigeon tries to get rid of it by tugging with one foot. As it repeats this motion several times, the string entangles the pigeon's beak and feet, and it forces the bird's body to curl up. Now the pigeon struggles to escape, trying to break the string or to fly away, with both feet stumbling. It flies a little, then crashes, and keeps trying until its foot gets severed or broken.

I find it painful to watch the crippled pigeons. They are always a little behind the group, alone, unable to find their way into the flock where the others find the food, only able to hop around while others stroll on top of the roof. The reason I remember Captain and Sooni together is because I had decided that they were a couple after observing them carefully. And I adored Sooni.

I remember the day I met each of them. When I put out the peanut food, a flock of pigeons who were waiting by the storage building flew over at once. They pushed and shoved each other to get to the best spot. The hierarchy among the pigeons was determined by strength, of course. But they were cowards, and they always acted as a group, never alone or just as a couple. Then one day, a handsome pigeon with pure white feathers came by himself. I cannot remember if it was before or after the usual feeding time. I guessed he had come several times before to my window to be fed with the group. The lone pigeon pecked on the plastic window as if he was knocking, and I opened it. Most pigeons flew away or moved to the side when I opened the window, but this one stayed there, faced me squarely, and cooed in a low tone. When I threw some self-made bird feed on the window ledge and the sill, he came in, as if he trusted me, and slowly ate his food. He rubbed his beak on the iron bar before he flew away. We repeated this a few times, him coming by himself and asking me for food by knocking on the plastic window, and I responding to his request. One day, Captain brought another pigeon. That was Sooni. Her feathers were pure white, and I knew right away she was a hen because she had a habit of looking down. Her modest posture was actually due to her lame left foot. Unlike other birds whose feet were severed, Sooni's ankle was curled up inward. When I gave them food, Captain stepped aside to concede the best spot to Sooni, and stood patiently, his chest puffed up, while she meekly pecked away. Only after Sooni had her fair share did he eat. Then they flew together to the roof of the storage facility and sat next to each other. When other pigeons came according to their usual schedule, they moved further away as if they were avoiding the crowd, and soon flew away.

After a few days, once I became familiar to her, Sooni sometimes came first, by herself. Standing there on one foot with her lame one curled up, she silently watched me from beyond the plastic window.

"There you are, Sooni! Would you like something to eat?"

She approached me only when I beckoned her, and she never ran away when I opened the window. The quantity of my self-made birdfeed varied, and there were times when I could afford to give her more, but she always ate just the right amount and left. On one rainy day, when I came back after being away from the cell, Sooni was sitting by the window, resting alone and waiting for me. Sometimes I saw her from the exercise ground. She would be sitting all by herself after the other birds had flown off to the kitchen area, looking for more food. Captain flew around freely and only came with Sooni near dinnertime. I had decided to separate their meal from the other pigeons'. But the others soon caught on to the special treatment the pair were receiving, and they began to follow Sooni to my window. Surrounded by the flock, Sooni was easily pushed away, and she never fought back, just flew to the roof of the storage facility and sat there alone before she disappeared altogether. It was different when Captain was around. He still knocked on my window, even when he was followed by the flock, and he ate alone while the others seemed to be waiting for him to finish. Once in a while, a brazen cock or two would come over and eat with him. Captain would ignore them at first, but the moment the other bird came too close, Captain opened his wing like an arm and slapped him. The pushed-away pigeon dropped from the window and flew back to the other roof. Captain ate just enough and flew away beyond the main building.

There were a few other pigeons beside Captain and Sooni that I began to pay attention to. There was Hoodlum, who always tried to hoard more food than he could eat, and who rushed about on the windowsill and started fights with other birds. Glutton still had the string from the hunters attached to his foot, yet brazenly came to the window if there was food for him. And then there was Fake Sooni, who looked so similar to the real one that I was fooled several times. She had white feathers, and she silently stood on the window ledge with her left foot curled up. I fed her a few times before I saw her with a perfectly fine pair of feet standing among the crowd on the roof of the depository building, hopping around and brushing her feathers using both feet. She had pretended to be a cripple! I guess she figured out, after accompanying Sooni to my window a few times, that I treated her differently, and she decided to copy her. So I decided to feed this smart, fake Sooni, too.

Perhaps even more strange, there was a pigeon I really liked at first, then grew sick of. I named it Quasimodo after the hunchback of Notre Dame. It was really an ugly-looking bird, and the only one whose sex I could never figure out. I guessed that something went wrong in the egg. Its body was about two-thirds the size of the other pigeons, its neck short and its body stout, and it looked more like a little quail than a pigeon. Its feathers were a dark and dirty gray, with brown ones like those of tree sparrows mixed in, and it looked shabby. And Quasimodo had the most tragic weakness for a bird: his beak was cracked open like a broken pair of scissors. There was no way for him to pick up the food properly; it was like he was using curved chopsticks. Around his beak and neck was grain dust from the pen, making Quasimodo look dirty and unkempt all the time, because it was impossible for him to brush or clean his feathers with that beak. Quasimodo seemed to try hard to conform to the flock. He pecked away at my window, but it seemed he never got one piece of peanut into his mouth. The other pigeons pecked at his head mercilessly whenever he approached them, so his head was covered with scratches and sometimes dried blood. But Quasimodo was unbelievably tenacious. He learned to visit me by himself. For Quasimodo, I saved whole peanuts and watched the bird pathetically trying to pick them up. As he pecked on the peanut with his cracked beak, the nut would roll away. Even if Quasimodo managed to pick it up, it was difficult to push it inside his mouth. The bird kept trying and trying and finally, by chance, he would swallow one nut. It was pretty obvious that Quasimodo's ferocity was related to the lack of food available to him and to hunger, and soon he became shameless. When I tried to feed him, Quasimodo was always in a hurry, and he pecked my hand in anger, puffing up his body in a strange manner and crying. I hated that twisted beak, and I felt sorry for him. Sometimes I just grabbed him and wrenched him hard. And gradually, I could not stand Quasimodo's ferocity.

One winter, on a snowy day, Sooni was killed by a cat right in front of my eyes. Viking, the striped vagabond, occasionally hunted pigeons. He patiently waited in the darkness below the storage building, aiming for the pigeons who landed on the open field in front of our building looking for food. Men awaiting trial, housed downstairs, sometimes threw a piece of bread or peanuts for the birds, and they hopped around down there. I saw a flock of pigeons landing on the snow-covered ground, including Sooni. She limped around on top of snow, but before long, something darted out from the shadow underneath the storage facility and attacked her. Sooni did not even struggle, she was just hung motionless from Viking's mouth. It was weird how calm and collected I was while witnessing the slaughter. The cat walked around the corner and disappeared behind the storage facility with his prey in his mouth, and I could not see anything any more. I did go and look behind the storage facility during my exercise hour. Before I even turned the corner, I could see that the ground was dyed red with blood, and the actual scene was even more brutal. There was blood everywhere on white snow, and all that remained were her feathers. The soft feathers were swept away by the wind and caught on the chain link fence nearby, where they fluttered as if they were still alive. The next day, and each day following until the spring arrived, I continued to feed the pigeons

twice a day, but I stopped naming them and singling any out. Attach-
ment is vain.

What were 1983 and 1984 like? Each year not so different from the year
before. I went on a hunger strike, kicked the door or banged metal cups
and plates on the iron bars, screaming slogans and singing combat
songs, and I was sent to the torture cell. This sequence was repeated a
number of times. I wanted a cellmate, even if we bickered and argued all
the time, even if we got sick of each other until we were about to kill each
other and fought over little things like food and insulted each other.
Eventually we'd get used to each other. The powers above knew how to
manipulate me, they knew it so well. They knew all too well that time
was everything. Through the Japanese occupation, the war, and all the
changing administrations, they had years of experience breaking prisoners. They always had a new deck of cards to play.

I forgot the details of the books I had once read. The only thing that
remained with me were the general principles.

16

In the spring of 1984 I went back to school. I was old enough to be called ma'am by other students but I still looked young. Eun Gyul had just celebrated her second birthday. I moved out of my mother's house and started graduate school. Jung Hee was an intern at the university hospital. I opened a studio on the second floor of a building in the university neighborhood and taught high school students who were preparing for college entrance exams. I did not want to work as a tutor, but I also did not want to depend on my mother, even if her business was booming. And I wanted to be alone and concentrate on doing my work well. Eun Gyul stayed at my mother's house. There was a live-in maid to help take care of her, and my mother was not as busy as she used to be, since she employed more staff now. She actually thought it would be better for Eun Gyul to stay with her.

I don't think you knew what was going on then while you were inside. At the time, the university neighborhood was cloaked in tear gas day after day. Many student activists who had spent time in prison or outside the campus in factories and night schools returned to colleges and universities. They were slowly roused from the shock of that May in Kwangju, and people were gradually coming together. Over one thousand political prisoners were released, but not one of the so-called lefties, like you. The Cold War was reaching its climax, and we half-expected there was going to be another world war.

Around that time, I got to know a man. Please, don't be disappointed, it was not like I fell in love with him or anything like that. It's just that he became my closest friend during your absence. And anyway, now that I think about it, how I felt about him was quite different from how I felt about you, but still, I liked him. I think I understand a little bit of what you were trying to preserve in there, staring at the walls. You were in that silence for a long time, but you would appear in my dreams every few years. There is nothing simple about living. Even your life in solitary confinement, wasn't it as grand and complicated as your own thoughts? We stood there on the edge of a precipice of social change. Some people were sliding down to the bottom of everyday life, some were carried up by their desires. As you had said, capitalism in South Korea was already on a roll, and it rumbled on by itself with little resistance, following the laws of motion. We never fought properly, we just argued about how to fight, looking for answers in textbooks, and we ended up losing in a few years what others took over a century to lose. This was the life that went on outside.

I think it was the early summer of '84. I went to see Jung Hee where she worked. I don't know why, but we had not seen each other for a few months. We talked on the phone once in a while, and we would arrange a date to see each other, but something would happen and we would miss each other at my mother's or one of us would cancel. I waited for her sitting on a bench in a corridor of the hospital, and Jung Hee finally appeared, wearing her white coat and looking tired.

"Have you been waiting long?"

"A little while. I'll go if you're busy."

"No, I have the night shift anyway. I asked already, we can have dinner together."

"That's good."

"Just wait one more minute. I want to go change."

Jung Hee and I slowly walked across the campus. The green of the trees and lawn outside was darkening but the wind was still refreshing.

"The truth is . . . I'm sorry, Yoon Hee, but I've double booked."

"What do you mean?"

"I was supposed to meet this person, I promised days before you called. Would it be okay if he joins us?"

"I guess so. Who is it?"

"My patient. A friend of his."

I knew who she meant when she said "his" like that. He was Park, a medical student a couple of years ahead of her, who was doing his mandatory army service as a medical officer. Later, he became her husband. Anyway, that is how I met my friend. Jung Hee did not tell me anything more about him.

We walked along the wall around the campus and then to a quiet restaurant, I think one of those serving casual, Western-style food. Jung Hee probably wanted a beer. Maybe she was stressed from working too much. I remember she was drinking a lot at the time. We climbed the stairs and pushed open a pair of French doors to enter the restaurant, and we saw a man sheepishly stand up from the corner by the window. I cannot remember my first impression of him, but I thought he looked like someone I knew. I think he was wearing a wrinkled shirt and an old dark suit.

"This is my sister," Jung Hee announced with no apology for my presence there, but he was very polite, bowing down to me at almost a ninety-degree angle.

"My name is Song Young Tae."

I felt a bit awkward, so I just nodded and mumbled something, never introducing myself. Jung Hee seemed to be intent on taking care of her business first.

"The results are very good, I don't think we have to worry about it too much. There was a cavity, but it's pretty faint now. Still, I think you need to keep taking your medicines. Let's get rid of it completely while we're at it. Your stomach didn't look great, but . . . well, I think that should get better, too, now that your dosage is a lot less than it used to be."

"Ah, glad to hear that."

"How are you these days? How do you feel?"

"I am still tired, but I don't have a fever anymore. In there, I was always a bit feverish."

"How long were you inside?"

"Three-and-a-half years."

"Really? Has it been that long already? It seemed like a while."

"Not really. It's about the same amount of time others rot in the military."

It was becoming more and more uncomfortable for me to sit there with them. What they were talking about did not sound foreign to me. In fact, it was quite painful to listen to them, because it reminded me of you. I figured he had just gotten out of prison, and based on what Jung Hee had said, he had tuberculosis or something like that.

"Park called and told me that he has a furlough coming up next week. He asked about you, so I told him that you're fine, just as I told you now. But you still have to be careful, okay? At least for the next six months. By the way, I heard you're going back to school."

"I'm a bit embarrassed to say so, but yes, that's the case."

"My sister is doing her graduate work there."

"Oh, really? Happy to hear that."

"She's an artist. She's not as boring as I am."

We ate dinner and emptied a few bottles of beer. I thought this Song Young Tae guy was very sincere, but he was not much fun because of his relentless sincerity. To make matters worse, he was a philosophy major. Philosophy? What good was that? I know, I know—look who's talking, what good was art, then? Song Young Tae was what we used to call a work in progress. He would never be impatient, he would simply try and try to persuade you with logic, sincerely, step by step by step.

I think I saw him again the following week. The evening was the busiest time for me, but that was when Song Young Tae showed up at my studio. During the summer, students had more time to practice their drawing skills, so I had almost twenty of them coming to my studio every night. I had to work until late at night, walking among the students as they sketched plaster casts, commenting on their work and correcting them once in a while. A college student, who I had hired as an assistant, came in and told me someone was waiting for me. There was a partition that separated the studio and the entrance area, and near the door was a sofa. He was sitting there, behind the partition. I probably would not have recognized him if he had not sheepishly stood up from the sofa, just like he had at the restaurant.

"Ah, it's you . . . How did you know I was here?"

"Yes, well . . . I asked your sister."

"Is there anything I can do for you? Actually I'm really busy right now."

At this point, any other man would have scratched his head and lost his nerve and mumbled something like, when will you be free? or when do you have time, maybe I should get going today. But his response was completely unexpected.

"I am not busy at all today. I can wait here until things slow down."

"It's going to take a while."

I tried not to be annoyed. I was old enough to be a mother and I thought I should be mature enough to control my temper. His eyes were smiling, narrowed into little slits behind his thick glasses. He seemed to be saying that he had nothing to hide, and he appeared to be nice, yet also confident, as if he had all the time in the world.

I could not firmly ask him to leave, so I just left him there and went back to my students. It was not just because he was somehow connected to my sister, but it was his natural ease that infected me and made me unable to kick him out. Even after I went back into the studio, I could not forget about him. I kept looking over toward the entrance. While walking among the students, I would stop at a spot where I could see the sofa and steal a glance. Song Young Tae had made himself quite comfortable; he had taken from his old leather bag books, papers, and a dictionary, and spread them out on a coffee table to work. From my vantage point I could see his bent back and the back of his head. His thick, curly hair was bushy and entangled like a madman's, yet he parted it so sharply that I thought I could see the crown of his head showing through. He was almost blind. Even with that pair of thick glasses he had to put the dictionary right up to his nose in order to read it. Somehow, it seemed like he had been working there in my studio for a long time. No, it was more than that—I almost had an illusion that he was the original owner of this space.

The students left one by one, and when I was done for the day it was after nine o'clock at night. I slumped onto a chair in the empty studio and was smoking a cigarette when someone's head peeked in. I thought it was the landlord from downstairs or the delivery boy from the Chinese restaurant collecting money, or one of the people who came in and out of the studio but was not related to me in any way. I turned my head and asked, "What is it?"

"It's me . . . It's me!"

Surprised, I did a double take.

"You are still here?"

He breezed into the studio. He had taken off his jacket and made himself comfortable, as if this was his own place.

"You didn't see me while you were pacing back and forth? I was sitting over there the whole time."

"Ah, I'm sorry. There were so many students here, I could not think of anything else."

"Aren't you going to offer me a cup of coffee or something?"

Now, I felt really bad.

"Sure, of course. Why don't you take a seat?"

He did not do as I asked, but wandered around the studio. He looked at the students' sketches as if he was a judge and pretended to look carefully at the small ornaments and handmade pottery on the bookcase and the dried flowers in a water jar. I placed a cup of coffee in front of another chair and began sipping mine.

"So, anything interesting going on in your life?"

"Huh?"

This time, he turned around with a dazed look on his face, like he was the one who had forgotten my presence. He looked really innocent when he smiled with his eyes disappearing into crinkles.

"Yes, something very interesting is happening."

Song Young Tae came closer and sat down to face me. He said, "I have decided to become your student."

"I don't know if that will work. I'm only accepting students who are preparing for the university entrance exams. And that is for two months only."

"Isn't there a special private lesson?"

"Depends. It'll be more expensive, though."

"That's fine. When can we start?"

"Whatever suits you. You don't need to come every day, so how about twice a week?"

"That's exactly what I wanted. We can start next week! So, let's see . . . Well, the thing is . . ."

He looked around and pulled a little datebook from his jacket's inner pocket.

"Wednesdays and Fridays are good for me. Does that fit into your schedule?"

"I'm okay if you come after six in the evening. By the way, why do you want to draw and paint?"

His answer came unhesitatingly, as if he were expecting me to ask him that question.

"Well, well, the thing is . . . because I want to be more flexible and open. In order to depict an object, you need various points of view and methods."

"That comes much later. First, you need to look at it correctly and capture the image as closely as possible."

"Still, I bet there are many differences depending on who is looking, what one sees and doesn't see. And techniques vary, too. Hey, aren't you hungry? Aren't we missing something here?"

"I already ate dinner."

"Ah, I see . . . Well, well, the thing is . . . How about this? Since you've decided to be my teacher, I the student would like to treat you the teacher to a drink."

I felt like a drink after my long day anyway, so I happily accepted his offer.

"Sounds good. This is my turf, so let's go to the place I know well."

We left the studio, crossed the street, and walked to the local marketplace. There was a couple who set up a street food stand under a large tent every night, 365 days a year. The husband was short and thin, while the wife was tall and plump, so the students who patronized them for night snacks called it the House of the Fat Lady and the Thin Man. Song Young Tae and I lifted a door flap and walked into the tent. It was quite full, and we had to squeeze into a small space where the narrow bar bent into an L shape. He dropped his head and studied the ingredients displayed on the bar as if to inspect them.

"Is your eyesight that bad? This is hagfish, and cow intestines, chicken gizzards, cow's heart. Well, I'll order anyway."

"Well, well, the thing is, I can't eat those things."

Song Young Tae was more fragile and discriminating then I had realized. I mean, it makes sense for a young girl who's just started college to be squeamish at a street food stand, but isn't it a bit silly for a man of our age not to be able to eat intestines?

"You have a very delicate palate?" I asked him in a mocking tone.

"Well, yeah, the thing is, I'm allergic to a lot of foods, so I just can't eat anything . . ."

"And how did you survive prison with all your allergies?"

He downed a shot glass full of soju in one gulp and grinned widely.

"I can survive uncomfortable situations."

"And what are the uncomfortable situations you're referring to?"

"Well . . . all sorts of things. Sleeping on the street, not eating for days."

"You've done all that?"

"I once spent a couple of months without any money in my pocket."

It was ridiculous, and I had no idea what he was talking about and what would happen in a few hours, but I did begin to feel closer to him. He said he was hungry, but he did not even touch the food, and kept emptying glass after glass of soju. At one point, I thought he would swallow the shot glass, too. I was beginning to feel uneasy when we had finished three bottles in quick succession. I probably had about a bottle. He ordered another one, and I tried to stop him.

"Enough, that's enough!"

"We're just getting started, and you've had enough already? Let's get just one more bottle and we can stop."

"Are you drunk?"

"What are you talking about? I may doze a little while drinking, but I never get drunk."

He managed to order one last bottle and drank it down as fast as he had before. When there was just a trickle left at the bottom, I found him falling asleep, just as he predicted. Ugh, how could I get out of this ridiculous situation? I was so angry, I wanted to slap the back of his head, still covered with those madman's disheveled curls, and leave him there, but I decided not to. I was embarrassed and annoyed, and I wondered what others might think, especially the couple who owned the place, but I could not abandon him there. So I dragged him back, somehow managed to get him up the stairs, and threw him down on the sofa. I was so angry, I sat across from him and lit a cigarette.

"What the fuck is this?"

But he seemed peaceful, slumped on the sofa, smacking his mouth. I calmed down a little as I smoked. I took off his shoes, because I did not want my sofa to get dirty, and his glasses. I put the thick windows through which he viewed the world onto my eyes. I could not see a thing, it was all blurred and cloudy. I placed the glasses on the coffee table and turned off the lights.

Anyway, Song Young Tae somehow entered my daily life. He was a year older than me, well, six months to be exact, and we started college the same year. From the beginning, he seemed like just a child to me. When I taught him to draw, I did not ask him to sketch plaster casts like the other students, but told him to draw everyday objects. I told him to take his shoe off and sketch that, and he did so meticulously. For the first month, he came twice a week every week, quite diligently, but later, perhaps because he was losing interest, he began to skip a day a week. At the end of the summer vacation, I was very busy with final evaluations for those finishing their two-month curriculum, and I barely had time to say hello to him when he did show up. I had no weekend, not even a free Sunday. But students would disappear like a low tide until winter, right before the college entrance exam season, so I had no choice but to work hard. And once the schools were back in session, I needed to go to my classes, too.

It was a Sunday afternoon, even busier than usual. When I walked behind the partition to answer the phone ringing off the hook, I saw him sitting there, taking over the sofa and working on a translation project like he always did. I had not seen him for almost two weeks.

"Well, well . . . It's been a while."

"Jesus, how many times did I tell you that you should not start every sentence of yours with well, well?"

"Sorry. I got into the habit of doing it while I was making fun of the head of security in the big house."

After I finished my phone call, I decided to chat with him a bit. I was trying to be polite, but I also needed a break, and I felt awkward charging him for classes that he kept missing. I studied his face and realized that it was completely sunburnt. His exposed arms were beyond sunburnt—they were peeling badly.

"Have you been somewhere?"

His answer was unexpectedly simple.

"We go on holidays, too."

I snapped, because I felt that his answer was too easy given the era we were living in.

"What a wonderful life you have," I said as coldly as possible. "Why on earth are you taking drawing classes? Trying to find a new hobby?"

"Well, and this is based on my childhood experiences, but the reason a slacker suddenly becomes interested in studying is usually the new female teacher at school."

"Since you're the laziest student in this studio, you're losing interest, I assume?"

"Not at all. It's just a different way of showing my interest."

It was so preposterous, I had to laugh. I had never considered him, not even for a moment, in that way. When I was at school, I talked as little as possible, answering only yes or no to the professors who always said the same things, and it was pretty much the same with my friends. At the studio, I talked to my students only when absolutely necessary, and after they left I spent the evening staring at a blank canvas. Sometimes it occurred to me to call my mother's house to listen to Eun Gyul babbling, or to talk to Jung Hee about our mother.

"By the way, what have you been working on all this time you've been squatting at someone else's place?"

I picked up the open book. I saw the title was in German.

"I'm translating."

"Did you find a job? Maybe I should charge you rent for office space."

"Well, well, the thing is . . . I've been mobilized to work as a free labor force."

"What's the title?"

"A few chapters from *The Poverty of Philosophy*. And some more from *The German Ideology*."

"This is for a publisher?"

He stared at me silently, then he gathered his books and papers and stuffed them into his bag.

"These are to be used as textbooks at a training center for professional activists."

"You shouldn't bring your conspiracy into someone else's workplace. Besides, what kind of change can be achieved with books?"

Song Young Tae took off his thick glasses and blew on them, then rubbed them gently with the end of his shirt and put them back on.

"There's a paragraph that I know very well. Well, well, it goes like this:

'Men should be aware of their own powers in order to organize them into a social force. When the man is not able to separate himself from that social force and no longer considers it a political power, he is truly liberated.'"

I do not know why, but I felt a sudden pain in my nose, and my eyes felt very warm. I thought of you. I couldn't even remember how long it had been. I felt as if I should write you a letter.

"Whose book is that?" I asked quietly.

"A man with a long beard, Marx. But he wrote this when he was still a young man. For us, this is only the beginning, too."

I got up quickly, trying to hide my red eyes. Because of the tear gas, I cried until my eyes were swollen every time I went to the university, even when I covered my face with a surgical mask, but there was no emotion involved in those tears. Human language is so powerful. I did not think those awkwardly translated sentences were poetic, but they reminded me of you all the same.

Years later, even when those sayings of Marx seemed ancient and trite, if I heard them spoken by someone else or read them in subtitles at the movies, or whenever I heard drunken students at a pub singing the "International," my heart felt colder, just as it did when I listened to songs from the past drifting out of an old record player. One night in Berlin, or was it early morning, I was silent as Mari scribbled something on the table with spilt beer, and the café turned into a festival, champagne bottles popping open. This was all later, years later.

"Ma'am . . ."

Someone said quietly, and I turned around to find him, still there, peering from behind the partition. I was actually a little happy to see that he was still there.

"What is it now?"

"Well, nothing much, just that tonight I would like to treat you."

"I am not going unless you take me to a really nice place."

Without knowing why, I took a look around the shabby and disorganized studio before I followed him down the steps. There was a dark gray car parked on the street. A chauffeur jumped out of his seat when he saw Song Young Tae and walked around the front of the car to open the back door.

"Get in."

Song Young Tae gestured like a doorman at a hotel, swinging his arm to point to the car. Confused for a moment, I still got in. When he climbed in and sat next to me, the car took off. It was a German car, rumored to cost as much as a small apartment.

"What is this?"

"I'm researching the basic conflict. I am borrowing it for a little while from someone, but he's not the real owner either. He stole it."

We went to one of the fanciest places at that time, the sky lounge at the top of a famous hotel. So many people were out and about so late at night. We sat by the window, looking down on the city unfolding below us like a field of stars. We ordered drinks. I kept silent at first while continuously sipping on my drink. Once I was a little drunk, I began to openly provoke him.

"Look, I want you to stop pretending, okay? I know who you are, I know exactly who you are! You are the son of a nouveau riche!"

He dared to talk back: "I know Mr. Oh very well."

"How does someone like you know an ascetic?"

"He is a friend of a friend."

I felt even more cruel, and I could not stop myself.

"Don't you dare show off in front of me. I heard from Jung Hee all about you. Your family owns how many acres?"

Unexpectedly, he gave up quickly.

"None of them belong to me. Listen, Yoon Hee, I'm just . . . someone trying to be aware."

"Awareness my ass. Your father was a member of parliament after the reforms in '72, wasn't he??"

Suddenly, he banged the table with his fist, and without the usual stutter, spat out, "Yes, he was, so what? An intellectual can choose his class. You want to accuse me of original sin?"

I just shut my mouth. I drank what was left in my glass in one gulp, as if it was ice water, and got up. My head spun around and I felt weak around my knees, but I put my weight on my heels and walked straight to the elevator. Since I did not see anyone in my peripheral vision I assumed he had remained in his seat. He was a bastard, and I didn't ever want to see him again. Pretending he was inarticulate.

I do not know how I got back to my studio. As soon as I walked in, I put a record on, took a beer out of the refrigerator, and drank by myself. Somehow my eyes stopped at my hand holding the beer glass; I saw my fingertips, and then I saw dark red paint chips under my fingernails. Drunk, I wondered if it was blood under my fingernails, wondered if I scratched myself somewhere without realizing why. Then I fell asleep.

The story of Song Young Tae is becoming a little boring and too long now, isn't it? No matter what, I did get to know him better and found out his many virtues and strengths. He was the only male friend I had. The foolish bastard, he ultimately made an outrageous decision. Kwangju could not be another Paris Commune, so what was the destiny of an intellectual of the eighties? I am thinking of the yellow sun setting on the empty field that fall, the year of his journey where he took a long round-about way to get to his destination.

After that night of bickering I ran into him one day, by chance, at the university. I was eating lunch at the cafeteria, and someone sat down in front of me, crashing his tray onto the table.

"Okay if I sit here?"

He was using the casual form of speech. Well, we already had done so the night we fought, so I assumed that's what we were going to do from then on.

"No one's stopping you."

"I'm sorry about that night."

"Why?"

"I know I acted like an asshole."

He was mumbling and I felt sorry for him, and thought maybe I had been a little unfair. But I also thought he deserved it and quickly hardened my face.

"Whatever you do, I hate anyone who shows off."

"Han . . . Let's be friends."

"You're not my enemy, so don't worry."

He grinned widely and began eating. I said casually to him, "I am a married woman."

He held his utensils in midair. He raised his head slowly and looked at me.

"Therefore . . . ?"

"I also have a daughter."

He did not say anything, he just kept eating, which made my confession to him a little pointless. Since I had started before he had, I was done before he was. As I tried to get away as slyly as possible, he grabbed his tray, even though he was not done, and followed me.

"I need to ask you a favor . . ."

As I walked out of the cafeteria and headed toward the library, he pulled me over to a bench.

"I have lots of books to read. I need to write papers."

"The studio is not too busy these days, right?"

"Yeah, I'm not accepting any students until winter."

"Would it be possible for me to use your studio as a gathering place for my friends?"

I did not have to ask any questions; I knew what it was all about.

"If it is for a study group or something like that . . . But I am going to tell you right now, I'll be out, or even if I'm there, I'm not going to play hostess. You bring what you want to eat or drink."

"Thank you. I'll call you tomorrow."

With that he got up and left.

It felt like there was more room to breathe on the university campus than before, and the battles of the previous semester had settled down during the summer vacation. Still, as soon as the new semester started, something was stirring on campus again.

On Saturday, I was studying at the library until late and left school after the sunset. I called my mother's house and got onto a bus headed there. The Harvest Moon Day was approaching, but I could not remember the last time I had seen Eun Gyul. I stopped off at a supermarket near the house to buy dried yellow corvinas, my mother's favorite fish, and also chose a few new clothes for Eun Gyul from a clothing store next door. Did I not even have time to go shopping at a nice department store for my own daughter? I think I spent those days not looking ahead, not even an inch. I somehow managed to attend classes, but I did not paint, and I did not make enough money. My heart began to race when I saw the blue gate and outdoor lighting of our house. I felt like a prodigal daughter returning from far away after committing many sins. When I pushed the doorbell, I heard a bird chirping, followed by my mother's low voice.

"Who is it?"

"It's me."

The door opened, the light in the entry hall came on, and my mother and her live-in maid appeared almost at the same time.

"Come on in. I think I was about to forget what you look like."

"How's Eun Gyul . . . ?"

From the living room I heard her voice, calling *Mommy, Mommy*. As we entered, Eun Gyul called for mommy with her mouth but stumbled backward and hid behind the maid. Me being me, I did not want to make a fuss in front of my mother, so I just stood there as I was prone to and watched her for a while.

"Eun Gyul, come here!"

I opened my arms wide, but she clung to the maid's skirt and buried her face. My mother mumbled, "You two are exactly the same."

The maid picked up Eun Gyul and put her in my arms, and I kissed her. Around that time Eun Gyul was able to utter simple words such as Mommy, bye bye, pretty and no, and the moment I kissed her she turned her head and pushed away my lips with her cheeks, clearly saying, "No, Mommy."

I held her tight for a while as I paced around the room. I felt her little heart beating and I thought of the time when she was still inside me. My mother had always been an unflinching person, so she pretended not to notice us as she looked out the window and then found the shopping bags that I had brought. She opened them, inspected the fish, and unfolded the clothes for the child.

"Mommy brought you some pretty clothes, Eun Gyul."

My mother changed her into the new clothes while I just kissed her over and over again, trying to appease her. After getting dressed in her new clothes, Eun Gyul seemed more comfortable, and she laughed and smiled, just being her adorable self. After dinner, however, she went to the maid, who she was more used to. My mother and I remained in the kitchen.

"Is it more comfortable for you to stay away from home?"

"It's not necessarily a comfort issue. I need to concentrate."

"It would be better for you to rent a real house or an apartment, as I've told you so many times."

"But I need to paint. I like it there."

"Jung Hee will be home soon."

"I didn't call her."

"I called her to tell her that you were coming home."

My mother pulled my hands and scrutinized them.

"These are not women's hands . . ."

She held on and stared at them for a while, then asked, as if it just occurred to her, "That man . . . Have you heard anything about him being released?"

"No. I did send a few letters, but I don't think he received them."

"He doesn't know . . . about her, then."

"Mom, stop it."

I pulled my hands away from her and gestured for her to stop, showing her my palms. She proceeded carefully, studying my face.

"I met that man, Lieutenant Park? The medical officer. He seemed to be a nice young man, so amiable."

I had heard from Jung Hee over the phone, so I just nodded.

"He'll be discharged soon, so I think they are going to get married sometime next year."

"He is a good guy. They seem happy together."

"And you . . . What do you want to do now?"

"Finish my degree, find a job."

"I used to think that way, too, when your father was in the mountains. I thought I'd live by myself, work hard and raise you two. But he came back alive, and after living together for a little while, I couldn't imagine ever doing it all by myself. I could not work out how on earth I thought I could do it."

"Wasn't Father a burden?"

"What are you talking about? The air in the house is different when the man of the house is there."

I was reminded of something I had not thought of in a while, so I told her.

"If formality is important, I can get married, too."

"What? With whom? How?"

"Obviously we can't have a wedding, but we can still get a marriage license, even when he is in prison."

"No. Never. A lifer has the chance for his sentence to be reduced only after twenty years or so, that's what I heard."

My mother counted with her fingers.

"It has only been three years. Life does not have to be so difficult. You don't have to do that. Do you love him that much? You can't forget him?"

I laughed.

"I don't know. I can't even picture his face anymore. Just leave me alone."

The doorbell rang, and Jung Hee came in with the maid.

"You're home, Yoon Hee!"

"You don't have to work today?"

"Off duty today. Where's Eun Gyul?"

The maid answered, "She just fell asleep, still wearing her new clothes."

"New clothes?"

"Your sister got her some as a present for the holiday."

Jung Hee sat down between my mother and me.

"Wow, what happened to you, Yoon Hee? You don't usually do that sort of thing. I also went shopping today and got her a few things from the department store."

My mother and the maid went to bed, but Jung Hee and I remained in the kitchen, sitting by the kitchen table and talking about things we hadn't had a chance to talk about lately. Maybe because she was working now, Jung Hee seemed more mature than I was in many ways. She was responsible and calm, and she knew how to listen. But what I liked best about her was that she did not possess the ignorant prejudice of many professionals.

"Do you know Song Young Tae well?"

"A little. He is a friend of Park, so he's not a stranger. Didn't I call before to tell you that he asked where your studio was? I thought I had told you a few things about him."

"Yeah, you did. He was in my year, did you know that?"

"He's considered a mutant in his family. Apparently he did pretty well at school before he got involved in all that."

"I can imagine. Why did he go to prison?"

"After that atrocity in Kwangju, he led the first protest in Seoul. He doesn't look like someone capable of doing such things, does he?"

"We had a huge fight."

"Why? Was he rude?"

"You know me. I cannot stand people feigning and posing."

"I did hear that his family owns numerous buildings in Kangnam. Did he act as if he was better than you?"

"No, it wasn't that bad. He can be quite charming sometimes."

Jung Hee seemed relieved.

"I thought . . . Do you like him?"

"I don't mind him. I don't know how, but we are becoming friends. After all, both of us are older graduate students, so it's a good thing. I need someone to bicker with."

Jung Hee's face became serious, and she looked straight into my eyes.

"Listen, Yoon Hee, I don't want you to become too close to him, okay?"

I smirked, "What are you talking about? You think I want him to be my boyfriend or something like that? He's such a baby, he doesn't know where his nose is. All he knows is how to memorize books."

"Yoon Hee, I'm sorry, he's a good guy, but he's a troublemaker."

"The whole place is full of troublemakers with good intentions. In fact, any young man with guts is a troublemaker."

"There are many people who do their job and live quietly, like me or Mr. Park."

"Even if you're not actively involved in it, you should be interested and witness it. That's how I feel."

"Ugh, I saw students clashing with the police during lunch hour. Tear gas exploding, Molotov cocktails flying . . . The police were hitting students with sticks, and their blood soaked their shoes. I am so sick of it."

"Jung Hee, I am thinking of visiting him before the Harvest Moon Day."

"Really? Of course, he's still in there. But only family members are allowed visitation rights, isn't that so?"

I nodded weakly.

"I know, but I still want to go. Who cares? If I can't see him, I'll deposit some money and clothes for him, I'll learn what the building looks like, what the guards look like."

Jung Hee neither agreed nor disagreed.

The next morning I got up and stayed in my studio. I was not doing anything, just sipping a cup of green tea, when the phone rang. I picked it up and heard the voice of Song Young Tae.

"Hello? Miss Han? This is Song."

"What do you want so early in the morning?"

"I told you I'd call today."

"Oh that. I have to be somewhere else today. But I can leave you the key."

"No, there's no need. Today's Monday? We'll be there on Wednesday."

After I hung up, I remembered something and looked through my drawers. I had once met your sister when I went to watch your trial. She gave me a business card with a phone number for her office at the university where she taught. I found the card and called her office. Soon I heard her say hello. Her voice was deep for a woman's.

"Pardon me, but . . . this is Han Yoon Hee. How are you?"

"Han, Yoon Hee? Ah, Miss Han!"

Stammering, I told her I wanted to visit you, and she told me she had not seen you for almost a year. I asked her where the prison was, how to get there, and what your inmate number was.

"I should go and see him too, but things are crazy before the holiday and I don't think I'll have time. How about this? Next time, let's coordinate and go together. If you're lucky, you two may get to see each other."

"Thank you."

After that, I had no choice but to actually go visit you at the prison. Suddenly there were lots of things to do. First, I went to a department store nearby and bought a couple of T-shirts with long sleeves and a thick winter sweater and a vest. I also got a couple of pairs of thermal underwear. The department store did not have thick winter socks yet, so I made a note to myself that I'd send some to you when your sister went for a visit.

I took an express bus, then a cab to the prison where you were. It was located in a secluded neighborhood right outside of the city. A straight, paved road lined by poplar trees cut through the rice paddies and barley fields. The first thing I saw was a tall white wall. On top of the wall was a watchtower, and in the watchtower stood a man with a gun. There also was a large searchlight and a loudspeaker. In the middle of the white wall was a giant iron gate painted blue. I asked a young man in an army uniform where the visitor's room was. I handed over my ID card, put on a visitor's badge, and walked through. There was another wall inside and a sign for the visitor's room. Inside the visitor's room was a large space just like the waiting room at a hospital. There was a place to register, and there were people sitting on chairs and waiting for their turn, staring at each other. I stood in line to register.

Finally it was my turn with the guard.

"Please hand over the request form."

"I haven't filled one out yet."

I was pushed to the side once again to fill out the form. There was a space for "relationship," and I debated whether to leave it empty. Finally I wrote the word "friend." I wrote your number and name, too. And then I got back into the line, and when it was my turn, the guard who had spoken to me before looked at me with clear eyes.

"What is your relationship with Mr. Oh Hyun Woo?"

"Just . . . A friend."

He smiled.

"Are you his girlfriend?"

"Well . . . Yes, yes I am."

I knew that when you were dealing with a government office or the military, the term "just a friend" did not exist. For them, there was a wife or a girlfriend, and there could be no other answer. It was fun to tease someone that his girlfriend had come for a visit, but a female friend would be too vague.

"You do know that only family members are allowed visitation, don't you?"

"We are . . . engaged. Is that not good enough?"

"I don't know, that is not my jurisdiction. Why don't you sit over there and wait a little while? I'll get the person in charge."

I waited again. It was only after I sat down that I began to pay attention to the other people in the waiting area. There was an old woman holding her grandchild, her eyes red and sore like she had been crying for a while. There were young women dressed in tight pants and colorful shirts or short skirts, and a woman with a sunburnt face who had fallen asleep with her baby still suckling at her breast. Almost all of them were women. The visitation rooms were behind a door on the right side, and I assumed there was another corridor behind it. A guard was sitting in the front, and whoever's name was called disappeared behind that door. Two women came out; the younger one was holding onto the wrist of a young boy about five years old, and suddenly she began sobbing loudly. The older woman cried with her and tried to comfort her by patting her back as she herself wiped away her tears with a handkerchief.

"Miss Han Yoon Hee," came from the speaker.

I got up. A guard standing by the door next to the reception area gestured to me. I approached him, holding the shopping bags. His hat had a gold line around it, and he wore a badge with a single flower to show his rank.

"Did you come to see Oh Hyun Woo?"

"Yes, I did."

"Why don't you come in here for a minute?"

He took me to a little room next to an office. There were an easy chair and a desk, and a framed woodprint of Daniel praying. Sitting behind the desk was a young guard with papers. It seemed like he was ready to record our conversation.

"First of all, I must inform you that Oh Hyun Woo is an important political prisoner who broke the national security law, and no one but his immediate family is allowed to visit him."

"I do know that. But I am . . . how should I say it . . . I'm like his fiancée."

"But your relationship is not legally bound, is it? We never received any special orders or instructions."

"Would it be possible for you to deliver a letter or note from me?"

"I'm afraid not."

He picked up a file from a desk and bent down to look for something.

"Furthermore, an accomplice or anyone connected to the case is on the list of people who are banned from visitation. Miss Han Yoon

Hee . . . Yes, here you are. You were arrested for harboring Oh Hyun Woo, were you not?"

"Yes, I was investigated for a short period of time."

"I see here that your indictment was suspended. There's really nothing more I can say."

I was not that angry or indignant, but tears rolled down from my eyes to my chin. I just felt powerless. I picked up the shopping bags and opened them. The paper bags crinkled.

"Can I at least deposit these for him?"

"Let's see."

He turned the bags upside down and emptied the contents on the desk. He looked through every piece of clothing, from the sweater to the vest to the thermal wear to the long-sleeved T-shirts, and then handed me a request form.

"Fill this one out. You have to list every item, including the size."

I wrote down each item carefully, as if it was a letter for you. While I was writing, he bent down and whispered to me.

"After you leave, I'll call Oh Hyun Woo over here and give him the clothes. I'll also tell him that you were here."

In a flash, I felt there was a ray of sunlight. I paused and raised my head to look at him and found his eyes smiling warmly. The younger guard who was recording our conversation was not there anymore. Formally, our interview was over. When I gave him the finished request form, he remained seated and kept talking.

"Oh Hyun Woo is doing very well in here. He seems to be quite healthy, no illness of any sort. Last summer, he began cultivating a vegetable garden in the backyard."

"What kind of vegetables?"

"Well, it's not that big. Little bit of lettuce, little bit of sesame plant, peppers . . ."

"He likes doing that sort of thing."

I did not know when he would stop talking, so I spoke quickly.

"Did he plant the seeds?"

"We planted lettuce and cabbage, but we got the seedlings for other plants from the nursery last spring."

"Did he grow them well?"

"They looked great," he said proudly. "Some inmates are selected to work at the greenhouse, where they can grow flowers. Of course, this is only allowed to model prisoners. A model prisoner gets extended exercise hours and also gets to work, so it's better for his health as well. Moreover, the time passes more quickly, and visitation rights are extended, too."

"What does he do for exercise?"

"He seems to either run or walk. After all, he spends so much time alone. Once you become a model prisoner, then you have access to various exercise equipment and that sort of thing."

Only then I realized the focus of the whole conversation had been the words "a model prisoner."

"How long does it take to become a model prisoner?"

"It depends. For ordinary prisoners, there's a series of steps they can take. In most cases it is possible for them to reach that status once they finish two-thirds of their sentence without reprimand. As for national security law offenders . . . There are no steps they can take, so what really matters is the conversion."

"A conversion?"

He nodded slowly and talked confidently.

"Yes. He can sign a paper recording his intention to denounce his past ideology and accept the new one."

I stared at him, not knowing how to respond. Suddenly, I thought of my father. Without realizing, my voice was getting louder.

"Who can interfere with what goes on inside his head? And doesn't that mean he has to admit his beliefs are against the law?"

"In other words, he should believe in freedom and the democracy of . . ."

"Doesn't a free democratic society means you can think and express things freely?"

"Well, that's enough. I have other matters to attend to."

I sprang up from the chair as quickly as he did, and I suddenly realized I was practically screaming. And I still had to leave you in there. On the spur of the moment, I bowed down deeply to him.

"Please, take good care of him."

He accepted it with a simple nod and pointed to the door. I left the room, unable to look back. I walked to the front gate and exchanged my visitor's badge for my ID card, then slowly walked down the newly paved road lined with poplar trees. I turned around and saw that the tall white wall was not so high anymore.

Up close, I had not seen the actual prison buildings, but now I saw them, lined up the hill like a staircase. When walking toward the building I hadn't noticed them, but now I saw little windows on the prison building and iron bars in front of them. I turned around and stood there idly, wondering if you were watching me. I heard the faint sound of a whistle blowing and someone barking orders. The black windows against the white wall looked like a pretty harmonica. But if I blew on it, only low, somber notes would come out. Or maybe they looked like the eyes of some sort of insect. And when I looked really closely, I realized that there were other colors, too!

They were clothes on the prisoners' laundry line.

The white wall seemed so lifeless, but there were washed clothes drying, evidence of lives. On the surface of what appeared to be empty cement buildings, multicolored laundry was flapping in the wind. There were more whistles and orders, followed by the clear sound of iron gates opening and closing, and a little later I saw human bodies moving past the windows. An arm or a pair of hands appeared at each window, collecting the dried clothes. Only then did I turn around and start walking. I did not want to look at those windows anymore.

I went back to the small city to take the bus. People, free to move around like I was, were crossing the street and going in and out of stores and greeting each other, so happy, yet to me the scene was mechanical and empty. It was as if I were watching a movie on videotape with the sound muted.

As I got back on the express bus to Seoul, I thought about you. I was thinking about our days in Kalmae, starting from the beginning. I thought that now I had no choice but to live my own life. And that I should do whatever I could for my art, even if that meant making my fingertips bleed. I decided I was going to walk that road all by myself, boldly. And I needed to figure out what kind of person I would be when I stood in front of you, sometime in the future.

The moon was not quite full. It stayed in my bus window for a while. Once in a while, we passed through small clusters of houses with bright windows. Under the moonlight, the empty roads in the little villages and the mountains and forests seemed even quieter and more lonely.

I decided to return to myself from that point on. Please, I pray that you never get sick or give up. Maybe one day, if I am reminded of it, I will go back to Kalmae, but I don't know. Maybe we will be utterly defeated in this battle. But so what? What the hell, I'll still look up to the sky even if I have fallen to the ground. I hope there is a thin line of afterglow remaining in one corner of the sky. Just like that dreadful, scary thing called hope that remains, no matter how small. Goodbye. Please, do not anticipate some sort of salvation within your gloomy, dark solitude.

17

I was taking a break after dinner. I had put a record on, and I was lying down in the small bedroom attached to my studio, leaning on a pillow with my legs stretched out in front of me, when I heard someone come in. He had called earlier, so I knew it was Young Tae.

"I thought no one was here."

He was peering into the room, still standing outside. I acted as if it was too difficult for me to sit up.

"Did something happen? Why are you acting like a pregnant woman?"

"Watch your mouth."

Young Tae sat down on the threshold.

"So did you go visit the prison?"

"Who told you that?"

"Jung Hee mentioned something," he said, feigning indifference. "Did you see him?"

"I couldn't, because I'm not a family member and I was implicated in the same case."

He remained silent for a little while.

"What the hell, we should get Hyun Woo out of there," he mumbled.

"How can we get a lifer out of prison?"

"That's why we have to overthrow this dictatorial government."

It was a line I had heard hundreds of times, and I did not say a word.

"So you came back with nothing. And that's why you're so down, is it?"

"No, it's because I ate dinner and I'm full. Look, just leave me alone, okay? And your cronies, where are they? Are they coming or not?"

"They'll be here soon."

"Fine, then I'm going to sleep in here, and you can wake me up when you're done, okay?"

I pushed Young Tae away and shut the sliding glass door. It was probably around eight at night when I began to hear people talking and pushing chairs and gathering in the next room. I guessed there were about twenty in there as they exchanged greetings. I heard Song Young Tae's voice.

"The reason we're gathered here tonight is to examine various problems we had during the first half of the year and to institute a set of tasks we need to achieve in the second half. First, I'd like to ask the preparation committee to analyze our current situation."

As if he had been waiting for that moment, a man jumped in, talking fast and without hesitation.

"Since the end of last year, the current administration had changed its course from absolute oppression to what they now call 'harmony with the people,' placating the citizens with education reforms. Our enemy is currently strong and we're weak, yet we were not able to see clearly why this placation is happening. Our so-called leadership committee came to a passive and defeatist conclusion that it was a trap, and that therefore we had to be circumspect in expanding our activities. In other words, we were hanging onto the education reform issue without the participation of the masses. As a member of the leadership committee, I should criticize myself first. The kind of system we have run excluded the opinions of the masses and therefore reduced space for the expansion and survival capacity of the voluntary movement. Though unknown to the enemy and working outside of the system, we needed to have constructed a centrifugal, representative student organization independently and to have simultaneously fought against the Student National Defense Corps in order to exhibit the fallacies of the liberation policy and their rhetoric of appeasement. In fact, the current appeasement is an external gesture to restore whatever legitimacy has remained since the Kwangju massacre, a palliative to avoid the politico-economic crisis evident in the nationwide bankruptcy due to 1.5 trillion foreign debt and the complete opening of the country to foreign investment last summer. But this crisis also gives us a chance to build a foundation to overcome the military dictatorship, not just from within colleges, but also in society at large. Therefore, it is essential to strengthen the departmental activities, which will become the nuclei of the mass student movement, and to utilize a large-character poster and pamphleteering strategy, which should center on students as active agents of propaganda. After taking over the mass student organizations, we should organize intra-collegiate resistance using this open space. Such allied action can maximize the political resistance in society and improve the movement capacity for what are currently relatively weakly mobilized universities."

Another, thicker, voice continued, "I agree that it is very important to obtain open democratization space in colleges and universities, and it is crucial to position resources externally, in order to mobilize the masses, who are the heart of any resistance movement. In order to reveal to them that it is the dictatorship that oppresses them and threatens their very survival, we need a framework of joint resistance for the protection of their rights."

A clear and high-pitched voice chimed in. "The Student Association has been restored, as expected, through the vibrant participation of our fellow students. We have debated the vanguard, or masses, issue since the late Restoration period. In fact, it should not be taken as a dichotomy, but as two sides of the same coin. It is important to cater to the mass consciousness and to mobilize them according to political contingencies, but we should be careful not to aimlessly follow or indulge them. It is necessary for us, the vanguard, to show them exemplary resistance, and therefore lead them. Without this combination, the motor of the democratization movement will not be started."

Song Young Tae's voice returned. "The blind spot of the closed leadership was that it tried to base the reconstruction of the organization on small groups within the universities. If the Student Association is to execute the everyday resistance that will mobilize the student masses, then the organization and activities of the vanguard must clearly exhibit the ideology and the purpose of a resistance movement in society. Therefore, I hereby propose a constitution for the organization that will fulfill these goals. As has become clear in the first half of the year, it is necessary to constitute an organization that can execute democratization as political resistance, and a permanent agency to coordinate the worker-student joint resistance."

The quieter, slower voice returned. "While we called ourselves the leaders, all we've been doing is controlling the Student Association and dealing with internal conflict. We have not even attempted to tackle the problems facing the whole nation, the whole of society; we've been confined within fences. Who placed whom in this position of leadership, which is illogical, and made them unable to set an example of self-sacrifice? We need to condemn this system of closed leadership and start all over again."

A female voice spoke, and sounded hoarse. "The organization is reborn again and becomes stronger through its struggles. We need to overcome our passivity and factionalism and regroup again. Furthermore, we should set up short-term goals that relate to specific situations, and for each instance reunite and redistribute in order to carry out our tasks. Our fight against the dictatorship needs to become a daily activity. I propose we begin with a committee which will eventually become a coalition."

The meeting went on and on, the discussions were endless, and I must have fallen asleep, because I only woke up when I heard the glass sliding door to my bedroom being pushed open. Song sat on the threshold like he had done before.

"I don't think you would notice if someone carried you outside. It's not springtime yet, how come you're so sluggish?"

"I don't know. I guess I was tired. I feel much better now."

"Why don't you come on out?"

I walked into the brightly lit studio. No one was there, but every fluorescent light in the ceiling was turned on. I hated that gloomy lighting, and the first thing I did after my students left was turn them off, leaving only the desk lamp on the table and the standing light in front of my record player. I quickly turned off the fluorescent lights. The studio was not completely clean, but it seemed to be neat. I took out a cigarette from Song Young Tae's pack, looked for an ashtray, and found an already emptied one. I looked around and realized someone had cleared off the table and had folded and stacked chairs neatly in a corner.

"Not bad. You cleaned up after yourselves," I said, lighting the cigarette

"Well we can't inconvenience the civilians too much, can we?"

"You sound like a warrior fighting for our independence, back in the '40s."

"Of course they left a mess. We cleaned up."

"We . . . ?"

"Yeah, she'll be back soon."

Before he finished his sentence, we both heard footsteps on the stairs. Her steps sounded quite purposeful, with her heels stamping forcefully. The door opened and someone came in. At first, with the studio lit and the doorway in darkness, all I could see was a silhouette. She was wearing a pair of jeans and a long-sleeved T-shirt, and she had bobbed hair. She put down plastic shopping bags on the table in front of us and tousled her wet hair with her fingers.

"What, it's raining outside?" said Song Young Tae.

"The fall rain keeps coming down quietly," she sang, tousling her hair.

I got up without a word, found a dry towel in a drawer, and handed it to her. She smiled as she accepted it.

"So sorry to inconvenience you so much. Thank you."

They even talked the same way? She nodded her head amiably and began talking to me.

"My name is Chae Mi Kyung. I went to the same school as Mr. Song over there, years later of course."

Her complexion was dark, her face round with thick eyebrows. She had big, dark eyes that twinkled with mischief. She looked like someone from Southeast Asia. It seemed like she knew who I was in a deeper way than just knowing that this was my place, so I just smiled back at her. I directed my praise for her effort to Song Young Tae.

"So, the perpetrator of this cleanup must have been Miss Chae?"

"Yes, well, I just picked up some cigarette butts and swept the floor and emptied the ashtray, that's about it. By the way, is it okay if I boil some water?"

"What, would you like some tea?"

"No, the truth is we haven't had dinner yet. I thought maybe I could cook some ramen noodles."

Only then did it occur to me to open the plastic bags and look inside. There were a couple of eggs, a few bags of nuts and other snacks, two bottles of soju, a few paper cups, and five bags of spicy ramen noodles. She snatched the bags from my hand.

"You want me to cook them for you?" I said, a little embarrassed.

"If you don't mind, I'll do it! I've been cooking for myself for so long, I know exactly when to stop cooking, so it tastes the best. Young Tae, what number do you want?"

"I'd be grateful for just number one."

"Here we go. Number one is ramen cooked in just water and spices. Number two has an egg added to it. And number three has chopped scallions."

Song Young Tae seemed to be enjoying bantering with Chae Mi Kyung tremendously. He was grinning as he waited for the next chance to butt in.

"And what's next? Please continue."

"Do not try to confuse me! The next is the special. Yes. Some chopped kimchi is added to all the above."

"Jesus, my mouth is watering. I don't need theories, I want real food!"

As I got up from my chair, Song Young Tae grabbed my arm and winked at me.

"Let her do it."

"I was just going to get some kimchi out of the refrigerator."

"I think she already knows where everything is."

"How?"

"She looked around while you were sleeping."

She was more brazen than Song! Still, I liked her immediately. I liked her brisk manners, and I liked that she was vivacious and honest. While she busied herself in the kitchenette I turned to face him. I was curious about her.

"What time is it?"

"It's almost midnight."

"Doesn't she have a home? Aren't her parents worried?"

"None in Seoul. She is from Busan."

"I can never guess the age of girls these days. She looks like a high school student, but who knows? In a different outfit, she could look like a middle-aged woman."

"What year is she in now . . . Hey, Chae Mi Kyung, what year are you in now?"

"Junior. I took one year off between high school and college."

"You're majoring in law, right?"

"Why do you have to mention that? It's nothing to be proud of!"

I could not just sit there and do nothing, so I got up to take the bowls out of the cupboard and the kimchi and other side dishes from the refrigerator. We all sat down around the table. She volunteered to serve the ramen noodles. I sat there quietly with an empty bowl in front of me and looked at her.

"To be honest, I'm a little hungry, too," I said.

"A midnight snack and soju, what a fantastic combination! And the autumn rain is coming down outside."

After serving ramen noodles to each of us, Mi Kyung shouted as if she was singing, "First, let's drink to the autumn rain!"

We raised our glasses and downed them at once. Mi Kyung jumped up from her chair and walked to the windows. She opened the drapes that were always drawn and began opening the windows one by one, something that I rarely did. There were creaking sounds, but every window opened wide like a miracle, and suddenly I could hear the rain. We were in the middle of a big city, but the wind that came in was fresh with rain. It seemed that Mi Kyung was just like that wind.

"What a wonderful idea!"

I was truly impressed. I had been locked in the studio, keeping the windows tightly closed and relying on artificial light. What did they say, that if you changed your thoughts you could change the world? The endless music of rain running down the gutters outside, the smell of moistened dry cement walls of concrete buildings, it all seemed like a miracle. Even the fluorescent lights on the ceiling were moving. And the plaster casts, frozen in the same spot for years, only casting certain shadows, now looked completely different with the shadows of dancing tree branches draped on them.

"Would it be okay if I stayed here tonight?" Mi Kyung asked as she cleared the noodle bowls.

"Huh? Why . . . ?"

"I have nowhere to go."

"That's true, Song Young Tae added. "She's renting a room at this house, and the owner just locks the door at midnight and goes to bed, no matter what."

I had no choice but to pretend that I believed the story.

"Really? Just tonight, then. Can't do it too often."

"I have this premonition that I'll be doing it quite often."

"She likes you," said Song Young Tae.

"Don't you dare. You think I have not realized that you two are trying to win me over to your side?"

"I thought you were already on our side," she joked. "I've heard a lot about you and Oh Hyun Woo, too."

Suddenly, I was irritated.

"What? How dare you? Are you making fun of me now? Do not joke about him in front of me, do you understand? And Song, you! I didn't know you yapped so much."

Both of them were caught completely off-guard by this sudden change in my attitude. Song Young Tae looked horrified.

"Really, Yoon Hee, this is a gross misunderstanding," he said, waving his hand. "The case of Mr. Oh is always mentioned when we study the history of activism from the early seventies. I just happened to mention your relationship to him because we were gathering here today."

"I am so sorry," Mi Kyung said. "We would not dare laugh at you and other people we respect behind your back. It's the opposite. Please, don't be angry."

I downed another glass of soju and remained silent for a while. Song Young Tae's face looked completely normal, he was not tipsy anymore. He stared at me for a while before speaking again.

"Han Yoon Hee, don't be angry, please. None of us can be cynical about the suffering we are all going through together. It was Mi Kyung's fault for mentioning his name so lightly, I know that. But she's still a novice, and she has a very clear definition of who's on our side and who's not. Inexperience can be charming, no?"

"Whatever . . . You guys have no idea."

But as I replied, I was already deflating.

Song Young Tae continued in the same tone.

"I find it ironic that I went onto graduate school as soon as I came back. But I am beginning to doubt that I will be able to finish it. Today, no one is free. Everything is connected, no matter what you do or how you live. Maybe years from now, when the world has changed so much, the lives we led will be completely forgotten. But now, all we can do is help each other, no matter how little we are, and try to make change happen."

"Song Young Tae! Just do what you have to do. I'm just trying to do what I have to do. I like freedom. Do not meddle with me."

Song raised his two hands as if he was trying to stop me.

"Fine, fine, I understand. You just concentrate on producing good paintings."

"What the . . . ? What is a good painting? I just paint, that's all. You better watch out from now on."

"What should I watch out for, ma'am?"

"Do not rush to fill up the void inside of you. You may overdo it. Especially since you know too many useless things. And you have too much money. Remember that."

Chae Mi Kyung murmured while tapping the table lightly, "That makes sense to me."

"So, Miss Han, you're not angry anymore?"

"No," I replied in a softer tone of voice "but you should leave now. There are plenty of taxicabs out the door. I plan to spend the night drinking with Mi Kyung."

"Phew! Thank God! Well, I should get going."

Song Young Tae lifted his arms as if he had just dropped off a heavy load, and patted Chae Mi Kyung's back.

"You silly little girl, why don't you ask her to make breakfast for you tomorrow morning, too? That way, she'll remember you for sure."

It was still raining heavily. I wondered if it was a monsoon in autumn. When the rain was over, the air would be cooler. After Young Tae left, I locked the front door and went back to the studio. I wanted to make amends with Mi Kyung.

"Want more to drink? I have some whiskey left."

"I'm okay. Would you like some more?"

"No, not really. How about something warm, coffee?"

"Sounds great. By the way, I was really scared just then. Look, I'm sweating!"

When I returned with the coffee mugs, Mi Kyung was going through my record collection. She carefully picked one up and put it on the turntable. I placed the two coffee mugs on the table and closed the window. I drew the curtains on top.

"You don't like the wind?"

"No, it's just that it's going to be noisy in the morning. And too bright."

We sat face to face, each of us hugging the coffee mug with both hands. I opened my mouth first.

"What do you learn at law school?"

"You learn how to protect the institution. It wasn't my choice, my father insisted on it. My father is a bureaucrat who started at entry-level and rose up to head of a department. A man of very few words. If he says no, that's the end of it. He's dreary and cold, like a character from a story by Kafka. I'm the first child, and . . . well, it's a big problem."

"How did you meet Mr. Song?"

"He used to coach my debate club, and we were at the same factory last summer."

"You were at a factory?"

"I worked as an assistant, and he was in the shipping department. He carried boxes for a month."

"Just the two of you?"

"No, there were more than twenty of us. We just happened to be assigned to this one place."

"How did you get in?"

"There were people in there already, working on a collective for students and laborers. Also the Christian missionaries who work with us."

"I thought he was on a holiday."

"He did have a holiday. He came to Busan when I was staying with my parents and called me to show him around. He treated me to sashimi and barbeque and buckwheat noodles, the whole lot. He rarely skips anything."

"I should have known."

"You know what? When the Bu-Am incident happened, I thought they were just crazy."

"When the what happened?"

"When the American Cultural Center in Busan was set on fire by students, remember?"*

"Ah, yes. It was incredible. I knew some people who were involved in that."

"It's continuous, just like water flowing."

"Well, shall we get some sleep now? There's a bedroom in there."

We pulled down the futons and lay next to each other. The light was out, but I could tell that Mi Kyung was still restless.

"Are you asleep?"

"No. Can't fall asleep?"

"Would it be okay if I came by once in a while?"

"Sure, just call me before you do."

"Can I tell you something? I did not register this semester."

"Have you told your parents?"

"I think I'm going to quit school altogether."

I did not want to say anything else. *Don't do it*, or *Go ahead*—anything I said would be futile. For a second, I thought of Jung Hee and her fiancé. In the same world were those beautiful men and women who led ordinary, normal lives. A few minutes later, I heard Mi Kyung breathing evenly. The bedroom was dimly illuminated with light seeping in from outside. I saw her hair, cut like a little girl's, spread all over her pillow. I pulled up the blanket that had fallen from her and tucked her in.

I woke up around noon, as was my habit. The curtains were still drawn, yet the room was bright. The space next to me was empty, with the futon and the blanket neatly folded. All the dirty dishes left in the kitchenette sink were gone, and the electronic rice cooker was on. There was a note left on the table. The handwriting was bold and leveled.

---

* In March 1982, protesting the US support of the Chun military regime, three student activists (two of them women) set fire to the American Cultural Center in Busan, the second largest city in South Korea. Inadvertently, another South Korean student was killed, and three were injured.

Dear Yoon Hee,

I was waiting for you to wake up, but you were in a deep sleep, and I had to go. I felt so ashamed this morning; I know I behaved like a little child last night. The rain has stopped. I have decided that I should live in a way which will allow me to face the next day's morning sun without hesitation, no matter what happens.

While I was waiting I got bored, so I took a peek through your sketchbooks. I realized that Young Tae was being impudent without knowing anything.

I made you a pot of bean sprout soup with fish stock. It's the perfect hangover soup. Of course, I had a bowl after I made it. I also put the rice cooker on.

I know you have a few side dishes but I thought you might want something more substantial. I braised mackerel pike with soy sauce and green peppers. Hope you like it.

I'll reappear again when you are about to forget me. And finally, I'm going to tell you one secret. My nickname is Black Bean.

It must have been about a week later, the beginning of October, when Song Young Tae came to see me. I was working, and I was not in the mood to joke around with him.

"I'm busy right now," I said without turning around.

"I know, I'll just stay here for a bit, I need to write something," he answered as he peered from behind the partition.

Instead of answering him, I kept moving my brush. I was about to wash the brush and change the color when I heard the phone ringing. As I turned toward the phone, I saw him jumping up to grab it.

"I think it's for me. Hel . . . Hello? Yes, that's correct, that's me. Yes, you can deliver to that address. Of course, I'll pay the whole lump sum. Thirty minutes? Okay, I'll be waiting."

I got curious, so I walked to the living room area.

"What was that? Didn't sound like you were ordering Chinese food."

"I did order something."

"So what is it?"

"Well, well, just wait and see."

I went back to my easel to resume working, but the brush seemed to be spinning in my hand. There were footsteps outside, then the door opened. Two men came in carrying a box the size of a small refrigerator. They were both wearing gray jackets with a logo on the chest, perhaps a company uniform.

"What is this?" I asked them, baffled.

"The copy machine you ordered."

"The copy machine?"

"We brought the electric typewriter, too. Where do you want us to set this up?"

Song Young Tae emerged from behind me and led them into the studio, his steps assured. Next to the refrigerator was a small table with a bamboo basket filled with dried flowers and fruit tree branches. Without hesitation he moved the table, the bamboo basket still on top of it, to the side, and gestured to the delivery men.

"Over here."

One man had already gone, probably to get the typewriter. The other began unpacking the box, and Song Young Tae helped him. They unplugged the refrigerator and plugged the refrigerator and copy machine into an extension cable. I did not want to make a scene, so I just watched them, my arms folded. The other man came back with a smaller box and put it down on another table. Young Tae paid them with a check and they wrote him a receipt.

"Here are the instructions. Would you like a demonstration before we go?"

"No, I've used it before, I know how to do it. Thanks."

"No problem. Call us if there's a problem, we'll be out here before you know it to fix it."

I began talking only after they were gone. I tried not to get angry. I tried to control myself.

"You planned all this, didn't you?"

"What . . . ?"

"Oh, so you didn't? You knew exactly where to put it, you knew where the plug was, everything."

"Yoo, Yoon Hee, the thing is . . ."

"My name is Han Yoon Hee, not Yoo Yoon Hee. I'm not saying this because I'm scared or anything like that. You should have asked for my permission before you did this. This is my space, after all."

"They are all yours. I'll just borrow them."

"Why do I need them? What am I supposed to do, make copies of my paintings?"

"Books are so expensive, you know, especially foreign art books. Don't you think it'll be great? You can make copies of your papers and all that."

I decided there was no point in getting angry.

"Alright, fine, I lose. I surrender. I know you got these to produce your seditious pamphlets, but what can I do now? Instead, from now on, you pay half the rent, understood?"

"That's a bit too much, don't you think?"

"At the very least, I should have an insurance policy."

Song Young Tae groaned and moaned as he unpacked the typewriter box, took the machine out, and connected it. After he had installed the ribbon, he rubbed his hands in anticipation.

"Well, let's give it a try, shall we?"

He took out a roll of papers from the inner pocket of his sports coat and spread them out next to the typewriter. Then he straightened one finger from each hand to form what looked like a pair of chopsticks and began pecking at the keyboard, one letter at a time. I glanced at the papers. He was typing up a magazine called *Torch*. How typical. All they can ever come up with is *Spark* or *Beacon* or *Fire on the Plain*, just variations of *Iskra*.*

"It's going to take you forever to type everything like that."

It was pitiful to watch Song Young Tae. In order to read the paper he had to look at it so closely that it touched his nose before he could type one word. Then he put his nose up to the paper again and typed another. I grabbed the papers away from him.

"Hey, hey, what are you doing? I can do it, I'll take one step at a time."

"Move over, I'll type them for you."

I pushed him away and sat in front of the electric typewriter. I began typing fast, as if I were a magician. When the typewriter reached the end

---

* A Russian word meaning "spark." It was the title of a political newspaper published by Russian socialists.

of a line, the roller made a cheerful sound and automatically moved to go back to the beginning of the next line. It made me happy.

"Nice machine!" I exclaimed.

"Wow, when did you learn to type?"

"You don't know that I was once a schoolteacher, do you? I used to type everything, from reports to the education department to letters to parents."

I was fumbling through the sentences and finally had to stop.

"What on earth are you talking about? 'In our struggle we were unable to take the initiative when unexpected events presented us with new opportunities. Instead, we recklessly exaggerated and stretched the situation and were buried underneath.'"

"It means what it says: 'Incurring a great loss by pursuing a small gain.'"

"And this was written for whom, and for what purpose?"

"To self-criticize."

"Among yourselves?"

"That's why this is really important. We need to set up a clear set of principles in order to continue fighting."

"So you plan to produce this regularly."

"Whenever there is an important turn of events, I want to offer a critical assessment."

I got up from the chair.

"You type, okay?"

"Why are you stopping?"

"I don't want you to expect anything from me."

"But you started it! Why don't you finish it?"

I ignored him and moved across the room. Song Young Tae began touching the paper with his nose again and typing with two fingers.

"Hello!"

Chae Mi Kyung came in wearing a skirt. I laughed.

"What a surprise. I was beginning to wonder where you were."

"You're so mistaken! We didn't plan this, I just came because I missed you."

"Hey," said Song Young Tae, turning to her, "do you know how to type?"

"Not much better than you do."

Young Tae groaned and moaned again and kept typing for a while, but he had to stop. He had finished only about half of the material.

"I can't do it any more. It's going to take too long for me to finish."

I had no choice but to push him away and sit in front of the typewriter again.

"Remember, next time write concisely and to the point."

As I quickly typed away, Mi Kyung exclaimed with joy, "My goodness, you type really fast!"

The first issue of *Torch* was done in about an hour. Song Young Tae stood in front of the copy machine and struggled with the instructions for a while, and then the machine started to work. Mi Kyung took the copies, put them in order, and bound them by stapling them into a pamphlet. It looked a lot more professional than any of the other handouts I had seen.

After they were done, Young Tae put the pamphlets into a duffle bag he had prepared. There were more than one hundred copies of it.

"Okay, I need to go now!"

He left the studio before I could yell goodbye back to him. Chae Mi Kyung took rice rolls from her bag and set the table.

"I haven't had lunch yet. I bought these from the market across the street, but I don't know if they're any good."

"So your nickname is Black Bean?"

Mi Kyung let out a hearty laugh, flinging her head backward.

"It's because my skin is so dark! At first they simply called me Blackie, but then changed it to Black Bean."

I thought the nickname suited her well, not just her appearance but her personality, reliable and quick.

"So you plan to continue publishing the pamphlet?" I asked.

"How did you know?"

"It's got Issue Number One written on it. So will there be a second, a third?"

"Who knows? I hope nothing happens until we do the tenth issue."

"The number of copies seems too small to affect the masses."

"Of course, it's not for them. It'll be distributed through clubs at each university. We want to enlarge the federation to the national level."

I could not help but laugh a little.

"Well, I guess I am in this too deep now."

"What are you talking about?"

"Isn't that the case? You guys are planning to continue producing the pamphlet here, aren't you? And I'll have to keep typing it for you, right?"

Chae Mi Kyung did not deny that that was their plan.

"I'm practicing, and I'm getting faster, I swear," she said.

I decided to ask her something that had been bothering me since he left.

"Young Tae seemed to have an appointment to see other people, but you didn't go with him. Why not?"

"We belong to different groups."

"How are they different?"

"Mr. Song belongs to Labor for Democracy, and I belong to the Coalition of Labor and Students."

"Is that why you said you want to quit school? To work at a factory?"

Mi Kyung blinked her big, dark eyes a couple of times, admitting that was her plan. I continued cautiously.

"I think school is the place you know best, and where you can work most efficiently. Do you really think you'll be able to help them a lot by going to work at a factory?"

"All I am doing right now is being a liaison between the school and other students who are already working at the industrial complexes. But I'm going to look for a real job as a laborer. I need to see the world through their eyes, that's why I want to work. I think I should just work for a couple of years."

"Unbelievable . . ." My words trailed off.

I think it was sometime later in October when Song Young Tae appeared again, this time dressed in a clean suit and even wearing a tie. He looked so different. He did not have that old, beaten leather briefcase that he always carried around, and there was no duffle bag for us to stuff with pamphlets.

"Wow, look at you! Do you have a date tonight?"

"Oh, please. All I've been doing lately is debating and arguing, my tongue is furred."

"I hope you keep quiet when you're here."

"We've started to debate our policies. If I can't convince them I have to accept it and go on."

"Yeah, well, by the way I haven't seen Mi Kyung lately. I'm curious . . ."

"She's in Boochun these days. She found a job."

"Really? So she disappeared without saying anything?"

"She's swamped right now, learning new things. Maybe she'll stop by next weekend."

He would not sit down, but walked around the studio, looking at his watch constantly. I told him as I pushed a chair toward him, "Please sit down. You are making me feel nervous, too."

"Miss Han, have you had dinner?"

"No, why? You want to buy me dinner?"

"I want to invite you as my date. You like Japanese food? How about sashimi?"

"Sounds good to me."

As I followed him out of the studio, I guessed that the dinner invitation came with an unspoken condition. He looked too different from his usual self. We were headed to a Japanese restaurant not far from my studio. On the first floor of the restaurant were a sushi bar and tables. Two men eating at the sushi bar turned around to watch us enter. We took the wooden stairway to the second floor, which was filled with private rooms, each enclosed by sliding doors lined in rice paper. We went into one of them, which was reserved under his name. He sat down without taking his jacket off, looking a little nervous. I found a floor cushion and placed it across from him when he said, "Sit next to me."

"You want me to pour you drinks? I can reach just as well from here."

"Sit over here, please."

I realized that he was not in a mood to banter, and it made me surer than ever that there was something else going on.

"I suppose more people are coming?"

A waitress came in to take our order, but he told her we were expecting more people.

"How many people are coming?" she asked.

"Two. First, bring us three bottles of beer, please."

Around the time the beer came, another waiter brought two young men, both of them neatly dressed in suits. One of them looked into our room and spoke over his shoulder to whoever was behind him, "Mr. Song is in here."

"Well, we see each other often these days, don't we," said Young Tae in lieu of greetings, and the two men studied me with razor-sharp eyes as they walked in. Song Young Tae looked beyond them through the open door and said, "Aren't there more of you?"

"Yes, downstairs. A couple of them came here half an hour ago for a safety check."

Young Tae turned to me.

"This is my benefactor," he said. "She's just like an older sister to me."

I had known this was going to happen, and I was not too angry. If there was a limit to how much one person can be shocked or angry, I had passed it numerous times by that point. I decided to be a bit shameless.

"I feel like I'm interrupting boys playing soldiers. I'm just here to eat, so don't mind me, please."

The two young men seemed to be asking who I was, without a sound. Young Tae said, "She's a painter. She has a studio in the neighborhood."

One of them bowed to me and said, "Ah, yes . . . I didn't recognize you. I've been to your studio once."

Then he turned to the other young man and whispered, "You know, Mr. Oh Hyun Woo's . . ."

The other young man, his hair short, tried hard to make his eyes penetrating and nodded his head. He was trying so hard to look serious that there was a deep line in between his eyes. The waitress came back to take our order, and all three men remained silent while waiting for the food to arrive. Maybe because he was getting bored, the one who had said he'd been to my studio began talking to me.

"What kind of paintings do you do?"

I thought for a minute how to answer.

"I don't paint apples or vases," I said, lazily.

"Then, what do you paint?"

"Nothing. An artist does not paint something every day."

"But still . . ."

I did not want to punish him, but he was the one who started it, so I decided to tease him a little.

"Well, it's my turn to ask you a question. What does your father do?"

"I'm sorry? What does that matter?"

Song Young Tae was grinning as he looked at the perplexed young man, but the other one's frown deepened as he glared at me. I turned toward Song Young Tae and asked him, relaxed, "Mr. Song, you're a student, right? Who pays for your tuition? Who gives you money to pay for tonight? Since being a student is not a job per se, isn't it important to question the student's background?"

The one with a frown quietly replied, "Yes, I admit, we're all from the petit bourgeoisie."

I ignore him and continued on.

"Just be humble, think of all this as part of learning about the world. I am someone who wants to paint, not somebody who stipulates what to paint."

They remained speechless, maybe reflecting on what I had just said. Fortunately, the food arrived. Song Young Tae offered them beer and then poured a glass for me, too.

"I'm sorry, both of them are underground. It would look too suspicious if there were just us, so . . ."

"I knew that, and I still came here, didn't I? Just be prepared to pay for dinner, alright? Order some abalone, too. Please, eat!"

As my attitude became friendlier, they all seemed relieved. Soon, Young Tae became serious.

"The formation of Labor for Democracy has just begun. We need to nationalize our organization. I think we should be ready by sometime next week, but the inauguration will have to wait until the beginning of the following week. What we need to do at the same time is form a network of activists who can carry out operations."

The one with the frown opened his mouth.

"The activists will be out in the open. However, the leadership circle and officials will have to remain undercover."

"Yes. Even among the activists, there should be two groups, offensive and backup. I think it's safe to assume that all offensives will be arrested and charged. Some of the backups, too, if they're unlucky."

"How many people are you estimating?"

"Only the best and the most dedicated ones, about fifty or more per school. From them, we will select a dozen or so as active and the rest will be the backups or demonstrators."

Song Young Tae poured more beer into the glass of the man with the frown and waited. He drank about half of the glass.

"And why did you want to see us?"

"I want you to select a few warriors from those in the underground, people who can lead a demonstration. And I want you, Mr. Cho, to be in charge of this operation."

"Has everyone agreed to your proposition?"

"There were fors and againsts, it wasn't unanimous."

"Those who were for it . . . what was their reason?"

"You've already been mentioned as a leader by those who were arrested last semester, so your arrest will not hurt other groups. And you have more than enough experience. And you've already done your military service, so at least you will not be dragged back there. And so on."

"What was your opinion, Mr. Song?"

"Of course I was for it."

"And those who were against it?"

"They said since you are already underground, you're already in a position to work there. That you should remain in school and mentor younger students. Things like that."

Mr. Cho raised his head; he seemed conflicted. His eyes became serious again as he talked.

"Okay, Mr. Song, I want you to be honest. I need to know the reason why I should lead this operation and go to jail."

"Fine, Mr. Cho. To be honest, you haven't achieved anything specific yet, but you're too well known to be useful underground. As soon as this organization is formed we need to be active. This operation, in truth, is not the real fight, but more of a provocation. If you're willing to sacrifice yourself for the movement, the organization will achieve success."

"If that's the case . . . I guess I should do it."

As soon as Mr. Cho answered, Song Young Tae extended his hand over the table and they shook hands. The other young man who said he had been to my studio put his hand on top of theirs.

"I'll join you, Mr. Cho."

I was beginning to feel so sorry for them, a lot more than I had at the beginning of dinner. I just sat there drinking beer and kept silent. After we all parted, Young Tae accompanied me back to my studio, and I could not resist telling him.

"If there's anything I can do . . . I'll help, too."

Song Young Tae regarded me from behind his thick glasses. In the busy section of the neighborhood, he looked like a modest salary man.

"You have already started."

I did a double take and asked, "What do you mean? What have I done already?"

"You belong to the publicity department, don't you?"

I could not scream, but I was so angry I had to say something.

"You bastard!"

18

I cannot remember what I was doing around the time that was happening. I was gradually getting used to living in a space the size of a little closet, becoming attached to little creatures within the walls and voluntarily erasing things inside my head. What were the principles I lived by? I made the decision to walk a straight line through the world where working people can be owners of their own lives. I thought I had just taken the first few steps. Since I was not there, the world did not belong to me. But maybe my survival inside added a little to the world, too.

I remember the hunger strikes. I did about thirty of them—we went on hunger strike in every season of every year, in memory of past events, to demand the abolition of the national security law, to demand an improvement in political prisoners' imprisonment conditions. The strikes were regular events, and each one lasted only three or four days, a week maximum. Still, a hunger strike creates a big fuss, and it is impossible for others to ignore it.

It begins with a declaration; you read out loud a prepared statement and shout slogans through the bathroom window, your only opening to the outside world, and you sing combat songs. When your voice is gone and your mouth is dry, use the rice bowl to make noises by banging it on the window frame; let everyone in the building know that this is a state of emergency. And finally, start kicking the steel door with two feet. If your feet hurt and you get tired, use the broom or the metal bucket.

If all of that fails to get any attention, open the tiny window through which the meals come in and make a speech, let it reverberate down the corridor. When you hear the guards running toward your cell, be prepare to defend yourself. Use a chopstick as a weapon and threaten to poke your own eyes out, throw the urine and feces you have collected, and block the door with the mattress. But soon enough, five or six guards will pounce on you and drag you out into the corridor, where they will fold your arms and handcuff them behind, bind your body with ropes, and put a gag in your mouth. The gag is made out of wood and leather strips, and when the large wooden piece is shoved into your mouth it presses your tongue down so you cannot swallow anything, not even your own saliva. The spit runs down your chin. Bound like that, you're taken to the cell with no window. Most inmates are locked in that thirty-three-square-foot space with six or seven others so that it is impossible to move, but a political prisoner is left alone even in there. Your legs are secured by a pair of shackles attached to a leather harness. Once your eyes get used to the dark cell, you can faintly see the small opening in the door, about the size of a fuel hole of a small stove. It can be opened only from the outside, and it is securely locked except when the meal is pushed through. Inside, you can see the toilet hole in the ground; the walls are covered in thick coatings of cement, and at the very top is a tiny opening for ventilation. You figure out the passing of time by the changing angles and varying degrees of faintness and brightness of the sunlight that somehow seeps in through the tiny opening. It takes a couple of hours to register the sudden change in your environment and grasp the still-existing world outside the door and the ventilation hole. By that point, the front of your shirt is soaked with your saliva, thanks to the gag in your mouth, and you think you are about to go crazy. Words are bubbling up inside of you, they fill up your heart and your throat, and you think everything will just explode if the lid is not removed. You try so hard to scream and yell, but the words cannot move beyond the tip of your tongue, and they slide back down to your throat. After about twelve hours, the little viewing window on top of the door is opened with a metallic sound and through it appears a pair of eyes that belong to the guard in charge of the torture cell. If the inmate's eyes are still full of hatred and rage, the viewing window is shut with pitiless speed, but it is most likely you are too exhausted to do anything but lie there by the time they decide to check on you. The door is opened, and the free wind from the corridor rushes into the cell.

"If you can keep quiet, I'll take the gag away. Can you be quiet?" the guard in charge says coldly.

You nod. You nod over and over again, begging him without words. A god's hand unties the leather harness and removes the gag. You open your mouth as wide as you can and take a few deep breaths, and you use your tongue, finally free, to lick your lips and teeth. The steel door is closed again. You bend your bound legs to raise your knees and sit down leaning against the wall, your hands still handcuffed behind your back.

It is strange, my regular cell is about the same size, but without the window the world shrinks even further. I feel like I am going to be weighed down by the darkness. I can't think of anything. It is just like the interrogation room in the basement somewhere, completely white and soundproofed, where my past is blank and I exist as an object. The pain is vivid when I press around the handcuffs with my fingers. There's a part of my back that itches, my twisted shoulders are cramping, even breathing through my nose and mouth is painful. I start tiny little movements to get out of my present situation where I cannot move, where I cannot lie down on my back or belly. These movements are the only thing I can do to pass time. First, I need to loosen my hands a little. More experienced inmates first try to find a nail or a wire. If they cannot find one in there, they wait for a chance, even if it takes a few days, to ask the guard's assistant and get it no matter what. Or they beg the guards to put the handcuffs on in front or release them for just a few seconds. When the handcuffs are adjusted the opportunity sometimes arises to turn the wrist at an angle and create a space. Back in the cell, the inmate rubs the dry hand with soap and then pulls the hand out from the handcuffs. When he hears someone approaching, he simply slips it back in and pretends nothing has ever happened.

Unlike other inmates, I cannot beg or bargain, so I crawl on the floor, studying every inch of it. If there is a spot where the wooden board is loose or jutting out, I keep pressing with my two feet. After about an hour, I find the head of a nail protruding a little. I lie down on my side and grab it with the tip of my fingers and do my best to pull it out. Sometimes they come out easily, but sometimes it takes a day or more. No matter what, the time passes, and pulling a nail out of the floorboard becomes more important than changing history. And then I get it. This little piece of metal is the key to turning me from a beast into a human being who can think.

It is almost dinnertime. The ray of sunlight has gradually moved to the left, and gotten shorter and shorter until it becomes a little spot right next to the ventilation hole before it completely disappears. The smell of soup with bean paste travels throughout the building, as does the sound of dinner carts wheeling down the corridor. My hands are still cuffed behind my back. I do not think this will be undone until the administrative office decides to see me, which usually takes three or four days. The key turns, and instead of the meal window, the whole door opens wide. The guard places a tray with three white plastic bowls right in front of the door.

"Eat your food, dog," he says.

If I was still on hunger strike I would kick it straight back into the corridor, but during winter I need to swallow my pride and eat in order to keep my body temperature up. I kneel in front of the tray with my arms and hands tied behind my back, and I bend over the tray and use my mouth to take a few grains of rice into my mouth. The food gets stuck to my nose and chin, but after a few tries I figure out how to do it. I push the rice into one side of the bowl with my tongue and pick up a small morsel with my teeth. As for broth, I pick up the bowl with my teeth and tilt it slightly by applying a little pressure, and I suck it through my teeth. Other dishes can be consumed with just my tongue and teeth as well. My jaw and clothes get wet, but I can eat everything. I wipe my mouth by rubbing it on my shoulder. The door opens again and the tray is taken away, and the guard confirms that the inmate is adjusting well by looking at the empty bowls. If the inmate is continuing with the hunger strike, they will get ready to force feed him. When this happens, the infirmary guard and his assistant arrive with a few other guards, then they open the door without warning and pounce. They put thin porridge in a rubber container and force a hose down the inmate's throat, and they continuously pump the rubber container to make sure that the porridge goes down. The pain of the tube in your throat, the feeling of porridge stuffing your throat and overflowing out your nose, is not the worst thing. You cannot help but feel violated, and you cannot help but cry because you are so humiliated. As soon as the door is closed you try to throw up everything in your stomach, but you cannot forget the silky texture of rice in your throat and the warm taste still lingering on your tongue. The line has been crossed.

The torture cell takes away from the inmate the very basic essence of human beings, the freedom to think. You don't have the luxury to think about anything. You need to have a goal, whatever that may be, and concentrate on accomplishing it. That is the only way to be sure that you are still alive. But I have a tool. I have to open the handcuffs. I fumble for the nail, which I have hidden in between the wooden boards on the floor, and I pick it up. With two hands bound behind and two arms trussed up with ropes, I cannot feel anything there, and my fingers are weak. First, I need to practice and relearn how to use my fingers by drawing a circle and a line and an x with the fingers holding the nail, getting used to the tiny details. Then, I am ready to push it through the keyhole and explore the complicated mechanism of the lock. I still remember the click—I would push and pull and twist it hundreds of times. I learn where to go, when to apply more pressure, I repeat it again and again as my fingers become more skilled. As I keep moving my fingers, my eyes are closed, and my thoughts wander away.

In the immense open field, tall barley plants roll like waves. Across the field is a little hill where gnarled pine trees stand, and the road I am walking on continues around the hill and across a bridge, where it bends behind another hill. Tall willow trees stand guard along the road, and I think I can hear them giggling as the leaves flutter in the wind. I am walking, but I do not feel anything uneven or jagged under my feet. The dirt road is moist enough to be soft like a pillow and it tickles my feet. As if in a dream, I walk soundlessly, sliding along the road.

Click! With a clear metallic sound, the latch is undone and springs up. Gently, I extract my hands. Now, it is the rope's turn to be undone. My fingers wriggle around the loops and knots and study them. At first, the knots are so tight that they feel like little stones, and it seems impossible to loosen them. I grope at them with my fingers, I try to pinch them, but my fingers keep slipping. After a while, it finally occurs to me that instead of untying them I should try to pull the rope from underneath the knots. As I wiggle around and struggle, the knot loosens a little. With one hand I pull the rope, while the other hand works on the knots. Finally, the knots begin to loosen, at first stiffly, but soon smoothly. The rope is knotted several times, but once the first knot is undone the others loosen automatically. It is so long, wrapped several times around my wrists, and I keep pulling it. It takes about an hour to undo the first knot, then it takes another hour to work on the rest. As the rope around my arms loosens, I tug it repeatedly until my wrists are free, leaving the coiled rope behind like a shed skin. I am exhausted by the time it is done, but I can lie down on my back. I open and close my hands, I scratch my nose, which I have been wanting to do for a long while, I lie down. There is a rectangular shape imprinted on the wall, the faint moonlight which has slithered in through the ventilation hole.

Somehow I fall asleep. Now it is time for the night guards to do the last inspection before their shift is over. I wake up to the sound of an iron gate opening downstairs and the quiet voice of a guard reporting, *All clear!* My eyes are wide open; I hide the handcuffs and rope under my body, put my hands behind my back, and pretend that I am sleeping on my side. It always takes forever for the footsteps to reach my cell. The sound stops in front of the door, and I hear the viewing window opening. As I lie down there, I open my eyes just a little to see the cap of the guard pass by. The footsteps go away again.

I am completely awake now, and I put my handcuffs back on. This time I lock only one side and leave one hand free, and I put the rope back on and tie it around my arms with my free hand to make it appear as close to as it was before. Finally, I put my free hand back into the loosely closed cuff. From now on, I can be free whenever I want. And I have the nail, too, which has been placed back in the floorboard where it came from. I feel victorious knowing that I can untie myself whenever I want to. The darkness in the windowless cell and the tightening walls do not worry me anymore. The first time is always the most difficult. After about a week, you get used to even the worst conditions. But if you are taken to the administrative offices for what they call counseling, you have to walk in the bright sunlight, and you suffer the aftereffects. The moment you leave the torture cell building to walk outside, you cannot open your eyes. Even with your eyes closed, the yellow light fills up underneath your eyelids, your head swims, and you stagger. The guard knows exactly what is happening, so he neither shoves you forward nor urges you to walk, he just sneers.

"So, does this feel good? Why don't you rot in there for a couple of months? I bet you'll turn into a model prisoner."

As I open my eyes and walk again, the white light gradually darkens, as if the light has faded away. Gradually, everything looks normal again. By the time I return to my torture cell everything looks beautiful with vivid and lustrous colors, from the trees to the sky, even the cement walls painted white. And now I dread going back to the windowless cell. Dragged back there, I am isolated in darkness, just like on the first day. The heavy iron door shuts behind my back with a loud bang, and the despair that sets in is that of a man who has lost everything. There are a number of phases in a windowless torture cell. The first ten days or so are spent struggling like an animal, trying to get used to your surroundings. The next phase comes when you return from the first outing, which confirms that your situation is as bad as it can be. And after hours of stagnation and tedium, the administration placates you by offering to undo the handcuffs or the rope, and offering conditions for your release, which is usually the writing of a statement of acquiescence and regret. You may think it is unjustified, and you still have enough hatred left inside that you do not want to consent, so there is a phase of resistance. Your administrator can impose the earlier conditions of punishment again, or he can try to placate you by prolonging the counseling period and therefore the walk outside. If the two sides clash for a long time, you may really lose your mind or be transferred to an even worse place. You acclimate one way or another no matter what. In the end, days such as these are dissolved in the modest eyes of a long-timer.

Most inmates try to rise through the prison hierarchy every chance they get. They try to find each guard's weakness, they act violently, and they nitpick at everything to annoy the guards. If they do not break during their first stay in a torture cell, they go back and forth for the next six months or so, making themselves the designated trouble-makers. The best way to attract attention is by injuring oneself. Some swallow sharp objects like a needle, a nail file, a nail, or a piece of broken glass, or they slash their belly with a knife made out of a can lid. One prisoner I know of sewed his perfectly healthy eyes shut with a needle and thread, saying he did not like what he saw, and there was another who sewed his mouth when he was told to shut up. Most guards give up at that point and let the prisoner be, unless he is at the beginning of his sentence. In this case, they will crush him until he changes his attitude, or transfer him somewhere else. But if it is at the end of his sentence, the guards overlook this sort of behavior, even if it is a hassle. Once the prisoner is allowed to grow his hair out, he is elated. And what does he get after all this? He may be assigned to slightly easier jobs, he may find more solid things in his bowl, or he may sleep in a cell with fewer inmates.

Imprisonment begins over and over again, as you get transferred to another prison, as your cell changes, as the administration changes. No matter how peaceful and logical the previous phase was, it all goes back to square one whenever something changes.

A political prisoner may start a hunger strike in prison because of what is happening outside socially or politically, but sometimes it is because of an issue related to prison life. A basic rule is that it has to con-cern other inmates as well, not just the political prisoner himself. What is considered inconsequential outside can be something worth fighting for, something worth risking everything for inside. You are willing to starve for days because you think the quantity of pork, served once a week, is not enough, or because you are demanding the warden's apology. All you have is your body, so you fight with your body.

My hunger strikes lasted one week at the shortest, three weeks at the longest. The how-to for hunger strikes has been passed down for decades by seasoned political prisoners. For example, it is better to do a short one during winter or to wait until spring, because you waste too much energy in cold weather. And you must gradually decrease the amount of food you eat for days before the actual hunger strike begins. What is even more critical for your health is that after the hunger strike is over, you have to be very careful what you eat. You usually declare at the beginning of the week, because the guards wait at least three days before they report it to their superiors. By Thursday or Friday there will be a response from the top, a compromise offered. If you go past the weekend, the guards will be rebuked by their superiors.

During one of the harshest winters, I started a hunger strike to protest against the censorship of books and letters. A week before, I began collecting salt and put every bowl and dish and any food bought from the prison store outside my door. First I drank salt water, then plain water. The first couple of days passed by quickly. An empty stomach minimized the effect of withdrawal, so I administered an enema to myself at night. I filled up a plastic bag with lukewarm water and secured a straw to it with a rubber band, and I filled myself up with as much water as possible. No matter how my stomach rumbled, no matter how weird I felt, I waited until the last moment. It seemed that things came out of my body endlessly. After repeating it three or four times, my stomach felt comfortable and the desire to eat gradually faded away as well. The problem is the third or fourth day—that's the toughest phase. There is a proverb that says no one can resist stealing after going hungry for three days. By the third night, every thought, every sense was directed toward food, and I could not do anything. Holding a book, no words could enter my mind. Around dinnertime I could hear the food cart approaching my door, and my sense of hearing and smell became very sensitive. The smell of cooked rice and bean paste soup wafted in so vividly. I could guess what the other dishes were simply by their smell.

The cart is traveling around my building, each cell buzzing with bowls and dishes clattering and inmates bustling to receive their dinner. I hear them eating and laughing together. I make sure that the little slot is closed and turn my back to the door. It feels just like it did when I would get sick as a child. After lying down in bed all day with a flu or a stomachache, I would hear the dinner table being set up on the other side of our house, and everyone except me would sit there to eat and talk, getting on so well with their lives without me.

The meal slot opens.

"Here's your meal," the prison assistant announces.

"Take it away."

"Why, are you sick or something?"

"Just take it away."

The slot is closed mercilessly. The rickety cart moves away. Since I already took salt in the morning, I drink plain water, just as I did at lunch, rolling it around my mouth as if I am chewing before I swallow. After about three bowls of water, the hunger fades away again.

The fluorescent light is so old that black spots appear at each end, and the buzzing noise I usually do not notice gets louder and louder. I am unable to sleep late at night. The metallic noise slices through my skull. This dim light that is always on becomes a sound that occupies my brain. My body disappears slowly, but my mind is more lucid than ever. This is the borderline phase of the third and fourth day, a blank page. After that, demands from my own body settle down and dissipate. I excrete nothing, not even the white water that came out before. All food smells revolting now. My body odor is fishy and fermented, and it soaks deep into my underwear and bedding.

I dream. Of all things, I always dream of an open field of grass and trees. Like the dream I had in the torture cell, I am walking on a dirt path across the field, I am grazing it like a wind or a cloud. After a couple of weeks I begin to feel cold all over my body, but it is not unpleasant. It is so warm and comfortable to lie down, just like lying in my bed at home after getting wet from rain. As the day passes by, I sleep less and less. In the middle of the night I wake up and spend hour after hour blankly sitting there. And like an old man, I reminisce. I sit there on my mattress and walk back into my past.

I see my little brother. For no reason, I think of the summer when I was about eleven years old. I am going fishing near an inlet with my friends, and my baby brother, who is four or five, wants to come with us. If I do not take care of him my mother will be angry at me, but I cannot trust him to keep the secret, that we are going to the inlet where we are not allowed to go. He is too little. I run away from him. I look back, and I see my little brother in the distance, flailing on the ground and wailing. I spend the day fishing by the river, and I only remember him when we return home, around sunset. Ah, my poor baby brother!

I think of the day I try to sneak out of the house to go see a Western movie, and he follows me again. If he cries I may get caught, so I have no choice but to take him with me. I grab his wrist and walk through the marketplace to the movie theater. In the dark my brother is scared and uncomfortable, so I offer him candies and soft drinks. He sucks down the sweet liquid as if he is drinking mother's milk. Still, he keeps fussing until I cannot take it anymore, so I drag him out of the theater and shout at him, kick him away and tell him to go home. His face is wet with tears, he disappears into the crowd of the marketplace. When the movie is over, I stand at the spot where I shouted at him, and my heart aches when I think of the sad little boy. His cry is still vivid to me today. At home, I find my brother sleeping in the corner of a room, his back to me and his face stained with tears. His bent knees and ankles are chubby. The memory stops with the face of my sleeping brother.

I remember journey I took by train to the end of the southern province. The long sound of a steam whistle is interrupted by the deafening roar of the wheels as it crosses a bridge. The sound still lingers in my ears, along with a sudden silence as the train reaches the other side and begins traveling on wooden rails. The abrupt change is like the unexpected arrival of death. The train is a passenger car converted from a freight train, with a very high ceiling and wooden benches. Heat comes from cast-iron stoves that use brown coals. The tin chimney pokes out through the window. As we travel through the plain, we stop at numerous stations, many of them so small that there is no attendant. People get in and out, going to and from the market. A chicken cackles and flaps her wings, unfamiliar dialects fill the air, and villagers brush snow from their shoulders as they climb into the train. Some people are roasting sweet potatoes and cuttlefish on the cast-iron stove, others open a bottle of soju. Somebody offers me a glass, too. The train does not skip a single tiny station; it crawls along the plain while the whistle screams loudly. A burning smell mixes with snow, and an old man who just came in and sat close to the stove to warm himself carries with him the odor of cattle dung and decaying straw. They never end, the little villages and frozen streams and rolling hills, and crows flutter like little pieces of black cloth on every tree we pass. As we get closer to the last stop, more people get off, and the train looks more like a marketplace or a public house at the end of the day with its empty chairs and the traces of people who occupied them. There is a series of iron bridges as the estuary widens, and the air on the other side of the river is hazy, enveloped in night fog. Snow is still coming down, but thinly, like pine pollen in the spring. The sun is still lingering above the ground, but inside the passenger car is dusky, and the yellow light is on in the little station where we stop. The carriage I am in is empty. Someone climbs onto the train. He is hugging a bundle, his head is wrapped in a cloth like a woman's headscarf, and hanging from his shoulder is an old military coat. He sits by the cast-iron stove, although the fire has died down by that point, and he peers at me every once in a while. His eyes seem so shiny, but I cannot tell if his face is dirty or tanned. I wonder where he is going. We are nearing the port city, the end of the land. I wonder where he is going. I wonder if he is returning to his hometown after losing everything in the big city. He finally opens his mouth, only when it is completely dark outside, to ask if I can spare a cigarette. I find a crumbled pack in my pocket and go to him. I offer him a cigarette. There are only two fingers left on his hand, enough to hold a cigarette. His nose is crumbling away, and he has no eyebrows. A leper. He gazes back at me without speaking. I strike a match and light his cigarette for him. He nods, still without saying anything. His perfect silence comforts me. I walk away from him but not too far, and I sit by the window and stretch out my legs. We can see the ocean now as the train moves slowly toward the port. After he finishes his cigarette he hums quietly, almost inaudibly. I cannot remember which song it was.

The night is so long. I wake up thinking I have slept for hours, but it is the night guard's footsteps that have awoken me. The buzzing noise from the fluorescent light begins again. My mind feels clear, like gazing into a burning candle. I clearly see the flame fluttering and the wick glowing as my thoughts sink deep inside of me. The fluorescent light gets louder in the silence; my conscience flickers. Why is it that the past becomes clearer as the stomach empties? The act of eating three meals a day belongs to a reality, the present. Maybe you leave the present when you stop eating. Old memories that were hidden somewhere in my brain slowly dissolve and spread throughout my body. But what is really strange is that my most vivid memories are of little mistakes I made and cruelties that I heaped upon others.

I think of the dogs we had. There was Mary, a nameless one with black fur, and many others. But the first dog I remember is Mary, who my mother got from a neighbor. Her fur was a mixture of gray and white, and I think she was a mix of a small dog like a spitz and a big one, a sheepdog perhaps.

Mary is smart. She understands people's words, and of all people her favorite is my mom, who feeds her every day. One rainy morning, I see Mary mating with a yellow dog about twice her size. I am on my way to school when I see the local kids surrounding them. The yellow dog does not care who is watching, he bares his teeth and growls as he mounts Mary. This is the first time for Mary, and she lets out pathetic yelps as she is pushed from behind. The scene is made even more pitiful when I see that her fur is wet, her ears are plastered to her head, which happens when she is scared, and her legs are flailing. I approach her despite my shame for her, but she is too stupefied to notice me. Kids throw pebbles at them and try to separate the two dogs by beating their connected behinds with a stick. A store owner comes out cursing with a bucket of hot water, and she throws it on them. At once they separate, and the yellow dog runs away and licks its still hard penis. Mary collapses to the ground, unable to move, still yapping. When the other kids move away, I pick up the stick they left behind and start beating her. I am disgusted with that little dog. Mary's legs give way and she crawls away as fast as she can manage back to our house with me chasing her. She hides under the little porch by the kitchen, and I poke under there with the stick, still furious. Mary cries and then snarls at me sharply. I throw away the stick and hurl insults at her, but when I finally calm down and look underneath, I see her meekly wagging her tail. She lives with us for seven or eight years. Then she contracts a horrible skin disease and someone tells my mom to treat it with boiling water and red beans, which only scalds her skin and makes her worse. A plasterer who has come to work at our house sees her and volunteers to take her with him, saying that she will not live much longer and that her owner cannot put her down. So my mother lets her go, but she tells us later that Mary resisted, that she did not want to go with a stranger. Not knowing what else to do, my mother comforted Mary and told her, *Listen, my little girl, I'm sending you away because you're really sick. When you get better, you can come back home.* And that is how Mary left our house, her leash pulled by the plasterer and the poor dog looking back toward the house several times as she walked away.

My black puppy comes when my mother has promised to get me a new dog as a prize if I am at the top of my class at the end of the first semester. When the report arrives I cry and swear and kick and scream for hours, and my mother cannot stand it any more. She takes me to the Youngdeungpo market and buys me the puppy. It lives with us for about five days. I torture the puppy. As soon as I bring him home I give him a bath with ice cold water and feed him steamed sweet potatoes, and he gets sick. I do not even have a chance to name the puppy. I come back from playing with my friends and there he is, already stiff, lying under the back wall in our backyard. I am so angry, I just roll his body up in a piece of newspaper and throw him into a river nearby. I still remember the newspaper and the dead body of the puppy floating separately and slowly drifting away.

After two weeks of my hunger strike, someone from the infirmary starts to visit me every other day to check my blood pressure. Naturally, my blood pressure is much lower than usual. Water tastes especially good. My beard is long and my skin dull, but my eyes are clear and bright. The guards come and go; one of them leaves me an apple, and the other opens a thermos with bean paste soup so I can smell it. Before they lock down the cells at night, I ask for permission to visit the administrative office and there return the food to them, untouched. They threaten to force feed me but I hold my own and tell them that I will file a complaint of torture if they do. Between the eighteenth and twentieth days, a resolution is offered. It is not exactly what I asked for, but close enough. This is the final critical point. If you want them to accept your request, you need to show them that you are not going to stop this until you die. This last phase is a long, tedious uphill battle. You know it can be over in a couple of days so you become impatient and your stomach begins to growl. All of a sudden, time stops. The day is long, the dark night seems to last forever.

Because of the cold weather you are emaciated, and you get frostbite on your ears and hands and toes from exposure to the cold. At first, it just itches, or you do not feel anything. I take off my socks and touch my toes, which are ice cold. I rub my hands together, I massage my toes, I caress my ears over and over again. After sleeping curled up under the comforter, its filling rolled up unevenly, and in a sleeping bag I made by sewing a blanket into a sack, my whole body is very stiff. No matter how hungry I am, I need to get up and run on the spot for at least an hour in order to loosen my limbs and let the blood circulate. Finally, they accept my conditions. After three weeks of enduring hunger, now I have to fight with myself again. Recovery is the most crucial and difficult phase. Twice a day, according to the infirmary's prescription, the prison assistant brings me a bowl of thin porridge. Sometimes it is accompanied by another bowl of bean paste soup with a couple strips of cabbage. The fragrance of rice and bean paste is wonderful. Now the memories of the past are replaced by the taste and smell of food. I write down everything that I want to eat on a piece of paper, and I start cooking the foods in my head according to my own recipes. Now I am back in the real world. After three weeks on a hunger strike it will take at least ten days before I can eat normal food again.

If there is one thing the inmates and guards agree on, it is how important eating is in prison. The political prisoners frequently demanded that the kitchen distribute a monthly menu, including quantity and price, but this was rarely carried out. When a menu was printed, it might have looked acceptable, but what was actually served would not have changed. The food budget was minimal, the kitchen was staffed by fellow inmates, and everything they cooked looked exactly the same. Everything was watery with little solid pieces. For example, the menu listed braised fish, but what was in the bowl was a murky liquid with crumbled fish bones. If you were at the top of the prison hierarchy, you could ask the kitchen to save pieces of meat or fish and cook them properly later.

The most popular items in the prison library were the supplementary cookbooks that are included in woman's magazines. I read all of them at the beginning of my prison life.

How about rice with mixed vegetables in a hot pot? Thinly slice carrots and sauté them with sesame oil and salt; blanch bean sprouts and season them with sesame oil, sesame seeds, and salt. Also thinly slice meat and season it with spices and soy sauce and sauté; halved and thinly sliced zucchinis are also sautéed with salt and sesame oil. Put oil in a pan and sauté the minced meat, then add hot pepper paste and water and sugar, and let it bubble away before adding pine nuts. This is the sauce. In a stone pot, put a layer of cooked rice and top it with the cooked vegetables and meat and cracked egg. Heat the stone pot until everything is hot, mix everything together with hot pepper sauce, and dig in.

If you jump into reading cookbooks too quickly, you only deepen the sense of deprivation. Since it is so cold, I pull my comforter up to my nose and close my eyes before I begin my cooking. My mouth is filled with memories of taste, and the memories of my family, of all the villages and streets I roamed around, of people I met.

Rice with bean sprouts tastes better with bean paste soup. They were my late father's favorite dishes, he ate them almost every weekend. Around lunchtime on Sundays, he would mumble, as if for the first time, *Maybe we should make rice with bean sprouts today.* Yes, let's make rice with bean sprouts. Right after the war, we raised our own bean sprouts in a dark pantry in an earthenware jar lined with cotton cloth. I remember my mother watering them often. When the beans sprouted and grew to the length of my little finger, they tasted the freshest and the most delicate; at this stage the yellow beans tasted nutty and the root hairs were not too long. I sat with my mom and helped her take the ends away with my fingernails. Meanwhile, my mom prepared fish stock by boiling a pot of water with a handful of dried anchovies. Later, when things were more plentiful, we used beef stock made of lean shank and added the cooked meat to the sauce, too. The next step is to layer rice and bean sprouts in a pot, add minced meat if you have some, and pour in the stock, using a little less liquid than normal. While the rice cooks, make the sauce. Add to soy sauce sesame oil, chopped scallions, red pepper, minced garlic, black pepper, and toasted sesame.

Now it is time to make the bean paste soup to accompany the rice. I think bean paste soup with clams goes really well with rice with bean sprouts. Freshwater clams were everywhere, all we had to do was just go to the river and walk around the soft sand and bring back a basketful. Using two fingers or just our toes, we found a handful of pretty little clams about the size of an adult's fingernail. As soon as we got to the house, the little clams would be soaked in salt water to clean out any sediment or sand, and then boiled twice, first just for a minute, and then in a new pot of fresh water until they were fully cooked.

When the clams open their mouths and the broth turns milky, add bean paste, but not the dark, crusty part from the top of the jar, use the golden yellow soft paste from inside. Add cubed tofu and scallions, and it is done. To make the soup more fragrant, add a few young stems of crown daisies at the last minute. When mixing the rice with bean sprouts, fluff the rice lightly. If the rice and bean sprouts get flattened by the serving spoon, it does not taste good anymore. Add the sauce little by little and mix it into the rice as you eat it.

Now I feel like eating *sujebi*, a humble soup of fish broth and torn dough. We ate that a lot right after the war. There was a brand of wheat flour called Handshake, packaged in a white sack printed with two hands shaking under a shield with stars and stripes. When we were evacuated to the countryside during the war, my mother used to make us whole wheat cake when she could get some of the dark brown flour. She mixed the flour with salt and water, measured it by the handful, and made each into an irregular oval shape. She steamed them in a cast-iron cauldron. I would take the dough and chew it in my mouth. We called it Korean chewing gum. The black whole wheat cakes were imprinted with my mother's fingers, like the grooves on the handle of a well-made tool. Sometimes she added black beans to the dough, and it would remind us of the special rice cakes we used to get on New Year's Day. The white American flour was so fine, I hesitated to touch it. With that soft flour she made a dough, threw little pieces of it into the boiling fish stock, and seasoned it with soy sauce. If she had kimchi, she chopped the cabbage and threw that in, too.

I remember going to my friend Kwang Kil's grandfather's house in the countryside when I was still in high school. Kwang Kil is long gone now. His house was in a little village miles away from the nearest train stop, so we had to walk for almost half a day along a winding dirt path beside a tiny river. It was wintertime, and the river, which was more like a stream, was frozen, and the dry grasses and trees were lightly coated with snow. I remember the first dinner at his house. There was no electricity, and

Kwang Kil's grandfather lit a lamp, which he usually did not. It was a simple dinner of rice cooked with radishes and soup with fermented soy beans. The rice was shaped into a little mound and served in an old porcelain bowl printed with two Chinese characters that meant life and fortune. It was a bit overcooked, but still tasted good. The radish was sliced thickly and cooked with the rice, and some barley was mixed in, too. There were various kinds of kimchi, made of cabbage or radish, some spicy and some not, and many, many side dishes that I had never seen in the city. The soup with fermented beans was thick and stinky like an unwashed sock. It was difficult to try it for the first time, but once I tasted it I could not stop eating.

Early in the morning, we were awoken by the sounds of Kwang Kil's grandfather coughing up sputum. It was before dawn, still dark outside, but his aunt was already up and had started a fire in the fuel hole. The courtyard was filled with the spicy smell of burning wood. It was cold outside, but the smell of smoke made us feel warm. Kwang Kil and I found a crude-looking army flashlight and an insect net that was used mostly in summer, and we walked into the bamboo forest behind the house. The tree sparrows were just waking up, and their chirping was almost deafening. I pointed the flashlight at a random spot and pushed the button. The spotlight surprised the birds, and they froze in place. Numerous tree sparrows stuck to each branch, forming a picture that looked like a fruit tree that needed to be harvested. Kwang Kil simply took the net and scooped them up, easily catching two or three birds in one motion. When they finally realized what was going on and tried to fly away, it was too late. With a little time and effort spent in the early morning, we were able to catch dozens of tree sparrows. We brought them back in a sack and roasted them on the embers in the kitchen fireplace. The kitchen was filled with the warm fragrance of cooked rice, and I remember eating the tender flesh of roasted birds with a little salt.

When my recovery was finally over, I could return to normal, everyday life in prison. My appetite was enormous, and no matter how regularly I ate, I was never satisfied, and I couldn't get rid of the persistent craving. January was the most brutal month in prison, and while trying to survive the month, suffering from cold and hunger, it was natural to feel that you were in danger. Like air escaping from a balloon, I lost almost twenty pounds. The Lunar New Year was approaching, and vegetables were scarce. But I had prepared for this with a prison assistant from my building since the previous autumn. The assistant, a model prisoner who got the job of doing menial work around the prison, knew me well. We got permission to raise napa cabbage in a vegetable garden in front of our building, and by early December we were able to collect dozens of large, fresh napa cabbage. We wrapped each one in a sheet of newspaper, stacked them in a plastic box we got from the prison snack bar, and stored them in a cool, dark spot under the stairway. This kept the cabbage fresh throughout the winter. They had to last until March, when fresh vegetables would be served again. We ate two out of three meals a day near the storage facility, and each of us ate a head of napa cabbage per meal. We took off the tougher outer leaves and dipped the inner ones in hot pepper sauce thinned with sesame oil. It tasted slightly bitter, but the savory fragrance was pleasant and palatable. The first couple of days were easy, and we had no problem finishing our portions, but after a few days I tasted grass in my mouth from just looking at the cabbage. But we had to finish the boxful of cabbage if we wanted to stay healthy. If we didn't take care of ourselves during the winter, our gums would become inflamed and we'd lose teeth later on. I remember my colleagues lost at least a couple of teeth each after they were released from prison. They told me how their teeth became loose and came right out after pushing them a little with their tongues. So I ate the yellow inner leaves of napa cabbage, I stuffed my mouth with the leaves and rice and the sauce and chewed, thinking all the time how much better it would be if there was a piece of meat or fish to go with it.

The lunches I shared with the prison assistant were infinitely more pleasant than dinner for an inmate in solitary confinement. They were times when I could actually see and talk to and argue with someone else. Dinner was served after the cells were locked down, so I had to eat alone. When the time came, I took out the white plastic bowls that I had washed well the day before and the wooden spoon and chopsticks I had asked inmates in the woodworking shop to make for me. I laid them out on a piece of newspaper and waited in front of the tiny meal window. The cart would arrive, the window would open, and in would come rice, soup, and a couple of side dishes. Even when I knew that nothing more would come in, I couldn't shut the window, I would wait for a while before I started eating. I sat facing the wall, took a spoonful of food, stuffed it into my mouth and chewed. My mind was blank; nothing kept my attention. There was music in the background, piped in from an old cassette recorder in the guard's office for meal times. They did it out of habit, not really to please us, and sometimes the guards played the same music, the same songs, for three days in a row. But no one complained, because no one could hear it very well. Over the music came the quiet murmurs of people eating and chatting from other cells. It sometimes felt like participating in a solemn church service.

One snowy evening, I was eating rice in a bowl of lukewarm broth when I suddenly felt a lump in my throat and my eyes began to well up. What was I looking at? In front of me on the bare cement wall was one of the calendars distributed by Christian missionaries. It showed twelve months on one page along with a picture of Jesus with a halo around his head and a long staff in his hand, standing on top of a grassy hill surrounded by sheep. Written underneath it was, *The Lord is my shepherd, I shall not want. He makes me lie down in green pastures, he leads me beside the still waters.*

It was not the words or the picture that made me cry, it was the numerous x-marks on the dates of the calendar. Each day of the past twelve months was crossed out, and a similar calendar distributed at the end of the year was hanging next to it with no mark on it. Whether they were crossed out or not, whether they were gone or still to come, they were meaningless days. What was it that I was trying to protect? What was I holding on to? I fought for more solid pieces in our broth, an extra piece of meat to reach the promised quantity, more exercise hours, less censorship of letters and books. I protested against abusive guards and remembered the prisoners who went before me. These amounted to an effort to keep myself sane, to somehow hold onto the little bit of dignity that was left to me. The tiny rewards that I received after everything I did were gone by the time the new season came, as the guards and administrators were replaced by new ones.

19

From the early winter of 1984 to May 1985.

In mid-November, Song Young Tae and his comrades attempted to take over the ruling party's headquarters. While the backup unit blocked the streets and stalled the police, the offensive unit, its members filling the complicated alleyways behind the building, ran inside and managed to occupy the headquarters for a while. They were armed with steel pipes and wooden sticks, and at one point they went all the way up to the top of the building. Song Young Tae was in a nearby tea salon, so he was neither arrested nor included in the wanted list published after the incident. From time to time he showed up at my studio, and he continued to produce pamphlets. I actually got caught up in this, and sometimes I would stay up all night, all by myself, typing and copying and binding.

I had completed two semesters of graduate school and I wanted to finish, even though I had gotten a late start. Then I would have accomplished at least my first goal. Remember? I wanted to live independently with Eun Gyul. The new semester started, and I met with my advisor once in a while and taught students at my studio. I forgot that it was springtime. I think it was mid-March when Song Young Tae came to see me in the middle of the night. As usual, I was slumped on a chair with a teacup in my hand in the empty studio when he came in.

"Hey, stranger, haven't seen you in a while."

"Yeah, I've been busy."

Instead of explaining his absence, he looked around the studio.

"I should take them with me."

"Really? Fantastic! Now I don't have to worry about anything anymore!"

"Well, I think it's little early for you to be so relieved."

I was swinging my arms wide, slightly exaggerating while I said, "I am free! I am finally released from the evil hands!"

There was the sound of a number of feet coming up the stairs outside, and three young men appeared at the door. The tall one was wearing a long coat like Young Tae's, another wore a leather jacket, and the last one a pea coat. They did not even look at me, let alone introduce themselves, but they came in and began moving the copy machine as Young Tae ordered them to. They took the manual press and the electric typewriter, too.

"Where are you taking them?"

"You'll see when you come with me."

"When did I say I was coming with you?"

He clasped his two hands like he was praying and begged in his most ardent, desperate voice, "Miss Han, please, just one more time, please help me. You're the only person I can rely on."

"Nope, I can't. I'm done, really I'm through."

"It's really important, and I don't have time to screen some new person. You've been cleared, so to speak."

Again, I could not stand firm.

"I guess something big is about to happen."

Song Young Tae stuttered when he was nervous and shuffled his words.

"Well, soo . . . soon, there's going to be . . . a tor . . . tornado."

"And why do I have to be swept into it?"

"Thi . . . this time, you . . . you can wrap it up."

I answered him by getting up without another word and putting on my coat. There was a small truck on the street carrying the equipment and waiting for us. One of the three men was sitting next to the driver of the truck, while the other two were in another passenger car. As we got into the truck, the car left. Soon we arrived at a tall building filled with studio apartments. This type of building, called an "office-tel," had just been introduced, and similar ones were growing all over the city like bamboo trees after rain. The elevator was loaded, and we went up to the eleventh floor. The studio looked nice, furnished with a desk, chairs, and a sofa, complete with a kitchenette and a bathroom. I looked around.

"How big is this?" I asked.

"They call this a 500-square-foot unit, but I think the actual space you can use is about half of that."

"It's nice. Good enough for you, I should say."

"The building isn't full yet. It's nice that it's so quiet, isn't it?"

After every item was put in its place and plugged in, the tall young man stood waiting.

"Mr. Song, anything else you want us to do?" he asked.

"No, that's it. Thanks for all the work. You can go now."

The young men did not say anything to me, but nodded before they quietly left the room. Young Tae looked at his watch.

"It's ten o'clock already? Man, he's always late."

"Is someone coming? Then I should get going."

"No, you can't! You said you'd help me!"

"What can I do with a stranger around?"

We heard somebody walking down the corridor outside, and Song Young Tae paused for a moment and listened. When it was clear someone was coming toward the unit we were in, Young Tae opened the door and cried out, "It's over here!"

"Ah, you're here already."

The stranger was a man in his thirties, wearing a worn gray suit without a tie and carrying a large yellow folder under one arm. It seemed he had not shaved in a while; he had stubble around his mouth, but he still managed to give an impression of propriety.

"Miss Han, let me introduce you to Mr. Kim. He went to our school a few years ahead of us, and he's a journalist who was recently fired."

The man in his thirties offered his hand, acting like someone older than he was.

"Glad to meet you. I hear you've been working hard."

I gave him my hand, but didn't say anything.

"So, you got it?" Young Tae asked him.

"Yeah, it was really hard to find. But I did get many different versions. Some of them are from the reporters who were there, but I also found a collection of witness and protester accounts."

"Let's see."

Young Tae was impatient. As soon as the man handed over a stack of papers, he gave part of it to me and went to sit down in front of the desk and began reading. I did the same, sitting across from him on the other side of the desk. Kim sat on the sofa by himself and smoked a cigarette while we read the papers.

"It's a little bit chilly in here. Is there no heating at night?"

"Ah, really? I have something here."

Young Tae took out an electric heater from under the table and plugged it in. Kim continued, "It's written by a number of people, and I marked the dates."

"The numbers in red ink, are those the dates?"

"They should be."

"Miss Han, let's make this easier to work with. We should organize them in order according to those numbers and then type them. Mr. Kim, I want you to select a few episodes that you think are more important than others. We can't include everything in one little pamphlet."

"I think all you need to do is record what happened in sequence. There are people working on a book right now, so a lot more details can be included there."

It was almost midnight when we came up with an outline. I got more materials from Young Tae and began typing. I had just read it, but the truth of the uprising and massacre of that May seemed to come alive at my fingertips.

Around seven o'clock, cars and large vehicles suddenly appeared from Yoodong, their headlights on and horns honking. At the front of the line was a fully-loaded twelve-ton truck that belonged to the Korea Express, Ltd., followed by eleven express buses and about two hundred taxicabs, filling up the Keumnam Street. On the truck were more than twenty young men, each waving our national flag, and the buses were filled with young men and women holding wooden sticks as weapons. The march of the cars continued in wave after wave of enormous rage. Their flashing eyes showed their unity, their sense of self-sacrifice, their stiff resolve that were the fruition of the May uprising, and this tidal wave swept through the city from the evening of the 20th to the next morning's sunrise.

I then typed what I believe to be the most impressive and touching moment in the pamphlet, the charge of the automobiles on the night of Tuesday, May 20.

Taxicabs gathered in front of the Moodeung Sports Complex. Some taxi drivers were already injured, their heads wrapped in bandages. By six o'clock in the evening, more than 200 taxicabs had gathered. The drivers parked their cars in orderly rows and shared what they had witnessed so far in the city, the brutal crackdowns, stories of drivers who were hurt and killed. They denounced the brutal and barbaric actions of the airborne unit and decided together to take the lead in breaking down the barricade. Each driver tied a cloth or towel around his head and drove his car to Keumnam Street. As the taxis arrived, many civilians who had been pinned in front of the blockade there cheered and wept tears of joy. Soon, the people there found whatever could be used as a weapon—a steel pipe, a wooden stick, a Molotov cocktail, a pickax, a butcher knife, or a sickle— and, throwing rocks over the cars, they charged again. Caught off-guard by this sudden turn of events, the army, acting under martial law, fought back by launching enormous quantities of tear gas. It seemed they were willing to suffocate the demonstrators. Tear gas bombs shattered the windows and windshields of the taxicabs, exploding inside. Unable to withstand the dizziness and suffocation, drivers in front had to stop only about twenty yards from the blockade. When they got out of the cars, the drivers were dazed and confused, lost in the thick fog of tear gas. They were crying and coughing, throwing up and staggering. The soldiers took this opportunity to attack. Three or four soldiers fell upon each driver, crushing skulls with their clubs, kicking and hitting drivers on the ground before hauling them away. Some drivers in the back were able to get out of their cars and escape, but dozens were arrested. The citizens who were shielding the taxicabs kept throwing rocks, hiding in the side streets or in between damaged cars. However, the soldiers belonged to the special attack corps, and they defied the rocks and continued their counterattack. Now there was a huge commotion, with cars crashing into each other because they were not able to advance. The windshields and windows of a few hundred vehicles were smashed. The soldiers were blinded by the headlights, so they broke all the lights with their clubs or rifle butts as they marched. The citizens retreated bravely, throwing rocks at the soldiers as they went. The soldiers were somehow able to push the citizens back to the end of the line.

"Wait, I have something that can be added there."

Kim interrupted me as he took a peek at what I was doing. Instead of saying anything, I stopped working and waited for him. He handed me what appeared to be a copy of a newspaper article.

"The article is dated May 22. It was censored."

I resumed typing, inserting the article into the witness account.

In the dense fog of tear gas, the protesters, led by buses, clashed with the soldiers. Keumnam Street near the Chunil Broadcasting Corp was filled with endless screaming and shouting. The clash lasted almost half an hour, and when it was over, among the buses and taxicabs with their motors still on, were numerous injured citizens, bleeding and unconscious. Two young women in their twenties dressed in bus attendant's uniforms wailed over the body of a man in his thirties. His skull was smashed. People carried the injured, crying, begging for an ambulance.

"Looking at all these papers and materials, I'd say we'll have to work for at least two days and nights. Let's try to finish half by tomorrow morning, take a break, and continue in the afternoon," Song Young Tae said as he shuffled papers. Kim seemed tired already; he kept yawning and rubbing his eyes. "I think I should get going. There's nothing left for me to do."

"Sure. Thanks, everyone will be grateful for this."

"You're very welcome. I'm just relieved to get rid of this stuff. Well, take care of yourselves."

After he left, Song Young Tae and I continued to work until dawn. I typed, and each time I finished a page, Song Young Tae made copies.

"It shouldn't be more than twenty pages. People have to be able to read it at one sitting and get mad. We plan to distribute it in the industrial areas as well. We need to produce about one hundred copies here, and then it will reproduce and multiply in others' hands."

Song Young Tae gathered the copies we had already made and counted them.

"Why don't we call it a day? That's exactly one half."

"Already? My goodness, the sun is up."

"I'll take you home. Let's get some broth, too."

"Broth? That's it? You're exploiting me!"

"Hey, calm down. You know what Mi Kyung is having now? A cup of instant noodles."

"Speaking of Mi Kyung, I haven't seen her in a while. It's better for me that she doesn't show up, but at least send a word so I don't have to worry, okay? Bastards."

"She's too busy right now, but she should resurface soon. Let's go!"

We turned off the light, made sure the door was securely locked, and left the apartment. The corridor was dark, the only light right in front of the elevator. While he had been natural and friendly in the studio apartment, Young Tae became completely silent now, dropping his eyes and never raising them to look at me while we stood in the cramped elevator. I felt awkward, too, and I tried to change the mood by joking.

"What, are you praying?"

Song Young Tae cast a glance at me from behind his thick glasses and gave me an embarrassed smile.

"Hmm? No, nothing."

We took a taxi back to my neighborhood and walked to the restaurant both of us knew well. It was busy all through the night with truck drivers and drunken students, but it was almost six in the morning now, and the place was not too crowded. We took a table in the innermost corner near the kitchen. All they served here was boiled pork, a soup with stuffed pig intestines, and a spicy soup with beef bones and cabbage. Young Tae took spoons and chopsticks from a container on the table and set them in front of me.

"I want the tripe soup, how about you?"

I hated how sometimes you'd find a hairy piece of lard in that soup, so I replied, "The other one."

Young Tae ordered our food, talking slowly.

"So . . . let's see . . . one soup with stuffed pig intestines, one with bones and cabbage, and a bottle of soju, please. And please make my soup spicy."

Until the food came out, he remained as silent as he had been in the elevator. I just thought he was tired; it did not occur to me that he might be behaving strangely. Why would I perceive him differently? The bowls were brought out with a bottle of soju and shot glasses. Without asking, Young Tae placed a glass in front of me and went to pour. I covered it with my hand and said, "No, I don't want it. I want to go home and sleep."

"Just one. I'll drink the rest."

I let him pour me a glass. He poured himself a glass, and without raising it to me, emptied it down his throat. I sipped from mine and took some broth. Young Tae was noisily stuffing his mouth, drinking the broth one minute and downing the liquor the next. Maybe I was not the type of person who could eat so late at night, or so early in the morning. My mouth felt coarse and the rice kernels refused to go down my throat, so I kept stirring my bowl with a spoon and took a few sips of the broth. Young Tae was already done with his soup, and he emptied the bottle into his glass to the last drop. He drank this last glass slowly, savoring every sip before putting down the glass on the table between us. After I put down my spoon and drank some water, Young Tae offered me one of his cigarettes, and even lit it for me. Then he lit one for himself, and after staring at his half-full glass, he emptied it into his mouth, as if he had just finished an enjoyable game. I wondered what he was doing. Now, Young Tae stared at me.

"Miss Han, what do you think of me?" he said.

Under normal circumstances, I would have just sworn at him or taken it as a joke, but he looked too serious for me to take it lightly. I figured, why don't I just smile back? For no reason, I looked at the dirty wall where the menu hung. "Well, what do you think?"

He banged the table with one hand. "I asked you first, didn't I?"

Frowning at his tantrum, I turned my head away from him. "Are you drunk after one bottle?"

"It's been almost a year since we met."

He was mumbling, then said out loud, "I think I'm getting used to you, Miss Han."

"You sound like a cheesy pop song. And stop calling me Miss!"

"I like you."

I could not say anything. I could not tell him that I felt nothing. I knew that without him, the past year would have been unfamiliar and endless. My reply was a bit harsh on purpose.

"Look, I like you, too, but it'll never be more than that, so forget about it. Do you understand that?"

"I'm leaving now."

He jumped up, went to the cashier to pay for the meal, and left. I remained in my seat, finishing my cigarette. By the time I had stubbed it out in the porcelain dish and left the restaurant, the market was already opening up.

I went back to my art studio. I walked into the unlit space of mine. There was a dim light coming through the drapes, and my furniture and other possessions appeared to be live animals holding their breath. Suddenly, I felt like the only dead thing in the room. The table was covered with an overflowing ashtray, scrunched-up cigarette packets, and coffee mugs, and the chairs around it were pulled back or turned around, still holding onto the shape of the people who had sat there before, carrying the now invisible past up into the empty air. I sat on the chair. I put my arms on the table. My right hand landed precisely on a coffee mug's handle. I picked it up and sniffed, and I smelled my own perfume. There would be a reddish imprint of my lips on it, too. I vacantly sat in the twilight. I felt like I was sitting alone in the middle of a burnt-down house or a ghost town.

I could not remember when I fell asleep. I was still sitting there on a chair with my head buried in my arms resting on the table. The daylight lit up the thick wine-colored drapes and came in through the gap. A ray of sunlight had landed directly on top of my head. I got up to adjust the drapes. Only after I shut the drapes did it occur to me that I should go inside and lie down.

The sun had gone down; it was dark again. I was still half asleep and remained motionless under the blanket. I was coming down with something. My throat hurt, I was hot, and my whole body ached. I wanted to drink ice cold water, but that meant getting up, walking out of the room to the kitchenette, and opening the refrigerator. I felt my eyes welling up, then a tear rolling down from my eyes down my cheek to my earlobe. I thought of my daughter. I missed her, and for a moment I thought about going to my mother's to see her, but then I thought about leaving her, turning my back to her and exiting the door as she watched me. I was tired of it. I thought of colorful laundry hanging from darkened windows on a white building. Then the few lines on a postcard from him. So he's going to be one of the stars out the window, is he? What star? It is just a black hole, neither the retina nor the pupil remaining. Much later, after the Berlin Wall came down, someone was talking about stars at a little bar in Budapest. Something about getting rid of stars somehow.

I must have dozed off again, still feverish. I dreamt of Hyun Woo. He is sitting there in my dark room, leaning against a wall. I stay in my bed, lying on my side, and look at him. For some reason, I cannot move one finger. He is smiling at me. *When did you come?* He does not answer. All of sudden, the room changes into the one in Kalmae. There is the paper-shaded window on the wall he is leaning against, and the low table and candles. Next to me is a small, rectangular futon for Eun Gyul, and our newborn baby is sleeping, her little fingers peeking from underneath her blanket, so thin and delicate like water. And there he is, sitting across from us and humming, I cannot remember which song. The room changes again; this time it is his tiny cell. So, this is where he lives. All I had seen before was a window from far away that looks like a hole punched through a wall. Eun Gyul is in there with us, too. He is lying right next to me, Eun Gyul sitting on his raised legs. He whispers to her, *The lady rides the horse, the lady rides the ox*, as he raises her up and down on his leg, and the baby giggles and laughs with every movement. He hands her back to me and quietly stands up. *Where are you going? Hold on for a minute!* I want to hold onto him, but I cannot move any part of my body. Eun Gyul crawls over to her father. All there is is a door, and there is no trace of him. Eun Gyul disappears, too, and I hear a baby crying from somewhere. I shuffle my body and look around, trying to find the child.

I opened my eyes. The phone was ringing persistently. Without realizing what I was doing, I sat up. My whole body was moist with cold sweat, and wet hair clung to my forehead. I wiped my chin and neck, covered with little beads of sweat, as I opened the glass sliding door and walked toward the studio. Only then I remembered that I had been in bed dying of thirst. Yes, I should get the phone. I walked toward the old-fashioned rotary phone ringing loudly on the table.

"Hello?"

"It's me. I called you so many times, and you never answered. What's going on?"

My heart slowed down and the unknown fear vanished, but I was also dejected. Song Young Tae's mumbling relieved me, but it also meant nothing had changed.

"Do you know what time it is now?"

"What time is it?"

"It's past eleven. I thought maybe I should go get you, but you didn't answer the phone, so I've been working by myself."

"I see. Well, I need to rest."

"You sound weird. Miss Han, are you sick?"

"I'm not well. I think I have a flu."

"Oh no! That's too bad. Should I get you some medicine?"

"It's not a big deal. I think I'll go to my mother's."

"That's a good idea. You want me to stop by early tomorrow morning?"

"No, I was about to leave. I'll see you later."

"Well, take care of yourself. I'll call you again."

Song Young Tae's voice went away. I stood there with the phone still on my ear, and the dial tone echoing from somewhere deep in the receiver sounded so hollow. I would not see Young Tae for a long time. *Shouldn't I stay with my mother?* I thought about it as I put a kettle on the stovetop so I could drink hot green tea. I changed my mind, because I did not want her to think that I was living alone and needed her pity. And I did not want Eun Gyul to catch whatever I had. I turned off the light and lay down in darkness again.

I was sick. No, it was more like the poisonous remnants of my twenties were being washed away with clean water. I did not move, I did not eat, but I did not despair, I just lay there like a piece of discarded clothing.

When I finally got out of the house, it was a blooming spring day. The magnolia flowers were already falling, the yellowed leaves drooping like corpses. I stood under the shower at the public bath in the neighborhood and vacantly stared at my naked body reflected in the mirror. Maybe there still was the trace of a baby around my waist. Water poured down on my body, and I soaped myself and stood under the falling water again. I asked the masseuse to scrub me. The muscular woman nudged me once in a while to signal that it was time to turn my body around. I remained on the table after she was done, blankly staring at the ceiling.

That night, I cooked dinner and ate by myself in the studio. I poured water onto rice and ate it with braised cutlass fish, kimchi, and a couple of other side dishes my mother had sent over. Like other people do, I turned the television on. It was so easy to slurp down the soupy rice. Something appeared on the television screen. *Wait, what was that?* A reporter was almost screaming. Protesters had broken into the American Cultural Center, condemning the American response to the Kwangju Incident. The protesters appeared on the screen. Each of them was wearing a headband with slogans on it, and they waved placards and hastily-written signs out the window. The leaflets they threw fluttered and fell like leaves from a tree. Their assertion that the US was responsible for the Kwangju Incident was something I was familiar with, I had seen it on numerous posters around the campus. On the screen, I recognized a few faces as those who had come to my studio with Song Young Tae. Those pamphlets we had made had been the beginning.

Song Young Tae vanished. It was more than two weeks after the American Cultural Center incident that I finally realized that. There had been periods when he did not contact me for a long time, but someone at school had always told me what he was up to and I was able to figure out where he was. But this time, there were endless demonstrations on campus and no one seemed to care where someone named Song had gone to. While I headed to the Mapo neighborhood in a bus, I saw the office-tel building that I had been to with him. *I think it was on the eleventh floor.* I walked down the corridor and turned a corner based on my guessing, and found a door with a little note attached with tape. It said *Translations*. I hesitated, then knocked. When the door opened, the face that appeared behind it was that of Kim, the man I met that night. When he saw me, he opened the door wider. Somehow, the studio apartment looked narrower than before.

"Come in."

He stood aside, as if he was waiting for me to enter. The office machines were organized differently, and there were a couple more desks, but the sofa was gone. I presumed that Kim's desk was the one closest to the window. Someone was sitting by the desk pushed to the left wall and scribbling. Before he sat down, Kim pointed to a folding chair right next to his.

"Have a seat, please," he said.

We were sitting side by side facing the door. I took another glance at the stranger and tried to sound as matter-of-fact as possible.

"It looks different."

"I'm sorry? Ah, yeah, we had to. I had to take over, not that I was planning to."

Kim turned to the stranger bent over the other desk.

"Mr. Chung, let me introduce you. This is a friend of Young Tae."

He nodded without saying anything.

"I'm saddled with it now since he disappeared. We couldn't just waste the rent, so we turned it into our workplace. We take turns coming here with work to make a little money."

"Something happened to Song?"

"Ah, you didn't know? He's wanted. After the American Cultural Center incident, even those who stayed in the background had to run."

I guess there is no way to contact him, and I have no desire to look for him either, I thought. Kim opened a drawer and took out an envelope. It was not the usual white one, it was an airmail envelope with blue and red stripes.

"I saw him here the day before he went underground. It'll be impossible to find him now. That pamphlet on Kwangju has been distributed in universities and factories all over the country, and the book has been published, too. It had been planned since last winter."

I put what I guessed was Song Young Tae's letter in my bag and began to leave, when Kim added, "Don't worry too much about him. He's a Little Lord Fauntleroy, I'm sure he's reading books somewhere with a view."

I was not too surprised. I did not take the bus again, but decided to walk slowly. The trees were turning greener every day; there were not too many people on the sidewalk at midday, and it was pleasant walking.

There was a brand new building with a bank on the first floor, and around the corner from it was a small acrylic sign. I found a shiny marble staircase leading to the lower level. Despite its appearance from the outside, inside was an old-fashioned tea room. I was a little disconcerted, but also relieved. If it was a new place with tacky decorations, I would have felt more uncomfortable. There were just a couple of old men who looked like real estate agents, and the interior was ridiculously large. There was a small aquarium and plastic plants and grapes, and the television no one was watching was showing a Hong Kong kung fu movie. I sat in the farthest corner near a wall. I waited patiently until the middle-aged waitress brought me the cup of coffee I ordered, then I finally took the envelope from my purse. *I need to see what nonsense he has written.*

> Dear Miss Han,
>   I should have visited you the day you were sick.

I had to laugh a little at his first sentence. It just sounded so classic. I mean, he decided to leave behind a letter. So antiquated. Even my old father was more elegant; all he did was tell you a story about unripe persimmons and leave it at that.

> But I could not go to your studio that night because I had to send everything nationwide the next morning. I know why you were sick, you were working too much. I think they started to look for us. I know more than anyone else so I need to go deep underground. Telephone calls are the most dangerous, so I'm not even going to attempt to call you. And too many people know that I frequented your studio, so I don't think I'll see you for a while, I don't know for how long.
>   I just want to reiterate that I truly admire Mr. Oh. Compared to what he's done, I'm just someone hanging around,

trying to figure things out. I haven't seen the stars yet, all I've discovered so far is a vague horizon. I have fantasized about raising his precious daughter with you. I knew about her from the very beginning, Jung Hee's fiancé had told me. Don't you think that we've worked together very well over the last few months? Before we knew it, we became comrades. I am writing this most sincerely.

Really, you like being sincere, don't you? I did not feel anything toward you, you know that. But one thing is certain. I felt comfortable with you. We were like brother and sister. I liked your naïveté, but unfortunately, I sometimes did not like that you were a little wanting when it came to things like appreciating people and nature, or beauty and sensitivity, things like that, the way I cannot do math. I know it is not a big deal. But still, a little disappointing.

I know this sounds like a cliché, but I was always happy and exhilarated when I was with you. That night at the restaurant, trying to express myself was harder than performing on a stage. Still, that is just a tiny speck of dirt. From today, I need to submerge myself deep underwater. I will have to hold my breath and close my mouth and eyes and fight my solitude. And I do think that I should never say these things out loud again, not until Mr. Oh is released. I'll always be near you. When we are able to see each other again, I will not mention this.

When you have a solo exhibition, I'll be there early in the morning when there aren't too many people to praise your brush strokes. If Mr. Oh is released, I may be a little bolder. For our little wishes to come true, we have to bring down the government. No matter how dark the night is, no matter how stormy, the sun comes up and the day brightens again. Just like that, the moment for revolution will come.

Revolution. What then? I think it's only possible in a no man's land, somewhere deep in the mountains where only ox-driven carts and donkeys pass by, or in a scene out of a Western movie where a rifle is the deadliest weapon. I remember a picture of a female guerrilla warrior in Nicaragua, carrying an automatic rifle and wearing a cartridge belt.

The mighty army parade sweeps through the plaza. A mountain of weapons is unloaded on the docks. The supersonic jets cut through the sky, a nightless city of radars and aircraft carriers, glass and steel skyscrapers. A group of executives touring the facility slowly walks by machines. Marching down the street arm in arm and falling down when the shots are fired. Such an innocent scene may still exist, but it is not the one of the revolutionaries taking over government offices and guarding their organization with arms; that scene does not happen anymore. And the possibility of it ever happening is becoming slimmer each day.

There will be endless debates and numerous arguments that will always need to begin from square one; compromises that no one's happy with will be made, and after a long wait will come some slight progress, which will most likely be distorted after a while. All there can be is a partnership or an election. It will be impossible to figure out how the threads got so entangled, you will be lucky to find the one you just missed. And everyone will resemble everyone else while holding onto the end of that one thread and arguing over it, never again able to go back to the starting point. While trying to destroy the system, they will form another system in order to destroy it. No one can remain a warrior forever. Even the revolutionary committee goes home after a day's work. At home, the wife takes care of the kids and complains that his paycheck is late again and nags that he is never home and whines that there is no more money. Again and again, they eat and drink and fight and have sex and sleep and wake up the next morning and change clothes and go to work and begin debating again. In between the land he had left and the sky of the far future there is an infinite black hole with its mouth wide open. A revolution? That is a frozen scintillation. If you are not banished like Oh Hyun Woo or murdered by bullets in front of a barricade like his brothers, you will have to live an exhausting life as an activist who has to commute to work. Still, even if that is the case, how beautiful a revolution is. Even if it makes your mouth dry, even if you end up quivering with disillusionment, it still electrifies you and reminds you that you are alive.

I tore his note into tiny little pieces until only a handful of letters were left. *I will never work for you, no, I will never go near you all again.* I decided to live quietly and simply, enjoying my work, even more so than my sister did. If the tear gas on campus makes me cry, I'll shed a tear then, but nothing more. Like the trees around the campus, I'll drop a few leaves and remain standing there, silent and unaffected.

20

It has been more than three weeks since I was released from prison, and I have spent four nights and five days in Kalmae. At first I was unable to fall asleep, staying up until the early hours of the morning to read Yoon Hee's notes and old sketchbooks and letters. In them was a life outside, the one I had missed. The heightened emotions of the first few days began to deaden little by little. What I felt, the bursts of rolling and kicking in the pit of my stomach, was never as specific as sadness or injustice, but more like a sensation on my skin, a feeling like dryness slowly moistening. It was like waking up from a nap at the end of a summer day when the sun is setting. Everything around me, the people, the mountain and the field, looked so vivid and clear and new that they appeared unfamiliar. I could see myself only as if through a mirror, and my eyes remained a pair of lenses viewing just this side while the world moved along on the other side, blind to me. I felt like smoke, a hovering spirit looking down at its body left behind like shed skin, watching family, friends and neighbors, unable to communicate with them and regarding them, detached. My fingers trembled and my stomach felt uneasy, like after taking too much cold medicine. I was afraid to stay in one place too long, and I kept distancing myself, separating my body and my spirit and studying every little movement I made, even breathing or picking up an object. This state of anxiety has continued for the past few days.

But now, in Kalmae, as I've met with the remains of Yoon Hee, I have found a partner. I can exist concretely here through her. What was locked up in solitary confinement was not Oh Hyun Woo, but Number 1444, just an awareness that in order to survive the worst of a situation you need to hold on to the convictions and actions of your past and preserve your human dignity. Now, I am returning to the world outside through my partner. According to the calendar I left prison just a little while ago, but it feels so far away, like something that happened many years ago. Eighteen years has become but a moment, like a scene in a disjointed movie. It is like trying to remember the dreams of my adolescence. I am an ancient Chinese man with magic eyelashes witnessing my various desires with foreknowledge of their transience and futility.

Just like any other day, I ate breakfast and left the little garden to walk down the narrow path toward the main house. Among the dry grass of the past winter were new green sprouts. I had thought about a few things the night before. I thought I should get a job when I went back to Seoul, even though it might be too late. I should meet Eun Gyul, even if she was now Jung Hee's daughter. I wanted to know more about her.

"Come in, come in. Did you have breakfast?"

The Soonchun lady was sitting on the porch. I was not wearing sweatpants, but a sports coat and a pair of slacks like I did the day I arrived here, so she asked again, "What, are you going somewhere?"

"Yes, I need to run some errands in town."

"Oh, that's perfect! We need to get a few things from there."

"Why don't you write them down for me?"

"Of course, of course, just wait one minute."

She came back with a piece of paper and a pen, and after a long time I finally managed to ask.

"By the way . . . you have the phone number for Jung Hee, don't you?"

"Hmmm? Beg your pardon?"

"The sister of Miss Han."

"Ah, yes . . . that's right, her name is Han Jung Hee. It's somewhere in here, I'll go look."

It took a while before she came back with a thick notebook. She pointed to one spot in the back of the notebook, where several numbers were written down.

"This is her home phone number, and underneath that is the number of her office. She always called a few days before she came down here."

"Do you have something I can write with?"

"Here's a pen, and you can take a piece of paper from that notebook."

I wrote the number down and tore off a little piece of paper.

"Come inside. You can call her now," she said.

"No, I'll call her later. Just give me the list of things you want me to get for you from town."

"Okay, I'll do that. My son went all the way to Kwangju to buy supplies, so he's not coming back until this evening."

It took her at least ten minutes to come up with a complete list, as she took frequent pauses to think hard.

"But how are you gonna get into town? There's no taxi here."

"I'll walk to the bridge and take the bus from there. I can get a cab on the way back, since I'll have to bring things back."

"Have a safe trip, then. And tell her to come visit us with the kids soon. We miss Eun Gyul, too, I want to see her! Maybe it's because I attended her birth, but I've grown quite attached to her."

I left the house and walked between orchards down the road. Today the tea salon seemed quiet. I had noticed that it got a little busy during the weekends but was mostly empty the rest of the week. It was before noon, but the Korean barbecue restaurant was already playing loud music. There were only three or four restaurants, but they made Kalmae looked like a big town with their ridiculously flashy signs.

I had wanted to go into the Soonchun lady's house and make the phone call right then, but I decided to wait because I hadn't decided how to start the conversation yet. Moreover, I did not want others to listen to that conversation. Imagining her voice over the phone, my heart began racing. Eun Gyul was almost eighteen years old, the same number of years as my imprisonment. If I had heard of her birthdays, her going to school and making friends while in prison, would it have been easier for me to endure?

Looking at the other inmates I met there, I knew that there were positives and negatives to having a family outside, as with everything in life.

You get to see the pictures of your children once in a while, and children grow up like bamboo. I do not know how it is for the family, but I think it would be another form of deprivation for the prisoner. A child whose father is taken away may consider himself tragic, but for me he is a picture of the father's past happiness. Looking at the photo of the child, I imagine the father taking that picture, or hiding somewhere out of frame, even if it was taken after his imprisonment. Through the picture of the child, the father is arrested in the happier past. But then, that child grows up, and appears as a teenager in another picture. We see already in his face that life is bitter. It may be just a shadow at the beginning, but soon he becomes a young man, and we can clearly see imprints of worldly anguish on his forehead. In many cases, a longtimer's face seems purer than those of his family going through the vicissitudes of life.

I saw many inmates suffering because of the absence of their family. I heard many of them crying in the middle of the night, no matter how hard they tried to stifle the sound. In the morning the prisoner might appear perfectly fine, but I would see him ceaselessly pacing around the courtyard during the exercise hour, pausing once in a while to look up and stare at the empty blue sky. If I had known that Eun Gyul existed in this world, I would have suffered agony once in a while, but I also would have felt unbelievably lucky. You cannot fear the moments when your heart is turbulent. Isn't life supposed to be like that anyway?

The neighboring town seemed even bigger than when I had seen it a few days before. There were tall apartment buildings everywhere, and downtown was full of automobiles. There were many cafés standing right next to each other or across from one another in small alleyways. I tried to imagine what the interiors would be like from their signs, hoping to find a quiet and accommodating place. One was called the Paradise Café. The old-fashioned name and the ancient Japanese-style double-story building made me think that maybe this one had been here for a long time. Then I realized it was the café Yoon Hee and I had gone into once to take a break from our shopping excursion. I took a steep staircase to the second floor. The creaking wooden steps were now carpeted, and I could not tell if the old steps were still there underneath. As I pushed the door open and walked in, I knew it was the same place. By the entrance I saw a makeshift barrier made out of a sheet of plywood that obstructed my view of the interior, but there was the familiar door to the restrooms. The round window just next to the restroom was also still there. Before, there had been a little console table and a pot with a bonsai tree on top of it. I remembered thinking then that the old Chinese juniper tree seemed too elegant to be placed right next to the restroom. And from the small window near the washstand, I could see the courtyard of a small, old-fashioned house with a gabled roof. I stood there by the entrance for a while, looking around, but no one came out to greet me. Was it still open? I took a seat in the center and lit a cigarette. On the inner wall of the kitchen was a set of sliding doors, and I guessed there was a room for the staff behind it. I cleared my throat to let them know that someone was here, and a woman appeared.

"Oh, I'm sorry I kept you waiting."

She was a plump lady in her forties, with a warm countenance that made her look like someone who should be working at a casual restaurant making bowl after bowl of rice and broth, not selling coffees and teas.

"I would like to order something to drink."

She did not even come out of the kitchen, just stood there.

"What would you like?"

"Well . . ."

I wondered if I should order something more expensive if I was going to ask her to use her phone. And I remembered that older men always ordered tea with medicinal herbs. I should treat the hostess, too.

"How about a cup of the medicinal herbal tea? And you should have one, too."

"No, I'm fine, thanks." Then she burst out laughing. "What is happening today? I guess you're quite old-fashioned."

"Why?"

"You're so generous to offer me a cup of tea."

"No one buys you a cup of tea these days?"

She laughed again.

"No one really comes here anymore, they order for delivery. For teas and coffees and girls . . ."*

---

* Many cafés or teahouses in the rural area (called Da Bang) double as brothels. Such practice became prevalent in the eighties.

It was my habit to keep my mouth shut when I really could not understand what was being said, so I remained silent. The medicinal herbal tea was almost a meal, the thick liquid mixed with egg yolk and dates and peanuts and sesame seeds. The woman answered the phone.

"Sorry, where? They already left for the co-op. Just wait a few more minutes, okay?"

The phone rang again.

"The Hajung village? Inner valley or the outer valley? Right, toward the inner valley . . . and on the field. Then our girl will pass by on a motorcycle, so you should call out to her to stop."

She diligently wrote the order down with the phone wedged between her ear and shoulder. Two young woman entered the café, followed by a young man wearing a motorcycle helmet. The older woman spoke to the younger ones.

"An urgent phone call from the co-op people asking when you're coming."

One of the girls, wearing a miniskirt that barely covered her bottom, a pair of long boots up to her knees, and long fake eyelashes, answered with no sense of urgency, "That's not us. We're just coming back from the real estate agency."

As she spoke, she stole a few glances in my direction, studying me. Soon she lost interest and took a seat by the high bar stool in front of the kitchen, her legs crossed. The other young woman remained by the entrance, looking in the mirror and playing with her hair. She wore a pair of leggings that clung tight to her legs and a baggy shirt over a tighter one that showed deep cleavage. The older woman ignored her.

"Young man, do you know the Hajung village?"

"Where the mill used to be?"

"Yeah, that's right. There are people working on the field toward inner valley. Seven cups of coffee."

She handed over a tray with a thermos and mugs wrapped in cloth.

"I think we really need a car," he grumbled.

"Listen, girls, one of you go with him. Take the backseat of the motorcycle."

"The road over there is not paved, it's gonna rattle a lot."

The older woman turned to the one sitting by the kitchen, "Hurry up and go, you'll be back in no time."

"No, I'm wearing a mini! I can't ride the motorcycle."

"Then you go," she said to the other one. "She should go to the Go club."*

"Well, I'm also going to wear a miniskirt tomorrow! This is such bull-shit."

They carried on bickering and grumbling as they left again, each girl carrying a tray wrapped in a pink cloth. Before I asked her to use the phone, I wanted to start a conversation.

"Your business is doing well."

"We manage to break even somehow."

"Bet you are making a lot of money."

"It's the owner who's making all the money. Me and the girls, we just get paid monthly. No, that's not correct. I get no tips, so I am worse off than them. The owner has three places like this, but all he does is collect money at the end of the day."

"There are so many cafés around here."

"A development boom! They're building apartments and factories . . ."

"Would you mind if I use your phone please?"

"Long distance?"

"Yes, I want to call someone in Seoul."

She agreed more easily than I expected her to.

"I'll give you some coins and we can add those to your bill."

She opened the cash register and took out a handful of change.

"It's one row of hundreds, so a thousand won. If you don't use them all, just give the rest back to me. See the public phone over there?"

I took the coins from her, walked over to the phone, and stood in front of it. I had used one a few times near my sister's house, but it was still unfamiliar. I breathed in and out a few times and looked at the piece of paper with the phone number, then began to dial. The coin dropped, and I heard a voice, "Doctor's office."

I was worried that I would get disconnected.

"Dr. . . . Dr. Han Jung Hee . . . please," I mumbled, adding a few more coins into the slot.

"May I ask who's calling, please?"

All of a sudden, I did not know what to say. I hesitated for a while.

"Hello? May I ask who's calling, please?"

---

* An establishment for men where they can play the game of Go.

I knew if I remained silent too long, the phone would be disconnected.

"This . . . This is Oh calling."

"One moment, please."

The voice disappeared and instead I heard music. It seemed to take a long time, as if they were having a sinister discussion behind the music. Then there was a different woman's voice, a little similar to Yoon Hee's.

"Hello."

"Is this Dr. Han Jung Hee?"

"Yes, this is she . . ."

The voice paused. I paused, too. She continued after she took a deep breath, loud enough for me to hear from the other side of the phone.

"You said Mr. Oh . . . are you Mr. Oh Hyun Woo?"

"Yes . . ."

I was at a loss for words again.

"I have never met you," she said calmly. "But I did read in the newspaper that you were released. My sister has passed away. Three years ago . . . cancer."

"I know."

"Ah, then you received the letters. I sent them to your sister's school around that time."

"I read them after I got out."

"That was about two weeks ago, wasn't it?"

"Yes, about that."

"And where are you staying now?"

"I'm in Kalmae."

She was silent. I had a feeling that she was covering up the receiver with her hand. Anxious, this time I called after her, "Hello? Hello?"

"Yes, so you're in Kalmae. I didn't go there for a while after my sister was gone, but finally Eun Gyul and I spent some time there last winter."

"Eun Gyul?"

Finally, we had reached the point I really wanted us to get to, and to talk about.

"I guess you know it all by now. She's seventeen, in twelfth grade."

"I see. I would like to stop by when I'm back in Seoul in a few days," I added as casually as possible.

"Sure. However . . . our daughter is preparing for her college entrance exams these days, and it's is more important than ever that she remains stable and calm."

I was at a loss for words again. I had no idea what to say. If the road is blocked, there is no need to drive straight through and collide with the barriers. There must be a way around them.

"I just wanted . . . to hear about Miss Han, and . . . her."

"Call us when you're back in town."

"Yes, well, thank you."

We exchanged goodbyes, and the phone call was over. I wanted to avoid the woman in the café, so I walked to the restroom instead of returning to my table. I glanced down through the small, round window. From here, all I could see was a part of the roof, neat rows of black gables, not the courtyard. I walked into the restroom. There should be a couple of stalls. Standing in front of the urinal, I saw the window opposite me, just as it had been before. And there was the courtyard. Under the March sunlight, washed clothes were drying. Under the shadow of the gabled roof was a row of pots full of plants and flowers, and on the other side of the courtyard was an orderly garden with a Chinese juniper tree, rhododendrons, and camellia trees in a neat row. I cannot remember what it had looked like before; the trees must had been younger then. But I do remember what Yoon Hee said merrily as she came back from the restroom. She said she saw a garden that looked very familiar. That there were four o'clocks and moss roses and cockscombs and morning glories. That the house's main porch seemed to be the perfect place to sit on a rainy day to eat scallion pancakes and drink rice wine. To spend quiet, ordinary days when nothing really happens.

I left the café and walked toward the marketplace. I went shopping, not at the market, but at the brand new supermarket, where I bought items on the Soonchun lady's list. I ate lunch and bought groceries for myself, too. It took me about ten minutes to return to Kalmae in a taxicab. I got out in front of Todam, where there was enough open space for the car to turn around, and walked up to the main house. The Soonchun lady saw me from the kitchen and ran out to help me with the plastic bags I was carrying in both hands.

"She just called!"

"Someone called me?"

"The sister. What's her name? Jung Hee."

"What did she say?"

"Well, let's see . . . She just asked if you were doing well here, if you were healthy and all that. She said she'll call back with Eun Gyul when she goes home. She wanted me to get you when she calls back."

"I see."

When I returned home, I did not bother putting things away in cupboards and in the refrigerator, I just lay down on the floor. Perhaps, I thought, she had gone over our conversation after we hung up and thought that I was in control of myself. I had no ill feeling toward her; in fact, I was relieved. Maybe she had decided to filter the inevitable shock through several layers. I had no intention of telling the child that I was her father. But I wanted to chat with her, about nothing and everything, and I wanted to see if there was a trace of Yoon Hee in her voice and manner of speaking. I cooked dinner for myself and ate it, and waited until half past seven before I went down to the main house. The Soonchun lady was waiting for me in the living room. She had brought out the phone already.

"They just called, and they want you to call back. Hurry!"

I took the piece of paper from my shirt pocket and repeated Jung Hee's home phone number to myself before I dialed. I heard the phone ringing, followed by Jung Hee answering it.

"This is Oh Hyun Woo."

"We were waiting for you. I've been thinking about a lot of things since you called me this afternoon. I was thinking of my sister, too. I don't think she was ever going to tell you about Eun Gyul. Maybe she had a premonition that you two would never see each other again in this world. I should tell you that we adopted Eun Gyul in . . . It was a year before my sister left for Germany, so it was '87. She had to start school the following year. Of course, she's all grown up now, and she knows who her birth mother is. But she calls us mom and dad, not aunt and uncle. And I am so sorry to do this to you, but there's something you need to understand."

Jung Hee paused and waited. I pressed her to go on.

"Please, tell me."

"Neither my sister nor me and my husband have ever told her about her birth father. At first, when she was younger, we told her that he was in America, and in the last few years, that he had passed away. After I talked to you, I was trying to think what my sister would have done in a situation like this. Now that you're out, I think we have to tell her the truth. But I think we'll need some time."

I decided to interrupt her there.

"I do believe you're right. She'll be an adult soon."

"She sure will be. Once she goes to college and into the larger world, it can happen more naturally, don't you think? I was talking to her just a little while ago. I told her that you were a friend of her birth parents who wanted to talk to her."

My heart was racing again.

"No, I just called to find out how she was doing."

"I already told her that you'd be calling tonight, so she's waiting. She's upstairs in her room, so I'll have to go get her. I am so sorry to make the whole thing so complicated and long-winded, but we love her so much. And I know you do, too, even more than we do. Please, don't hang up, wait for her. I'll go get her right now."

There was the sound of the receiver being placed somewhere, followed by a faint electronic sound. I put the receiver to the other ear and then switched it back to the first one, the voice still echoing.

"Hello? Mr. Oh?"

"Yes, I'm here."

"Here she is."

"Hello?"

That is her voice. My mind was blank, and I just repeated back like a recorder.

"Hello."

"How do you do? I'm Park Eun Gyul. My mom told me about you."

"Ah, did she? I am a friend of your father. I knew your mom, too. So you're in twelfth grade now?"

"Yes."

"It must be tough for you right now. What do you want to study when you go to college?"

"Something in the liberal arts. I'm not sure yet."

"And how's studying? Are you doing well?"

"It's alright, I guess. I heard that you spent many years abroad."

"Um, yes."

"In what country?"

"I, I immigrated to America."

"My father passed away in America. Since you were his friend, you saw him often in America?"

"Yes, I did."

"What . . . what was he like?"

"Nice, a very nice man. A little naïve."

"When are you coming back to Seoul? I heard that you were in the countryside."

"Yes, I am, but I'll be back in a few days."

"Call us when you are back. I'd really love to meet you."

"I promise I'll call. I want to meet you, too, Eun Gyul."

"Goodbye. Here's my mom."

Eun Gyul's voice was cheerful, and it went up a little at the end of each sentence. She sounded very positive and self-possessed for a girl who grew up without her birth parents. Jung Hee's calm voice returned.

"Thank you so much for calling. When you're back in Seoul, just call my office."

I mumbled some words of gratitude and farewell, too, and the phone call was over. I remained in the living room for a while, my head empty. The Soonchun lady came out of her bedroom, wiping her eyes with her sleeve. "My goodness, you can be so coldhearted. How can you be so collected while talking to her? I tried hard not to eavesdrop, but I couldn't help but hear you talk. I bet she knew who you were, she's so smart, she has always been since she was a little girl. Why didn't you just tell her, Mr. Oh? Why didn't you just say that you're her father?" I just smiled a little and looked up to the dark, empty space above. Before she could mention Eun Gyul again, I got up and bid her farewell. "Thanks for letting me use the phone."

"That's nothing . . . Are you going back already?"

"Yes, I'm a little tired."

I walked back on the little dirt path toward the house. It was dark, but I was used to it. The door was bright, lit from behind by the fluorescent light I had left on. From outside, the lattice work on the door appeared more clearly. It seemed like someone was in there, about to open the door and come out saying, *You're back!* I took off my shoes and climbed up to the porch, then opened the door and confirmed that no one was inside. Instead of going inside, I collapsed on the porch and watched the embroidered springtime night sky. A shooting star fell. Maybe someone just passed away. A lonely dog was barking from far away. Even if you are alive somewhere, the absence of the other person who used to be there beside you obliterates your presence. Everything in the room, even the stars in the sky, can disappear in a second, changing one scene for another, just like in a dream.

21

I think it was sometime in the autumn of 1985 when, for about a year, they began to allow long-term political prisoners a couple of days of furlough, or what they called "visitations." As oppression turned into appeasement in the outside world, the regime's effort to "convert" political prisoners also changed, from brute force to more conciliatory tactics. During the 1970s, many political prisoners died because of the endless torture; many of those who survived the torment committed suicide. They began to "convert" me as soon as I was transferred to the prison. They sent me to the torture cell for weeks after weeks for no reason, and I had to eat like a dog. Two different departments within the prison bureaucracy—education and security—competed to produce the most converts. They pestered us continuously. It didn't matter if we had broken the National Security Laws or the Laws of Public Assembly, or been involved in the fabricated espionage cases; they wanted to change what we thought, our ideology.

There was a machine to see inside the human body, so why couldn't they come up with a machine to see through the brain and mind as well, to easily identify whether we were red or blue? I myself was not really sure if I was red or blue.

My crime was that I was opposed to the killing of innocent civilians by a military government that had seized power by force and enjoyed the support of an industrialist monopoly that attached itself to the dictatorship in exchange for privileges and spoils. After what happened in Kwangju in May 1980, how General Chun Doo Hwan's soldiers opened fire on the demonstration against his new regime, we learned who was on our side and who was on the other. Our eyes were opened, and we realized our enemy was not the North. Certain writings were brought in from foreign countries at the beginning of the eighties, things that during the sixties could have landed you on death row simply for possessing them, and we read them in secret, holding our breath. Was my friend Choi Dong Woo on the Left since he collected these kinds of papers and reproduced some of their content in our own papers? As I stayed in prison, the outside world changed, and all of this became unremarkable and commonplace. Things do balance themselves out. *See? It really wasn't such a big deal.*

"Listen," I said. "How many times have I told you? I am not an agent from the North; you know that better than anyone."

"It's just a piece of paper, that's all. All you need to do is sign it, and everything will change in an instant."

"It's only a piece of paper! Then why do you want me to sign it so badly? I never followed their ideology, so how am I supposed to turn from that to this? Or, do you want me to admit that I am a Communist? Do you want me to certify the political maneuvering and the violent oppression of this dictatorship?"

When they realized that they could not achieve much on their own, they began to use people from outside. They brought in members of our families to beg us to sign, people who had not been allowed in for visitation for a long time. When that failed, they used the violent criminals to torment us. Then it was the turn of volunteers from religious organizations who wanted to "help" us, bringing armloads of food and writing long letters to us. It seemed they wrote to us political prisoners every other day. Letters from our families were limited to just a few hundred words and were confiscated after three days. Mostly the volunteers' letters were about their religion, asking us to change our minds. Fortunately, I did not have to suffer through it too long.

Shortly after our uniform was changed from short sleeves to long—it must have been the beginning of October—the chief of the prison's education department stopped by my cell with a couple of dissident university students and said we were going to be allowed a special visitation. No matter who it was, a visitation usually meant food.

It had been a hard summer. The mosquitoes and flies and hellish steam from the cement walls were gone, and we could hear crickets at night. A breeze would come in through the meal slot and escape through the high window over the toilet; it tickled my whole body as it passed. We were always hungry and would borrow cookbooks from the guards so we could "eat out," and fishing and hiking magazines let us "go on a trip."

"Okay, who has the special issue on the Solak Mountains?"

"I'm still reading it."

"I want it back, now!"

"Hold on, I haven't even reached Hankaeryung yet."

"Bastard, when are you going to reach the mountains? Stop hanging around the outer valley."

A special visitation during such a season made our mouths water, and we all wondered what they brought us this time.

One of my neighbors, in for forming an illegal organization, said he had a visitation coming up later in the month and had seen Christian women with bags of food. "I hope they have some sticky rice cake," he whispered to me. His face was covered in scabs and he hadn't been able to shave. He rubbed at the stubble.

"You're not supposed to have any special visitation, are you?" said my other neighbor, the president of the student union. "I bet they're trying to get you to sign something."

"Let's not argue with them if they give us a sermon, okay?" said the first.

"Just stuff your mouth and belly as much as you can."

"There is no free ride in this world. We should at least argue a little, shouldn't we? You'll see; this is just the beginning."

A section chief of the education department, who called himself "the Professor," had me brought to his office. He appeared affable enough on the surface, but was cunningly determined to advance his career. He was an entry-level officer who had climbed up the ladder and had no plans to go back.

"I had many younger siblings, my father was sick and bedridden, my mother supported all of us by peddling on the street, and I dared not dream of going to high school," he would begin. "In those days, if you finished middle school and knew a little about the law, you passed the exam and became a civil servant. We're the real people, not you guys. You guys were so full of it and so spoiled that you didn't study as you were told and ran around protesting this and that. To be honest, I really resent you guys.

"During the Revitalizing Reform period, we suffered a lot, too, did you know that? There was no heating in the corridors, no desks, no chairs, nothing. We had to do the night shift standing up the whole time. Walking around the cell block freezing to death, we'd look into your rooms, you know I actually envied you guys. At least you got to sleep under a blanket! Sometimes I just wanted to go in there and lie down next to one of you. We were afraid we'd break our noses by falling asleep while standing up and falling down on our faces, so what we came up with was a hook. You bend a wire into an S-shape and attach it to your belt and go to work. When you get sleepy, you could just hook yourself to the corridor, lean on it, standing up of course, and go to sleep. If you hear the boss's footstep, you get up, take off the hook, and walk around.

"And then I met people working here in the education department, and I really envied them. They got to wear civilian clothes instead of uniforms, no night shift, no inspection, and they got to meet civilians from outside, too. And what can be more patriotic than purifying Commies? Before, they used to say, an ideology for an ideology, and the education department preferred Christians. So you know what I did? I went to the seminary at night. And I took that qualifying exam, too. Did you know that I'm in graduate school now? And that I teach at the school, too? I've read a lot about the other side, too, so don't even think about bullshitting in front of me, understood?"

The Professor called me into his office, which was located right next to the waiting room.

The two section chiefs shared a room, and connected to it was the office of the department chief, whose position in the prison hierarchy was only second to that of the warden. "Mr. Oh, can we talk for a minute?" The Professor asked me to sit down in an easy chair next to his desk.

"You should have something to drink, since you came all the way here," he said, feigning kindheartedness. "What would you like? Hey, come over here, what can we serve to Mr. Oh?"

The prison assistant, who was most likely a convicted thief, quickly came over to us.

"We have all different kinds of drinks here at the Education Department Café. As for traditional teas we have green tea, ginseng tea, citron tea, goldenseal tea, and adlai tea. We also have coffee, English breakfast tea, and various other beverages including Coca-Cola, Sprite, and energy drinks . . ."

"Stop, stop, stop. Are you nuts? How come there are so many choices?"

"Most of them are donated. Some are supplied by the purchasing department."

The Professor seemed satisfied with the explanation. "Well, what would you like? How about a cup of coffee? I bet you haven't had that in a while."

"Sounds good to me," I said.

"Hey, make sure you get the biggest mug and fill it to the brim, do you understand?"

The Professor bent down toward me secretively. "Mr. Oh, I need to ask you for a favor today. I want you to listen really carefully, okay? A very famous minister is visiting us today, and I've specifically recommended you."

I knew exactly what he was talking about. "You mean one of those educational lectures, right? So you can report to those higher up that you've done something, that you've observed my attitude, and things like that. Isn't it just a waste of time?"

"Oh, come on! What can I do? They keep sending me notices that we should carry out the fall program and report back as soon as it is over."

He had included the dissident students. "They can write an essay afterward."

"I don't think they'll write what you want to hear."

"Doesn't matter, we can always edit and rewrite. That's not the issue.

I just want to ask you one thing, and that is, please, at least pretend that you're listening when the minister talks, alright?"

"For nothing?" I joked.

"Hey, we know better than that. We've prepared a buffet, of course. And above all, the reason why this program is so important is that— don't tell anyone else—there are evaluations going on right now, and some lucky National Security Law offenders may get a furlough."

After my interview with the Professor was over, the two students were called into his office as well. We were taken to the Special Visitation Room, which was furnished with comfortable armchairs and a large conference table covered with food: heaps of fried and glazed chicken, various rice cakes, and yes, the sticky rice cake with bean flour that my neighbor had craved, and refreshments. An old man was waiting for us, and he greeted us with a raised hand.

"Welcome!"

The Professor introduced us to "the most venerable Reverend So and So" and made us bow to him. We were each introduced by name, the crime we had committed, whether it was against the National Security Law, the Law of Assembly, or some other law, our sentence, and how many years we had left to serve. It did not seem to matter to him that there was a total of three of us in there. The Professor stood up, clasped his hands, and attempted an official opening address.

"Well, it is my great honor to welcome you to the fall lecture series. Our speaker today, Reverend Kang, began his work in the purifying operation for Communists during the postwar period, and he has served with distinction for many years. He has turned many, many National Security Law offenders toward humanism. He has taught so many bloodless, cruel Communists to repent and to regret, and shaped them into good citizens. He is a true patriot, and . . ."

The preacher interrupted him. "Listen, listen, that's enough. They must be hungry, so why don't we let them eat first? This is not a lecture, I think a discussion with open minds would be much better, don't you think?"

"Of course, of course. Well, I should leave you to it. I hope everything goes well."

Then the Professor turned to the two students and threatened them,

"Don't you dare be disrespectful. Listen to the reverend, do you understand?"

As soon as the Professor left, the tall one quickly picked up a piece of rice cake, threw it into his mouth and chewed. The president of the student union punched the tall one's arm, but the reverend did not seem to mind too much.

"Don't worry, that's fine. But why don't we say a little prayer before we begin? Now, let us pray."

He gathered his hands and bowed his head down. The two students stayed seated, but did not otherwise acknowledge his praying. I did not want to appear too insolent, so I put my head down but kept my eyes open. The reverend seemed to be quite experienced with such situations, and he chose not to notice.

"Dear God, the Almighty Father, we're gathered here today, with the food you've blessed us with, to ascertain the value of the family that you've given us. These men in their youthful ardor once fell under the spell of Satan, but they have realized their mistakes and they are ready to repent. It was not their fault; they were misled by Satan, so please guide them back to the righteous path. As they eat this food today, please let them realize how much their families miss them, that the still empty spaces at their dinner tables are daily reminders to their families of their absence. Let them each realize the grace of their country and family, and realize also that they will be born again as your faithful children."

He added a few words and said "Amen" by himself. Only then did he open his eyes and look around at us. We remained silent, and the reverend raised both his hands and offered, "Please, help yourselves. We're not a rich church, so I know this may not be enough, but we did prepare it with our hearts."

Before the reverend stopped talking, the two students were on the chicken. I joined them and picked up a chicken leg. I could not remember the last time I had eaten chicken, and my stomach was so eager that the meat slid down my throat before I could chew. The chicken had been fried, glazed with a spicy garlic sauce, and roasted. The two students were already reaching for their second piece, and I glanced at the reverend who was looking down at an open Bible with a pair of thick reading glasses perched on his nose. In minutes, the chicken was gone and only a few bones were left on the plate. As we began to attack the mound of rice cake, the reverend began to speak.

"Why don't we talk as we enjoy our food? Mr. Oh, you've been sentenced to life. What do you think of religion?"

I thought about it for a bit and then mumbled, a little self-mockingly, my mouth filled with sticky rice cake, "Now? I am grateful."

"What do you mean by that?"

"You brought all this wonderful food."

"You were born in the South, correct?"

"Yes."

"Then how and where did you learn about Communism?"

I smiled as I replied, "I know nothing about that."

The president of the student union, who was also chewing on a mouthful of sticky rice cake, added in a cheerful voice, "Don't you know, minister? It's all fabricated!"

"Then isn't it even easier? All you need to say is that you changed your mind; they'll let you go home right away."

"Let us go?" The student was incredulous. "That's a lie. It's like they are hitting someone first and then asking him to admit to the reason why he was hit."

"You also broke the National Security Law, correct? No matter what, it is not right to divide public opinion when the puppet state in the North is watching for every opportunity to start the war again."

The tall student joined in. "The bloody dictatorship, by killing innocent civilians, divided public opinion. They should be in here, not us."

The table was empty of food. The reverend began to tell the familiar story of hardship and oppression in the North, but the president of the student union interrupted him.

"Stop talking about what's going on in someone else's house. I told you, we don't know anything about them. We would willingly curse them, too, but we know nothing about them. We should find out more about them before we do."

I could see where this was going and interrupted: "Reverend, maybe there will be a chance for me to go to your church and pray as one of the believers. Thank you so much for this wonderful food. I think we should all go back to our cells now and read the Bible. Why don't you say a closing prayer now?"

This kind of visitation happened a couple of times a month. The young ones who stubbornly talked back at the first meetings eventually resigned themselves to the routine and learned to pretend to listen to the lecture while stuffing their faces nonstop.

Furlough was a big deal. None of the real Communists ever stood a chance of seeing outside the prison, but those with family outside or deemed as possible converts were sent outside, one by one. Escorted by prison guards in plainclothes, they took a train or bus and visited cities far away, where they ate the food their family had prepared and had a chance to talk to them in private. They'd spend the night in a jailhouse nearby and come back. It took two, maybe three days, but it took a long time to forget the warm homemade meals and the equally warm laughter of their families. When someone returned from furlough, we all hung onto the viewing window and asked questions as quietly as possible, always aware of the footsteps of the guard on duty down the corridor.

That autumn many prisoners' sentences were reduced, and the dreamy experience of a furlough was too strong a temptation for all of us. Even the guards in charge of our cell block tolerated all the communication among prisoners, and they sometimes looked out for us by standing at the end of the corridor to make sure no one else was coming.

"Mr. Yi, where did you go?"

"We left here and took the express bus."

"Is the bus station far from here?"

"No, just across the bridge, right outside of the town. It doesn't take long at all, maybe five minutes."

We all paused for a moment. I could see it in my mind. If you take a car and go through the gate, and drive on the road lined with poplar trees and cross the bridge, there's the bus station.

"Were you still wearing your prison uniform and handcuffs and ropes?"

Someone butted in from another cell, "What are you talking about? They give you normal clothes and a baseball cap for the furlough. You can't tell something's off unless you looked really close."

"They gave me a jacket, too!" said prisoner Yi.

"I guess they'd feel a bit ashamed, too, if everyone knew . . ."

"Anyway, the express bus is just like it used to be, right?"

"It was my first time," Yi said. "We didn't have that in the fifties."

"Did you eat lunch at the rest stop?"

"Yeah, beef soup and what is it, this fried hot dog thing on a stick."

"A corn dog! And then?"

"We got off in Seoul first. My home is in Kwangwon province, actually."

"It's still the same, isn't it?"

"I wouldn't know. All I know in Seoul is the central station and the Great South Gate. Anyway, there were so many people, I thought something was happening. There were more than I've seen in pictures. We were waiting for our train in this big area, and maybe all people do these days is take train trips, but there were just so many of them walking back and forth."

He tells us how he sits down by the window in a train. The river flows on the right, and there are high mountain tops and forests. Once in a while, the train passes through an unfamiliar village. The high-rise apartments are like empty castles in a daydream. The guard is sitting next to him dozing, and every time he leans over the tip of his gun brushes against Yi's ribs. The other guard, who is sort of a team leader, keeps blabbering. "Look around, isn't this a great place to live? It's all up to you. Your wife is waiting for you. Your children are big enough to grow old with you. Didn't you see in the picture? You have five grandchildren!"

They get off in a rural area, and as they leave the station house he recognizes the landscape. The small village looks just like it used to, maybe a few buildings and roads have changed just a little. The point where three streets meet, where the mill used to be, looks the same, and so does the village's civic office building, built during the Japanese occupation with plywood boards covered in cement. He sees people running toward him. An old woman wearing dark baggy pants with flower prints and a faded short-sleeved T-shirt gives him a bear hug.

"My dear . . ." she says and begins to cry.

Reflexively, he hugs his wife's shoulder. Beneath his chin, he sees her white hair gently swaying in the wind. On one side of them is a farmer in his forties, his face tanned dark; he stinks of cigarettes. On the other side is a middle-aged woman.

"Father!" they say.

The guard in a suit takes them away, and the team leader grabs his arm and moves with him, too.

"Let's hurry and get you home before anyone else sees you," says the one in the suit, while the team leader shows him the paperwork to reinforce the conditions of furlough. As he walks into the house, he notices the rotting floorboards and the ripped paper on the sliding doors. It was all much worse than the houses he saw from the train. High up on the living room wall is a frame filled with yellowed and faded photographs, including one of him wearing the uniform from the last years of the Japanese occupation. He is squinting in the sun. His young wife is wearing a white cotton top, her hair in a bun secured with a stick. Next to her is a boy wearing a school uniform, and on her lap is an infant. He realizes time has stopped only for him.

Mr. Yi's voice trembled as he told the story of his furlough. It had happened so recently that he could not quite figure out the sequence. Someone helped to stir up his memory.

"You already told us about the lunch you had with your family at a Chinese restaurant before you left."

"Yes, that's right. It is an old place called San Dong Ru, although the owner was different."

His mind slips back to the long-gone past. The story he tells now is about the first time he ate noodles with black bean sauce when he followed his father into the village on a market day. It is a story he has repeated many times during exercise hours. No matter how recent, everything a prisoner experiences is like a fluttering dream. Memories can be perfected only when he is free. The story is that he swallowed the whole bowl of noodles as if drinking a bowl of soup, in one breath, and sat there still wanting more, and his father put his own noodles onto the young boy's bowl.

When the story is over, each of us returns to the tiny window by the toilet in our cells and stands there. It is the spot where you feel to your bones that you are alone. There is a faint white moon in the early evening sky, a handful of stars. You hear something from the faraway corner of the sky where the red sunset still remains. A flock of birds takes flight, just like they did yesterday. You picture the tall trees on the river bank over which the birds will fly.

About ten days after the reverend's visit, I got a chance to visit the outside. The weather was getting colder every day, and the old-timers had already received thick comforters from the laundry department. The filling was synthetic, which meant that it rolled into little balls over the years so there were lots of empty pockets, which did little to protect the sleeper from cold air. The experienced inmates asked for permission to use a larger cell when it was empty during the day as its occupant went to work. There they spread the comforters out on the floor, found the little balls inside the covers, and spread each one of them. Once every ball was rolled out, they could mend various parts of the comforter. Some sewed together two blankets to make a big sleeping bag. Some asked the concession worker to save cardboard boxes and lined the floor with them. The cardboard was often wet by morning from the damp concrete. Old woolen socks were used as sleeping hats. Uncovered ears and noses got so cold they would wake the sleeper. And if you tried to read for too long in your cell, your hands would go numb and couldn't hold onto the book. Mittens were only good for exercise hour. So we'd stick two pairs of the cotton gloves issued to working inmates, one inside the other. The approach of winter was a busy time for the inmates.

I was in the middle of my various preparations for the coming winter when I was summoned by the chief of the education department. The office was very warm; there was a gas stove in the middle of the room. The Professor was waiting for me. He offered me a cup of hot tea.

"Mr. Oh, you were selected for a couple of days of furlough. I just want you to know that it was I who recommended you strongly."

"I guess I should say thank you."

"There is one condition. You need to sign an agreement before you go, and you have to write a report when you come back."

It seemed so bothersome, and I felt helpless, so I just mumbled back, "Well, then forget about it."

"Oh, come on, you may never have a chance to go out again! I already wrote out the agreement, all you need to do is write your name and stamp it with your fingertip."

He showed me a typed paper. I was supposed to pledge that I would abide by the rules both inside and out of prison and that I was aware of the punishment if I would break such rules; things like that. I took the pen the Professor handed to me and wrote down my number and my name, which looked unfamiliar once I put them down on the paper.

Then I put red ink on the tip of my thumb and stamped the paper with my fingerprint. I felt like I had done something I should not have, so I kept rubbing my thumb even after I took off the red ink with a piece of tissue. The Professor gestured for me to follow him.

The chief of the education department was a fat man in his fifties with drooping eyelids that made it look at if he was always sleepy. His voice was thin and sounded tired, but his gaze under those thick eyelids was still piercing. The Professor presented the agreement to the chief with both hands.

"This is the inmate selected for the short furlough," he said.

The chief glanced at the piece of paper for one second, uninterested.

"I must say, you've been a model prisoner, and . . . we still cherish the hope that you will develop a better, more proper ideology regarding our country, and I think you'll realize what you need to do once you see how much our country has changed, how developed it is. Therefore, Number Fourteen Forty-Four, I look forward to reading a great report when you come back. Do you understand?"

"I don't know . . . This is so unexpected . . ." I was feeling truly overwhelmed.

"So, is he the only one going out?" the chief asked the Professor.

"Yes, the others did not meet the requirements."

The chief nodded. "For how long?"

"He'll leave tomorrow morning at nine and stay one night. In total, thirty-two hours."

"What? He gets to sleep outside?"

"Well, a home visit lasts for three days. His is not getting a full one, but Number Fourteen Forty-Four is from Seoul, so the schedule had to be set that way."

"Wow, the warden has given you a special permission. Now I am really looking forward to a good result when you come back."

It still did not seem real as I walked out of the office. Tomorrow, I would be in Seoul, near my home. My heart was beating fast, and I felt dizzy. As we walked back to my cell block I mouthed the slogans decorating the bare walls. *You do not know what life is until you eat your bread with tears. Do not follow, take the lead. What did I do for my family today? Mother, your son will be born again.*

"Can I go visit my family?" I asked the Professor as he escorted me back.

"It's not a visit to your home," he said. "Think of it as a field trip to society."

Then he did add, as if he felt quite generous, "But you never know, it all depends on your behavior. Maybe there will be a special visit or something like that."

As soon as I walked into my cell, I heard inmates all around me talking and asking questions.

"Mr. Oh, I heard you're going out! Congratulations!"

"So you're staying the night, too?"

"Where are they taking you?"

The guard in charge of the cell block must have known before I did and had told the other inmates after I left my cell, so the news was already out. Somehow I felt sorry for the others, and I was careful not to seem too enthusiastic.

"I don't know, I think it's just for one day. I bet they'll just circle around the neighborhood a few times and bring me back here."

"They didn't tell you what the schedule is?"

"Well, I do know that I'm leaving tomorrow morning, but apart from that . . ."

Since I did not appear to be too excited, the others were soon deflated, and disappeared back into their cells, away from the viewing windows. I lay on my mattress, arms crossed. It was not some imaginary trip with a map, nor was it a memory trip to the past; it was real, my body and spirit together leaving this place. I did not know then that this was another form of torture.

The old-timers say that there is a turning point between the third and fourth year into your sentence. After the fifth year, things get easier, and the next crisis comes around the tenth year. But with time, the gap between each crisis gets wider, until the prison becomes home. Like the slogan on the corridor said, "You are reborn as someone else."

Only once before had I been allowed to go outside. I had a terrible ear infection that the infirmary couldn't handle and I had to go to a big hospital in the city to see an ear, nose, and throat specialist. I had been having a cold wash in my cell, pouring water on my head, and some of it got in my ear; whenever I tapped my head, it sounded like there was a wooden gong inside. I should have known better and let the water come out on its own, but it was still there after an hour so I poked around in my ear with a stick, which made everything worse. The next morning, I had a fever, my cheek was swollen, and it was very painful. At first it was bearable, but soon I was begging to be taken to the infirmary, where they applied some antiseptic and gave me a few antibiotic pills. After two nightmarish nights, they finally sent me to the hospital.

Before we left for the hospital, I was strip-searched and given a gray uniform, denoting that I was a prisoner being transported, and a pair of open-backed rubber shoes. My wrists were handcuffed and my arms bound with rope so I couldn't move them. One of my two guards, now dressed in civilian clothes, held the end of the rope that trailed behind me like a tail. I was given lunch before we left. I would not be allowed to eat outside. Without their caps and badges, the guards looked like my old neighbors.

A jeep was already waiting for us at the front gate with its engine running. I got in the back with the lower-ranked guard holding the rope. The senior guard took the passenger seat next to the driver. The gate had been opened and we drove out. The guard next to me took out two sticks of chewing gum, unwrapped one and put it in his mouth. He unwrapped the second and put it in front of my mouth, which I opened so he could put it inside. I was getting a taste of freedom, and it was spearmint.

We crossed a bridge. It was in the middle of summer, the rainy season, and the muddy river had risen close to the top of the levee. It was a cloudy day, but no longer raining. I studied the new car models and their occupants; I regarded them intently on purpose so that they might turn around and look back. No one did. They talked to each other and laughed, or they stared straight ahead. The only person to meet my eyes was an old man waiting for the light to change at a pedestrian crossing. Our jeep had stopped. When our eyes met, he quickly turned his head, but he could not resist too long, and turned toward me again. His gaze was intense. The light changed, and the jeep moved on. The old man hadn't moved.

"Stop here," the higher-ranking guard ordered the driver. "There's no parking space in front of the hospital. It'll be harder to park there."

"Isn't it far from here?" the other guard asked.

"Not really. About a hundred yards, tops." the higher-ranking one answered, opening the car door.

The guard next to me wound the rope a few times around his hand and pushed me in the back. "Get out."

Since I could not use my arms, it was a struggle not to fall, and the other guard stood by the door to help me. Once out, one guard stood right next to me while the other followed from behind, tightly holding the rope. I looked around at the shops and restaurants as we walked down, and I soon noticed the large glass entrance to the hospital. A young woman pulling a child by his wrist came out of a jewelry store. He was crying. Abruptly we were facing each other squarely on the sidewalk. The child stopped crying immediately when he saw me. His mother watched me, too. I heard my backless rubber shoes slapping the ground. I had to walk with slow, tiny steps so that they would not slip off. The child shook his mother's arm.

"Mommy, what is he?" I heard him say.

The woman did not answer her child, just grabbed his hand and walked fast to pass us. I could not resist turning back. They were standing there, next to each other, watching me. I smiled at them, the woman grabbed the child's wrist again and hurried in the opposite direction.

In the waiting room at the hospital, a row of chairs and a large sofa in the shape of a square with one side missing faced the receptionist's window. I was directed to sit in the innermost part of the sofa, as the senior guard went to find the assigned doctor. The occupants of each of the chairs pretended not to notice us; likewise those sharing the sofa. Our section had plenty of seating, but no one joined us, preferring to stand, facing straight ahead, faces devoid of expression. Two teenage girls came into the hospital loudly talking to each other and, oblivious, walked toward the sofa. About four of five steps away they stopped talking and exchanged looks of "What's this?" "Come on, let's go sit somewhere else."

I told myself I was not a criminal. All I did was oppose the dictatorship. I refused to cooperate. But there are no markings on the gray uniform. I could have been anyone. Even Number One-Four-Four-Four sounds like a stranger to me. I am not here. No one sees me. I have been erased.

Now I am going outside again. For what? To reassure myself of my absence? They are verifying the way back for me, they want me to practice.

"Let's change your clothes before we go, shall we?" said the higher-ranking guard. The lower-ranking guard handed me a folded pile.

"I just got these from the laundry department, but I don't know if they fit. Number One-Four—I mean, Mr. Oh Hyun Woo, I think the medium is too small, so, large?"

The dark gray top and pants had lots of pockets. It was called a Saemaul uniform, an outfit that became popular during the New Community Movement of the 1970s, led by President Park Jung Hee. Many bureaucrats wore it as a kind of uniform, like the Chinese wore the Mao suits.

"Here's a hat for you."

On top of a desk was a cap in a similar shade of gray with the word "Saemaul"—the New Community—embroidered on it. There was a belt, a pair of sneakers, and cash, too.

"It's 30,000 won from your deposit," the senior guard said. "You keep it. Now, shall we go?"

Like the time I went to the hospital, there was a jeep waiting for us. This time, there were three guards to escort me, all of them in plainclothes—two in suits and one in a windbreaker. The jeep took us across the bridge to the new bus station that Mr. Yi had told us about. When the leader of my escort spoke to me, his voice was different from the one he used inside the prison.

"Mr. Oh, it's been a while since you last took the bus, isn't it?"

"Are we taking the bus all the way to Seoul?"

"That's the most convenient for us, it's nonstop."

One of the lower-ranking guards, the one in the windbreaker, took out the bus tickets from the inner pocket and checked the time. "We have about ten minutes left."

We hadn't drawn any attention at the bus station and I sat down near a television; the guards sat a little bit away from me. The television was showing a professional baseball game. I didn't watch the players, but instead the people filling up the stadium, wondering if, by any chance, I might recognize one of them. The fans were cheering; the ball flew, they got up from their seats, and they cheered some more.

"You wanna taste this?"

The leader held out an ice cream cone. I had eaten ice cream before, of course, but somehow it looked so unfamiliar that I just held it for a while, looking at it trying to think what I should do with it. *That's right, I need to take off the wrapping first.* As I tore off the wrapping paper in a spiral pattern, the ice cream cone studded with cookie crumbs appeared. Sometimes, the taste of food can be so sharp. It touched a part of my brain that made me remember the first time I tasted ice cream. Like Mr. Yi's noodles with black bean sauce. My mom bought one for me on a sports day at school. The ice cream man strolled around carrying a container filled with ice that had a smaller spinning container in it, and he kept yelling "Sweet, cool ice cream cones!" After sucking out every drop of ice cream, kids would sneak up to other unsuspecting kids and stick wet pieces of the cone onto their backs.

Maybe it was because I ate something cold, or maybe because I was nervous about traveling, I needed to pee.

"Can I go to the restroom?"

"Number one or number two?" The leader didn't wait for a reply. "Escort him to the restroom, both of you."

The two guards got up, frowning, looking nervous.

"Walk," the windbreaker said.

I slowly walked toward the restroom, avoiding the crowd in the waiting area. Uneasy, the windbreaker walked right behind me.

"Watch out, Mr. Oh Hyun Woo, I am armed," he said, walking quickly.

I went into the restroom. One of them stood behind by the door to guard it while the windbreaker followed me and stood at the urinal right next to mine. He opened up his jacket and showed me what was around his waist.

"See this?"

The other inmates called it the chicken head, and the gun was hanging heavy in a leather case. We were two faces talking to each other in a mirror. "I don't really want to do this, but I don't want you to do anything stupid," the face said.

I smiled without saying anything. Afterward, I walked back through the crowd, concentrating on finding the place I had been sitting before, as if I was going back to my prison cell.

When we finally boarded the bus, they pushed me to the very back.

"What, we have to sit at the back of the bus, too?" the windbreaker complained.

This is the best spot for us," said the leader.

"I get car sick. It'll shake too much back here."

As soon as he said that I started to feel sick to my stomach, like I was car sick, too. The bright sun of the clear autumn day made me dizzy, but above all I was exhausted from being among so many people.

The bus is moving. There is new road after new road, and finally we go onto the Seoul-Busan Expressway that I am familiar with. I see the red and blue roofs of farmhouses and the faraway hills that I missed, now appearing with a purple hue and hovering in the sky. The field has been harvested already, and cut rice plants are tied and lined up around the field like soldiers on parade. A forest dotted with orange-colored persimmons flies by the window like a picture fluttering in the wind. Even a magpie, something I see all the time in prison, seems freer here as I watch it fly away into the distance. Like a scene from a movie, I want to jump out of the bus and disappear into the purple shadow of the rolling distant hills. The three men are sleeping. Only the leader opens his eyes a little from time to time, whenever he feels the bus slowing down a little, looks around to figure out where we are and takes a quick look at me, then he closes his eyes again and falls back asleep. I cannot sleep. I am absorbing the landscape all at once. When I get back, I'm going to feast on these pictures compressed into my brain and my heart, nibble on these stored nutrients little by little.

I am back in Seoul. I can feel it from a long way off. The open fields disappear, replaced by crowded little buildings that look like blemishes or wounds covering the roadside and rising up the hills. All the cars seem to be headed in one direction. It is not a cloudy day, but there is something hazy hanging in the air. I no longer see flying birds.

Women are walking around on the streets. From her calf and the hem of her skirt to her hip, from her hair to the high heels on her feet, a young woman is freedom. Especially when you look at her from afar. I see a young man slowly pacing in front of a building; he has a cigarette in his mouth and is wearing a shirt without a jacket. A small crowd waits at a bus stop. This is the world from which I was kicked out. Without knowing if I will ever return. I can only participate from behind the glass window of a moving bus.

I remembered Nam Soo's grumbling about Seoul. It was at the very beginning of his underground days, and he did not know the city at all. I was one of the people assisting and guiding him until he got settled, and I had to keep an eye on him day and night. The first few days went by with us talking and exchanging news of other friends, but within a week we had run out of things to talk about. One day, I had to run errands without him, so I took him to a small movie theater close to the place where we were staying. I estimated it would take me about three hours to return.

"Go in there and catch a couple of movies in a row," I told Nam Soo, pointing at the theater. "By the time you're done, I'll be waiting for you out here."

Nam Soo, grinning as he usually did, scanned the posters and promotional pictures hanging next to the box office. "There's a Chinese war movie and a romantic comedy. Today's cultural event combines both the literary and the military!"

Life in Seoul was always hectic. Once you turned around you forgot what had happened only ten minutes before, and thought only of the present right in front of your eyes. It took me more than four hours to finish my errands and, when I got out of the bus and walked toward where we were supposed to meet, it was already dark, and the street was crowded with people going home from work. The movie theater was still a distance away, but I stopped walking and glowered. There was Nam Soo, sitting alone on the steps leading up to a pair of large glass doors, staring into space. I felt sorry, but I was also annoyed at the pathetic figure he made, so I got mad at him as I approached.

"Why are you sitting here? Do you know what time it is now?"

"Well, I finished the movie with fighting and kicking, but I left the one with kissing and hugging and crying as soon as it started, so I guess I've been sitting here for a couple of hours."

"Look, the motel where we're staying is close to here, and you know that I would have gone there if I hadn't seen you here."

"I don't know how to get there."

"Oh, come on, try a little. Look, that street right over there? That's the street you walk up and down every day. You just go up the street, and then you'll see the red neon sign for the motel."

I did not like that he was sitting right in front of the movie theater where everyone could see him, so I continued to gripe. "What if you were seen by those who are looking for you? You know it is not just about your own safety."

Nam Soo grumbled nervously as he followed me, walking quickly. "Seoul is too complicated, I'll never figure it out. There is no east or west or north or south."

I remained unsympathetic and annoyed. "They say an activist should know the city. I'm not just talking about the geography. There's something in that complicated mess."

Still behind me, Nam Soo mumbled as if he was talking to himself, "Fuck that . . . I don't need to know it, we'll just forget it later."

The bus arrives at my station, and other passengers grab their bags and carry-ons from the shelf above, but we remain motionless at the very back of the bus. When most of the passengers are off, the leader walks down the narrow aisle first. I follow him, with the two guards closely behind me. I am too anxious to even take one step without the escorting guards holding the rope. It has been a long time since I had to navigate such a large space with so many paths all by myself. At the bus station, in the crowded area inside the station building, I keep losing my sense of direction and have to pause.

"What's wrong?" the guard in a suit asks from behind.

The windbreaker gently pushes me. "Do you see the chief over there? Do you see the back of his head? Just follow that, okay?"

Among the waves of people coming and going I find the closely cropped head of the leader and run after it.

"Just imagine that this is no different from the inside," the suit says. "Then it'll be much easier."

I do not reply, but I agree with him. It is true; I have returned to a larger prison. As we leave the bus station we find ourselves in the middle of a gigantic city. The leader is standing there waiting for us, and as we gather around him he checks his watch and says, "Let's see . . . It's time for lunch already. What should we do?"

"What do you mean? We should just follow the schedule."

"The schedule . . . Here, I have it."

The leader reads his pocketbook. "Today's schedule is as follows: lunch, visit the old palace, go to a movie, and then a department store, and that's all. What would you like to do first?"

I can't quite remember what places he just listed. On the bus from the detention center to the court house, every suspect fights to sit by the window, to look through the meshed windows and see if they recognize any street that passes by. But no matter how hard you look with your head sticking to the window, nothing sticks in your brain. What you are looking at is a place you have already left, a place where you cannot be anymore.

"I don't know, I can't think of any place I'd like to go first."

My answer is indecisive, so the windbreaker says to the leader, "I don't think we can visit all these places today. Let's eat first, and then we'll figure out what to do depending on how much time we have left."

The leader starts walking ahead of us, having made the decision. "Let's take a cab."

We wait in line like any other good, ordinary citizens, and we get into a taxi cab when it is our turn. The leader takes the seat next to the driver.

"The Dan Sung movie theater, please."

Then he turns his head back to tell us, "I checked the movie schedule already. After all, there's nothing like a Hong Kong martial arts movie to pass time, don't you think? We can eat after we get tickets."

The streets in Chongro are as jam-packed with people and cars as ever, but I am much more used to walking now than I was at the bus station. The suit gets the movie tickets and tells us that we have about an hour before it starts.

"What do you say, how about some grilled beef for lunch?"

The leader looks around the street, where the two big movie theaters face each other. "Let's see if we can find a decent restaurant around here," he says. "I think it'll be easier to find one on the other side of the street."

They lead me across the large avenue. It is lunchtime, and the restaurant is pretty crowded. The truth is, I was eyeing an old Chinese restaurant next to a fire station and craving noodles with black bean sauce, but the moment I heard the word "beef" I easily gave up that idea. What is strange is that whether you are in prison, or in the military, you never fantasize about really fancy, expensive food, maybe because the gap between your imagination and the reality is too big. When "eating out" while reading a cookbook, you skip the pages with elaborate dishes made by chefs, but linger on the ones you ate all the time at home. I used to think of large meat dumplings, each the size of a man's fist, served at a dark Chinese restaurant with dirty tables. Sometimes you found a piece of pork fat, the hair still attached to the skin, among the vegetable filling. Or I'd desperately crave the noodles with black bean sauce. I could almost hear the chef banging and kneading the dough to pull the noodles, and I could smell the pork and vegetables and the sauce being cooked in a wok engulfed in tall flames. Whenever the inmates talked about food during the exercise hour, they inevitably ended up comparing the noodles with black bean sauce from their own favorite restaurants, boasting that each one of them knew the place where they served the best bowl of noodles. I once saw two young criminals in a fist fight that left them both with bloody noses, because they couldn't agree which dish tasted better—sweet-and-sour pork or stir-fried noodles. But why had I never thought of grilled beef?

The four of us walk down the hallway, take off our shoes and sit around a low table in a large room. As the marinated meat cooks away on a small grill on the table, the windbreaker uses a pair of chopsticks to place a few pieces of it on my plate.

"Well, well, this prisoner's life ain't so bad, is it?"

The leader gives him a look, frowning.

"Stop the bullshit. Help yourself, Mr. Oh, eat as much as you want. We eat this all the time."

I put a piece of meat in my mouth and chew. The texture is so tender, and my mouth is soon filled with the flavors of garlic and honey and soy sauce. It has been a while since I have tasted any seasoning. The kimchi at the prison looks red, but it is never spicy, just salty.

"It's much better outside, isn't it?" the suit mumbles.

My eyes are burning, and I bend my head down because I do not want them to notice anything. When I put my chopsticks down on the table, the leader asks, "What's wrong? It doesn't taste good to you?"

"No . . . It's just . . . a little . . . spicy."

"I guess so; you haven't had food like this in a long time. By the way, you should have something to drink, too. What do you like, soju or beer?"

"Beer?"

He orders it. Cold bottles are brought to the table, and a glass with the white foam up to the brim is placed in front of me.

"Well, congratulations!"

The windbreaker raises the glass to me. Confused, the suit raises the glass and asks, "What? What are we celebrating?"

"Congratulations on your release! Well, let's call this a rehearsal."

After a few glasses of beer, my face is enflamed and throbbing. And I finally relax. I almost think for a moment that I am, indeed, released.

In the darkened movie theater, I feel like I am spending a holiday with friends. For a Buddhist monk or a soldier, or for any young man who does not have a regular job, the movie theater is the only point of contact with the rest of the world. What you are watching may be a story from a different world or a scene from a foreign place, but you are participating in what others are also seeing and feeling and remembering. The newspaper is not as vivid an experience, but I still remember the shock, which remained for months, when newspapers and magazines were allowed again after a long time. The world was thriving without me, as if nothing had happened.

It is still bright outside when the movie is over, about half past three in the afternoon. My eyes are blinded by the autumn sun's dazzling rays. All the colors on the street, people's clothes, everything is so vivid, it looks like there is a festival going on. People push past me, indifferent.

"Look, we don't have too much time," the leader says. "Can you think of some place else to go besides a department store?"

The suit asks me, "How about a marketplace?"

"The market? That'd be too tricky to escort, no?" says the windbreaker, looking at the leader.

"Yeah, but the Great East Gate market is nearby. We can just walk around there, I guess."

I am just standing here, at the intersection, listening to their blabber. Since I remain silent, they take my silence as agreement and head toward the marketplace. While walking, I become convinced that it is actually a good idea to visit the market. There are four of us, so the leader and I walk in front while the suit and the windbreaker follow us. We wander around the market place, zigzagging through the numerous stalls and vendors, "Choose one, only 1,000 won for a T-shirt!" "5,000 won for a pair of pants!" "Come on, take a look! It's practically free!" "Down parkas, bonded goods!" "Watch out, heavy load, out of my way!"

The noise at the marketplace sounds like little children chattering behind a glass window at the end of a room. Only the voice of the leader rings clearly, sometimes loud, sometimes soft, as my ears are slowly unclogged.

"Mr. Oh, don't you wanna buy something? Go ahead, you have money from your deposits, remember?"

Ah, that's right. I finger the three 10,000-won bills folded in half in my pocket. I keep one hand in my pants pocket while I look around.

"But you should know you can only get what is allowed inside," he says, "or it'll be confiscated when you go back."

Only then do I remember my friends left behind. I stand in front of a stall selling underwear. During the exercise hours we wear boxer shorts, but the officially distributed ones are always white and easily stained. On cold winter days, the prison fashion is to put on boxer shorts over thick thermal underwear, as if we were imitating real boxers. Although it does not really look like we are walking outside wearing only underwear, we cannot help but laugh at each other, pointing out each other's odd appearance. I pick out some large-size boxer shorts, with stripes or dots, and long-sleeved cotton T-shirts to wear under the prison uniform. Only four colors are allowed—gray, navy blue, white, and black. No printed letters or elaborate patterns. I spend 30,000 won. I pay with my own hand.

"Well, the day has come to an uneventful end," the leader says as he looks at his watch.

"Let's go, hurry!" the suit adds.

"I'm not staying there tonight," the windbreaker says.

"Where do you think you're going?" the leader asks. "You're still on the job until we go back."

"What? We have to sleep there, too?"

"What's wrong with it? We shouldn't spend all our traveling expenses. But I guess it'll be okay to have a drink after we check him in."

"Are we going somewhere else?" I ask him, finally.

"Didn't you know? According to the rule, you have to spend the night in a prison. But I can tell you now, you should look forward to tomorrow."

"Aren't we going back tomorrow?"

"We just need to be back before the lockdown."

The group grabs a taxicab again, and once settled in the passenger seat, the leader tells the driver, "We're headed to Anyang."

The taxi driver quickly glances back at us through the back mirror. "Where in Anyang?" he asks.

"The prison. We're escorting a prisoner, so push on that gas pedal, will ya? Don't worry about the traffic."

Sitting in between the two guards in the backseat, I remember the night I was sent to the detention cell. It was the middle of the night and raining. I remember the cool metal of the handcuffs tight around my wrists, too tight. We get out in front of the prison gate and walk in through a small door. As we walk into the other side of bleached-white walls, I smell cooked rice. A speaker blares the sound of a trumpet, announcing the end of the daily schedule.

"We made it just in time," says windbreaker.

We walk past another wall to reach the main building. Things are busy, hectic. The shift is changing, some guards getting ready to go home. We wait like peddlers among the bustling uniforms. The leader appears with a section chief, who is holding onto paperwork and studies me up and down. He asks to the leader, "Did you feed him dinner?'

"We didn't have time. Can we order him something from the staff cafeteria?"

"Sure, not a problem. Take him to the visitation room, he can eat there first and then you can lock him up."

He assigns me a new guard.

"I bet you're tired," the leader says. "So go eat your dinner and rest. And I'm telling you, we have a surprise for you tomorrow."

The windbreaker and the suit remain seated, but they raise a hand as I leave. I follow the new guard to the second floor and reach the special visitation room furnished with a single coffee table and a couple of couches. The young guard does not say anything to me. The only time he asks me something is after he calls the cafeteria to order my dinner.

"So what, a home visit?" he asks.

"No," I say, "just a field trip."

While I eat my dinner of soup with cabbage and rice, he stands in the corner holding a small tape recorder, and an earphone in one ear. It seems he is learning a foreign language, because he keeps quietly repeating a few words. When I am done with dinner, he makes me walk in front of him, directing me with curt orders, like I am a bull being driven into his pen. "Forward!" "Left!" "Right!" "Turn!" "Stop!" "Attention!"

I am taken to a special cell where prisoners spend the last few days of their sentences before being released. It is a large room with a heated floor, and the walls are not bare, but covered with wallpaper, although the pattern is tacky. The floor is already quite warm, so they must have been heating this room for a while. The young guard pushes me in and slams the door. It looks just like any other cell door. He bolts and locks it and shouts to the guard stationed midway along the corridor, "One additional prisoner for the night!"

It is still a prison cell, but I feel like I have traveled far. This cell is so unfamiliar that I actually miss my little cement cell. I lie down under a blanket and stare at the ceiling. The mildew is different, so are the images I see. There is a lot of writing on the walls: dates of release for the prisoners before me, quick notes on their thoughts and feelings. They are written all over the walls in tiny handwriting. Did they want to leave behind some evidence of human existence in here?

"My darling Sook, I'm coming to you tomorrow."

"Thirteen years of bloody tears."

"To my late father, your son is finally coming home."

"Park Kap Joon, screw you! You're my enemy until the end."

"It is all gone, my youth."

"My fellow brothers, do not ever commit a crime. This place is a trash can for human beings."

"Money is the problem. Have no money, then guilty."

Deep sea divers need to decompress as they emerge from the ocean so their bodies adjust to changing pressures. And in an old myth, there is a river of oblivion between this world and the next; one forgets everything by crossing. Most inmates spend two or three days in this cell. It is still

in the prison, but there's one more wall that confines the general popu-
lation. Here, the inmate is halfway out, and within a few days he begins to
forget all about what happened inside. Once released and sent home, he
faces a new reality, yet soon finds that he is still naturally connected to
his own past—and prison becomes just a gap in his memory. However,
he is mistaken if he thinks that nothing has changed. The world is like
flowing water and it has moved on, while he thinks that he has landed in
the same spot, that he is soaking his feet in the same water as before.

I do not sleep well, maybe because I am not sleeping in my own cell.
Just like at any other prison, the daily activities begin as soon as the sun
is up. The guards have changed, but the same young man opens my cell
door. I walk the same corridors as I did the day before and go to the visitation room. The leader and the windbreaker are not there; only the suit
is waiting for me.

"Did you eat breakfast?"

"Yes, they already served it."

"The chief will be here soon. Guess who's coming to see you."

I have been thinking that someone is coming for a special visit. The
suit continues in a whisper, "If only you wrote down something, then
you could have gone home, too. It's not a home visit, so a special family
visitation during the field trip is a privilege among privileges."

"Family?"

As I say this, the leader, still wearing the same clothes as yesterday,
walks in with another guard from this prison. All of a sudden, he uses a
polite form of speech.

"Mr. Oh Hyun Woo, your sister is here to see you," he announces in a
dignified manner.

Behind them, the door is tentatively opened, and my sister's face
appears in the widening gap. Then I see the familiar hat my brother-in-
law always wears because he is bald. Dumbfounded, I get up from the
chair. "What are you two doing here?"

My sister grabs both my hands and shakes them, and her eyes behind
her glasses are already turning red.

"Please, take a seat," the local guard says. "Since this is a special visitation, you have plenty of time. So take your time, enjoy."

The leader signals to the other guards from my prison and takes a place on a folding chair in a corner while the suit leaves the room. My sister is carrying two large shopping bags.

"Those bags were inspected at the front?" the leader asks.

"Yes, don't worry. It's all food."

My sister looks as if she still cannot believe that she is facing me directly, without an iron grill or an acrylic panel to separate us. They came to see me last spring, so it has been more than six months since the last time we saw each other. A prison assistant brings us drinks on a tray and leaves after placing them on the table. I really don't know what to say. Nor do my sister or her husband. The leader, sitting there with a visitation record book in his hand, waits with a pen held in midair.

My sister breaks the silence. "I heard that you looked around the city yesterday."

I nod. My brother-in-law opens his mouth, too. "We got the word just yesterday morning, out of the blue, and your sister was not able to sleep at all last night."

"I am so sorry. I'm always such a burden to you."

"Just take care of yourself . . ." she says, "and join us soon."

She opens the shopping bags.

"I made a few dishes for you. And you need to get ready for the winter. I deposited two sweaters and two pairs of thin thermal underwear, just like you wanted, and a few pairs of thick socks."

The leader chimes in from behind, as this is one thing he is sure of.

"We have them. When we go back, we'll register them and hand them over to you."

My sister takes out dish after foil-wrapped dish, spreads them out on the table, and peels each of them open.

"Look at this. Rice rolls, just like Mom used to make."

I know them well. All of us went to school picnics and festivals with those rice rolls. Whenever she made them, we surrounded her and fought each other for the chance to nibble on the ends, where the filling stuck out. We all knew her recipe by heart. First, you lightly toast and brush some sesame oil onto the dried seaweed sheet. Spread the rice on it, making sure it is not too sticky, and arrange the fillings. The filling is the key. Minced meat is stir-fried with sweet and salty seasonings, spinach is blanched and dressed, the old-fashioned pickled radish is sliced long and thin, eggs are whisked and cooked into thin sheets on a hot pan. If even one thing is missing, the rice roll won't taste good and that is the end of it. My mother used a bamboo mat to roll all of them into a round log shape and, with a knife rubbed with sesame oil, slices the roll into pieces of precisely the same thickness.

After the rice rolls comes beef cooked Seoul-style with the meat pounded before being seasoned and cooked on a charcoal grill. Then braised short ribs and various dishes of vegetables and mushrooms, sautéed and seasoned. There are tiny fried oysters and meatballs, pears and persimmons, which are in season, and a dessert drink with fermented rice in a thermos.

The taste of the rice roll reminds me of the house we lived in, the one in Youngdeungpo built by the Japanese with many built-in closets and an indoor bathroom. Only then it occurs to me ask them about my mother.

"How's Mom?"

My sister is looking down at the table and does not raise her head. No one says a thing. The last time my mother saw me was more than eighteen months ago, and that was through an acrylic panel.

"Come on . . . eat," my sister says, her eyes redder than before.

"You told me she was not healthy, but it's not a big deal, is it?"

"So-so. Please, eat some more," she says reluctantly.

I stuff my mouth with rice rolls. Fortunately, I had no appetite for my prison breakfast after the previous day's splendid meal in the city. Now I was ravenous. I cannot remember what we talk about for those hours. I just remember eating until I can't swallow one more bite. I am so full, I can't breathe, and I think even my throat is filled up with food. When it is time for them to leave, the leader allows me to accompany them down the steps. My sister grabs my hands again to say farewell.

"Be strong. Outside, they're making a huge fuss that we're hosting the Summer Olympics and the Asian Games and all that. Who knows? Maybe things will change when these things happen."

"Don't worry, I'm actually doing well."

It is my brother-in-law's turn, and the usually reserved man of few words mumbles, fingering the brim of his hat without putting it on, "The thing is . . . I have something to tell you . . . Hyun Woo, the truth is, your mother passed away. It happened last September, and . . ."

My sister, who had turned away, now pours out the information. "She had cancer of the vertebrae. Last winter, she fell down when she slipped on snow and could not get up after that. The doctors said there was nothing they could do and so she came home, but she only lived for another six months. We took care of her funeral."

I stare at them both blankly.

"Did she say anything?"

My sister is now smiling.

"She made us promise that we'd marry you off. Well, we should get going now. Please, take care of yourself."

As they walk across the courtyard toward the front gate, the leader says, "We should get ready to leave, too."

In the afternoon, we board the bus heading south. It is windy, and the sky is an angry-looking gray. I can summon no emotion. The leader asks how I feel after the furlough, and I answer without hesitation, "The day before you go on a trip is always more exciting, isn't it?"

I do not think he understands what I am talking about, but I have always been like that, ever since I was a child. There is no special day, everything is unexciting and ordinary. Only right before it happens is there a little flutter in my heart. Whether it was a school field trip or New Year's Day or my own birthday, nothing seems too special when it happens. After spending a summer Sunday at the riverside, having fun fishing and swimming, what I thought about at the end of the day was the next day, Monday, a rainy day that I would have had to spend at school. After a field trip there are exams at school, and after New Year's Day or my birthday are many more colorless days that are all a little spoilt like left-over food. I know that this short trip will become a long-lasting wound. This memory will be an ache in my body and heart on rainy days.

22

That fall, in the middle of October to be precise, Jung Hee got married. Her husband-to-be was Dr. Park, of course, who had finished his military service as an army surgeon. The day she told me about the wedding, I met her at a café near the university hospital where she worked. Dr. Park had returned to the university to finish his medical degree, and he was working at the same hospital. I arrived on time, but she was already there waiting for me.

"What is going on today? You're not too busy?" I said.

"He doesn't have to perform surgery today, which is unusual. He told me to wait for him here."

Jung Hee looked very different. Before, there were always little lines of exhaustion around her eyes. She usually wore comfortable pants, and she didn't think twice about leaving the hospital in wrinkled and stained scrubs. But these days Jung Hee was blooming. At twenty-six years old she was not a young girl anymore, but she could still pass for a first-year college student. Her face was rounder than mine and she appeared more feminine than me. I looked at her eyes and lips and guessed that she had applied a fresh layer of makeup before she came to meet me. My hair was in a messy ponytail and I was wearing a pair of jeans spotted with

paint and a thin cardigan, but Jung Hee was wearing a black dress acces-
sorized with a necklace and earrings.

"Look at you! I think I'm going to just go home after our drink."

"What are you talking about? Dr. Park said he's treating us to dinner."

"I don't know, I feel like I'm intruding on you two."

"To be honest . . . we have something to tell you."

I was preparing for my solo exhibition. If I did not keep myself busy,
I knew I was going to either blow up or collapse. Eun Gyul had grown
up enough to say things that adults could actually understand.

"We're getting married," Jung Hee blurted it out.

"Of course you should," I replied matter-of-factly. "He's done with his
military service and now he has a job. Did you tell Mom?"

"Mom is the one who first suggested it. We met his parents last
month and set the date."

"What? So all the decisions are made and now you tell me. I'm the last
one to know? When is this happening?"

"The sixteenth."

"That's just two weeks away."

"Sorry. I'm sorry that I'm doing it first."

I had to snicker as I lit a cigarette.

"There's nothing to be sorry about. As I told you before, I'm used
goods. Anyway, congratulations."

"Mom wanted me to tell you."

For whatever reason, people close to me were being cautious and
uneasy, and it caught me off-guard. I thought I would be fine, but I was
actually feeling a little hurt.

"Mom can be quite old-fashioned sometimes," I grumbled.

Jung Hee picked up her teacup and drank the warm liquid, carefully
puckering her lips so as not to leave a trace of her lipstick on the cup.

"Yoon Hee, after the wedding I want you to move back in."

"Hmm, should I?"

"You can't leave Mom and Eun Gyul by themselves."

"She'll be five next spring. We should send her to preschool."

"You can spend your days at school and in your studio, but you should
at least have dinner with them at night."

I sincerely tried to picture such a scene in my mind.

"It makes sense. I'll talk to Mom."

Jung Hee continued, "I think I've spent more time with Eun Gyul than you have. You have no idea how much I care about her."

"That spoiled little brat!"

It came out of my mouth without me realizing. Jung Hee seemed to be taken aback.

"What, are you jealous?"

"No . . . She is just as stubborn as her father. How should I say it, I think I'm a little frustrated."

I thought of what had happened when I went to see her the week before. I arrived there around dinnertime, and when I walked in the maid had already left, and my mother was watching television by herself in the living room. When she saw me, she put her index finger on her lips and said, *Shhh.* As I asked *Why?* without making a sound, I noticed that the volume of television was also lowered to that of a whisper.

"Eun Gyul is asleep."

"Already? I told her on the phone that I was coming to see her."

"She went out with Jung Hee in the afternoon."

I had not seen her in a while, but Eun Gyul was sleeping peacefully, as if that did not matter to her. I went into her bedroom to see her sleeping face, and I found her curled up on her side with the blanket kicked away. I kissed her cheek and was walking out when I tripped on something on the floor. It made a rattling sound. It was a little ball made out of a soft material. It had come with a baby dress Jung Hee bought when Eun Gyul was about three months old. I think it was imported from Japan. There was a little bell inside, so it made a noise when shaken. Ever since, Eun Gyul had to have the ball all the time. She fingered it while she took her bottle, she needed it when she was falling asleep. She was almost five, but she still played with it even though it was really worn out and had been mended several times. The cotton filling poked out here and there, and I thought, *How hideous, I should get her a new one.* Without thinking too much, I picked it up and threw it into the trash can. I slept at my mother's that night and was woken up by an uproar in the living room the next morning. Eun Gyul was screaming and crying. I walked out, still in my pajamas.

"Eun Gyul, look! Mommy's here."

She did not even look at me, she just kept kicking and screaming on the floor, "No! I don't want Mommy! I want my friend!"

My mother was trying to calm her down.

"I saw it when she went to bed last night, so where is it?" she muttered.

"What are you looking for?"

"Ugh, I don't know what else I can do. She just can't live without that ball!"

I quickly ran to the trash can by the foyer and found the ball.

"I once threw it away, too, and I had to pay for it. I guess she's really attached to it," my mother said.

Eun Gyul put the ball next to her cheek and rubbed her face on it.

"I hate Mommy," she shot at me.

My eyes filled with tears.

"We're here." Jung Hee waved, and Dr. Park strode across the café to get to our table. He was a tall, charming looking guy. Before he sat down, he bowed to me with great courtesy.

"I haven't seen you in a while. Hope all is well?"

"Well, not everything's well, I have to say," I replied curtly, and he seemed confused.

"I just told her," Jung Hee said.

"About . . . what?"

"That we set the date."

He pretended that he was shocked. "What do you mean? You haven't told her until now?"

"Oh, please, I know you two are in this together."

I looked at them out of the corner of my eye, as if I was really angry.

"Let's see how you treat me tonight, and then I'll decide to either forgive you or to ruin everything."

"Gee, I guess we're in big trouble."

That night, I ate and drank my fill with the couple and went back to my studio, alone, and I thought of Eun Gyul again. Well, it's all my fault, isn't it? I was her mother in name only. Have I ever remembered her birthday? Have I ever bought her something she liked? And when was the last time I slept next to her? I cannot remember. I did feel guilty, but that was it. I was scared to see my own daughter because it was so heart-breaking and frustrating. I was always by myself.

Two days before Jung Hee's wedding, I finally got my suit from the dry cleaners and went to my mother's house, still wearing paint-covered jeans and a sweater. The house was wrapped in joyous commotion. Various aunts and cousins and children were there, all overexcited and running about. I looked for Eun Gyul, but she was busy running from one room to the next. I smiled and said hello to some relatives, none of it heartfelt, and I escaped to Eun Gyul's room, locked the door, and smoked a cigarette. A new dress was hanging from the head of her bed. I picked it up to study it, front and back. It was a beautiful white dress embroidered with white roses and trimmed with lace around the neck, at the cuffs of the sleeves, and on the hem of the skirt. The skirt would almost reach the ground when she wore it. And there also was a small bouquet of silk flowers, the right size to fit perfectly into a small child's hands.

It's like she's the one getting married! I was uncomfortable and cranky, but I had to stop when two things came to my mind. The first thing was the wedding of a friend of mine who had been living with her boyfriend and their children for a long time, who finally decided to hold a wedding ceremony just because she did not want to regret not having one later. Both children were girls, three and five at the time. The bride in her mid-thirties still looked beautiful in her wedding dress and professionally applied makeup. It was quite unconventional at the time to see the couple enter together, hand in hand, led by their two little girls. The second thought that came to mind was a scene from the wedding of Eun Gyul, all grown up. In a flash, I gathered myself. I remembered once again giving birth to her in Kalmae with the help of the Soonchun lady. No one had predicted it, no one had desperately wanted it, but I could not erase it either. Eun Gyul's birth was an unexpected surprise. In life, there are so many unexpected surprises.

I remember Jung Hee's wedding with a few photos. I did not frame the family picture. I just put it up in the studio by the desk with a push pin on the wall. Jung Hee's head is slightly bent toward her groom, as if she is about to lean on him. I guess the photographer told her to pose like that. Maybe the photographer also touched up just the bride and groom in the darkroom, because other than the couple of the day, everyone else looks a little dull and unattractive. Only Eun Gyul, looking so alert standing in front of the couple and holding the bouquet, appears to be as brilliant as the bride and groom. In the background, in the farthest corner, is me, looking like a teller in a small country bank, tilting my head and looking over at something. I can't remember what I was looking at.

Until the summer of 1986, I kept busy preparing for my solo exhibition and writing a qualifying paper for my MFA. If I wanted to find a job somewhere, even if it was an instructor position at a small college outside of Seoul, I had to work hard. After Jung Hee's wedding, I moved back into my mother's house. As Jung Hee predicted, the three of us were able to live peacefully together, each leading her own life. My mother now owned a good-sized building in a busy marketplace where she ran a textile manufacturing and distribution business, and her daily life was not as tiring as it used to be when she went to work at the break of dawn and came home around bedtime. Now she left the house in the early afternoon and came back before dinner. Eun Gyul was still only four, but she seemed to be precocious and smart, so we decided to send her to a preschool. She spent her mornings there, and we took turns picking her up around noon, my mother or our maid or me. In between, I went to school or locked myself in the studio.

At school I observed from afar what was happening with the activists who were, as you might say, dealing with ideological conflicts. Like most educated and concerned citizens, I could not stomach their neatly itemized slogans. Whether the issue was antifascism and autonomy, or democratization and constitutional amendments, these were, after all, basic principles. So why couldn't they be more flexible? Throughout the first half of 1986, not one day went by without demonstrations and protests. I particularly remember the large-scale demonstration in Inchon, flooded with slogans and flags.

On a hot, humid day during the summer vacation, I was working in my studio. Eun Gyul had gone to the beach with Jung Hee and her husband, and my mother was visiting a Buddhist temple in the mountains with her friends. After a few days in the empty house with our maid, during which I did not talk much to her, I decided to return to my studio. At the time, I was becoming interested in wood prints, especially those in the style developed by the circle of people influenced by the Chinese writer Lu Xun, and I was sticking to simple lines and shapes. As I burrowed into the velvety surface of the woodblock, the studio was filled with gentle sounds and the fragrance of trees. Around the room I had hung finished blocks and prints on the wall. I had worked until late and was debating where to go for dinner when someone knocked on my door.

"Who is it?"

No reply came. Curious, I opened the door.

"Oh my God, who is this?"

"It's me. Do you remember me?"

I actually did not recognize her. I could guess who she was from the familiar voice.

"Wait, are you really—Mi Kyung?"

"You do remember."

"Come in, please, come in."

We sat face to face on the sofa by the entrance door. Slowly, I studied Chae Mi Kyung's appearance. Her hair was bobbed right under her ears, just like a high school girl from the seventies, and her face was haggard. It seemed like she had not applied moisturizer, let alone makeup, in a long time. Her deep navy blue T-shirt looked too hot for such a humid day, and her cotton pants were baggy. She looked ordinary and inconspicuous, like she would disappear quickly if she walked outside and stood among the crowd. Mi Kyung did not look like a student anymore. I nodded.

"Yes, I remember now," I said. "So you're still working at a factory?"

"Uh-huh, I finally finished the apprenticeship. I'm a technician now."

"A what? Jesus, you make it sound like you've passed a bar exam or something like that."

Mi Kyung was as cheery as ever.

"Well, it is a new life for me, isn't it?"

"What kind of factory is it?"

"An electronics one. I was a trainee for six months, and I've been working for almost a year after that, so I'm a pretty seasoned professional, I must say."

A thought came into my mind. I wanted to ask her something, but I did not mention it.

"So, what brings you here after all this time?"

"Well, I live in Inchon now. I trained in Boochun before that, so I really didn't have a reason to come back to Seoul. I just happened to have something to do around here so I was in the neighborhood and then I thought of you! I always felt bad that I disappeared on you without saying a word."

I knew she was making it up.

"Well, I was about to leave because I haven't eaten yet," I said.

"I haven't had dinner yet either."

"Good, let's go get something to eat."

Chae Mi Kyung glanced at her watch nervously.

"It's only half past six. Do you have any other plans for tonight?"

"Tonight . . . ? Why?"

"I wanted to take you back to my place."

I looked at my watch, too. I had worked hard all day, and I knew I would not be able to sleep until late since it was still so hot. *Why not,* I thought.

"It'll take some time before we get to Inchon. What if we get even more hungry while getting there?"

"Food tastes better when you're starving."

We first took the bus to go to the subway station where we would take the Number 1 line. Outside, it felt like a steam room. Inside the subway train was worse, filled with body odor and heat. I was beginning to regret the whole thing. After we had been traveling for a while she spoke, still looking out the window.

"I met Song Young Tae today when I went out," she said.

I knew it. That was why I had decided to follow her.

"So he is alive? What is he doing now?"

"He's living in Inchon, too. He has lost a lot of weight."

"I'm sure he's never had to work so much in his life."

Mi Kyung's neighborhood was a slum filled with shacks, near where the refugee camps during the Korean War used to be. The sun had set, and it was finally getting dark. As we walked through the narrow alleyways, Mi Kyung finally confessed.

"I'm sorry, Yoon Hee, please forgive me. We just wanted to see you. This was the only way to do it."

"We?"

"Song Young Tae is waiting for us at my place. He told me to bring you here without telling you why. In the underground we call it docking."

I was not too surprised, and I could respond without changing my facial expression.

"Then wait, we should do some grocery shopping."

"Don't worry, I'm sure they've prepared everything already."

"Why? Today is a special day?"

Mi Kyung grinned, "Well, it doesn't mean much, but . . . it is my birthday."

"I see. Wait, I see a store over there. And I bet that red light means it's a butcher."

I simply ignored Mi Kyung pulling my arm and bought beef and vegetables.

"You said he lost a lot of weight. Isn't he here to get some food into his body?"

"My friend and Mr. Song already went grocery shopping. I bet they're done cooking, too."

Mi Kyung and I walked into a long, dark alleyway. There was not a single streetlight around, and following the steep slope, the alley was lined with the outer walls of small house after small house, so that it looked like a narrow corridor. We reached an old house plastered with cement. The front gate was so low that Mi Kyung simply reached over it and undid the crossbar with one hand. It had a traditional layout, a square with one side open, but it was hastily built with unevenly applied cement plaster. In the courtyard, some women wearing slips and thin underwear were sitting on a flat wooden bench and cooling off in the evening wind. There seemed to be at least ten rooms in the building, and there was a young man or woman in front of each door. Mi Kyung greeted each one of them. She seemed to be familiar with everyone in the house. They, in turn, shot brief, furtive looks at me. All of sudden Mi Kyung, who had been walking in front of me, disappeared, and I was lost in the middle of the courtyard. As I stood there, I heard Mi Kyung's voice coming from somewhere right above my head.

"Yoon Hee, I'm over here. Come on up!"

I looked up. I could never have imagined adding a room in a place like that. There was a room built with cement on top of a structure used as a storage shed. I saw a steep iron ladder, and, carefully, climbed it. All I saw at first was a tiny room containing a kitchenette and a space to take your shoes off. Someone was standing in front of another door, the indoor light illuminating him from behind.

"It's good to see you, Miss Han."

It was a familiar voice. No matter what, I was happy to see him again, and I felt like crying a little. I thought of making a joke out of it, too, but I decided to just grab his hand.

"Well, you look well."

I followed him into the living quarters. It was actually a lot larger than it looked from the outside. In one corner there was a plastic closet, a desk, and a chair, and a small bookcase was in the other corner. Mi Kyung, who was standing right behind me, screamed, "My goodness, what is that?"

In front of the window on the right side was a clothesline from which various pairs of underwear and boxer shorts hung. The men in the room appeared to have done lots of laundry while Mi Kyung was gone. Song Young Tae just stood there and grinned while the other guy took them down.

"The kids in the room by the gate were using the laundry machine," he said. "So I thought we might as well use it, too. Why not?"

"Hey, they're still wet!" said Song Young Tae fingering the clothes piled in the other guy's arms. The young man took a look at me, put them in a large plastic basin, and took them outside.

"We're about to eat, so . . ."

"What, is laundry garbage or something? Why can't we eat with wet clothes hanging to dry?"

In the middle of the room was a round table with a large pot, bottles of soju, and glasses. Mi Kyung took the lid off and sniffed.

"Imbeciles! What kind of food is this?"

"I don't know, Mr. Song made it. It's good, actually."

"Did you decide to experiment, using my birthday as an excuse?"

Song Young Tae was shameless as ever.

"What's your problem? It is a dish called mapa tofu. Don't complain about it until you've actually tried it."

"Mapa tofu? I see pork and tofu, but what is this?"

"Oh, we bought some fish cakes but we didn't know what to do with them, so I just added them in there."

Mi Kyung gave them a look before she went out to the kitchenette. I was thoroughly enjoying this little commotion while I walked around the room. The window over the courtyard was small, but directly opposite it was a larger window, and the room was quite cool, thanks to the breeze. I stood in front of the larger window that had been revealed when they took down the wet clothes. We were pretty high up, and I could see clusters of slate roofs below and the brightly lit office buildings further away.

"Do you see the line of lights beyond all the neon signs? That's the ocean. You can see it clearly during the day," said Song Young Tae as he stood behind me.

"It's better than what I expected," I whispered.

"Isn't it? Mi Kyung found an ideal spot. So I come here from time to time to escape the heat, even though I have to suffer her abuses."

I saw that Mi Kyung's boyfriend was sitting on the floor leaning against the wall.

"Have things calmed down a bit?" I asked.

"Who knows? I'm a missing person. Everything's different now, my name, my job."

It was a story I had heard before. Hyun Woo had told me in detail what he did when he had to go underground, so the neighborhood and the atmosphere did not seem so unfamiliar.

"What are you doing these days?"

"Working at a factory. I'm a lathe technician. I've got the license, too."

"And you're about to stir things up again?"

"No, no, that's not it. I don't want to rule over anyone. I'm just a friend who can assist them. I want them to stand on their own and be the owners of their lives."

Song Young Tae finally introduced me to the young man sitting on the other side of the room.

"This is Ki Hun. He works at the same factory as Mi Kyung. They're the same age, too, and they're friends. This is Han Yoon Hee, my friend."

Ki Hun smiled shyly and nodded. I continued to question Song Young Tae.

"You've been here for a year now?"

"No, I was actually in Anyang learning how to use a lathe with friends."

"And you never contacted your family?"

"I sometimes sent a word or two, but I haven't done that in a while. No news is good news, as far as they're concerned."

"But are you really okay? I mean your health."

I looked at his hollow cheeks and his coarse, dry skin. Song Young Tae flexed his muscles to show off his biceps.

"I eat well, I feel better, I think I'm actually healthier now," he said.

"Well, I guess that's a good thing then. So you plan to live here for a while?"

"For a while? I'm going to spend the rest of my life here," he replied in a lighthearted tone.

Somehow, his cheerfulness sounded ominous to me.

After that night, I did not see him again for a year or so. When we parted he promised to keep in touch through Mi Kyung, but she did not call me, not even once. They were busy, conspiring. Later I found out that they were managing numerous study groups and clubs in the industrial area. They even led a demonstration in their neighborhood under the banner of Laborers and Students United.

They were able to march all the way into downtown Seoul, even to the front of an American army base. I thought I could find my way back to Mi Kyung's house, but I knew that I should not visit them unless they asked me to, for their safety.

I finished my degree in the spring of 1987. And I found a teaching position at a college in a small city, where I spent two days a week. That spring, strikes and demonstrations seemed to go on endlessly, and by early summer the whole country seemed to be protesting, denouncing the government for the death of a young university student called Park Jong Chul who was tortured to death, and demanding an amendment to the election law. By June, the resistance was reaching its climax. Urged by my classmates, I joined a cultural organization and was asked to participate in many protests and demonstrations. From old men with white hair to young woman like me, we all marched together in downtown Seoul, the crowd flooding every street corner. I did not know that I had the energy left in me, but I screamed and yelled with the others. We covered our mouths with masks or plastic bags to withstand tear gas and pepper spray, and we threw bricks, even though they did not travel very far. All over the country, millions of people from all walks of life rushed into the street. We were full of hope at the time. We thought we could remove the military dictatorship and build a new world where everyone could live like human beings. When the government took one step back and declared that a presidential election would be held later that year, the resistance quieted. That was the beginning of our failure. The laborers' struggle for their rights was just beginning, but the masses did not participate. For them, the only thing that mattered was the election of a new president and a change of power in government. When the June resistance was over, the summer vacation began. That was when Song Young Tae called me.

"Miss Han? It's me, Young Tae."

"Hey, how are you?"

Although it had only been a year since Mi Kyung had helped us see each other using her birthday as an excuse, it felt like a decade. We spoke like survivors inquiring about each other after a war had ended.

"Are you still staying there? I guess not much is going on these days."

"Well, something's going on. I'm at a hospital."

"Why? Are you sick?"

"Yeah, the same thing I had before. I'm a lot better now, though. I've been wondering how you are."

"It's about time you come back to the big wide world. You should go back to school, too. Where is the hospital? I'll come see you."

So I headed to a sanatorium run by a Catholic organization outside of Seoul. Because of my commute to work I had bought a car, and I had gotten quite used to driving on highways. I liked that I could be so mobile, going wherever, whenever I wanted. And I liked the solitude of driving on an empty road. The machine once more confirmed what an individualist I was, how much happier I was not having to mingle with too many people. It was weird imagining Song Young Tae at this clean and quiet sanatorium located among rolling hills. Many nurses were nuns, and one of them took me to the exercise room.

Song Young Tae was dressed in a T-shirt and a pair of hospital-issue pants, and he was absorbed in a game of ping-pong. When he saw me approaching, he put down the paddle and forfeited the game. While others stared at us, he came up to me and extended his hand for a handshake. I felt a little awkward, but I accepted it.

"You look good," I said.

Song Young Tae took me to the garden in front of the hospital. We sat on a bench under a tree, looking out over an open field. I knew he had had tuberculosis in the army and in prison, and I remembered that Jung Hee had told him she saw something in his X-ray when we had first met.

"They tell me it's gotten a lot worse," Song Young Tae said. "I need to rest and take medicine for at least a year."

"That's a good thing, a chance for you to take a break."

"I can't stand it. I feel like I just ran away from it all."

"Isn't it almost over? There's going to be an election."

"The fact is, this is only the beginning. Nothing has changed yet."

"What is it that you really want?"

"For the people to have real power. To get rid of the Yankees and their puppets."

"You should just take care of yourself now. I don't want anything anymore, just for Hyun Woo to come back."

"You'll probably have to wait for a while. The transitional period will last longer than people expect."

"How are your friends? Are they all well?"

"Many in the core have been arrested. But I think there are still plenty in the field. I just don't think I can go back there again."

"No, your job from now on is to take care of yourself and live well. Who can object to that? You did everything that you could."

"Maybe I should go back to school, concentrate on studying."

"No one can deny that you have the potential. I bet your parents are relieved, too."

He blinked a few times, then rubbed his eyes as if he had something in them. Then he started to cry.

"Hey, hey there, big guy, what's going on?"

"I just . . . I just regret . . ."

Without thinking too much about it, I put my arm around his shoulder, and he buried his head in my chest. We sat there, just like that, for a long time.

"I think I should go." I patted his back a few times and got up. I did not want him to feel awkward about it, so I stared down at the ground and avoided meeting his eyes.

The summer vacation was ending, and I was preparing for the fall semester when I received a thick envelope delivered to the college I was working at. On the outside was written "From: Chae Mi Kyung."

> Dear Yoon Hee,
>
> It's me, Mi Kyung. I'm still at the same place, alive and well. As for Mr. Song, I believe you may know by now what happened to him. He was working all through the night at the factory when he threw up blood and fainted. We discussed the situation among the group and collectively decided to hand him over to his family. I was going to contact you as soon as it happened, but he did not want me to, saying that he would do it himself. I think he must have contacted you by now.
>
> Everyone's so tired and exhausted, I don't know if we can go on. But we do believe that this summer was a crucial turning point, and we've been preparing diligently for the last few months to form a labor union. It is not the decisive moment yet, but we think each factory should develop a core group at this point.
>
> Here in my factory, four of us former students were sent in by last year. But the higher-ups decided that only one unit should take the lead, while the rest of us had to remain undercover, careful not to be exposed while remaining spectators. This was not the case everywhere, but quite similar things have been happening everywhere, including in heavy industry where Mr. Song was working. The workers put up a tremendous fight this summer. They were totally prepared

for it, too. They are not the submissive, meek workers of the past. They're determined to claim their rights, and some of them are taking a step further, ready to go beyond forming a union and become a real political force. We did not have to spend a long time changing their minds and educating them as we did in the past.

We started by distributing newsletters to various groups and clubs within the factory. There are 2,500 employees in our factory, and about 400 of them are female. We make refrigerators and washing machines, and we've started producing air conditioners as well. If you're a man who has graduated from a vocational school and finished his military service, you get paid 5,300 won a day, but if you're a woman it is 3,700 won a day, no matter what. If we meet the quota there is a 50 percent bonus, and there is something called a special allowance for risky operations, which never gets distributed among the floor workers. The old-timers and section chiefs split the money among themselves. The average overtime per month is about one hundred hours, and two days out of the week are all-nighters. If there's a deadline for delivery, we go into special overtime, which happens at least a couple of times a month. If the overtime lasts longer than four hours, we get bread as a snack, and during the all-nighters they serve us rice or milk. There is no holiday except for Sundays. We're supposed to get a couple of vacation days per month, but that's in name only. Untaken holidays are covered with extra allowances, and no one gets to rest.

At least the working environment is not as dangerous as it is for others, since we deal with electronics. Most accidents result in slight injuries, unlike other places dealing with steel or chemicals, where something disastrous happens every week. Instead, it's dusty in the factory and there is very little air circulation. There is a locker room with showers, but no one trusts the water quality, and I have never seen anyone actually using them. For fun, there are various circles and clubs, such as a soccer team, a baseball team, a hiking club, a fishing club, and the women's club. And then there's the kusadae union, the "company protection unit." They don't mingle with the rest of us, and they call themselves a union even though they work for the benefit of the owners, not the workers, and they are the first ones sent to clash with us on behalf of management.

Through these various groups and clubs, we met experienced and insightful workers whose thoughts were similar to ours. They became the core, and we hoped for them to lead us. We guided them toward analyzing the political situation and studying the labor law or reading certain books, while they told us about what kind of life an ordinary worker had and how to organize them into a force. It is amazing progress compared to four or five years ago, when our predecessors had to operate alone and in secret, unable to accomplish much before they were fired and arrested.

You remember Chung Ki Hun, the man you met when you came to my place? He is my colleague and comrade. He did not even graduate from elementary school. His mother passed away when he was young and he was raised by a stepmother. He left home when he was in fifth grade. After he got to Seoul, there was not a job he did not have, from delivering Chinese food to working at a sweatshop. When he was fifteen he committed a petty crime, and he was sent to a juvenile home where he passed high school equivalency exams. Sometimes, a good thing can come out of the worst situation, too. I think that even in the most horrendous circumstances, certain people turn out differently due to their natural intelligence and their effort to live correctly. He's been working here for about three years now, and he is considered a good technician. Remember how profoundly moved we were by the life of Chun Tae Il? But here, I've met so many Chun Tae Ils.* They are not the workers of the past.

* Chun Tae Il (1948-1970) was a factory worker and a labor activist who set himself on fire in protest of working conditions at an industrial complex. He is considered to be a pioneer of the Korean labor movement.

When I first started working here, Ki Hun was my team's leader. One day, out of curiosity, I gave him one of our pamphlets called *The New Road*. I just wanted to see how he would react. The next day, he left me a letter. It was just a sheet from a notepad, but it was filled with what he thought of the pamphlet. He criticized it, saying there were too many difficult words for an ordinary factory worker to understand, that the reality of everyday life was not reflected in its writings and that the discussions of working hours and wages did not reflect the current situation. He also suggested that we should avoid mentioning the political issues too directly, since this might cause suspicion. I was surprised when I asked him to recommend someone for the job of distributing pamphlets and Ki Hun volunteered to do it himself. He took about thirty copies to distribute among the members of the hiking club he belonged to, then he invited us former students to join their regular outings. Up in the mountains, after hiking for a while, everyone gathered around to take a lunch break, and naturally people talked about everything. When people talked about their work and the factory, it was very easy to bring up the matter of a labor union. Most of them were young men in their twenties, the oldest in his early thirties, and they were close. I became very close to Ki Hun. And he also introduced me to a new friend, Shin Ja, who would become my confidante. A graduate of a night school run by the big companies guaranteeing education and employment at the same time, she was one of the most experienced workers at the factory and all the young girls trusted her.

Our little group began publishing newsletters that mirrored the views and opinions of the factory workers. The previous spring, the organization had made the decision that two former students should take the lead in our activities at the factory, and I was not one of them. Since I had never been arrested, I got the job using my own IDs, but the two student leaders had used fake ones and were under the constant threat of exposure. Me and another former student who got the job legitimately had to remain undercover as long as possible and support them.

On the day of an operation, we prepared thousands and thousands of copies of our pamphlets, placed them all around the factory, and distributed them as the workers came into the cafeteria for lunch. By 12:30, the cafeteria was at its busiest, crowded with people. The two leaders ran up to the front with a hand mike and read the pamphlet aloud while the rest of us clapped and shouted slogans with them. Soon the managers and guards came in and tried to take them away as we whistled and jeered. But most of the workers remained passive and uninvolved as the management condemned the leaders as Communists and student activists only pretending to be workers. We all hung back a little at the time, but I know that this incident left a strong impression. You want proof? When the Miss Kwon incident happened,* we distributed copies of the written arraignment, and everyone at the factory, men and women, was talking about how disgusted and horrified they were by the government.

Dear Yoon Hee, the world we lived in was filled with oppression and lack of freedom, but at least on the surface there was the appearance of a civilized society. But this place, it is bound by double layers of shackles. Even if the outside world were to see a ray of sunlight, the absolute darkness of this place wouldn't change much.

Last June was glorious, but for us, it was just one sunny day during a long rainy season. There is no denying that the power of the people's movement became a strong foundation for our fundamental struggle. We started to prepare for the strike in July. All over the country, workers began to stir and rally to fight for their basic rights.

---

* Kwon In Sook was a young college student who was arrested in June 1986 for using a fake ID to work at a factory near Boochun. While in custody, she was sexually harrassed and physically abused by the police. In July, she was able to get her story out to a group of lawyers, who pressured the government to prosecute the police. In 1989, Moon Kwi Dong, the policeman who was the principal offender, was sentenced to five years in prison.

There were various signs that people at the factory were changing. The first thing I noticed was the women's club. Sometimes, the team leaders and section leaders were worse than the people in the administrative offices. They wanted to show off the little power they had by acting more author-itarian than their bosses, and it was worse when it came to their manner toward women. They didn't care if she was younger or older; they would order her around and swear and talk down to her. I'm not saying everyone was like that, but sometimes those who used to be factory workers and had climbed up the ladder treated their colleagues worse than management did.

Around two or three o'clock in the afternoon is the hardest time at the factory, when the body is languid after eating lunch and efficiency is at its lowest. There was one middle-aged woman, I think she had her period. She had already gone to the restroom after lunch, and the second time she left her position the team leader, who was a man, said something to her. But she still could not hold it any-more, and when she attempted to leave her position for the third time the team leader yelled at her, "You bitch! Either you don't drink water with your lunch, or you stop coming here starting tomorrow!"

We had all heard worse before, and the woman just froze where she was, her head down, unable to say anything back to him. But Shin Ja jumped up and ran up to him, grabbing him by his throat and yelled back at him.

"You! Don't you have a mother and a father? Do you think you are allowed to talk to your elders like that? If you are a human being, you shouldn't act like that!"

Preposterously, he slapped her face. The rest of us were just watching them, breathless, when the middle-aged woman who started the whole thing, who hadn't moved until then, picked up a steel pipe and ran toward the team leader. She said she was going to kill him. He ran away. Every woman in the room began to scream and shout, *Get him!*

Get him! He ran around the room and only barely escaped. We stopped the machines and began a sit-down strike. We demanded that the team leader apologize and that a new rule be implemented to prevent any manager from using abusive language and violence. A couple of vice presidents came down, apologized, and made excuses and a big fuss, but it did little to appease us.

Then, a few days later, there was an accident in the middle of the night. We had been ordered to work an unscheduled all-nighter. It was the season for air conditioners, and since spring we had had frequent all-nighters to meet the demand. While working, a man fell asleep and his hand was cut off by the conveyor belt. After he was rushed to the hospital, all the men in that section stopped working and demanded that all-nighters on weekends be abolished. It was a small compensation, but it made everyone realize the power we had.

Yes. You set yourself aflame and melted away at the crossroads in front of your factory, but your last letter remains. Mi Kyung, I took the long road back here and I am finally ready to write a belated reply to your last letter.

What is a life? At first, it is just eating enough to survive, something so easy and simple. I bet we all used to wear grass skirts and spend most of the day, from dawn to dusk, doing not much else, just enjoying each other and making love. Around dusk on an early summer's evening, you'd find your mate and go to bed. You would wake up when the sun rose and collect clams by the water or berries in the forest. Only the minimum amount of time would be wasted on supplying food. And then you'd play. I am also sure that there was no strong sense of possession among men and women, and all children were raised by everyone, together. But the evil shadows appeared from outside of the forest. They came from below the horizon, from a place where life is not so easy and plentiful. And they wanted to trade. Every evil in the world begins with a merchant. They are so clever and powerful, like a snake with wings.

Dear Mi Kyung, let us consider what art and revolution are all about. It is our maddening effort to return life back to what it once was. In order to do that, to resume our lives at dawn, we try to destroy what has been built during the day.

Let's return to the matter of food. Even beautiful young Jesus chose the only way to return to where he began, to restore the most humble and selfless meal on earth, offering himself as wine and bread. The Last Supper before his death was in fact the new beginning, as death is the rebirth of all living things. He said his farewells and promised to see his friends again. So many painters have tried to capture the scene of his Last Supper. A meal that consisted of stale bread and sour wine.

Mi Kyung, I can never see you again. You stupid little girl. Love shouldn't be like lipstick you apply on your lips, something that hovers on your tongue like a witty saying. Nor should it be something too abstract and grand. Well, they say they will be together until death drives them apart. Nothing really shocks anyone anymore, and the words are becoming more violent. Love is what? About one half of it is a body, like food, about one quarter of it is daily life, like breathing in and out continuously, and the rest is completed by the people around you. It is only there if we can grow old together. We all fail before half of our life is over and spend our last days in lonely isolation. Maybe we should think ourselves lucky if we make it to the midpoint, maybe we can finish everything else in the afterlife.

One more story about food. Someone told me about his father. Right after the war was over, there were hailstorms and droughts during summer, and the food had run out by the beginning of winter. All people could do was stay at home and try to keep themselves warm. He said the evenings were somehow bearable, but the daytime was really intolerable. One day, his father got up and went out to the empty field, staggering and stumbling, and began digging the soil with a hoe, just like a hungry horse or dog would if it was hungry. He continued sweating up a storm, even though he was burning the little energy that was left in his body. How do you overcome hunger? With work, which created everything in the world.

Dear Yoon Hee,

Five days before the strike, we reviewed our pamphlets one last time, and made the decision about how to carry out the strike.

Two days before the strike, we went to the union office, which was really a union in name only, and demanded that they fight for ordinary workers. We thought this would justify our action and reassure the rest of the workers. And we were going to start a campaign seeking signatures from those who wanted to form a new union. We were going to ask those who were fired from the factory before to come back and distribute pamphlets, which would help them to understand our goals and the meaning of this strike. So that was our plan, to ask other workers to join us and let them be the center of this strike. But we were too circumspect and did not realize that they were at a breaking point, that they were ready to burst into flames with the slightest touch.

There were seven of us and also four laid-off workers, and we visited every section of the factory to distribute pamphlets. During the morning break at around 10 a.m., Shin Ja took a portable hand mike and read the pamphlet out loud, emphasizing the necessity of this strike. We did not expect the response we got. People wanted to start the strike right away. So we got together hastily and made the decision that we should rise together at lunch hour. After we ate, around 12:30, about fifty people gathered in a courtyard in front of the cafeteria. Ki Hun took the mike and began chanting.

"Let us come together! Let us unite and show them how strong we are!"

Management came out. They were caught off-guard and unable to stop us. As we marched around the factory, they trailed behind us, begging, "Don't you think that's enough? You can disband now, and we'll talk."

By the time we reached the sports field, the marchers numbered over a hundred. As the crowd swelled, those who were hesitant at first seemed to be encouraged to join the group, which soon rose to one hundred and fifty. By the time we had marched through the factory and visited each section, there were at least one thousand workers gathered at the front entrance. Naturally, Ki Hun, who was holding the mike, took charge. He suggested that we form a committee for the strike and that each section select a member to represent it. This had not been planned, so people called out a name or two at random, and Ki Hun asked them to join him up front and lined them up. We all thought a lively debate would begin concerning how to carry out the strike and whether they had confirmed their own representatives, but everyone just stood there, looking at each other and not saying a word. Finally, Ki Hun took the mike again.

"Everyone! If you agree with what you've just read in the pamphlet you're holding in your hands, put your hands together and show us your support!"

People were clapping and screaming, so much louder than we expected. Encouraged, Ki Hun pushed on.

"Then I want to hear now if you accept these men and women in front of you as your representatives!"

There was more thunderous applause from the crowd. Right there and then, we formed various groups in charge of negotiations, security, food, and public relations, and we declared a full strike throughout the factory. Banners and headbands were made and distributed, lyrics were copied and handed about, and as the top representatives decided, a few people went to the management office and kicked out the office workers. Forklifts were parked in front of the gate as barricades and guarded by people from the newly formed security department. That was at around half past three in the afternoon, and we quickly proceeded to a public debate on our demands during the strike. We also made up our slogans and practiced screaming them, one group leading the chorus while others followed.

We deserve compensation for our sweat and labor!
Let's build a democratic labor union, we want labor to
*   be liberated!*
Victory for the united fight of 10 million workers!

Time passed quickly and I felt almost spiteful. I truly understood what it meant to have no time. Our demands were soon organized and listed, and we rushed into forming the Committee to Propel the Democratic Labor Union. The resolution was adopted unanimously, with very little resistance. A chair and two vice chairs were selected, as well as an auditor, and the representatives for each department were retained as before. It seemed like heaven was helping us.

We also decided that we needed to set up rules and regulations to prepare for a prolonged strike. First, there was to be no drinking and no leaving the factory grounds. Everything was scheduled, from the wake-up call to bedtime, and daily activities were organized systematically, from three meals a day to debates and assemblies, protests and even breaks. If there was no interference, everyone should follow the schedule, but we also had to be prepared for an emergency if the situation changed suddenly. Each department came up with a guideline for its members. When negotiations began, there were to be two representatives from those who began the strike, joined by the chair. We were using the cafeteria as a conference room, and when it was time for dinner, some women got up to cook without being asked to. It was half past eight by the time everyone was able to eat something. We had collected a little money to buy food. It was not a fancy meal, and no one was able to go home for the night. But we all sat down together, and some men even admitted that they had to hold back tears as they took their first bite.

The next day, the first negotiations began. A vice president showed up at the front gate with a few managers. The security department prohibited them from entering the grounds, and they hastily made up a conference table right in front of the gate, bringing over a table and a few chairs. As they took their seats, all of us gathered around the gate, surrounding it with rows of people, and we shouted our slogans and sang songs to raise our spirits. They appeared to be less confident than the last time they had shown up. Our representatives began the meeting, but their offer was so far off from our demands that we broke off the meeting and left the table. That day, we also came up with a new policy. It was not easy to assemble four or five hundred people in the cafeteria every morning, and there were other workers who agreed with the strike but did not stay in the factory. Although the machines were stopped, they were still coming to work every morning as usual. So we decided to carry out the strike at each of our work stations, each of us going back to the department we belonged to. This was the best decision we had made. We were able to greet other workers at the bus station and bring them in and encourage them to join the strike. As we walked back and forth and talked to others, it was a perfect chance to carry out our "agitation propaganda," not only among the workers, but also with ordinary citizens who lived near the factory.

On the third night a commotion broke out. There were over a hundred workers gathered in the cafeteria, plus over two hundred divided into groups and getting ready for bed all around the factory building. All of sudden, we heard people screaming, glass breaking, and loud footsteps approaching, and then women screaming.

"The kusadae is here! Line up!"

Men were screaming with hoarse voices. We ran out of our workstations and picked up whatever could serve as a weapon, a wooden stick or a steel pipe, and we ran to the cafeteria. The lights in there were switched off, and it was pitch dark. The barricade by the front gate had been penetrated, and we saw dark shadows running out of the cafeteria. There were about seventy or eighty of them. They must have thought that all the strikers were gathered in the cafeteria. There were more of us than they expected and we fought back fiercely. They ran through the front gate and disappeared into the darkness. We found almost twenty injured in the darkened cafeteria. Many were able to escape, but those who were caught were beaten. After administering first aid, we called ambulances and sent them to hospitals.

The next morning all of us gathered by the front gate, those who were on the factory ground the night before and those who had just arrived, and we held a rally denouncing violence. The company union, the bogus organization controlled by factory management, also gathered on the other side and used a mike to disrupt our rally. They claimed we were a vile and improper organization and urged people not to be fooled into joining the strike. But there were more people than ever gathered on our side, over fifteen hundred. Ki Hun, who did not belong to the committee but who had begun the strike, stood in front of everyone again and made a speech. I am writing down whatever I can remember.

"Maybe they think they can stamp us out with violence. Maybe they think they can break our solidarity and halt our efforts by killing hundreds and locking hundreds in a cold, dark prison. But that is their biggest illusion. A tiny spark can burn down the whole prairie. In the hearts of 10 million workers, the hope for a democratic labor union will never die. No, it will burn and erupt like a volcano as long as we continue our struggle. My dear brothers and sisters, it's not over yet. No, it cannot end yet. We'll continue to fight until we form a democratic labor union and regain our rights!"

You were able to withstand for two more days. Your coworkers finally entered the management office, something you had all decided to wait to do. Once there, they trashed the place, throwing computers and other office supplies out of the windows, destroying the sofas and chairs, all that was so neat and clean and proper, and breaking all the windows. I later learned that the committee did not order them to do this. It was just some young men who were unable to take it anymore and did not listen. I can understand why they would be inflamed, comparing the inferior and deteriorating environment of their own work spaces to the clean office furnished with air conditioners, water purifiers, and vending machines. During the negotiations, the representative of the labor department informed you that the committee, unapproved by the government as it was, had no power to censure management. Then things began to fall apart. During one week of the strike there were three negotiations, and when certain compromises and agreements were made, the committee, unable to carry on, folded.

Soon afterward, the police stormed the factory and arrested a number of leaders, including you. You were all fired, naturally, but you, Mi Kyung, were not charged, since you had no record of falsifying personal information in order to get a job at the factory. You were released after a month. Your letter ends like this:

> My dear Yoon Hee,
>   A few of us, Ki Hun and Shin Ja and some people from the hiking club, go to the factory every morning to protest the firings. We are poor, but still thriving. Whatever little savings I had are all gone, but our friends bring us all sorts of things. We have boxes of ramen noodles and more than enough briquettes. Come what may, I think I am staying here. I was once able to break out of the thick and foolish shell of illusion, so how am I supposed to turn my back and return to an untruthful life?

It was too late by the time I found out that you no longer existed in this world, a world that is like an ocean full of hardships and tribulations. Winter had arrived again. People scattered and went their own ways. The young ones with shy eyes who were so excited that now we could actually vote, that we had achieved a democratic state, the ordinary citizens who clenched their fists and rose up, the distinguished personalities with white hair and faces filled with rage. All of us were out of our minds. Were we drunk? I feel like it all happened a long, long time ago. Our once boiling blood cooled down in our veins, and we just bowed our heads or smiled bitterly, unable to hate, and each of us went his or her separate way, as if we never wanted to meet again. Scattered on the cool road after the tempest of an election were pamphlets and printed papers, wet from the frost of the night before. That was it, that's where we had arrived.

I met Song Young Tae, the man you would have followed to the end of the world. I know it is all in the past now, but I do want to say this. There's nothing between us, Young Tae and I. I think of him as a friend, and I feel comfortable when I am with him, as if we grew up together. And both of us were lonely at the time. Don't you think he is so immature? I mean, he's not an adolescent anymore, but he still passionately detests his father. And I was tricked by him into serving as his stenographer, but it was worth it. It was a chance for me to remember to be my daughter's father. I guess both he and I have now moved a certain distance from a simple yearning for each other.

When Song Young Tae told me about your death I just could not believe it. It was the second time I saw him put his head of unruly hair down on my lap and cry. He is doing a lot better at the hospital. My dear Mi Kyung, I think of your youth, which did not have enough time to express itself. I think of how your face lit up at the mention of him, your eyes smiling and squinting with pride.

I have been there. I stood on top of that building, the one across the street from the factory's front gate, where you poured a bottle of chemicals all over yourself and fell as a ball of flame. There was a restaurant on the first floor, a café on the second, a billiard room on the third. I tried to be as inconspicuous as possible as I climbed up the steep cement steps and reached a small steel door. When I pushed the rusted door it opened quietly, like magic. I took one step and stood on the flat rooftop, so desolate. There were empty soju bottles rolling around and a strong smell of urine. I was able to stand exactly where you stood, where you could see the front gate directly. I heard that it happened during the rush hour, when laborers were done with the day's work and left all at once, crowding the street. I wonder what you looked like. Probably not like a flower. Perhaps, the pamphlets you threw into the air might have looked like petals. But you just dropped to the ground, a burning object that landed with a thud.

If I were there, even though we are all daughters, I think I could have been your mother. But if I could have caressed you, your singed hair would have broken into pieces. Your fingers would have been the remains of burnt twigs.

I walked down the stairs again and into the restaurant with aluminum sash windows. I ordered a spicy stew and drank soju by myself. The day was short, and it was soon dark as night, illuminated by pale streetlamps in front of the factory. Dim traces of human forms began to appear and soon filled the street. Under the bleary light in their drab clothes, they looked like water flowing through darkness.

When will they stop and form an ocean? How far do they flow?

23

Hello. It's me, Han Yoon Hee.

I just came back to Kalmae.

I feel like one thousand years have gone by.

As soon as I returned, I bought our house. It looks the same, but is more of a ramshackle. It was filled with bags of fertilizer, and the wallpaper and floors were covered with mold. Still, it's not overrun with weeds, as they say in fairy tales. The water pump is red with rust. The Soonchun lady told me to take down the old structure and build a new one, but I want to leave it as it is until you come back. So I've just fixed the floor and redone the wallpaper.

I came by myself this time, but I will bring Eun Gyul here next winter. It is 1993, and Eun Gyul is almost twelve. She starts junior high next year. Her breasts are budding already, and she looks like a woman. She resembles you a lot. She is my daughter, but then again she is not. Sometime around the '88 Olympics, Jung Hee and her husband adopted her. She had to go to school, and I was still unmarried. She calls me Mom, of course, but I think it feels more natural to her to call her aunt mom.

That was an unbearable period for me. Why? More hardship and pain were waiting for me, but that was the most difficult time I faced. The hope that you might return one day began to fade away, as did every value

I had held onto in the past. A quiet disillusionment was spreading from the bottom of my heart, making me wonder why I still kept on painting.

I said I just returned, right? For the first time in five years. Starting today, I will record the last five years of my life. I have written down a few words in a sketchbook that I had left here.

The road that brought us here can be the road by which we return. No one's journey has ended. I am here, again, where once I was, absent. I am him, always. I come to meet him. Nothing has changed. Since the beginning the way was set.

I wanted to leave this country, especially after sending Eun Gyul to Jung Hee's house. My sister also has a son who was almost three years old at the time. I decided to study abroad. Maybe I wanted to examine myself and this place from far away. I thought New York would not suit me. For me, whether it is food or clothes, if it is too complicated, it is not comfortable. As for Paris, I confirmed later that it was a city where liberty was once flaunted like a festival but now looks more like wet bunting fallen to the ground. Indifferent, I headed to Berlin. A wet and gloomy city from espionage movies.

All I could picture of Germany was beer and bread. When I first arrived in Berlin I was planning just to visit, but I liked the city. The early winter is cold and windy. It is either drizzling and foggy or sleet falls for days. Sometimes, incredible thunder and lightning tear the sky apart. By three o'clock in the afternoon it is dark, and the city is empty by six. I took a train from West to East Germany, and even I, who was so used to things like this, got a little nervous. I have lived too long in a land where too many things are forbidden.

Berlin was just like an island. Through the train window I saw the white branches of birch trees and an old tractor, abandoned in an empty wheat field that looked like a ruined battlefield. Guards wearing red clips and leather straps around their shoulders, and long boots on their feet, came into the car and examined my passport. I entered the occupied city surrounded by tall walls.

The Ku'damm was crowded with young people, but the narrow streets and alleyways were mostly empty. Paint was peeling off of old unkempt apartment buildings, and a yellowish smoke from coal fires filled the cloudy sky. Berlin is like our demilitarized zone, or a corridor where two different buildings face each other. It is a buffer zone. I decided I liked this city of neutral temperaments. North and south are opposites, like front and back, but east and west are the same, aren't they, two sides of one? The sun rises on one side and it sets on the other, but dusk is not too different from dawn.

I spent the first day in this city where I knew no one sitting at an unremarkable café on a street corner, and then at an ordinary Italian restaurant, staring out at the street, my mind empty. I had no desire to be impatient and busy, to visit the museums and galleries as most travelers do.

The nervous silence in front of Brandenburg Gate seemed to be even deeper than that of the plaza in front of the city hall in Seoul when martial law was proclaimed. I only found out much later, after the wall came down, that it was actually a window into the other world, forbidden to East Berliners from the moment they were born.

I was staying at a small guesthouse near the wall whose owner I thought was an Arab. The interior was decorated with tapestries with arabesque patterns and huge pottery vases in primary colors. There weren't many people there, just a few English students backpacking and a Turkish couple I sometimes saw during breakfast. I remember the shocking moment when I opened the window facing the street in my bedroom. First I had to open a set of heavy drapes, then the dark tinted glass window, then still a pair of wooden shutters. When I pushed them open, cold damp air rushed in and an enormous gray wall emerged in front of me. It stretched as far as I could see from left to right. I cannot forget how helpless and suffocated I felt, as if someone had just punched me in my chest. It was as if the opposing views and thoughts of a people had materialized as an object in reality. I have never been to the demilitarized zone in our country, but I do remember that feeling of helplessness whenever heavily armed soldiers climbed onto a bus I was in and inspected everyone.

The wall appeared to be stubbornly asserting the fact that it was an inorganic thing. It stood there, curt and gruff, with not a crack or a hole. There was no decoration; it was a gray rock that blocked the street with iron rods poking out of it here and there. I left the guesthouse and went down an alleyway to look at the wall more closely. It was a dead end, blocked by the buildings on the West Berlin side that had been in the shade for so long that they were covered with moss. Garbage cans lined the entrance, and it looked as if people never used this side. Not a single flowerpot decorated the windows facing the wall. I found that what appeared to be just gray from a distance was actually covered with graffiti and drawings and posters. Some of them were really carefully applied paintings. I was moved, witnessing this unusual art exhibition. On top of this cement structure that so mercilessly covered up any feelings, dreams, hopes, and memories, there were traces of life. In tiny holes where the cement had crumbled, dust had gathered, and tiny wildflowers were growing in this miraculous soil. My eyes filled with tears and for the first time in ages I thought of you.

My German was poor, but I wanted to stay there. I liked the attitude of the young people who disliked both the Yankees and Russkies who occupied the city, and since I had just left the place of abstinence, I thought it would be better for my mental health to stay at a place similar to a church with a cemetery or an old school instead of suddenly moving onto a brighter, vicious place. Berlin was a forgotten place, and it reminded me of the view I saw when I went to visit you, when I had stared at dark windows and hanging laundry from far away before turning around. Maybe I wanted to put myself in exile here.

One day I met someone I knew at the currency exchange booth in front of the Berlin Zoo. She was a couple of years behind me at university, and although she was not a particularly talented artist, she was a really nice person with no prejudices, and she had many friends. I had not seen her for a long time, since we graduated, but I found out she was studying here in Berlin. She had married a German, a lawyer at that, as she put it. I cannot remember her name. It is hovering somewhere in the back of my brain, but I just cannot say it out loud. I think we saw each other about three times while I was staying there. Anyway, thanks to her fluent German, I was able to interview with a professor at an art school, and I made an appointment to see him again when all the paperwork was ready. I asked my friends and Jung Hee back in Seoul to send over the certificates I needed, and I prepared a portfolio of my work. After the final interview, I was admitted to the school. At the time, the real estate market in Berlin was quite favorable for renters, and it was easier to find a cheap but spacious place there than it was in Bonn or Frankfurt.

This may sound unfair to you, but to be honest I've been relatively lucky in my life except for my relationship with you. I was able to find a studio with a really reasonable monthly rent near the Bundesplatz. It was only three U-Bahn stops away from downtown Berlin, and only one stop away from a large park with trees and grass and a lake. From the square, five streets stretched out like the spokes of a wheel, and each street corner was lined with convenience stores, groceries, and little ethnic restaurants. A farmer's market opened there every weekend, where I was able to buy fresh vegetables, fruit, homemade cookies, sausages, and hams.

The place I found was over a hundred years old, built during the Prussian period. It used to be a factory building but was converted into a dormitory for laborers after the war. Each floor was about twice as high as an ordinary apartment. The front gate was large enough to let a truck through, and next to it was a row of nameplates with unit numbers and a buzzer next to each one. When a visitor pressed my buzzer, they could let me know who they were, and I could open the small side door next to the enormous iron gate. Inside, right next to the door, was an old steel switch to turn the light on. The dark corridor along the courtyard was lit with a row of single lightbulbs on a timer, which would turn off automatically by the time the visitor reached the entrance to the building. Inside the building, there were doors in every direction, but the center of the building was a shaft of open space all the way up to the third floor. In the center of this space, a wrought-iron stairway coiled up in a spiral around a pillar. Although technically the third floor was the top floor, the building was actually six stories tall, since each floor was a duplex. I remember how I would push the light switch at the bottom of the stairway and start climbing. When I was carrying nothing my steps were lighter, and the light would stay on until I got to my apartment. But on days I came back from shopping, the lights would switch off without mercy and I would have to fumble in the darkness to find the next switch on the landing. I always wondered how much energy they saved by doing that.

The previous occupant of my unit had left behind a drape hanging across the ceiling, perhaps because she did not like looking at the high ceiling. It was made of white broadcloth printed with blue seagulls. Next to the entrance was a built-in closet to store shoes, umbrellas, and coats. There was no door into the room, only curtains draped on each side, which had also been left behind by the previous occupant. At the front of the room the ceiling seemed very high, and there were many windows with white cotton drapes hanging languidly upon them. The lower part of the windows could be pushed open, but the upper part was fixed shut. Actually, I did not mind looking at the ceiling, which was supported by an absurdly large I-beam. Shaded light fixtures hung from the ceiling, while the loft created a shelf and occupied about one third of the space. A steep ladder was attached to it. The loft was my bedroom, furnished with a low bed, a night stand, and a drawer to store my underwear. I brought up a low table for the empty corner and stacked up books I wanted to read. I would read lying in bed before I fell asleep. Under the loft was a pair of long folding chairs, the sort usually used at the beach, and a sofa bed. On the left side of the apartment was a round table and two wooden chairs, a desk and a chair, and a large easel and a midsize one that I bought myself. In the middle of the wall with windows was a gas stove that looked like a radiator. A pilot light the size of a candle flame was always lit, and when it was turned on a row of flames spread out to the left and right and heated it up. On the right side of the apartment was a huge built-in closet, and on the left was a door to the kitchen. Right behind that door was a small bathroom with a water heater, a toilet, a shower, and a little window.

Through the little window I could see the courtyard with pine trees, white birches, and zelkova trees. Right in front of my window stood a large horse chestnut tree with abundant green leaves whose flowers would float into my studio every spring. Just under the window was a small table for one, covered with galvanized iron, and a matching chair. I ate most of my simple meals there and became friendly with the horse chestnut tree. This long and narrow space lined with a sink and refrigerator was much cozier to me than the empty apartment, which looked like a storage room. Coming back home, I would sit there and drink warm tea mixed with liquor in order to warm up my cold body in wet clothes.

The reason I am describing all these tedious details is because this was my world. Finally I found that I was able to escape from the self-consciousness that had so oppressed me back home. I was able to work a great deal among people who did not know me.

As I said, once the laborers left after the war and moved into new apartments, the building had been used as a storage facility. The city had purchased it and turned it into studios for poor artists, renting them out for a low price. I found it through a friend, a musician from Czechoslovakia. People still called asking for the previous tenant. My answer was, *Call her in Prague.* I had also kept her tattered tablecloth and a small framed picture that hung in the kitchen. The tablecloth was an ordinary cotton one, and I guessed it once belonged to her because each corner was embroidered with daisies. Maybe she forgot to pack it. The frame hung above the table, right in front of my eyes when I sat down. It was a lithograph by Käthe Kollwitz, a self-portrait. Because of this one print, I decided I liked the previous occupant. In the 1920s, Kollwitz was already an old woman. Her eyes are filled with tenderness and compassion, yet under them are deep lines of suffering. She is looking out with an expression of a mother worried about her child. I did not hang anything else on the wall, but I did put up a poster next to the door, something I bought from a gift shop selling imported goods at the Kaiser Wilhelm Church. It was a picture of an American Indian warrior, and the photograph looked more like a charcoal drawing; maybe it was a gravure photo, or maybe just an old photograph reproduced carelessly. The warrior is standing on top of a crumbling bluff, and he is spreading a handful of something over the open field below. Looking at the feather on his head, the quiver on his back, and the axe in one hand, I was quite sure that he had just returned from a battlefield. I do not think he was throwing seeds or soil. Maybe it was the remains of someone who had been cremated. Underneath the photograph was a German sentence printed in black letters, "The motherland is sacred!"

I like the winter in Berlin. There were some really cold days, but most of the time it just drizzles. You just wrap a long scarf tightly around your neck, and if an umbrella is too cumbersome, you just put on a hat. It is not like a summer shower that pours down noisily. It just continues endlessly. And the fog rolls in, turning the space around each streetlamp misty. The bone-chilling cold slips in through the openings around your neck and the ends of your sleeves and reaches all the way up to your elbows.

One day I carried a sack full of laundry to the laundromat across the square, and I made a new friend there. I liked the laundromat; with a few coins you could do everything from buying some detergent to washing and drying your clothes and ironing, and there was always music playing and books and magazines around, even vending machines and coffee machines, so it was not too boring to sit there until the laundry was done. That night the laundromat was pretty empty because it was late in the evening. I was sitting in front of the washer when the door opened and an old lady entered. She looked as if she was coming back from an outing, because she was wearing a black suit with a silver pin on her chest, a necklace, and a pair of earrings, and her face was carefully made up. She was carrying a large leather bag in one hand, brown with brass fastenings, and I thought it looked very classy. But then out of that bag came her underwear. I could not help but watch her with interest, trying to be as discreet as possible. She put coins in the slot, opened the round door of a washing machine and stuffed in her laundry, then she took a seat across from me. When our eyes met she uttered a greeting, *Guten Tag*. I nodded my head in response. She sat there for a bit, then her shoulders trembled. She took out a small tin flask from her bag, the kind that so-called drink lovers or, if I'm really honest, alcoholics, always carried around in their pocket filled with cheap whiskey or brandy. She unscrewed the top, threw her head back, and took a generous gulp. She smacked her lips and raised the flask toward me.

"Would you like some?"

I was going to shake my head, but I decided to join in her loneliness and reached for it, accepting it with a *danke*. The moment I put the top to my lips I knew it was German brandy, very similar to French cognac. The taste and scent of it was quite nice.

"Can I have some more?" I asked her.

I guess she understood my poor German, and she answered of course I could, and I took another shot. She took another one, too.

"I'm Frau Mari Kline. I am your neighbor."

"Really? I'm Han."

"I know, I saw the nameplate at the door."

I had no idea who was living across the hall from my room, but perhaps she had been observing me from the day I moved in.

"My husband was an artist, too. He's long gone. He loved Asia. I still have a few pieces of Chinese pottery he liked. I could show them to you later, if you like."

Other students once warned me to be careful with lonely old neighbors who lived alone, but I did not care. Most of them lived with a dog or a cat as a companion, to whom they talked endlessly, as if to a family member. I was told that they were almost pathologically curious about other people's affairs, and once you talked to them, they tried everything they could to continue the relationship and meddle in your daily life. But the truth was that I felt like I was about to go crazy. I needed a neighbor, whoever it might be. As we spoke, sometimes neither of us understood a word the other was saying. Sometimes we had to mix in English, and by the time our laundry was done, we had emptied the little flask. I was the one who remembered it first.

"So can I see that pottery?"

"Oh, of course."

We walked back to the building together, each of us carrying laundry under one arm, as if we had known each other for a long time. We climbed up the spiral stairway, now one of us ahead, now the other. We lived on the same floor; my unit was on the right, while Frau Kline's was on the left. She opened the door and went inside first to turn the light on. It was identical to my unit except that there was no loft. The first things I saw were the paintings that almost completely covered the wall and the pottery displayed on top of a wooden chest of drawers. The room was sparsely furnished with a large bed at the far end of the room, a dining table with two wooden chairs in the middle, and a single easy chair. She turned on two lamps, and the room glowed warmly, as if lit by several candles. But nothing could hide the fact that it was the home of a poor, lonely woman. I walked to the chest and carefully studied each vessel that she showed me one by one. Two of them were Japanese, ordinary liquor bottles that you find in souvenir shops. A couple of jars with wide mouths and a calabash-shaped bottle were from China, perhaps more than a hundred years old. I realized these were the pieces of pottery she had been talking about. Still, they were just everyday vessels that were probably from a small antique shop in Hong Kong or another port city, and I bet there were many others just like them. The rest were earthenware, all of them produced for tourist shops.

"Aren't they nice?" she whispered. "My husband bought them for me. This one we bought together when we went to Japan."

I picked up the calabash-shaped bottle to look at the landscape painted on it.

"If you want it, I'll sell it to you."

"Well . . ."

I just smiled at her.

"How much do you need?"

Frau Kline thought about it for a little while.

"It's probably worth more than 500 marks, but I'll accept 300."

I nodded. I had not been to her kitchen yet, but I guessed that her pantry and refrigerator were empty. It seemed like she was on welfare, and she could probably survive a few days on nothing but liquor. She did not offer me a seat, but I sat down on the chair in front of the table.

"I think I have some tea. Should I add some whiskey to it?"

"How about just whiskey?"

"That sounds about right."

She went into the kitchen then came back with a small bottle of whiskey, half-filled, and two glasses. She poured each glass about half full and sat down on the easy chair facing me. Frau Kline raised her glass toward the calabash-shaped bottle.

"Goodbye, my dear," she muttered.

"Was it something you cherished?"

I knew it was just an inexpensive object, but I did not want to hurt her feelings.

"My husband was a very famous artist."

"When did he pass away?"

"Ten years ago."

"The paintings on the walls are his?"

"They are what's left, everything else went to galleries and museums."

I got up to walk around the room and study each painting on the wall, starting from the entrance area. Frau Kline remained in her easy chair.

"Actually, he died almost twenty years ago."

I turned my head toward her.

"He worked a lot for about eight years, until the mid-sixties, then he went into the hospital."

What I saw were the traces of the abstract expressionism of someone who wanted to escape from our fixed ideas and the rationales of the objective world. Using a knife or the rough strokes of a brush, a thick line was drawn from the top to the bottom, or paint was clumped together like a child's scrawl. These were familiar, like the paintings I had seen at many graduating student's exhibitions. On the second wall, the paint was more thickly applied and spread as if still wet. Various colors overlapped or separated or met again. On the third wall, up to the middle of it, was one with abstract characters roughly scored on a simple background. At the end of that wall was the largest painting in the house. Runny paint was mashed and squashed by fingers drawing numerous circles and lines. The color was not vivid, but muddy, as if someone who did not know how to apply paint was using too many colors and losing the original shades. In an attempt to remove the painter's thoughts and compositions and plans, he had actually left behind numerous imprints of his own hands and fingers on the painting. I was very happy. I stood in front of it for a long time, holding the glass in my hand and sipping from it little by little.

"That is the best one, isn't it?" she said.

I wanted to throw the question back at her.

"Why, is that what you think, Frau Kline?"

"You can call me Mari."

"Okay, I'll do that."

"He earnestly concentrated on wasting his talent. We had no choice. After the war, what was left were just piles of bricks and rats. Both of us detested this country."

"What did you do during the war?"

"You know the Hitler Youth? Even now, all Germans are soldiers. They're very good at lining up."

"Then why didn't you leave this place?"

"We were too poor, so we just lived here."

I spent about an hour talking to Mari and drank a couple more glasses before I got up.

"You want to come over to my place?"

"Will that be okay?"

"I should pay you for the pottery."

My room was three or four steps away, but she put a thick red shawl around her shoulders. I walked into my house with her close behind me. When I realized that I had her eyes following me, all of a sudden my house seemed unfamiliar. The first thing Mari did was look at the poster by the door and read out loud the words printed on it. *Mother. Land. Sacred.*

"A great image. But in Europe we killed the mother a long time ago."

I pretended that I did not hear her, grabbing my purse from the table to take out my wallet, and Mari walked over to the table to look at Kollwitz's self-portrait.

"Haven't seen this face in a long time. We are no longer able to produce something like this, not anymore."

"Ah, that's not mine. The previous renter left it here."

"Did you see the original in Cologne?"

"Not yet . . ."

I paused for a bit, then I added, "On one hand, I am so sick of people that I am trying to get rid of them and run away. On the other hand, I'm doing my best to find them."

Mari was not just an alcoholic old woman. A faint trace of a smile appeared around her mouth.

"That sounds very familiar. Stephan died at the national sanatorium. He lived there for twenty years with no idea who he was."

I took the money out of my wallet and handed it to her.

"Here, 300 marks."

She accepted it, counted and checked each bill like an old woman at a store making sure that the money was real, and put it away in her pocket. I watched her walk into her apartment from my doorway, and I placed the humble calabash-shaped bottle she left behind on the table and stared at it blankly. For a second or two, I thought I should put a couple of roses in its empty mouth.

I thought about how Mari and Stephan probably met in the middle of postwar ruins, at a studio or an art school or maybe a makeshift exhibition space in a warehouse. I do not think they came from East Berlin or had any intention of crossing to there. But I still think they had a hard time adjusting to postwar West Germany, where freedom was plentiful but it was that of the occupied, a freedom rationed by Americans. It was also the case for many East German artists who had been stuck with the mannerisms ingrained by propaganda, which had forced them to cease to be individuals, but who had finally managed to awaken from their disillusionment. As soon as he was released from the sharp teeth of the swastika, young Stephan might have been attracted to the Americans' sense of naïveté, their wild freedom. After all, every desire begins with a reaction against something. By the time they realized that their generation had been caged and domesticated behind the Iron Curtain, it was too late. He probably often drifted off to a place of spring naps, like the place painted on the exotic bottle he brought over for Mari, and he gradually forgot the way back to his humble home in Berlin.

How can I start again? I cannot be another Mari, whose life stopped twenty years ago, self-anesthetizing myself, can I? According to her, Stephan was little known in the art scene because his friends, now the establishment, bought his paintings and donated his work to public museums. But what I felt looking at the modest works he left behind, hanging on the walls of her house, is how small we are, that a person's ideals, life, and work could be just a little bubble. I could see the last traces of his hand when I went back to Mari's house, but I began to think that they were actually his beginning.

The reason I wrote down details about Frau Mari Kline is because she was one of my closest friends during that time. And she is also the only person who knew the intricacies of my sad relationship with someone else.

Wait, there is one thing I forgot. Just like you and me, they lived together freely without the legal union of marriage. They lived for ten years in a warehouse in Kreutzberg, now a Turkish neighborhood. Mari sent her man, who had by this time forgotten how to speak, to a sanatorium and visited him once a month. She gave up painting and worked as a caretaker of the elderly during her middle age, and then as an hourly maid when she got older, barely making a living.

Much later, I saw her drawings and sketches. She would go to Tiergarten near the Zoo station, always clean and neatly dressed, and sketch with a pencil on a small pad the size of her palm. Numerous lines overlapped each other, and they seemed simple, yet complex. I was barely able to make out objects like a bicycle and a house, or a bathtub and a pair of shoes. I knew for sure that there was a female figure, repeated in similar shapes, perhaps herself. A circle for head, and a few pencil lines behind the circle to denote hair. I asked her about it once.

"This . . . what is it?"

I asked, pointing to a figure that looked like a tangle of wool.

"Oh, that's Hans."

"Who's that?"

"Stephan's dog."

"I guess there's a story here."

Mari pointed to something else that looked like a showerhead.

"It's a mop, used to clean a room. I beat Hans with that mop."

"You don't have a dog."

"He died a long time ago."

"Ah, so what you're drawing at the park is not from the present. You're drawing memories."

Mari stuck her red tongue out between her wrinkled lips, like a little girl whose important secret has been revealed.

"Why did you beat Hans?"

"Because I hated Stephan. It was his dog, after all. I think it was the winter of 1970. He was not painting anything at the time, not one single painting. I was working as a caretaker for sick people. I would come back early in the morning after working all night, and he would have finished a whole bottle of cheap schnapps and be sleeping. Of course he did not think of feeding the dog. Hans would get crazy, whining and jumping all over, so I punished him really harshly. After that, Hans didn't like me. Yuni, you probably don't know what the year 1968 was like for us."

That's what she called me, Yuni.

"A little bit."

"Here was worse than Paris. The young people thought that everything had to be destroyed so they could start all over again. After that, there were two choices left. Go back to the countryside and the primitive lifestyle, or become a terrorist."

"What does that mean?"

"There's not much of a difference. One lot was thinking in the long term, the other thought there was not much time left. They wanted to change the methods of production and consumption."

"After the war, we all wandered about like Stephan, in Japan and in my country. Even the paintings are similar. The brave avant-garde. Now, we're much better than that."

Mari's eyes were turning red.

"These days I wonder what he really wanted to do. I just live by remembering little things."

The eighties went by so fast. Some other Korean students in Berlin who were my age got together once and talked about it. They said it was just like we went to the outhouse for a few minutes, and when we came back a decade had gone by. In Mari I saw myself, and in the disappeared Stephan I saw you and Song Young Tae and most of all Mi Kyung.

But where was the snowman we all made together, so merrily and with such care? Under the daylight of one afternoon, the original shape melted away. The coal eyebrow and red pepper nose fell from its face. The hat was blown away by the wind. The head melted on top of the body and formed a small mound of snow, soiled by dirt and dust. The children's joyous laughter is no longer there, and all that is left on the street is a little life, muddied by wheels and footsteps.

24

Then as now, I do not feel I have to apologize to you.

Unexpectedly, I fell in love with a man. For a long time, you were not a reality. To me, Eun Gyul was like that, too. As prison was a part of your life, the love that came to me somewhat late in my life in a land so far away was also a very important part of mine.

It was May 1989. May was the most glorious season of the year, a blessing. The chill and misery melted away with the low, dark clouds, and the clear blue sky opened up. So many flowers bloomed at once that people allergic to pollen walked around with bloodshot eyes wearing masks and blowing their noses nonstop.

I took the U9 line, which started in Steglitz, to Tiergarten. I thought I would take a walk along the Landwehr Canal, where the memorials for Rosa Luxemberg and Karl Liebknecht were, or look at the ducks and swans on the lake before taking a long walk around the park and going into the city center. Sometimes I bought a bratwurst at a stall nearby. The memorials used to sear my heart whenever I looked at them, but now they were just words that always stood there, like signs on any street. The bourgeois party had built the memorials to honor the very same people they had killed. To get to them you take the little round bridge in the shape of a rainbow across the canal, then walk along a narrow path and reach a forest with almost no one else around.

Anyway, what extraordinary thing can happen on the subway? In Berlin's subway, there was no one who checked your ticket at the entrance or in the train. But everyone carried around a pass or bought a ticket. If you thought you could try and get away with riding trains without paying, you might get caught when train guards unexpectedly boarded the train and demanded to see your pass or ticket. You would be embarrassed and have to pay a hefty fine.

Since I was a student, I had a pass. I got a discount, so it was a good deal. I always kept it in my purse, but I had never met a guard on a train before, so I sometimes forgot whether I had it with me or not. But other students told me plenty of stories about their humiliating experiences, so I tried not to forget. Once in a while, I ran back to my studio when I realized that I had left my pass in there. At the Berliner Straße station, four men in uniform got onto my train.

They began checking people's tickets, two on each end of the car walking toward the center. I was not very surprised, I simply opened my purse to look for my pass. *Oh no, where is it?* I could not find it. Already, my face was turning red and I could not stand still. The man in uniform knew what it meant, and he looked straight into my eyes and opened his hand toward me. I stuttered, "I . . . forgot to . . . bring my pass."

"You have to leave the train at the next station."

Two young men and an older gentleman in that car were caught as well. I was still hoping to find it, and I kept rummaging through my purse. I found everything else but the pass. Now I was worried about the fine. All that was in my wallet was a little over twenty marks in bills and coins. When the train arrived at the Güntzelstraße station, the officers gathered those of us who were caught in front of one door and directed us to get out. That was when he approached me from behind. "Don't worry, it's no big deal."

I glanced at him, but I did not have the time to look at him properly. You had to show the officers your ID, pay the fine, and get a receipt, or if you didn't have enough money, confirm your address, promise to pay the fine later, and sign a document stating that you had ridden the subway train without a pass. It was my turn, and of course I did not have enough money. Once again, I heard the voice from behind. "Do you have enough money to pay the fine?"

It was only then that I realized something and I turned around, not just my head, but my whole body, to face him. Both times he had spoken to me in Korean. He looked much older than me. He was wearing a dark gray trench coat, and it seemed like he had not shaved in a few days, because stubble covered his chin here and there. But his eyes were warm and smiling. I took out one ten-mark bill and two five-mark bills from my wallet and showed them to him. He simply nudged me aside, asked the officer how much the fine was, paid for it, signed the receipt, and pushed me out the door.

"Let's go. They're busy, too."

We hurried out of the office. He took the stairway leaving the station and I followed him, still confused. He was tall. And he swung his slightly bent shoulders as he walked. When we climbed up the stairs, we were right next to the wide Bundesallee, where cars were speeding by.

"Um, excuse me . . ."

He turned around.

"I know, you owe me," he said.

"I'm sorry, I think I left the pass at home."

"That happened to me, too, I know how that feels. If you're unlucky, you can get caught twice in one month."

"If you give me your address or phone number, I'll pay you back later."

"Ah, here's the receipt."

He took the fine receipt from his coat pocket and handed it to me.

"You look like a student, what do you study?"

"I'm at the art school."

I took the receipt but I could not part ways with him; I began walking with him because he was moving again without giving me a chance to say goodbye.

"How long has it been," he asked, "since you got here?"

"I came last year. And you . . . what do you do here?"

"I'm a research fellow here at the engineering school. By the way, where . . . Are you going home now?"

"No, I was going to take a walk."

"Oh, that's good. I am invited to a dinner. Why don't you join me?"

"Well, that's a bit . . ."

I was slowing down my steps, but he kept moving forward, and then he raised one finger and shook it at me.

"You won't have another chance to pay your debt."

I sped up to walk with him again. "Where are you going . . . ?"

"To the home of a friend of mine who is studying here. Don't worry. Don't you wanna eat bean paste stew?"

Maybe it was the thought of the fragrance of warm bean paste stew, or maybe because his invitation seemed so natural, but somehow I found myself walking with him toward Rosenheimer Straße. He told me his name, Yi Hee Soo. I gave him mine. He had been an assistant professor at a university in Korea. He had gotten a degree in Korea and now he was trying to experience different cultures, to do some research and add something to his resume. Anyhow, I felt more at ease. Forty-two or -three, or maybe forty-five years old? But he could still pass for someone in his mid-thirties.

I felt a little awkward as I visited a student's apartment with him. There was just a couple, Mr. and Mrs. Shin, no child. The husband seemed to be reserved and sincere, but the wife was belligerent and high-strung. When she became tipsy, she talked to us in a casual form of speech, swore at her husband, and in general acted quite rowdy, but she did not make us feel uncomfortable. It seemed like she was exhausted from supporting her husband in a foreign country, yet she was not condescending. We stuffed ourselves with kimchi, bean paste stew, lettuce wraps, pork belly, garlic, and soju.

We left that house around ten in the evening, and by that time I felt like I had known Mr. Yi for a long time. He was an environmental engineer, but there seemed to be more to him than someone who just knew about machines. He actually seemed to know a lot about many different things. He was studying how Germans disposed of their domestic and industrial waste. But he was not as radical as my other friends in Korea. He carried on a conversation with humor, not confrontationally, and he was sensible. I had never met a man like him before, so balanced. I could bet that he grew up in a conflict-free middle-class household, a houseplant placed by the window where there was plenty of sunshine and fresh air.

With the excuse that I had to repay him, we met once more sometime in mid-May. I treated him to dinner at an Italian restaurant called Roma near where I lived. I forget what we talked about that night. I can remember every little thing I talked about, so many years ago, with my father or you or Young Tae or Mi Kyung, but why is it that I cannot remember that conversation with him? We did exchange some personal information that day. He had gotten divorced three years before. He had a teenage son who was living with his mother. I did not want to tell him my story. He knew little about me, less than my neighbor Mari. Of course, eventually he would learn everything.

The day after our dinner date, Mr. Yi called me in the afternoon. He invited me over for dinner at his house. It was such a beautiful day, and the park was colorful with kids and families, young men and women sunbathing, elderly people walking their dogs. My heart was fluttering for no reason, and I had been out twice already in short sleeves and cotton pants. Through the open window, the murmuring sound of the horse chestnut tree leaves dancing outside the window floated in. Someone was practicing the flute in the opposite building, and the clear sound drifted in and out.

When I got to the phone, Mr. Yi said he had already called several times. I wrote down the address he gave me, and still excited even though I had seen him the night before, I changed my clothes. I had only a handful of occasions to dress up in Germany, and this was one of them. I think I still have that dress. A simple, light brown dress that reached the middle of my calves. It was loose, and there was a cord that I could tie around the waist. I cannot tell you how comfortable that dress was. It was made out of Indian cotton, as thin as gauze. Is it weird for you that I'm going on and on about a piece of clothing? I found it among the piles of clothes at a flea market in front of the city hall.

Once, we had to cut down a rose tree in our garden because it was infested with aphids. All that was left after the winter were short stubs of dried brown branches barely visible on the ground. No one in the family mentioned the roses from the previous year. Why would we? It was just a tiny thing sticking out of the ground. In spring, we planted other annuals, the seeds of moss roses and four o'clocks and zinnias. Tender sprouts came up, and soon the pale green turned dark as the garden blossomed into a lively flower bed. But one morning as I watered the garden, among the competing flowers I found a few small buds, rose buds. Among the vibrant annuals, I saw a green branch growing right next to the brown sticks, straight and ready to bloom.

Before I left the house, I studied myself in front of the half-length mirror in the entranceway draped with the seagull-patterned cloth. I thought I saw something wet, something shiny in my eyes somewhere. My heart was racing, as if I'd had several cups of strong, dark coffee. Outside, the darkness was still faint, but the antique streetlamps of Berlin were already on, lighting the evening mist. I was carrying a thin sweater and I decided to drape it around my shoulders.

His house was in an old three-story apartment building in Wilmersdorf with high ceilings like mine. His unit only had one bedroom, although the living room and the kitchen were quite spacious. I sat down in front of a large table that was both a dinner table and a desk. There was a computer and a bookcase and not much else in terms of furniture. Mr. Yi was wearing an apron that covered his chest, and he was struggling in front of the oven.

"What are you doing?" I asked as I approached from behind. He gently pushed me away.

"Hey, women are not allowed in the kitchen."

"What, are you playing a game of opposites?"

"Haven't you heard of neo-Confucianism?"*

He pointed to the table. "Please, sit over there. Tonight's special is— have you ever had lamb?"

"Of course. You need lots of spices for that."

Mr. Yi opened a cold bottle of Mosel wine, filled a glass with it, and gave it to me. "A palate cleanser before dinner."

I put the cold glass to my lips and sipped a little from it. I walked around the house with the glass in my hand and saw a framed black-and-white photo of a sculpture of Maitreya sitting with one leg up and meditating with a mysterious smile on his face. Then there was a brass Buddha, about eight inches tall, standing by the window, and a tapestry next to the bathroom door depicting a thin and elongated Buddha.

---

* There is an old Korean saying that men are not allowed in the kitchen.

"There are a lot of Buddhas here."

"Well, I like it over there. I cut out that photo from an airplane magazine. The brass one I brought over with my books, and the tapestry was a present from a friend of mine, Martin."

He brought a plate of skewered lamb and peppers, eggplants, and onions to the table. There also was a basket of rye bread and another bottle of wine.

"They look great."

"I learned from a friend."

I ate very well. The appetizer of thinly sliced ham and melon was wonderful, too. After the dinner was over, we drank a trocken wine with a slightly bitter taste, and Mr. Yi offered me a hand-rolled cigarette. I took a puff, and the smoke was stronger than a normal cigarette, yet the original fragrance of grass, so pleasant and sweet, remained and complimented the bitter taste of the wine.

"This is a cigarette, isn't it?"

"They sell it at the Turkish shops. I think it's from Pakistan."

"It's more rustic than a cigar."

If I had seen a scene like this in a movie, I would have shuddered at the corniness of it all. But such a reaction would have been an overstatement, too, don't you think? So what if we pretended a little? The next day, the midday sun would rise again, bleaching out all our props and scenery.

"So why do you like that over there?" I pointed at the Buddha hanging on the wall with the cigarette.

"That we're all one; it sounds so nice and peaceful."

"It is easy to interpret the world in the simplest terms."

"Who's doing the interpretation? People attach meanings to seasons and things like that based on their own lives. The world exists alone, unrelated to all that."

"We should change the world, shouldn't we?"

I sounded just like my friends. And he, the quiet one—his eyes widened and he threw the question back at me, a little indignant.

"Change? For what? It's a tiny wave in the ocean. Each life is so short. Why can't you stop thinking that humans own this world? Over there, the idea seems to go against physical reality at first. But through meditation, you get rid of your desires, you become nonexistent, and you humbly disappear. You don't come back or go to another world, or anything like that. To use the language they use, you escape forever the chains of transmigration and reincarnation. That is the way to exist for the world."

I did not reply, although I wanted to ask about war, poverty, and hunger. Mr. Yi continued, "They say the enlightened Buddha does not reincarnate, but I think reincarnation is not such a bad idea. Of course, everyone firmly believes that they'll come back as a human being. But it is said that such a reincarnation is only possible after millions of eons. Why not as an insect, or if you want to be a bit fancier, a pine tree standing on top of a hill? The leaves dancing in the wind. East or West, manmade cities and industrialization are hell."

"Indeed, it hasn't been that long since we appeared on this Earth. But I am, right now, a human being."

"We know that we took the wrong course, that of technology and progress, and we're inevitably headed toward the waterfall of self-destruction. We humans are supposed to be the most intelligent creatures, but we're less responsible than other feeble creatures who don't want more than they already have, aren't we?"

I was beginning to feel stifled, but I remained patient. "First of all, we need to correct the relationships between human beings."

"Nothing would change how it's been done so far. Life itself has to be transformed."

I could feel my voice getting louder. "How is that possible? The means of production, the methods, the actual power, they are all firmly established already. Who's going to do it? How? Shall we start a new movement?"

"The argument for system versus culture is not easy, and it cannot end tonight, even if we start now."

My words were becoming harsh and biting. "I saw the flag of the Green Party here, and it was purple. Blue painted over the red. If that is not reformism, what is? Revolution is impossible, so let's try a movement for a new lifestyle and see what happens in the long term, isn't that it? Someone once defined it as . . . absorbing the opposing force. With a lot of money, anything can be planned and controlled."

"It is a natural process. The abundance of summer causes a forest to become thick and overgrown, but then the monsoons and floods arrive to get rid of the elements of decay and corpulence. And finally the fruits and grains of the harvest season arrive. A civilization can be transformed only through the united efforts of nature and humans. If you change what's inside, the shell will fall apart or change its appearance. If only quantity is valued and everything is judged according to numbers, then the more important aspect, the quality, is ignored. As everything becomes too specialized and divided and standardized, and if, on top of that, due consideration and awareness are lacking, then the production becomes bigger and more complicated, the need for money becomes greater, and leads to violence. Whether it is socialism or capitalism, both start from an obsession with production. A plentiful society, a society where that abundance is wasted, cannot be a model for the rest of the world. A plentiful society's rule tells the rest of the world that we can all live well if we follow its technology and development. But that would be a disaster for everyone. We need a different model. Without fundamental changes in favor of something that is humbler and simpler and more vital, the system cannot change. Our humanistic approach toward labor and capital will remain within the system, and therefore it will never gain the strength to transform the system itself."

I could not agree with everything he was saying, but I was attracted to the fact that he was passionate about something and that he knew what he wanted to do. Unlike us, he was keeping a certain distance from reality. And at the same time, his words sounded very abstract. Either way, he was to become my closest friend in that foreign land so far away from home.

The weather was quite unpredictable in June, and I got really sick. And I did not feel good about it. Whenever a change was about to happen to me, I always got really sick and had to suffer through it. A child grows and matures whenever she goes through an illness, but for an adult like me, maybe it was just a shortcut to aging and decline. But then I didn't really think that was the case. There is a difference between a light spring rain that softly encourages new sprouts and a heavy autumn rain that strengthens the roots deeply embedded in the soil. I wished I could sink lower and deeper into my heart.

I could not leave my bed in the loft. I wrapped myself with a thick sleeping bag and two blankets, but my teeth were still chattering and my body shaking. My neighbor Mari figured out what was going on, and she brought over hot onion soup and chamomile tea spiked with whiskey. She wrapped a thickly knitted scarf around my exposed neck.

"Now you're becoming a real Berliner."

Here, I had been told, you suffered from both allergies from May flowers and from the flu, thanks to June showers. The weather was unbelievably capricious. Rain in the morning, sun for a few minutes at noon, hail or snow in the afternoon, then thunder and lightning at night. The phone kept ringing, but I could not leave the loft, so I let the answering machine pick up. From down below and far away, I heard Mr. Yi's voice.

"Hi, it's me, Yi Hee Soo. I called you several times but haven't heard back, so I was just curious. Are you traveling? Anyway, call me when you get back, please."

When the phone rang again Mari happened to be at my house.

"Mari, can you answer the phone for me?"

She answered the phone, then covered the receiver with one hand. "Yuni, it's a man named Yi."

"Aaah, tell him I cannot come to the phone because I'm not feeling well."

Mari conveyed the message in German to him and hung up the phone.

"Who is Yi?" Mari asked as she came back up to the loft with a cup of hot chamomile tea.

"A boyfriend I acquired recently."

I took the mug from her, which was so heavy that my wrist could barely hold it up. I took a sip but it did not go down smoothly.

"Ugh, you put too much whiskey in here."

"Drink it. It'll warm you up."

Not wanting to disappoint her, I forced the tea down my throat, one sip at a time.

"Please, try to cut down the liquor. And don't forget to eat real meals."

"Yes, I know. I started drinking just at night before I went to bed, to save on heating bills, but the quantity just kept growing. So, tell me about this boyfriend of yours."

"I don't know him that well yet. He's forty-three, divorced with one son."

"That sounds like information for government officials."

I smiled meekly, "What do you want me to say?"

"I think both of you are interested . . ."

"How do you know that, Mari?"

She tapped on her wrinkled nose with her index finger and said, "Through here. Even in complete darkness, I know if it's vodka or schnapps or cognac in the bottle. Just like liquor, love has a very distinctive scent."

"Did you ever have relationships with men after Stephan went to the sanatorium?"

"Of course, a few of them. There was the doctor, an ordinary guy, and the theater director who was really poor . . . Can't remember when the last one was."

"Was he still alive at the sanatorium?"

"Yes, he was. That's very different. You're thinking of that man in prison now, aren't you? But consider how we dream. No one dreams of one thing all night long. When we awake only certain images stay with us clearly, though no one can predict where a dream will go. We do not know how our lives will end. But without the intertwining of disparate elements, we would die without knowing which were the important parts."

Maybe it was the whiskey in the chamomile tea, but my eyes became heavy and I felt sleepy. Mari tucked me in. "You can't have the same dream all the time. There will be others. Goodnight."

When I opened my eyes again, I could not tell how long I had been asleep. The cloth draped across the tall windows was still dimly lit, but I could not tell what time it was. The early summer sun stayed up longer, but the window also remained bright when the terrace above was lit. Then I realized the bell was ringing. And someone was shouting, "Yuni, wake up, open the door! Someone's here!"

The bell kept ringing, and I took one rung at a time, my legs shaking, down the ladder. I turned the light on.

"Mari?"

Someone else, not German, replied, "It's me."

I opened the door. Mari, wearing her nightgown and shawl, was standing there with Mr. Yi.

"What's going on?" I muttered as I hid halfway behind the door, like a scared child. I was wearing big, baggy pajamas that looked like a man's, my hair must have been clumped, disheveled, and sticking out, and my skin shadowed and sickly yellow with an expression of total misery.

"Are you really okay?"

Mr. Yi pushed the door and was about to enter, but he stopped and turned around to nod to Mari, "Thank you, ma'am."

"*Bitte schön.*"

Mr. Yi shut the door firmly. He was carrying something in his hand, and he put the other hand on my shoulder without hesitation.

"Go lie down. There's no real medicine for a flu. You just keep your body warm and sleep as much as you can."

It was strange, but listening to a man's voice speaking my own language made me feel so warm, yet also made me want to cry. I did not dare go up the ladder to the loft and leave him. I found a blue tartan blanket that I normally used in the park and sat down on the reclining chair. He was about to enter the kitchen, as if he had been to my house several times. I was barely able to speak but I managed to ask in the softest whisper, "What are you doing?"

"Oh, I bought a few things from the Korean grocery store. Let's treat this illness our way. A warm and spicy soup with bean sprouts, and since they didn't have abalone, I'll make you pine nut porridge."

Amazed, I had to laugh a little. He stuck out one finger and shook it, just like he did when we first met in the subway.

"I'm not going to let you laugh at my hobby. Stay there, don't do anything."

"Fine. What time is it anyway?"

"A little after nine in the evening."

The kitchen door was closed, and through the crack I saw him turn the light on. There was a clattering noise, the sound of cupboard doors and drawers opening and closing, the rhythmic beat of the knife moving on the cutting board, all of them made me fantasize that I had returned home. The sound of water flowing from the faucet, and the low whistling, too. I don't know how long it took. Something smelled good, just like the smell from the kitchen at home. The door opened and I laughed so hard that I began to cough.

He was wearing my apron. It was something I grabbed at Ikea and decorated with various-sized strawberries. Mr. Yi set the table with different bowls and dishes, remembering to place a cork potholder under the pot. I could not resist the smell anymore, so I slowly dragged myself to the table, still wrapped in the blanket.

He took the lid off and filled a bowl with a ladle. It was a real miracle, the soup with bean sprouts, and white porridge with pine nuts, and two kinds of kimchi—where he found them I had no idea. As I took a spoonful of hot broth, I exhaled involuntarily. The broth was seasoned perfectly with red pepper flakes sunken to the bottom. He sat across from me and grinned as he watched me, like a parent. I just kept drinking the broth. Mr. Yi took a spoonful, too, and said, "Here, there's a different word for a flu."

"What . . . ?"

"Loneliness."

"That sounds about right."

"Most illnesses can be cured at least halfway by just eating Korean food."

The bowl of soup was done, and then so was the porridge, accompanied by the crunchy, savory kimchi.

"What are you, a magician? Where did you get the kimchi?"

"Would you be disappointed if I told you that I bought it from the store?"

"No matter what, the soup was just amazing."

I wiped the beads of sweat around my nose with a napkin.

"Well, it's time to clean up."

He got up to get the dishes, and I tried to stop him.

"Please, don't. I'll do them later."

"When you volunteer, you might as well go all the way. Then the gratitude will be as plentiful as your offer."

Again there was a clattering noise, the sound of water, him whistling. My body felt so warm and relaxed, and I fell asleep before I knew it. When I opened my eyes again, the lights hanging from the ceiling were turned off, only one lamp by the wall was on. It was so quiet. I got up and sat down. There was the sound of someone breathing. I looked around and found Mr. Yi sitting on what looked like a beach chair, his legs stretched out, asleep. He had found a square pillow, placed it on his belly, and was hugging it with both arms as he slept. I picked up the tartan blanket that I had wrapped myself with, and I approached him as quietly as I could to cover him with it. I quietly chuckled a little, too. Because I put the blanket on top of the pillow, it looked like he had an enormous belly. I went into the kitchen. My goodness. In the plastic dish rack, dishes and bowls were arranged according to their sizes, each one of them washed and dried perfectly. Then I found a note attached to a shelf.

> I brought over some spices, so I organized them a little. It will be easier for you if you label them later. As for soy sauce, I combined it with what you already had and put it in the cupboard under the gas stove with the oil. Arranged on the top shelf, in order, are: red pepper flakes, black pepper, dried parsley, garlic powder, bay leaves, bouillon cubes, salt, and sesame seeds. Bean paste and fermented bean paste are in the refrigerator. It's not from the store, Mrs. Shin provided them.

He must have thought that after I fell asleep he would clean up the whole kitchen and go. When he was done, he would have tiptoed around the house to turn off the lights and thought he would take a little rest, and then he must have just fallen asleep. I did not wake him, I just went back up to the loft and lay down on my bed. He did not snore, but he smacked his lips from time to time, as if he was eating something in his sleep, like a child. For the first time in a long time I felt safe and not alone, and it felt really nice. That was how we spent our first night together.

Many people left Berlin in July. They went to the beach, the mountains, southern Germany, or abroad. Students went back home or to West Germany, where there were more summer jobs available. Many Korean students also went home for the summer, and only the elderly and their dogs remained in the parks. The days got longer and longer, and the dark blue of dusk was still visible at ten at night. I would often think that it was still early in the evening, but if I checked my watch it would be quite late at night. I told you that I got quite close to the horse chestnut tree outside my kitchen window, didn't I? Its thick branches hung heavily next to my window, and on windy days the branches and leaves touching my window sounded like they wanted to talk to me. Often Mr. Yi would appear with groceries and a plan to cook something delicious. One hot summer evening, he came with thin noodles and young radish kimchi in one of the large, round jars that the Germans used to store fruit jams. I was so surprised, because all I could find at the groceries, even in the Turkish stores, was napa cabbage, Chinese napa cabbage at that. Where did he find young radishes? He told me that there was a Korean man who came to Germany as a miner. He had rented a parcel of farmland nearby, and he was growing all sorts of our vegetables there. The bestselling item in summer was the young radishes. Of course, the person who bought the young radishes and turned them into edible kimchi was Mr. Yi Hee Soo himself. We all know that you need to salt the vegetable first and add lots of seasonings. But that day I found out for the first time that you could season it by submerging it in saltwater with a cheesecloth pouch filled with a mixture of glutinous rice powder and red pepper. Afterward, you use this liquid from the kimchi and mix it with stock for the noodles, but you never use meat, as it's not refreshing in summer. Using large dried anchovies with the heads and innards trimmed, sauté them in a dry pan, then start cooking them in cold water and take them out when the water boils. That way, the stock is not too fishy, just mildly flavorful. Mix the cooled-down stock with the kimchi liquid. Cook the thin white noodles and rinse them in cold water, place them in a bowl with young radish kimchi on top, and then add the liquid. We sat facing each other, so close that our heads were almost touching, around the tiny table by the window. Behind the glass the horse chestnut tree danced with the wind, and we ate the cold noodles. I remember that summer in Berlin, slurping endlessly, with no pretension whatsoever, it all tasted so good. As the tree moved, it sounded like it was laughing out loud.

The midpoint between our houses was where Volkspark intersected Bundesallee, and we would leave our houses and meet at the grassy area near the children's playground. Already, he and I had entered into each other's daily lives.

One day at the end of that summer, we had to go back to his house from Volkspark. The rain was pouring down, so we were waiting for the rain to stop, and I stayed there overnight. The sound of thunder was really loud. Even the windows shook. Both of us were startled and flinched a little, shouting, *What is going on?*

It became colder and I put on a large sweatshirt that he handed me. As the water flowed down the drain, it sounded as if we were near a brook. From the sweatshirt, especially around the neck and the chest, came the scent of his aftershave and cigars. Such smells were already familiar to me. I was sitting on the one easy chair in his house, the one covered in corduroy, with my legs up, and Mr. Yi was sitting a little bit away from me, by the wooden table with his feet on it. We drank freshly brewed coffee in large mugs, each of us holding our mugs with both hands. With the first sip, my throat warmed up but a chill went down my spine. My lower belly ached a little, and I wanted to pee. I did not finish half the cup of coffee before I went to the bathroom. After I emptied my bladder, I wanted to soak in hot water.

"I'm going to take a bath!" I shouted to him through the closed door.

I turned the water on, took off the sweatshirt permeated with his scent, and poured some bubble bath in. He knocked on the door.

"Yes?"

What was really not like me, when I thought about it later, was that I was not surprised or taken aback. Already, we were that much part of each other's lives.

"Here," he mumbled from behind the door.

I opened it a little to let his hand in. It was holding a glass full of red wine. He leaned through the gap. "It will relax you. Make you feel better."

I took the wine glass and went into the bathtub filled with white bubbles. The water warmly enveloped my whole body. I put the glass down on one end of the tub and enjoyed the feeling of my body unwinding little by little. I took a sip from the glass, and then another sip, and as the slightly bitter sour taste lingered at the tip of my tongue I felt my body awakening. For a long time, I had been asexual. I had sometimes felt certain urges, maybe a few times a year. But I always just went back to sleep, lonely and weary, like a patient recovering from surgery imagining all the wonderful things to eat but just drinking a cup of water to appease the appetite. I had never told anyone about this, but for a long time I slept with extra pillows in my bed. It just felt so empty. I placed them all around me, and as I tossed and turned I hugged them with my arms or legs.

After the bath, I wiped the mist on the bathroom mirror, and in an instant before the steam covered it again, I saw my body, flushed like a child's. I did not put the sweatshirt on, instead I took the white terrycloth robe hanging on the door. His robe was too big for me, the hem reached the ground, and I had to roll up the sleeves a couple of times.

I lay down on a chair for a while, and although I could hear everything I could not move, as if I was under hypnosis. I knew he was near me because of the scent of his cigar. Neither of us said a word, we just touched and confirmed each other's intentions and made love. I was afraid. To me this was just like the wall that stood somewhere in Berlin, obstinate and unavoidable. Knowing that the way ahead would be blocked I would turn even before I could see it. We started that way, two people wandering along an endless wall.

The first night I spent with him, I could not sleep deeply. I kept waking up, and telling myself to sleep, then falling asleep again, opening my eyes and realizing a couple of hours had passed with no trace, like I had a light fever. As I tossed my head on his arm and saw behind his shoulder the dawn seeping in through the window, I realized how much I wanted him. We could not spend a day without seeing each other, and ran to our respective apartments whenever we could, so that sometimes we would end up missing each other. Sometimes I would just confirm his presence at his house by watching the light come from his window, and then go back the way I had come.

What did we do until that autumn? We did not even notice that the season was changing. He and I formed a single universe. In a short period of time I got to know most of his friends, from his fellow researchers and school friends, to Korean-German acquaintances and waiters at the Korean restaurants and shops, to his neighbors.

It was October. Now that I think about it, it was just a few weeks before the wall came down. I had returned home to find several messages on my answering machine. I was listening to them halfheartedly as I filled the coffeemaker with water, put the filter in, measured the ground coffee, and pushed the button, when suddenly a very familiar voice caught my attention.

"Miss Han, it's me, Song Young Tae. I've been here in Germany since last summer. In Göttingen. I've been meaning to call you, but it took me a while to settle down, so I kept postponing it, and now hopefully it's not too late. I'm planning to study here for a few years. Jung Hee said you're doing well. I'll call you again soon."

I went back to the answering machine to hear his voice one more time. At his first words of *Miss Han, it's me*, my eyes welled up. And at that moment, I thought of you, something I had not done for the past couple of months, and I thought of the building with a billiard room from which Mi Kyung fell, and I thought of Seoul. It was like coming back home from a long trip to find your personal belongings still there, unchanged. I realized how long I had been gone. Lovers lose all sense of time and space, but it is just an illusion. It is like death. Everything was still there, except us.

November 9, 1989. Berlin.

I was there that day. The music was on, I turned up the volume, and I was eating dinner by myself. I cooked a sausage from the refrigerator, and I boiled a potato and ate it with salt. I was eating a piece of dark bread and cheese with a small bottle of beer when the phone rang. I thought it was Mr. Yi, who was on a business trip to Frankfurt with his friend Martin.

"Hi, it's me."

"Miss Han?"

"Huh, who is this?"

"Who did you think I was? It's me, Song Young Tae."

"My goodness, that's right, you called before once. So you're in Göttingen? What on earth are you doing there, you little monster?"

"I'm studying, of course, what else? I have to go to Berlin, can I stay with you?"

"Of course, no problem. My place is decent enough. But what are you coming here for?"

"You don't know? Turn the television on."

"I don't have such a thing. What, something's happening?"

"The whole of Germany is going crazy. The East German government declared the removal of the Berlin Wall and free travel between the two sides. It is the beginning of Germany's reunification. The wall will be useless from now on!"

"Is this true?"

"Yes, it is! Go out and witness everything for me. I plan to be there tomorrow."

We ended the phone call after exchanging our addresses and phone numbers. Finally, I heard noise from outside. I tried to look out, but my studio faced the courtyard and I could not see the street from there. Then the doorbell rang. It was Mari.

"Yuni! I was just watching TV and they said the wall is coming down! Everyone is going toward the East!"

"I just heard. We should go to Brandenburg or Potsdam, Mari."

"I was just about to."

The phone rang again, this time it was Mr. Yi's voice. "Yoon Hee, did you hear the news?"

"Just now."

"What an enormous change it will be! I'm almost there. We should be able to get into the city in about an hour. Why don't we meet at that café in front of the train station?"

"Let's do that. I was just about to leave."

As I hung up the phone and got ready to leave, Mari asked me, hesitating, "Look . . . do you have money?"

"For what?"

"Let's get a bottle of champagne."

"Champagne?"

"Yes. This will probably be the last party for me."

I put on a trench coat and walked out the door with Mari, who was wearing a thick winter coat and even a hat. At a convenience store we bought a bottle of champagne, and as we crossed the square we saw people honking their car horns and young people shouting and blaring party blowers. As we got closer to the city center, the crowd got bigger, so big that the large boulevard was packed with people singing, laughing, hugging, and screaming. It seemed like every Berliner was out on the street. They were all walking in one direction, toward East Berlin.

I looked for a taxicab. I took them once in a while if I was coming back from the KaDeWe department store or when the weather was bad. Across the square was a public telephone booth, and right next to it was a taxi stand, where normally two or three cars were standing by until late at night. I squeezed Mari's arm as we walked toward the taxi stand, saying, "Let's get a taxi."

In Berlin, you cannot simply raise your hand and grab a taxi on the street. Each block has a stand, and you have to wait there until an empty one arrives. We were not waiting for too long, but I must have seemed anxious during that moment I could not find one. I could not stand still, I felt so restless.

"It'll be here soon, Yuni. Why are you in such a hurry?"

"What if it is over before we get there?"

Mari laughed.

"Over? This is only the beginning. I can feel it. When we lost the war and the Americans and Russians were coming, it was very different from this. I was hiding underground behind a crumbling wall with my mother and sister."

"Did Berliners know this was going to happen?"

"Last summer, many East Berliners asked for asylum in the West, and some went to West Germany via Hungary. This fall, there was a demonstration for free travel in Leipzig, and one million gathered in East Berlin—that was just last week. But a few million held an antinuclear rally in Bonn, and there are demonstrations all the time in West Berlin, but nothing happens, you know."

"Yes, I remember reading about that demonstration in East Berlin."

A taxicab arrived, and when we asked the driver to take us to the Berlin Wall, he replied, "It's all jammed around Brandenburg. There are too many cars and people. I'll take you if you can get off at the Philharmonic Hall."

We agreed. As we drove past Tiergarten, we had to slow down, and sometimes stop, as there were too many cars going in the same direction. Somehow we made it to the Philharmonic Hall, and we got out of the car and walked among the crowd. It was softly drizzling like on a spring evening. We were headed toward the Reichstag, but every street was completely filled with people. As we approached the wall itself, we saw that a part of it had already been penetrated, and cars and people from East Berlin were coming through while the West Berliners were greeting them, clapping and screaming. The young and impatient ones were hammering and chipping away at the wall, and some of them had climbed on top of it. There was a young couple who walked through the wall and hugged each other, and a man slowly driving through, his young family in the car waving their hands out the open windows. The border guards wearing uniforms and leather boots and armed with guns, and the officers in long coats, watched in silence. People were singing in chorus, here and there. Mari had managed to open the bottle of champagne and took a few sips directly from it, then offered it to me. I took it and drank from the bottle, too. People who came out of the wall and people who stood on the street hugged and greeted each other endlessly. Something violent was bursting inside of me, and I just started to cry. My hair was already wet from the drizzle and so was my face, but my tears felt hot.

"Why are you crying?" Mari asked me.

I turned around and saw her crying, too. "I was thinking of my country. Why are you crying?"

"Can't feel anything . . ."

"What do you mean? Give me that bottle."

I took the bottle again, and this time I drank quite a lot from it. The tip of my tongue was fizzed, and there was a sweet aftertaste. Mari took the bottle back and took a big gulp. She wiped her mouth.

"Those people don't know that this party will be over in a little bit. But it is always wonderful to see a barrier falling away."

Other people were also drinking wine or champagne, pouring it for others or splashing it on the wall, shouting and singing. Looking around, I realized that I was surrounded by white faces, that I was the only Asian. When everyone else is so happy, you cry because of your own sorrow. We stood there for about an hour, and people continued to come through the wall.

"Look over there," Mari said as she tugged at my sleeve. Across the street, young men with shaved heads and men in leather outfits were lined up, raising their hands at an angle, in that motion familiar from movies, as they greeted people. It was the Nazi salute, borrowed from the old Roman army, and they were singing something that sounded like a marching song. People jeered at them from one side but they kept singing louder and louder.

"Let's just get out of here, please." Mari pulled my arm, as if she were begging me. We crossed the square, almost carried by the crowd. From different corners of the streets, firecrackers and fireworks, usually kept for New Year's Eve, were going off.

"The East was not an exemplary society, but it was still the mirror to the West. Now, no one has to be cautious anymore. They'll do whatever they want to do."

"Did you like Socialism?"

"The Stasi were bad, but there were some great works of art produced over there."

"Stasi?"

"The secret police. But what does that matter to me, especially now."

This time, Mari took out her handkerchief to blow her nose and wipe her eyes.

"It's all people can do."

"Let's go, I'm supposed to meet Mr. Yi."

We walked along Bismarckstraße for a long time before we could find a taxi, which we took to the Europa Center on Budapest Straße. Across the street from it was the café I had been to several times with Mr. Yi. I cannot remember the name of it, but it was right on the street, a good place to watch people on a nice day when the tables were out. But it was the middle of the night and raining, so everyone was crowded inside. I had never seen the café so full. Almost everyone was drinking beer or wine, talking loudly and cheering. I looked around and saw Mr. Yi Hee Soo and Martin already there, at a table near a window where it was less crowded. He raised his hand and asked as soon as we sat down, "Where are you coming from?"

"We were near Brandenburg."

"We drove around Checkpoint Charlie and Brandenburg. So, what do you think?"

I thought for a little while before speaking. "Well, I don't know yet. It was just strange, and then I just wept."

"Utopia does not exist. See what will happen now. One side of the scale is gone, so it is off-balance. It'll take some time, but things will have to change."

Mr. Yi turned to Martin. "Yuni says she cried. How about you?"

"I was shocked. History seems like child's play. Until yesterday, no one had any idea that the wall would come down like that, like a sand castle."

We drank draft beer until three o'clock in the morning. Mari ordered schnapps separately and sipped it quietly, without saying anything. We left Martin and went back to my studio, supporting Mari. After taking her to her house, just the two of us, we sat on the reclining chair, leaning onto each other.

"If one valley is blooming with flowers, the other valley's snow may start melting, too. "

"I don't think that'll happen," I said adamantly. "I think things are going to get tougher. This is not the solution. At least they had the correct beginning, didn't they?"

"After how things ended here, it'll take too much effort to just hold onto things as they are and there will be change. And Mr. Oh will be released, too."

"Ah, let's not talk about him."

I must have been really irritated because my voice was rising. Even though I had drunk quite a bit I was sobering up, yet I wanted to act as if I was still drunk.

"I'm not having a fling here, Mr. Yi Hee Soo. What is your plan for the future?"

"Who knows? I am thinking about it. I don't want to go back to the university, so maybe I should open my own school, a small one, somewhere remote. Live with my son and my mother. And with Miss Han, too."

"What makes you to think I'd do that? I may end up staying here."

"Go to bed. I'll rest a bit and leave when the sun comes up."

I pulled on his shirt collar. "No, you have to tuck me in."

As I dragged him up the ladder, staggering, I missed a rung and almost fell down, but he caught me from behind and firmly pushed me up. He took off my shoes and coat and sweater, and lay down next to me.

I slept with him many times. I remember his voice, his coarse chin where he had shaved, and his rough skin. His sensibility and stability were immensely comforting. And he was affectionate. I kept some memories of the feverish passion, but isn't it pleasant to be in the shade of a tree on top of a hill on a sunny day?

He was like a shadow that quietly took a step back when we said goodbye, never leaving me soaked with blood of grief and sorrow. I wanted to be a woman generously turned to look in the same direction, just like that woman in my dad's story of the persimmons. It would have been better if we had not had to separate, if we could have lived together for a long time.

Song Young Tae arrived the next afternoon, after Mr. Yi had left. He called from the Zoo station and asked me to meet him there. I used to tell visitors from other cities to meet me at a restaurant in the station, because it was easier that way.

I took the wrought-iron stairway that led into the station, and I saw him facing the waiting area. All I saw was the back of his head in the distance, but I knew it was him right away.

"Mr. Song," I called to him in a small voice. It did not feel right to call him Young Tae. Maybe I felt removed from the close relationship we once had. He turned his head around slowly and looked up at me.

"Oh, I didn't know you'd be coming from that direction."

I sat down across from him. We sat there for a while and stared, as if verifying each other's existence. Young Tae looked very different. Maybe he had bought it here in Germany, but he was wearing a long brown leather coat, and his glasses were not the big, horn-rimmed pair I was used to seeing, but small, round ones with gold frames. That's right, he was the son of a wealthy man, wasn't he? And now I supposed he had been released from the burdensome affiliation with his comrades. On a table he had placed a map of Berlin and a camera, but I did not see any luggage.

"Did you take the train?"

"No, I drove on the autobahn. I thought it would be the easiest way to find this place."

"So you bought a car?"

"Yeah, I needed to get around, so I got a used one."

"Have you been admitted to a school?"

"Not yet, I'm just learning the language now."

"Did you eat lunch?"

"I ate something at a rest stop. Come on, let's get out of here."

"Wait, I need to catch my breath a bit."

His car was parked at a parking lot in front of the Zoo station, a nice deep hunter green–colored sedan.

"Well, well, well, look at that, a BMW. What a special treat."

"It looks nice on the outside, but it had to be serviced twice already."

Song Young Tae and I sat next to each other in the front.

"Still, it was flying on the autobahn," he said, starting the engine. "It just keeps on going faster and faster. You know the way around here, don't you?"

"I usually get around underground, so I just know the main roads."

"What would be the nearest . . . Okay, let's go to the Brandenburg Gate."

As we drove from the Zoo station to Ku'damm and Budapest Straße, we saw every street and square crowded with people from East Berlin, West Berlin residents, and onlookers from other cities.

Whenever we see North Koreans on television or in a foreign city's airport, we can tell where they are from simply by looking at the way they are dressed or the way they carry themselves, and it was the same with East Germans. They just seemed awkward and ungainly, like people from a remote village coming to the city for the first time. It had not been a day yet, and all they did was wander around the busier sections of the city. West Berliners welcomed them with a smile as they experienced the new atmosphere. Within a month, however, the West Berliners would regard them with disdain and consider them bothersome, while the East Berliners would turn their attention toward foreigners, whom they thought would be easier targets.

The East Berlin guards were still standing in front of the Brandenburg Gate, but people were taking pictures in front of the wall and climbing it. East Berliners were relatively free to visit the West if they used one of the several checkpoints and U-Bahn stations, but those who wished to visit East Berlin still had to go through the clearance at Friedrichstraße, and those with cars had to register at Checkpoint Charlie, guarded by West German and American soldiers. All these walls would later be dismantled by citizens and the government.

We went to a little park next to the Brandenburg Gate, a tourist attraction complete with observatory platforms. No one was standing there on the platforms. The coin-operated telescopes had already become use-less. Near the platform was a barbed-wire fence hung with white crosses, names and dates written in the center of each.

"What are those?" Song Young Tae asked.

"People who were killed while trying to climb the wall."

"Propaganda? Like in those underground tunnels at the DMZ."

"I think . . . this is a little different."

"What is so different about it? I can hear the same yelling and screaming to condemn the enemies of freedom."

"Whether it's a human being or an animal, if it is alive, it should have freedom to move to a place that is better suited for it."

"Freedom is not an abstraction! Once you have some needs, you are trapped. Where can you find freedom without money? Freedom should be something above that, shared by all the members of a society, but they have degraded it."

"This side was not a paradise, but neither was the other side. Now we will see that clearly with our own two eyes."

"We still have to carry out the promises this century has made."

Song Young Tae and I talked oil and water as we walked around. It was completely dark by four o'clock in the afternoon, but the city center was still festive as we entered it. In front of us was a couple taking a walk with their young children, and we knew right away that this was a family from East Berlin soaking up the new air. Both adults held onto a child's wrist tightly, and they were walking cautiously on the inner side of the side-walk. There were many more people like them in the city center. As usual, all the stores were closed at six o'clock, but the lights were left on in their windows where mannequins stood among various goods, with no trace of a living person. We used to call those brightly lit windows with their mounds of material goods the windows of capitalism. Ah, it was the per-fect name for them. The people from the East stood in front of those display windows like a crowd in front of a street performer, mouths shut tightly, arms crossed or holding onto a child's wrist, and just kept staring.

Mr. Yi once said that as more and more nonessential products are brought into the market, the essential well-being of the people disap-pears. There were so many lingerie stores, clothing stores, accessory and cosmetics stores. In the display windows of an electronic goods shop, more and more new things were presented in more windows, and on television screens. The East Germans were a little shy at first, admiring these products of the new world as if they were an art installation or some new landscape. Then the West German government decided that any East Germans visiting West Berlin could receive 100 marks per person from any bank, as long as they showed ID. One hundred marks per person. East Germans brought over all their family members and friends. Five people meant 500 marks, which was a lot of money, even in West Germany. In a few days, Berlin turned into a grand marketplace. People were coming from the farthest corners of East Germany. The first thing they bought was electronics. Everyone was carrying around a television set or a cassette radio. In order to learn about the West as quickly as possible, you needed to attend the new school, the television. And then they were buying fruit. Fruit wasn't imported anymore under the controlled economy of Socialism, where all they got were strawberries and apples, available only at certain periods throughout the year. The most popular item now was California oranges with Del Monte stamped on the skin. And then boxes and boxes of toilet paper. Later, it would become impossible to buy used cars, thanks to East Germans. What was really funny, however, was how poor West Germans or foreign students rushed to East German supermarkets and cleaned them out, buying meat and bread and dairy products. Over there, the cost of food was only about one-third that of West Germany. And books were so cheap! This strange economy continued for a couple of months until there were no restrictions on travel. In order for the two economies to unite, the West German government decided to exchange East German currency for the West German one at the same rate, as long as the total amount was reported. Naturally, black markets thrived. Some immigrants from Southeast Asia or Turkey went to East Berlin and bought unreported East German currency at a much lower rate, then brought it back and exchanged it at the full rate. All this happened over the next few months, until, as everyone knows, West Germany ended up absorbing the East the following year.

I decided to take Song Young Tae to Mr. Yi Hee Soo's house. I called Mr. Yi and explained the situation, and he willingly agreed to host my guest.

First, I took Young Tae to a German restaurant and treated him to a dinner accompanied by Berliner Weisse, the beer mixed with syrup. At the end of the meal I broached the subject.

"When we're done, I'll take you to where you'll sleep tonight."

"What are you talking about? Aren't we going to your house?"

"Well, it's a studio, so it won't really be comfortable for you."

"You bragged that you'd be the host! What is this, are you shy or something? So whose house are we going to anyway?"

"Someone I met here. He's really nice," I said as casually as possible.

Song remained silent and then whispered, "I guess . . . it's a good thing that you found a friend."

He stuffed his mouth with several Nuremburg sausages at once and chewed for a while, his head bowed down. I waited, quietly.

"What does he do, is he a student?"

"No, a professor. He works at the research center here."

"You like him?"

Instead of answering, I nodded. Song Young Tae wiped his mouth with his napkin.

"Well, let's get going then. If you like him, I bet he is a decent person."

"How long are you staying here?"

"Don't worry. I want to go to East Berlin tomorrow to buy some books, and I'll have to leave in the afternoon."

It would be the first and the last time Song Young Tae met Mr. Yi Hee Soo. As was his nature, Mr. Yi was gentle and warm, while Young Tae remained stiff. The next day, the three of us went over to East Berlin together. We left Mr. Song's car at the parking lot across the street from Mr. Yi's apartment, and we took the U-Bahn to the Friedrichstraße station, where we went through customs. It was the first time for me, but Mr. Yi said he had already done it a couple of times. I put my passport under the window, and it came back with a pass allowing me to stay in the East for thirty-six hours. I was told that there were a lot fewer people at the station than before. We walked around the neighborhood near the wall. The buildings were old, and the streets were quiet, as if everyone had gone to visit West Berlin. Once, while driving on the highway, I had made a rest stop on the East Berlin side. It was incredibly filthy and the service horrible. I am not even going to tell you how bad the restrooms were. I was told that that was the case because no one owned the place. In East Berlin, there were no places to drink coffee other than at hotels run by the government. Song Young Tae knew exactly where he wanted to go; he went directly to a bookstore on Unter den Linden, near the entrance to Humboldt University, and bought complete sets of Marx and Hegel. Even I could tell that he was buying them for almost nothing, compared to what he would have paid in the West. In the center of the city, we saw the familiar flag with a star in a circle and walked toward it. Looking at the sign that said Democratic People's Republic of Korea, we were delighted and uncomfortable at the same time, and we walked around the building once before walking away. Trailing behind us, Song Young Tae slowly approached me.

"Maybe I should go in there. Get some information."

"You can get a lot at German university libraries."

"Miss Han, do you know what really shocked me after I left home?"

"Besides the wall coming down?"

"That we were living in a bubble. That North Korea is really near us, closer than Europe or America."

"But that is so obvious."

Mr. Yi did not say anything, he just smiled. He rarely said what he was thinking. Anyway, it only occurred to me after we returned to West Berlin how far off track we'd gone. After sharing a late lunch, Song Young Tae was leaving. As he stood outside his car I spoke to him.

"I'm sorry that I didn't do more for you after you came all the way here."

He did not look at me, but turned his eyes to the street.

"I missed you, Miss Han. Take care."

Mr. Yi and Young Tae shook hands. Then Young Tae raised one hand toward me, and drove away. Finally, I was left alone with Mr. Yi again, just the two of us. I put my hand in his coat pocket, held his warm hand tightly, and began walking.

"Where should we go?" he asked.

"Let's go to my place tonight."

25

By December, the crowds in West Berlin had become an everyday occurrence. The subway resembled those in Seoul and Tokyo during rush hour, filled with tourists, East Germans, and even Poles and Czechs. Near the Reichstag, flea markets sprang up. There was a huge increase in automobile theft. It was around this time that something unforgettable happened to us.

On a rainy winter evening, a young man crossed over the wall. It was more like he seeped through the crumbling wall. Alone, he got off at the Zoo station. He bought a sausage to eat, and carrying an old umbrella, he wandered around the city among the huge crowds, stopping to look at the display windows or the pictures in front of a peep-show booth. East Germans had quickly learned how to use peep-show booths, and they would line up to go in and use bags of coins. From what I heard, there is a pair of holes where you can place your eyes, and next to it is a slot to put coins in, like on the binoculars at tourist attractions. A timer starts the moment the coin is inserted. You see a small room and a door, through which a woman enters to do a strip show, taking off her clothes, one article at a time. When the time is up, something clicks and you cannot see anything anymore, and you have to put more coins in to watch the show again. This young man used only one coin and was furious when he left the place. The city lights were too bright, and he did not know that the U-Bahn trains had stopped running. He went back to the Zoo station, but all he found there were homeless people. In a panic, he ran around, checking the numerous platforms, but all he did was confirm that the tracks were empty and that he had lost his way out.

Not knowing where he was going, he crossed a street and saw women standing on the street wearing short skirts and heavy makeup, watching the cars passing by. When a car stopped, they would go over to start a conversation or borrow a light for their cigarettes. Using his poor German, he asked the women which way it was to East Berlin. One woman sneered that there were no more trains going there, that he should stay here one night and go back tomorrow, that she'd take him. Because he did not understand a situation like this, he asked how much it would cost to stay one night. She answered 100 marks, a real bargain. What else could he do but recoil and run away? One hundred marks for one night of sleep? He made sure his two crumpled twenty-mark bills were still in his pocket. The young man returned to the square in front of Europa Center, illuminated like a fairyland with Christmas lights and decorations. He sat on an empty bench near a fountain, which wasn't running because it was wintertime. When he saw an Asian couple pass him by, he hesitated, but managed to ask for a light for his cigarette. The man with the light asked him in German if he was Chinese. *No, I'm Korean*, he answered, and the man laughed out loud and said in Korean, *I'm Korean, too.* For a few seconds, a loaded silence prevailed among the three Koreans. The man and woman were Mr. Yi's friends Mr. and Mrs. Shin. The young man hesitated, but spoke first, breaking the silence.

"Is there no train going back to East Berlin?"

Mr. Shin was the first to realize what had happened.

"Ah, you cannot go back now. The train will start running again tomorrow morning, so . . . you can stay with us if you like."

The young man looked so young, he could easily have passed for a high school student.

"We live very close to here," Mr. Shin added. "You can rest for the night, and we'll bring you back to the station tomorrow morning."

He followed them without protest. They walked three blocks down the now almost empty streets to the Shins' place on Rosenheimer Straße.

When they got there, however, the young man refused to go upstairs. Staying on the street, he said, "Where are we?"

"This is our apartment."

When Mrs. Shin answered, the young man added, even though they already knew, "I'm a student from North Korea."

"Really? We're students, too. Come on in."

I heard this story from Mr. Yi three days after it had happened. Mr. and Mrs. Shin had brought the young man to him. I knew that even two nights would have been really inconvenient for the Shins. They lived in a studio apartment where the bed and the kitchen and the living room were all one open space. So they did what they usually did when friends came for a visit. They made a bed for him on the sofa and drew a curtain around their bed.

The young man was twenty years old and from Pyongyang. His name was Cho Young Soo. He had started studying at an engineering school in East Berlin only eight months before. After serving him breakfast, Mr. and Mrs. Shin took him to Wannsee and to the museums and the botanical gardens, and then they showed him West Berlin, wondering how he would react. He followed them around until dinnertime and then declared that he would not return to his dormitory in East Berlin. At first they were just trying to be nice, but now they had begun to panic. This was a politically explosive problem. They fretted and worried and thought about it, and then they brought him to Mr. Yi Hee Soo.

When I got to Mr. Yi's apartment, the young man from North Korea had already spent the night there, and he did not appear to be nervous at all. Mr. Yi introduced him to me. I felt like I was looking at my youngest brother. Young Soo was wearing Mr. Yi's corduroy pants and green sweater. I set the table with bread, ham, and cheese that I had brought over, and wanting to appear friendly, I cracked a joke.

"You don't have horns."

"Pardon?"

His eyes widened, and I put two fingers on top of my head.

"Horns, don't you know? In the South they say North Koreans have horns."

"We were told that all South Koreans are special agents."

Mr. Yi interrupted, "Mr. Cho here says he won't go back to East Berlin."

"What are you going to do if you don't go back?" I asked him.

"I want to live in Germany."

"What if Germany doesn't accept you?"

"Then I'll go to another country."

"Then there would be so many people you'll not be able to see again. First of all, you won't see your mom."

Mr. Yi, who was standing behind him in the kitchen, gestured to me not to say anything more. He brought over plates and put them on the table.

"Well, you don't have to decide anything right now," he said. "Let's eat first, then we'll take you to the department store."

Mr. Yi and I took Young Soo and spent the whole day at department stores and shopping malls. As we walked around, whenever I had a chance, I whispered to Mr. Yi, "Can you please tell me what you intend to do with him?"

His answer was quite simple, "Send him back."

"Why? What for?"

"Would you want me to report him to the immigration authorities, or to our consulate?"

"Just leave him alone. He should make that decision on his own."

"Listen, it's like there was a heavy rain and the levee was broken. So many things were carried down to another lake because of the flood, and one of them was a baby fish. But this is a completely new environment and there are too many big fishes here. It's not going to be easy for the baby fish to survive."

"Who knows? Maybe he'll decide that there are more things to eat and more water plants here, and that this is a better place to live. Living is taking risks, wherever you are."

"You yourself said that he'll never see his mother again! Young Soo is only twenty. He's just a runaway."

Mr. Yi bought Young Soo a thick windbreaker with a hood and new underwear and socks. It was almost Christmas, and the interior of the department store looked like a palace with all sorts of decorations and lights. After looking at the picture of Santa Claus in his red suit and white beard riding a sleigh led by reindeer, and after finding a man dressed in the same clothes standing by the toy section, Young Soo asked

Mr. Yi who he was. I found his answer simple and funny. Do you know what Mr. Yi Hee Soo said? He said it was the department store's monster. We went back home to have dinner, after which Mr. Yi started talking with Young Soo.

"I think you will be with me for a while, so what do you want to do most here?"

"Take the train, go wherever I want to go . . . travel to other countries in Europe, too."

"Then when are you gonna go back?"

"I know it's been a few days, but I cannot make up my mind. Every night, I think I'll go back to my dormitory the next morning, but when the morning comes I change my mind."

"Are you afraid that you'll be punished when you go back?"

"I want to live as I want in a new world."

"How can you live just as you want? That's too easy, and nowhere in this world is it that easy. You won't be able to see your mother and father and sisters. Ten million people have not seen each other for the last fifty years. I don't know the world you grew up in, but I can guess that many people believe that you'll one day become a great engineer after studying abroad, and that you'll pay them back by bringing back new ideas and technology. Things are difficult over there. Just think of how many workers you will teach."

"But a man has the right to choose his own happiness!"

"Sometimes, unfamiliar things just look better. But if you cannot resolve the problems in your own home, you cannot be successful in someone else's home. You're not an adult yet. It's like you just ran away from home. I want to send you back to your family, but of course, it is something you have to decide. You don't have to do this right now, but think carefully. Was there anything that you were not happy with before?"

"Nothing happened the way I wanted it to. It's not like I chose to study mechanical engineering."

"Hmm, that's not right. But I bet there were many other young people who wanted to study abroad, isn't that right?"

"Of course. I haven't even served in the army yet. The exam's really difficult. Only one out of sixty or seventy gets chosen."

"I don't know much about politics, but I'm worried about someone using you. Whether you're in the North or the South, life is very precious to everyone. If you're in danger and it's impossible to live, anyone can become a refugee, even in this rich country. But if you struggle together with your family, don't you think you'll be much happier later in life?"

Mr. Yi went on talking to Young Soo with the utmost sincerity. I knew he was a serious person, but I trusted him even more after watching him trying to resolve what he could have considered merely an annoying problem with such fairmindedness. Each side likes to brag about who came over and who chose what, but I also think that my life is the product of South Korea and that I have to do my best there. Didn't you say that once, too? On the other hand, that's what people in the North should do, too. Wherever we are, I think we have to do our best to transform ourselves from within. That is the first condition of our country's division.

The next day we did not accompany Young Soo. We gave him a map and a little money and sent him out on his own. For three days, Young Soo traveled around the city riding the trams and buses, and by his tenth night in West Berlin he seemed to be in a very different spirit.

"Why don't you go see him?" Mr. Yi whispered to me. "He's in his bedroom, and he's not coming out."

"Maybe he's sleeping because he's tired."

"I don't think that's it. He seemed to be really depressed from the moment he walked in."

I opened the bedroom door quietly and found Young Soo sitting on the bed, his head bowed.

"Can I come in?"

"Yes, of course."

As I walked in and took a seat across from the bed, I saw Young Soo quickly wiping his eyes and turning away as he hid something underneath his pillow.

"Did something happen?"

"No, nothing."

"What's that? Show me."

"It's just a picture."

"May I?"

He held the small picture, but I snatched it from his hand. It was a black-and-white photo of a family, five of them standing in line in front of a weeping willow tree. The man wearing a suit with buttons up to his neck must have been Young Soo's father, and the woman with tightly permed hair wearing a traditional Korean dress his mother. In between them stood a boy wearing a white shirt and shorts and a Youth Group scarf around his neck, perhaps a third grader. I knew for sure that this boy was Young Soo just by looking at the face. Two girls wearing middle-school uniforms were likely his older sisters.

"You were looking at your family picture. Where was this taken?"

"We had a picnic by Daedong River."

I gave the picture back to Young Soo.

"Listen. I'm going back tomorrow," he said, taking the photo.

"I think that's a good idea."

"I called the school dormitory today, while I was out."

"Who did you speak to?"

"A friend who's studying here, too. He said everything will be fine as long as I go back, that I should just come back as soon as possible."

"If you did something wrong, there will be penalties. But just be honest, tell them everything and be candid about it."

"I think so, too."

"Let's eat dinner."

When I brought Young Soo back to the dining table, Mr. Yi had already set it up. I opened my mouth before he could.

"Young Soo is going back to school tomorrow."

"Really? We should take him back, then."

As the three of us ate dinner, we did not have much to say. I cleaned up and made some tea. The two men sat quietly and drank the tea, and then Young Soo finally opened his mouth. "What happens if you ask for refugee status here?" he asked.

"I'm not sure, but I guess you have to get a lawyer and report to the government. There will be an investigation and you have to spend some time at the refugee camp. Since you do speak a little German you'll be able to find a job soon, and then . . . something like that."

"I can't imagine what it would be like living here. Germans seem so lonely. Everyone is on their own."

"Everyone's in charge of their own lives. Isn't it so wherever you go?"

"They just work and make money and buy things."

The next morning, we took Young Soo to a discount store nearby and bought him a few presents. I chose a wool scarf with a British label and a pair of gloves, and Mr. Yi found him shoes. Right there and then, Young Soo wrapped the scarf around his neck and put the gloves on and changed his shoes. We took the train to Friedrichstraße, where one side of the railway was West Berlin and the other side was East Berlin. Our plan was to drop him off at customs, but he asked us, practically begging, "Please come with me. They'll come get me once I call them."

I followed them while Mr. Yi wrapped one arm around Young Soo's shoulder and went downstairs to the underground passage. We passed through the crowded station and crossed a road to Potsdamer Platz. In the middle of the square was a poorly maintained field. There were benches all around the square, and a public phone booth.

"Call them," Mr. Yi told Young Soo.

When he came out of the phone booth after a long telephone call, his face was flushed.

"They'll be here soon."

Potsdamer Platz was quiet, with few people walking through. Across from it was a government-run hotel and a busy street beyond. We sat on a bench facing the hotel and waited for more than half an hour. A car turned the corner and two men got out. Young Soo stood up. He took a few steps forward and stopped, and the two men who were looking around the square were now headed toward us, walking on the lawn. As they approached us, Mr. Yi got up from the bench, too.

"I should get going. Take care, both of you," Young Soo said.

"Goodbye. Study hard!"

"Bye-bye."

As he walked across the square, Young Soo looked back at us several times, and Mr. Yi and I waved to him. We took the train from the Friedrichstraße station and went back the way we came.

At that time, Eastern Europe was changing fast. In Hungary the Socialist Party took over, in Poland the Solidarity Trade Union, in Czechoslovakia the Civic Forum, followed by Bulgaria, Romania, Yugoslavia, Albania, and Croatia. Eventually European socialism was revealed to be a failure.

It was inevitable that the system switched from national socialism to the free-market economy of capitalism. We did not know it at the time, but 1989 was a turning point in world history.

The dream that my father and you shared, the one that I supported deep down in my heart, had to return to the starting gate. The whole world had to start all over again. We all knew very well the current way of living was not right, and so the countless poor and powerless people had to begin all over again in this changed world.

During the 1990 summer vacation Mr. Yi Hee Soo went back to Seoul for a visit, but I stayed in Berlin. I considered making a short visit, too, but I knew that all I would gain from the trip would be some weight, thanks to my old mother, who would feed me as much as she could. The thought of having to go to Jung Hee's house to see Eun Gyul also dissuaded me. In order to teach at a Korean university as a real professor, I needed to go back with a title, but the art school here did not offer acceptable degrees. A diploma was sort of a master's degree, but we art students had the option of doing a *Meisterschule*. I was lucky that my professor was quite favorable toward my work, which tended to be neoexpressionist. I was planning not to go back to Seoul until I was done here.

It was one of those late summer evenings at the end of August. During summer in Berlin the sun lingers until around ten at night. It is the opposite of winter, when it gets dark at three in the afternoon. In summer I would open all the windows wide at dusk and enjoy the tranquil hours of faint light. One evening the doorbell on the front gate rang. I asked who it was. It was Song Young Tae. I pressed the button to open the gate. A little later my doorbell rang, and there was Song Young Tae. In both hands he was carrying suitcases and bags and other things. In his navy blue suit, white dress shirt, and red tie, sweating heavily, he looked like a country bumpkin visiting the city for the first time. I could not resist laughing out loud but then I covered my mouth.

"What is this, are you going on a date or doing an interview?"

"Can I have a glass of water, please?" he said, as he entered my studio and dropped his luggage. I took out a bottle of water from the refrigerator and he finished it in one gulp. He collapsed onto a sofa.

"Where have you been?"

"Can't you tell? I'm arriving from somewhere far away."

"Somewhere far away?'

"I have just crossed over Eurasia."

"Pfft! Who hasn't flown in a plane these days?"

"But I bet only a few have crossed the Ural and Xinganling Mountains."

Young Tae was loosening the tie around his neck and undoing one button. He put a shopping bag and a box on the table.

"What's all this stuff?"

Without saying a word, he opened the bag and the box and took out several things. A bottle of ginseng liquor, another bottle of liquor made from the azaleas in the Baekdu Mountains, Younggwang cigarettes, and cultivated ginseng roots. It was only then that I figured out where he was coming back from.

"What do they mean . . . all these things . . . ?"

"I'm coming back from Pyongyang."

"Why did you go there?"

"Because everyone said it's the one place we can't go, so I thought, why not?"

I was not too surprised after all the things that had happened in the last few months, but this did seem to be quite a sudden leap.

"Really, it's about time you stopped acting like a desperado, don't you think?"

I was pretty certain that Young Tae had been to the big event organized by Koreans from both sides and all over the world. He probably went with Korean-Germans.* I found my wallet and walked to the door.

"Let's go get some dinner."

"Aren't you gonna cook for me here?"

"Didn't you have enough Korean food over there? And I'm tired. Can't you just eat what is offered to you, please?"

I took him to the Italian restaurant Roma, across the Bundesplatz. I wondered why there were so many elderly couples in the neighborhood restaurant every evening. The food was really good there. The owner still wore an apron, but he usually greeted and talked to customers out

---

* In 1990, a rally for the reunification of the Korean peninsula was held in the North with attendance by Koreans from around the world. The South Korean government refused to recognize the event and went on to arrest hundreds for their suspected involvement.

front instead of staying in the kitchen. We took a table in the innermost corner and ordered red wine. Before our food arrived, I tore up the freshly baked bread that still smelled like flour and began interrogating Young Tae.

"How was it?"

"It's complicated. I can't describe it in one word. I'm both impressed and depressed."

"What kind of doubletalk is that?"

"It made me cry to see the resourcefulness of those who survive despite the harsh conditions, but it is depressing to see the absolute control there is over everything.

"That's what I would have expected anyway, none of that's new, is it? I once read that they call themselves a porcupine whose quills stand up to imperialism."

"You say it as if it's about some foreign country! While we were rolling in the lap of luxury, they were doing what we should have done."

"What are you talking about? We weren't standing still. It took a while, but we've been crawling diligently, like a tortoise."

"We'll change, too. But the transition could take decades."

"What are you going to do now? This is a big deal. You don't expect that you'll be able to go back to Seoul without getting into huge trouble, do you? How stupid are you, to do this at a time like this?"

"I just decided to be on their side, okay? Besides, I'm just a nobody. I'm not going to be of much help."

I told him the story of Cho Young Soo, and Young Tae listened to it patiently without interrupting. I ended the story by telling him, "Of course, it cannot end like this. Even if it takes time, it should not be resolved the way it was in Vietnam or here. It's a fight that has continued for over a hundred years since we opened up the port."

"I am just sick of this place now. It's like everyone prepared for the meal for a long, long time and just when the table is set they turn the light off. Even though the hunger is still fierce."

"I'm told that's human nature."

Both of us stopped talking. We ate and drank, smoked cigarettes, paid the bill, and left the restaurant. I could not bring him to Mr. Yi's place this time, so I had to take him to my studio. I went up to the loft and got into my bed while he slept on the sofa at the foot of the ladder. As I tossed about, the mattress spring made small metallic sounds. Out of the blue, he spoke. "Do you ever think of Chae Mi Kyung?"

"Once in a while . . ."

Then this time, it was me who suddenly raised my voice, "Why are you so stupid? She was in love with you. I knew from the moment I saw her."

He did not answer. He remained silent for a while then asked again, quietly, "Miss Han . . . Are you really in love with Mr. Yi Hee Soo?"

I was angry he was doing that again, and I didn't think I could stand it. I remembered that early morning at the humble restaurant, where he spoke in low tones as if acting in a romantic movie. But my heart was beginning to ache as well. Really, our lives were so difficult. I did not answer. And then he brought up what I was afraid someone might ask.

"What about Mr. Oh?"

"And what makes you think that you can ask such a question?"

I sat up in bed. Inside, furious words were bubbling up wildly. Ten years ago, a shadow of my father's youth came to me, asking for my protection. We tried to lean on each other, despite the guilty conscience that every young man and woman of that time carried within themselves. He disappeared behind a darkened window, and he was erased by time, dust, and wind, like words written carelessly on a wall with a pencil. He is still there. But he's there as something missing, an absence. I wanted my life back, a quiet life where no one interfered. The bubbling words could not flow out my throat, but sank down slowly into my heart, like water going down the toilet.

"I just . . . I thought I would ask," Song Young Tae whispered, barely audible.

I lay down again, and finally I realized that you had come back to me.

The next day, after I dropped off Young Tae at the train station, I paced around the house, my heart an empty vessel. I went over to see my neighbor Mari. I pushed the doorbell several times but no one answered. I was about to go back to my studio, but then I banged on the door with my fist. I thought I heard someone's footsteps inside and felt that someone was watching me through the peephole in the door. The door cracked open a little, and I pulled it wide open. Mari was standing

there in a bathrobe like a ghost. Her white hair was let down and she had
no makeup on, and she was swaying because she was drunk. I did not
feel like making light of the situation, so I just supported her walking
back inside and helped her sit on a loveseat. I sat down next to her, too,
and saw a half-empty bottle and glasses strewn on the table. I had
already decided a long time before not to criticize her about the
drinking, so I just sighed.

"Mari, have you eaten anything?"

"Yes. I ate a lot."

I did not bother quarreling with her, I just went into her kitchen and
opened the refrigerator. A little bit of sausage and milk and butter. No
dry cereal, but I found powdered grain, and I mixed it with milk and
brought it to her. I placed the bowl right under her chin and fed her a
spoonful at a time. Although she frowned and turned her head away at
first, she began taking the liquid after the first spoonful.

"Did you drink all through the night, alone?"

"No . . . I . . . drew something."

Under the sofa, I found the small sketchbook, opened to a random
page. I noticed a few pages with drawings I had seen before, followed by a
few empty ones, then I found writing in German.

> *The life of a human being is like poetry, there is a beginning
> and an end. It's just that that is not all.*
>   *Would lovers be scared in front of the dead? Ah, the dead,
> please let her rest.*

After the writing were drawings in pencil and pen. I had seen her
drawings many times before, and I knew the several important clues to
them. A circle with several lines growing behind was Mari herself. Like
in a child's drawings, there was a triangle underneath the body, perhaps
a skirt. Meanwhile, Stephan had a round head and a long body but no
triangle, so he must have been wearing a pair of pants. Here he was a
long stick man lying down below a straight line and among slashed ones.
Maybe this was dead Stephan buried underground. In another, Mari was
standing on top of another straight line, and there was a ball of wool, too.
The winding line looked like a leash. It seemed like she was visiting

Stephan's grave with Hans. But above the ball of yarn was a small cloud. I pointed at it with my finger.

"Mari, what is this?" I asked.

She chuckled with a hoarse sound, and when she spoke she did not sound like herself at all.

"That's a hat for Hans. The one that the dead ones carry around with them."

A halo. It was Mari taking dead Hans to the grave of dead Stephan—in the end, it was a drawing of Mari left alone. Mari gazed at her own drawing, her eyes vacant.

"Hans lived for a long time, until he was fifteen years old. But I never took him to the sanatorium. Stephan didn't even recognize me, and I had to take a train. Hans died before Stephan did. Turn the page."

Mari with the triangle skirt was pointing at a straight line with an arrow. I thought the straight line meant the ground, and next to it was a group of snail-like circles with tails and a rectangle. I turned the sketchbook around to figure out what was going on, but I did not get it.

"What is this?"

This time, Mari answered curtly, "Just lines."

"What is this arrow?"

Without saying anything, she took a glass and poured liquor into it. I knew what she was going to do, so I grabbed the glass from her.

"Stop it. I'll take this one."

"Oh, Yuni, if you get as drunk as I am we'll understand each other."

"I don't think so. My drinking is different from yours."

I took a sip and gave it back to her, and she took the rest in one gulp. She looked at her own sketchbook over my shoulder.

"The arrow is a shovel. In the box is Hans. I wanted to bury him in a garden filled with daisies—"

"Is that all you think about these days, Hans?"

"About the baby."

"He was a dog."

"I came back from a night shift and the dog was sleeping. I opened a can and put the dog food in a bowl and pushed it over to him, but he stayed there, his head buried between his legs. I must have had a drink after that, because I was really drunk by the time the sun came up. I touched him, and he was stiff. I wrapped him in a plastic bag and carried him in a cardboard box, and I walked for a while to a park. Then I saw the yellow garbage truck. I staggered over and threw the box in the back of that garbage truck, then came back home and slept as if I were dead. When I woke up in the afternoon, Hans was gone. It took me a long time to remember that I had thrown him away that morning."

"Stop it. So what? I'm tired of your story about the dead dog."

"Once, Stephan and I got pregnant. I had an abortion."

I turned to the next page and saw a body of a square and a triangle overlapping with the circle with sprouting lines. On top of Mari's skirt was a box. Maybe this was not the box containing Hans, maybe it signified the death of a child. I didn't ask her.

"I heard that old age may be lonely, but it's peaceful."

Mari laughed again.

"That's a lie. You just pretend that that's the case. You look different but what's inside is the same as ever. Like the desire to sleep with a man. But there is something you do finally learn."

"What is that?"

"The best time of your life. And love."

"Are you talking about Stephan?"

"The baby. I am an old woman who almost became a mother. And Stephan also became my son."

At that moment, I felt a shudder coursing through my body, as if I were being electrocuted. I thought of the portrait of you as a young man that I painted that summer, how it still remained in Kalmae covered with dust.

It was autumn again. Mr. Yi and I became more of a routine. Instead of running through the park looking for him, I concentrated on working, producing a piece a week. I did not tell him about it, but around that time I began to think of you again. I would sit at the tiny table in my kitchen drinking tea and watching the brown leaves of the horse chestnut tree fall, and there you would be, pacing around in the courtyard. Of course I knew it was not really you, that it was just an illusion. If I felt guilty toward someone it was actually toward Mr. Yi Hee Soo, not you. I loved him because it was comfortable. He was near me, like a glass of water on the bedside table. But the strange thing is that he had to leave me around the time you were coming back to me. I wonder now if I was being punished.

The reunification of Germany was complete by October that year, as expected. Mr. Yi was nearing the end of his stay in Germany and was getting ready to go back to Korea. For a little while, I thought about giving up and going back with him. It had been exactly one year since the wall had come down, and the cold weather rushed in so quickly that I was always wearing a thick down coat.

Mr. Yi Hee Soo went on a business trip to somewhere near Frankfurt with Martin. He was planning to visit a small community there. He had a dream of opening a beautiful little school in his hometown when he went back to Korea. I knew very well that he missed the little village he had left when he was a child, and we used to talk over and over about the bridge and the elm tree and the ponds as if I myself had been there, although I had just heard about them from him. It had been almost a week since he'd left, but he had not called. I was a little worried and wondered what was going on.

In the morning I went to my school and called the research institute at the engineering school. Naturally, they told me he was not in. I asked for Martin, and they made me wait for a long time. Somebody came back to the phone and asked for my address. It seemed a little odd, but I gave him my address and asked what he needed it for. I guessed he was a German research fellow or an assistant there, but all he said was that someone would come see me. I was baffled, but decided not to think about it too much. But no one came, and no one called me the following day. I stayed home all morning, then invited Mari over for lunch. We reheated Korean mixed noodles and frozen spring rolls and we ate them all. I went out to buy paints and brushes, then saw a Korean movie I had heard had won some awards. It was intriguing to hear the lines in Korean but to see the subtitles in German. I don't remember much of it, but I do clearly remember the scene of a child monk picking up a tiny bird that had fallen from the nest. And the funeral of the old monk, his body on top of a woodpile in flames. I sat alone at a Viennese café, drank a cup of cappuccino and a glass of cognac, and stayed there a while neither thinking nor doing anything in particular. When I came back to my neighborhood near Bunde-splatz, it was already dark. I slowly climbed the stairs and was about to turn the key and open my door when Mari appeared at her door and said, "Yuni, you have guests."

"Guests? For me?"

She beckoned me in with her head. I went into her apartment as if I were being sucked in. When I entered, I saw an older lady sitting on the sofa where we always sat down and relaxed. A young woman stood up from the wooden chair next to the table. Mystified, I just stood there and looked at them. The young woman, who seemed to be around my age, spoke first.

"Are you Miss Han Yoon Hee?"

"Yes, and you are?"

"I'm Yi Hee Soo's sister. I heard so much about you from my brother. This is our mother."

Only then did I bend my body and bow to them. I took them back to my studio. The older lady collapsed onto the sofa.

"Please excuse me," she mumbled. "I need to lie down."

I quickly found a pillow and placed it on the armrest.

"You should rest your head on this."

The older lady lay there with one arm covering her face, and the sister remained silent for a while, sitting with her head down. Something was not right.

"Did something . . . happen?" I finally managed to ask, and almost at the same time the sister covered her face with two hands and cried, "My brother is dead."

I just stared at her. At first, I could not understand what she was talking about.

"He hasn't come back from Frankfurt yet."

The moment I said so, I knew it was wrong. The sister took her hands down from her face and shook her head as if she wanted to brush off something, and she took a deep breath. Now, she was looking straight at me and continued in a much calmer tone.

"We got word last Friday. We were in Frankfurt until yesterday. We came to Berlin to pack up his belongings."

I was not surprised. It felt like my head was completely empty. Things had been moving too smoothly, hadn't they? I had known something was going to happen. A faint sneer spread from under my chin and brushed my lips before it went away.

"When? How?"

"The first day of the trip. There was an accident on the autobahn. His friend, the one he was traveling with, got badly hurt, too. He told us about you when we saw him. We've been calling since yesterday but we couldn't reach you, so we decided to come today."

Listening to her now calm and collected voice, I could not feel much of anything. Still, tears welled up in my eyes and rolled down my cheek.

Martin gave me the details much later. It was snowing lightly from the moment they left Berlin, but the road conditions seemed okay. Some spots were icy, and the snow continued until they got near Frankfurt, where cars were slowing down considerably. At the autobahn interchange near the city of Hanau, a container truck coming the opposite way crashed into the median and flipped. The dislodged container crashed onto the other side and slid down, blocking the road and causing a series of crashes. Five cars in total; several people died at the scene. Martin lost consciousness. The ambulance came and managed to get the two men out of the crushed car. Even several months later, I could not ask Martin about Mr. Yi's last moment and what he looked like.

I looked straight back at Mr. Yi's sister with my wet cheeks.

"Where, where is he now?"

"We closed the casket yesterday and sent it to the airport. I am so sorry to bother you, but do you mind bringing us to my brother's place? My mother has not been able to sleep at all. We'd like to rest there and then pack, since we have to fly back tomorrow."

"Of course," I mumbled, stupidly. "I have the key."

I crossed Volkspark the way I always did, and the two women, quiet, their heads bowed, followed behind me. That night was freezing cold. The streetlamps in the park looked like they were frozen blue. The windows at Mr. Yi's place were dark. He would never come back here again. I remembered how sometimes we would talk to each other on the phone and I'd come over here and wait for him to return from a local bar or from a walk through the park. I used to look at the darkened window with a sense of warm intimacy. Or I would come over here after he had gone to bed and ring the doorbell. I would wait for a while until I heard his sleepy voice through the speaker and saw the light turn on.

Entering his place, I easily found the light switches in the dark and faced his belongings in that house, things I knew so well. Humbly, I stood by the door and waited patiently while his mother and sister looked around the room and studied and caressed the objects, still holding onto his touch.

I don't want to go on and on. I could not join in their sorrow in that room. As I was about to leave, before I bowed to the two women, each now sitting in chairs far away from each other, I had to ask the sister, "Would it be okay if I took this with me?"

She turned her head, following my fingertip. She probably was not in a state of mind to realize exactly what it was I meant, whether it was the little Buddha sitting on the windowsill or the Tibetan holy scripture in German next to it, but she quickly nodded her head.

"Of course, please."

I tried my best not to look at anything else and walked straight to the copper sculpture the size of my palm. I took it, turned around, and left.

When I came back home, the moment I sat down on the sofa, I began to cry as loudly and as much as I could. Mari later told me that she heard me cry that night, but she did not take one step out of her room. Westerners are usually circumspect when it comes to getting involved in other people's emotions. They only have a fixed amount of emotion. I knew what time their flight would be, so I went to the Tegel Airport the following afternoon. The two women were again sitting apart as if they did not know each other. I went over to the sister and sat next to her. Unlike the day before, her face was made up, and she had changed her clothes, so that now she looked like a different person.

"We packed up everything. The people at the research institute said they'd send everything over later."

I imagined his room empty, white sheets covering the furniture.

"Were you going to marry my brother?" she asked.

If I had answered honestly, I would have said I was satisfied with the way we were in Berlin, and I did not think about the future. But I did not answer honestly.

"We were thinking of going back to Korea together," I said.

"He always had the worst luck."

She calmly opened her purse to take out a handkerchief and wiped around her eyes. They were walking to the gate when Mr. Yi's mother, who had not said a word until then, turned around to look at me and then took a few steps toward me.

"I just wanted to apologize on behalf of my son," she said. "I am so sorry. I wish you all the best."

26

Another year passed. With the attempted coup of August 1991, the Soviet Union was completely dismantled, showing the whole world the birth and death of a constitutionally socialist state.

The death of Mr. Yi Hee Soo passed with an unexpected quickness. It is not that I felt the time I spent with him was wasted, it just felt like it was not real. I did not remember it as the recent past but as a fleeting moment from a long time ago, like a spring day when I was a little girl playing by the levee, making necklaces and bracelets out of clover flowers and violets and lying on the ground chewing foxtails. Certain parts are vivid, but some things are vague, no matter how hard I try to remember. The tiny unimportant details remained with me for a long time, and now everything is just an unimportant detail. Only the little brass sculpture I took from his place, that now rests on my desk, remains the same.

Now it was time to say goodbye to Song Young Tae.

He called me from time to time, sometimes acting serious, sometimes explaining that he was doing something very important, sometimes angry. Still, he was one of the few close friends I had in Germany. I once went to see him in Göttingen. We went out to the countryside with his friends to drink and barbecue, and we sang throughout the night to release ourselves and made the neighbors angry.

From the outside, I did not appear depressed at all. Since I had been working hard for a while, I had more than forty paintings to show, including eight large canvases. I had a solo exhibition at a gallery near Tiergarten. I think it helped me complete the *Meisterschiller*.

The exhibition began with drawings, continued with large and small canvases mixed together, and ended with the most recent work, which was somewhat different from my past work. To be honest, I was greatly influenced by Mari's childlike graffiti with simplified lines and expression. But I tried to be more specific and also to appropriate the simplicity and abbreviated forms of folk art. I did not want traces of the past to be the starting point; I wanted to start within my own style. The subject was hidden inside the form, and the objects were shown as certain symbols that were highly stylized. The audience looking at them would reinterpret and translate according to their own views. The figures were distorted and overlapped and clumped together, but they were still bound by certain rules of geometry. My bigger canvases followed this set of rules even more strictly, depicting simplified figures bubbling up, as if they were about to burst.

The exhibition was pretty successful. Several media outlets covered and reported on it, and offers for exhibitions in other cities followed. I spent every single day surrounded by strangers. The last day, I stayed late at the gallery after it was closed to take down the paintings with Mr. and Mrs. Shin. Well, maybe it was not so late, perhaps half past seven, around dinnertime on a summer evening. A man with glasses wearing an unbuttoned white shirt and a loose cardigan walked in. He was pulling a large suitcase with wheels behind him. I took a hurried glance at him but turned back to take a painting off the wall, and then the familiar voice came from behind. "Can't you take them down after I've looked at them?"

Turning around, I realized it was him, Song Young Tae.

"You can't complain. You're too late!"

But I was happy to see him. Somehow he always managed to reappear when I was just about to forget him, and of course he always presented a new set of problems every time he did, which was taxing. I stepped back and waited until he had walked around the gallery. I introduced him to Mr. and Mrs. Shin, and he helped us clean up and pack everything. Temporarily, the paintings were to be kept in the gallery's storage room. We went to a Greek restaurant nearby to eat dinner. We talked about the absurd failure of the coup in the Soviet Union and about the depressing prospect of worldwide capitalism. There was nothing new or radical about our conversation; we were saying things students were saying in cafeterias everywhere. After we bid farewell to Mr. and Mrs. Shin, Young Tae and I took a taxi back to my studio because of his cumbersome suitcase.

"What on earth is this? Where are you going now?" I grumbled, as he put the suitcase into the trunk of the taxicab.

"I'm going back," he replied casually.

"And you'll give up your studies?"

"Miss Han, why don't I buy you a drink to celebrate the successful end of your exhibition? We can go out again after we drop off my suitcase."

"There's no need to go out. I have plenty to drink at home. There's a case of beer and a few bottles of Mosel wine. Let's just drink at home. I don't want to go out."

"But I want to buy you a drink!"

"Next time."

I dragged him back to my studio. I knocked on Mari's door and invited her, too, and we had a little party. Sometimes we talked in German, but mostly in our language. Mari lifted her glass and said, "Congratulations on your solo exhibition."

Young Tae also raised his glass, so I had to as well, a little embarrassed.

"Yuni, there was one painting that I really liked," Mari said.

"Which one?"

"The one with cream sprouting from a long rectangle and touching the numerous triangles above. That one. The large canvas on the first wall of the last room."

It was a painting of a human figure, transformed into a soft, melting shape, reaching out one hand from the confines of walls and trying to catch a butterfly, which was in the form of two overlapping triangles. Outside of the rectangular frame were numerous butterflies with triangular wings. The only nongeometric form was that of the human being, melting and caked within the walls. Mari had read it as a lump of cream. Unlike her, I did not translate my own painting for her.

"Your paintings were incredibly depressing," Song Young Tae muttered in his usual peremptory manner.

"Really? In what way . . . ?"

"They refuse to communicate, they are egocentric, and they seemed to be saying that the world is determined not to change anymore."

"That's how I feel these days."

"Let's go on a trip together."

Since he was so unpredictable, I had to reply, guarded, "Where, back to Seoul?"

He rustled around and took something out of his back pocket.

"Tickets for the Trans-Siberia train. I heard about it from my grandfather many times. How about we commemorate the end of the Cold War with this trip? Let's go."

"Where did you get that?"

"Several travel agencies are going crazy now. I got them from a Japanese one. We'll be part of a tour group."

What I still cannot understand now is that there was not one thing suggested by Song Young Tae that I ever turned down. Maybe he was trying to leave me an imprint of himself and our time together. I studied the ticket and the travel brochure with pictures of the Siberian landscape. When we told Mari about the trip she said, "When we were young the continent was blocked and divided into several pieces. Even the sky was divided into two."

I had no choice but to accept.

"Looks splendid," I said.

Song Young Tae and I left Berlin in early September. We had to arrive in Moscow on the date the travel agency had specified. We made preparations based on our own research. Did you know, for example, that there are only two months of summer in Siberia, and that the first snow arrives by late August? We made sure we had enough instant noodle packages. From the last U-Bahn stop at Berliner Straße we took a bus to the airport. The Schönefeld Airport was once an international airport in East

Germany, with flights to Eastern Europe, the Soviet Union, and other socialist states in Asia. Of course, there was a flight to North Korea, too.

When we arrived at the Sheremetyevo Airport in Moscow via Aeroflot, it was raining insistently. The airport was enormous but almost empty, with only a handful of passengers, maybe because the high season was over. We took a bus to our hotel, which was near the Red Square and the Moscow River. It got dark early, and the streetlamps were misty in the rain.

That night, we went out in the rain and wandered around, then had dinner and stayed at a café until late drinking beer. On our table were two brass candleholders, a red candle in each one, and because it was dark I did not realize how drunk Young Tae was. Both of us had been pretty quiet from the moment we began that trip. I had followed him without too many questions because I had fantasized for a long time of traveling through a continent without barriers. The city was not as scary or disquieting as I'd imagined it would be, but even our modern hotel was gloomy. It felt like a gigantic but deteriorating government building. The faucet leaked rusty water and drunk people staggered along the alleyways outside. The airport was full of austere officials with over-bearing manners and female volunteers who were fat and brusque. At least I could understand the bare stores, and the expressionless faces with tightly closed mouths in the long lines outside every store, no matter how little or insignificant the merchandise was. The locals, who did not care for the tourists, probably felt less discomfort than we did. They could at least retreat to their own tiny apartments. Song Young Tae poured more beer into his glass with a trembling hand.

"This is really ridiculous. How can a country with one-sixth of the landmass of the whole world be so poor? The whole place is like a crumbling wall. The building has been abandoned for too long without maintenance, and the concrete parts are falling down. How can they take such poor care of people?"

"Are you talking about buildings or people, Mr. Song?" I asked. "Everything is made by people, and in the end people are the problem," I said, without too much of emotion. "It's like dreaming of an ideal woman and then discovering her dirty underwear."

"Is there any place not like this? An island or a mountain or a village, still untouched and undiscovered at the end of the world?"

Suddenly, the few months you and I had together went through my mind, followed by the beautiful open school Mr. Yi Hee Soo talked about. I saw how the candles dimly lit the space above the small table.

"From now on, the material world will dominate. The market will demand uniform production from everyone on Earth, and it will say that this is civilization, that people will have to accept it if they don't want to collapse. Everyone will turn into a pair of brilliant crystal eyes, a product with no imagination, only responding to money."

I remembered the helpless sneer that spread around my mouth when I heard the news of Mr. Yi Hee Soo's death. I felt the same way now.

"Whether you like it or not," I spat, "this is the world we live in. There is not much I wish for anymore."

"I don't think you really loved Mr. Yi."

"I guess you can say whatever you want now, since we are in a foreign place. It's not like I can leave you here."

"You just wanted to escape to someplace else, like I do now."

"Is that so . . . ?"

I replied with fatigue in my voice.

Another day was beginning on a continent where only a hollow shell remained. In the morning, our tour group gathered in the hotel lobby. The tour guide did roll call and lectured us on how to behave and what to expect. Most of the tourists in our group were Japanese. Most of them were young, but there was an elderly couple, too. At two o'clock in the afternoon, we went to the Yaroslavl train station in front of Komsomol Square. The Trans-Siberian train headed to Vladivostok was departing at three o'clock. Before the departure, Young Tae and I went to a *berioska* on the other side of the square to buy food, as we were advised by the tour guide. We got three bags filled with everything from cigarettes and vodka to salami and ham and instant coffee. At that time, no solo foreign tourist was allowed to change route or get off the train and stay at a city during the transcontinental trip, but tourist groups were. It took one week for the Trans-Siberian train named Russia to complete its tour. Our schedule included a night's stay at a hotel in

Irkutsk and another at Khabarovsk, and then the group was to disband in Vladivostok. The train was an electric locomotive painted green with a red star, and there were only two passenger classes, first and second. All foreigners were to use first class only. A female attendant dressed in a light blue shirt and a navy blue skirt and tie greeted us at the entrance. Like in Europe, a passenger train had compartments furnished with a pair of seats on each side that could be used as beds. The window was draped with curtains, a table suspended underneath it, and the floor was carpeted. The attendant distributed blankets, pillows, sheets, and towels to each compartment.

The train began moving, and as soon as it left the city we saw white birch trees everywhere. Even in the darkness, pale trees were visible as they passed. It would be the beginning of autumn in other places, but here it was already deep into the season, the leaves darkened to the deepest shade of brown. The train crossed over the Moscow River headed toward Kirov. Until you cross the Ural Mountains, you're not in Siberia yet. In darkness, the black wall of forest sprouted up like irregular teeth beside the endless fields.

I began to realize how beautiful this enormous land was when I saw the sunrise on the great plain dusted with frost. The train moved without stopping, and the low sun would be revealed then hidden again by tree branches. Little villages, rooftops, and fences were scattered on the endless field. They looked like tiny blemishes on Mother Earth.

The sunshine turned the yellow and brown leaves of the birch trees into golden fragments, and the larch leaves had started to turn yellow. Beyond the grassy fields and wetlands, the evergreen forest of fir and spruce and pine trees stretched on. The forest touched the distant horizon, which we never seemed to reach even though we were moving all day long. We spent the first couple of days just watching the overwhelming land, both of us looking out the window without saying much.

We saw the morning sun reflected on the surface of a river or a pool of water in the wetlands, creating a pattern like a silver net on it, or a group of ducks and birds flying over the fields of reeds. Among the weeds, the fertile black soil of Russian land exposed itself and coursed down along the tracks. No one was working on the unharvested wheat fields. Only a rusted tractor stood in the middle of them. The train passed several small stations in the middle of wilderness, never stopping. They were old wooden structures whose color had faded to gray, and the staff, wearing black uniforms and hats with a red stripe, would stare at us while holding a flag. Or there were robust railroad workers wearing orange vests waddling away while carrying a railroad tie.

We used the first-class bathrooms at each end of the car to wash our faces and sometimes our bodies with hot water. Then we ate breakfast. This usually consisted of dark bread and ham, and we bought warm milk from the cart pushed around by a train employee. Lunch was served in the restaurant car, the only meal served during the day. We started with borscht, a vegetable soup made with beets, carrots, potatoes, and cabbage and topped with sour cream, accompanied by tough and sour rye bread. Then came a stew with pasta and meat and peas, and we laughed as we ate it, calling it a different version of our beloved noodles with black bean sauce. It was actually quite good. The beer bottle had a Russian label, and its slightly sweet taste and fermented smell were so lively that we called it a version of our rice wine. When the train took a break at a crossroads, which happened rarely, we went out to find women selling food. The passenger car was warm, but when we stepped out it felt like the cold air was cutting through our backs. The sunlight was so bright and the sky was so blue, but the cold air made it feel like early wintertime. Women wearing scarves on their heads and sweaters or vests were calling and beckoning to us. They offered homemade bread and cookies, hardboiled eggs, still steaming boiled potatoes in a pot, fries, toasted sunflower seeds, ugly little apples, and scallions. Young Tae and I bought the hot potatoes for snacks. The woman wrapped them in newspapers and gave us a bunch of scallions. It was only later that we found out you were supposed to dip the scallions in a sauce as you ate the potatoes. Our train car attendant was a plump young woman named Tania, and we communicated through hand gestures most of the time. She did not speak a word of English or German, but if Young Tae looked through the Russian dictionary and tried to speak a word of Russian, she quickly understood what we were trying to say and even corrected his pronunciation. Thanks to her bringing us hot water in a samovar, we were able to eat ramen noodles for dinner. Of course we offered some to her, and Tania ate them, almost crying because it was too spicy for her, but still exclaiming, "*Karacho!*"

Dusk on the plain was magnificent. Birds flew over tall birch trees, and the mist rose from the earth and filled the air as the temperature dropped. The sunlight faded into muted shade, and the sun turned red and appeared misshapen, like a watercolor whose colors have spread. The earth and the forest, the sky and our train, even our faces looking out the window and our clothes were colored red. Hills and mountainous regions began to appear, and far away we saw tall mountaintops covered in white snow, protruding like sharp teeth. As she passed by, Tania pointed out the window and yelled, "Ural! Ural!" That night, with the Ural Mountains as the border, we said goodbye to Europe and crossed over to Asia. Siberia was a wholly different world, another mighty land.

Moving through three nights and days, the train crossed the Ob River and arrived at Novosibirsk. It was around eight at night. The train stopped for about an hour at the station, and I woke up Young Tae, who had fallen asleep earlier, and went out to get fresh air. Since we had been sitting down for so long, the passengers tried to get out and walk on firm ground, no matter how much the attendants tried to stop us. We saw a small crowd gathered outside, near the exit where the cargo was transported. There was a big street market there, larger than any we had seen, and men approached us to exchange US dollars. Others were selling hot bread filled with smoked salmon and chicken soup with noodles as thick as my finger. I chose chicken soup, because it reminded me of the bowl of noodles I used to eat at Daejun Station.

We arrived in Irkutsk the following afternoon, and had to leave the train with all our belongings. We were to stay there one night, tour around the city and Lake Baikal, and then switch to a different train. From our hotel I could see the Angara River, and I remember the moment I opened my window to let in the sky, the river, and the forest colored by the red sunset. The following day, we were transported in a tour bus all over the city and up to Lake Baikal. I can barely remember the walkway along the river in front of our hotel and the Museum of Decembrists, but Lake Baikal looked like an ocean, and all around it looked like a village in the Alps. I did not want to leave the warm bus to be swept up by the freezing wind coming off the lake.

"They were the heroes and heroines of *War and Peace*," said Song Young Tae as we passed by a row of wooden houses. I knew the Decembrists were actually aristocrats who led the first revolt against the czar and the system into which they were born. As Napoleon stirred things up across Europe, the idea of a republic spread like dandelion seeds blown in the wind. The five leaders were executed, and more than one hundred aristocrats were sentenced to life and exiled to the lumberyards and mines near this city. The wives and fiancées of these men came through the snowstorms to be with their loved ones. Some of them were reunited, but sometimes the man died or the woman didn't survive the journey. The women worked as laundresses or maids while they waited for the men to finish their sentences, suffering the insults and scorn of the guards and judges. Tournetshaya, a duchess, did not stay in Irkutsk, but went into the mountains to the village of Nerchinsk to be with her husband. Madame Borkonkaya found her husband among the mine gang, and instead of embracing him, she kissed the chain around his feet. It took more than thirty years for them to be pardoned and released from hard labor, and those who managed to survive never returned to Moscow or St. Petersburg. Many revolutionaries went through here afterward, Lenin and Chernyshevsky among them.

I remember the two of us walking along the Angara River talking about them, stepping on the yellow leaves carpeting the ground. I was wearing a windbreaker, and Young Tae was in a thin winter coat and a wool hat. On the riverside road were mothers pushing strollers and young lovers taking walks.

"After all that sacrifice and effort, the modern age was barely able to hold the barricade of the antiestablishment for seventy years. The bourgeoisie has taken over again. The whole world is in the process of being colonized."

As in Berlin, Young Tae constantly wanted to return to talking about current events, but I did not want to be disturbed on this very personal and lyrical journey. I think I was very tired. At the Museum of the Decembrists, before the humble objects and other traces of those exiled to a lonely life here, I thought of the dark windows I had seen when I tried to visit you in prison. For an instant, my eyes felt warm. Looking up the tall, straight body of the white birch in front of the museum, I shook off that memory. And what I regret most now is that I did not try to understand Song Young Tae at that moment.

"You should call it a change. Everyone and everything under the sun changes."

"Look at how those whities got together to bash everything in the Persian Gulf! The only place that's left is the North or Cuba. Maybe I should go to the Caribbean and try to get along there? But it's too far."

"Look at that baby!"

I approached a baby who must have been two years old, sitting in a stroller and laughing out loud at her mother's hand gestures. The mother had taken a ribbon from her hair and was shaking it in front of the baby, and as it fluttered in the wind the baby laughed. Young Tae remained in front of the concrete barrier on top of the high bank facing the river. The mother did not seem to mind that I held the baby's fingers and gently shook them. I kissed the baby's cheek and returned to Young Tae.

"Look, there's one, and there's another. There are lots of moms and babies here."

"Didn't you see a lot of them in Berlin, too? What are you fussing about?"

"Nothing. You don't like family, do you?"

"I hate my father."

"Then how can you survive anywhere? The two places you talked about are only persisting because of a central father figure."

"I hate the fascists and the bourgeoisie."

"Your father was one of those?"

"He was in parliament and a member of the ruling party, someone who served the dictatorship for a long time. You know that."

"I think I've finally begun to understand my father," I said, but I was thinking of something else. I was not sure which was correct, his hatred or my understanding. And each of our beginnings was so different, like heaven and earth. I mumbled as if I was still talking to myself, "There are so many people like them, just ordinary people all over the world. Who's going to protect them now?"

"Aren't they the ones who resisted their protection, who wanted to go back to the old days? The market will swallow them."

"Competition is bad, of course. But government control is just as bad."

"It's futile to go on about things that don't exist."

We returned to the journey that had consumed our lives over the previous few days. But how irresponsible it was, the traveling. Like the wind, we passed fields and villages and houses of people. But this road was a path across the continent that brought me closer to my own dividing lines. To my country, which was divided in the middle, where so many people had sacrificed their lives for their dreams and now were exposing the wounds all over their bodies before the onslaught of change.

As we passed Lake Baikal and traveled into East Siberia, a range of mountains appeared at the far end of the great plain, and we began to notice long winding rivers and hills. The coniferous forest of taiga continued, with spruce trees and cedars and larch trees with elegant brown leaves, and what seemed like every birch tree in the whole wide world, unendingly following the railroad. The Trans-Siberia train followed the course of the Amur River, the life source of this continent that greets the rising sun and guides it until it sets. Riding nonstop for two nights and days, Young Tae and I could no longer bear being on the train. We usually had a little bit of vodka as a nightcap, but the night before we arrived in Khabarovsk we were drinking more. At first we were just a little bit tipsy, but things accelerated, thanks to Tania, when she brought us a hunk of pork and Russian sauerkraut, so similar to our own kimchi. The day before, I had given her some pairs of pantyhose as a present. We began drinking in earnest. The nighttime air was cold, but we kept the window open. The refreshing fragrance of trees and the river drifted in. Each of us talked and sang and chattered, not necessarily to each other, and Tania left after a few glasses since she was still on duty. Song Young Tae and I had not lost consciousness, but we were slurring. At one point we started to calm down, and soon both of us were quiet in his or her own thoughts, as we normally were.

"Why are you weeping?"

Only when Young Tae pointed at me with his finger and asked did I realize that I was crying while staring into the darkness outside the window. I was thinking that I wished Mr. Yi was with me right here, right now. This was completely different from the absence of you, still alive.

"I was thinking of Mr. Yi."

"A selfish individualist . . ."

"Hey, I am no 'ist' of any kind."

"All you care about is yourself. And your paintings are awful."

"You think you're better than me? All you do is talk, talk, talk. Why don't you just do something instead of talking about it? Or do one thing well and forget about the rest."

Song Young Tae's mouth was twisted, he seemed to be sneering.

"You're hopeless. You never loved anyone, not even yourself."

Tears were gushing down my cheeks. About half of it was the effect of the vodka. I was crying, but I didn't feel despondent and I wasn't screaming. It was my turn to attack.

"You bastard, you knew what was happening! And what did you do to Mi Kyung?"

"It was that kind of time," he murmured.

"Don't you dare blame the times," I shouted. "Admit that you made a mistake!"

Suddenly, his face became curiously contorted, and he began to weep as I was. "I can . . . disappear . . . if that's what you want."

That made me loathe him even more, so I climbed into my bed and closed the curtains. The rhythmic sound of the train wheels on the track continued. Was it true that we did not love anyone? Or is it just that we did not know how to love? I think I fell asleep. The curtain was opened stealthily. The light was out, but I was able to make out the upper torso of Young Tae standing right above my head. He bent down and kissed my cheek. I did not know what to do. My head was a jumble of thoughts. He got up quickly and left, closing the curtain again. I turned toward the wall. As always, the rhythmic sound of the train wheels continued, and the restless train moved into the night.

When we arrived in Khabarovsk, the first snow of the season was falling on the Amur River. The strange thing was that the snow was coming down while the sun was dimly shining on, like rainfall on a sunny summer's day. We unpacked at a hotel near Lenin Square. This was to be the last city we would stay in. The next day, we would go to Vladivostok, and the group tour was to end there. In the hotel lobby, there was a ticket office for a cruise on the Amur River. In our itinerary, a cruise at sunset was already included. Young Tae's face was puffy, and he had not said much all day. The hotel looked out over the square and the grand avenue named after Karl Marx. We got into a tour bus in front of the hotel and went north on the grand avenue to the harbor. The sun had set, but it was still a little early for the white sunlight to turn red. The first floor on board was the cafeteria and the second floor the deck, and everyone tended to stay on the deck. We stood among other tourists on the right side of the deck and looked down at the river, leaning on the railing. Far away were the dark mountains and forests of China. There they call the Amur River the Black Dragon River, the name we are more familiar with. This magnificent river flows through most of Eastern Siberia and into the Sea of Okhotsk at the northern part of Sakhalin. The cruise ship was to travel slowly down the river to the iron bridge of Khabarovsk and then turn back, which would take about an hour and a half. The sun was going down on the other side of the river, and bands of yellow and red appeared in the sky. Like an ignited tree, the bands widened into a wide swath that colored the surrounding area, the sun falling fast as it burned into a red flame. The river was also turning red. The water closer to us was a darker shade of blue, and the color faded as it moved away from us. When it finally met with the red sky there seemed to be no boundary between the two.

"The sun is going down again," I thought I heard Young Tae mumble.

I watched his face as he stared down at the river.

"Are you feeling better?"

"What . . . ?"

"You said your stomach hurt before."

"Hmm, I'm really hungry now. Thanks for asking, though."

I regarded him in silence.

"I really appreciate that . . ." Song Young Tae said to me in the voice that I was so familiar with. "I really appreciate that you came on this trip with me, Miss Han."

"I've enjoyed it."

I hoped a few words like these might clear the air. When the cruise was over and the tourist group dispersed at the harbor, the two of us went to a Chinese restaurant we had seen from the bus. We ordered four dishes and ate rice for the first time in a while. Then we went to a café, and that is where he disappeared. After he ordered coffee, he got up and left as if he was going to the restroom. He still had not come back long after I'd finished mine, and I simply assumed that he had become sulky again and had gone back to the hotel by himself. I ordered a cocktail and stayed longer, listening to a chamber music group playing there. Alone, I felt rather free and unencumbered after being obliged to accompany someone for more than a week. I was alone again, thank God. And even if I'd still been with him, would I have been able to stop him from what he was about to do? After spending about two hours there, I slowly walked down the grand avenue back to the hotel. The moment I walked into our room I saw that his bag and clothes were gone. Somehow, I remained calm at that moment. I looked around and found a piece of notepaper leaning against the vanity mirror. Hastily scrawled onto the paper were his words:

> I was going to leave as soon as we arrived here, but I decided to stay and have at least one more dinner with you. My dear Miss Han, I am going to the most secluded village in this world, and I won't be coming back from there. The north of the peninsula is perhaps the most isolated and difficult place in the world right now, but I can't stand idly by . . . or kill me! I'll never forget this trip. Dasvidanya!

At first, I had no idea what this extraordinary action of his really meant. The next morning, I simply told our tour guide that we would be ending our trip here, and I stayed at the hotel for one more night. Of course, he did not come back. After spending a whole day in an unfamiliar city all by myself, it finally dawned on me. He had had a different destination in his mind since the beginning of this trip.

27

After I returned to Korea, I came here for every vacation. This place has changed a lot, too. The intoxicated noise of drunk people singing karaoke and the smell of fatty meat grilling have replaced the gentle sounds of the brook and the refreshing fragrance of the breeze.

I am now a professor at a university outside of Seoul, and I live by myself in an apartment near there. The world has changed but nothing seems different here, and people are even more individualistic. They seem to think that they have achieved everything now, and they are more obvious than ever about their selfish nature and their obsession with money. Wealth has become the most important basis for relationships, not just among friends, but among family, between parents and children and among brothers and sisters. I wonder what they would do if all at once they were stripped of their material wealth. I just know that they would have to pay for it one day. The people are mired in inertia, the youth have lost their idealism and now only seek pleasure. The fastest way to win in politics is through hypocrisy and opportunism, and the media openly continues to fabricate and distort information. This corruption is an open wound from the violent rule of the past. After living in a restricted society for too long, it is said, people are afraid of creative power or spiritual fulfillment, and they come to detest change. While we still have a long way to go, and you are still in the same place, all the values are mixed up, and those who hold power are still the strongest.

Yet, I love this place and I am proud of it. I lived through an era with people who achieved some progress, inadequate as it is. From this pile of poor and miserable rags, we will weave beautiful new clothes.

When I came back two years ago, I bought this house and the land around it in our names. And finally this year, 1995, I renovated the house. At first, I did not want to touch anything, because I did not want to spoil anything you might remember when you came back here, but things were deteriorating. I had to fix the roof and the bedroom, and I updated many things, too. As I am writing this, I hear the owl's hoot as we used to. Around dusk, I heard the cry of turtledoves, too. Do you think they are the same birds as before, who have somehow survived until now? Or are they the spirits of dead ones, united with all the things that we have lost?

Once, I was criticizing a friend and I screamed in despair that we did not love anyone, that we did not know how to love. But now, I want to correct myself. On this Earth, at any given moment, there is love. How it appears to others may differ depending on the era. I watch our friends being worn down by everyday life like pebbles being washed away and slowly disintegrating in seawater, and I hope that they are not regretting anything. I want them to respect the depth of meaningful, plentiful life that still remains in their hearts, and I hope that they will be able to embrace their pasts and their futures with more mature love.

I am not feeling well these days. I think I am too tired.

Summer vacation came to my rescue, but at the end of the
semester, I was supposed to monitor an exam and almost
collapsed in the classroom. I was standing up front for a
while, then I took one step and was about to turn to the
window; maybe it was because of the bright light, but I felt
dizzy and stumbled. I somehow managed to grab the windowsill, and I remained standing there, my eyes closed.

A similar incident happened while I was taking a bath. I
was sitting down, letting the water run down my back, and
all of sudden there was a sharp pain in my lower abdomen.
Not knowing what else to do, I grabbed my sides and twisted
my body as I moaned. It took a while for the pain to go away,
like waves calming. Recently I have lost a lot of weight, and
I always had pretty pronounced cheekbones, but now they
seem to protrude even more.

I have been thinking about motherhood, a perennial topic
of mine. The one that begets all others. Rosa Luxemberg's
foundation for criticizing tyranny and bureaucracy was
motherly love for the masses. The modern world has been a
dreary and bleak era of males, filled with conflict and
anguish. Like the life of an old secret policeman who used
to torture his prisoners but is now in hiding somewhere, it is
devastated and lonely. Look at those dreary eyes, glaring
with determination to hold onto the hegemony that he may
lose, and to regain the power he has already lost. Look at
that insipid smile that he is trying to pass off as warm love,
and the cold eyes that want dominion over everything and
obedience from everyone. They cannot be hidden beneath
the sinisterly warm expression.

I am once again looking at Käthe Kollwitz's woodcuts from
her later years. I had forgotten about them. Now I keep
going back to her self-portraits, as I did when I was a student, especially those from when she was an old woman
whose face was filled with empathy, roughly delineated with

crude knife lines. Reflected in her face is the long, agonizing journey, starting with her son's death on a battlefield during World War I, to her sympathy for the underprivileged, and the persecution that she and her colleagues suffered, to the death of her grandson on the Russian front during World War II. While I was in Berlin, Mari Kline once said that we are living in a world that would not allow us to work the way Käthe did. I think I said something like, "Here, people are sick of each other, they chase each other away or avoid one another, but there are other places where people are desperately looking for each other."

Well, this place has become the place Frau Kline was talking about.

I'm thinking of the last time I saw Mari. In the winter of 1992, the last winter I spent in Berlin all by myself, she was taken to a nursing home run by the government. Even in the eyes of our building manager, she was severely alcoholic. Right before she left I saw her, thin as a piece of paper, sitting on her bed. Her studio had been cleaned up, and there was a single suitcase, small and worn out, placed next to the bed. She was wearing a gray suit that was too baggy on her now and a felt hat, and she looked like an actress from an old silent movie. I had brought her yellow roses, and she took them close to her face and inhaled deeply. And then she did not say anything, and just smiled gently.

I want to go back to Käthe's last image, the lithograph that is considered by some people to be her last testament. It is an image of a mother hiding three children inside her coat. The mother's face, which looks almost androgynous, is strong and powerful. Her hair is swept back, her mouth closed, with hollow cheeks that emphasize the cheekbones. She is raising her arms to protect her children, and it looks like her head is connected to her shoulder with no neck. Her eyes are determined and unafraid, looking up as if to say, *So, what are you going to do now?*

Under her raised arms, two children are facing to the left

while the last one is facing forward on her right side. The little one on the right is lifting up the mother's coat and peeking out with a mischievous expression while the larger one on the left is looking up to where the mother is turned, with a startled face. The other child right beneath him also peeks out, about to cry. The title of this lithograph is *Seed for the Planting Shall Not Be Ground*, a line from Göethe's poem. It is so powerful and realistic that it is difficult to believe a seventy-six-year-old woman did it. And it is a simple image, maybe too simple for the artists of today, who tend to consider everything they do so complex and sophisticated, even though all we all do is paint. Well, I finally began to get an inkling of what living is all about after I turned forty. Here, I want to write down a few words of Käthe's.

> *A mother is someone who doesn't think about anything else; her entire life can be summed up in the life of another. Old people internalize things and remain indifferent, it's true, but I should add that this introverted quality can be just as pure as a mother's oneness.** *

> *As always, when I bury a person I mourn them, but I don't cry too bitterly because I am always overcome by the feeling that I must live on. "Who knows what might not be possible tomorrow. So I must live today." Everything has its due time. It is beautiful. But all things must pass.*****

As I bid farewell to a century of wars, of men killing men, I think of the maternal instinct that's been murdered with these men. I killed mine. I was forced to, when you were taken away from me. But, I am determined to regain that great essence.

---

* Käthe Kollwitz, *Die Tagebücher* (Berlin: Akademie Verlag, 1989), p. 586.
** Ibid., p. 693.

It is snowing outside. Jung Hee drove me to Kalmae. Another year is about to end. Last month, I wrote my first letter to you. Of course I did not send it to the prison, but to your sister, even though I do not know when you will be released. I did that because I may not be here in this world when you finally regain your freedom.

As I wrote in my letter, I am sick. I have been to the hospital. I knew something was wrong, my skin felt like the skin of a dried fish. I was sitting on the toilet to urinate but felt something warm gushing out. I looked down and saw red filling up the toilet. It did not hurt, but there was the blood. When I called Jung Hee and told her about it, she came to me right away and took me to a big hospital. The results came back; the doctor was hesitating and Jung Hee was already crying, so I knew it was something grave. I was actually quite serene, maybe because I have gone through so many shocking incidents throughout my life. Before we finished the registration process and I was assigned to a single room, I spoke to Jung Hee, calmly and without anger. I told her, if it is serious or hopeless I should be told first, before anyone else, so that I may tidy things up with some dignity. So it is cervical cancer. I have received radiation and chemotherapy, and the pain has lessened, but I am not too hopeful. I am losing weight at an alarming rate. I think I will stay here in Kalmae for three days. I had to cry and beg, saying that I thought I would get better instantly if I came to this beautiful place with its clean air, saying that they should think of it as my one last wish, the one thing that they could do for me. So I think this will be the last time I write something from here. Maybe I will write another letter and send it to your sister when I go back into the hospital.

I was never able to be a real wife to a man or a real mother to a child, and in my forties it finally dawned on me that I truly want to be a mother. As a failed artist who has accomplished nothing, I was finally beginning to understand the meaning of motherhood and the way to look at the world as a mother, and now I have a disease that takes away the root of motherhood. Life can be so strange.

I need to ask you for one thing. I do not know when, but by the time you finish reading all my writings in Kalmae you will learn about our child, Eun Gyul. I did not want you to know about her while you were in prison, but there were times I just wanted to take her there and push her through the iron bars and show you her smiles. And there were times when I wanted to escape from her, and from you. Everything that I cannot teach her or give to her in the future, I want you to do for your daughter.

I guess you are an old man now. Everything that we wanted to protect, the things that we endured so much for, are shattered now, but they are still shining through the world's dust. As long as we are living, we will have to start over again and again. What did you find within those lonely dark walls? Did you walk through the path in between rocks and find a place suddenly bright, blooming with a multitude of flowers? Did you find our old garden?

Yoon Hee's note ended there. The last letter among the ones my sister gave me was dated the summer of 1996. I remember her last sentence.

You in there, me out here, that's how we spent a lifetime. There were difficult times, but let us make peace with all our days. Goodbye, my darling.

It took me a few years in solitary confinement to realize, painfully, what our era had meant once it was over. Our various attempts to take control of the government had become outdated or unnecessary. The antiestablishment ideas that were formulated from within the system of capitalism and materialism were distorted during the process of realization. Instead, like a skeletal steel frame still standing among the ruins, a few remaining propositions are more important than ever. In any society, the most lively legacy of the last few hundred years is the defense of democratic principles and the return of sovereignty to the people. They are like the handful of belongings saved from a burnt-down house. There should be a continuous challenge to authority for change and reform, and groups of ordinary people should form an alliance to reclaim what was taken by the state inch by inch, like a children's game, and enlarge the territory to the level of practical equality.

One summer's day, I went out to the exercise field and found a commotion everywhere on television, on the radio, and in the newspapers. In the middle-class neighborhood south of the Han River, which has prospered since the seventies, a bridge and a department store had collapsed one after the other. Around that time, the government appeared to have changed to a civilian one, but it was in essence only a controlled transition from military dictatorship at the conclusion of more than thirty years of modernization. For days there were accounts of people who died, or who somehow persevered under fallen concrete and dirt until they were rescued. The media blasted the owner of the department store, who had illegally altered the structure, continued to operate the business despite warning signs, and made no attempt to evacuate the customers until the very last minute. Then various stories about his past came out. Apparently, he had been an agent for the Japanese during the occupation. The details of his activities were not clear, but he evidently became an officer at the Japanese consulate in Manchuria. After the liberation, he came back to Korea and worked for the American occupiers, and during the Korean War he became an interrogator of Chinese POWs. Fluent in Chinese and knowledgeable about anti-Japanese activities in Manchuria, he was considered one of South Korea's top experts. He was involved in forming the South Korean intelligence agency, served as an intermediary to the American army, and managed to win the bid on the choicest parcels of land where the American army depot used to be. He became a real estate mogul, building apartment buildings and department stores. Everything was detailed in the newspapers. In the South, the era of government-controlled development and modernization was coming to an end, while starvation and a mass exodus had begun in the North. It was the beginning of the last chapter in this divided land. The chaos and changes could go on for a long time on a much larger scale. Would there be anything else left for me to do? If so, it would be a struggle in everyday life.

In prison, I had a habit of living in the future, getting ahead in days in order to erase them. At the beginning of each month I crossed out the whole month on the calendar, and on New Year's Day I drew a circle around the new year. But the present dragged on so slowly. The news of the changing world outside quietly soaked in from time to time, like the season's passing shown by dandelion seeds or the yellowed leaves of a willow tree floating in through the iron bars. The news might arrive late, but we knew very well what good and evil had transpired in the outside world before the year was gone.

We must return to the revolution of June 1987 that was so long anticipated, yet ended up being cursed for years to come. Everyone had been hopeful, but then they lost their hope, and, despondent, we splintered into too many fragments. The laborers, the farmers, the students, the intelligentsia, the religious, the poor, the unemployed. The list was endless, and we even had to add the white-collar workers to it. Still we did not find ourselves, not realizing that the true birth of citizenship would occur only when we all got together.

It has been less than a month since I was released from prison, and the whole country is going through a serious economic crisis. All I had were a few pairs of underwear that I'd brought with me from solitary confinement, and I could not imagine what it meant to be poor. The little sparrows sitting on the wire might fly away at once when others approach, and when they come back they try to reorganize in the mist of confusion. Those who do not quickly participate in this momentary reorganization fly away, and are scattered all over the place. Maybe I am not alone.

The sixth morning in Kalmae arrived.

I packed my bag, and I included Yoon Hee's notebooks. I made breakfast, and I washed the dishes and mopped the floor, like I used to in my solitary cell. Before I left the house I looked at the portrait of two people whose paths had crossed. I do not look at my younger self, but at Yoon Hee, the older mother standing behind me gazing beyond my shoulder,.

When I close my eyes, I see the flowers of seasons that are now gone.

Walking on the ridge between the vegetable fields, the cold morning dew soaking my ankles, I spot the pale pink flowers of bindweed peeking through green leaves here and there. A thistle is shaking in the wind with its numerous prickles that look like fur. Pampas grasses are swaying on top of the hill with the blue sky in the background. With a whoosh, one magpie flies through tree branches, while a pair sits on a gently swinging branch with their tails touching once in a while. Just one step away from the bindweed flower is the tip of her white rubber shoe, and I see her long fingers plucking the thistle. She is walking through the pampas grasses. Her shirt and the hem of her skirt appear then disappear among the white plumes. The magpies are sitting on the branch of a persimmon tree, and Yoon Hee is leaning against its trunk. Suddenly, it is dark and prison bars are draped in front of my eyes. Above the white wall encircled with barbed wires, a searchlight brightly illuminates the night, and beyond the wall is a persimmon tree guarding the road. At first she does not appear, but soon Yoon Hee is there, standing under the tree. Someone stands by the bathroom window and sings the same song over and over again. He is out of tune and making up the lyrics as he goes along, but he continues to sing quietly and cautiously, taking a short break once in a while. Look, it's snowing! The rhythmic sound of footsteps walking down the corridor. I open my eyes, and the black-and-white pictures disappear.

Did you find that place? Yoon Hee asks me. I will answer that I am on my way back home. That I have climbed the mountains and hills to look for the house. That I started to see the village lights and smoke coming out of a chimney far away. That I started walking, swaggering, following the road you traveled before. I stand on the side where she is looking out from behind my young face, and I murmur, "I'll come back."

Like a man leaving the house he grew up in, I looked around once more, and then I left the house. I said goodbye to the Soonchun lady, her youngest son, and his wife. I walked down the narrow road through the orchard to get a taxicab by the bridge, and I left Kalmae, as I had returned to it.

Eun Gyul is wearing her school uniform, a tartan skirt and a short-sleeved shirt. Her long hair is parted in the middle, and it rolls up slightly at the end, just like her mother's did. When I push open the glass door and walk into the bakery, she politely stands up from her chair and waits for me to approach. I remember Han Jung Hee's concerns, and I try not to show my emotions.

"What was my father like?" she says.

"Did you like your mom?" I ask.

We speak almost at the same time. We smile, followed by a moment of awkward silence. Like a good child, Eun Gyul makes the concession and answers first.

"I liked her but I could not understand her."

"What does that mean?"

"She only cared about one thing."

"Just one thing?"

Eun Gyul averts her eyes and pauses, as if she is choosing her words carefully, "You must know people who are like that. An avid collector, or someone who always takes the same road . . . Like possessed, or something like that."

"That doesn't sound like the person I knew. Maybe she loved the world in a different way than you do."

"There were times when I was younger when I did not like her, but I grew up to like her in the end. And now, you have to give me an answer, too."

"What was your question . . . ?"

"My father. You were with him in the United States, weren't you?"

"To borrow your words, he was also someone who cared about only one thing."

Again, she acts like a good child and declares, "I guess it's not such a bad thing to be passionate about something."

Eun Gyul and I find seats on a bench in a park. She and I watch little children run around and play in a sandy playground with a slide and swings. An old man is pushing a little girl on a swing. As he pushes her with a bit of force, the swing goes up high and the little girl shakes her tiny legs and giggles with delight. There is the creaking sound of iron chains. We sit side by side and eat cotton candy. I fumble with my tongue through the soft texture of spun sugar, which keeps sticking to my lips.

I take out a handkerchief and wipe the pink stain from Eun Gyul's cheeks. She has already figured out that I am her father.

"When I was younger, I wished I had a father who would play with me like that."

"Weren't you close to your mom?"

"It's not that we didn't want to be, but . . . how should I say it, our timing was off."

"Then what did you do?"

"I just played by myself. And she spent time by herself, too. And it became harder to spend time together, and if we went somewhere together for a special occasion, like to an amusement park, it was too tiring for both of us because we were both too considerate toward each other."

"Why was that?"

"We were both frustrated and then felt sorry for each other, so we tried to overcompensate, and then we both realized what the other one was doing, and we repeated it again and again."

Eun Gyul answers her cell phone, and hesitating, she gets up.

"I have to go now. I hope we'll see each other often, Dad."

In a flash, all these scenes disappear. Outside the bus window, the earth in springtime passes by. Blooming forsythias cover the hill, and the field is dyed light green with brand new sprouts.

I go to the place where we decided to meet over the phone. She will be there with her aunt. It is a café in a busy area overlooking a square with a fountain. It happens to be the lunch hour, and people who work in nearby buildings are taking a break, sitting on benches and steps. At one corner of the square, a brass band is playing "The Blue Danube," and water is sprouting from the fountain. I stand on the sidewalk to look for the meeting place, and when I see the crowd sitting on the marble steps in front of the building I sigh. Out of the blue, I am drenched in cold sweat and my legs are unsteady, like the day I left the university hospital. I try to calm down by leaning against a marble column, hiding from the people going up and down the stairs. I walk around the column to go down the steps, and Yoon Hee is standing at the bottom of the stairway. I cannot tell if she is wearing white or the palest blue, but there is a faint smile on her face as she watches me. I stagger down toward her. I knock into people climbing up, I shake them off with both hands, and I move my feet quickly, flustered. I could see her but now she is gone, maybe she has been swallowed by the crowd. Would it be possible to rewind the film and repeat the trace of her that was just here? I take out a handkerchief to wipe my face, and I inhale and exhale a couple of times to steady my breathing. Across the street I see the sign for the café and its French doors.

And fly from?
Everyone
And bound for where?
For nowhere
Do you know what time they have spent together?
A short time
And when they will veer asunder?
*Soon**

---

* Bertolt Brecht, *The Rise and Fall of the City of Mahagonny*, trans. by W. H. Auden and Chester Kallman (David R. Godine: Boston, 1976), pp. 72-73.

"More has been expected of Hwang Sok-yong than almost any other Korean writer of the past quarter century. Ever since the early 1970s, when Hwang began to write stories about the nameless millions on whose backs the Korean 'economic miracle' was realized, he has been regarded as a champion of the people," writes Bruce Fulton in *The Columbia Companion to Modern East Asian Literature*. Indeed, Hwang Sok-yong has witnessed many of the tumultuous events of modern Korean history and drawn artistic inspiration from his own experiences as vagabond day laborer, student activist, Vietnam War veteran, advocate for coal miners and garment workers, and political dissident. The works of Hwang Sok-yong have consistently reflected the trials and tribulations of Korea's modern history.

Hwang Sok-yong was born in 1943 in Zhangchung, Manchuria, where his family found refuge after the Japanese occupation of Korea. When Korea was liberated in 1945, they returned to Hwanghae province in what is now North Korea, then moved again to an industrial suburb of Seoul in 1949, just before the start of the Korean War. In July 1953, an armistice was signed that definitively divided the country into two states, a division that still haunts the national psyche.

Mr. Hwang debuted as a writer in 1962 while still a student at Gyeongbok High School when his short story "Ipseokbugen" (Near the Marking Stone) won the Promising Young Writer Award sponsored by the journal *Sasanggye* (Intellect).

In 1966, Mr. Hwang was drafted into Korea's military corps in Vietnam, and reluctantly fought until 1969 for the American cause, which he saw as an attack on the Vietnamese liberation struggle:

> What difference was there between my father's generation, drafted into the Japanese army or made to service Imperial Japan's pan-Asian ambitions, and my own, unloaded into Vietnam by the Americans in order to establish a "Pax Americana" zone in the Far East during the Cold War?

In Vietnam, he was responsible for "cleanup," erasing the proof of civilian massacres and burying the dead. Based on these experiences, he wrote the 1970 short story "The Pagoda," which won the Korean daily newspaper *Chosun Ilbo*'s New Year prize.

His novella, *The Chronicle of a Man Named Han*, the story of a family separated by the Korean War, was also published in 1970, and is still relevant today as tensions between North and South Korea have forced some separated families to travel to a third country to see long-lost relatives.

Mr. Hwang published a collection of stories, *The Road to Sampo*, in 1974, then became a household name with his epic *Chang Kil-san*, which was serialized in a daily newspaper over a period of ten years (1974–84). Using the parable of a bandit from olden times ("parables are the only way to foil the censors") to describe the contemporary dictatorship, *Chang Kil-san* was a huge success in both North and South Korea. It sold an estimated million copies, and remains a bestseller in Korean fiction today.

Hwang Sok-yong also wrote for the theater, and several members of a company were killed for performing one of his plays during the 1980 Kwangju Uprising, a bloody confrontation between pro-democracy supporters and Republic of Korea Army General Chun Doo Hwan's dictatorship. During this time, Hwang Sok-yong went from being just a writer revered by students and intellectuals to becoming a political activist.

In 1985, he published a substantial and award-winning novel based on his bitter experience of the Vietnam War, *The Shadow of Arms*. It was translated into English in 1994 and into French in 2003.

In 1989, Mr. Hwang travelled to Pyongyang in North Korea as a representative of the nascent democratic movement:

> When I went to North Korea I realized that writers from the North had read poems and novels by progressive writers from the South. The main reason for my visit was to promote exchange between the Association of South Korean Artists and the General Federation of North Korean Literature and Arts Unions. I suggested starting a magazine that

would feature works of Northern as well as Southern writers. That was how the *Literature of the Reunification* magazine was born, and how many works from Southern novelists and poets were introduced to the North.

This border crossing was a violation of South Korean national security law, so Hwang Sok-yong was forced to live in exile in New York, later in Germany during the fall of the Berlin Wall.

In 1993, he returned to Seoul—because "a writer needs to live in the country of his mother tongue"—and was promptly sentenced to seven years in prison for breach of national security. While in prison, he conducted eighteen hunger strikes against restrictions such as the banning of pens and inadequate nutrition. Organizations around the world, including PEN America and Amnesty International, rallied for his release, and he was finally pardoned in 1998 as part of a group amnesty by the then–newly elected president Kim Dae-jung.

After his release, Hwang Sok-yong published his first novel in ten years, *The Old Garden*, in 2000. The story of two lovers separated when one is sentenced to eighteen years in prison for his political activities in the Kwangju Uprising has been highly successful and won the Danjae Award and the Yi San Literary Award. In 2005, it was published in German by DTV, and in French by Zulma. The English-language edition will be published in September 2009 by Seven Stories Press, and subsequently in the UK by Picador Asia.

The Guest, a novel about a massacre in North Korea wrongly attributed to the Americans, which was in fact a battle between Christian and Communist Koreans, was published in 2001. The "guest" is a euphemism in Korean for smallpox, or an unwanted visitor that brings death and destruction, and it is used in the novel to describe the twin horrors that Christianity and Communism became when introduced to Korea. The English-language edition was published in 2005 by Seven Stories Press.

In 2003, Hwang Sok-yong wrote *Shim Chung*, a novel based on an old Taoist tale about a girl who is sold to Chinese merchants so that her blind father can regain sight. Seeing a similarity between Chung and the "girls and women workers of South Korea who went up to Seoul to seek jobs in factories and end up eventually ruining themselves during the period of modernization in the 1970s," Hwang used this well-known Korean folktale about filial piety to illustrate how the body and soul of a young woman changed during the imperialism of East Asia in the nineteenth century.

Mr. Hwang followed with another strong and globe-trotting female protagonist in his bestseller *Princess Bari* in 2007. Named after a famous Korean folktale about a princess who saves her world, Hwang Sok-yong's Bari loses her family to famine in Korea in the 1990s, travels to London as an illegal migrant worker, and weds a Muslim man. Amid global violence and conflict, such as 9/11 and the July 7 terrorist attack on London, Bari sets out on a quest for true reconciliation that transcends nationality, religion, race, culture, and ideology.

In an effort to connect with a younger generation of readers, Hwang Sok-yong wrote his next novel entirely on the Internet.

> I want to tell young people not to be too disheartened by all
> this pressure. They should not be afraid to break the mold,
> to break out of this system and find their own way of life.

From February to July 2008, he serialized *The Evening Star* on his blog. The site received over 2 million visits and hundreds of comments each day. The printed novel went on to sell over 500,000 copies, and its success prompted other renowned writers to do the same.

Today, Hwang Sok-yong is working on a new grand plan: to set up a peace train that will travel from Paris to Seoul in July 2010, passing through Ulan Bator and Pyongyang for the sixtieth anniversary of the onset of the Korean War. He has recruited an international team including the great North Korean novelist Hong Seok-jung (winner of the prestigious Manhae Literary Prize in 2004) and Nobel laureates Jean-Marie Gustave Le Clézio of France and Orhan Pamuk of Turkey.

> This train that will run from the European continent to the
> Far East will be a symbol of the end of the Cold War and a
> bond between the two Koreas after more than half a century
> of hostility.

ABOUT SEVEN STORIES PRESS

SEVEN STORIES PRESS is an independent book publisher based in New York City, with distribution throughout the United States, Canada, England, and Australia. We publish works of the imagination by such writers as Nelson Algren, Russell Banks, Octavia E. Butler, Ani DiFranco, Assia Djebar, Ariel Dorfman, Coco Fusco, Barry Gifford, Hwang Sok-yong, Lee Stringer, and Kurt Vonnegut, to name a few, together with political titles by voices of conscience, including the Boston Women's Health Collective, Noam Chomsky, Angela Y. Davis, Human Rights Watch, Derrick Jensen, Ralph Nader, Gary Null, Project Censored, Barbara Seaman, Gary Webb, and Howard Zinn, among many others. Seven Stories Press believes publishers have a special responsibility to defend free speech and human rights, and to celebrate the gifts of the human imagination, wherever we can. For additional information, visit www.sevenstories.com.